KIMBERLY LOTH

NINA WALKER

NEW WORLD SHIFTERS

THE COMPLETE SERIES

Editing by Ailene Kubricky

And Cookie Lynn Publishing

Cover Design by Mibl Art

Paperback Omnibus ISNB: 978-1-950093-47-2

Addison & Gray Press

NIGHT OF THE WOLF MOON

NEW WORLD SHIFTERS
BOOK ONE

KIMBERLY LOTH

NINA WALKER

Chapter One

Fourteen minutes.

It seems a trivial amount of time--but had I been born fourteen minutes earlier--I'd be the claimed one instead of my sister.

"It's going to be okay," I whisper in Willow's ear and tighten our hug even though I know it won't be. Nothing will ever be okay after today. "You're stronger than anyone I know."

The soft wind blows, rustling through the cotton field behind us. We've come to the edge of the village because we don't want the wolves getting anywhere near our homes. I'm the only sibling here today, and that's because I insisted on coming. The rest of the field is sprinkled with voyeurs pretending to be supportive, three sets of parents, two claimed daughters, and one unlucky son. Mama, Willow, and I don't stand too close to the other families, or anyone, for that matter. There is no solidarity among us--we're all here because we had no choice.

Willow starts to shake, fists clenching against my back, but not because she's crying. My sister doesn't cry when she's afraid. She gets angry.

"I love you, Poppy." She steps back, practically peeling us apart, and addresses Mama and me one last time. "Goodbye."

Only I can see the slight tremble in her limbs that indicates that she's on the verge of losing her courage.

She turns her back on us and marches across the barren field toward the other two claimed, Charlotte McKenzie and Devansh Patel. We call this the taxing field because nothing will grow here, and that's what the claimed are, a tax on our people. Some say nothing grows because of what happens here with the monsters, that this land is cursed. Others insist it's from radiation even though we've been assured there's no radiation near our village, but if there's no radiation, then why is this field so desolate? I tend to err on the side of science. I mean, once the wars got bad enough, the nukes took out most of the cities, and stray bombs ended up all over the wilds. I was born decades after the wars, but evidence of them is still everywhere. Barren because of radiation or not, the taxing field is the last place anyone wants to end up. Tears stream down my face, and Willow's figure blurs in my vision. We're opposites like that. Where she burns with anger, I freeze with despair.

Willow and I have always had a bond deeper than anyone could understand. We're two parts to the same whole—like soulmates. But despite the closeness we share, we've suffered through our adolescence with the bitter knowledge that we'd be separated one day. She's to go to the city where the monsters live; I'm to stay here in the village, and that will be the end of *us*.

"Knowing something is going to happen and having it happen are two entirely different things," I whisper to Mama. Having it happen hurts a hell of a lot more. If life isn't cruel enough after the fall of civilization, try being the second half of a twin sister pairing where the first is claimed.

I step forward to go after Willow, but Mama is quick to snatch me back. "This is the way it has to be," she hisses in my ear, voice pleading. This is why Mama and Papa didn't want me to come along today. They knew my emotions would get the better of me. But I had to come. I knew that I'd never be able to accept Willow leaving me unless I saw her go with my own eyes.

I swallow hard, wanting to run anyway, but I stay on our side of the field because Mama is right. If I run after her, they'll kill me. At least, that's what everyone says. I was here once before, last year. Nobody was killed that day, but it certainly felt like it. I wasn't supposed to come, but I did anyway, staying far enough back to avoid notice. I'd watched them take Knox, my boyfriend. Willow had begged me not to fall for him because he had been one of the claimed, and our relationship was doomed from the start, but try telling that to my heart. It didn't listen, and I did fall. Willow had held me for days after that while I mourned his departure. Who will hold me now?

This is the way it has to be. Mama's words echo in my ears. I wish I could silence them, that they weren't the truth.

If Willow and I were identical twins, I'd take her place. Over the years, I've wondered if I'd have the courage to switch lots with her had we been given the genetic opportunity, and now I know the truth. I would. I love Willow more than I love myself. She isn't meant for a life of oppression. Neither am I, for that matter, but this will either break her or kill her. She's *too* strong, and she'll never submit to them, not like I would.

But Willow and I are not identical, so it would be impossible for me to take her place and not have anyone know it. To break the law would mean both our deaths. To give her a chance at survival, I have to let her go. I hate myself for it.

Mama squeezes my hand. She's crying. Papa and little Evan aren't here, but I'm sure wherever they are, they're crying too. They said their goodbyes back at the house because neither could bear to come along for the claiming. I guess some people would rather not witness their worst fears come alive right in front of them.

But I'd rather see the truth—no matter how bad—than spend my life wondering.

Those of us who aren't claimed stand along one end of the field that marks the edge of our village. The unlucky three who must leave during their eighteenth year on the morning of the harvest moon are gathered at the other end. Willow, Charlotte, and Devansh have all prepared for this. The girls have known they were claimed their entire lives since they were given their lot at birth. Devansh could have been spared if his parents had ever birthed a girl, but his mother was blessed with boys only, same as Knox's. So Devansh is the claimed, allowing his family to continue living in our village. Still, being prepared doesn't make this any easier. If Knox was hoping for a little sister to come along and take the burden, he never once showed it publicly, nor privately to me. Devansh doesn't show it either. Some things are simply what they are, and there's no changing it.

My eyes flit from Willow's back, where her long strawberry blonde hair sways side to side over her new green dress, to the tall men barking out orders and lining the claimed up like cattle. These men offer us their protection from the monsters roaming the wilds even though they're also monsters themselves. Monsters and jailers as far as I'm concerned.

Willow's shiny hair is almost pink in this September morning light, and it catches the eye of one of the men—the leader. He grasps it, running a lock between his greedy fingers, before reaching down to grope her backside. Willow twists from his grip and slaps him across the jaw. The sound echoes across the field like a cracking whip.

Silence.

No.

She didn't just do that.

Mama grips my hand, and our neighbor Mr. Fernsby appears in front of me. He's one of the voyeurs, come to "support us," but I shove him aside, holding my breath and watching helplessly. The man standing in front of Willow shifts into a full-blown wolf. His body transforms with the ripping of clothing as his human flesh deforms into that of an animal. His fur is dark brown, nearly black, and in his wolf form, he's a head taller than my sister. I've never seen the wolf shifters in their wolf bodies, and here one is, standing over Willow, saliva dripping onto her cheek.

Willow doesn't move. She just stands there with her fists clenched tight and her stance wide, as if prepared to battle. "Oh, let them have mercy," Mama whispers. A few of the other men move closer to my sister, but they don't shift into their wolves. They just watch, like me.

The wolf growls, and the guttural sound tears across the field. My insides turn to ice.

"Close your eyes," Mama mutters next to me.

But I don't listen to her. Even though I know what's about to happen, I cannot look away.

He opens his jaws wide, and I will her to run. But Willow's never been a runner. She's a fighter. She's looking straight ahead, even as the razor-sharp teeth come down on her.

The jaws clamp on her head, and I let out a squeak. Mama squeezes my hand again. The wolf lifts Willow into the air, and her body hangs limp, blood gushing from her neck. I should close my eyes now, but I can't. Instead, I watch as he shakes her side to side. Her body flings this way and that until it finally separates into two pieces and goes flying. The wolf drops her head, her pretty pink hair now bright red with blood. Her body lies ten feet away from him.

A scream releases through me, ripping my soul in half. Mama clamps her hand across my mouth. Mr. Fernsby grabs my arms and forces me to turn away. I blink wildly, staring at the dead earth, muffled sobs racking my entire body. My heart aches. I'm weightless and a million pounds all at once. The stench of Willow's coppery blood wafts across the breeze so thick I can almost taste it. I tear away from Mama's hand and fall to my knees, vomiting into the dirt.

This isn't real. This can't be happening.

"Submission," a male voice roars, "subservience, and obedience. Those are the three rules for the claimed."

Three words that all mean the same thing.

I turn on my knees to gaze back over the field, careful to keep my eyes up and away from what's left of Willow. Grief hasn't hit me yet, only shock. But it will.

The man has shifted back from his wolf form. He's naked and is slowly pulling on a pair of pants that one of his underlings has handed him. He's back to being a man, or what appears to be a man. *Father* is a man. *We* are men and women here in our village. Humans. Those wolfish beasts are not men––they're monsters––demons sent to plague us.

"If you want to survive," the wolf shifter continues, addressing the two remaining claimed who stare at him with horrified expressions, "you will follow those rules as if your life depends on it. Because it does." He points to the rest of us across the field. "And so do theirs. Do not forget that your friends and family get to live because of our protection. We could just as easily take all of you as slaves or leave you to the lycans." He smiles sickly as his bronzed skin gleams under the stark light and his shaggy black hair whips in the wind. "But we're far too generous for that."

His companions chuckle.

Hate burns me alive from the inside out. All I want is to destroy him, to kill this disgusting *thing* and every other *thing* like him.

One day, I will.

They're different from the grotesque lycans: they have a pack, they can change at will, they're born *wolf shifters*––not humans infected with a virus that turns them mad at the full moon like the lycanthropes. But to me, they're just as bad as the lycans. Maybe they're even worse.

Things used to be so different before the wars.

Monsters used to hide in the shadows while humans controlled everything, and from the stories, life was good. But then the monsters got tired of hiding––that's when the wars started, and everything changed. There are many whisperings of what happened, of why all of the supernaturals died but shifters didn't, of how lycans came to be, but those are just stories to us now. We don't know what's real and what's not. Maybe too much time has passed, and nobody knows the truth anymore. Or maybe it's like what my father says, that the victors get to choose how history is written.

And that certainly wasn't us humans.

"Now, who are the parents of this defiant little waste of flesh?" The shifter kicks at Willow's slumped body and strolls over to her decapitated head, frowning down on it. "Too bad. She was rather pretty."

My tears have dried under all this fiery hate, and all I can see is red.

Red blood.

Red hate.

Mr. Fernsby shuffles away from where he's been blocking Mama and me. So much for neighborly love and support. Everyone turns to stare at us, their heavy gazes mixed with accusation, fear, and pity.

Mama grips my hand so tightly I might scream. "No," she whispers. "No, no, no, no."

Our village is small—only twenty families—and as long as I have been alive, this has never happened. The firstborn goes to the wolf shifters, and the rest of us work the fields and try to find meaning in our simple lives. I have no idea what happens if a firstborn dies on the day of her claiming.

"Mama, what's going on?"

The wolfman stalks toward us. I can practically hear his heavy feet pounding the dry earth. His bare chest is streaked with blood and dirt, and his muscles ripple with the clenching of his fists.

Mama tightens her grip on my arm. "If the firstborn daughter dies before she is claimed, then the second-born must take her place." Her voice sounds hollow.

A lump forms in my throat, but before I can let a scream loose, the man stands before us, breathing hard. His chest glistens with sweat and the red sheen of my sister's blood. He stares down at my mother. "Your daughter defied me and denied us a claim. What was her name?"

"Willow." Her voice is strong, and I don't know how she could fake that.

His lips thin. "Hmm, pretty name. And who is your second-born?"

"Poppy, my lord." Mama pushes me forward an inch. The wolfman leans down and sniffs my neck. I shiver.

"She smells of age. How is that possible?"

She looks around for a minute, as if willing the others to save us. But nobody says a word. Who would dare?

"Twins, my lord." She closes her eyes for a moment, holding back tears. When she opens them again, she's emotionless, and not one single tear falls. It sends a shiver of warning down my spine.

I look up at the man, hating him even more. An evil smile twists his lips. "How fortunate for us." He shoves his face right in mine, his ice-blue eyes studying me like a map. "Your mother knows how to be respectful to us. Do you?"

I take a small step back and mutter, "Yes."

"Yes, my lord," Mama hisses next to me. Her tone feels like a slap.

The man just stares, and I clear my throat. "Yes, my lord," I say louder than before. My heart is drumming against my ribcage, but from fear or anger or shock, I still don't know.

"Good. Then we won't have to kill two of you today."

He grips my arm, nails sharp as claws, and drags me away from Mama. I cry out and reach for her, but she gives a quick shake of her head. If I want to keep my life and protect what's left of our family, I have to go without a fight. I understand, and I don't even blame her though it feels like a betrayal, but I'm still not prepared for this.

My sister had been attending classes for nearly a year with the other claimed from our village and the villages around us. They were taught how to behave around the wolves, the names of their leaders, and the nuances of shifter culture. I am going in blind. Willow never told me what she learned, and I never asked. It's not that I didn't care. It was just that I didn't want to be reminded that she was leaving me or to think about Knox anymore.

The man dumps me next to Charlotte McKenzie. She's beautiful with her long golden hair braided intricately down her back, her cheeks and lips painted rosy pink, and her virginal white cotton dress perfectly pressed. She and I aren't friends, never have been. She liked Knox, and he liked me, so naturally, she hated me. But she reaches for my hand--I'm no longer her enemy.

Today we are in this together.

Chapter Two

They must really like blondes. There are sixteen wolfmen here, ranging in age from older teenagers to adults, and they all stare at Charlotte like she's a juicy meal and they want to be the first to the table. Growing up, her golden hair and rosy complexion made her stand out in our village. She always loved the attention, which was one of the qualities that bothered me most about her. Today, however, her confidence is crumbling under their hunger.

I whisper in her ear. "Do you know what comes next?"

"Silence," the same male who killed Willow barks at me. He's at least fifteen feet away from our walking line. Is his hearing really so good that he could hear my question? Or maybe he just knew I'd spoken. "We will complete the Harvest Moon Ritual by nightfall, and then we'll show you all to your new home."

So he did hear me.

I blink away the tears. It hits me that I'll never see my real home again. I didn't even get to say goodbye. Papa and Evan will be absolutely devastated by the news, and there's nothing I can do to comfort them.

I don't know how long we've been walking. An hour? More? My mind is clearing from the cloud of shock, and all I can think about is everything I've lost.

I open my mouth to ask another question, but Charlotte stops me with the squeeze of her hand and the widening of her eyes. She shakes her head, and images of Willow's decapitation rip through my mind. I can still smell the copper of her blood; I don't know if I'll ever forget it.

I don't speak again.

We walk for what feels like hours, Charlotte and I still gripping each other's hands for stability. The sun rises high in the sky and burns my cheeks, but I can't be bothered to care. My muscles ache. I'm not dressed up like the other women. I'm in brown canvas farming trousers and a button-up shirt used for field work. Our village is harvesting the last of the cotton for the season, and normally, I would be joining the others to work in the fields. In a few weeks, we'd be sitting about in groups and chatting and singing songs while spinning the cotton into fabric. It's hard labor, but it's all I know. What will become of me now?

Eight villages surround the wolf city, and ours is only the second to have been claimed for the day. We're one of the smallest villages, so we have to work extra hard to keep up with the cotton harvest. I don't mind. It's better than this endless walking. We go from village to village, and I always turn away, desperately trying not to listen to the muffled crying as the claimed join our group. By the sixth village, I'm numb inside and out. I'm not holding Charlotte's hand anymore, either. I don't even know when that fell away.

Our walking group has grown. Now there are nineteen of us, fifteen women and four men. Only two more claimings to go––the textile village and the distillery.

Every village has a purpose, from farming to making clothes to raising livestock. Our village grows the cotton and makes the fabric, sending it on to the textile village where they dye it and fashion it into clothing. We share with each other and take care of ourselves despite most of what we produce getting handed over to the wolves. Though, that isn't as bad as losing firstborn daughters or those few oldest sons to them. We do it because the shifters protect us from the lycanthropes who rove the wilds. As bad as the wolf shifters are, at least, they haven't succumbed to a virus that's made the lycans beholden to the moon phases. Lycans will decimate an entire village during one full moon night if given the chance.

It's a steep price to pay but better than losing our entire population in a night. The claiming always takes place during the day of the harvest moon in September. Rumor has it that one time, when I was too young to remember, the textile village had a family who refused to hand over their oldest daughter. As punishment, the shifters did not protect them, and the next day, all but two families in that village had been slaughtered by the lycans.

No one has refused since.

We wait on the outskirts of that textile village now. It's still very small since they lost most of their people years ago, and most of the population is made up of young married couples from the surrounding villages who were trained to make clothes, so they rarely have a child of age to send. I'm a little surprised we stopped, actually. I've been bringing fabric here for years with Papa and don't remember seeing anyone my age.

The men pass around a skein full of water, and we all drink. Charlotte and I haven't left one another's side. More women have joined us like we've all gravitated toward each other, same as lambs do. The men then take out a bag and hand us each an apple, a dry roll, and a chunk of cheese. I guess they don't want us passing out on the way to the city——how thoughtful. I can't help but roll my eyes.

"Do you know their names?" I whisper to Charlotte. We both turn to study our jailers. I hate them all for what they did to Willow, but I'd like to put a name to the one I hate the most, the middle-aged looking one with the bronzed skin and dark hair, who thought he could grope my sister and then kill her for having enough self-respect to slap him.

Charlotte swallows a bite of her apple and locks eyes with him. He nods at her, and she wipes her palms on her dress between bites. "We learned about some of them during our classes. The one in charge is Anders. He's a beta and the alpha's second in command." She jerks her head toward the one who's been paying the most attention to her, his silver eyes never straying from her for long. He's attractive——with dirty blonde hair and a summer tan, and he's younger than the other men here, maybe no older than us. "His name is Grady, and he's also a beta. He's in charge of defense around the villages and is third in command. The rest I don't know."

We finish our meal in silence with the men all still staring at Charlotte's honey blonde hair. That's when they're not staring at the rest of us. I can't stand their attention even if it's fleeting, so I keep my eyes on the dusty ground.

Anders returns a few moments later with a girl who definitely did not dress up for the occasion. She wears a ripped black t-shirt that is so short it doesn't even cover her stomach and denim shorts that are cut off at mid-thigh. Her dark hair is cut severely short, and it looks like it's been hacked off with a kitchen knife. Charlotte sucks in a breath, and I know what she's thinking. While the claimed men have to razor their hair as short as possible, the claimed women aren't allowed to cut their hair shorter than the bottom of their shoulder blades.

This girl must've cut hers last night. I'm surprised she's still alive.

I like her already.

Anders shoves her in line right in front of me. I glance at the rest of the men and see that Grady's expression has changed from a persistent scowl to one of utter shock. Anders brings his hand to a section of the girl's hair and gives a hard yank. "You'll pay for this in the city. If we hadn't already lost one today, you'd be dead."

"Better dead than a slave to you." Then, she spits in his face. Anders is not having a good day. No one moves for a moment. Fur ripples across Anders's arms, and before I know what's happening, Grady is there, shoving Anders hard in the chest.

Anders growls. A flash of a wolf face comes and then goes.

"She's mine," Grady yells. "No one touches her." He crosses his arms and glares at the rest of the wolfmen.

"I belong to no man." The girl scowls at Grady. "Especially not an animal like you."

But Anders immediately relaxes and ignores the girl. Then, he guffaws, and I'm completely stunned. I thought for sure I was going to see a repeat of Willow's death. Why had no one stood up for Willow, but this girl is still alive? Guilt barbs deep because it should've been me who helped my sister. Anders doubles over in laughter, but no one else seems to understand the humor. He pulls himself together and places a hand on Grady's shoulder. Grady hasn't moved from his spot. "You have fun with that one." He walks back up to the front of the line. "Moving out," he calls.

Grady grips the girl by the upper arm and drags her out of the line despite her kicking at him. He eventually picks her up and carries her on his back like she weighs nothing. I have no idea what just happened, and I want to ask Charlotte, but I know I'll get into trouble if I do. Somehow, I don't think any of these men will care to save me. I'm not uniquely beautiful like Charlotte, nor am I dressed to enhance my femininity like so many here. I don't have a resilient spirit like the girl Grady has taken a liking to, and there's nothing about me that shines as she does. I was never supposed to be claimed, and maybe that makes me less worthy than the others. But why should I care? None of this is right, anyway.

My feet are achy, and my head is heavy as we head to the last village, the distillery. It's the only village that we don't have a lot of regular connections with. It's the largest in the area––fifty families. They have the most wealth and nearly all the amenities that the wolf city is rumored to have. Papa always told me to never go near the distillery boys when they came to our village to trade goods. The boys from other villages would attend our dances so the young people could court, but I was never allowed to dance with the ones from this place. And when we arrive in the village square where they apparently do their claiming, I think I understand why.

Their girls are nothing like our girls.

There are six of them. It's a lot. They're not dressed in long cotton dresses like the rest of us--or, in my case, ugly trousers. These women are proudly showing off their skin with short and tight outfits that I've never seen the likes of before. Some appear to be made of leather and others the sheerest cotton that leaves nothing to the imagination. How did they even get such clothes? I blush and look away. Every girl at this claiming proudly displays her cleavage and has painted her face with more rouge and charcoal than I've ever seen on a single person.

And none of them are crying. Not one.

In fact, their expressions are smug, like going to the wolf city is the best thing that's ever going to happen to them. But the two claimed men from this village look just as dejected as the rest of us, with their downcast eyes and slumped shoulders.

What do the women of the distillery know that I don't?

Chapter Three

We round a bend, and the wolf city appears on the horizon. I'm a bit underwhelmed. Not that I was looking forward to it or anything, but the way Papa described the cities, I always thought they would have large, looming buildings. This one doesn't. It's shoved full of buildings, but aside from a few spires, they all appear short and squat.

We stop at the edge of the river. There is a large bridge, but it's got a gaping hole right in the middle of it. I wonder how we are going to manage to cross it safely. An image of myself falling through crumbling concrete and into the rushing water flashes through my mind, and I forget to breathe. Fortunately, we sit down in the tall grass to rest. The humidity wraps itself around me like a wet blanket, and I wipe the sweat from my forehead. Grady passes around the skein of water once again, and Anders disappears down the embankment.

I count the number of the claimed to distract myself from the unknown. I have no idea what's coming, and I don't want to think about it. There are twenty-eight total now, twenty-two women and six young men. Twenty-eight people who have friends and family back home, who had full lives before the claiming changed everything.

The women from the distillery village are all flirting with the wolf-men. They're laughing and touching them on the arms, acting in a way that the people of my village would find scandalous. I shiver and look away. I will never willingly touch one of these men. They are monsters. *This* is monstrous.

Anders returns. His black wavy hair hangs over one eye, and when he brushes it away, I notice a lot of the girls are watching him. He's older than most of the wolves and has at least ten years on us, probably more. There's an experienced edge to him that these women seem to find appealing. But what if I told them about what he did to Willow? Would they still look at him like a prize, or would they see him as a curse, as I do?

"The boats have arrived," he calls out. "The claimed men will follow Grady, and the women will follow me."

Devansh Patel stands as if to be first to the boat, but then he makes a run for it, heading straight toward the river. He jumps in, splashing water in an arc as he swims wildly, almost like he's trying to rescue a drowning man. Maybe he is––but it's not someone else's life he's after saving; it's his own. Where he thinks he's going, I have no clue. My heart aches as I picture his family back home. What will happen to them now that he's run from his obligation? Charlotte and I exchange worried glances.

Anders laughs. "He does realize it's a full moon tonight, right?"

Grady shrugs. "I guess he'd rather drown or be killed by lycans than be claimed by us." Then, Grady sighs, annoyed, and flashes his eyes toward the textile village woman he was carrying earlier. "Don't even think about trying the same thing."

She folds her arms over her chest and glares right back.

Grady points to one of his men. "Take care of this, please." The man tugs off his clothing and shifts into a massive gray wolf. He paws at the ground, snarls loudly, and then darts to the river's edge. He runs along the bank, faster than the water itself, until disappearing into the horizon.

I don't know how Devansh is going to die, but I'm certain his death is imminent. I look away to the boats bobbing against the shore and will my mind to think of something else. He wasn't necessarily a friend, but we still lived parallel lives. That said, I can't handle his death along with my sister's. I just can't. As selfish as it is, I force the Patel family from my mind.

"Let's go," Anders calls out to us women, and we don't dally.

Papa has a small rowboat that he sometimes takes out to catch fish on the river. I've gone with him a few times, but I get sick on boats. Willow went with him more often. She loved the water. Mama called her a fish and me a bird. Now, Willow's dead, and I'm being escorted to a cage, but at least I'm alive. My heart tightens to think of her like she was on those days we went to the river. I still can't believe that she's gone.

These boats are much larger than Papa's rowboat, and we all fit on one of them easily. A young man stands at the rear of the boat. He's way too scrawny to be a wolf. He must be one of the claimed slaves. If this is what's in store for me, I can handle this. It wouldn't be a life I choose, but I could drive a boat. It might even be more fun than growing cotton.

I let out a sigh of relief. I've been imagining all the horrors the wolf shifters could do to me, but now I realize that the claimed probably just become their servants. It wouldn't be any harder than the work we do in the cotton fields. Either way, they own us. The worst thing on this side is that I'll never get to see my family again.

A roaring sounds from the back of the boat, and we shoot off faster than I thought was possible. I cover my ears, and Charlotte laughs. "What's that noise?" I ask, speaking louder than I have all day.

"It's an engine. The cities have more technology than we do. We were taught about it, but seeing it is entirely different."

We both gape in awe as we fly down the river. We bounce on the waves, and I hold on to Charlotte's arm, certain we're all going to be flung off this thing. The sun is setting, painting the sky orange, and the city up ahead is lit with strange colored unnatural lights. The houses perch on the river, all squished together and painted bright colors. Men hang off of balconies and hoot as we pass.

If I weren't here under these circumstances, I might enjoy myself. The other girls are. One of the distillery girls has an arm looped through Anders's, and she's pointing to things on the shore while he's speaking animatedly to her. He turns his head and catches my eye. I hold his gaze, hoping he can see the hatred in my stare. He killed my sister, and someday he will pay. As if reading my thoughts and finding them entertaining, his lips curl up into a sadistic smile, and he winks.

Charlotte unhitches my arm from hers and scoots away.

Anders laughs and breaks our gaze. He slows the boat, pulling up to a dock. It's painted with a bright turquoise paint that's peeling along the edges. We climb out and line up on the shore. I'm the only girl in work pants, but maybe that's not such a bad thing. Maybe they'll give me a job that will keep me busy. I don't mind hard work. Plus, I'll need to stay busy if I'm going to survive the grief of losing my family, not to mention the entire future I had planned for myself.

Anders waves his hand at someone approaching us. My breath catches. Dread and longing swirl in my chest. I'm frozen, staring. He's the tallest young man I've ever seen, at least six-foot-five, with broad shoulders and a commanding stance. But it's not his height that stops me. It's his beauty. He is without question the most stunning boy I've ever seen, with a sculpted athletic build, piercing blue eyes, honey bronzed skin, and jet-black hair that curls down around his shoulders. As he walks past, the other wolfmen bow to him. Next to me, the girls stand taller.

"Say hello to the alpha," Anders says before bowing along with the others. "This is Prince Ryne Tremaine."

We're a chorus of breathy hellos, and I'm suddenly wishing I were dressed like the other girls or had Charlotte's blonde hair or just something, *anything*, to make me stand out. I mentally pinch myself. What is going on with me? I should hate him––I do hate him. If it weren't for his men, Willow would still be alive. If he's the alpha, then maybe that's the explanation for why I find him so attractive, for why I want him to notice me so much––surely an alpha is born with a natural presence. But it doesn't matter because Mama always said it's what's on the inside that counts, and I can guarantee that whatever is inside this creature is rotten. I need to stay far, far away from him.

His eyes survey us, unreadable, until they catch on mine and grow curious, then hateful, and then . . . He turns on his heel and storms away.

Anders chuckles. "Sorry, ladies, he must not like the looks of this year's claimed." His eyes roam over us and lock with mine. My chest burns. I don't know when, and I don't know how, but he will pay for what he did to Willow. A slow, creepy grin slides over his lips, and he winks at me. "I do though. Perhaps I'll choose my mate from one of you." His eyes never leave mine. Titters come from the distillery girls, and I break his gaze. All of the girls are glaring at me like I killed their cat. I drop my eyes to stare at my scuffed boots.

"What's he talking about?" I hiss to Charlotte.

"I have no idea," she whispers back.

A vehicle pulls up with a long flatbed trailer behind it. "Up you go," Anders says, and the men corral us up on the trailer. I wish I had some clue as to what was going on, but nothing makes sense. At least we don't have to walk anymore. Anders and his men sit on the edges of the trailer, and all of us girls congregate in the middle.

The distillery girls fluff each other's hair and yank down their shirts so even more of their cleavage shows. One tries to sit next to Anders, but he shoos her back to the rest of us. The ride is rough, and Charlotte and I cling together so we don't tumble over. Darkness has fallen, but lights line the street. A few men walk along the edges of the road, but it's mostly empty.

Up ahead I see more lights and crowds. There are far more people here than in my village. More bodies in a single spot than I could've ever imagined. Charlotte grips my hand tightly. She's been hot and cold with me all day, but I don't mind. At least I'm not the only one who doesn't know what's going on. We turn a corner and are met with music blaring and lights strobing. I've never seen anything like it. I wonder at the bright lights but have to cover my ears to the unnaturally loud thumping music. The truck drives slowly down the street so everyone can get a good look at us. The sidewalks are full of extremely tall, muscular men, most of whom are shirtless. They howl as we pass. I suck in a breath and catch the scent of alcohol and sweat.

Something is very wrong here.

The distillery girls all start dancing and blowing kisses, lapping up the attention. The rest of us huddle closer together, uncomfortable and afraid. A man lunges for the trailer, but Anders jumps off the side and shoves him back. "The claimed aren't for your taking. Not yet anyway."

The man growls and steps back, but his eyes linger on us, and a hungry smirk crosses his scarred face.

"What does he mean by that?" I ask Charlotte again, but I think I might know. I also think I might be sick.

My initial impression of just being servants might not be correct, and I'm nervous because these men are acting like they want our bodies. Knox and I had kissed plenty, so I have a general idea of what it means for a man and woman to be together, but I can't imagine being with one of *them*. Is that what we are?

Whores?

That's what my mother called girls who didn't have husbands and would spend their nights with different men. I'd never met one, but Mama warned me about becoming one. Especially when she saw how much time I'd been spending with Knox. "Poppy," she'd said. "That boy is claimed and will never be able to be your husband. Don't go whoring yourself out to him." Then I made the mistake of asking what whoring meant.

I never asked Mama a question about it again. Now, seeing what I might have to do, I wish I had. I can't help but wonder what Willow would think of all of this. No doubt she'd tell the distillery girls off for their behavior and challenge the wolves for engaging in whatever this is. No doubt she'd be the center of attention through it all, even more so than Charlotte. Her strawberry hair and fiery personality always made the boys crazy.

We continue down the bumpy road, coming to a halt in front of a large stage.

"Follow me," Anders calls to us, "and be careful not to get bit."

Chapter Four

"He's joking, right?" I squeak and reach for Charlotte again. This time, she rolls her eyes at me and peels herself out of my grip, rushing ahead to walk with the distillery girls. I know we weren't friends back home, but it wasn't like we were enemies either. Her rejection stings.

"Probably not joking." The girl from the textile village hooks her arm through mine. "Will you getta look at these sickos?" She grimaces at the leering men. They're all ages, from young teens to adults, and they're acting like we're the only women they've ever seen, but that can't be true.

I swallow hard. "I don't understand."

She turns with a pitying look, honey-colored eyes creasing at the corners. "What village are you from? You never heard the rumors?"

"We help grow and harvest the cotton," I say. "Northwest."

"Ah . . ." She frowns. "Well, in Southeast, let's just say we're close enough to East to see and hear a lot of things that go on between them and the wolves."

East is the official name for the distillery village. The eight villages go by the geographic location to the city, either that or what they're known for making. I always assumed we all led similar lives and only interacted with the wolves for the claiming, beyond them protecting the borders, of course.

"What goes on?" I ask, but I'm interrupted by Anders ushering us onto one side of the stage. I look away from the crowds and up into the sky.

The harvest moon hangs low above the buildings. It appears closer than I ever remember, the orange glow mesmerizing. If I were where I was supposed to be, I'd be sitting outside our modest home with my family and neighbors, missing Willow and wishing her the best. Papa would've built a fire to keep us warm while we exchange stories with our friends, who'd be trying to cheer us up after the claiming.

I look away. I can't be bothered with the moon tonight. I'll never look at it the same way again.

Anders raises his hands and howls--actually howls. The crowd of men follows suit. It's so deafening I have to cover my ears again. The alpha strides onto the stage, and my eyes lock on his face. He's smiling, and it feels like the first time I've ever seen a boy smile. Ryne, his name is Ryne--it dances around my head like lightning bugs in summertime. But then I remember what he is, and I can hardly think of him as a boy, let alone as someone I should be attracted to.

"Welcome to the harvest!" he bellows over the crowd. Their howls transform to cheers. The buzz of anticipation is so intense I can hardly breathe.

The textile girl tightens her grip on my arm and ignores the crowd. "I'm Joanna, by the way. What's your name?"

"Poppy."

The howling stops, and everything goes silent. I can practically hear my heart thundering in my chest. I wonder...can the monsters hear it too?

"The harvest is always a favorite time of year for the pack," the alpha continues. "Are you ready to see who your new girls will be?"

Another howl from the men, and I swallow. I don't like the looks of this at all. I drop my eyes so I don't have to see the crowd. We're hidden on the back of the stage, but I have a feeling we'll be thrust front and center before too long. What comes after that is anyone's guess.

"Ladies," he calls, and I jerk my head back up. He's not pointing at us. He's waving a group of girls over from the other side of the stage.

They are dressed quite differently from us. Each wears a shimmering ball gown that is cut extra low in the chest to reveal their figures. The dresses are made from beautiful fabrics I've never seen before, certainly nothing that can be found in Northwest. These come in a rainbow of colors, and they flare out at the knees. The fabric trails each of them, actually dragging along the stage. Mother would be shocked at the wastefulness. There are nine women in total, and with the exception of different colored hair, they all look so similar from where I'm standing.

They stop near the front of their stage, shoulders arched gracefully. I can't see their faces, so I don't know if they are smiling.

"Four of my betas have chosen to retire this year. Come and choose your mates," the alpha says.

It's then that I notice a large group of muscled men. Some are standing on the far end of the stage, and some are down in the crowd. Anders and Grady stand with the ones on the stage. They've cleaned up and are now wearing black pants and jackets with white shirts underneath. There are so many men that they blend together in a sea of black and white.

But there are four who stand apart from the rest, four who stare at the women as if they're about to enjoy a long-awaited feast. My stomach hardens.

"Who are they?" I hiss to Joanna.

She snorts. "Don't you know anything? Those are the betas. Some of those men hope to make us their wives, though we're all going to end up as babymakers––that's for sure." I just gape at her, and she rolls her eyes, continuing on. "Listen up, there are one hundred betas in all. When they retire from leading lower ranked wolves, they take on an advisory role and get to choose a wife."

"Babymakers?" I'm still caught on that word.

"Yep. But trust me, it's better for us to be married off to a beta than not being chosen at all." She looks out to the other men in the crowd, the ones who aren't dressed up, and scowls.

"Make your selections," the alpha bellows.

Four of the men each choose a girl by pulling her into his arms and kissing her deeply. The crowd loves it. When the couples are finished, the men take their mates and disappear. Five girls are left. One of them falls to her knees and breaks out in sobs. An older woman rushes forward, peeling the crying girl off the floor. I catch a look at her face and gasp. I know her. She's Julia, a girl from my village. She went through the claiming last year when Knox was taken. Our eyes meet, and she screams out, "Get away while you still can, Poppy!"

That does it. Anders is there in an instant, striking her down. Blood arcs across the stage. She sobs even harder, her mouth now dripping with blood, as the older woman ushers her and the other girls away.

"They will be at the mating houses by midnight." The alpha continues speaking to the crowd as if all this is completely normal. "And you lot won't have to wait any longer."

More howls.

Bile rises in my throat, and my stomach clenches. I'm horrified by what is happening even though I don't fully understand what it is. A blinding spotlight shines on us, and I flinch.

The alpha waves his hand toward us. "I'm pleased to introduce the new crop from this year. We've had our most fruitful season yet. Wouldn't you agree?"

Ryne just called us crops, and now I definitely don't like him. I glare his way as we're pushed out onto the center of the stage. He doesn't even notice.

"Betas, who wants to claim their bride from this group?"

The distillery girls smile and wave at the remaining men in suits. Charlotte is now among them. She's pulled her dress down lower too. Joanna snorts. "Fools."

Grady steps forward immediately and gives Joanna a hearty smile and a wink.

"I think he likes you," I whisper.

"He said we're fated, but he's delusional. I'm going to escape before he can get his hands on me."

"Escape?"

"Yep. You wanna come with?"

Hope burns in my heart, but the image of Willow's head flashes through my mind. I have no idea what running away would look like or what would come of it. Tears sting my eyes even to imagine the idea. "I don't know," I whisper back. What would that mean for my family? And how would we even make it out of here alive, let alone survive the wilds?

Anders steps forward, his eyes heavy on me, and I shiver. I could never be with him. If that is my fate, then I will run away with Joanna, fate be damned.

Three more men step forward who were not on the journey to retrieve us.

"Five. Not bad. And we have twenty-two claimed, so don't worry, men. You'll have fresh meat soon. The Wolf Moon Festival isn't far off."

Another howl from the alpha sends the rest of the crowd into a frenzy. The sound is deafening, but something instinctual tells me not to cover my ears or let my fear show. I don't flaunt it like some of the other girls, but I stand a little taller and shoot the alpha a scowling glance.

He's looking back at me, not so angry this time, but maybe a little intrigued. He sees my expression and smiles. Part of me wants to rip that smile right off his face, and the other part can't help but wonder how he became the alpha--the other part wants to know his whole story. He looks younger than most of the betas. And he's strong and big, but he doesn't have that razor edge that Anders has, nor the cruel energy that lives among his pack.

"He's the sickest one here, you know?" Joanna hisses low. "You'd be smart to stay away from him."

"You're right. I will." My voice cracks. I want to believe her, but for some inexplicable reason, I don't.

As if he heard us, he chuckles darkly and nods once toward Joanna.

Something guttural screeches above us. I peer up at the buildings just as a flash of gray catapults from a nearby roof and onto the stage. The creature's eyes are bloodshot. Its mouth rears open to reveal teeth as long as fingers. His form hulks twice as large as anyone here as he extends up onto his hind legs.

"Lycan!" Charlotte cries seconds before it lunges toward the alpha.

<h1 style="text-align:center">Chapter Five</h1>

The alpha dodges his attacker and immediately transforms into his wolf form, letting his clothing fall in torn strips on the stage. His wolf self is nearly as tall as his human self, with sleek black fur and glowing eyes the same bright blue. He growls at the lycan––a sound so dark and haunting that I'm certain I'll remember it forever. All of the men follow their alpha and shift into their wolves. Good thing too because three more lycans crash onto the stage. The last is the biggest, and the impact sends splinters of wood flying in all directions.

All the girls scream and huddle together as the battle erupts around us.

The lycans stand on hind legs and swipe their claws and teeth at the wolves. The wolves are large animals, but the lycans are something else. They're a mutation––half-human, half-wolf––and entirely grotesque. The wolves may be smaller, but they're faster and organized. They move together in quick formations, almost as if they can communicate telepathically. Perhaps they can.

I find myself on the outside of the circle of girls along with Joanna and Charlotte. Most of the distillery girls are in the middle. Many are already crying. Joanna grabs my hand. "We should run away," she hisses in my ear.

"Are you crazy? They'll kill us."

"This might be our only shot."

I shake my head. She might be right, but there was no way on earth that I was about to run away with lycans on the loose. I've always called the shifters the monsters, but the truth is staring me right in the face now. The lycanthropes are the ones who come in the middle of the night and kill humans like it's a sport, so they're the true monsters. I'll take my chances with the wolf shifters.

Joanna breaks away from us, and immediately, a lycan leaps after her. He's twice her height with dark gray fur and wicked-looking claws. He lunges, but before he can grab her, a light golden-brown wolf leaps in between them, throwing the creature off balance.

Joanna stumbles back to my side, gripping my hand as the wolf and lycan fight right in front of us. The lycan slashes at the wolf, but he's too fast. The lycan changes tactics and lunges for our group, exposing his side, and the wolf sinks his teeth into its throat, tearing the flesh away. The lycan drops to the ground, and the brown wolf positions himself right in front of Joanna. I'd bet my life that he is Grady, but I don't tell Joanna that.

"Are you okay?" I ask her.

She nods even though she has a death grip on my hand. The entire stage is shaking with the fight. Down on the ground, wolves snarl and slash at the remaining lycans. I question whether I'm going to make it out of here alive tonight, and that makes me press farther back into the group of girls. Everywhere I look, there are claws and teeth and blood. Even the crisp air smells of copper.

The stage rumbles beneath my feet, and I bring my gaze up to watch the biggest lycan break away from his fight with the alpha and charge straight for us. He jumps high and lands right on top of our group, knocking us to our backs. Girls scream, but I don't. A stillness settles over my mind, and I decide I'm *not* going to die today. I push at the rough fur, unsure of what part of his body is over me. Joanna and I break away by crawling on our hands and knees. Blood soaks into my pants, and for a second I worry that it's mine, but I don't think it is. The light brown wolf appears right next to us, his muzzle nudging Joanna along. She swats at him, but he doesn't let up. I expect him to turn back and go after the lycan, but he stays with Joanna.

A streak of black rushes toward the lycan, but before the alpha can reach him, the monster grabs one of the claimed girls and takes off with her. A smaller lycan disengages from his fight and grabs another girl who's cowering near the edge of the stage. She lets out a shrill scream, and then she's being dragged away as well. The wolves howl, and I have to cover my ears. Most of them take off after the two lycans who grabbed the girls, but the light brown wolf still stays by Joanna's side.

Silence descends on us. Compared to the cacophony from before, it's quiet enough to hear a pin drop.

No one is fighting anymore. People are bloodied and bruised. I'm certain a few of the wolves have died, but everyone on stage seems alive.

Joanna's wolf shifts back into his human form, and of course, it's Grady. I avert my eyes. He's naked.

"What the hell were you thinking?" he growls at Joanna.

She crosses her arms and smirks at him. She seems unabashed by his naked body, but several other girls stare or look away with reddened faces. "That I didn't want to be killed by a lycan. I thought I'd take my chances away from where they were fighting."

A young man brings Grady a pair of pants, and he jerks them on. "You're lucky I was here, or you'd be dead. Or worse, turned into one of them." He hovers over her, his nostrils flared. Joanna never breaks eye contact. She doesn't thank him or cower. If he's a beta and used to being in charge of a couple hundred underlings, then perhaps he's met his match in someone as stubborn and confident as Joanna.

Prince Ryne jogs over wearing simple pants that hang low on his hips. The muscles of his chest ripple under the smears of blood, dirt, and sweat. I can't seem to tear my eyes away from him. *This* is his element--war, pain, protection. What does that say about me, to be so attracted to him right now? But part of me hates him, so I try to cling to that part.

"Were any of you bitten?" It's the first question out of his mouth. I think I know why.

The boy who handed Grady his pants raises a shaky hand.

Ryne hangs his head low. "I'm so sorry, pup."

"What does that mean?" one of the girls whispers. But we all knew that a single bite from a lycan would turn you into one of them. I don't know what it will do to a shifter.

"Nobody else was bitten?" he asks. We shake our heads no. "Good. A lycan bite will turn a human," he confirms, "but it will kill a wolf. Either way, the outcome is . . . gruesome." He flinches on the last word. Emotional, not because he's afraid but because he's regretful. I'm completely mesmerized by him and once again disgusted with myself for it. Why does this keep happening to me? Remember, this man keeps traditions that caused Willow's death. He's enabled rituals that have caused us claimed girls to be standing here tonight under the full moon instead of safe at home with our families.

I knew the wolves hated the lycans as much as we did, if not more so, and now I understand why. Wolves are nearly invincible and live long lives, but if a lycan bite can kill them, then perhaps they're almost as vulnerable as humans. The wolves are mostly back in their human form now, and they seem shaken. They aren't nearly as confident as they had been before the lycans attacked.

The young boy kneels before his alpha. "Please, Prince Ryne, have mercy."

Grady hands Ryne a long, silver sword. The glint of it flashes orange under the moonlight. I've heard silver can kill the lycans, but what is he going to do with it to this young shifter? Clearly, the pup is no lycan.

He answers my question with the swing of his arm, the sword arcing toward the boy to sever his head from his body. It rolls to stop at my feet.

I scream. I scream in terror, but mostly, it's anger that shreds my throat. "How is that merciful?" I can't help the accusation bursting from my lips as I try to ignore the decapitated head. "How can you do such a thing to a child?"

Ryne strides forward and catches my face in his hands. His fingers are coated in blood, and his grip is tight, fingertips pressing into my cheeks. He's inches from my face, those blue eyes peering right down into the very depths of my soul. "That pup would've died an excruciating death akin to lethal poisoning. The lycan venom would have cooked him from the inside out and taken days to slowly eat away at his body and sanity. Now, tell me again that I wasn't merciful?"

I can't breathe. I can't blink. I can't move.

Charlotte elbows me, and I snap out of my defiance, nodding against his fingers. "No, my lord. You gave him a painless death."

"That's what I thought." He releases me and steps back, surveying the lot of us. I immediately miss his hands on my face, and it's all I can do to not reach out for him. Again, this must be some kind of draw to him being the alpha. Surely, even humans can't help but react to pack hierarchy when it's so strong like this. I quickly glance around, and the rest of the girls seem just as enthralled by Ryne as I am.

So that's it. I force myself to go back to hating the man.

There were twenty-two claimed females, and now there are twenty. The two taken by the lycans are likely already dead.

"I apologize about tonight, ladies." The alpha straightens, and his expression relaxes. "The lycans don't often make it past our guards, but sometimes accidents happen. They've managed to attack your villages in the past, have they not?"

We nod our agreement. It happens. I'm pretty sure it happens anyway, though a lycan attack hasn't been seen in my village since I've been alive. Our wolf shifter guards do their job well, or maybe our village is small enough that the lycans want a bigger target.

"You'd be wise to be alert during every full moon." He looks around at the aftermath of the battle, runs a hand through his long, disheveled hair, and then sighs. "Welcome to the Carolina Wolf Pack. You're one of us now."

Chapter Six

R yne waves Anders over. "Get them to the house as quickly as possible. Be on the lookout for any rogue lycans. We've already lost two girls tonight. I don't want to lose any more."

Anders gives a nod. "What about the dead?"

"I'll have the other betas gather them. We'll burn the bodies in the morning."

Anders heads for us. I scoot closer into the middle of the girls and find Joanna's hand. She stiffens at first but then squeezes mine back. I'm used to being close to another female because of Willow, and now that she's gone, I can't help but seek Joanna out. Grady still stands on her other side and watches her like she's made of porcelain. I don't know why he's determined to protect her, but I know that if I stay close by her side, I will be safer by association. Charlotte comes up along my other side. Her shirt is soaked with blood.

"What happened to you?" I ask.

She gapes at me. "The same thing that happened to you." She points down.

My trousers and shoes are splattered with blood as well. "Ugh, that will never come out."

Charlotte loops her arm through mine. "It doesn't matter. They will give us all new clothes anyway."

She's been so fickle with me today, but I don't have the energy to care.

"How do you know that?" Clothing takes a lot of time and work.

We're supplied with it in exchange for growing the cotton and turning it into fabric, but even then, we only get three new outfits a year.

"We were to bring nothing with us but the clothes on our back." She rolls her eyes. "They told us at the claiming meetings."

Well, I wasn't at the claiming meetings, and Charlotte knows exactly why. Maybe she's not really interested in being my friend, or maybe she's not thinking and wouldn't deliberately try to hurt my feelings. I decide to give her the benefit of the doubt and let it go.

We shuffle off the stage and back to the trailer we rode on. Will I be considered ignorant because I did not attend any of the meetings? I know nothing that I'm supposed to. I should've been a better sister and talked to Willow about what went on in those meetings. I know she'd have told me everything I wanted to know, even if she wasn't supposed to. We never kept secrets. My heart aches to know she died with all of my secrets hidden away inside her. So many are lost now--years and years of memories--just gone.

The trailer rumbles down the cobblestone streets. The sidewalks are empty now, and I stare at the houses as we pass. They are all different colors, three or four stories high, long and narrow. Most have lights on in the windows, but the curtains are drawn. I still can't believe they can light up like that. I've heard of electricity, but we don't have it back home. I feel like I've stepped into an entirely different world.

I wonder which house will become ours and if we will stay together. I may not know Joanna very well, but I like her better than any of the other girls, and maybe next time there's a chance, I'll have the courage to run off with her. Even as I think it, I worry I'm not brave enough. That was always Willow's job.

The trailer stops near the water, away from all the houses, and I spot the boat from before. I groan. "Not another boat ride."

"It's the fastest and safest way," Grady replies. "Don't worry. You'll get used to them." For the first time, I wonder what Grady's underling did with Devansh Patel, assuming they caught him. Maybe Devansh got away and won't have to be a claimed boy after all. Knox's pretty face pops into my mind, and I push it back down into the mental box I've used to lock away that particular heartbreak.

We all scramble onto the boat; it roars to life and flies up the river this time. The moon is so high in the sky, so bright that I can hardly see the stars. It casts yellow light on the many houses and buildings along the river, but as we get farther away from the city, the houses get farther and farther apart. I can't help but keep a look out for lycans. What if there are more out there, hunting us right now? I tuck my arms tight against my body and try not to shiver.

We come around a corner, and I spot a massive, brick plantation home. There are a couple of these back in the village, but nobody lives in them. They're used for meeting spaces. I've always wondered what it must have been like years ago when they were used as homes. I never thought I would get to live in one myself, and given the circumstances, I wish I wasn't about to find out.

Smoke curls out of its many chimneys, and soft light glows from every window. The boat slows and heads for the dock near the house. A rusted sign with moss growing along the edge has words written across it, but I can't read it.

"Drayton Hall," Joanna says in a whisper.

Charlotte turns on her with a little gasp, "You can read?"

Joanna sighs. "I guess mine is one of the only villages left that still cares about education, but I suppose I shouldn't be surprised."

Charlotte huffs and glares at her. "We've never had anyone who could read to even teach us, so get off your high horse." She gives me a little look like she wants me to get mad at Joanna too, but I hold my hands up. I'm not getting between these two.

"Typical." Charlotte pushes past me to join the distillery girls. That just may have been my last chance to befriend her. But honestly, if it wasn't going to happen during the eighteen years we lived in the same village, it wasn't likely to happen today just because we've been thrown into a traumatizing situation together. I smile at Joanna and hope she doesn't ditch me. I've never *not* had someone.

"This place." Joanna nods to the house and whispers, "it has a dark history. Do you believe in ghosts?"

I roll my eyes. "No. Do you?"

"No, but if I did, I'd definitely think this place was haunted. Do you know about what the humans used to do here hundreds of years ago?"

I shake my head.

"They kept slaves," she whispers.

A haunting chill creeps through my awareness as Anders leads us to the front of the three-story square house. It's a dark red brick with four gleaming white columns up the front. Two identical staircases lead up to the front porch, and we climb them without slowing. Anders knocks on the door while we stand huddled together on the checkered flooring. I stare at my work boots. The tips are covered in mud and blood and will surely make a mess in a place like this. The massive home is made from different materials than I'm used to back home. Out in our village, we live in little three-room houses. We don't have running water or electricity. We do our cooking over fires, not that we have a lot of meat. It's mostly boiling vegetables. We get our water from a well. We trade with the villages for bread and other necessities. Living in Northwest, we never had anything like this. Life was simple, but at least we were safe.

The door opens, and I immediately recognize the woman standing in the doorway as the same one who had escorted last year's girls onto the stage before us earlier tonight.

"Hello, ladies!" She beams at us as if our horrible night hadn't even happened. "Please, come in! It's getting cold out there."

We shuffle into the entry room. Same as outside, this room has two intricately carved staircases on either side that lead up to the higher levels. The floor in here is polished wood and gleaming without a speck of dirt. The walls are painted a soft greenish-blue, and the ceiling is white with carved detailing unlike anything I've seen. It's stunning.

"You must be exhausted." She claps her hands, and a couple of other older women appear. "Please take the claimed to their sleeping quarters," she tells them and then levels us with a knowing look. "You've had a big day. It's going to be hard, but please do try to get some rest. Tomorrow, we start your training."

"Training for what?" Joanna juts out her hip in challenge.

Grady chuckles low. Her insolence only seems to make him like her even more. I'll admit I like it too. It makes me feel stronger to be next to her.

The woman isn't fazed one bit by Joanna's outburst. "What's your name, dear?"

"Joanna." The girl is fearless.

"Ah, our one claimed from the textile village of Southeast. It's nice to meet you." Joanna says nothing, and the woman continues. "Well, Joanna, what do you think the word claimed means?"

"That the patriarchal wolf society has enslaved women into forced breeding."

The room falls into a hushed silence. I don't know what that word means, patriarchal, but from Joanna's tone, it can't be good.

Anders rushes forward, his arm outstretched to strike Joanna down, but Grady pummels him to the ground. We scream and scatter out of the way. Not Joanna though. She doesn't move a muscle. "Well," she huffs. "Am I wrong?"

The older woman does the opposite of what I expect. She smiles. "You're not wrong."

Anders growls, shifting right there in the middle of the crowded room. I press my back against the wall. The older woman throws open the door and yells, "Get out! There is no shifting allowed in this house."

Anders snarls at her but leaves. Grady stands, wiping blood from his chin and leveling Joanna with a look. "I won't always be here to protect you, mate."

She glowers. "I'm not your mate. Now leave, and join the rest of your dogs!"

The energy is so intense I can practically taste it. Grady shakes his head, chuckling again, and leaves.

The older woman tuts heavily and brushes her hands along her skirt like this is all normal in her world. Maybe it is. "You can call me Madame Delphine. I was planning to discuss this tomorrow, but Joanna is correct. You are here to mate with the wolves."

My mind races to put all the puzzle pieces together. I should've known—there were so many clues—but the shock still hits me hard. "Why?" I squeak out.

The distillery girls laugh.

Delphine catches my gaze and holds it. "What's your name, honey?"

I can't tell if she's normally this warm or if this is a trick. "Poppy."

"Well, Poppy, have you noticed any female wolf shifters since arriving in the city?"

My mind combs through the events of the day. "No."

"That's because the wolf shifter genes predominantly produce male offspring. Only one in a hundred shifter children are born female. That's a problem for them, don't you think?"

I nod, my face growing hot.

"And so, you, Poppy––and all of you––are here to be the solution. The sooner you accept that, the better."

"And if we don't accept it?" Joanna snaps, her eyes narrowed in challenge.

"Then you die."

Chapter Seven

The room is so quiet that I can hear the clock in the corner ticking away. Delphine takes a deep breath. "Well, ladies, I think that's enough for tonight. Vivien and Lucille will take you to your rooms. They will also instruct you on what to wear and where to meet in the morning."

Vivien and Lucille are like copies of Delphine, all middle-aged women with slightly graying hair tied back in a bun and donning puffy maroon dresses with white lace stitched around the collars. I start for the left staircase, the other girls all following.

"Poppy, could you stay behind, please?" Delphine instructs.

A nervous tension coils in my stomach. "Sure."

Joanna stands at my side. "Do you want me to stay with you?"

"You will join the other girls, Joanna. You have nothing to fear from me. I am no wolf."

Joanna sniffs. "No, just the mother of the most high."

I have no idea what she means, but Delphine glares at her. "Go on upstairs. I'll send Poppy up in a few minutes."

Joanna gives my hand a squeeze, then barrels up the stairs after everyone else. I look down at my dirty boots because even though this woman isn't a shifter, she still makes me nervous. I've ruined her perfectly mopped floor.

She sets a hand on my shoulder. "I was given a list of all the girls who were coming, and your name wasn't on it."

I swallow. "I know. My sister Willow was supposed to come."

"And why didn't she?"

"She slapped Anders after he . . . after he . . . touched her inappropriately."

"I see. And so he killed her?" She says it like it's the natural response to being slapped, like there's no surprise my sister was killed.

"Yes." I bite back the words I want to say, things about justice and decency. I don't know that I can trust this woman. I probably can't.

"Your sister and you were twins?"

I jerk my head up. "How did you know that?"

"Because otherwise, you wouldn't have been of age." I catch a regretful expression on her face before she turns and starts up the stairs, lifting her long skirts so she doesn't trip over them. "Come. I will show you to your room."

I follow her, my steps in my clunky boots so much louder than hers.

"Were you and your sister identical?"

"No. Not at all."

"So you are not the same size?"

"She was six inches shorter than me and had a much larger chest."

She was curvy and beautiful, looking like a woman years before I even sprouted breasts. I didn't mind though. I've never cared for unwanted attention. Besides, most of the boys in our village wanted Charlotte.

Except Knox. I hope I get to see him soon even though I know it will be torture. I hope he's okay, that he's alive and doing well in his new role here, whatever it is. What will he say? What will I do? I swallow and push my first love from my mind. It's a lost cause, really. This city is huge, and Knox is one insignificant claimed man.

Madame Delphine continues. "Well, then we are going to have to find you some different clothes because everything we had made was in her size. I'm sure we've got something that will work. I'll have Lucille take your measurements before you go to bed. Now, tomorrow you will wear a black tank top, shorts, white socks, and sneakers. Meet out on the lawn at six. We do physical fitness for an hour every morning. Then you will shower and change into your uniform. It is the black, fitted dress. You will wear stockings and heels."

I wring my hands together, trying not to panic. I've seen heels in old magazines and on the girls who were on the stage, but I'd never worn a pair myself. Willow and I used to laugh at the absurdity of them. Who can walk in those? I'm certain I'll twist my ankle within minutes of putting them on.

We hit the top of the stairs and enter a massive room with squishy couches and several low tables. Shelves filled with books line the front and side walls, and the back wall has wide doors that look like they open onto a porch.

I stroll over to the books and run my fingers along the spines. Maybe Joanna can read some to me. I've never really cared that I couldn't read before, but now I feel as if I've missed something important.

"This is the claimed's sitting room. There are four bedrooms on this floor and four up in the attic. You sleep two to a room. As there are a lot of you this year, the east room on this floor will sleep four. We had a room set up in the basement for two more, but I understand we lost two to the lycans, so we will not have to use that room. You are lucky enough to only have one roommate. Yours is the west chamber on this floor." She points to a door near the porch. "Between you and me, that's the best room." She winks. "Go on in. I'll send Lucille up in a few moments for your measurements, so don't fall asleep just yet."

I stare at the door. There are two small signs with names scrawled on them. One says Charlotte and the other Willow. I squeeze my eyes to fight back the tears.

She's really dead.

And I'm really about to become a shifter babymaker.

"Madame Delphine?" I ask the question before I talk myself out of it. "Those women you were with earlier tonight, last year's claimed, were they living here before us?"

"Yes, dear. It was their year, just as I was in my time many moons ago. And now it is your time. This is the way of things..." Her voice trails off as if in thought, as if she wants to add something else, but then she turns and walks away.

With a deep breath, I push open the door and find Charlotte inside. Her back is to me as she changes into pajamas. She glares at me over her bare shoulder. "A little privacy, please?"

I can't help but snort as I turn to face the wall. "You didn't seem concerned about privacy when you pulled your bodice down to show off your cleavage to the betas."

She laughs bitterly. "Judging me now will only make you a hypocrite later." She brushes past me. Our room has lavender paper fastened to the walls, two small white beds piled high with cotton bedding, a small chest of drawers at the end of each, and a closet where Charlotte is busy flipping through a rainbow of dresses. "I'm going to do whatever I have to in order to survive this place and make it tolerable," she huffs. "Trust me, Poppy, you're going to be right alongside me soon enough."

The scary thing is she might be right.

I take the bed that Charlotte has left for me and open the drawers, finding my own sets of pajamas waiting. The next drawer contains the neatly folded exercise clothes I'm to wear tomorrow morning. Considering how late it must be, that's going to come fast.

A knock thumps on the door, and both Charlotte and I jump. Lucille pokes her head in. "I've come to get your measurements."

She holds up a long wide string with marks on it. She uses it to find the length of my legs, how wide my hips are, and the size of my chest. She marks them all down in a tiny notebook. Not only does she know how to read, but she can write as well. I find it fascinating, and suddenly, I *do* want to learn to read. She takes a few more measurements, and I study as she scratches out each number. I know the numbers, but the letters mean nothing.

"I'll have a uniform for you after physical fitness. Your shorts have a drawstring in them, so they should work even if they aren't the right size. Goodnight, ladies."

She exits the room, and I peer up at the light affixed to the ceiling. I have no idea how to turn it off. It glows a soft yellow, but if I look at it for too long, my eyes start to water.

"Get into your pajamas, and let's go to bed," Charlotte says. "I need to get my beauty rest."

I'm still staring at the light. "But how do we turn it off?" I'm not even sure if we can. The thought of trying to sleep in blinding unnatural light sends a wave of exhaustion rolling over me.

Charlotte rolls her eyes but smiles ruefully. "Madame Vivien showed us how to do it." She walks over to the wall and points to a little white switch. She flicks it, and the room goes instantly dark. It catches me so off guard that I squeal, then giggle, and then Charlotte turns it back on, and I have to give it a try for myself.

A few minutes later, I tire of the electricity enough to change into my pajamas and fall into the bed. I don't think I've ever lived a longer day in my entire life. The darkness is the only familiar thing about this place and I hate it. Charlotte even breathes differently than Willow did. The events of the day catch up to me, replaying themselves over and over in my mind until I eventually drift away into nightmares of lycans and shifters and blood and death and the two bluest eyes that I've ever seen.

Chapter Eight

"My shirt is so much looser than yours," I complain to Charlotte as I pull the drawstring tight on the shorts.

She shrugs. Her clothes fit her perfectly, but my tank top hangs low, and my shorts are so short I can feel a breeze on my cheeks.

"I look ridiculous," I say.

"You do," she agrees with a triumphant smirk, the kind that lets me know, in no uncertain terms, that we are *not* friends. Why did I have to room with her and not Joanna?

Charlotte and I are the last ones out the back door. The field behind the house is vast and dotted with massive oaks reaching out with their gnarled limbs. We had an oak in the middle of our village square. The kids all loved to play on it. Willow and I used to sneak out at night and climb as high as we could. It was there that we shared our hopes and fears. She was scared of what would become of her when she was claimed, and I was scared of what would happen to me when she was gone.

Now, I know how foolish we were to act as if we had any control over our fates.

I spot Joanna and make a beeline for her, leaving Charlotte behind. The distillery girls snicker as I pass, but I ignore them.

Joanna stares at my legs. "Dang, girl, what happened to your shorts?"

"It was my sister who was supposed to be here, not me. She's short."

"And had boobs." She knocks her finger into the armhole of my shirt and gives a tug. "Here, let me fix this for you." She pulls the drawstring out of her shorts––because they fit fine without it––and uses it to bunch my shirt in the back and tie it up. "There. Now none of us can see your bra. Can't help the butt cheeks though."

I tug on my shorts, but it doesn't do anything. "Thanks for helping me with the shirt. My entire wardrobe is pretty much useless."

She points to herself. "Hey, I'm from the textile village, remember? I am good at altering clothing. I can help you, but we'll have to ask for some supplies."

Relief sweeps through me. "Thank you."

"No problem."

Well, Charlotte may be out, but at least I have Joanna. "How's your roommate?" I ask her.

She sniffs. "Her name is Faye, and she's a distillery girl. I hate her."

I'm grateful Charlotte is not one of them, but from the way she's been kissing up to them, I'm not sure if it would've made a difference. She's practically one of them now. She's currently standing in their little huddle, sending dagger-gazes toward Joanna and me. What did we do to them? Nothing. But it doesn't matter.

My heart sinks a little. This place is going to be rough.

Madame Vivien jogs out in front of us. She's short and athletic with silvery-ginger hair tied back in a ponytail and wearing almost the exact same thing as the rest of us instead of that puffy maroon dress the other house mothers wear. In spite of her age, she's incredibly fit and toned. So are most of the women from my village back home, but she doesn't have the hardness around the edges like they do. I bet her hands are soft as butter.

"Welcome, ladies. I hope you all had a pleasant sleep. I know you had a late night, so I'll go easy on you today, but know that this will not always be the case. We're going to stretch and then jog around the field."

We spread out and all follow along with her stretching. Then Joanna and I set a pace in the middle of the group as we run. The morning air is heavy with humidity but not hot yet, so it's not too bad. Joanna and I chat about our families as we run.

We reach the house and pass it. "One more lap, ladies," Madame Vivien calls after us. We pass a few distillery girls that were behind us before.

Joanna snorts. "Looks like they've never run before in their lives."

"They probably haven't." Joanna and I both spent our days doing manual labor. I worked in the cotton fields, and she would've been assigned to churn swaths of fabric in giant vats of water and dye. Compared to that, this run is nothing.

We approach the house again, and I slow. Madame Delphine stands on the front steps, but this time, she's not alone. Ryne is with her. His head is dipped low, and he smiles at something she says. It's the first time I've seen him smile in the daylight, and it's beautiful. My stomach flutters––maybe I've taken the sun for granted all my life.

Joanna hits me. "I know he's hot, but stop gawking."

I drop my eyes, my face heating as we approach Madame Vivien. A few of the girls are already there, but many are still far out in the field. I sit on the ground and stretch out my legs. Joanna crouches next to me. "Don't look, but he's staring at you."

I quickly glance up under my eyelashes. Sure enough, it's like he's studying me. There's no anger in his eyes nor attraction––there's curiosity. "Why?" I whisper to Joanna.

She snorts. "Probably because of your shorts."

I flush and stand, moving behind her. Ryne tears his eyes away from me, kisses Madame Delphine on the cheek, and escapes back into the house.

I let out a breath. At least, I don't have to hide anymore. The rest of the girls finally return, and Madame Delphine joins Madame Vivien on the field.

Madame Delphine makes eye contact with each one of us. Did she hold my gaze a few seconds longer than everyone else's? "Good morning, ladies. Today begins your training. I know this is all new to you, and while some of you have a good idea exactly what you are training for, most of you don't. In any case, I want to clear up any misconceptions you may have." She stares at the distillery girls, and they all drop their eyes. Perhaps they aren't as well informed as I thought.

"If you are lucky, you will be with me for a year," she continues. "In that year, I will teach you all that is necessary to be a good wife and mother to shifters. You will become physically fit, learn to read, and think logically. You will learn to be obedient, subservient, and submissive to your husband." Those three words are a trigger, taking me right back to when Anders stood over Willow's body and announced them as if they were gospel. "You will learn to fight in case you must defend your young. You will be trained in the best way to care for and raise a child." She pauses for a long moment as if to drive her point home. "Our traditions go far back, encouraging the betas to enjoy young women who are well rounded and pleasant to be around, but also cultured and elegant. As a lady, you will learn softer things as well, like how to paint and sing. You will learn how to walk properly and how to groom yourselves so that the men will enjoy your appearance." She holds up a finger. "But do not mistake me. Your purity must stay intact until you are given to the wolves, whatever that may look like for you."

I grimace, knowing exactly what she's speaking of. Mama made sure I knew of holding onto my virginity when Knox and I were dating, because he wasn't going to become my husband. And she spoke of it often to Willow since purity was part of the rules for the claimed. The wolves even sent a doctor to our home to check that her virginity was intact before she came to the claiming. She wouldn't have broken her promise though, not when it would have condemned our family and ended up with her dead. Little good it did her.

Joanna crosses her arms and sniffs. "I'm going to be just the opposite," she whispers so that only I can hear her. "I'm not going to be Grady's *lady*."

Madame Delphine glares at her but doesn't acknowledge the comment. "This is a competition, and not all of you will get to spend a full year here. While all of you train, there are only five betas who will take a bride this year. One is already fated to Joanna." Everyone stares as Joanna bristles, and I catch many of the girls shooting her death glares. "That leaves four for the rest of you."

That's nineteen girls vying for four men. My gut twists to think about what the next year is going to mean for me. If these men want a beautiful lady, then where does that leave me? I like to work outdoors. I'm tall and too thin to have curves. I don't have golden hair or sparkling eyes, and I never say the right thing.

"So we just have to impress a man?" Faye, Joanna's roommate, who I gather is the leader of the distillery girls, juts out her chest. "That's easy."

Madame Delphine tuts. "Sex appeal will only get you so far. You must prove to us that you can be a respectable lady. It's our tradition that the women who marry the betas hold themselves to the highest caliber. Each day, you will find scores posted in the entry hall. These will be given by your teachers. Every three months there will be a festival during the full moon where the two girls with the lowest scores will be cut from training and sent off."

Faye's face turns stony.

"Sent off where?" I ask. I can't believe I just asked that, but I'm riveted and horrified by what she is saying.

Madame Delphine meets my eye. "Many years ago, when the wars first ended, and the packs took over the remaining cities, humans and wolves mated freely so that humans could have protection, and wolves could breed faster. But as the genes mutated and female wolf children became rare, the claiming was established." She takes a deep breath and lets us in on the terrible truth. "Those of you who are not claimed by a beta will be sent to mate with the lower ranks of deltas and gammas. There are far too many of them to be able to pair you off, so you will mate with more than one man, blessing our community with many children."

"But-but how will they know who their father is?" I whisper.

"They don't have a father or a mother. Those children are raised by the pack."

Her words spin in my head. All of this had been hinted at since I left home, but now that I understand exactly what's expected of me, tears spring to my eyes. I look around at all the other girls. I don't stand a chance.

Madame Delphine continues. "You will do your morning chores after your workouts and before you get dressed in your gowns. There is a chart in the hall with the chores listed. Each day, you will rotate responsibilities. They will prepare you for life after this year of training."

Joanna crosses her arms. "Most of us already know how to do chores. Besides, what good are they going to do any of us? We're just going to spend the rest of our lives on our backs with our legs spread."

I gasp at Joanna's boldness. If she weren't fated, would she still talk like this? Somehow, I think she would, and I like that about her. She reminds me so much of Willow.

Madame Delphine gives Joanna a curious stare. "Well, I guess you probably don't need to learn the chores since it is very clear that you are a fated mate and will not have need of the skills that chores will teach you. Grady will see to it that your household has an adequate staff, which you will be expected to manage. But I do hope you'll do your part while you are with us as Grady is not allowed to take you until the next harvest moon. You may be mated, but he still has to convince his alpha that you are right to be a beta wife."

"That's not what Grady said--"

"All marriages come down to the alpha's approval."

Joanna stiffens and shakes her head, but Madame Delphine ignores her.

"As for the necessity of the chores, with the exception of the four other ladies, most of you will be house servants in the hours that you are not. . . how did you put it, Joanna? Ah yes, on your backs." Her expression turns sad. "Which you will be, more often than not."

She purposefully left out the crude part of Joanna's phrase, but still, our purpose here has become terrifyingly clear. There's nothing any of us can do about it but try to keep our scores high and impress a beta enough to become his wife.

We get sent off to our duties for the morning, and unfortunately, Joanna and I are separated. Madame Vivian insists that Joanna go with her to get her hacked-off haircut fixed. I'm paired up with Charlotte and Faye, and we're sent to collect vegetables from the gardens for dinner tonight. We're to wash them and bring them to the kitchen. I wonder if cooking is another skill we will learn this year. I've always been a terrible cook.

I don't mind gardening since I love working with plants and being outside. Maybe instead of being a house servant one day, I can get a job doing that instead. If I focus on that idea, then I don't have to think about the rest of my duties. I purposely keep the idea of mating locked away in my mind. I don't want to think about it. I can't.

"Fated mates," Faye scoffs as she stomps through the garden. "We'll see about that."

Charlotte huffs along with her. I keep my mouth shut and my ears open.

"What are fated mates?" Charlotte asks.

"Apparently it means that she's destined to be with Grady. It's some weird wolf shifter thing, kinda like our idea of soul mates but stronger." Faye is a short and stunningly curvy girl with big, fawn-like brown eyes and long curly auburn hair. Her looks kind of remind me of Willow, if Willow were to spew venom from her mouth every time she talked. "But he can't choose her until next year, and he has to convince Prince Ryne that she's good enough to be a beta wife." She chuckles low. "And a lot can happen in a year, if you know what I mean."

Charlotte nods.

I whip around, waving the carrots in my hands as I growl at her, "Is that supposed to be some kind of threat?"

Faye glares. "Maybe it is, and maybe it's not. Either way, it's none of your business."

"Joanna is my friend, so that makes it my business."

Faye laughs, turning her insults on me. "You're never going to be selected by a beta." She runs her eyes up and down my body. "Shifters like their women with something to love and hold onto, you know? Like actual boobs and a butt. You might as well be one of the claimed boys. You're so flat-chested."

Charlotte laughs, and my face burns hot. Part of me is hurt by Faye's harsh words, but more than that, I'm upset that Charlotte is going along with this. She's the only person I have left from home. She's my roommate, and I still wanted her to be my friend. Despite the evidence to the contrary, I was clinging to the hope, as stupid as that was. Well, that hope is gone now.

"You don't know what you're talking about," I say, trying not to sound defeated.

"Really?" Faye pops her hip. "The shifters have had tons of interaction with my village for years because they like us better than the rest of you." She juts out her full chest and runs a hand down her perfect hair as if to make her point. "We have good genes." She winks at Charlotte. "But I think you have a great shot, hon. You have the best hair of any girl this year, and your eyes are so pretty. You really stand out."

"Thanks," Charlotte beams.

"Let's take these inside. Ryne's in there." Faye brushes past me and snatches the pile of carrots right out of my hands as she goes, plopping them into her basket. She opens the garden gate for Charlotte and slams it closed before I can follow.

I glare, but she just tosses her hair over her shoulder and leaves me to manage the rest of the gardening alone. No wonder Joanna hates her. I hate her too. And not only do I have to live with her and girls like her for the next year, but I have to compete with them to get a mate. If I fail, my life will be miserable. I gaze down at myself, judging my body and finding it severely lacking. Maybe she's right. Maybe I don't stand a chance.

Chapter Nine

The river is much sleepier along the bend where the manicured lawn of the estate kisses the water, nothing like it was back where Devansh jumped in. Here it's actually quite peaceful, even though it makes me think of him and wonder if he's alive. I shake the depressing thought from my head, pushing ahead of the rest of the group, and focus on the sunrise as it casts a gorgeous golden glow across the landscape.

We've started off another day with a morning run, and today I use it to collect my thoughts. We're a week into training, and I'm still the fastest one here. Exercise is the one thing I'm actually decent at. Joanna is a close second, so I slow down to her pace. Being the fastest probably isn't a good thing, considering I'm a gangly lightweight with muscles and hands that look like they're used to manual labor. Those traits aren't attractive to the beta wolves picking out a mate, so what good is any of it going to do me here?

Still, I let myself enjoy this one thing I have over the other girls. I'm strong, fast, and I love the feel of blood pumping through my veins. The sun warms my skin in the exact same way it did in the cotton fields back home. If I were to close my eyes right now, I could fool my mind into thinking I was there instead of here. The first smile in days creeps onto my lips.

Two hands shove my back, and I lose my footing, tripping over my feet and plummeting into the river. The cold water shocks me and fills my mouth and nose. I come up sputtering, desperate to get the water clear.

After a terrible coughing fit, I stand in the shallow water and find Joanna in it right next to me. Mud drips down her face and clings to her short hair. If she looks like a drowned rat, then what do I look like?

"Who did that?" she screams angrily, but it's useless. The group of girls has passed us, and every single one of them is laughing hysterically. Somehow, over the last few days, it's become the two of us against the eighteen of them. Except Joanna is fated to Grady, so even though she's got my back, sometimes I feel like it's me against the world.

I've never been so lonely.

I climb the steep shore, and Joanna and I help each other out of the water. Mud suctions to my shoes, and some of it runs down my arms and legs.

"Let's go get changed," I grumble. At least Joanna's hair looks cute in the short cut. Madame Vivien did a good job fixing it. Mine is a knotted mess from the river water.

By the time we make it back to the house, the rest of the girls are waiting on the lawn, but they're not alone. The betas are here. Ryne too.

"Great. Perfect timing," I sigh.

"What happened?" Grady growls, stalking toward us like Joanna is in mortal danger and not simply covered in muddy water. "Are you okay? Who did this?" He cups her face and peers into her eyes as if he's already madly in love with her.

She scoffs and shoves him away. "Who says anyone did it? I fell into the river."

He glowers at her. "No one falls into the river by accident."

"I do," she spits out, running her shaking hands over her hair.

Grady turns on me and grips me hard by the shirt. "Did you do this to her? You two get in a fight or something?"

I can't breathe.

Joanna claws at his arm. "She didn't do anything. She's my friend, you idiot."

Grady is ripped from me and thrown to the ground. Ryne stands over him, his eyes blazing with anger. Then he turns that glare at me, and I feel as if the earth just swallowed me whole. He takes a few deep breaths and reaches out to help Grady up. "You know you can't hurt any of the girls. Don't be foolish."

Grady brushes off his pants. "Sorry. I got carried away." He meets my eye. "I apologize, friend of Joanna. What's your name?"

"Poppy," I whisper. "And it's okay."

Although, it's not really okay.

He pats me on the back. "So we're good." He waggles his eyebrows and falls back into line with the other betas. Anders watches me with hungry eyes. Ryne sniffs and scrunches his face as if I smell like a swamp. I'm sure I do.

He grumbles something under his breath that I can't hear and addresses the group. "This is a competition. We like competition. We encourage it. But that said, we don't tolerate sabotage, especially if it puts someone's life at risk. Do you understand?"

The girls agree in unison. Faye's shout of yes is heard above the crowd. I roll my eyes. I'm certain she was the instigator.

Ryne turns on me. "You don't agree, Poppy?"

"Oh, I do," I croak. "It's not like I pushed myself into the river."

"I thought you fell." His eyes flick to Joanna.

She stiffens.

"That's what I meant. We fell." I meet his eyes in defiance and immediately regret it. The ocean blue color is now stormy with frustration.

He steps back. "Another thing we don't tolerate is lying." He points to the house. "Now go get changed, and, Madame Delphine, please deduct points from Poppy's score today."

I gasp. Are you kidding me? I glare right back at Ryne, matching his indignation with my own. I don't give a crap that he's attractive or that because he's the alpha, I'm naturally drawn to him. This hot and cold attitude is confusing and rude, not that there has been a whole lot of hot except for a few lingering looks. Maybe it's in my head, and he's just cold.

If I were brave like Willow or Joanna, I'd challenge him. But I don't like talking to the wolves, especially not the alpha. I know I have to get used to this, and later in the year, we're even going to have to go on dates with the betas so they can get to know us better, but right now I doubt I'll get that far. I'm pretty sure I won't make the first cut. I really am terrible at all this, and considering those deducted points will now put me at the bottom of the leaderboard, I don't think I'll be able to fool any man into wanting me. And now that Ryne seems to have it out for me, I'm in big trouble.

I brush past him and try not to blush as the five betas stare after me. Joanna has been altering my clothing, and Madame Delphine has brought in a few new things for me, but the exercise gear is still the same ill-fitting and overly revealing stuff that was made for my sister. I can practically feel Anders's gaze on my butt, but I'd rather die than mate with him. If he picks me, I'll refuse him. I don't even know if I can, but I will, even if it means death. So, who do I have left? Three men who I haven't met yet and who haven't looked twice at me.

Joanna and I go up to change. Each day we're assigned our outfit--usually a dress--and today is no different. I pout at the hot fabric and then hurry back down the stairs to join the others. Joanna is waiting at the door.

"I can't afford to lose any more points today," I sigh.

"I know. I'm sorry." She's upset because there's nothing she can do to help me. "I understand if you don't want to be my friend anymore."

"What?" I stop and turn on her.

"You'd probably have better luck if you took Faye's side. You know, like your roommate did. I'm just going to bring you down. I'd be dead right now if that idiot Grady hadn't decided I'm his mate." Her facial expression is calm and collected, but her eyes shine.

"First off, Charlotte's a brown-noser. Secondly, Faye's a jerk. And third, there's a reason that you're the only friend I have here." I pull her into a tight hug. "I wouldn't trade you for any of those girls." When she hugs me back, I can feel her worries begin to ease.

She might be right, but I can't bring myself to ditch her just to save my own skin. It probably wouldn't help me anyway. I already know how this ends. Besides, I really like her, and I wish I could be half as brave as she is.

"You know," I go on, "maybe I can be a servant in your household with Grady." That's when I'm not being forced into mating, of course.

"Don't think that way," Joanna hisses. "We're going to get out of here before any of that happens."

How she thinks we're going to get away is beyond me, but I nod and follow her the rest of the way down the stairs. I'll let her worry about escaping. Right now, I need to worry about getting my scores up.

We get through our morning chores and are sent back outside. When we walk out onto the lawn, and I see what our activity is for the day, my heart drops. Will I never catch a break?

Twenty art easels have been set up in the grass. Back in my village, we have an artist named Laurel. She always manages to find bits of charcoal to draw with and makes paint out of plants and crushed stone. Every home in our village has a painting from her hung on the wall. Once a week, she teaches the village children how to draw, paint, and sculpt. I always went to her classes because it was a break from our normal labor, but to say I'm a terrible artist would be a massive understatement.

Everyone always "oohed" and "aahed" over Willow's art, while Laurel would put a hand on my shoulder and say, "Maybe next week we'll find your talent." I'd laugh, thinking it was nice of her to imagine there was any artistic talent hidden somewhere in me for her to find. Years of lessons, and she never found an ounce. But back then, it didn't matter. It was just for fun. And now it does--I certainly won't be moving up the scoreboard after today's lesson, that's for sure. Too bad running doesn't count for much. It should. They were the ones who said they wanted women who could defend their young as well as be proper ladies.

Madame Lucille stands in the middle of the easels and waves us toward her. "I will be your art instructor. Once a week, you will spend a few hours with me, learning how to paint. The betas enjoy the finer things in life, and they'll like mates who can create beautiful things for their homes."

My eyes flick to where the betas are grouped up on the porch, observing us from above like overlords. Grady is taken, which leaves Anders, Justin, Cade, and Nico. They're attractive enough, but every time I look at them, all I can see is what they represent.

The girls hang on Lucille's every word. Charlotte has a small smile on her face. Most of the girls here have probably never even picked up a paintbrush before. Charlotte and I are at an advantage, thanks to Laurel. Well, Charlotte is, but not me. I might even be at a disadvantage because I already know how bad I'm going to be, and my hands are starting to shake.

"Today, I would like to see what kind of artist you are so I can help cultivate your natural talents. Perhaps you are good with portraits, or maybe your skills lie in landscapes and nature. Others of you will lean toward the more abstract arts. Paint me a picture today that tells me who you are."

Joanna and I snag easels right next to each other. "Have you ever painted before?" I ask her.

"Not paint, but I can draw. I'm a fairly skilled designer, and if I hadn't been claimed, I would've probably been brought closer to the city anyway to design dresses and things for the beta wives." She digs out the colored pencils from the basket next to the easel and starts to sketch.

I study my own basket. There are several different kinds of art materi-als. Laurel would be in heaven. I wish I could give the basket to her somehow. She'd do it justice, and then I could go back to running, the only thing I'm even remotely good at, the only thing that clears my head and allows me to forget where I've ended up. But no. With a resigned sigh, I find a tube of black paint and grab a wide brush. I smear the paint right on the canvas. Then I dig the brush into it, jerking to the left, leaving a wide swath of black paint. Then I paint up and down. Anger courses out of me, and I dig the brush in harder.

I smear red onto the canvas. Willow is dead.

Then I do blue. I'm doomed to a life of whoring against my will.

Next comes yellow. Ryne has it out for me.

Then purple. So does Faye and her gang and maybe even Charlotte.

I brush this way and that, not really caring how it looks. Tears start, and I can barely see what I'm doing.

Willow is dead.

Dead.

Dead.

Dead.

A hand falls on my wrist. "Poppy, stop." Joanna jerks my hand away from the canvas, and muddy brown paint splatters all over her shirt. I drop the paintbrush and fall on her shoulder, sobbing.

Chapter Ten

The days blur together, much like the paint did on my canvas during that first art lesson, and really, every subsequent lesson since. I'm depressed––it's not something I've ever experienced before. Oh, I certainly thought I was after Knox was claimed, and I definitely thought I was during the final weeks with Willow, but nothing has even come close to this level of despair. It's like I'm living with a knife in my stomach that nobody but me can see. My life has become hopeless and painful and numbing all at the same time, and that knife twists deeper each and every day.

I should be home, grieving my sister with my family. I should be out in the fields with Papa or baking bread with Mama or telling bedtime stories to Evan. Instead, I've spent the last two weeks since that art lesson trying to force myself into a mold that I'll never fit.

It's pointless.

"Are you not even going to get out of bed?" Charlotte snaps at me early one morning while shimmying into her workout gear. Her back is to me, but even in the shadows, I can tell her body is perfectly curved and exactly what the betas want in a wife. I'm pretty sure she's going to end up with the tall blonde beta named Justin, based on the way he looks at her, which is fine by me, but I still grumble and roll away.

"Joanna is worried about you, you know," she huffs. "She thinks you could get a beta if you were to actually try. Not that I think that, but you know, she does. Attitude is everything, and this mopey one of yours is not attractive."

I do know that. I know that I'm a mess. I know that I'm not trying. And that Joanna thinks I have a chance. But the woman is also under the delusion that we're going to be able to run away and somehow survive out in the wilds, so it's not like her judgment can be trusted.

"Tell them I'm sick," I finally murmur. I roll back over to face the wall. I usually enjoy this part of the day because I love physical exercise, but it's only one measly hour, and then hell starts. I can't be bothered anymore.

I may as well give up now. Either way, I'll be shipped off to the mating house come the Wolf Moon Festival in January. I've literally been near or at the bottom of the leaderboard every day since we arrived here. I close my eyes and drift back to sleep. I dream of home, but it's wrong. Nobody can see me, and it's like I never existed.

Rough hands shake me awake. "What?" I sputter, trying to pry my eyes open. My body is heavy, and my mind is filled with cobwebs.

"Come on." Madame Delphine leans over me. "You have to get moving."

"I can't today. I don't feel well."

She presses her hand to my forehead and tuts. "You're fine. Now, come on, there's something I want to show you."

"If you take a special interest in me, it's only going to make the other girls hate me more," I groan.

"That's funny because I didn't think you cared."

She's right. I've been too sad to care what *anyone* thinks.

Madame Delphine is obviously not going to take no for an answer, so I peel myself from my mountain of warm blankets. She leaves, and I dress in my gown for the day—a pretty navy-blue one with a sweetheart neckline—clean my face and teeth, and brush out my long hair. When she returns with a shiny green apple, I take it because it's the only breakfast I'm going to get this late in the day. I don't even know what time it is. We head downstairs, and I half-expect her to lead me to the classroom where the other women are taking a singing lesson—another talent that's escaped me—but she doesn't. We walk right past their closed door and out the front.

A couple of the betas are hanging out on the porch, and my face reddens because they must know I'm being forced to get out of bed today. I feel ashamed, and I hate that feeling and refuse to own it. They go silent, watching as she directs me into a waiting car. It's black and shiny and belongs to Ryne. I've seen him dropped off in it a couple of times, but never thought I would get to ride in it. When I slide into the backseat, and he's not there, I'm thankful but also a tad disappointed. He must be in the house somewhere. Why is he here so much? He's not a beta, but I guess he's invested in making sure his men end up with suitable wives.

Madame Delphine slides into the backseat next to me and shows me how to strap myself in safely, using what she calls a seatbelt. It's restrictive and cuts into my neck. My stomach rumbles, so I bite into the apple and look up just as the driver catches my gaze in his mirror. Time slows to a stop.

I know those eyes––those honey-brown eyes––those kind farmers' son eyes.

I fell in love with those eyes.

"Knox," I whisper and cough on the apple chunk.

"Are you okay, child?" Madame Delphine asks, patting me on the back.

Knox looks away. But it's him. *It's him!*

"Fine," I squeak.

I knew there was a possibility that I'd see Knox at some point, but I wasn't expecting it today. My heart beats so loudly that I can hear it thumping in my ears. I drop my eyes, studying my hands. I want to look at him again, but I can't, or we might both get into trouble. It's very likely he has no idea why I'm even here. I wasn't supposed to be. I'm not Willow. Or maybe he's already overheard the whole story. If he is Ryne's private driver, he probably hears a lot. But does Ryne speak of me? Maybe Ryne doesn't even think of me when he leaves here. Knox could be just as stunned right now as I am.

"What do you know about our children?" Madame Delphine interrupts the storm of emotions whirling through me.

"Our children? Are you a shifter then?" I ask without thinking.

She chuckles. "Goodness no, but I did mother one."

"Just one?"

"So you don't really know about their kind at all? I thought they taught you lessons before you came."

"They do, but I wasn't supposed to come, remember? My sister took the lessons, not me."

Madame Delphine pats my hand. "I am sorry about your sister."

"It's not your fault."

"I know, but I hate death of any kind."

This surprises me coming from a woman who teaches girls to be subservient to men.

I stare out the window and watch the shells of houses go by. A few have been cobbled back together, but not many. Mostly, it's just trees and fields of weeds. Part of me would like to clean it up, to make it beautiful, but the shifters don't deserve beauty.

"Anyway," she continues as if my prolonged silence isn't awkward. "How much do you know about the moon virus?"

I clear my throat and try not to meet Knox's gaze even though I want to. I can tell he's looking at me again. "I know that many generations back the humans and supernatural creatures were in a huge war for control of the world. The humans bombed just about everything, trying to get rid of the supernaturals, but it didn't work." I think about the wasteland between my village and the next. "It only made it worse. Humans were close to becoming extinct until they released a lab-created virus." My voice trails off.

"Go on."

"Well, all I know is that it was airborne and lethal, and humans were immune to it. It killed most of the supernaturals off except for the ones that had mostly human blood in their veins––the lycanthropes and the shifters."

"That's correct," she continues. "We believe it was that virus that altered the wolf shifters fertility. They can still procreate, but it doesn't happen frequently, and there's still the problem of only producing male offspring ninety-nine percent of the time. As you can imagine, only having one percent of shifters being born female would eliminate their race pretty quickly if they couldn't breed with humans."

I stiffen and try to push the anger down. "So they created the claiming."

"As a way to protect humans from the growing lycan population and as a way to keep the shifter numbers strong." Her tone isn't defensive. It's matter-of-fact, like of course the claiming only makes sense.

I turn on her. "But why can't all the claimed have one mate? It's not right what they're doing."

Her eyes turn sympathetic, but she still defends the wolves. "You have to understand. Most betas will only have one or two children during a woman's fertile years. That's not enough to keep the pack numbers where we need them to stay protected."

I'm putting the pieces together, finally getting what she's saying, and my stomach is sick with the truth of it. "So they take additional mates..."

"Yes. If a woman has no child by the age of thirty-five, the beta returns to guarding the city and can elect to take another mate whenever he chooses. At that point, he will no longer be married to his first wife and will leave her for his second, or third, and so on."

"And if she does have a child?" I ask.

"Then she is allowed to raise him, but once he comes of age and joins the pack, her time as a mate is done, and the same process continues. Unless of course if they are fated mates, then they will stay together for her lifetime, even if they aren't blessed with children. But those are rare cases. Joanna is the first one I've seen in my five years as house mother."

So she's only been doing this for five years. Interesting . . .

"Then where do the beta wives go after they are no longer good for bearing children?" Maybe I shouldn't be curious about this, but I am.

"They usually take jobs overseeing the children's homes, but a few have other roles in the city. Some manage the girls in the mating houses or run a shop. Others simply live a life of luxury and do nothing. They are not required to work if they are married to the betas, so they only do if they wish to stay busy." She frowns. "In fact, there is a group of them that get together and gossip as if it's their job."

"These are just the beta wives, right? What about the rest of the girls?"

I have to know because that is likely my fate. It's good to know that I won't be stuck doing it forever. I look up front to where Knox is driving, wondering what he's thinking of all of this. I wish I could include him in our conversations, could get his opinion on everything, or even gain just one look to know his thought process.

But he doesn't look back at me again.

"They stay in service until they're no longer able to bear children," she explains. "Then most of them go work with the children, helping to raise them in community houses and sometimes acting as wet nurses for the infants. It's assumed they will birth children from the lower ranks of gamma and deltas, but there are betas who frequent the mating houses as well, so who knows, really." I can't help but grimace at that. She's saying that these men get to have a wife and countless mistresses at the same time, and it's fine because it's in the name of growing the pack. The whole thing makes my heart hurt, especially since those children aren't even raised by their own mothers. "Mating house girls are much more fruitful than beta wives, with most having twelve to fifteen children in their time."

My jaw falls open. I remember the sounds Mama made when she birthed Evan. It was painful, bloody, and it quite honestly scared me. I've never known any family back in the village to have that many children. "How is that possible if the shifters are so infertile?"

"Most girls have four to five partners a day." Her voice sounds regretful, but I can't quite be sure if she honestly cares, considering her job is to prepare us for these horrors. "It doesn't take long at that rate. Once they are pregnant, they go live in a birthing home with other pregnant girls, where they are pampered to no end."

"Oh, so now that she's pregnant, she has value to you?" I snort. "Got it."

"A woman *always* has value here," she sighs. "But we want to protect those babies. Our future safety depends on them growing up into warriors. Don't forget what the wolves do for the humans out in the villages."

I bite my tongue, because all I can think of is what Anders did for my family.

"After the child is born, the woman is given a month of recovery time and then must return to the brothel, where, if she is lucky, she will only be a month or two before she is pregnant again."

"Why do you do this?" I can't help the question from spilling out.

"It's exactly as I said. We need to grow the pack for everyone's protection."

"Fast enough to require forced breeding?" I haven't felt much besides grief lately, but right now, I definitely feel anger, and that anger is forcing life into me again, so I welcome it.

"The lycans--"

"Are there *really* that many lycans?" I cut her off. The first I'd ever seen of one was at the claiming ceremony. And yes, it was huge, but there were countless shifters ready to take it and its companions down.

"There are," she says, her voice growing cold and frustrated, "and they are building their army every full moon." She unbuckles her seatbelt as the car slows to a stop. "Enough about that. We're here."

Chapter Eleven

I miss my father. He described cities like this to us kids, his stories having been passed down through the generations. Of course, he'd never seen one in person, but hearing him speak so confidently of them always made me wonder if maybe he had. He often talked of the tall shiny structures reaching into the sky like glass fingers, exactly like these. I gaze up at the blue and gray and brown buildings that seem to reflect every color of the rainbow and try not to smile. It's unlike anything I've ever seen before, and it makes me feel small and insignificant but also excited all at the same time. We'd seen so little of the city when we arrived. I hadn't realized we'd missed so much.

It's only when Knox opens my door and takes my hand to help me out of the car that I'm knocked back into reality. He squeezes once and then drops it, turning away. Meanwhile, a million memory seeds bloom within me. Growing up with him flashes behind my eyes––our few school classes together and how he hated the art workshops same as me, working the fields next to his large family of boys, the first time he showed interest *in me* with that dimpled smile and those kind brown eyes, our first kiss beneath the summer willow trees, the first dance around the community bonfire, and the day I had to say goodbye . . .

And now, he's here and a slave, and soon I will be too.

"This way, dear." Madame Delphine threads her arm through mine. Thankfully she's missed the connection Knox and I have. Will he and I ever get to talk at all? "It's time for you to see why you need to get out of bed each morning and fight for a beta." She begins pulling me toward one of the buildings.

I catch Knox's expression as I go. His face has gone gray, like he's about to be sick. So am I, for that matter. I don't want to be mated to a beta or sent to a mating house. I want to fall back into Knox's arms and forget about this nightmare. I want us to go home, to be normal teenagers.

I hadn't realized how much I missed him until now.

Several cars pass by, and I jump. Even after riding in one, I'm not used to how fast they go. Madame Delphine chuckles. "I remember when I first arrived at the city. Everything terrified me. You'll get used to it."

We step inside the shiny doors, and I'm immediately disappointed. The only thing inside is a long, bright white hallway with a few glass doors along the walls. Madame Delphine walks swiftly through the hall, and I peek through the glass. All I see are a few women sitting at desks and shuffling papers around.

At the end of the hall are four wide metal doors. Madame Delphine pushes a button, and there is a loud ding, but nothing happens. "What's that?" I ask.

"An elevator. It will take us up to other floors."

I turn the foreign word around in my head in examination, wondering how an elevator is going to work.

"What are those women doing back there?" I question.

"They are coordinators. They make sure that every child is matched with a caretaker and plan the children's schedules and meals."

I think that would be a job I could do someday. It certainly would be better than raising children who aren't my own. Though it probably requires reading, and I'm not good at that. Maybe if I'm able to stay in the house longer, I'll be able to learn.

There is another loud ding, and the doors in front of us slide open. We step inside what appears to be nothing more than a tiny metal room, and Madame Delphine pushes a button with the number four on it. The doors close, trapping us inside. The little box of a room lurches up, and I grip the nearest handrail as my weight shifts. Madame Delphine smiles.

In no time at all, the box stops moving, and the doors slide open to a cacophony of sound. I press my hands to my ears as we step out. The whole space is wide open with tons of equipment for children to play on.

Little boys are everywhere, laughing and playing. A few are tussling, and a woman runs over to break it up. If I had to guess, I'd say they were all around the age of three or four. And to think, they're all shifters, all going to grow up to be part of this wolf pack.

Madame Delphine puts a hand to her chest. "Goodness me, I forgot how loud they were at this age."

I nod and lower my hands. "My little brother was loud, but there was only one of him." I hate that I'm thinking of him in the past tense, but chances are I'll never see him again.

An adorable curly-haired boy runs up to Madame Delphine and wraps his arms around her legs. "Hi, lady!" he looks up to her. She pats him on the head, and then he jumps over to me and does the same to my legs. I laugh down at him and smile while a woman approaches.

"Madame Delphine, what brings you to our home?" The woman curtsies a bit and pries the little boy away from my legs. I have to admit I wish I could get another hug.

"I'm here to show one of my girls how the children are raised. I thought she might appreciate it. Poppy, meet Nana Eliza. She and I were in the same claiming year."

"Oh, how nice. Were you a beta wife before coming here?"

Eliza's eyes go sharp. "No."

I'm instantly ashamed of my assumption. Madame Delphine doesn't say anything. I figured since they are friendly, they'd run in the same circles during their child-bearing years, and she must have been a beta wife. But apparently not. "Oh, I'm sorry."

Nana Eliza doesn't have time to stand around and talk. There are so many children here and so few caretakers that she's immediately pulled back to her job. We circle the large playroom, talk to a few of the little boys, and then go back to the elevator.

This time Madame Delphine pushes the number for fifteen. "We group the children born of each mating house together. They're then separated by age. Once they age up a year, they go to live on the next level. Each level has sleeping, eating, bathing, and learning quarters for the children. Age fifteen is the last year they'll live in this particular building. At sixteen they are assigned delta or gamma class. They will join the army or be given other assignments and move to new quarters. Those first two years are grueling work, but it's how the boys become men. And at age eighteen, they're permitted to begin mating with the women in the mating houses. They will mate until they grow old and pass away, though many don't make it to old age because of the lycans."

So that's why she brought me here. To see who my potential mates will be one day. I shiver to think of just how old these shifters can get, not wanting to imagine what mating with someone old enough to be my father or grandfather would be like.

The door opens, revealing how high up we are. The view of the city from here makes me want to jump back into the elevator. Just like before, it's noisy, and boys are everywhere.

Much, much older boys.

They're all standing around in what appears to be an open empty room, save for a few floor mats. If I could count them, I'd guess there'd be over fifty boys, and they all turn to look at me at the same time. I want to disappear.

"Hey, pretty mama," one of the closest ones calls out loud enough for everyone to hear. He waggles his eyebrows and then grabs his crotch. "Wanna practice on me?"

"That's enough, Klein," an older man barks out, stomping forward and whopping the smirking kid across the back of the head. "Talk to the women that way in front of me again, and you'll earn yourself a lashing."

I swallow hard and glare at Klein, but when he catches me looking, he blows me a kiss.

"Madame Delphine." The older man steps forward to shake her hand. "To what do we owe the pleasure of your company?"

"One of my girls needs a lesson in how our pack works." She gestures toward the boys. "Carry on. Poppy and I will observe from here."

The man nods once and returns to instructing the boys in combat methods. And then two by two, he directs them to shift and fight each other on the mats. When they begin stripping down so they can shift without ruining their clothes, my cheeks heat, and I drop my gaze to my feet.

What comes next is bloody. And loud.

I didn't expect it to be so awful. They growl and snarl at each other, claws and fangs sinking deep into their opponents. They're evenly matched and don't hold anything back as they battle one another. For the first time, I wonder if wolves within the same pack kill each other. Dominance is *everything*.

I press myself against the cool elevator doors. "Can we go, please?"

"Do you see now, child?" Madame Delphine says. "One way or another, you will bear the wolves' children. In one case, you will get to raise them and love them as your own. In another, you won't even know them. They grow up here and belong to the pack."

I nod but don't say anything. There's nothing else to add.

I hate that the betas are so special to warrant a real family unit while the rest are raised in groups, but I can see now that's all part of the control. Make a wolf beholden to the pack and his fellow wolves his brothers, and he'll do anything for them, even die for them. The pack becomes more important than family when the pack *is* the family.

So why let the betas keep their children?

There must be a reason, but I'm still not sure what it is.

The doors open, and I stumble back into a broad chest. Large hands steady me, and I turn back to stare up into the blue eyes that have infiltrated my dreams each night since the harvest moon. "Mother, what are you doing bringing her up to this floor?" Ryne hisses. "You said you were taking her to see the children."

Mother?

Ryne's warm hands stand me upright, and I turn to take Ryne and Madame Delphine in, suddenly very aware of the resemblance between them. Madame Delphine is Ryne's mother––the *alpha's* mother––and I had no idea.

"She hasn't been trying."

"I'm aware of that."

"So she needs to know exactly what she's getting herself into," Madame Delphine continues coolly, not the least bit phased by the alpha. "Quite frankly, all the girls do."

Ryne glares for a moment, then motions for her to join us in the elevator. When she does, his face goes stony. "Fine, Mother. If that's what you want, then let's take her across the street, shall we?"

Madame Delphine stiffens.

"What's across the street?"

They don't answer me.

Chapter Twelve

"I'm going to head home. You two go alone," Madame Delphine insists. "Knox will have time to get me there and back before you're through."

My eyes widen. She's leaving me alone with him? Ryne softens and runs a hand through his black hair. It tumbles back around his shoulders. "Maybe she's learned her lesson and doesn't need to see what's in there. I can send her back with you." He turns on me. "If you promise to try harder."

Something about that causes a fire to rise within me. "You wanted me to see what's across the street, so show me what's across the street."

"She needs to see it for herself," Madame Delphine cuts in and levels a hard look at Ryne. "That is your fate if you do not win a beta." Her unreadable expression and the fact that she said words clearly meant for me while looking at her son is confusing, but I don't ask questions. Not when I don't know if I want to know the answers. If anything, today has made things worse, not better. I think I would rather die than live among these beasts.

"Of course, Mother. I'll bring her home when we're done." His tone is regretful, but nobody changes their mind, and so I follow Ryne across the street.

We enter another tall shiny building, and my ears are immediately assaulted by the loud music. This isn't like the music we made ourselves back in the village. This is something else entirely, something foreign and wild. The lights are dim, but I can still clearly see most of the vast room. I immediately wish I couldn't. Girls are everywhere and in various states of undress. A few wear no tops at all. Mother would be horrified by all of this--most people would! I desperately want to go home and forget this nightmare exists.

Ryne puts a hand on my back and bends low to whisper in my ear. I can't help but feel secure under his touch, and I hate myself for that too.

"This is the Broad Street Mating House. It's the worst of the lot. Don't leave my side while we are in here. My wolves are allowed to do almost anything they want with women inside this particular brothel. They won't bother you if you are with me though."

It's too hot in here. A bead of sweat trickles down the back of my neck. Ryne leads me through the crowded room to an empty round booth near the back. He slides in, and I go after him. I sit a little apart from him, but close enough that he could protect me if I needed him to.

Ryne waves down a woman in a black uniform. "I want a scotch and a glass of wine." The woman is older than the other women here--too old for bearing children. That must be why she's been assigned this job. She nods and disappears.

"What do you think?" Ryne asks.

I take in the scene. There's a lot of dancing or standing around, and with bodies so close together, it's sometimes hard to tell where one ends and the next begins. Most of the men have women hanging all over them, as if they want to be with these vile men. My heart hurts.

"I don't understand why the girls would go after the wolves. I wouldn't."

The waitress comes back with the drinks, and he thanks her. Ryne hands me the glass of wine. I've never had anything with alcohol in it before—Mama wouldn't allow it—but I don't tell Ryne that. I just take a sip of the bitter liquid. I don't like it.

"Actually, you would. Most of the girls want to get pregnant."

"Why?"

"Probably to get a break from here," he mutters and downs his drink.

Couples come and go from various doors, and I shudder to think what is happening behind the closed ones.

We don't say anything more. I just sip at my wine and watch. That's what he wants me to do, isn't it? To see what will happen to me if I don't try harder. A lot of the women are laughing, but they have dead, soulless eyes. The men mostly seem pleased with all the attention. It's not a life I want, not at all. I want to be in control of my body and my fate. I want love and a real family. I want to work in the fields and go to bed feeling accomplished with dirt under my fingernails. I want to grow old without ever having known this place existed. But I was born a human girl in a shifter's world, and that will never be the case.

The wine leaves my body feeling calm, and I start to think that this wouldn't be so bad, to be desired by so many. And then I shake my head. I can't think like that. It's a trap.

"I think if I were here, I wouldn't dress like the others," I announce.

Ryne eyes me, the blue seeming to glow in the darkness. "What do you mean?"

"I would cover myself from head to toe and hide in a corner. Then I wouldn't have to do anything or get pregnant to get out of here."

Ryne scowls. "That would be worse for you."

"Why?"

"Not all of my wolves are gentlemen. Some like to be rough, they like to be challenged, and they seek out women who are hiding. Sometimes the new women try to hide like you said, but after a few days, they're acting just like any of the others in here."

Almost as if to illustrate Ryne's point of wolves not being gentlemen, one storms across the room and rips a woman out of the arms of the man whose lap she's sitting on. The man with the empty lap growls and stands, fur rippling on his arms, but the first man towers over him. They circle each other, and it reminds me of the teenagers from across the street. This is a show of dominance more than it's about one particular female. The man who lost the girl finally backs down, and the other throws the woman over his shoulder, stalking from the room with her. She doesn't fight him.

Ryne waves the waitress down. "Another scotch and wine, please."

"Why didn't the other guy fight?" I ask.

"Because he's a gamma, and the other is a beta. Gammas can challenge a beta for their place in the pack, but they rarely win. If and when they lose, they'll either be killed in the fight or sent out to the wilds to try and make it as a lone wolf. We don't survive on our own. We're not meant to be separated from our kin."

And nobody survives in the wilds.

I think about the beta man and the rough way he handled the woman, yanking her around like a piece of property. I'm glad he's not one of the monsters I'm supposed to compete for this year. "And to think, a lot of the girls at the house believe your betas only take one mate. Oh, to be married to a beta, what a dream." I roll my eyes.

He snorts, "They only take one wife at a time, that's true. But many betas are unmated, so they visit the brothels just like the gammas. And while they usually stop while they're married, some do not."

"Maybe you can answer a question for me." He hums to himself and I'm not sure if that's a yes or a no, but I ask it anyway. "Why let the betas have families at all?"

He goes still. "It's a perk for the betas and a goal for the new woman."

"Right. Some goal. And what about you, Ryne? Do you visit the brothels?" I have no idea why I'm being so bold. It must be the wine. Or maybe it's the fact that I'm pissed off.

"I do." He rakes a hand through his midnight hair and gives me a challenging look. My mouth pops open, and I suddenly feel a flicker of betrayal, which is ridiculous. I have no claim to this alpha. He catches my sour expression. "I do what is expected of me, but I am also a man. Your judgment doesn't bother me."

Then why does it sound like it does bother him? "And what kind of man are you? Do you violently take the women, or do you let them come to you?"

The low red light from the lamp above us shines on the black hair that hangs around his shoulders, framing his face in lurid shadows. He levels a heated gaze on me, and it does things to me that I'd rather not admit. "I take what I want, Poppy. Don't you ever forget that."

"You didn't answer my question."

"No, I'm never violent with women."

"And what about allowing others to be violent with them? You're the alpha. You make the rules, don't you?" I fold my arms over my chest and lean back into the padding of the booth. I need to put space between us.

A sardonic frown tugs at his lips. "I don't make the rules. I enforce them."

"Alright, then who makes the rules?"

"My father." He sighs heavily. "The alpha king."

It never occurred to me that his father was still alive, considering Ryne's the alpha of this pack, but then again, Ryne is a prince, so it would stand to reason that his father is a king. "And where's your father?"

"So many questions." He chuckles darkly, takes another sip, and then looks off into the distance as if lost in a daydream. "He runs the Chicago Pack."

"And he's okay with violence toward women?" I'm growing braver by the second. "Your beta killed my sister, and now I'm supposed to pursue him as my future husband. Why do you think I've been so depressed?"

"If you end up here," he snaps. "Anders will have you anyway. He does not care to be loyal to a wife and will continue to frequent the mating houses often." Even though it's what I've been learning today, to hear it so bluntly rocks me to my core. "Your best bet is to go for one of the other three betas choosing brides this year. And yet, I haven't seen you try. Do you even remember their names?"

My face reddens. He has me there. I do know them, but he's put me on the spot, and my mind is more muddled than ever.

"Cade, Nico, and Justin," he spits out.

"I knew that!" I wave at the scene unfolding around us. "But you need us. Without human women, you'd have no pack. So maybe you should punish those of you who kill innocent women." My eyes narrow. "Anders shouldn't get off so easily."

He leans back against the leather bench and stares at me until my stomach twists and tiny hairs dance across my arms. I don't break his gaze. I'm right. I know I'm right.

"Your sister was replaced by you before your arrival, so Anders wasn't punished," he finally replies. "But I assure you that if any of these women in here are killed by one of my wolves, the wolf responsible will be sent to the wilds."

"Anders should be sent to the wilds."

"Anders is the highest-ranked beta and my number two." He tenses. "Be careful to remember who you're talking to."

I glare. "So that's what it's like being an alpha, huh? You make it okay for someone to murder my innocent sister just because the guy's your little lacky?"

Something unreadable crosses his features, and he turns away. He has nothing to say, probably because he knows I've caught him with the truth. Sometimes the truth hurts, but not as bad as watching a beloved sister be ripped apart by the very thing that was supposed to protect her. I want Ryne to hurt about this, as if that will take away some of my pain.

It won't.

A woman approaches our table. She's tall and pretty, with wide blue eyes and long sleek blonde hair. She wears a tight short skirt and a plunging crop top that shows generous cleavage. Nearly downright modest compared to what everyone else is wearing.

And silly me, I didn't even know clothing like this existed.

She slides into the booth next to Ryne and puts a hand on his chest. "Ryne, we haven't seen you here in forever. Did you come back because you missed me?"

He extracts her hand, and she leans up and bites his ear, trailing kisses along his neck. I look away and stare into my drink, my chest burning. I can't tell if it's jealousy or just embarrassment for him. But also, I kind of hate him right now, so the last thing I want to see is him enjoying himself because of a system that is broken and wrong. And besides, I have absolutely no reason to be jealous. Ryne is the alpha. I'd never land him in any kind of way that would be meaningful. Not that I want to. He's enforcing all of this, after all.

When he kisses her back, hot bile rises to my throat, and I want to claw the two of them apart. What the hell is wrong with me? I do not want Ryne!

A hand slides up my thigh, and I jerk my head up. A man has managed to sit beside me without me even realizing it.

"You are a pretty thing," he says, alcohol hot on his breath.

I close the distance between me and Ryne, sliding an arm behind his back without thinking and gripping his waist with my hand. The only thing to save me here will be if this man thinks I'm with Ryne.

Ryne jerks away from the girl, reaches across me, and grabs the man by the throat. The table topples over, sending our drinks flying. The other girl disappears.

Ryne gets right into the man's face. "Don't you dare touch her. She's with me. Do you understand?"

The man's eyes widen, and he nods. Ryne drops him and holds out his hand to me. "I think we've seen enough. Let's go."

Chapter Thirteen

The next day I'm out of bed before Charlotte. I put on my workout gear, head downstairs, and step out into the warm, humid air. Today's exercise is yoga, but I want to get a run in before we start because I always feel better afterward.

I stop dead on the deck. Ryne stands there with Madame Delphine, both talking in low whispers. Neither has noticed me.

"Father would never allow it," Ryne says.

"You can't deny fate. He would be forced to understand."

Ryne gives a low chuckle. "No, he wouldn't."

I step forward loudly so that they don't think I'm eavesdropping, and Ryne spins around. "Poppy, what are you doing here?"

A small thrill goes through me at the way he says my name, drawing the end out a little. I clench my fists.

"I wanted to get a run in before the day began. That's allowed, isn't it?"

"Of course," Madame Delphine says, stepping aside. I slip past her and Ryne, and I try to ignore their eyes on me as I take off across the field. Soon, I find my rhythm, and all my turbulent emotions disappear.

I finish my second lap and find the rest of the girls already outside stretching, so I go and join Joanna.

"Glad to see you up and at 'em. Whatever they showed you yesterday must've made an impact." She was a little bitter that I wouldn't tell her, but I didn't want to relive the day. All I know is that, in spite of not wanting to be a part of this at all, it's time for me to fight for a beta because the alternative is too horrific. I've got a year to get myself from the bottom of the charts to the top. And I'm going to do it for Willow. For myself. Joanna still talks of running off, and if she finds a way, I'll join her, but I'm not counting on it.

Madames Delphine, Vivien, and Lucille all stand at the bottom of the stairs in tight black tank tops, leggings, and boots. I've never seen Madame Delphine out of a dress. She looks ten years younger, not to mention fierce and deadly. I wouldn't want to get on her bad side.

"Today we have a special training exercise for you. We will take you into the basement. There will be no talking once we enter. Silence is a must, or points will be deducted. This is not the day to test us."

I quickly glance at Joanna, and she raises her eyebrows. We enter the basement through the cellar door, and all fall silent as we descend the stairs. This place has a creepy energy, and I'm reminded of the haunted feeling I had when I first came here and learned of its history.

We're led into a larger brightly lit room despite the lack of windows. The floor is covered in squishy black padding. Ryne stands at the front of the room, with the five eligible betas along the walls, but it's not just them. There are around twenty or so other wolves as well. They all stand on the edges of the padding. We huddle in a circle in the middle. The Madames go and stand among the wolves.

I want to whisper to Joanna about what is going on, but then I remember what Madame Delphine said, and I can't afford to lose any points.

Ryne leans against a bench and stares at us with crossed arms. His gaze lingers on mine for a few seconds longer than everyone else's, and he nods once, as if he's trying to tell me something. I'm completely captivated by him, and my stomach burns with that thought.

Someone hits me from the side, and another pair of forceful hands shove me to the ground. A boot kicks my ribs, and I curl into a ball as fists pummel me. I'm in shock. What is going on? What do I do?

"Help," I scream out. "Please!" I cover my head, but I'm still being hit and kicked from all sides. Through the flurry of arms and legs, I spot the rest of the wolves holding the other girls back. "Help," I scream once again.

"Fight back," a fierce voice whispers in my ear. It's Grady. His familiar voice is all it takes. I kick out, and my foot connects with a shin. Then I send my arms flailing, scratching and clawing anything I can reach. An elbow slams into my mouth, and I taste blood.

And then I'm alone, lying on the ground, breathing hard. Anders, Grady, and Nico retreat.

Ryne stands over me and holds out a hand. I take it, allowing him to hoist me up. He leans down low. "Are you okay?" he asks.

I take stock of my body. In spite of the pummeling, nothing hurts but my shoulder where I hit the ground and my mouth where I bit my lip when Anders's stupid elbow hit me. "Yes."

"Then come with me."

He takes my hand and leads me to the front of the room. My breathing is still rapid, and my heart races, but other than that, I'm fine and refuse to show weakness.

The rest of the wolves are positioning the girls around the room so they are all spread out. Joanna struggles against Grady's grip, but I'll be honest that she doesn't seem to be resisting his touch as much as she's enjoying it, and he's definitely smirking.

Ryne drops my hand and addresses the girls.

"Who can tell me what changed? Why did they stop beating on her?"

Joanna thrusts her hand up in the air, her expression fierce.

"Joanna?" Ryne calls on her.

"She kicked Anders."

"That's right. She started to fight back. As you can see, she is fine. While it looked like she was getting beat up, my wolves were careful not to hurt her. Today we not only have the betas who are your potential mates but also several others." I look around at the men I don't recognize. I count fifteen who've been added to our usual group. "Some are already mated," he continues, "and others have not yet decided to take a mate. They will assist with your training today. Five of you will be lucky enough to become a beta wife. That means that you will bear our children and raise them in your own homes. You must learn how to protect not only yourselves but also your children in case we are not around. Our wives must be warriors as well as ladies."

"Oh, is that all?" Joanna tuts.

I'm sure she's going to get points deducted right here on the spot, but Ryne simply ignores her. "Today, you begin your combat training. We will return once a week to work with you, but most of the time it will just be the five of us, so take advantage of the help we have today and soak in everything we teach you."

I stand a little taller, assessing the group of men for who I think will be the hardest to beat.

"Now, the reason we attacked Poppy first was because she wasn't paying attention to her surroundings. Let that be your first lesson."

Not paying attention? I was distracted by *him*. Fury burns in my chest. I hate him.

"Poppy, you may rejoin the others."

I wipe blood from my mouth and glare at the infuriating man as I take the empty space between Charlotte and Faye. I want to go stand by Joanna, but she's too far back, and if I were to trek back there, I would draw too much attention to myself. The last thing I want is to get blindsided by these brutes again.

Ryne continues to address us. "Today is a test of endurance. You fight until you drop. The last one standing gets top points for the day. You are allowed to fight back as fiercely as you wish." He smiles. "My advice? Pace yourself, but don't hold anything back either."

Sounds like a contradiction to me.

Not a moment passes before the wolves are on us, shoving and hitting. Anders has come after me, singling me out as he often does, and I fight him with every ounce of energy I have. None of his blows cause me much pain, but he's relentless. I want to hurt him, to punish him for what he did to Willow, but I'm no good at this. Time passes, but I don't even know how long. Ryne walks among us, observing, sometimes calling out instructions, but never touches anyone.

Faye is the first to fall and not get back up. I don't see much, but the next time I catch a glimpse of her, she is sitting along the wall, sipping out of a bottle of water with an apple in her hand, scowling at the rest of us.

My arms tire, and most of my blows don't seem to faze Anders, so I use my foot to kick out, and he doubles over. He glares at me and lashes out, his fist connecting with my face. My head snaps back, and stars blur in my eyes. When my vision clears, Ryne is standing between me and Anders. "We don't hurt them," he hisses. "I thought that was clear."

Anders gives a nod. Ryne turns around. "Are you okay? Maybe you should go sit down."

I shake my head. Half the girls are already out, and I'm not ready to join them. "I'm fine."

He purses his lips. "As you wish. Anders, you walk around and see how everyone is doing. I'll continue here with Poppy."

Anders chuckles to himself but leaves, and Ryne spins, hitting me across the ribs. His blows are softer than Anders had been, more controlled, but he's faster, and I find myself tiring quickly from the constant defense. Our eyes lock as we fight, and something powerful yet beautiful ignites within me, like a lightning strike connecting with sand, transforming it to glass. I'm focused on Ryne's every movement, blocking as often as I can. My muscles beg for rest, but I use it as fuel to keep going. I won't give up.

I don't know how long the fight continues before Ryne steps back, his hands up. "It's over."

I shake my head. "No. I can keep going."

He chuckles, and pride lights his eyes. "Everyone else is on the floor and has been for the last ten minutes. You are the last one standing. Good job."

Madame Lucille brings me a bottle of water and a banana. I remain standing, not wanting to look weak, but my legs shake.

Ryne doesn't move far from me as he addresses the group. "I need you all up and facing your opponents once again." There is a collective groan, but the wolves help the girls up. Once everyone is back on their feet, Ryne continues. "While you may see us as your enemy today, we are not. We care deeply for your welfare. Every week we will fight, and then you will leave with a hug to remind you that we are not your enemy."

Could've fooled me.

Ryne pulls me close. He smells of man and wolf, and I'm strangely attracted to that. I wrap my arms around his waist. I don't want to allow myself to relax, to let him think I trust him or care to be here, but it's like a string within me snaps, and my knees go weak. Ryne shifts and just holds me for a moment. Something changes between us in that hug. It's not sexual by any means, but there is a form of affection there. It's strong and comforting. Is it friendship? Respect? I'm not sure, but I melt into it, wanting to stay here with him and forget about everything else.

There's a light tapping on the door, and I look up as Knox steps into the room. Fire flares in my belly. His face is an unreadable mask as he takes us in, our bruises and all, his gaze finally landing on me like a pile of rocks. His eyes flash cold just before he looks down at his shoes.

"What's this slave doing here among our women?" Justin sneers and spits at Knox's feet. Faye beams at the guy like his behavior is to be admired.

Ryne holds up one hand and keeps me tucked against him with the other. "Careful, Justin, this slave has earned a place as my right-hand man, or have you already forgotten the night he defended me before many of my own betas?"

There's a story there. I'm dying to find out what it is. If only I could sneak away with Knox for a few minutes so he could tell me everything. I was hoping we'd get a moment alone in the car yesterday so I could explain myself, but it never happened. He drove Ryne and me back to the house without acknowledging my existence. Ryne didn't let me out of his sight. Even though he didn't stay at Drayton Hall after he dropped me off, it became apparent that human women are not allowed even a second alone with the slave men.

"Prince Ryne, please forgive the interruption." Knox looks up again, his pretty eyes saying so much more than his words alone. "The alpha king is here."

Ryne's arm squeezes me closer.

"Do you know why he came to the city early?"

"No, but he insisted his son come to see him at once."

Ryne nods. "Thank you, Knox. I'll be up shortly."

Knox leaves. The energy in the room has shifted. The betas seem more intense than ever, looking to Ryne for direction. Ryne drops his arm and steps away from me. He squares his shoulders and adopts the same jovial facade he used the night of the claiming ceremony. It's the professional version of himself. I don't know what the real version is, but I suspect it's not this.

"Thank you, ladies, for your hard work today. I'm sure I can speak for my betas when I say we are very pleased." His smile is magnetic, and everyone stares at him, a bit of awe in all of our faces. "I hope we didn't frighten you too much, but it's important that you know how to protect yourselves and your pack. Your scores will be posted after dinner. As a reward, you may have the rest of the day off."

Many of the girls squeal with approval. We haven't had free time since arriving here. Every day it's exercise, chores, lessons, meals, sleep, and repeat. But despite the excitement, there's something unsettling about the suddenly open afternoon. I don't think this was part of the plan. The alpha king's arrival has changed things, and I want to know why.

Chapter Fourteen

Even though the women's sitting room is next to my bedroom, I've barely had a chance to spend any time here until today. I share a big plush armchair with Joanna in the corner. We've got a book between our laps, and I'm trying to concentrate on the adventure story as she quietly reads it aloud. To me, the letters are still a bunch of squiggles, but I can't wait to be able to read these stories for myself one day. Books may be my only escape. But even after a few weeks of reading lessons, I can't read more than a few words. I'm the worst out of all the girls. Though only Joanna can read books fluently at this point.

Well, except for Bailey. That girl picked up reading like a fish to water and has had her nose in a book ever since. I sometimes wonder if she even knows what's going on in the real world, because all she seems to care about is reading. I have to admit, I'm kind of jealous. I'd love to be able to escape into a fantasy world right now. And if I don't make it past the Wolf Moon Festival in January, I'll never have enough time to learn. Maybe I won't get a beta, but I hope to at least get reading down before I go.

On the other side of the room, Faye and the rest of the girls sit around on the couches and gossip mercilessly about the betas. So far, we've had little time to really spend with them, so I don't know why they're going on and on about them, as if they really have anything substantial to say. The betas watch us during our lessons but barely talk to us. Madame Vivien let slip that starting next month, we'll have to go on dates with them. I shudder at that thought. I don't want to spend time alone with any of them, especially Anders.

My mind goes back to this morning and the hug Ryne gave me. He's probably the kindest shifter I've met so far, which is odd considering he's the alpha. It's pretty apparent that he wants me to get claimed by a beta, but I can't figure out why he cares so much. I'm one of twenty women here, one of many who come through Drayton Hall every year. Maybe his mother put him up to it so that I'd stop moping around.

Outside, rain pummels the house, but even that isn't enough to drown out the other girls' incessant chattering. Of course, on the one day we have off, a storm blows in, effectively hiding the sun and locking me inside with a bunch of women who hate me. Madame Delphine sent us up here for some "bonding time," but Joanna is the only one who's shown me a shred of kindness and is the only one I'd like to actually bond with.

"Has anyone been kissed yet?" Faye says extra loud so that Joanna and I can hear the question. A few of the girls had the betas paying closer attention to them, but none as much as Faye. The men all seem to try to steal moments to talk to her. But a kiss? It seems unlikely.

Joanna groans and closes the book. "Okay, Faye." She takes the bait. "Tell us who kissed you so we can get back to our lives because we all know that's what this question is really about."

Faye rolls her eyes. "Well, maybe if you weren't such a stuck-up bitch, Grady would've kissed you by now."

"Who's to say he hasn't?"

He hasn't. Joanna doesn't want him to, and I'm sure she'll avoid him for as long as she can, but the pink in Faye's cheeks is totally worth the lie.

Faye straightens her shoulders and tosses back her shiny auburn hair. It's the kind of red that changes with the light, and right now, it's all dark and sultry and perfect. "How about we play a game, Joanna. If you can guess who kissed me on your first try, then I'll do your chores for a week, and if you can't, then you'll do mine."

Joanna scoffs. "Easy, that would be Justin." He's had his eye on Faye since she arrived, and we saw him pull her into an empty room a few days ago between lessons.

Faye smirks. "Nope. You lose."

"Then who?" Charlotte giggles. "Tell us!"

Faye's eyes land right on mine. "Ryne."

"You're lying," I blurt. I shouldn't react to her—this is exactly what she wants—but I can't keep the anger from flaring. Ryne hasn't touched any of us, nor shown her special attention. I know she's lying. She has to be. It's like she's intentionally trying to goad me, not anyone else. Though maybe it was because I fought with him during our defense class this morning. Maybe she noticed our intimate hug.

She leans back in her chair and puffs up her chest. "Ryne is twenty-three years old, Poppy. He's obviously very experienced with women, and he's here all the time. Why do you think that is?"

"What are you implying?" Joanna cuts in. "That he's here for you? Because I haven't seen him so much as utter a word to you." She sets down the book and stands. "You're jealous."

Faye rolls her eyes and stands as well. She walks right up to Joanna. "What would I have to be jealous about?"

"That Ryne--*the alpha*--is paying extra attention to Poppy."

All the girls turn to look at me, and heat begins to crawl up my neck, coloring my cheeks. Is Ryne paying me extra attention? He did show up when I was out with Madame Delphine, and today he cut Anders off to spar with me. When it was all over, he held me. Everything else can be explained away, but that hug. I shake my head. Everyone got hugs, right? So what if ours felt special? Maybe all the girls felt that way about their hug. There is no way Ryne cares one iota about me. And even if he did, it wouldn't matter. He's the alpha prince, and he's not claiming a wife this year.

Faye is slowly turning the color of a ripe tomato, and I realize Joanna is right. Faye is jealous. It sends a shock of pride right through my center.

"Oh please," Faye sputters. "Ryne's still a young alpha. He's not here for a wife. He's here to make sure his betas get what they need and maybe to get a few of his own needs taken care of. Which *I* can easily take care of for him."

"Oh, and is that a good idea considering you have to keep your virtue intact to land a beta?" I shouldn't continue to goad her, but I can't help myself.

"You're going to get yourself kicked out of here, and it'll be your own fault."

Faye rolls her eyes. "Ryne has the mating house for *that,* but it doesn't mean he can't get a taste of his favorite claimed girls every once in a while." Faye grins wickedly. "Why do you think he kissed me? Because he knows I will keep things interesting. Poppy isn't pretty enough to get anyone's attention. Ryne just talks to her because she fights like a man." She glares down at me, and I can't take it. I get up and join Joanna.

Now that I'm standing, I'm able to look down my nose at Faye, and I'll admit it feels good. I ignore the comment about me not being pretty because I know she's right. I'm plainer than all the other girls and don't have the same curves they do, but so what? Charlotte and the other girls giggle. This is the best entertainment they've had in a long time.

"So does Ryne kiss you, Poppy?" Faye presses, batting her long dark eyelashes to taunt me. "Does he corner you behind the willow tree and run his hands all over you and kiss you like you are the only woman in the world, or is that just me?"

Heat burns me up. I'm embarrassed and angry, confused and defeated, and I'm just standing here like an idiot. What can I say? Nothing. I shouldn't even care that she's making out with Ryne. He's of no consequence to me.

Faye smirks. "That's what I thought. You don't even belong here. I heard what happened to your sister. I guess I shouldn't be surprised that she turned out to be even more pathetic with men than you are." She turns, her long shiny hair flipping.

I can handle rude comments about myself all day long, but I won't stand for insults about my sister. Red pulses through me, and I grab hold of Faye's stupid hair and pull. She screams as I twist her toward me, yanking harder. She reaches for me, but I dodge her, so instead of my face, her hands grip my wrists, nails clawing. I hiss and release her.

"What is wrong with you?" she screeches and dives for me. I catch her against my stomach and wrench my knee up into her ribcage. She growls and bites my arm——actually bites me! I scream and push her away, but only so I can get her in the position I need to swipe at her face and draw blood.

Hands grab hold of my upper arms, pulling me back. Joanna.

"Stop!" Madame Delphine yells as she and Madame Vivien burst into the room. "What's going on here?"

"Poppy attacked Faye," Charlotte explains, and the other girls nod vigorously. I give Charlotte the nastiest glare possible. *Traitor.*

Madame Delphine turns on me. "Is this true, child?"

"She provoked me."

"No, I didn't!" Faye insists, standing and brushing herself off. Crocodile tears shine in her eyes, and blood drips down her cheek. "We were just talking about the men, and she blindsided me."

"That's not how it happened," Joanna interjects. She drops her hands and stands in front of me like a protector. It's something Willow would do.

"Yes, it is." Charlotte gasps, and my glare deepens. "What is wrong with you two? You've banded together to hate the rest of us from day one."

"They think Grady will persuade one of his buddies to choose Poppy," says one of the girls who I've never even talked to. She speaks like she's the authority on friendship with Joanna. Her name's Ivy, and she came here from the distillery village, so it's no surprise that she's backing up her friend. I feel like I should tell Madame Delphine Faye's comment about Willow, but the words stick in my throat.

"I think I've heard enough." Madame Delphine sighs and levels me with an exasperated look. "Violence toward your fellow claimed is strictly prohibited. I don't care if Faye provoked you. You cannot start fights. You had managed to get out of last place today, Poppy. You were the top girl this morning. And now look at what you've done. I have no choice but to deduct points."

I'm so angry that I don't even care about the stupid leaderboard right now. "This is what Faye wanted." I point at her. "You couldn't stand that you placed last at combat today and that I won."

Faye is always at the top of the board, but today, she dropped down three places because she can't fight to save her life. Joanna snagged the top spot. She seems to be good at everything. And I jumped up from the twentieth spot to the sixth. So much for that lasting.

"You're crazy!" Faye has the audacity to look totally shocked and a little bit afraid.

I smile at the angry red scratches marring her otherwise perfect face, hoping they leave a scar. She deserves to be as ugly on the outside as she is on the inside. "Stay away from me, and never say another word about my sister."

I storm to my bedroom, slamming the door behind me so hard that the walls rattle. I can still hear when Faye yells after me that I'm a delusional freak who will never land a beta.

She's right. I know she's right. This argument isn't even about Ryne because he's not interested, and anyway, he angers me every other time we interact. This is about fighting for a life that isn't complete hell. It's what Willow would want me to do. I'll never forget what I saw yesterday at the mating house, and I'm not going to give up on my future. Nor am I going to let Faye win. Not again.

Chapter Fifteen

On Fridays, whoever is at the top of the leaderboard gets the afternoon off, and today that happens to be Joanna. The rest of us are usually assigned extra study in whatever subject is our weakest. For me, that's everything except for combat and exercise, and I normally find myself alone with Madame Vivien or Madame Lucille, working on art or reading or my worst nightmare––singing.

After lunch one Friday in late October, Madame Delphine asks me and Joanna to stay behind as the girls head off to their extra lessons. I wonder if we're in trouble.

"Grady has requested this afternoon to take you out, Joanna."

Joanna crosses her arms and glowers at Madame Delphine. "I was at the top today. That means I get to choose what I do this afternoon."

"Actually, it doesn't. It just means that you don't have to do extra lessons. He will be here in twenty minutes to pick you up. He also requested that Poppy accompany you. I think perhaps he thought you'd be more willing that way."

Joanna considers it for a moment, and I hope she'll say yes. I don't want to do extra lessons, and I like the thought of getting out of the house. Maybe we'll have fun.

"Okay, but only because Poppy is coming with."

"Very well. Madame Lucille has laid out appropriate clothes for your outing. And, Joanna, perhaps you could help Poppy with her hair and makeup."

Joanna nods vigorously and drags me up the stairs. Our gowns brush against each other, and she loops her arm through mine, whispering excit-edly. "You know what this means, right? It means that he's bringing another beta. Oh, Faye is going to be so jealous that you got the first date. We're not even supposed to have them until next week."

"What? No." Faye and I have kept away from each other, and I have the sinking feeling that if Joanna is right, then Faye's going to lose her mind.

"You heard Madame. She wants you to look pretty. You know, I'm not convinced that Ryne wants you like Faye is obviously worried about, but Madame Delphine seems to have a soft spot for you."

Yeah, and she's Ryne's mother. But I don't think any of the other girls know that. Joanna knows though. The first night here she called Madame Delphine the mother of the most high. I asked her about it later, and she said that because the textile workers sometimes come into the city to do fittings, she learned the truth of this place through the whisperings her mother heard. It's how she knew about what the claiming really meant and why she resisted coming here.

"Was your mother at the claiming?" I frown.

She shakes her head. "I refused to let my parents come. They probably would've got themselves killed. They hate the claiming more than I do."

And my mother pushed me to Anders after he murdered my sister.

Thoughts of that day swirl around in my head as I quickly remove my gown and change into a white tank and tight black pants with tall leather boots. I wonder what would have been different if my people of North-west knew the truth of our claiming––if my mother had known the truth. Would it have made a difference? I remember the way she gave me away so easily, how she called Anders "my lord," and my chest burns.

Joanna knocks on my door, and I let her in. She's in a matching outfit that looks incredible on her. "We must be doing something active. Other-wise, Lucille would've set us out more stupid dresses. Now sit and let me fix you up."

She puts my plain brown hair back into a fancy braid and puts all kinds of stuff on my face. I've never even worn makeup before, but it makes my eyes look bigger. I've always thought they were a muddy cinnamon color, but right now, they shine like bright amber. I smile to myself and thank her.

"You make a great canvas, Poppy. I only accentuated what's already there."

I don't have anything to say to that. I've never believed I was beautiful. I still don't, but at least I'm presentable now. We manage to make it back downstairs in just under twenty minutes.

Madame Delphine appraises us both. "Good job, Joanna. She looks beautiful."

I flush, knowing it can't possibly be true, but secretly hope the others will think I look semi-decent.

"Thanks," Joanna says, smiling at me. "She *is* beautiful."

"Now. Grady will have you both back here just before dark. It's the full moon, so everyone will be locked up tight, and several betas will guard the house."

I've been dreading this night. Full moons always come with anxiety, but our village never got attacked, so it was easy to pretend nothing would happen. Now that I've seen first-hand what the lycans are capable of, I'm never going to let my guard down during the full moon again.

Outside, Ryne and Grady lean against the shiny black car. When they see us coming down the steps, they stand straight and grin. Joanna groans, and my eyes lock on Ryne. He's staring at me. I hadn't been expecting him. Is he my date? No, that's silly. He's probably dropping Grady off or something. I'm sure one of the betas will be my date. Hopefully not Anders. Maybe Justin, Cade, or Nico. I need to get to know them better.

Knox gets out of the car and stops short when he sees me, the color draining from his face. My heart races, and I wish more than anything that I could save him from this life of servitude.

"Can't have her, man," Grady laughs, patting Knox on the back. "She's mine." They think he's looking at Joanna, but I know the truth.

Knox laughs along and opens the door for us. When Joanna and I climb into the back, he shoots me a pleading look. Grady slides in next to Joanna, and Knox closes us inside. Ryne sits up front. Knox gets behind the wheel, and away we go.

Joanna elbows me in the side and mouths, "Ryne is your date."

I shake my head. It can't be. They're just giving us a ride somewhere. Maybe I don't have a date after all, or maybe one of the other betas is meeting us somewhere. Whatever it is, I'm sure it's not a date. Dating is what people do when they're looking to find the right person for marriage. Ryne doesn't date the claimed. He goes to the mating house and leads his pack and nothing more.

The car ride is thick with tension. Joanna won't talk to Grady, and Knox and Ryne both keep checking the rearview mirror to look at me. I don't know which boy to give my attention to, so I mostly stare out the window and try to keep from blushing. I need to get a good look in a mirror soon because apparently, whatever Joanna did with my hair and makeup is working.

When we arrive at the large barn-like structure and get out of the car, the scent of animals and grass and crisp autumn sunshine sends a wave of happiness through me--happiness and longing for home. Vast fields with horses lie parallel to either side of the dirt drive, and the trees in the distance are sprinkled with reds, yellows, and oranges.

Everything I thought I knew about Ryne clashes with the relaxed man who laces his arm through mine. I guess he's my date after all. I should be disappointed. I should be wanting him to be a beta, but I'm not. A thrill of excitement races through my bloodstream, despite everything I should be feeling. I'm on a date with Ryne. How did this even happen?

"Have you ever ridden horses before?" His voice is playful. I've never seen this side of him.

I shake my head.

"What?" Joanna gushes. "We're riding horses? I've always wanted to!"

"Good, because I'm going to teach you." Grady puts his arm around her shoulders, but she scoffs and pushes him off. She's not angry. She's just being Joanna.

She walks ahead of him into the barn, and he smiles after her like she's the only woman in the world he could ever want, like she's perfect because of her prickliness and not despite it.

"Why me?" I ask before I can stop myself.

"What?" Ryne asks, but he's watching Grady chase after Joanna.

"Why did you ask me to come along?"

His lips twitch. "Maybe I like you."

I snort. "That's absurd."

He stops and stares down at me. "Why is that absurd?"

"I'm hardly pretty like Faye or Charlotte."

Ryne chuckles and continues walking, pulling me along. "It's true that you look nothing like them but trust me when I say that you are very pretty. Just in a different way. Besides, there is often more to desire than just looks, and I happen to enjoy your company more than theirs."

I flush at the compliment. I shouldn't enjoy this, especially since being out here in the fresh air on a farm feels too much like home. We had horses in our village, but I was never allowed to ride them. They were work horses. Maybe today I can just be a girl out with a boy and forget all about the reality of my situation.

Reality can come back tomorrow.

"Thank you," I whisper. My lips twist into a little smile.

He laces his fingers through mine. I can't breathe as we walk the rest of the way in silence, but it's the best feeling.

In the barn, Joanna is bouncing up and down in front of a dark chestnut horse with wide light brown eyes. The coloring of the horse matches her coloring perfectly, like this horse was made for her. Ryne extracts his arm from mine and disappears into a stall. Joanna squeals and drags me closer to the horse.

"Isn't this exciting?" she asks. I've never seen her like this.

"Yeah."

"I've never been this close to a horse before. Do you think it will bite me?"

I chuckle. "No, silly, horses don't bite." At least the ones in our village didn't. I reach my hand up and pat the nose of this one. "See."

Joanna's eyes widen, and she does the same. The horse lets out a snort, and Joanna jumps back, giggling. This is a totally new side to her, and I'm a little in awe.

She loops her arm through mine. "I can't believe it's Ryne out with us. Faye is going to have kittens."

"We aren't telling Faye or anyone else. I don't need another reason for them to attack me."

Joanna's eyes dance. "Fine. We'll keep your little secret. But let's make a deal today. I'll kiss mine if you kiss yours."

"Joanna! No."

Grady returns carrying a large saddle, and Joanna skips away from me, peppering Grady with questions. Who knew that all it would take for Joanna to fall for Grady was a silly horse?

He helps Joanna up into the saddle and then hoists himself up behind her. Joanna is happier than I've ever seen her, and Grady is beaming from ear to ear as he talks her through handling the reins.

"Are you ready?"

I spin and find Ryne next to a black horse with white feet that I swear is twice as tall as the one Grady and Joanna are on.

"That's a big horse," I say. I let out a slow breath and try not to imagine falling off that thing.

Ryne pats the animal's neck. "He is, but he's my favorite. Come on, I'll help you up. He's more docile than Grady's horse."

"Do you ride often?"

"I do. It's peaceful, and it gets me away from the city." He waggles his eyebrows. "My preferred way to roam the outskirts of town is in my wolf. There's really nothing else like it."

"I can only imagine." I remember when he shifted, how natural and powerful he was in that form. But I don't let myself linger on that thought for long.

He places his hands on my waist and easily lifts me up so I can fling my leg over the other side of the horse. I clutch at the saddle; afraid I'm going to fall right off the other side. Ryne climbs up behind me and pulls me close to his firm body. Heat blisters my cheeks. I've never been so close to a man before.

Knox and I were close, and we kissed sometimes, but we mostly held hands and talked. Our bodies never made contact like this. It's both comforting and thrilling all at once.

Ryne kicks the side of the horse, and it starts to walk. I yelp, tightening my grip on the saddle as Ryne chuckles at me. I eventually settle in, allowing myself to enjoy the experience. We spend a while going in circles in the corral, learning the ropes of equine safety. Ryne is a great teacher and comfortable on a horse, even if his body pressing into mine is rather distracting.

"Ready to try something fun?" he asks.

"This *is* fun." I grin. "But sure."

"Hold on." He kicks the horse harder than last time, and the animal begins to gallop. It's not like we're going that fast, but I grip the saddle horn and squeal as adrenaline races through me. Across the corral, Joanna and Grady do the same. Her joyful laugh echoes through the space. We slow, and then Ryne hands me the reins so I can control the horse. It's different when I'm in control. I feel like the horse and I are connected somehow. And when we start to gallop again, it's as if we're about to fly.

We slow, and the stable hand opens a gate to allow us to ride the horses outside into the pasture. The sun is still high in the clear blue sky but will be approaching the horizon soon. By then I'll be safely back at Drayton Hall with the other girls, but I want this moment to last. I want it to be the middle of summer when the sun is generous with her time and not autumn when the nights are long.

"What do you think? Shall we race?" Ryne nods toward Grady and Joanna. She's got the reins, no surprise there, and it's clear that Grady couldn't care less. He's smirking like a love-sick idiot, obviously using this as an opportunity to wrap his arms around her body and get as close as possible. Joanna letting him is a huge step in the right direction for the couple.

I attempt to hand Ryne the reins. "Okay, but you steer the horse."

"Are you sure?"

"You know, for an alpha you sure are quick to hand off control to me."

"Maybe I want to lose control sometimes."

I can't see him, but I can hear the confession in his tone and feel the heat of him against my back. When he takes the reins from me, his hands linger against mine. It sets my belly on fire. How can something that is wrong feel so right? Ryne is a bad person. He's not safe. He isn't even one of the eligible betas. I shouldn't be enjoying his touch.

He calls out to the others, and we're off. I lean down, gripping the saddle, my face close to the horse's mane, and Ryne leans down with me. Our horse is bigger and faster than theirs and shoots out into the lead. Its hooves thunder against the earth, and bits of dirt and grass fly up around us. Cold wind rushes past me, kissing my cheeks. The movement of the animal brings Ryne and me even closer together. It's the most exhilarating moment of my life.

We come to the edge of a wooded area, and Ryne slows us, pumping his fist into the air in victory. He whoops, and I can't help but giggle.

"You won that time," Joanna calls out, "but we'll get you on the way back!"

We ride to a clearing within the trees, and the guys help us off the horses and tie them up. A large, red, checkered blanket is sprawled out in the center with a basket of food and wine sitting on the edge.

"Who's hungry?" Grady announces.

Joanna lights up. "Me! I'm famished."

"Are you hungry?" Ryne asks. I shake my head. I'm really not. We ate lunch before we came, and I'm still wired up from the race. "Me neither. Want to go for a walk?"

I shouldn't want to be alone with him, but I can't keep myself from nodding. He takes my hand, intertwining his fingers with mine, and leads me farther into the forest.

Fall is in full swing, and I pick up a red leaf that has fallen to the ground. Ryne clears his throat. "Did you spend a lot of time outdoors before you moved here?"

I nearly snort at the idea that I just moved here like I had a choice, but I answer his question anyway. "Yeah. Our homes were small and cramped, and we don't have electricity, but I'm sure you already know that. We all liked being outside, but I guess myself more than others. I enjoyed working in the fields and climbing trees."

Ryne pats the trunk of an old oak. "You mean like this one?"

I gaze up. The nearest limb is five feet off the ground, but I could probably swing myself up onto it.

"Yeah, like that one."

"Come here," he says, pulling me closer to him. He places his wide hands on my sides, just above my hips.

"What are you doing?" I ask.

"Helping you up." He hoists me high into the air, and my squeal nearly drowns out his chuckle. I grab the limb and swing myself up onto it, much like I did on the horse. Then I find the branch above it and pull myself up even farther. Ryne is close behind me as I make my way up the tree. I finally reach a wide limb and sit, my back to the trunk.

Ryne is close behind and sits across from me, straddling the limb. His eyes dance as he studies me. "That was fun. We'll have to climb trees more often."

"My sister, Willow, and I spent a lot of time up in the trees." My voice cracks a little at her name.

Ryne shimmies forward and brushes the hair out of my eyes. My skin burns where his fingers touch. "I am sorry about your sister. Anders's temper gets the best of him. If I had been there, she'd still be alive."

I nod, not wanting to think of that awful moment again. But I can't help the tear that slides down my cheek.

Ryne scoots even closer and brushes it away. "Hey, don't cry. I'm sorry. I didn't mean to make you upset. Tell me more about what your plans had been before coming here."

I pause, because it's not something I'd thought of often at home. In the months leading up to the claiming, I'd been solely focused on Willow leaving me. But I had come of age as well.

"I suppose I would've found a husband and continued working the fields like everyone else. But I also probably would've grown my own garden and helped increase our food supply. I liked working with my mother in hers, but she never had enough time to expand it."

"Why not?"

"Her own duties and general housekeeping. Plus us kids kept her on her toes. I have a little brother too, by the way. My mother's life probably would've been my fate as well."

He's quiet, and I wonder what he thinks of my past. But I don't ask.

The wind rustles the nearby poplar leaves like wind chimes, but I can scarcely focus on that when Ryne's pretty blue eyes stare into mine. This close, I can see the dark rims and the flecks of white. His black hair is tied back today, accentuating sharp cheekbones. There's something so manly about him, so foreign and alluring. Our eyes lock together, and my mind blanks.

He dips his head, moments away from kissing me.

I push my hand against his chest. "Stop."

"What's wrong?" His eyes go cold, and he scoots back. The moment is ruined. I don't understand what he is doing with me.

"What are your intentions?" I blurt.

"Umm––" He scratches the back of his head. "To kiss you."

He says it so plainly, and my stomach lurches.

I summon the courage to tell him exactly what's been on my mind since he slid into the car with us. He's toying with me. "Ryne, if you kiss me, and this becomes a thing between us, then what happens when we get back to the manor? Will your betas still think of me as an option, or will they consider me taken? I know I'm not as desirable as the other girls, but I have to at least try to escape the mating house. Isn't that why you took me there in the first place? To show me what my fate would be if I don't get a beta."

He's quiet for a minute, considering my words carefully. "My betas know I'm not taking a wife anytime soon. This won't matter. In fact, a relationship with me might even make you more desirable to them. It's an honor."

That fire in my belly from before turns to smoke. "The keyword there being might. Have you dated one of the claimed girls before?" I hate to ask the question because the answer might hurt, but I feel like I have a right to know. Willow would be proud. I'm a little surprised at myself as well.

A hard mask passes over his features. "You're right. Let's go back."

We don't talk after that, and I take his non-answer for a yes. He's the alpha, after all. He can take whatever woman he wants just as easily as he can discard her. And what if he takes her virtue also? Does that mean she's ineligible to marry a beta? He won't speak of past relationships with claimed girls, which probably means that whatever happened to them was not a happy ending. If every girl he dated ended up with a beta, then he wouldn't have backed off since that was my whole argument.

But truth be told, it is more than that. I don't want to date him and won't be okay when he gets bored. I have no idea why I caught his eye, and it doesn't matter. What matters is landing a beta so I can still have that family and garden and a semblance of a normal life.

"I think I'm hungry now," I say in a soft voice.

We scramble down the tree, and he helps me out of it but quickly drops his hands from my waist. We walk back to the clearing in a rather awkward silence, only to find Joanna and Grady kissing. Grady holds her like she's the most important thing in his entire world, and I'm faced with the stark truth. They're fated. We're not. Grady will never ever do to Joanna what Ryne is willing to do to me.

He just wants to kiss me and then hand me off to someone else. I don't want that. Even if he could promise that I'd end up with a beta after dating him, I don't think I'd do it. I have more than my body to guard. I have my heart as well.

Chapter Sixteen

"You will be sleeping downstairs tonight," Madame Delphine announces during dinner. We're seated at the dining tables with a bigger feast than normal and immediately cease chattering at her announcement. "Now, girls, I know this may seem a little extreme, but I assure you it is a customary precaution for all humans living in the city to spend full moons under lock and key. The only exceptions are the celebratory moons, but even with those, most humans choose to stay inside." I exchange a worried glance with Joanna, and she grimaces. This doesn't sound good. We were never this locked up in our village. It seems strange that we're in more danger here in the wolf city than we were there.

"It is much easier for us to lock up one or two rooms than to try to board up the entire manor," Delphine continues. "God forbid a lycan got past our border patrols and came here. They would kill you without hesitation."

My stomach goes hard, and I put down my dinner roll. Since the moment Joanna and I were dropped off late this afternoon from our double date, I could think of little else, but now visions of bloodthirsty lycans take over my mind. I'm sure I'll have nightmares tonight, and it's not something I'm looking forward to.

"So chop-chop." Madame Delphine claps her hands. "Finish up and then go get into your pajamas and meet us downstairs."

Charlotte is the first to leave, dashing up the stairs to our bedroom. By the time I go up myself, she's already changed into silky pink pants and a matching button-up. She leans across the vanity with her face inches away from the mirror, staring intently into her eyes. Her cheeks are bright pink as if she's just returned from a run. Sweat beads along her hairline.

"Are you okay?"

She jumps and turns on me with accusatory eyes. Maybe she's getting sick and doesn't want to be left out of the safest spot in the house tonight, but having us all sleep in the same room might not be a good idea.

"I'm fine," she snaps. "Mind your own business." And then she storms away like I've offended her.

"I'll mind my own business when you mind yours," I growl to nobody as I get dressed and head downstairs.

Maybe Charlotte isn't sick. Maybe she's angry about my date with Ryne. I'd hoped to keep it a secret, but that seems to be impossible around here. The second we returned this afternoon, everyone already knew. Their distrustful and jealous faces said it all. I decide to let the Charlotte thing go for now, but I'm going to avoid sleeping next to her just in case she's ill or up to something.

I glance at the board on the way down. My name is third from the bottom. It's not the best position to be in, but at least I've moved up a couple of places.

In the windowless battle room, twenty-three cots are set up, each piled with a fluffy white blanket and pillow. The room's big enough to fit us all plus Madames Delphine, Vivien, and Lucille.

"The rest of the staff left for their own homes hours ago," Madame Delphine says once everyone has arrived. "We will all be staying in here. If you need to use the restroom, one of us can escort you, but please, I'd rather not open this door once it's locked, so I hope you've emptied your bladders already."

A couple of the girls raise their hands sheepishly, and Madame Lucille ushers them out. Everyone seems nervous with their worried eyes and thin lips. Even Faye and Joanna, opposite sides of the same tough-girl coin, are a bit jumpy tonight. The girls from the bathroom run are quick to return, and then we all settle into our beds. Madame Delphine lights a small lamp and turns off the overhead lights before locking us in. She doesn't use a key. She slides a metal barricade across the door that slams shut with a bang.

A few of the girls gasp.

"This is all customary," she assures us. "Lycans rarely make it into the city, but we're being extra careful, especially after the harvest moon last month. Not only are there wolves stationed all over the city and at the borders to the wilds, but your betas are outside, prowling the grounds at this very moment. They'll be out there all night in their wolf forms."

As if on cue, a series of howls echoes outside. Inside, some of the girls start to cry.

"That's our men, isn't it? Not the lycans?" Faye speaks up.

"Yes," Delphine says. "Lycanthrope calls are less . . . organized. They sound more like guttural screeching than actual wolves. And they're much, much louder. Not to worry. Again, this is all normal. Please, let's all try to relax. You're welcome to talk among yourselves for a half-hour, and then it'll be lights out for everyone."

I turn in my bed, ignoring the cot's squeaking, and face Joanna. "Are you scared?"

"No," she whispers. "If anything, I think this would be the perfect time to escape."

"Are you crazy? There are wolves everywhere. And lycans in the wilds. Besides, I thought you liked Grady." I whisper even lower. "Ryne and I totally saw you two kissing."

She scrunches her cheeks and sighs dreamily. "He is rather nice, isn't he? Better than I thought . . . But he's still not my plan."

"So then what's the real plan here, Joanna? I still don't understand it. Where do you think you'll go?"

"I can't reveal anything yet, but I'm working on it. Besides, we have eleven more months until the claiming. Give me time."

If anyone can find a way out of here, it's Joanna, but that only makes me afraid for her. For as much as that woman is determined, the wolves are too, and they have fangs and claws. Part of me wants to go with her when she escapes, but another part is stuck in the fear of the unknown, and that part might keep me planted right here.

"So what happened with Ryne?" Joanna whispers back. I close my eyes for a second and try to figure out how to respond.

"He tried to kiss me, but I didn't let him."

Her eyes widen. "Why not? He's gorgeous and the alpha. He could help you."

I disagree, but even if she's right, it still doesn't change the fact that I don't want to be used, especially not by someone who could break my heart on a whim.

"Okay, ladies, lights out." Madame Delphine turns off the lamp, plunging the basement into blackness. A few of the girls squeal and giggle. Joanna reaches over and grips my hand. I squeeze back.

"Now, calm down. It would be good for you all to try to get to sleep before the howling of the lycans starts. It'll be much harder then."

The howling of the lycans? We rarely heard their howling back home. This city must be their target, so maybe that explains why they don't come around the villages anymore. But if they're smart enough to have a target, then are they as unhinged as we've been led to believe? If lycans only want human flesh, why go after the wolf shifters at all?

A hush falls across the room, and I replay my afternoon with Ryne again even though I know I shouldn't--the more I push them away, the more the memories flood me. Maybe I should've let him kiss me. He was nice, and his very touch caused my heart to race in a way I've never experienced before. Why did I deny him? I know there were many logical reasons, but here in the dark, I can't think of them.

A howl pierces the silence. It's guttural and screechy, sending warning prickles across my skin. I clamp my hands over my ears.

The howl didn't come from outside.

<h1 style="text-align:center">Chapter Seventeen</h1>

A clatter followed by a scream comes from the other side of the room. I spring from my cot and find Joanna's hand. "What's going on?" she asks. It's pitch black. We can't see anything.

"I have no idea," I shout over the noise. Girls are screaming. At first they sound surprised, then frightened, but it's the horrified wails of pain that will forever be etched into my memory. Joanna and I move away from the noise and run into other girls doing the same. Something loud and metallic sounding slams against a wall.

"Don't step on me," Faye's voice growls, and she shoves me hard.

The lamp light flicks on, momentarily blinding me. I squint to let my eyes adjust.

Then I scramble back. A fully grown lycan towers over Madame Lucille. It's so tall that its head brushes the ceiling. Its grotesque limbs are covered in matted gray hair, and saliva drips from its snarling mouth.

Madame Lucille holds up her hands. "No, no, no," she gasps. The lycan bares long bloody teeth, snapping them shut around Madame Lucille's neck. Blood spurts around the monster's mouth as it gives a mighty shake. Madame Lucille's body goes flying one direction and her head another, an arc of blood between them.

More screams.

The lycan crouches onto all fours and turns on us, surveying the room with bloodthirsty eyes. They shine like the pale white of the moon. We're all dead.

Madame Delphine scrambles at the door, fumbling with the lock.

Time seems to slow as she flings it up and pushes the door wide. A gust of wind blows into the room, and the lycan stands up on its haunches and sniffs. Madame Delphine swings around to hold the door open from behind, and we all will it to run out.

It doesn't.

It takes a slow walk around the room. None of us move. The lycan sniffs at Faye, its muzzle grazing her auburn hair, and a trickle of urine slides down her leg. I'd do the same if I were in her shoes. Joanna and I are pressed up against the wall, but the creature is so close that we can smell its putrid breath. It moves even closer to Faye, its mouth slowly opening. It's going to bite her.

I don't think. I just react. "Hey!" I yell. "Over here!"

It turns its head, eyes narrowing in on me. Oh no, what have I done?

I let go of Joanna and inch along the wall toward the door. I keep my eyes locked on the lycan as it stalks toward me. I need a weapon. Something. Anything. But there's nothing. We're trapped in here with this monster and now it's picked me as its next victim. It lowers onto its haunches, readying to pounce. Fear twists my stomach, and I think I might vomit. I can't let it touch me. I won't die tonight.

It dives for me, but I roll out of the way at the last second. Its long claws decimate the floor right where I was standing moments before. Adrenaline urges me to keep moving. If I can just get out the door, maybe I can find something to fight it with. This is our sparring room, but there are no weapons in here. We were told we'd be learning weapons training later, but I can see now that to have us wait was completely foolish. We're not going to be fighting hand-to-hand combat against *lycan*. If only there were something here. I'm suddenly on my hands and knees, crawling as fast as I can for the exit, but there's no way I can outrun the monster.

Another lycan howls from outside the house. Ours jerks its head around and lets out its own higher-pitched howl. My ears ring, and the monster turns back again, coming right for me. I scream, sure this is going to be the end. I hope my death is quick. I know it won't be painless. I ready myself to fight to the bitter end, but it passes me, taking off out the door.

Madame Delphine slumps against it.

"What are you doing?" Madame Vivien hisses at her. "Shut the door."

Footsteps pound down the stairs, and six wolves race into the room. The girls are yelling to close the door. Madame Delphine slams the door shut and locks all of us inside. The room is a mess. There's blood everywhere and a tangle of bodies on the far side. Joanna appears next to me and wraps her arms around my neck. "Are you okay? Did it bite you?"

Before I can answer, the wolves shift into men--our betas and Ryne--and I avert my eyes at their nakedness. Grady races over to us and jerks Joanna away from me. He hugs her tight, and she squirms in his arms. "Let me go."

He obliges, but he keeps her close. "Are you hurt?"

She keeps her eyes planted firmly on his face. "I'm fine. Now would you go put some clothes on?"

The other wolves are with Madame Delphine by a chest of drawers. She hands them all loose black shorts for them to dress into, though I don't think they care. Grady drags Joanna with him to the others and gets himself a pair.

Ryne meets my eye but doesn't come over to me, and I don't move either. He's covered in dirt and blood, anger contorting his handsome face into something unrecognizable. He puts a hand on his mother's shoulder and whispers something in her ear. She whimpers, a tear streaking down her cheek, and nods. She whispers something back to him, and he looks at me for a long moment.

Ryne speaks to his betas loud enough for us to hear, even over the sound of all the girls crying. I'm one of them—I can't help it. I've never seen so much blood, and now that it's over, the reality of it hits me square in the chest. "Anders, inspect everyone for bites. Nico and Justin, take the bodies away and burn them."

I blink at that word, bodies.

Plural.

I don't want to look, don't want to know who else the lycan has killed.

Ryne turns to Grady and Cade. "We're going after her."

"Who?" the question slips from my tongue.

Ryne levels me with a sullen expression. "Charlotte."

I gasp, and my thoughts quickly fill with shame. I should have known. I spent the last month in the same room as her. How did I not see it before? *She was bit!* That night at the Wolf Moon Festival, she was bit . .
.

And she didn't want anyone to know, least of all her roommate.

Grady gives Joanna a quick hug but ultimately does as his alpha instructs, sprinting out of the room. Cade and Ryne follow. Nico and Justin begin carrying the bodies out and I can't help but look this time.

The two girls who had been sleeping on the other side of Charlotte have been shredded to bloody pieces. They're in worse shape than Madame Lucille even, and she's been decapitated.

Now that I'm looking, I can't stop staring.

Someone tugs on my arm, and I turn to Faye, who swings her hand, slapping me clean across the face. I screech and fall to my butt. "She's from *your* village! She was *your* roommate. Why did you protect her?"

I shake my head. "I--I didn't know." But I should have. She wouldn't change her clothing in front of me. She was cagey and withdrawn. She was meaner than I've ever known her to be, and she even looked sick tonight. How did I not see it?

"Faye, you should be grateful for Poppy. She saved your ass tonight," Joanna cuts in. She storms across the room and comes to stand between me and Faye.

"Not when it was her fault to begin with!" Faye snarls back.

She's right. The signs were there.

Faye lunges forward past Joanna to get to me, but Joanna catches her, and the two start clawing at each other. Madame Delphine is quick to pull them apart. "Enough. We'll make inquiries later. Right now we have to inspect everyone for bites. There's no time to waste."

"That's right." Anders strides to the middle of the room. "Everybody strip."

"Excuse me?" Joanna barks. "I'm not stripping for anyone."

Anders narrows his icy eyes. His bronzed skin is covered in sweat, and the lines around his eyes and mouth are deeper than normal. He's not playing around. "If you don't let me inspect you for bites, then I will assume you are infected, and I will kill you myself."

"But Grady--"

"Grady isn't here," he roars. "And this is a command from the alpha, so Grady wouldn't be able to stop me."

Joanna looks to Madame Delphine, who nods in confirmation.

Anders laughs and opens his hands wide. I think his expression is an attempt at being charming, but I find it severely lacking.

"If anyone needs help removing their clothing, that can be arranged," he jokes.

Nobody laughs.

We do as we're told. I'm shaking, embarrassed, and hating my lack of curves even more now that I have to undress in front of other girls who've spent the last month belittling me. But maybe we'll all be too traumatized by what happened tonight to remember much of this come morning. No. It will be an extra dark stain on our time here at Drayton Hall, one we'll want to forget, but I'm sure we won't.

Cool air wraps around my limbs as I stand naked, one hand over each of my private areas. Anders takes his time inspecting every inch of the girls. He takes extra time with Joanna just to make her mad, and of course it works. Her cheeks flame, but she stands tall, refusing to back down. He tugs at her short hair, and she snaps her head back. He shakes his head and moves on. When he gets to me, our eyes lock. Even though his are hooded in shadow and almost impossible to read, the lust swirling with them is unmistakable.

"Drop your hands," he says slowly.

I swallow hard and release them from where they're covering me. What I don't expect is his touch. I flinch away. "You didn't touch the other girls," I breathe.

"Don't move," he says slowly. "And don't talk either. I like you better when you don't talk." And then he runs his sweaty hands across my torso and around to my lower back, his fingers edging along the top of my cheeks. My stomach churns. All he would have to do is move them a few inches lower to cup my butt and it would be the exact same move he did to Willow. I should fight back as she did, but before I can channel my dead sister's bravery, his hands are gone, and he steps away to inspect the next girl. Humiliated, I turn away and hurry back into my pajamas.

"Please, don't," the girl whimpers.

I swing around to watch, assuming he's doing the same to her as he just did to me, but I'm wrong.

A wolfish growl rips through the room as he picks her up, naked and all, carrying her away. "She's been bitten," he calls to us. "I'll be back in five minutes. Don't move."

"What's he going to do to her?" Ivy asks.

Faye snorts bitterly. "Kill her and burn her. Same as they do to any human who's been bit."

Joanna makes for the door. "Not on my watch. It's not her fault."

Madame Delphine and Madame Vivien block her path.

"Move out of my way!"

"Get back in line, Joanna." Madame Delphine sounds bone tired. "There's nothing anyone can do. He'll make it quick and as painless as possible." Her sad eyes travel across the lot of us. "And then he'll finish his inspection on the rest of you."

"Has anyone else been bitten?" Madame Vivien asks gently. Her face is streaked with tears. I've never seen her like this. She's normally such a professional woman. As an instructor and house mother, she has a quiet and stern way about her. "It would be better if you told us now," she continues. "We should have inspected you after the lycanthropes attack at the harvest moon festival. We made a grave mistake that has cost us five lives." Tears brim in her eyes.

First to go were Teresa and Lily, but at least they were murdered in darkness, where we didn't have to watch it happen. But I'll never forget the way Madame Lucille died so similarly to Willow. And now Belinda has gone with Anders to die. I hope they're right, and that he'll make it quick, but I have my doubts.

"Who's the fifth life?" someone asks.

"Charlotte, of course." Madame Delphine sighs regretfully. "They'll hunt her down and kill her. But even if she somehow manages to get away and can find a way to survive in the wilds, she's lost to the lycanthropic virus. Charlotte as you knew her is gone."

I plop down on the cot and bury my face in my palms. It's no secret that I never particularly liked Charlotte, but she didn't deserve this. She should have told someone about the bite. But then what would have happened? She'd have been sentenced to death, no questions asked, no way to plead her case. Nothing. She was probably scared out of her mind all month long. Maybe if I'd been a better friend to her, she would have confessed the bite to me, and I could have somehow helped her. None of these people had to die. All of this could've been avoided.

Faye was right to slap me.

Anders strolls back into the room and zeros in on the girls who haven't dressed yet. "Who's next?"

Chapter Eighteen

After it's over, we're sent back to our bedrooms, and more betas are called in to stand guard at our doors. Joanna and I lie there in the dark, neither one of us able to speak. She took Charlotte's bed because she didn't want me to be alone. The memories of tonight scrape through my mind like the edge of a knife, and I don't think I'll be able to sleep. I can't help but stare at the darkened window. I'm not safe in here either, but I don't have anywhere else to go.

Sometime later there's knocking on the door, and I'm jolted awake. Sunlight filters through the curtains, just like any other morning.

"No workouts today." I hear Madame Vivien through the door. "Get dressed in your gowns and come down for breakfast."

Joanna has altered all my outfits by now, and the ones that we weren't able to make use of, Madame Delphine switched out for new ones. I choose my simplest gown. It's black and unadorned with lace or jewels, but it's still tight in the bodice and flares out at the waist. It's uncomfortable, and I'd give anything to swap these gowns out for my ugly work clothes back home. I wonder if I'll ever wear farming clothes again.

"I'm going to wear black too," Joanna says. "We all should." She sits me down and begins brushing my hair out for me. I didn't have to ask. She just knew I needed her help today. "It's not your fault, you know."

"Isn't it?" I let out a breath. I can still smell Charlotte's rosy scent in this room.

"No, it isn't," she insists. "It's the wolves, and it's the lycans, and

Charlotte's. And I'm not going to let anyone blame you for it, not even you."

I reach out and pat her hand, holding her gaze in the mirror. Her brown eyes hold mine and I find strength there, as if she's giving it to me from sheer force of will. I've never had a friend like her——someone who feels like blood even though they aren't. "Thank you."

Joanna finishes up and then leaves to get herself dressed. As she goes, I notice little brown specks of dried blood on the back of her silk pajamas. I don't think anyone got out of that room without some kind of stain, visible or otherwise.

Breakfast is a solemn affair. Most of us can't even eat. When the perimeter is declared to be safe, we're sent outside to an art lesson. I sit and stare at the white canvas but don't touch a single drop of paint. The betas don't join us, and nobody speaks to me.

That night at dinner, Faye asks Madame Delphine the question we're all wondering. "Excuse me, Madame," she says, between sips of water. "Did they ever find Charlotte?"

"Not yet," Madame Delphine replies. "They lost her scent at the river. She's probably to the wilds by now."

I wonder what she's feeling. Is she afraid? Angry? Regretful? Does she even remember what she did to us? Did she know she was going to turn? Maybe she thought she wasn't infected. Maybe she did, and she wanted to hurt us. I'll never know the answers to these questions.

The next morning it's back to business as usual. We meet out on the lawn. Madame Vivien is there to give us our workout assignment.

"Poppy," she calls to me. There's a darkness in her eyes——something I've never seen there before. "Come here."

I go to her, and she glares down at me. She's one of the only women I've met who's actually taller than I am. "You and I are going to be doing a one-on-one workout today." She looks to the others. "Go ahead and do whatever exercises you'd like."

Whispers erupt, and a few head off to run while most stick close by, their eyes never straying too far from me and Madame Vivien. "Do one hundred pushups." She points to the ground. I stare at her for a second. "Now. Go!"

I drop down and start. My muscles are tired, but I endure and go as quickly as I can. I have a feeling this is just the beginning of what's going to be an intense hour. A minute later, someone drops down next to me.

"What are you doing, Joanna?" Madame Vivien asks.

"You said we could do whatever exercise we wanted," Joanna hisses. "So I'm going to stick with my friend and do what she does. If you want to punish her for something she had absolutely no control over, then you can punish me as well."

I can't believe Joanna is calling her out like that. Apparently, Madame Vivien can't either, because she huffs out a breath and stalks away. But she's back as soon as the push ups are done and tells me to get up and do a hundred burpees.

"I don't know what that is."

Her face goes red. "Watch carefully." She drops down, extends her legs back, brings them in again, and stands back up. "Now, go." She smirks at Joanna. "Both of you."

We start, and I quickly realize these are ten times harder because they combine cardio with pushups, and my arms are already screaming. The rest of the hour continues much the same way with a series of difficult exercises, many of them new to me, but I don't mind. Maybe I deserve to be punished, maybe I don't, but I like the way my thoughts go numb. Every muscle screams for relief, but I don't let up. I have to be stronger. And whenever Madame Vivien gives me a new exercise, I treat it like a challenge. Sweat pours from my body, and I gasp for every breath. I need water, but I don't ask. My only regret is that Joanna is doing this with me, but she never once complains.

"What's going on here?" Grady's voice cuts through the cool morning. Joanna and I turn from where we're doing sit-ups with Madame Vivien looming over us like a mountain of rage. He stands with Ryne, and both of them are staring.

"These girls are getting a personal training session from me," Madame Vivien says. "You do not need to concern yourselves with their physical fitness. That's my job."

"It looks like you're trying to hurt them." Grady storms over. He hauls Joanna up and tucks her under his arm. "Do they even have water?"

"I assure you that I know exactly what I'm doing," Madame Vivien snaps.

"Go inside." Ryne steps forward, his eyes leveled on our house mother. "We will finish up with the ladies."

She huffs and stomps off.

"Let's get you something to drink." Grady walks Joanna toward the back of the house where the kitchen door is located. Ryne and I stand there, staring at each other. My breath starts to slow, and now that I've stopped moving, my mind begins to let the troubled thoughts in.

"Why did you do that?" I ask. "I had it under control."

He folds his arms over his broad chest and glowers at me. "I was trying to help you."

"Madame Vivien doesn't need to be ordered around on my behalf. If I'm ever going to get her to respect me, then I have to show her I'm strong."

"The woman lost her best friend of many years," he challenges, "and she was taking it out on the one person she has left to blame."

So he blames me too? A wash of regret prickles through me, and I turn away. He reaches out and snatches my hand. I don't turn back. "Hey, I didn't mean it like that. There's no logic behind blaming you, and I don't, and I'm sorry if others do. If anyone's to blame, it's me. I'm the alpha of this pack. Protecting this manor is my job."

I scoff at that, ripping my hand from his and walking toward the house.

"Why are you angry with me?" he asks.

"I agree that you should protect us, Ryne," I say, flipping back around. I wipe the sweat from my forehead, but not because I care what he thinks of me right now. All my guilt has balled into anger that I want to hurl right at him. "What is the point of our combat training, huh? We fight you guys hand to hand. That does nothing to prepare us for a real attack."

"There's a method––"

"Well then, your method's crap! We should be fighting you in wolf form, in your *strongest* form. And we should be learning to use weapons."

He shakes his head. "These things take time. Once we get through the first two rounds of cuts, we will spend the second half of the year working with weapons. But our men will not turn into wolves to fight you. It's too dangerous."

"Why are we bothering with this becoming-a-proper-lady nonsense when there's a real threat out there? We should do everything I've suggested, and we should do it now."

"No." His word is hard and fast, like a slap to the cheek.

I'm filled with disgust. "Every single woman who comes to the

Carolina Pack deserves to learn how to protect herself." My throat goes raw. "Especially the ones who are sent to the mating houses."

His face stills, and his eyes narrow. "You don't trust me."

"No, I don't." And then I turn and run away toward the kitchen. I need to find water and a chance to breathe, but most of all I need to get away from him before I say something else I might regret. Because as soon as I blurted that I didn't trust him, deep down I knew I was lying. I shouldn't trust him, but for some reason I do, and I still can't figure out why.

Chapter Nineteen

I wake up gasping. Sweat beads along my hairline, reminding me of the blood that haunts my dreams every night. I sit up in the dark, clutching my chest. *Another nightmare.* It feels like it's been ages since I slept soundly, and with the next full moon coming up in only a week, I don't know how I'll ever sleep well again. I look over to Charlotte's bed, relieved to find a mound of short dark hair on the white pillow instead of Charlotte's long blonde curls. Joanna moved in to get away from Faye, but also, I suspect, to comfort me. At least I didn't wake her up with this latest nightmare.

The weeks since that terrible full moon have passed by in a blur. They never found Charlotte. I worry that she'll come back for me. It's gotten so bad that every night I end up dreaming about lycan fangs and pooling blood and horrible, horrible screaming. The rest of the girls hate me more than ever. Faye keeps telling them I must have known, and that I was hoping Charlotte would take out my competition. There's no use defending myself because the girls refuse to hear me out. Madame Delphine and Joanna believe that I didn't know anything about Charlotte, and I think the betas do too, but no one else does.

I've heard the girls talk about their own nightmares. Nobody is going to get over this easily. Our lessons have continued as normal, with Madames Delphine and Vivien filling in for Lucille. Out of everyone, I'm still certain that Madame Vivien hates me the most. A few times a week she singles me out again, and I endure her workouts without complaint. I'm getting stronger and faster, and I keep hoping

I'll gain her respect, or at least her forgiveness, but nothing changes. She looks at me as if I'm the lycanthrope, as if I decapitated Lucille myself.

I don't have the heart to tell her that I enjoy the punishing workouts. It's the only thing that clears my head. And besides, they're all probably right to hate me--I should've seen the signs. But then again, Charlotte should've asked for help, and the wolves should've checked for bites the first time. Ryne was right when he said he's to blame too. There are many of these "shoulds" floating around the manor these days, but none of them can bring the dead back to life.

It's Saturday morning, so we're permitted to sleep in, but I can't handle being in this room for another second. I need another grueling workout to empty my mind. I peel myself away from the bed and peer out the window. The waxing moon is still in the sky, getting bigger every day, but the sun is rising. That's all I need. I quietly slip into my workout gear and head out for a run. On my way, I stop in the entry to catch up on the scoreboard.

Now that four more girls are gone, I've dropped back down into the bottom of the group. I'm not surprised, not after the past seven weeks I've had struggling with letters, failing at music, and even leaving my canvas blank during most of the art lessons. I haven't given my all anymore when we've had combat training on Thursdays. I've tried to bring up my very valid points again in front of the other girls, hoping they'll back me up, but the men continue to tell us to be patient and *trust the process*--which has to be the most infuriating phrase on the planet. All around, I'm disappointed. My name being in the bottom placement is expected, but it still stings.

What am I thinking? I shake my head to snap myself out of this downward spiral.

I'm being selfish. There are only sixteen of us now. It's hard to believe we've already lost six girls, but we have--seven if we count Willow, which I do. I should be grateful to be alive, not wallowing over my low score. I need to get my determination back. I need to find my grit again before I end up in a mating house.

"I know you were trying harder," Madame Delphine says, and I jump. "But you seem to have lost your spirit again."

I spin to find her watching me from the top of the stairs. She's already dressed for the day in the ugly maroon gowns the house mothers wear. She comes down and stands right next to me. She looks older and softer than I remember with more creases around her eyes and more gray hairs. I see her daily, but that doesn't mean I really look at her. I've been in my own world so much lately that I hardly notice anyone anymore. And right now, there's something in this woman's eyes that appears to be sympathy. I try not to read too much into it.

"Looks like I'm at the bottom again." I frown at the scoreboard.

"I know." She pauses. "What happened with Charlotte has been hard on you."

"Yeah, and I only have about a month to move up." I squeeze my hands into fists. "I don't want to go to the mating house."

"You are a strong woman. I don't think that will be your fate."

I snort, wishing she'll prove to be right. "Even if I manage to climb farther up the board, none of the betas are going to choose me at the next harvest. I'm not pretty enough."

"Honey, if it were just looks the betas were after, we'd place you all the first night."

"Well, I'm not talented either. All these lessons--singing, dancing, music, art, reading. I am terrible at everything. And I just don't get why it's so important."

"It's the custom," her voice trails off and then lowers. "But it's also a way for them to keep the pack strong. The hierarchy among the human women mirrors much of the hierarchy among the wolves. The mating houses aren't created equally, and it's no secret that the beta wives get to enjoy luxuries that aren't afforded to the others."

I think about that for a minute, tying together what she's saying with what she's not saying. If they make us earn our spots in the upper class, make us fight tooth and nail to get a husband, then maybe we'll help them keep this system going instead of trying to dismantle it. Things are starting to make sense now, and my stomach hardens.

Madame Delphine clears her throat and steps back, donning her professionalism once again. "The betas also want women they can relate to and enjoy spending time with, women who are strong against our enemies and who will be loyal to their husbands, no matter what. Who wouldn't want to hold an intelligent conversation with their spouse? You're very smart, Poppy, more so than you give yourself credit for."

"Thanks," I whisper. I didn't know how much I needed the compliment until it was mine.

"These are all areas that you shine in. I believe Anders already has his eye on you, and I'm certain once you start spending time with the others, your score will go up."

I swallow hard. I don't want Anders and can still feel his grimy hands on me. The one good thing about the last few weeks since the full moon is that we haven't seen the betas as often, and the dates were postponed. Nobody will tell us why, but I believe it has something to do with the war going on between the wolves and the lycans––something happened that night, and our men have been extra busy ever since.

"We're starting the dates today." Madame Delphine pats me on the shoulder. "And the betas get to add points for your behavior. I'm certain you'll do well."

The front door opens, breaking the otherwise still morning, and Madame Delphine and I spin around. Ryne sticks his head in, followed by a very pretty woman. Appearing perhaps in her late twenties, she has wide blue eyes and long blonde hair that falls in soft curls around her face. I wonder if she's the wife of a beta. She certainly looks the part.

"Mother," Ryne says, kissing her on the cheek. The woman gives a slight curtsy. "I've brought you Lucille's replacement. I think you will find her very capable."

Madame eyes her warily. "Oh my, you're young. When did you retire?"

The woman clears her throat. "Yesterday."

I expected her voice to be breathy or soft, but she speaks with command and authority. She'll have no trouble gaining our respect, but she still seems too young to be staff here compared to the other house mothers.

"Welcome to our home. Meet Poppy, one of our girls."

"Hello, Poppy." The woman smiles and then flicks her eye up to the board as if she's done it before, which I'm sure she has. She scans it until her eyes land on my name, then holds out her hand. "I'm Nova. Perhaps I can help you escape my fate. We will see what we can do about getting you to rise up on the scoreboard."

I nod, liking her already. "Thank you. I can use all the help I can get."

Ryne won't look at me. He hasn't said a word to me since our argument, and that feels like eons ago now. He stands near me though, and his musky smell lingers in the air––hinting of snowstorms. We only get a few snowfalls each year, but the smell is so unique, so clean and crisp. It covers the rest of the world. That mixed with cedarwood is Ryne's scent, and I have to fight the urge to close my eyes and breathe it in. So instead, I study his black hair and the way it's tied back at the nape of his neck, accentuating his high cheekbones. His jaw clicks, and his shoulders stiffen. He knows I'm watching him.

Madame Delphine clears her throat, and I snap my eyes back to the ladies, my cheeks instantly going hot.

"It's nice meeting you, Madame Nova." I turn and head out for my run. I can't stand being near Ryne and not talking to him, let alone finding myself wrapped up in his presence when he can't even be bothered to look in my direction. I slip out the door, the scent of snowfall all around me despite the amber sunrise.

Joanna fluffs up her hair. It's getting longer and is close to hitting the top of her shoulders. It still looks great, but I can tell she's bothered by the odd length.

"How do you think she managed to leave the mating house so young?" she asks.

I shrug. "I don't know." Everyone has been talking about Madame Nova all day. We didn't have any lessons with her yet, but she observed all of them. She sat next to me in reading class and helped me sound out words. I still can't read full sentences, but something about her enthusiasm made me think that maybe I'm not a lost cause.

"Why am I even bothering to get ready? I should be helping you," Joanna says.

She retrieves a navy-blue gown from the closet and holds it up against my body. It's got a plunging v-neckline in the front *and* the back. I'm not sure how comfortable I'll be wearing something so revealing, but it should draw attention, and isn't that the point?

We're doing our first group date this evening, and all the girls are in a frenzy. The betas are taking us out for dinner, and we were told to dress our best. The entire house is a flurry of activity as the girls get ready. Thankfully Joanna and I have this room to ourselves.

"I don't even want to go on this date. What if I get stuck with Anders?"

"Then you get stuck with Anders. It's better than the mating house."

"Joanna! You saw him grope me. You know how he killed my sister?" My voice shakes. "He touched me in the exact same way that he touched her."

"That's brutal." She frowns. "But I still think being with Anders is better than living in a mating house. Anders is the type to go to the mating houses even when he's married. But if you're at the mating house, he'll be able to do whatever he wants with you, but so will a thousand other men."

I glare at her.

"You know I'm right," she huffs. "Don't shoot the messenger. Now sit. I'll do your makeup."

We spend the next hour doing hair and makeup and then head into the foyer with the rest of the girls. The betas haven't arrived yet. There are sixteen of us but only five betas, so the tension grows thick with each new girl to walk into the foyer. Joanna is dressed in black--she purposely didn't choose her best gown, but she looks amazing anyway. She gets Grady all to herself, so the rest of us will be going in groups of four. The top four girls on the scoreboard get to choose their dates. The rest of us will be chosen by the betas.

Madame Nova comes up next to me, now wearing the maroon dress the house mothers wear. It looks odd, aging her at least ten years. "What beta have you had your eye on?"

I let out a breath. "Anyone but Anders."

She raises an eyebrow. "Okay. Good to know."

The door opens, and Ryne walks in first. I didn't realize he would be here, and my breath picks up speed. His eyes land on me, traveling down my neckline and back up again. They lock with mine, and I hold them, daring him to be the first to break eye contact. He does, quickly shifting his gaze to the rest of the women. Anders is just behind him, followed by Nico, Cade, and Justin. They're all dressed in suits and look great, but I can't seem to pay them any attention when Ryne is in this little room, especially not when he is dressed up like that.

The men scan the room, clearly enjoying the array of beautiful young women. Nico stiffens and lunges across the room toward me. I yelp and stumble back just as he grabs Madame Nova, studying her face as if committing it to memory. "Mine," he says and smashes his lips against hers.

Gasps erupt across the room. Anders is there in seconds, ripping them apart. Madame Nova breaks away breathless. Her eyes shine as she looks up at Nico.

"Nico, she's barren," Anders hisses. His face has gone red, and his entire body is so rigid that I'm certain he's about ready to explode into his wolf form.

"You think I care?" Nico scoffs. "Have you ever heard of a wolf denying his true mate?"

Ryne raises his hands with a little frown, and Anders deflates. Everyone turns to Ryne, waiting for him to say something. All the while, Madame Nova hasn't said a word, but her face has drained of color. "She won't be able to bear you children," Anders says, as if that should outweigh a man's fated mate.

"We don't know that," Nico replies. "Maybe since she's my fated, she'll be able to bear my children. But I don't care either way. I'm taking her." He turns to the alpha. "Will you stop me?"

Ryne shakes his head.

"I thought I was done doing sexual favors for wolves." Madame Nova snaps out of it and pushes back against Nico.

Joanna snorts. "Go, Nova," she whispers.

Madame Nova glowers at Ryne. "You promised I would have this post. I do not wish to be anyone's wife, fated or not. Are you going to break your word to me?"

The tension grows thick as everyone holds their breath. Nobody challenges the alpha, let alone a woman. It makes me like Nova even more. "I cannot deny any wolf his fated mate," Ryne says at last. "It's pack law."

"And how do you know I'm truly his mate?" she questions. "He could be lying."

"It's not possible to speak a lie about someone being a fated mate to another member of the pack," Ryne says simply. "Our pack bond wouldn't allow it. I assure you that Nico *is* your mate."

Madame Nova turns her glare on Nico. "I cannot bear children, and I do not wish to be with another man for the rest of my days."

"But it's meant to be." Hurt crosses Nico's expression, like she's breaking his heart even though he doesn't know more than her name. The bond of mates must be more powerful than I thought. I can't imagine looking at someone and instantly knowing I'm supposed to be with that person for the rest of my life. But I also can't imagine turning into a wolf. There are a lot of things about shifters that don't make logical sense.

"Please," Nova relents. "It would weaken the Carolina Pack to take me as your mate." Her hand sweeps toward the rest of us girls. "There are many here who want nothing more than to be your mate. Wonderful girls who would be able to bear you a brood of boys and make you happy. Choose one of them and leave me alone."

Nico runs a hand through his mess of chestnut curls and finally lets out a growl. "Fine."

But I don't believe him.

I don't think any of the girls believe him.

Come time for the harvest next fall, Nico won't be selecting any of us as his mate if he can help it. But he's also one of the kinder men here, and he's not going to force himself on anyone against her will.

"Under one condition," he adds, inching closer to Nova. "You come live with me for the rest of this year." If there were any last shreds of hope in the room, they evaporate. These two are practically a done deal, and even though her mouth thins and her eyes narrow, we all know it's only a matter of time until she gives in to fate. That's the way these things go. "I don't expect you to touch me," Nico continues. "You'll have your own room, and you can spend your time as you wish. If you hate the life I have to offer you, then you can leave, and I will choose one of these claimed at the next harvest festival. I'll never bother you again."

She juts her chin. "And what of my post here?"

"I'll bring you here each morning and take you home each night." It's an easy solution. "I'm here often, and besides, a lot of the staff come and go for their shifts. There's no reason why you should have to live here to do your job."

She considers his words. "You promise that if I refuse you at the next harvest, you will never bother me again?"

He reaches his hand toward her to seal the deal. "On my honor as a beta."

They shake hands.

But it's pointless. They're *fated,* and Nico is charming and handsome. Nova may seem determined now, but Nico's got nearly ten months to chip away at her resolve. Look at Grady and Joanna. She insisted she'd never let Grady touch her, but by the next full moon, she kissed him.

The rest of us girls exchange frustrated glances. Our eligible betas just went from four men down to three.

As *my* fate would have it, I end up on the date with Nico. All the girls at the bottom of the list got stuck with the least desirable beta--the one who's gunning for someone else. There's no point to this date. We're fill-ins for the real thing, and Nico can't even be bothered to pretend. Not that I blame him. I don't want to pretend I have a chance with the guy, either. I saw the moment he realized Nova was his fated mate––it was as if he'd woken up for the first time in his life. Nobody will ever compete.

At least the next date will be rotated to one of the other betas. Hopefully, Justin or Cade. I want to avoid Anders for as long as I can, on the chance that he'll fall for one of the other girls and forget all about me.

After the situation with Nico and Nova is decided, we get our date assignments and are driven to a tall colonial red-brick building overlooking the river. Inside, we discover that our betas each have a floor to himself to entertain his group of girls. We're on the third floor, and though the view of the sparkling river at night is stunning, I'm jealous of the laughing and chattering coming from above and below. Our sad group sits quietly eating, because whenever one of us tries to engage Nico, he mutters a flat yes or doesn't respond.

Pointless.

I twist the noodles on my dinner plate around and around my fork, sighing heavily until I can't take it anymore. "If you'll excuse me." I rise from my chair. "I need to attend the ladies' room." Nico brushes me away like an annoying gnat, and I hurry from the table. I head down the wide curving staircase to the main level and stop short to find Knox bounding toward me. He's alone.

I press myself against the wall.

He stops too, looking around for a minute to make sure we're really alone. "I would hug you right now, but I don't want to die."

To hear his voice directed at me is like a slap across the face.

Tears well in my eyes. "Are you okay? Are they treating you well?"

"Better than most, but that's only because Ryne took a liking to me a few months after I arrived last year." He bites his bottom lip and lets out a deep sigh. "Are you okay?"

I shrug. I'm not okay. I'll never be okay. But Knox has enough burdens to carry and doesn't need me added to his load.

"Listen," he whispers low, voice growing urgent. "I hear things in that car, and there's something you need to know about Ryne."

"What?"

Footsteps pound the stairs below, and he grimaces, shakes his head once, and then continues up the stairs to disappear around the corner. My face burns, and my mind races. I want to chase him down and demand answers. I want to forget this moment ever happened.

I can't have either.

Ryne appears on the stairs. He doesn't smile. "What are you doing, Poppy?"

I swallow hard as my heart skids. I'm afraid to say the wrong thing, but lying to Ryne also feels wrong. "I was just heading down to use the bathroom."

"There's one on each floor."

"Oh, I didn't know that. I only saw the one on the main floor." I turn back around, Ryne joining me as I head back up.

"How's it going with Nico?" He digs his hands into his suit pockets. He's dressed as nicely as the betas, which is strange considering he's not the one dating us. I don't know why I wish he were. It's impossible and stupid. And anyway, I'm supposed to be mad at him for not giving us the proper defense training we need.

"About as well as you'd think dating someone who is fated to another would go," I deadpan.

I don't know why, but I expect him to offer condolences or to at least have something else to say to me, but he doesn't. He veers off at the second floor like I'm nothing of importance and leaves me without another word.

Chapter Twenty

Knox's words haunt me the next day—or rather, what he didn't get a chance to say. What would he possibly think I need to know about Ryne? Not to mention those first-love feelings came roaring back during our brief moment alone together. My dreams were filled with memories of our stolen kisses and the way his hands felt on my body, of the dances we shared and the good times we spent with our families.

It's confusing, especially considering what Ryne does to me, but I don't want to think about Ryne right now or ever. Seeing Knox didn't have a big effect on me until he talked to me, until he *looked* at me, and now everything feels different.

I don't want a beta. I want Knox and the life that was stolen from us.

And I can't have either.

The girls congregate in the entryway staring up at the scoreboard. Our points from the dates must've been added in. Joanna and I hit the bottom of the stairs and find our names. The betas could give us anywhere between zero and ten points.

Of course, Grady gave Joanna ten. She's still at the top. Faye squeals because it looks like Justin gave her ten points as well. All the girls who had dates with Nico got zero points, so we're all still at the bottom, and everyone else is lightyears ahead of us. How is it fair that Nico even got to rate us at all? He doesn't care about us.

Joanna frowns at me. "We gotta do something about this. You can't go to a mating house at the next festival."

"I'm trying."

She pulls me to the side and whispers, "I know, but maybe we need to sabotage the other girls."

I step back and gape at her. She's serious. I don't like that idea at all. She isn't talking about sabotaging Faye or the girls at the top, which happen to be the meanest of the bunch. It would be Callista or Ivy. They are the closest to the bottom and my date companions with Nico. Ivy is a distillery girl and is close with Faye, so she hasn't been too kind, but it's not like I want to go out of my way to hurt her. As much as I don't want to be sent to the mating house, I don't want to be responsible for sending someone else either.

"I can't do that," I respond. She opens her mouth to argue, but I shake my head. "I couldn't live with myself."

She tuts. "Why do you have to be such a good person?" We laugh and head outside for our workout.

I was hoping we were running today, but yoga mats are spread out across the lawn. I hate yoga. It's the one physical activity that I'm not good at. I don't have the patience for it, nor am I very flexible. The doors open behind us, and the betas all walk out, wearing workout clothes. They don't normally exercise with us. Double groan.

Madame Delphine stands in the middle of them. "Your dates will still be on Saturday evenings in groups until after the wolf moon, but during the week, the betas will be pulling each of you out for one-on-one time. They will integrate with your lessons. Today they've decided to join us for physical fitness. Tomorrow will be art. We have worked out a schedule, so you will each get individual time with at least one beta every week."

Nico is near the back, talking with Nova and ignoring the rest of us. She's stiff and standing at a distance, but I can already tell she's warming toward him. Her cheeks are pink, and her eyes look brighter than when she arrived here yesterday. I hope I don't get stuck with him again and end up with more low scores.

Justin skips down the stairs and stands next to Faye. They grin at each other, and I'm pretty sure she must have kissed him to get her ten. It's not lost on me that someone as awful as her would already have a beta after her. I wonder if we can count him out now as well. This keeps getting harder and harder.

That leaves Anders and Cade. I search Cade out, finding him hanging back from the others. He hasn't taken an interest in anyone yet, from what I can tell. He's not so bad. He's attractive enough, muscled and tall, with dark skin and black curly hair. He has a stunning smile when he actually uses it. I try to catch his eye, but he doesn't notice me.

I take a step down the stairs, ready to head to the mats closest to him, and a hand grabs my arm. I jerk my eyes up.

Anders stares down at me with a hungry look in his eyes. "You're with me today."

I bite my tongue because I can't afford to lose any more points. At least there isn't much talking we can do in yoga. It's a pretty solitary sport.

I give him a curt nod and head to a spot in the middle of the field so we'll be surrounded by everyone else.

He chuckles. "Wait. I know you don't like yoga."

"How do you know that?"

"We've been watching all of you since you arrived. I know that you enjoy running and hand-to-hand fighting. You hate reading and are an abysmal artist. And Ryne told me you like horses. It just so happens that I have horses at my home." He straightens. "Most of the betas live in town, but I have my own estate farther out. I hope to show it to you someday."

I blink at him. I don't ever want to see his estate, and I certainly don't like to think about Ryne talking to any of the betas about me, let alone this one. But this is not the Anders that I know. He's acting almost nice. "Why are you telling me this?"

He leans forward, and his brown shaggy curls fall into his eyes. He's older than the rest of the men, but not so old that I wouldn't find him attractive. If things had been different, if *he* was different, then I could see myself going for him. "Come on, Poppy, you know I like you." When he smiles, a dimple appears in his left cheek.

A sense of foreboding crawls up my spine, and my inner voice screams at me. I want to tell him to leave me alone, but that would probably make him want me more. I bet he's one of those guys who likes a chase. If I start acting sweet toward him, maybe he'll tire of me, and I can score some good points in the meantime.

He places his hand on my lower back, and I worry that his hand will travel farther down, but he's a perfect gentleman as he guides me away from the yoga mats. "Why don't we run today?"

I step away from him and force a smile. Running doesn't require any touching. "That sounds nice." Excitement shifts in his icy eyes, and I immediately wish I hadn't agreed.

A hand slips through my elbow, and Joanna stands there with Grady.

"Are you guys jogging? We'll come with you."

I release a sigh of relief.

"This is supposed to be one-on-one time," Anders growls.

"Relax, man, we're all just talking," Grady says with a grin. He winks at me, and I wonder what Joanna has told him about my hatred of Anders.

I'm tired of all the chit-chat. I extract myself from Joanna's grip and take off in a jog, figuring whoever wants to come with me will.

Anders quickly catches up and runs next to me. Joanna comes to my other side with Grady next to her. No one says anything. That's fine by me. I don't have to talk while I'm running.

"I heard that the girl who changed into a lycan was your roommate," Anders says.

My jaw tightens. "Yes, and I should've seen the signs but didn't."

Grady snorts. "There are no signs. I doubt even Charlotte knew except for the bite. She would've had zero symptoms until the night of the full moon."

"That's not what everyone thinks. They're all mad at me, even Madame Vivien."

"That's not right," Anders says. "We'll talk to her. Maybe we should do a class on the lycans and explain how they can hide in plain sight."

He smiles, and that damned dimple appears in his left cheek again. His sweetness is throwing me off guard. I'd much rather he be his true self around me than put on his act.

"Yeah," Grady agrees. "I want Joanna to be able to fight them."

"I already can, you moron. I wasn't helpless at home, you know."

"I know. But extra training can't hurt. You have to be able to protect our pups."

She growls. "I'm not having your babies."

Grady rolls his eyes, and I almost do the same. Joanna likes him— she's admitted as much to me. "You were singing a different tune on our picnic. Didn't you tell me that our first child would be named Daniel after your father?"

"No. I told you *my* first child would be named Daniel. You are such an imbecile. I don't know why I even kissed you."

Grady chuckles. "Because you looove me."

She punches him in the arm, which only makes him laugh even harder as they fall behind. They keep their eyes on me but give us space.

Anders has grown quiet.

"Do you wonder if you'll ever find your fated mate?" I ask.

He scoffs. "I doubt it. It's rare. The fact that there have been two this year is a miracle. And I'd rather not be fated. I'm not ready to settle for just one mate for the rest of my life."

At least he's honest.

"Isn't that the point of betas choosing a mate?" I already know the answer is no, but I want to hear it from the source.

He snorts. "The point is to keep the pack hierarchy stable, but after our women retire from childbearing, I'm free to choose a different one."

I have to force myself not to roll my eyes. "Have you had a mate already?"

"Yes. Three actually. My last one retired a couple of years ago. I have eight children. Nico is my son."

I stop abruptly and gape at him, trying to wrap my head around that. This news leaves me shocked, and I thought nothing could shock me anymore. He doesn't look much older than Nico.

"I know what you're thinking, Poppy. But shifters age slower than humans. Our average lifespan is close to two hundred years." He shrugs like it's nothing.

"So how old are you?"

He puffs out his chest and edges closer to me. "I'm ninety." Old enough to be my grandfather! And he only looks about a third of that age by human standards. It makes me wonder how old Ryne is, but I don't ask. Faye said Ryne's twenty-three, and I'm inclined to believe that, but what if he's older? What if he's already had a mate who is now retired too? My mind swims with questions, and I'm suddenly filled with suspicion that the wolves have been lying to us about everything. I don't know who to trust anymore or what to believe.

"How do you feel about Nico being fated to Nova?" I ask, my voice cracking.

That angry streak of his flashes across his face, and then something else. Love? No. Not that, but some kind of twisted version of love. "Nico wasn't born a beta. That honor went to my eldest who's already with his second mate. Nico is my youngest, so he's always been special to me. He joined the lower ranks when he turned fifteen and had to claw his way to the beta rank, which took nearly a decade of hard work. He was driven by wanting to bring up sons of his own and make me proud. And now he's drooling over a barren woman like some kind of virgin pup. It's despicable. He should contribute to the pack and carry on our family legacy, but I can't do anything about a fated mate."

I swallow hard and step back. Anders scares me. I hate him for killing Willow and I'm afraid for anyone who has to be near him. He can go from violence to charming within a matter of seconds. I'm suddenly very aware that Grady and Joanna aren't paying us any attention. They're farther back on the path, kissing against a tree, wrapped up in their own world.

"Ryne told me that you frequent the mating houses." I blurt out the first thing that comes to mind, instantly regretting it. I don't need Anders thinking about a mating house while he's practically alone with me.

"I do. Just because we betas have a mate doesn't mean we have to give up the other pleasures of life."

Bile rises in my throat. This man is disgusting. He could have had Willow either way. He could have chosen her for his mate, or if no one else did, he could've had her at the mating house. But she fought his roaming hands, and he killed her for it. And now, what does he think? That I'm going to be with him? That I'm going to forgive him for ruining my life? For destroying my family? And if I am with him, that I'll just stand by so he can sleep with other women--women who are being forced into sexual slavery?

I turn away and begin jogging again. I can't stand to look at his face a moment longer. He catches up and runs alongside me as if he has no idea what I'm thinking, or maybe he does, and he simply doesn't care.

Or maybe he likes it.

"I'm sorry about your sister," he says at last.

My heart twists in surprise. "No, you're not."

"That's not true." He grabs my hand and tugs me to a stop again, giving me an earnest expression. His icy eyes shine. Regret is not something I've ever seen on his face, and I hate him even more for it now because I know it's nothing but a practiced manipulation. "I lost my temper. Emotions were high with the harvest moon and the claiming. They got the better of me. Once we shift into our wolf form, we become more animal than man. I regret my actions."

"What am I supposed to say here?" My cheeks burn.

"Do you think there's a chance you could ever forgive me?"

No. That will never happen. I can't forgive murder, especially one so brutal, especially my twin sister. But I don't say that because even though it's true, two can play this game. I have to think of my future. Perhaps he'll help my score if I'm nice to him. "Maybe."

"I'll take a maybe." He smiles again and pulls me into a tight hug. He smells of sweat and wet dog and everything I hate.

I hug him back and force myself to sink into him. It takes every ounce of self-control that I have not to rip away.

He needs to think he's winning, that I'm one more woman he can control. He can't--this isn't over. I will never forgive him for murdering Willow. He's a bad person who cheats on his wives and replaces them when they can no longer bear children. He kills the women who resist him; I'm sure Willow isn't the first and won't be the last. When the moment is right, when he's least expecting it, I vow to return the favor.

Chapter Twenty-One

The full moon comes and goes without incident, and the following month is a blur of dates and lessons. Luckily we're still doing group dates, so I don't have to be alone with Anders. My scores aren't improving enough to keep me out of the bottom. Every morning I check the board, only to be disappointed. I'm trying to stay positive––I'm working hard––but the fact remains that I'm not cut out to be a beta wife.

"Today we're going to have an important lesson on pack hierarchy," Madame Delphine says one morning during breakfast. "Finish up. There are outfits laid out on your beds. Please go change and meet back in the foyer."

We're only a week away from the Wolf Moon Festival, and my name remains on the bottom. The madames constantly remind us during lessons that the bottom two girls will be sent off to the mating house the night of the festival. It's meant to motivate us, but I'm starting to panic.

"You can still get your score up. There's still time," Joanna whispers to me as we rise from our seats. I nod once and glance over to Faye and Ivy. Ivy's also at the bottom. They exchange a conspiratory look and then turn on me, both of them smirking. I'm not willing to sabotage other girls, but I can't say the same for everyone else.

"Don't worry about them," Joanna says. "I won't let them hurt you."

I sigh, wishing she could guarantee that.

Many of our lessons are in the classroom, and I expect this one to be the same, but the outfit I find on the bed is a long red cotton sweater dress with a sophisticated white hooded wool coat to layer on top. Thick black tights and little black booties complete the look. It's all brand new, as if it were made specially for today.

"Okay, we can definitely make this work," Joanna gushes, picking the dress up and pressing it to her chest in a little hug. For as much as she hates this place, she adores the clothing. I guess that makes sense given her background.

We hurry to change and go to the foyer where Madame Delphine leads the lot of us outside. The sky is dreary and overcast, which explains the identical warm outfits. We near the river to find the same boat from our first day waiting for us. The engine rumbles gently in the water, sending ripples into the wake. We climb inside and sit on the rows of wooden benches. It's not as crowded since there are four fewer of us than there was the night of the harvest moon. One more week, and two more will be off to the mating houses. Unlike last time, there is no sense of excitement today. Not even the distillery girls are into it. The only thing I can read on their faces is dread. Somehow we all know today isn't going to be a good one. Maybe the dresses were meant to placate us, or maybe they were meant to make us easily identifiable.

"Where are the betas?" Ivy asks.

"We'll see them there," Madame Delphine says. "Madame Vivien will be staying back at the house." Madame Nova is the last to climb into the boat, and even she looks worried. "So it's just me and Madame Nova here today. Please don't stray from our group once we get to the city."

I force a smile on my face and sit up taller, catching Madame Delphine's eye. Others may not be happy about this day, but I've got a score to increase. If faking a positive attitude and sucking up to the house mothers is how I'm going to do it, then so be it.

We're off, and it gets even colder. I huddle close to Joanna as we bounce across the water. It feels like forever until we finally dock in the historic part of town. It's beautiful here, the history well preserved and untouched from the years of neglect like other parts of the city. I can almost picture what it must have been like before the wars. I can imagine the human families who lived here, free from fears of lycans or shifters. This is nothing like the tall shiny buildings with the mating houses and where the pups are raised. It's nothing like the outskirts of the city where things are falling apart, or like the villages where life is simple. It's similar to the area where we gathered for the harvest but nicer. I didn't know homes like this existed anymore.

We're instructed to walk down the sidewalk in a single file line, to keep our heads high, and to smile. As we pass several of the homes, women and their male children peek out. Some of the people wave at us, and we wave back.

"These are the betas' residences," Madame Delphine announces. "Some of you will live in this neighborhood."

"It's amazing," Faye gushes. "Can you tell us which houses belong to *our* betas?"

"We'll leave that for another day," Madame Delphine replies with a sly smile. "Come along, now."

Madame Nova heads up the rear of the group, and Joanna and I slow down to chat with her. "So you're living with Nico in one of these?" I ask. "What's that like?"

Her mouth thins. "It's nowhere I belong. I'll be staying in Drayton Hall full time soon enough."

"Right . . ." Joanna's voice dips into sarcasm. "You do know that he's been marking all his dates with zero points, don't you? He has no intention of marrying one of these claimed girls."

"Our agreement isn't about what he wants. It's my choice." Nova brushes a bit of lint from her dress. "Don't worry about Nico. And anyway, you have Grady."

"Yeah, and Poppy here has nobody."

I elbow Joanna in the ribcage. "It's not her fault."

Madame Nova frowns. "I'll see what I can do. I'll talk to Nico about what he's been doing with the scores."

"It won't help Poppy. She already went on her date with him, remember?"

Our group stops in front of a white home. It's by far the nicest one in the neighborhood, with plastered walls and tile roofing. I've never seen a home with these kinds of materials, and I instantly fall in love with it. "It's called Spanish style," Nova says, as if sensing my thoughts. "There's a few like this around here, but this one is by far the biggest."

I peer up at the three stories of arched windows and terraces, columns by the front door, and the towering palm trees in the yard, and something twists inside of me. It's immaculate, and I long to know what it looks like on the inside, but I know that even if I do, it won't matter.

"Which beta lives here?" One of the girls asks the question we're all thinking.

"This is the alpha's home," Madame Delphine supplies. "It belonged to Ryne's father, but since King Tremaine runs the Chicago Pack now, Ryne lives here alone."

So that would mean Madame Delphine used to live here too. She only had one child as far as I know. I wonder what it was like for her to be with someone who left her when her child grew up. She went from living in this beautiful home as a lady to running Drayton Hall for the claimed young women. There's definitely a story there.

"But we're not going inside Ryne's residence today," she continues, pointing across the street. "This way, please."

We cross the little cobbled street to an open area with grass and trees--a park. We have one at home in the village, but it's nothing as grand as this. There's even a playground that's laid out like a castle--ours was a single slide and swing set. Little boys play on it, some in wolf form, others as humans. We keep walking to the far end until we come upon a crowd of men and a few women who are so dressed up that they must be beta wives. The crowd is loud, and a nervous energy seems to crackle through them. Something important is happening.

We walk toward the crowd, but before we reach it, Madame Delphine stops, gathering us around her.

"Who can tell me the hierarchy of the wolf pack?"

My hand shoots into the air. The madames occasionally question us, awarding points to the girls who answer correctly.

Madame Delphine nods to me.

"The alpha king lives in Chicago, ruling over all the shifter cities. Each city has its own alpha; Ryne is ours." I pause for a moment. When I lived in the village, I would've never thought of the pack as part of my life. I would have called him their alpha, not ours. And now, it's practically all I think about. "Below him are the members in the Council of Betas, who are all mated. They advise Ryne and oversee the unmated warrior betas."

"And who are below the betas?" She raises an eyebrow.

This is where it starts to get tricky, but I'm pretty sure I have it. "Next are the gammas. They are the defensive warriors who protect the wolf city and the surrounding human villages. And then below them are the deltas. They have the greatest numbers. They can be hunters, but they're mostly the offensive warriors who leave to fight the battles out in the wilds."

"Very good. How many are in each class?"

My hand shoots up again, but so does Faye's. Madame Delphine calls on her instead. "The council usually has between twenty and forty betas. That depends on how many are currently mated. The unmated warrior betas are always one hundred. When a beta moves up to the council or dies, a gamma takes his place."

"And do any of you know how many gammas and deltas there are?"

This time, Ivy's hand is the first one up. "There are exactly three hundred gammas, but the alpha can assign more if he feels the pack needs extra protection. The rest are deltas, and I think there's got to be at least a thousand of those by now."

I swallow hard, trying to relax. I had no idea there were so many wolves. They act like they're so outnumbered by the lycans, but I can't imagine that's actually true. And to think, the girls in the mating houses have to sleep with any man who wants her, an endless parade of partners who care for nothing but sex and growing the pack. They don't even know who their own children are most of the time.

It's not right.

I raise my hand, and Madame Delphine points to me. "So, if most of the children are raised by the pack, how do they choose which ones become deltas or gammas?"

Her lips thin. "That's a good question. There are levels to the mating houses, which helps keep things organized from birth, but there are also opportunities for the boys to compete for the gamma spots during their fifteenth year."

"And what about the girls?" I can't help but ask. "You said one in a hundred wolf shifters is born female."

She nods. "If she's born of beta parents, she'll be permitted to stay with her family. If she's not, she'll be sent to Chicago to be raised in a special boarding house overseen by the king."

I look around, noting the surprised faces of some of the other claimed. Either they weren't paying attention, or nobody told them the truth. Maybe I shouldn't have asked my questions——it'll only create more competition——but we all deserve to know what will happen to the children we'll one day have.

The shyest girl of the bunch raises her hand. Her name is Bailey, and she mostly gets by because she doesn't have any enemies, and she keeps her nose in a book most days. "So I know the children are raised by the pack, but when do the mothers get to visit them?"

Nova bristles. "Never," she grumbles. "And you'll be right back to mating after you recover from childbirth."

The mood visually shifts, some girls staring at their shoes and others with mouths hanging open like fish.

Someone needs to stand up to the alphas. Not just to Ryne, but to his father. I want it to be me, but to think things will ever change is laughable. There are far too many wolves, and what are humans supposed to do about it? My family doesn't even know what's happening in this city. They think I'm some kind of servant. If they knew what service I was training to provide, they'd be horrified.

"Enough about that." Madame Delphine clears her throat and continues. "Two more questions before we join the crowd. How does one become a warrior beta?"

Lexi, the teacher's pet type, beats me to it. Which stinks because she's not far above me in the rankings, and those points could've moved me up one slot, but then again, I'm starting to feel sick to my stomach and don't care to talk anymore. I want this lesson to end.

"Any wolf wishing to vie for a spot above them in the pack hierarchy has to fight for it," Lexi says. "In this case, several may fight for the spot of beta, but only the last one alive gets it."

I frown. The wolves are so desperate to grow their packs that they'll harvest human women, but then turn around and fight each other to the death? It seems like such a waste.

"That is correct to a certain degree. A wolf may surrender during a fight, but if they do that, they will be cast out to live as a lone wolf in the wilds. It's the greatest shame that can happen to a wolf, and most would rather die." She levels us all with a steely look, but I can't understand why. "It's the same process for those deltas wishing to move into the spot of a gamma. Gammas typically live longer lives because they get to stay closer to home. They also get better accommodations and are permitted more visits to high-quality mating houses."

The fact that they put us into different levels of mating houses is disgusting, as if women need to be ranked. It reminds me of the farm animals that get entered into competitions at some of the villages that surround ours. Every spring Papa would take us to see the winners. Bile burns in my throat, and I have to relax my face to keep the anger from showing. There are over a thousand wolves just in the delta class, and I wonder how many mating houses there are. The one Ryne took me to was large, to be sure, but there couldn't have been more than twenty or thirty girls there.

"We will be visiting the battle arena later this evening where the deltas, gammas, and warrior betas fight each other. Now, last question. How does a beta become an alpha?"

I answer before she can even call on me. "They challenge the alpha to a fight. If they win, they take over the pack, but if they don't, they die. There is no option to surrender."

"And how do they win?"

"They kill the alpha."

"You girls have been paying attention. And now you are about to witness a challenge on our alpha."

"How often does this happen?" Faye asks.

"It's rare now. Maybe once a year. Sometimes not even that. Ryne is a strong alpha. You are lucky you get to see him fight."

We follow her toward the crowd, and all I can think is that I certainly don't feel lucky.

Chapter Twenty-Two

The crowd of wolves parts for us as we approach the circle. They all nod to Madame Delphine, but a few sneer at us girls. Madame explained that challenges against the alpha are always in the park near Ryne's house because he gets to set the time and place, and he likes to go home afterward and rest. I also wonder if it's a way to intimidate his challengers, as if he can't even be bothered to battle in the arena. This is his home turf.

We shuffle forward until we are right in front. Ryne stands shirtless at the far end of the circle, and he gives his mother a tight smile. The wolves in the crowd are restless. Joanna squeaks next to me, and I look over to see that Grady has come up behind her and wrapped his arms around her waist, pulling her back into his broad chest.

"Are these all beta wolves?" I ask him.

"Yes. Only warrior betas today. Except the two standing behind Ryne. They are council betas sent to witness."

"Who challenged him?" Joanna asks.

"That idiot Braden. He became a warrior beta less than a month ago. He doesn't stand a chance. But he's not the risk to Ryne. It's those who will challenge him afterward."

"What do you mean? Madame Delphine made it sound like it'll only be one."

"That's how it starts but fighting weakens him and wolves can be opportunistic. Ryne will probably fight four to five betas tonight as more come forward to try for a shot at alpha. I don't know why anyone would risk it. Ryne is a monster. He's unbeatable. The real fun comes later. We'll go down to the arena and witness the brawl that will bring in the new warriors."

"That sounds barbaric," I say.

"It is. But it's part of our world. Yours now as well." He squeezes Joanna tighter. She shakes her head but doesn't say anything. I sure hope she doesn't think this is *fun*.

Ryne steps forward, and a hush falls over the crowd. A young guy stomps from the onlookers, his fist pumping in the air as if to get them to cheer him on. Nobody does, but it doesn't deter him. He smiles wickedly and flexes large muscles as he rips off his shirt. This must be Braden.

"Do you challenge me?" Ryne asks him with an annoyed glare.

"I do," Braden replies haughtily. He puffs out his chest before crouching into a fighter's stance.

Both men release guttural screams and shift into their wolf forms, their pants ripping to shreds in the process. Ryne's wolf is unmistakable—I'd recognize that perfect inky black fur and those glowing sapphire eyes anywhere. He's actually smaller than Braden's wolf. Braden is raggedy with tufts of brown fur mixed in with the gray, but he's massive and rippling with excitement. They growl and circle each other for only a moment.

Ryne makes the first move.

He pounces, landing on Braden's back and sinking his teeth into the hide around Braden's neck. Braden wails and tries to buck him off, but Ryne holds fast.

The crowd is cheering now, egging Ryne on. Braden falls to his forearms and then flips over, putting himself on top of Ryne. It works long enough to get Ryne to release his hold, and then the two are back up and circling each other again.

Blood drips into the grass. Braden is hurt. He growls and lunges for Ryne, this time swiping at his shoulder and getting a hit. Ryne isn't the slightest bit deterred. He attacks again, the anger rolling off his wolf in waves of absolute dominance. It's obvious he's done this many, many times before.

It doesn't take long.

Ryne gets his mouth around Braden's neck again and shakes violently. Something in the gray wolf cracks and dislodges, and Braden tumbles to the ground. His body is completely limp. He never even had time to shift back to his true self, not even in death. Or maybe this wolf is his true form, and the human form is the lie.

Ryne howls and then shifts back. He's naked. His muscled back is to me, and blood drips from the wound on his shoulder. He calls out again. "Do you challenge me?"

Another man tears from the crowd, shifting instantly into a scrappy gray wolf. Ryne shifts again, and the fight is on.

"I guess a council beta decided to end his life today." Grady sighs. A middle-aged woman screams obscenities the entire time, begging her husband to stop, but before long, it's Ryne she's begging to stop. Of course, neither do until the gray wolf joins Braden in death.

The woman falls to her knees, her dress billowing around her. Her sobs will probably be heard for miles as she's carried away. Once again, Ryne shifts back into his human form and calls out for more challengers to come forward.

"Nobody would dare," Joanna asks Grady, "would they?"

But before Grady can reply, two more men step forward in answer. They appear to be very young, and they're obviously identical twins. They're both fair-haired and lanky. My heart does a little twist. They remind me of me and Willow.

Ryne's shoulders slump. I can tell he doesn't want to do this. "Who's first?" he snaps. "Or would you like to die together?"

And that's all it takes.

The boys shift into identical honey-colored wolves and circle their alpha. I almost expect him to make them fight one at a time––that's fair––but he doesn't.

He shifts into his wolf form once again and goes for the closest of the two, ripping into the much smaller wolf with unrelenting teeth and claws. He's so fast that, even with two of them, they still don't stand a chance. One jumps on his back, but Ryne is quick to shake him off, slamming the young wolf to the ground. The wolf whimpers and then shifts into his human form.

"I surrender!" the boy calls out.

A dissatisfied murmur ripples through the crowd.

The other wolf uses the opportunity to pounce on Ryne. He lands on the alpha's back, getting a tight hold of Ryne's neck and biting down, same as Ryne has done to the others. Ryne roars and shakes the wolf off, but not without taking a deep gash to his neck first. Blood glistens on his black fur.

Ryne turns on the wolf and delivers the killing blow. He clasps his jaw down on the exact right spot to split open an artery. It ends his opponent in seconds. As his lifeblood spills, the wolf turns back into a boy. He looks barely old enough to be here. Maybe sixteen at most. His twin crawls over to the dead brother, looking up at Ryne with blood on his face.

"Please," he begs. "I shouldn't have listened to my brother. It was his idea. I never wanted to do this. It was stupid. Please, please have mercy."

The crowd goes silent. Ryne is still in his wolf form. He looks up and catches the eye of a man I hadn't noticed until now. The man is standing at the far end of the crowd and is surrounded by massive betas who could be bodyguards. He's dressed in a black suit, but even without that, power would still radiate off of him. He's clearly someone of importance.

He also looks just like Ryne, if Ryne were a little older.

"That's the alpha king," Grady whispers, confirming what I was thinking. "Name is Thorn Tremaine."

"I knew it," Joanna whispers back.

"My sons are fools." A middle-aged man steps to the edge of the circle. "I beg you to spare my child, but I know that you probably will not." He kneels down. "Still, I must try. Please."

Ryne stands there, still in his wolf form, leaning over the crying boy. The alpha king nods once to his son. That's all it takes. Ryne acts, swiping a claw along the boy's neck. It slices clean through the flesh and ends him quickly. There isn't even time for the boy to scream.

Chapter Twenty-Three

The alpha king smiles and melts into the crowd of betas.

The man who was moments ago begging for his son's life crawls forward and holds his dead children in his lap, crying silently. Never once does he blame Ryne. There is no anger in his eyes, only deep regret.

"Disgusting," Joanna whispers.

"This is the way of things," Grady replies, his voice clipped. "We're wolves." As if that's justification.

Ryne stands firm in the middle of the crowd and howls. It's starting to get dark. The sun is setting fast. We all wait to see if another wolf will step forward in challenge as minutes pass. No one does.

Ryne changes back into his human form. Sweat streams down his chest, and blood is everywhere. I drop my eyes and immediately regret it because now all I see are the four dead souls strewn about the grass. Anders hands Ryne a towel, and he wraps it around his midsection.

"Go enjoy the brawl. I'll see you all tomorrow," he calls out to the onlookers.

He stalks toward us, and the crowd parts, letting him through. As he walks past me, making eye contact for a half a second, I have an overwhelming desire to go to him. I step forward, but Joanna grabs my wrist and jerks me back.

"What are you doing?"

I don't answer her because I can't explain it. I hate him, but I can also see the pain in his eyes and can't help but want to comfort him.

Once he's past the crowd, the spell breaks, and a sickly kind of excitement fills the air. Grady drops a kiss on Joanna's cheek. "I've got some business to take care of. I'll see you at the brawl. Save me a seat."

She sniffs. "Fat chance." But I know she will.

Madame Delphine waves us over. "We'll ride over to the brawl with the rest of the betas. Feel free to mingle among them. They will behave. I promise." She winks. "It's time you started to get to know more than just the four who might be your mates. We will meet back at the boat after the brawl."

Joanna pulls me back. "Now is our chance," she whispers so low I almost miss it. "By the time she realizes we are missing, we'll be long gone."

"What are you talking about?" I ask.

"You are at the bottom of the scoreboard. In a week you'll be on your way to a mating house. We can't let that happen."

"But you're at the top. Plus, you're so in love with Grady. You can't leave him."

"I am not in love with him. It's an act. I don't want to be here. Never have."

My mouth drops open. She had me fooled, and I can't help but wonder if she's lying to herself. I see the way she looks at Grady.

"I won't let you go to the mating house, and you'll never get away on your own. Now come on," she hisses.

I need to be stronger, braver, smarter––this is my chance. A few weeks ago, I'd never have taken it, but now a strength is rising inside of me, one that started as a flicker and is building to an inferno. Joanna is right. It's time to run.

I don't think as we melt into the crowd, our group of girls getting farther and farther away. I have no idea where we are going or how we'll get there, but at least it won't be a mating house. My fear of the wilds is nothing compared to my fear of living in one of those places.

We slip away from the crowd under the cover of darkness and into the shadows of two quiet houses. I loved this outfit when I first put it on, but now I hate it. It makes us stand out. I can only hope that it's dark enough, and the wolves are preoccupied enough, that our red dresses and white coats won't become a dead giveaway.

"Let's stay here until the boat leaves," Joanna says. We listen to them laugh and carry on as they all get on the boat. There's more than just our group as many betas have joined in. The boat is packed. It rumbles to life and begins to move down the river, disappearing into the night.

"Do you think anyone saw us?" I ask.

She shakes her head. "They would've come after us if they did." The lights in the houses next to us are both off. I didn't think when we decided to escape, but now panic is setting in. If they catch us, they'll kill us.

"Maybe we should go find help and pretend we got separated from our group," I say. Nerves are eating away at my belly. That and we're wildly unprepared. We haven't eaten for a while, we have no food or water to take with us, and we're in these stupid dresses. This is a terrible idea.

Joanna grabs my arm. "No. We'll be fine. Trust me."

"Do you even know where we can go?"

She doesn't say anything.

"You don't have a plan?" I'm having a hard time keeping my voice down, and I'm already regretting my moment of courage that led me here.

"Of course I have a plan," Joanna hisses low. "I just can't tell you everything in case we get caught. I know where we are going, but I'm not telling you."

Her words sting and it bothers me that she doesn't trust me, but then again, I lost my nerve and argued for going back. Joanna grabs my hand and tugs me out of our hiding spot. I feel exposed, but there is no one around.

"What if someone sees us?"

"Then we pretend we're wives of betas."

"And if the people we run into know all the wives?"

"Stop worrying. We'll get out of here. I promise." Her voice is growing frustrated and impatient. She tugs me down the street, approaching Ryne's house. Every light is on, and I shrink into the shadows as we pass. Joanna sniggers a bit. "You know, if I didn't know better, I'd think you were sweet on him."

"What? No." And besides, I think the alpha king is in there. That man scares me.

She loops her arm through mine and tugs me closer to her as we walk down the street. If anyone saw us, they would just think we were two friends out for an evening stroll. I'm glad Joanna has a good head on her shoulders because if it were me, I would just flat-out run, which would look suspicious.

We make it a couple more blocks, and the knot in my chest releases. We're getting closer to freedom. Has Madame Delphine realized we're gone yet? Probably not. There were so many people piled onto that boat, and she said we would all meet back *after* the brawl. She's not keeping track. We have hours until the brawl is over. At least I hope we do.

A lone man walks on the sidewalk, heading straight for us. I tense.

"Relax," Joanna says. "We'll be fine. Just don't make eye contact."

I drop my eyes and giggle like Joanna has said something funny. The man slows as we approach, coming to a stop. Joanna keeps our pace, which is good, because I would've frozen. He doesn't say anything, and as soon as we pass him, I hear his footsteps start up again. I let out a breath as he disappears.

"That was close," I say.

"Nah. Not even. He didn't even notice us."

"Then why did he stop?"

"Because he assumed we were beta wives and was being respectful." Her voice drops an octave. "We will have to cross the river. That's going to be the hardest part."

"Do you mean like swim?" I gulp. I'm a good swimmer, but it's freezing cold in January, and the current is strong. Visions of drowning wash through my mind.

"What do you think I am?" she scoffs. "There are people who will help us. Trust me."

I don't know why I never thought someone would help us, but I truly didn't. The idea that there are people out there who feel the same way we do, people who would risk their lives to get us out of this city, gives me hope like I haven't had in months. A smile plays on my lips, and adrenaline pumps through my veins, encouraging me onward.

We pass several dark houses, and out of nowhere, a hooded man steps out from between two of them. Joanna and I both stop, and then Joanna gives a nervous laugh. "Goodness gracious, man, you scared us."

My heart thunders in my eardrums, and I ready myself to run.

She moves to step around him, and he lashes his hand out, gripping my arm. "Where are you going?" he growls.

I know that voice. "Ryne?"

Joanna pales. Ryne uses his other hand to peel away his hood, and his ice-blue eyes glare at me. My breath catches, and I try to wrench away, but his grip is impossibly tight.

He drags me back down the street, and Joanna jogs to keep up. I want to tell her to run, to get away while she can because Ryne obviously doesn't care what she does. He's singled me out. I don't know what will happen to us now. Hopefully Ryne won't kill us, but I don't really know. Is this it? Is this the end? Maybe he'll throw me in the mating house and be done with it. I've certainly caused him enough trouble, and it would be easier to get it over with. But as he marches me down the sidewalk, I think it's more likely he'll kill me.

"Are you taking me to the mating house?" I bite out.

He snorts but doesn't say anything.

"Please, Ryne, you don't understand," I press on. "We can't live like--"

"Shut up," he finally hisses. "Don't say another word."

It takes no time at all for us to reach his house. He pulls me up the porch steps and shoves open the front door. Joanna stumbles in after us. Knox stands in the entryway, his eyes wide. His face drains of color, and I wish for so many things in that moment--for him to help me, for him to get away from me, for him not to have seen me like this at all.

"Is my father gone?" Ryne snarls.

Knox nods. "He's left for the brawl."

"Good. Go fetch Grady, but don't tell him why I need him. No one knows these two are here but you and me."

Knox disappears out the door. I'm overcome with betrayal. I know it's stupid, and Knox can't do anything for me now, but his loyalty to Ryne stings.

Ryne tosses me down onto a couch that is way more comfortable than any I've ever sat on before. Joanna sinks down next to me. There's a long pause that seems to go on forever. My breath slows, and my mind starts to relax. Maybe he's not going to hurt us. I close my eyes tight and count backward from ten, then open them and allow myself to look around. His house is stunning. The style dates back to well before the wars. It's gorgeous with dark wood and papered walls. Beautiful paintings adorn the walls. I run my fingers along the edge of the white couch pillow--the furniture is upholstered with a mix of white linens and creamy leathers. I suck in a breath and catch his smell, that winter and cedar scent. It does something to me I don't like, so I close my eyes again. I'll never be in a room this nice again in my life. He's going to send me away to a mating house. I can feel it. And if for some reason he spares me, I'll end up there in a week anyway.

Joanna elbows me in the ribs, and I open my eyes to see Ryne pacing in front of us. His hair is wet and hangs around his face, hiding much of his expression. He pinches the bridge of his nose. There are still scratches all over him, and blood is seeping through his shirt.

"Explain," he finally says.

My mouth goes dry.

"We were leaving. I couldn't stand around and let Poppy get sent to the mating house," Joanna says matter-of-factly. I'm surprised she didn't try to lie to him, but Joanna is a straight shooter when she wants to be.

"So you decided to run away?" He curses under his breath.

"It's not like we had any other options. Poppy has been at the bottom of the board for weeks, and the festival is coming up."

"You would've died out there."

"We were willing to take our chances. Better dead than forever raped by wolves."

Ryne doesn't speak; he just continues pacing. "I get it," he says at last. "I don't like it, but I get it. Joanna, do you have any idea how devastated Grady would be if you left? You can't mess with him like that."

He claims to get it, but then he cares more for his friend's feelings than our own. I fold my hands over my chest and glare. "What's our punishment? Because if you are going to kill us, please just get it over with."

"Now she speaks." He snorts. "I'm not going to kill you, but if you ever try this again, I will bring your family to the city and kill them in front of you." He stalks over to me and leans down close. "Do you understand?"

My stubbornness is shattered to pieces with his words. I cower away from him and let out a clipped yes.

"Good. You're damn lucky nobody else knows about this because that's exactly what would have happened if you'd been caught by someone else." He stands back up. "Don't you get it? I wouldn't have had a choice."

I think of Mama and Papa and little Evan, and my stomach goes hollow. "You would punish them because of me?" I'm choked up. I can't help it. It's so wrong.

He shakes his head angrily. "There are things about being an alpha that I can't control, and I'm not going to be able to keep protecting you if you keep making reckless choices like this."

Protecting me? He's done nothing to protect me.

"Now, the reason you ran away was because you don't want to get sent to the mating house, yes?"

I nod meekly.

"Okay. Then I will tell Madame Delphine that Grady wanted to spend some time one-on-one with Joanna and that I requested you join her. I will instruct Madame Delphine to give you just enough points so that you are third from the bottom after tonight. You have a week to not screw that up. Do you think you can handle that?"

I have no idea why he's decided to be nice to me. I feel like there is a catch here somewhere, but I can't find it.

Joanna scowls at him. "Why are you being so nice to her?"

Leave it to Joanna to say what we're all thinking.

"Because I want Grady to have a shot with his fated mate, and that seems to only be possible if Poppy's around."

Something inside of me deflates. Again, he's only "protecting" me because it's important to his beta. Ryne looks out for his friends, and normally I'd find that admirable but not in this case.

Joanna crosses her arms and smirks. "Damn right it is. You hurt her, and I will raise hell."

I mean, it's a nice sentiment and all, but I can't help but feel that's not the reason Ryne is helping us. There's got to be something else going on, but for the life of me, I can't figure out what it is.

Knox comes back into the room with Grady in tow.

"Joanna?" Grady asks, shaking his head. His sandy hair catches the light, and his silver eyes darken with worry. "What's going on?"

"They tried to run away."

Grady's face pales, and in that moment, I swear I can see his heart break.

"You what?" he says, still staring right at Joanna. Then he brings his gaze back to Ryne and swallows. "Would you like me to get their families?"

Ryne shakes his head. "We're going to keep this between us for now."

Grady visibly relaxes. "And what are we going to do about it?"

"I'm not going to do anything. Whatever you wish to do with Joanna is up to you. We have an hour or so before we have to head to the brawl."

Grady grips Joanna's arm, pulling her up from the couch.

"Hey, let go of me. I'm not your property."

"You have no right to speak to me in that tone right now," he yells. "What were you thinking? You could've been killed! I should kill you myself!"

Joanna cowers. It's the first time I've seen her scared of any of them. Grady drags her out of the room. I want to chase after them, to defend my friend, but somehow I know Grady isn't going to harm his fated mate. Of all the betas, he's the kindest, and he's obviously in love with Joanna.

"What will he do with her?" I ask, just to be sure.

He shrugs. "He won't hurt her, though her pride may be bruised a bit by the time he's done. My guess is they'll be making out the next time we see them."

Knox leaves and comes back into the room carrying a steaming bowl of water. He holds my gaze, his eyes full of intensity. The energy in the room shifts, and Ryne jerks his head around. "Leave it. Poppy will clean me up."

Chapter Twenty-Four

Knox gives a wordless nod and sets the bowl down on the little table next to where I'm sitting. He pulls a couple of wash-cloths and bandages out of his pockets and lays them next to it. And then he's gone. I have to admit I'm disappointed, but I understand; Knox is trying to survive the same as any other human, and I doubt Ryne wants him around while I handle this. Guilt washes through me when I realize I don't want Knox around for it either. I'm pretty sure Ryne doesn't really need my help. I mean, he's been through this how many times now? Regardless, I gaze at the first-aid supplies, deciding where to start. I've doctored up my little brother plenty of times and even Papa once when he cut himself in the field.

But I have no idea what kind of care Ryne expects.

He unzips and shakes his arms out of his jacket and then peels off his bloody t-shirt, muscles rippling in the process. He's clean from the shower, but there's a lot of blood seeping from his wounds. Aside from a nasty gash on his neck, everything looks minor.

He sits down next to me. I don't move.

Ryne looks at me for a long moment before clearing his throat. The side of his lips curves up playfully. "Poppy, will you please clean my wounds? I'm not good at it myself, and I just sent away my man."

"Oh, yes."

Heat prickles over my skin. I dip one of the rags in the water and set to work on the worst areas. I clean up the big gash on his neck, only to find a wound right cutting across his stomach as well. My fingers graze over the hard ridges as I work. There is something strangely intimate about this, which leaves me feeling unnerved, and yet I can't help my attraction to him. Why does he have to be so alluring? Why do I have to both hate him and want him at the same time?

He hisses as I wash the stomach wound, but he doesn't complain. I rub some ointment over it, then place a band-aid on top and set to work on his arms. The cuts are much smaller here and don't need much. Never once does the man move. It's like touching a warm statue.

"You know what Joanna said about the mating houses?" His voice is low and soft. "About being raped by wolves? I wish it wasn't that way."

"You would do away with the mating houses?"

He shakes his head. "We have to have them in order to procreate, but I wouldn't force women there. We would recruit from the villages but allow women to volunteer and be paid. I actually expect we'd have more women than we do now if we did it that way. I told my father that once, but he thought I was joking."

He's wrong. I can't imagine anyone volunteering for that. Well, Faye maybe. But his words surprise me.

"I didn't realize your father had so much control over you."

He sighs. "You have no idea. I am an alpha to others, but my father is the alpha to me, which often means I'm just as trapped as you are. I have no control over who my mate will be either. He'll choose her."

"Why?"

"Because he wants a strong mate for me. I understand it, but I don't like it."

I move back in front of him, washing away the rest of the blood from his chest. He locks eyes with me, taking my hand in his and peeling the washcloth from my grasp, then pulls me closer to him. My lungs tighten. Traitorous excitement spreads through me like hot liquid.

In spite of all logic screaming at me to run away, I don't. I allow him to pull me down into his lap. He stares deep into my eyes with his stormy blue ones before leaning forward and placing a soft kiss on my cheek. I let my eyes flutter closed and revel in the moment. Tonight I'm not a claimed woman waiting for a man I'll never love. Tonight I'm just a girl enjoying the touch of a man I'll never have but desperately want.

I marvel at how quickly he can take my emotions from one end of the spectrum to the other. He moves his face up and gently kisses both of my eyes. My heart leaps. He feathers his lips down the other side of my face and runs his nose along my neck. I bring my hands up and twist my fingers through his hair.

He lets out a little moan and pulls me closer to him.

Bringing his lips to my ear, he whispers, "I know you don't think this, but you are the most beautiful girl I've ever laid eyes on. From the moment I saw you, I wanted you. But I can't have you."

"Why not?" I squeak, and my cheeks warm.

"There are plans for me that don't include you, but I swear on my life that one of these days, I will kiss you."

I gasp, longing to pull his lips to mine.

He sighs. "But that can't be tonight. I don't want to make you a target."

I swallow and try to make sense of his declaration. Up until now, I've been denying my feelings for him, but I can't anymore. I know who he is, and I want him anyway.

"Okay," I breathe out. I don't want to agree. I want to demand he kiss me and put us both out of our misery, but I'm not brave enough.

He pulls away and sets me to the side, lifting me off his lap as if I weigh nothing. I instantly miss his touch.

"Poppy, I promise I'll do whatever it takes to keep you out of the mating houses. I don't know how yet, but I will. That means you'll end up with one of my betas, but that's better than the alternative."

I swallow. "Thank you." But I don't mean it. Anything short of being with him will be wrong.

He lies back on the couch, and a wicked smile crosses his face. Before I can blink, he pulls me on top of him again. He holds me and plays with my hair. Our bodies are pressed close, and neither of us says another word. At first I'm filled with electric need, but contentment starts to creep in, and I relax. We lie there for who knows how long until I drift in and out of consciousness.

Someone clears his throat, and I bolt up. Grady stands there, smirking, and Joanna's eyes are wide. I notice a distance between them that has never been there before. They must still be mad at each other.

"We have to go," Grady says. "Or Madame Delphine will send out a search party for them."

Ryne runs a hand over his face. "Knox, bring me a shirt," he calls out. I force myself off of him, not wanting Knox to see me so close to his captor. Ryne takes the washcloth again and cleans up the last of the blood. His wounds have completely healed. I knew the shifters healed quickly, but to see it myself is shocking.

Knox enters the room holding three different shirts. I can't meet his eyes. Shame sweeps over me, and I've never felt so confused. Ryne grabs a black t-shirt, slipping it over his head.

"Come on, let's go."

I stand and follow them out the door.

"Where to, boss?" Knox asks. I wince at Knox's cheerful tone because I know it's fake.

"We have to take these women to the brawl. It looks like they're going to have to meet my father after all."

We ride across town in the back of Ryne's car. Grady is still seething mad, so he chose to sit up front in the passenger seat. He doesn't look back or speak a word to Joanna. She's folded in on herself and staring out the window, equally angry. I don't know what happened between them tonight, but whatever it was only made things worse. I'm squashed between Ryne and Joanna, and every inch of my left side burns with the memory of the time we just shared. It's an odd feeling, wanting to lean into him with Knox only a couple feet away. He drives us through the city, and when I catch his gaze in the rearview mirror, he quickly averts his eyes.

Is he mad at me for trying to run away? Is he upset that I got caught? Or can he sense my draw to the alpha?

I'd give anything to have a moment alone with Knox, just to talk. I'm afraid that will never happen. The incident on the stairs was bittersweet. Sweet because we were finally alone together, and bitter because it ended so fast.

Ryne shifts his weight, and his arm presses against mine. I can't help but study his smooth tanned skin. It's a marvel, really . . .

"What?" he asks.

"Your cuts and bruises. They're gone so fast."

He nods. "Benefits of being a shifter. The only thing we can't heal from is a lycan bite."

"Not the only thing," Joanna murmurs.

"That's right, Jo," Grady speaks up. "We're not immortal. We bleed. And we die. Just like what would have happened to you tonight if Ryne hadn't saved you."

"Saved me?" she growls. "That's a funny way to put it."

"Enough," Ryne interjects. "You will behave. We're here."

Sure enough, we slow to a stop outside of a large structure unlike anything I've seen before. It's tall and concrete, curving around the edge, with bright lights at the top. I'm not sure what it is. Knox jumps out to open the doors for us, and we climb out. I gaze up at the building, feeling small.

"It's a football stadium. Used to be used for human sports," Knox says.

Ryne shoots him a scathing look, and Knox backs away, holding his hands up. "I'm sorry, Alpha. I forgot my place."

Ryne doesn't say anything. He takes my hand and tugs me after him. "Is Knox not allowed to speak to me?" I ask.

He stops short and tilts his head, giving me a suspicious look. "How do you know his name?"

White-hot fear shoots through my body. "You've used his name many times in front of me."

He frowns. "Right. Sorry."

I don't want to get Knox into trouble. They'll kill him if they think he's trying to start something with me. I'm certain of it. Everything they do here is about growing the pack. A claimed man cannot have a claimed woman. They're here for labor, and that's all. There aren't many of them since only the human families who never had daughters have to give up a son, but I hate that any of them are here in the first place. As far as I'm concerned, the deltas could be doing these jobs, and the human men could be spared from a lifetime of slavery.

And a lonely existence.

Knox gets back in the car, and his face disappears behind the dark glass.

Joanna and Grady walk on either side of us as we head toward the stadium entrance. They won't even look at each other. I'm sure it won't last. Joanna can hold a grudge until the end of time if she wants, but Grady is smitten. He'll forgive her and work his way back into her heart. At least, I hope that's what happens for both of their sakes.

As we go inside, the first thing that hits me is the noise. The men holler and cheer so loudly it's like walking into a wall of sound. The next thing is the smell, crisp winter night mixed with sweat and blood and alcohol. And the third is the blinding light. I blink rapidly until my eyes adjust. I wish they hadn't because what I see is horrific.

Chapter Twenty-Five

The building is open to the dark sky and shaped like an oval. Most of the seats are empty, but there are still globs of people cheering from the raised seats all along the sides. In the middle is an open field of grass with bodies strewn across it.

Too many bodies to count.

Wolves and naked men lie sprawled out, many with their entrails exposed. Tears burn my eyes, and I drop them to stare at my shoes.

"Looks like it's over," Ryne says with a twinge of something in his voice that's either regret or relief. Regret that he missed it or regret that it even happened? I wish I knew.

"Are you sure you don't want to go down there?" Grady asks.

"Yes. Let my father announce the new rank advancements. He loves it."

"He'll be sending the ones who surrendered out to the wilds," Grady says, spinning to Joanna. He grabs her chin, turning her to look at a line of four men on their knees on the far side of the field. "Do you know what would have happened to you if those rejected wolves had come across you out there?"

Her face turns stony, and she jerks away.

"Come on," Ryne says, "let's go sit down with the other claimed."

We make our way down several sets of stairs until we come across Madame Delphine and the others sitting in rows near the edge of the field. Our girls are intermixed with the betas, some who are courting us and some who are not. All the girls have smiles on their faces, but even I can tell that most of their smiles are fake. I wonder what atrocities they witnessed tonight. I'm suddenly grateful for Joanna's impulsive heart, even if it meant we got caught. At least we didn't have to watch all these men die.

We join the others, and Faye shoots me a disgusted look before sitting on Anders's lap. A few rows above, I catch Justin's longing gaze on her. I somehow know that her attention toward Anders is all part of her master plan. If she can make Justin jealous, then he'll want her even more. Nova and Nico are sitting side by side, their heads bent toward each other in a deep conversation. Nova can say she's not going to marry him, but there's no getting between those two already, and it's only been about a month. Cade is in the middle of a group of six girls, all vying for his attention. From the satisfied smirk on his handsome face, he's obviously loving every moment.

I glance at Ryne, wishing we could be public with our affection here. I want it to be like it was back in his house when we were alone, but one look at his pained expression, and I know that's a foolish thought. I'm not supposed to want him. He's bad for me. Even he's starting to come around to that fact.

The four of us sit down with the others as Ryne's father struts onto the field. He announces the new positions to a wave of cheers from the audience. When I don't immediately react as the others do, Ryne elbows me in the side. "Play along," he whispers against my ear. "It's for the best, trust me. If my father doesn't like you, you're as good as dead."

I clap and smile and fake it along with everyone else because when the alpha king wants you to clap, you clap.

When the time comes for the four surrendered wolves to be exiled to the wilds, things take a dark turn. "I've never had respect for cowardice." The king's smooth baritone voice rings out over a speaker, echoing through the stadium. He sweeps his hand around to all the bodies. "At least these men died heroes. You four are a disgrace to this pack." He stalks toward the four cowards so angrily that I think he's about to shift into his wolf and end them himself. "I've decided it's only fair that you battle each other for the right to live. The last one standing will be allowed to go to the wilds. The rest will die along with your more courageous brothers."

The men look at each other with shock, but it doesn't take long for the battle to begin. They dive for each other, their forms turning from man to wolf in midair. The crowd loves it.

"This is new," Grady says low over the roar of cheers.

Ryne is stiff as a board beside me.

"Carolina is your pack," Grady continues to him. "Are you really going to let him change the rules like this?"

Ryne's wolf growls from within, and he turns on Grady. "Not another word, beta."

Grady shrinks back. "Apologies, alpha."

Joanna looks between the two and rolls her eyes, a little bit of her personality thawing underneath the icy attitude. For the first time, I realize that Ryne may be afraid of his father, and I want to know why. I peer over to Madame Delphine, but her face is an unreadable mask as she watches the field. The poor woman has to watch the man who was once her lover and her husband and the father of her child, and act as if he is nothing to her now. I don't blame her for hiding her emotions. She gave him an heir and an alpha, and what was she given in return? A new job grooming the upcoming claimed. Madame may well be a respected title, but she's not living the life of an alpha's wife, and certainly not the life of an alpha king's wife.

The entire time the four men battle, I keep my eyes downcast. I can't watch. I only know it's over by the way the crowd cheers louder and the people around me stand and jump and scream. I stay planted in my seat, and Ryne stays with me.

"It's over, Poppy. You'll be able to go home now," Ryne whispers. The word home hits me like a punch in the gut. "I'm sorry about this. I wish it could be different."

"Why can't it?" We're surrounded by standing, cheering people, who are paying us no attention, and somehow it feels like we're the only ones here. I stare at him, taking in the tangle of long raven hair around his tan face, the high cut of his cheekbones, and the deep blue of his eyes. It's a face I could stare at forever, and right now, I think he understands. More than that, I think he might agree with me. He cups my cheek and wipes away a tear that I didn't realize was trailing down my skin.

"It just can't." He peers into my eyes, pleading for me to understand. But how can I ever understand? He claims he's just as trapped as I am, that he doesn't have control, but I don't really believe that's true. He has a whole pack of shifters who will do whatever he asks.

"Hello, son," a gravelly voice interrupts us. "I didn't expect you to come out tonight." Ryne drops his hand from my face and turns as the voice continues. "Are you going to introduce me to this woman who seems to have stolen your attention?"

The crowd parts to reveal the alpha king standing not three feet away from us.

Chapter Twenty-Six

Ryne moves away from me as we stand. I'm not sure why he doesn't want to be seen with me in public, but I'm certain that whatever the reason is, it'll hurt me. If it didn't, then there would be no reason to keep secrets. I frown at that, wishing I were better at guarding my heart from him.

Joanna is at my side, looping her arm through mine. "Tonight," she whispers in my ear, "you are going to tell me exactly what is going on between you and Ryne."

I nod, too distracted by the power dynamic between father and son to pay attention to what she's saying. They're standing toe to toe, neither one saying a word.

We're all watching.

Waiting.

The alpha king is still dressed in the same pressed black suit from earlier, though he's loosened the tie, and the sleeves are a little rumpled. Like most of the wolves, he has shoulder-length hair. It frames high cheekbones, same as his son's. There's one streak of gray in the front, but otherwise it's also black as ink. He has the same cerulean eyes as Ryne but with a few added wrinkles around the creases. The resemblance between Ryne and King Thorn is uncanny——nobody could argue Ryne's parentage. Thorn is quite attractive for a middle-aged man, but then again, his middle age isn't the same as ours.

How old is he, really?

Anders doesn't look much older than Nico, and Anders is Nico's father. Not only that, but Nico is Anders' youngest son. So that must mean the alpha king had Ryne when he was much older than when Anders started having children. Maybe King Thorn went through several wives before he found one who could give him an heir, or maybe Ryne has brothers that I just don't know about. Thorn is definitely the oldest shifter I've seen, so maybe that's how he rose to his position. In fact, I don't think I've seen *any* wolves yet who actually look older than forty. Odd, because if they live to be twice as old as humans, wouldn't they at least look elderly by the end of their lives? Maybe the shifter genes don't work that way, or maybe most of the wolves don't make it to old age because they kill each other so haphazardly for rank. Was Thorn Tremaine a shifter during the wars? Did he help fight the final battles that ended the human governments? Did he help establish the claiming of humans?

I'm filled with questions I'm far too afraid to ask.

"I see you've brought along this year's claimed." The king speaks, breaking the tension and glancing around at the girls. When his eyes travel across me, my cheeks prickle. "How many will marry a beta?"

"Five."

"Good thing it's not more. I have to say, son, your houses are lacking a little. You have too many men and too few women. It's time for you to either lower the claimed age or take two from each family like we've done in Chicago."

I force myself to hide my horror. If they took two, that would be twice as many women fighting for the betas. It would not be pretty.

"Perhaps. But I still think you're going to run into human population problems, father. I don't think that's the solution."

"Then what is?" His father chuckles, but he's clearly not amused.

"Maybe it's just time for me to expand my territory. The Savannah panther pack is weak." Ryne sounds so sure of himself. "We could take them out and gain all their humans."

I blink rapidly. Panther pack? I thought only wolf shifters lived in this area. I've heard whisperings of other species of shifters out there, but to realize an entire pack lives close is a revelation.

The king raises his eyebrows. "You would take another city? But, son, that is the stuff of kings, not princes. Are you saying you want to usurp me?" His tone is joking, but his eyes are razor-sharp on Ryne.

"Not at all, I only wish to grow your territory as well as mine. You mentioned that we don't have enough women. If I expanded down to Savannah, I would have twice as many villages to claim from."

The king claps him on the back. "Don't apologize for ambition. I'm glad to see a little initiative from you. Now, tell me. Who's heading to the mating houses on the wolf moon?"

Faye slides forward and loops her arm through Ryne's. Her cheeks are rosy, and her smile is triumphant. She's certainly getting around tonight––the girl thrives on attention "That would be Poppy and Callista."

My jaw drops. I want to punch her square in the nose and rip out all that pretty auburn hair. Joanna squeezes my arm, and I'm sure she wants to do the same.

The alpha king narrows his eyes at Faye, biting his bottom lip suggestively. "And you are?"

"Faye Donovan, Your Majesty. Top of the board. At the harvest moon, I will be a proud wife of one of the betas." She bats her eyelashes. "Unless there's an alpha who needs a mate?"

He chuckles. "I like you . . . So where are Poppy and Callista?"

His eyes roam the crowd, and Callista inches toward the king, her hands shaking. I move as well, but Joanna holds me back. "I have to," I hiss.

I step forward, and Ryne shifts a little so he's standing between me and his father. The alpha king's eyes flash with mirth, but he doesn't say anything. He simply strides around Ryne and places a finger under my chin, forcing me to look in his eyes. No, these are not like Ryne's eyes after all. They are cold and unforgiving and laced with evil thoughts.

"What's one week?" He puts an arm around my waist and tugs me into him. "Poppy will come home with me tonight, and I'll drop her off at the mating house before I leave town."

Ryne bristles. "That's not how things work in my pack, father. Callista and Poppy have one more week to prove themselves, and I owe it to my men to let them have the first taste of the women if they fail." The two men face off a moment before Ryne adds, "Besides, Poppy moved up the board today. Give her a week to see if she can hold her spot."

Callista clicks her tongue, and some of the other girls send me scathing looks.

I know Ryne's trying to protect me, but his words still make me shiver. And now everyone knows he's willing to stand up to his father when it comes to me. I don't know if that's a good thing or a bad one, but I'm leaning toward bad.

The alpha king stares at me for the longest time, and I'm certain he's going to refuse Ryne's wishes. My heart speeds, but I stand tall. "I suppose so," he says at last. He leans down and whispers low in my ear. "I see the way my son looks at you. Next week, when you inevitably enter the mating house, I'll come back for you. I will have you before he does. That's a promise."

He straightens and slips away into the crowd of gawkers. It takes every ounce of self-control I have to not collapse into Joanna's arms. I am now under the alpha king's nose, and I don't see how I can possibly get out of it.

"Delphine," Thorn hollers.

She rushes to his side, curtsying low. "Yes, Your Majesty." It's the first time I've ever seen her completely submissive. She always stands up to all the wolves, but right now she's not even looking this man in the eyes.

"I would love to escort you and your girls back to the manor. Then you and I have things we need to discuss."

He holds out his arm, and she slips her hand through. I wonder if I'm the only one who sees the slight tremble. Joanna grabs my hand, jerking me back to her. Grady stays with us as we make our way up the stadium stairs.

Faye has not left Ryne's side, and she giggles at something he says as they walk ahead of us. He looks just as easy with her as he had been with me, and my chest burns with jealousy. Perhaps whatever happened between us was nothing.

But it didn't feel like nothing. It felt real. Even more real than what Knox and I had.

And he did just stand up to his father for me. That has to count for something.

"Are you okay?" Grady asks. I jerk my head toward him, surprised. I would have expected the words to come from Joanna, not him. He's barely said anything to me as long as I've known him.

"I'm fine. Why wouldn't I be?" I'm careful to keep my face blank, wishing I could believe my lies.

Grady doesn't say anything more. We walk from the arena through a few city blocks until we're at the river's edge again. We climb into the boat and find seats, and Ryne joins his father. The rest of the betas say their goodbyes. I have a feeling Ryne hadn't been planning on going with us, but he doesn't want to leave us alone with the king. To think that he's the only person in this entire city who can stand up to Thorn is terrifying.

We're all tired by now, the long day bearing down on everyone. Exhaustion clouds my mind, and my eyes want to shut it all away. Joanna sits next to me at the back of the boat, wrapping an arm around me. I wrap one around her too. We don't speak. The boat starts to move––I'm used to it by now––and soon we're traveling up the river. It's dark enough to see the stars since the moon is barely beginning hanging over the horizon. The breeze and mist from the water are icy cold, but I don't mind them because they wake me up.

I watch Ryne––I can't help myself.

He's sitting between his father and Faye. The girl practically has herself in his lap, and his arm is around her back, but he doesn't seem to be paying her any attention. His eyes keep tracking back to me. Even though he's cast in shadows and sitting all the way across the boat, I can still make out his features under the half-moon. I know he's watching, and I like it.

He's beautiful. On the outside, of course, but there's light hidden within his inner-darkness, trying to get out. I want to find it, to show him that it's okay to be good.

Maybe he really does want me. Maybe he really will protect me.

I remember what he said earlier about kissing me one day, and my heartbeat picks up. I can picture us now, can feel the softness of his lips and the hardness of his muscles as he wraps me in an embrace. Everything else seems to melt away, and longing rises up inside of me unlike anything I've ever felt before.

He must sense it because he narrows his gaze, and even from here, I can see the same thing mirrored back in him. Our future kiss is inevitable. We are inevitable. We must be. We have to be. I can't help but smile. For the first time since coming here, I actually feel like I matter and that maybe I'm special.

That's when Ryne breaks our gaze, turns to Faye, and kisses her.

Chapter Twenty-Seven

I'm frozen, unwilling to believe what I'm seeing, but unable to look away. He's really kissing her, and for everyone to see.

For me to see.

Joanna's arm stiffens around my side, and she curses under her breath. "Don't look, Poppy. He's not worth it."

I rip my eyes away, and my heart shatters. It shouldn't. This is stupid. He's not mine. He's the alpha, and there was no way he was going to keep me around anyway. He would've just used me and spit me back out. He even said that he'd help me get with a beta, and never once did he say I would end up with him. At least I hadn't kissed him. It would've made this worse.

Maybe not though, because then I'd have the memory.

The moment we shared at his house was more intimate than a kiss, though. At least I thought so. I drop my eyes to the boat floor, and my mind swirls. I can feel my face burning as a few of the other girls look back at me.

Ryne keeps kissing Faye.

Joanna puts her other arm around me and holds me close. I have no idea what's happening to me, but tears threaten. I will them away, not wanting Ryne or anyone to see me cry. The betrayal is too much.

Finally, I brave a glance back up. Ryne releases Faye, and she positions herself under his arm, smirking. He doesn't look at me once as he turns to his father, starting up a relaxed conversation. It's like I don't even exist.

Resolve swells in my chest. I've let myself become distracted. If I want to stay out of the mating house, I've got to be focused on the betas. Justin or Cade are the only ones I can even hope to win, and if they were here right now, I'd channel all this emotion into them. I'd get up right now and go flirt with them. I'd let them know that I was interested. My choices are slim, but either of those men would be a million times better than a life in the mating house.

Faye meets my gaze and blows me a little air kiss. She's gloating.

There's something about her that draws men in like a magnet, and whatever it is, I need to find it inside myself. I need to step up and prove to everyone that I'm capable of being a beta wife. Cade would be easier to ensnare, seeing as he isn't already set on Faye, and I'm pretty sure Faye is still planning on Justin. Although, if I were able to snatch Justin from under Faye's nose, that would be justice well served. First, though, I have to work my way up the board.

I hope Ryne keeps his word and gives me enough points to at least be out of the bottom two, but I can't count on anything from him ever again.

Why did he kiss her? The question pops into my mind, and I shove it aside.

The boat docks at our house, and I refuse to jump out of my seat and race off the boat in front of everyone. I walk slowly to the house, my shoulders back and head high, and don't stop until I'm in my room. I strip off my clothes and climb into bed. I don't think I'll be able to sleep, but I have to pretend so I don't have to talk to Joanna when she comes in.

I close my eyes tight, and all I can see is Ryne's lips on Faye's. Despite my best efforts, tears wet my pillowcase that night.

I stop at the scoreboard on the way to breakfast the next morning. Sure enough, Ivy has bumped down a spot, making me third from the bottom. Only two points separate me from her, and ten points are between me and Katelyn for the fourth from the bottom spot. As awful as it is, I'm not too worried about Callista. She doesn't have strong alliances in the house, and none of the betas have shown her any interest. She's just as helpful in the classes as I am, but she's not good at exercise or fighting either. The poor girl doesn't stand a chance.

I can focus on overtaking Katelyn later. For now, I just need to stay above Ivy and Callista. My heart twinges a little because I know what that means for them. I wonder if they truly realize exactly what's in store if I succeed. I'm certain none of the other girls have paid a visit to the mating house because if they knew the truth of it—if they saw what I saw—they'd be fighting tooth and nail to stay out.

Joanna loops her arm through mine in that familiar way of ours, and we enter the dining room. We're the last ones in, and I jerk my eyes over to Faye. I expect her to be crowing about the kiss with Ryne, but she's not. Her eyes are red rimmed, and there's a cut on her cheek and a yellow bruise under her eye. I can't tell from here, but it looks a little like a bite mark. She's got her eyes on her grits and isn't saying a word to anyone.

"What happened to Faye?" I whisper.

"Oh, I forgot you went to bed before everyone. The alpha king wanted to take her home. Ryne refused, so the king took her on a walk instead. The stupid girl went willingly, of course. I was still in the library chatting with Bailey when Faye came running up the stairs. She looked a mess and was crying. I have no idea what happened, but whatever it was, it wasn't good."

I don't want to feel sympathy for Faye, but I do. I can only guess at what the king did to her. That man is cruel down to his center.

"If he took away her virtue, does that disqualify her from marrying a beta?"

"I don't think anyone would dare question it since she was with the king."

What did Madame Delphine have to endure in her years with him? Maybe she's happy to be running Drayton Hall. Maybe this was her out from a lifetime at his beck and call. I look around for her, but she's not here. It's just us girls this morning.

Normally, Faye has her sidekicks surrounding her but not today. It makes me feel doubly bad for her. Just because someone is popular doesn't mean they have true friends. True friends are there for you no matter what, especially when things get uncomfortable. Right now, all of Faye's friends are staring at their plates and pretending she's not here, which would explain why the only seats left are at her table. Joanna and I sit down and start our breakfasts, but I can only pick at mine.

"I'm sorry about whatever happened to you last night," I say to Faye. I can't help it. I don't like her, and she doesn't like me, but I feel terrible for her. No woman deserves violence like that, and my mama raised me better than to look the other way.

Faye scoffs and drops her fork against her plate with a clatter. "Do you mean the part where Ryne kissed me?" She raises an eyebrow, and the cut on her cheek stretches. "Because yeah, I figured you'd be sorry to see that. But guess what, Poppy? I'm not sorry."

My stomach hardens. Okay, maybe I don't feel so bad for her.

"Why do you have to be such a bitch?" Joanna cuts in. "She was trying to be nice."

"By rubbing it in my face?" Faye glares at me. "Don't make comments on things you'll never understand, little girl."

"Don't talk to her that way."

"Oh, and what's she going to do about it? Poppy is weak."

That comment cuts the deepest because I know she's right. I am weak. I have been ever since I got here. But I'm tired of being weak. I want to jump across the table and show her just how strong I am, but I've realized something lately. Being strong doesn't mean being violent or stooping to her level. Being strong means standing up for yourself.

"I'm not going to sit here and take your abuse. I tried showing you kindness. I'm done." I push back my chair and gather my dish to take it to the kitchen. A wave of relief washes over me. Whatever happens to me, it won't be because of Faye. She has no more power to make me feel bad. The fact is we're in this terrible situation together. She's a victim too. She's really good at making herself seem like the villain here, but she's not. The villains are the Carolina Pack, the alphas, and the whole damn system.

"So that's it?" Faye hisses. She's right on my heels. "You're just going to walk away from me? What about last night?"

I turn on her. "What about last night? Facts are that Ryne kissed you, and then his father hurt you. I don't know what else you want me to say here."

"Do you want to know why he hurt me?" She steps closer. "Because you didn't accompany him to the mating house like he asked." She points to her bruised face. "As far as I'm concerned, this is your fault. It should've been you."

Heat ripples across my skin. "You'd rather I'd be the one with cuts and bruises? That I endured that and who knows what else?"

"Yes."

I shake my head at her. "Why? Honestly, give me a reason why."

"Because I'm going to be a beta wife, maybe even Ryne's alpha wife." She spits at my feet. "And you will be nothing."

Chapter Twenty-Eight

The week passes faster than I thought it would. Before I know it, the morning of the wolf moon dawns. There are no classes today, but tonight we'll head back into the city for the celebration where the two lowest scoring girls will be sent to the mating houses. Just the thought of it makes me shiver. Dread twists me up inside, but so does relief because at least by tonight, we'll all have some answers.

I throw on a pair of running shorts and lace up my sneakers. This week was good to me––it felt like I could do no wrong. Madame Vivien eased off on her personal training sessions and had us run for physical fitness. In combat class the betas were busy, so we fought each other. I didn't get to throw a punch at Faye, unfortunately, but that's okay because I was the last woman standing. And thanks to Madame Nova and Joanna's tutoring, I'm finally able to read a little bit. The only iffy class was knitting. My scarf turned out completely lopsided, but I still managed to turn out a better one than Ivy's. And both Callista and Ivy are horrible at combat. It doesn't make me feel any better sending women to the mating house who are terrible at defending themselves, but that's not my fault. I can't keep feeling guilty for other people if I'm going to survive this place.

I stop and stare at the board on my way out the door, expecting to see our scores. Instead, there's a note written across it. *Final scores to be revealed tonight. Good luck!*

I take a deep breath and tell myself not to worry. Yesterday morning I was third from the bottom, and I had a perfect day, so there's no reason why I shouldn't be safe. After this, I'm going to work harder than ever to climb up the board and win a beta. The betas have stayed away this week, but Madame Delphine said that was only because they were initiating their new warrior betas and preparing for the wolf moon festivities.

The front door creaks open, and Nova slips in. Dark bags line her eyes, and her lips are pressed tight together. She sees me and forces a smile.

"You're up early on your day off."

"I like to run in the mornings."

"Can I join you? Running is good for thinking."

I glance at her maroon uniform dress, and she chuckles. "I'll change if you'll wait for me."

I nod and slip out the back door, stretching my legs. I like Nova a lot, and she's been generous with the points she's given me, but we haven't really talked much since the day she arrived, besides the extra tutoring sessions. But then those aren't really about talking, they're about learning.

She joins me, and we start slow. I don't know what her pace is, and I don't want to leave her too far behind, but she speeds up a little, and I follow. Neither of us says anything on the first lap, so I startle a little when she speaks up just as we pass the house.

"Nico wants to take me as his mate tonight."

"I thought they only did that on the harvest moon."

"That's what I thought too, but Nico said they can do it at any festival with the alpha's approval. Grady wanted to do the same thing with Joanna, but Ryne told him no. He said Nico and I could make things official, though."

"Do you want that?" I hadn't realized they'd gotten so close. She was so adamant that she wasn't going to be with another wolf again.

A soft smile brightens her face. "I do. But I feel guilty. That's one less beta for you girls. If I agree to be his mate, then I'll be condemning another girl to the mating house. I would never wish any of you to go through what I did." We slow to a walk and catch our breath. "Nico is a good man. He's kind and gentle, and he doesn't care that I'll never be able to give him children. I'm stealing one of the good ones. That's not fair to you guys, and I'm not sure if I'll be able to live with myself."

"But do you love him?"

She wipes a few tears off her face. They've made her blue eyes bright, and when the sun catches her blonde hair, it lights her up like a halo. She looks young and in love.

"I do." She lets out a cathartic laugh. "I've not said it out loud yet. But I really do. I know it's only been a short time since I met him, and it sounds crazy, but this fated mate thing is impossible to explain."

"Try? Because I'm curious."

She shrugs. "I can't not be with him."

"Then I don't see that you'll have any choice. Will you still work here?"

"Yes. We talked about that. Since I probably won't be able to have kids, then it makes sense that I do something with my time. I like working with you girls."

I nudge her. "We like you too."

"But a lot of the girls will resent me."

"Probably, but I won't. And you know what you can do for us?" I sigh deeply. "You can prepare us for the mating houses, not just the betas. Because most of us will end up there, and I don't think these girls have any idea what's in store for them."

Her face pales. "That's true. Maybe I can help. I'll have to be discreet about it, of course."

We jog in silence for a while.

"What beta are you going to try for?" she asks at last, eyeing me with a tilt to her lips.

"I haven't decided yet. I'm not even sure I'll make it past tonight."

She grins. "Actually, don't tell anyone, but you're fourth from the bottom right now. You're going to be fine."

Relief sweeps through me, and I let out a little laugh. "Thank you for telling me."

She nods. "So, back to the betas. Who's caught your eye?"

I think about that for a minute. "Cade is a safer bet, but if I get Justin, I can rub it in Faye's face."

She chuckles. "I've noticed that you two don't get along."

"That is the understatement of the year. I don't know how to win over a man though. Will you help me?" I can use all the help I can get. And, well, she *did* work at a mating house.

"I'm not supposed to show favoritism, but I always love an underdog. Next week, we'll do a makeover, and I'll teach you how to woo a man." She giggles and suddenly sounds as young as she actually is. She can't be more than ten years older than me. Her hard life has aged her, but maybe things are about to change. Maybe they're about to change for me too.

"And I'll also see what I can learn about Justin. The more you know about him, the easier your job will be."

Now it's my turn to laugh. "All I know about him is that he's all about having fun and flirting with the pretty ladies."

"Good. Then you'll be perfect."

We're taken to the Wolf Moon Festival by boat an hour before the sun is supposed to set. The pale moon has already risen over the horizon even though the sky is still indigo. As we zoom across the water, the moon looms over us like a promise.

The lycans will be out soon.

I wonder if Charlotte is still out there somewhere and if she made it through the last two months in her new life. I'm sure I'll never see her again, and even though I'm still angry at her for keeping such a big secret, right now, I can understand why she did it.

Because I'm terrified.

Even though I'm in the fourth slot, I still feel like something bad is going to happen tonight to snatch that away from me. Maybe it's this place and this whole messed up process, but I've lost my trust.

"You did it." Joanna squeezes my hand. That girl is good at reading people. I already told her the news, but she can tell I'm still freaking out. "Don't worry. Tonight you can relax and have fun. I hate to say this because it goes against everything I stand for, but I think you should flirt with the betas tonight and really put yourself out there. This is your chance to make an impression and show them how special you are."

I smile weakly. I'm one of sixteen girls and ranked in twelfth place. I don't feel so special.

"I'm serious," she adds. "And besides, you look incredible."

I do like how I look. I'm dressed in a sparkly pale blue dress. My brown hair is curled in loose waves down my back. I've got makeup on—red lips, black lashes framing my brown eyes with blue sparkles across the lids, and white shimmery dust on my collarbone. Nova snuck in at the last minute to apply those last two touches. She even sprayed me with perfume that smells like a perfect summertime night, making me hope for better days ahead. Even though we're all dressed up, none of the other girls got her added touch.

We dock, are loaded onto a bus, and a few minutes later are dropped off in front of the most gorgeous building I've ever laid eyes on. It's three stories tall with white columns all across the front. A monument outside of it reads "Hibernian Hall, established 1840," and I smile because I actually read those words without trouble.

"At least we're going to be indoors," I say to Joanna.

"No kidding. It gets cold and dark fast in January," she agrees. She lets out a little puff of breath that instantly crystalizes, proving her point.

We're herded inside and are met with a blast of welcoming heat. I gasp as I take in the decorations. This place is even prettier inside than it is on the outside.

Huge pine trees are set up with tiny snowflakes and silvery blue wolf ornaments hanging from them. In our village we celebrate Christmas, but not here. The day came and went just like any other. But this feels like Christmas, even though the decorations are all blue and white. We girls are released to the ballroom, and I stroll through the trees, running my fingertips against the prickly needles. Maybe tonight won't be so bad.

"Your dress matches the decorations." Ryne's familiar scent of spicy earth surrounds me, and I clench my teeth. I tell myself that he is the last man I want to talk to, but I know it's a lie. I don't turn around, but I feel the heat of Ryne's body close to mine. I shouldn't, but I want to lean back against him and feel his arms around my waist.

"I'm sorry about Faye," he whispers, his breath caressing my ear. "I had to throw my father off your scent."

I clutch at my dress, and a weight lifts off my heart. He was protecting me. Why would he do that? Part of me doesn't want to believe him, but the bigger part desperately does. "Is your father here tonight?" I brush my fingers along the edges of a snowflake decoration, and glitter sticks to them.

"No," he breathes, resting one hand on my hip. "You look beautiful. I have half a mind to take you as my mate tonight."

I can't help it. I spin and stare into his gorgeous blue eyes. They're framed by his dark lashes. His black hair hangs around his cheeks, begging for my hands to run through it. I don't understand this man.

"Why would you do that?"

He chuckles and runs a finger down my cheek. "You are clueless as to how captivating you are, aren't you?" He sighs. "As much as I want to, I can't. It will not be easy watching you go with one of my betas, but it will be better than the mating house."

"Just not Anders. Please. Anyone but Anders."

A frown forms on his lips.

"Did I say something wrong?" I ask.

"I foolishly hoped that maybe you felt the same way about me and would beg me to take you instead. But I guess I was wrong." He steps away and disappears into the crowd. I stand there for a moment feeling thoroughly confused. If I had begged him to take me, would he have? He isn't the type to want a desperate female. Or maybe he is, and I completely misread him.

"You know, I heard about your sister." Faye's familiar drawl grates on my ears. I don't respond, still watching Ryne's retreating back. "She was killed because they found out she whored herself out before they came for her. Beta wives are meant to be virgins. You must be so ashamed."

Anger bubbles up in my chest. I spin around to face her. "That is not true. She was killed because Anders is an asshole who couldn't keep his hands to himself, and she wasn't taking it."

Faye let out a laugh. "Likely story. How long did it take you to make that up? I bet that's why Ryne likes you."

"Shut your mouth, Faye."

"Oh honey, you only wish I'd shut up because you know I'm speaking the truth. Deep down, you know Ryne only likes you because he's hoping you're a slut too." She pokes my chest with each word that follows. "Just. Like. Willow."

Fury burns behind my eyes, and I slap her across the face without thinking. Hearing her say Willow's name was too much. She holds a hand to her face, her eyes wide.

"You little bitch." She reaches over and pulls my hair so hard that my eyes water. I scratch at her arms, but she doesn't let go. I stomp down on her exposed toe with my heel, and she screeches. She lets go but lunges for me, her hands flapping.

This is not the combat I know, but I can't manage to punch her when she's thrashing at me with nails and teeth. Instead, I grab at a flap on her dress and pull. It makes a satisfying ripping noise. She gasps and tackles me. My back hits the floor hard, but I manage to hold my head up so it doesn't crack on the floor. I struggle underneath her but can't move very well in my dress. I scratch at her face and yank her hair out of its careful updo. She claws at my dress and then goes for my hair too.

She's suddenly lifted away, and everything stills. A livid Madame Delphine towers over me. Grady holds a struggling Faye back, and Joanna helps me up. One strap of my dress is torn away, and there is a rip from the bottom clear up to my thigh.

Ryne stands a little ways away, his arms crossed and lips twitching. He thinks this is funny! Madame Delphine does not. Her face turns as purple as a Christmas plum, and she looks back and forth between us. Faye calms down, and Grady lets go of her.

"Never in all my years of running Drayton Hall have I seen such a spectacle. Fighting is never allowed among my girls, and to do so at such a public event is unforgivable." She swallows hard. "I'm sorry, but I can't see any other way to proceed. You will each lose fifty points."

My shoulders fall. Fifty points is a lot. Now it's going to be even harder for me to work my way up the board, but at least I made it for tonight.

Faye smirks at me. "When will the points be taken, Madame?"

"Immediately."

My world closes in around me in slow motion.

"So does that mean that Poppy drops to the bottom of the board right now?"

Madame Delphine's face falls for just a second before responding. She straightens her shoulders, avoiding my eyes. "Yes."

Bile rises in my throat, and I seek out Ryne's gaze once again. He's not laughing anymore.

Faye presses on. "So Poppy is heading for the mating house? She's got to be at the bottom of the list now."

Madame Delphine purses her lips. "Yes. I suppose that would be the case. I'm so sorry, Poppy." Her face is ashen. "The most disappointing part is that you did this to yourself."

After all that hard work, my worst nightmare has come true.

Chapter Twenty-Nine

Joanna clutches at my arm. "But you can't do that. She was fourth from the bottom when we left the house."

Madame Delphine sniffs. "How did you know that? The points weren't posted today."

I open and close my mouth, wanting to reveal what Nova told me but knowing that I can't get her in trouble. Besides, it would be pointless now anyway.

"Never mind." Madame Delphine shakes her head. "Whatever the score was, it was before that despicable display. I hope the rest of you girls will learn from Poppy's mistake."

I want to defend myself and explain how Faye goaded me into it, but I don't because it won't do any good. Fifty points for Faye just bumped her to the middle of the board, but I'm a goner. When we left tonight, everything looked so hopeful. And now, it's all gone. This isn't fair.

I glance around, taking in the crowd of elegantly dressed party guests. They're all gaping at me. It's the full moon, so not every beta is here, but it certainly feels like it. And the ones that are married have brought their wives along. The women are nothing like me. They're polished and perfect and glaring down their noses in my direction. They must think I'm pathetic and want me sent away this very minute. There's not an ounce of compassion among them.

Madame Nova appears at my side, gripping my elbow. "Come on, let's get you cleaned up."

I jerk out of her arms. "Why? She just started what they'll finish." I nod to the pack of wolves who now all eye me hungrily. They didn't know who was headed for the mating house when they arrived tonight. Now I'm fresh meat.

She drags me away from the crowd anyway, and Joanna grips my other arm. We enter a bathroom that is designed in entirely cream marble and warm lights. Madame Nova grabs a few fluffy white hand towels and wets them in the sink. Joanna gets to work on my hair.

I catch sight of myself in the mirror. I'm a mess. My hair sticks out in all directions. Dirt and blood cover my face and shoulders.

"I need you to listen to me," Nova says, each word a careful directive.

I jerk my eyes down to meet hers.

"I'm going to talk to Nico and ask him to speak to Ryne on your behalf. We need to see about getting you sent to either the Pennsylvania Alley or Church Street mating houses. Church street would be best, but all the women want in there, so it's harder to get into. Once you are there, ask for Flora."

"At which one?"

"Doesn't matter. It's a code word for help, and the girls there will take care of you."

"How are any of the mating houses better than others? Seems like they would all be terrible."

Nova snorts. "Each house has a reputation, and the men go to the ones that cater to their needs. Broad Street is the worst. If you get word that they are sending you there, run. Death is better than the horrors they'll inflict on you there."

"Church Street is the best because it feels more like dating. The men that go there want the girls to want them, so they rarely take a girl without her consent. A few girls there have long-standing relationships with warrior betas, and some are even monogamous. Pennsylvania Alley is similar, but it's not quite as good."

Panic builds in my chest. I don't want to do any of it. I want to run right now, but that means Evan and my parents would die, and I don't want that either. I rub my sweaty palms along my ripped dress but find them too shaky.

I bend over, breathing hard. "I can't do this."

"You can, and you will. Poppy, you are strong, and this won't break you. Now, you have to go back out there and pretend like everything is fine. That is the life of a claimed woman. I'm going to find Nico and see what I can do for you." She puts both of her hands on my shoulders and forces me to look at her. "Don't let them know they've gotten to you. If they sense weakness, it's all over. Be strong, Poppy."

Joanna grips my arm and leads me out of the bathroom and back to the party.

I don't feel strong at all.

There's dancing, but it's a blur––the music, the couples, the laughter, the smells, the food, the enjoyment––none of it matters anymore. And then I'm dancing too, being passed from beta to beta, but it's only my body on the dance floor because my mind is elsewhere. I don't hear what they say or register much of what's happening.

I look up to find that I'm in the arms of the man whose fault it is that I'm here tonight. Anders smiles down at me with a sinister grin and brings his lips to my ears. "I had hoped that you would be my wife, but this way I get you earlier. I'll be sure to find you at your new mating house."

I don't say a word. I can't. His hand on my back slips lower and lower, but before I react the same way Willow did––and I should, death would be better than what I'm about to do––Grady cuts in and pulls me close.

"Are you okay?" he whispers.

I shake my head.

"I wish I could say something that would make this better, but there's nothing to say. I can, however, keep you from having to dance with creepy men."

I clutch at him, grateful for this one small mercy. "Thank you."

We fall into an easy silence as we dance. All I can think about is going to the mating house tonight. I'm terrified they are going to send me to Broad Street.

The king may not be here at the dance, but he promised he would find me at the mating house, that he would have me before his son. And if Nova is right about different houses having different reputations, then he will make sure I am sent to one where he can abuse me all he wants. Nova said she'll have Nico try to help me out, but I can't cling to the false hope.

I glance over to where Faye is dancing with Anders. She's smiling at him as if she hasn't a care in the world. The wound on her cheek healed this week. She said she wished it were me who had been beat up, and now it will be. I know she is awful, but I never thought she would do something like this. She goaded me with fake gossip about Willow, and like an idiot, I fell for it. Now she's middle of the board, and I'm done for. At least Ivy is probably saved, though I have no doubt Callista is at the bottom with me. I look over to where Ivy is dancing with Justin. She's a follower, going along with whatever her friends want. She's like a pliable clay in Justin's hands. Too bad he's not interested. His eyes aren't even on her. They're on Faye as she laughs at something Anders says.

Faye will end up a beta wife if she doesn't somehow nab Ryne. And just because Ivy escaped the mating house this time doesn't mean she'll survive the next cut in three months or the two after that. I may even see her at a mating house if we get sent to the same one.

Where will I be in three months? With any luck, I'll already be pregnant and waiting it out in the birther's house. I always wanted a family. Being a mother one day was a given. A fact of life. Now I'll be a womb and nothing more.

A tear slips down my cheek, and Joanna is instantly at my side, leading me away from the watchful eyes. I catch sight of Ryne. He's staring at me with the same kind of intensity he used in his battles. Is he angry at me? I think so. Well, I'm angry at myself too.

We escape the massive ballroom and wind through a few back hallways until we end up in a kitchen. The staff is busy refilling the trays of food and sending them back out with the servers. There are no human men here. Only older women, the ones who aren't of child-bearing age anymore. They've all been in my shoes, and they look at me with knowing pity but don't say a word as Joanna leads me to the sink and helps me mop up my tears.

At last, she hugs me. "I'm sorry," she whispers in my ear, so quietly that nobody else can possibly hear. "Nova will get you sent to a good mating house, you'll see. Just go along with it and keep a low profile. Wait for a message from me. I am going to get you out of there as soon as——"

I step back and ask bitterly, "When are you going to give this up? There's nothing you can do to save me."

"I'm serious," she continues, looking around her to make sure nobody is listening. She pulls me back into another hug and whispers low again. "You don't understand. I'm part of a network of people who are fighting this system from within, and we're going to help you. Remember to ask for Flora." She lets me go.

I blink at her, a million questions swirling in my mind. She shakes her head once. It's not safe to talk about it. Not here. Probably not anywhere.

But it all makes sense now. I wish she had trusted me with this information sooner. I hope it's real. I hope she can help me. And hope is all I have to cling to. There's nothing else left.

"Where is she?" A male voice rips through the room. Joanna and I jump.

Nico appears with Ryne on his heels. His hair is disheveled, and his eyes are mad with panic. He turns to us. "Have you seen Nova?" His voice pleads.

I frown because I thought she was going to find him.

"We'll help you look for her," Joanna chimes in. "She's probably just in the bathroom or something. She helped Poppy clean up after the fight."

"No." Nico shakes his head. "We looked everywhere. We've turned this place upside down. The kitchen is the last place to check." He looks around helplessly, and the women scurry out of his way as he starts tearing through the cupboards, as if somehow Nova could be in one. It's irrational. But then again, so is love.

Ryne spins him around and forces Nico to look at him. "Pull yourself together."

Nico's face falls. "But she was supposed to become my mate."

"I know. But she probably got cold feet. You gave her a year and then drastically upped the timeline. I'm sure she's back at home waiting for you. You need to give her more time. She's been through a lot with the mating house and everything."

"I thought she loved me."

"She does. I've seen you two together, and I know she does. But she just needs a little more time to get used to things. You owe her that."

Nico nods, but he keeps his shoulders slumped, avoiding looking at any of us.

Ryne meets my eyes. "It's time. Madame Delphine is probably looking for you two. I'm going to pretend I didn't see you trying to run away again."

Joanna scoffs. "We aren't trying to run away. Poppy just needed a place to cry, you asshole."

He gives another stiff nod.

"Nico, do you know what mating house I'll be sent to?" I have to know.

He and Ryne exchange a guarded look and then leave without answering. My heart rate quickens as we follow them back to the ballroom. My feet feel like they're filled with lead. Joanna and I are going up on a stage with the rest of the claimed, and then once again I will be forced from my home and taken to a place I do not want to go.

I wonder how long it will be before the others join me, but there are many mating houses. Maybe I'll never see any of them again.

Even though I tried to walk slowly, before I know it, we're up on a stage with Ryne standing several paces in front of us, howling at his betas. It seems so strange to see them acting so uncivilized when they are dressed in tuxedos. But there's nothing civilized about them. They are monsters, all of them.

Joanna clutches my hand. We stand in the middle of the claimed women. I wish I could stand in the back, but there is no back. We are lined up, all in full view of the betas before us.

"Tonight, two of the claimed will join the mating houses. Would you like to meet the girls who will serve at your pleasure?" Ryne asks.

Bile rises in my throat, but I swallow it down. Nothing will save me now, and vomiting in front of all of them would just be embarrassing.

Ryne walks the line and pulls out Callista. She whimpers as he leads her to the front of the stage. This is no surprise. We all saw this coming, especially Callista herself.

"Meet Callista. She will be joining the Rainbow Row house."

A cheer goes up in the back of the crowd, no doubt from those who frequent that house. Rainbow Row was not one that Nova mentioned, so I have no idea what that means for her. I can only imagine it's not good. Surely the girls at the bottom of the crop are sent to the least desirable houses.

And then Ryne is in front of me, grabbing my hand and pulling me forward. I squeeze his hand, not wanting to ever let it go. Tonight my whole world will change. I've had months, but I'm still not prepared. I'm not ready to give up my innocence to violent men who will simply move on to the next girl once they've tired of me. I'm not ready for any of this.

Ryne slides his hand across my back, and I hate that I love the way it feels there. "Meet Poppy. She's scheduled to head to Broad Street."

My head begins to spin, and the only thing holding me upright is Ryne's arm. Nova told me to run if they sent me there, but my feet are frozen. I can't move. My life is over.

Ryne squeezes me a little tighter. "But it wouldn't be a Wolf Moon Festival without a few surprises, right?"

The crowd howls again, and my brain races to comprehend what he's saying. He spins me around so I'm facing him and brings both hands to my cheeks. There is something in his eyes that I can't place. Something that looks like fear and longing.

He inches his face closer, and my eyelids flutter shut. Then he presses soft lips against mine, and everything inside me snaps.

Chapter Thirty

It's him and me and nobody else. The rest of the world fades away as his lips caress mine. He presses closer, fingers clawing into my hair, mouth demanding in the sweetest way possible, and I lose myself. This is so much more than simply lips against lips. It's his soul exploring mine. It's each of us having a missing piece that we didn't even realize was lost until this very moment––the moment that we find that piece in each other.

I find myself in him.

How can that be? He's the alpha of the Carolina Pack. He's powerful and tortured and sinful and everything wrong for me. I'm just a simple farm girl who wasn't even supposed to come here. But I am here, and I can't deny this feeling.

It's not attraction or lust. I don't know if it's love, but it feels like it could be.

It's fate. Of that, I am absolutely certain.

Too soon, Ryne releases me and stares deep into my eyes. His are like a terrible storm finally parting to reveal the clear blue sky. He has no more questions about us either. He feels it too––knows it too.

We're fated mates.

My heart leaps for joy, and I can't help but smile. "It's you," I whisper softly.

He frowns, breaks our gaze, and turns back to the crowd. There are no cheers. It's dead quiet. Everyone is staring, suspicion and confusion evident on their faces. I lick my bottom lip, just to taste him one last time, and realize everyone is watching me too. I'm sure they saw everything and are judging me. My feelings are laid out as if my chest has been ripped open, and my wild heart is on display for everyone to sneer at. Who am I to be fated to Ryne? I'm nobody to them. But maybe they don't matter. Maybe all that matters is what Ryne thinks. My cheeks burn, and I sink behind his broad shoulders, trying to hide myself.

"That was fun." He laughs the kiss off. "You all know the only way a claimed can be saved from the mating house on a festival night is a kiss from the alpha. I don't think the girls knew that though."

A gasp goes out among the girls, and the crowd chuckles knowingly. We definitely did *not* know this rule. And I don't understand. I thought Ryne kissed me because he wanted me. I thought we were going to be together now. Didn't he feel what I did? Aren't we fated? Maybe it's both––maybe he saved me because we're fated.

The betas don't say a word, so Ryne continues. "I've never used it before, even though my father loved using that particular loophole to get the ladies all worked up on festival nights." He smiles ruefully, and the crowd chuckles again. Many of them must have known the previous alpha before he became king. "That said, I think you might want to understand why I saved Poppy." There's a low murmuring of interest among the crowd. "She'd make an excellent beta wife, but there is one beta in particular who practically begged me to save her. Anders, you owe me."

Ryne laughs. The men cheer. The women glare. And Anders grins wickedly.

Wait––Ryne only kissed me to save me for Anders? If I'm fated to Ryne, then surely I'm to be *his* wife. But maybe we're not actually fated. Maybe I made the whole thing up like pathetic, wishful thinking. But no. That can't be. I know what I felt. So why didn't Ryne feel it too? I thought for sure that he had when he looked at me, but he did frown . . .

My eyes burn. I can't help it. He rejected me and is pawning me off on Anders. The man who killed Willow. The man he *knows* I want nothing to do with. This is nearly as painful as watching my sister die all over again because I know that every time I have to look at Anders is another time I have to be reminded of her death. I can't stand it. I need to get out of here. My hands start to shake, and my vision blurs with tears.

"But I didn't just do this because Anders asked." Ryne goes on. "I did it because Poppy deserves it. She's the best fighter of the bunch and the most physically fit. She's innocent, pure, and obviously beautiful." That one gets a few whoops. "Yes, she needs to work on some of her other skills, but she's also humble. There are several instances where she should have earned more points but never demanded them, not as some of her fellow claimed have done."

His gaze lands on Faye for a long moment, and she squares her shoulders. Did Faye demand more points? I wouldn't put it past her.

"For example," he continues, "what many of you don't know is that one of her classmates turned into a lycan during a full moon a few months ago." The crowd grows uneasy at this news. "When the other girls tried to protect themselves, she did the opposite. She tried to save the other claimed and put herself in mortal danger. That proves that she has the kind of bravery my men need in a wife."

The crowd shifts gears, and they cheer again. It shakes me from my heartbreak, and I give them a little smile. Their applause is for *me*. I can hardly believe it.

"Now I know many of you men have been waiting patiently for new recruits, so our third-place woman will be joining the Broad Street Mating House. Poppy will continue on at Drayton House with the others. Anders, I expect you to make sure my kiss was not given in vain. You treat this girl right, do you hear me?" Anders gives me a smile, and I want to gag. Does this mean I have to be his wife at the end of all of this? It's pretty clear Anders has made his intentions known. At least I'm not going to the mating house today, but the thought of Anders has me in knots.

"Ivy," Ryne continues, "please come forward."

Madame Delphine appears at my side and ushers me off the stage without a word. Reality sinks in as the crowd parts to let us through. Ivy is standing with her friends, her mouth open and her head shaking. She sends a pleading look at Faye, but Faye shrugs and steps back.

"I tried to help you," Faye hisses. "You should be grateful I sacrificed points for you."

Leave it to Faye to make this about her.

"That isn't fair," Ivy gasps. Someone pushes her out into the center of the floor. She stumbles over her silver gown before righting herself. She's all alone, but not for long. Two men come for her. "No! I'm third! Poppy can't do that."

"Poppy didn't," one of the men snaps. "Our alpha did."

"Then your alpha is wrong!"

"Don't you dare question our alpha," he growls. Brown fur flashes over his arm, ripping open his suit jacket. He's about to shift, to attack, but he gathers himself together and stays in his human form.

She shakes her head until her hair pops free of one of the clips. It falls in a long dark curl down her back, and the other man snatches it between his fingers, lifting it to his nose. These are betas I don't know, betas who might even be married already, but there's a cruelty inside of them that is unmistakable.

"Get off me!" Ivy screams. It's the first time I've seen any real fire from the girl, but it's too late. She fights with her nails and teeth when the men grab her and haul her from the ballroom. I don't blame her for defending herself, but she shouldn't fight them. Fighting will attract violent men to her bed. She'll live to regret showing this side of herself to all these betas. That's if she lives through the Broad Street house at all. I suddenly wish I'd have sat the girls down and explained what I knew about the mating houses––competition be damned. Hopefully, Ivy and Callista will be pregnant with a stranger's baby by the next full moon. What an awful thing to hope for.

Guilt rakes through me. Ivy is right. This isn't fair. But I'm also so relieved that it's her and not me, and that alone makes the guilt even worse. I can't allow myself to hold on to it. It's misplaced guilt. It should be anger, and it should be directed right back at the men who created the mating houses in the first place.

Madame Delphine keeps a tight arm around my shoulders. "Come, ladies, it's time to get out of here. The real festivities begin at midnight, and it's no place for a lady."

I don't know what's about to happen, but we've left Callista and Ivy in the men's clutches. They will not be the same after tonight.

We are led outside, Madame Delphine staying at my side. There are guards everywhere, most in their wolf forms and way more than when we first arrived. I gaze up at the full moon and shiver. It feels like we're risking so much being outside right now. I feel exposed and vulnerable, and I just want to be safe. I don't know if that will ever be possible again. The wolves walk with us on all sides, but it doesn't help. Somewhere in the distance, one of them howls at the moon. For a second, I imagine it's a lycan's screech and not a wolf's call.

Joanna keeps pace with me. "Are you okay?"

I shake my head.

"At least you're not in a mating house."

"Is that any better than being promised to Anders?"

"It's not promised, exactly. There's no guarantee."

"Um, I'm pretty sure he called dibs tonight, and Ryne helped him do it."

"Be grateful, child," Madame Delphine says emphatically. "This is infinitely better than where you were headed. I know you don't like Anders, and I know he killed your sister, but one cruel man is better than hundreds. Trust me."

I don't say anything because she would know. She was the wife of likely the cruelest one of them all. But the thought of sharing kisses or a bed with Anders fills me with dread.

The thought of sharing kisses with anyone but Ryne feels wrong at this point. I shake my head. I must've imagined that connection. He was just a good kisser. I'll move past that kiss. And hopefully I'll be able to find a way out of the marriage with Anders. Just because Ryne wants me to marry him doesn't mean another beta can't claim me. I'll just have to work extra hard to make that happen.

Nova will help me get Justin. I wish she'd have stayed instead of going home early tonight, but I don't blame her. The festival probably brought up a lot of bad memories. And if her disappearing tonight means she's not ready to accept Nico as her husband, then he needs to respect that. But I know she loves him. She'll be his wife by the end of the year. And in the meantime, she can be my friend and ally at the house. The others may want to push me off on Anders, but I'm certain Nova will be on my side.

Once we reach the path back to the boat, Madame Delphine lets go of me, and Joanna takes my hand. Grady jogs up next to us. "Look at that, you girls get to stay together after all. You'll both be beta wives."

Joanna scowls at him but doesn't say anything. We reach the river, but the boat isn't there yet. The girls all mingle among themselves, but I wander down to stare out over the water. It's dark, and lights from the surrounding buildings cast an eerie wash of color over the whole thing. There are two moons now, the one in the sky and the one reflecting in the water.

I have no idea what the future looks like. Does this mean I'll no longer have to worry about points if Ryne can kiss me at festivals to keep me reserved for Anders? Is the threat of the mating house a thing of the past?

Something floats out in the river just below me, and I creep closer to get a better look. A log. My voice catches in my throat. That's not a log. It's a body.

"Help," I finally scream and scramble down the embankment. "Help!"

Footsteps pound behind me, but I splash into the water. It's a woman wearing a pretty pink gown. No. No. This can't be happening.

I flip the body over and let out a whimper. Nova is staring up at me with very bloodshot, very dead eyes.

I hear splashes behind me, but I don't move. I just cling to the dead body of a woman I've come to love. She cared for me in a way that the other house mothers did not.

Grady reaches past me and takes Madame Nova into his arms. "Come on, Poppy," he whispers. Nico stands on the shore, his face a mask of horror. Grady reaches him before I do and hands him the body. Nico lets out a gut-wrenching cry. It transforms into a heartbroken howl, and the other men join in. We girls just stand there, staring, broken, disbelieving.

How did she die? She wouldn't have killed herself. She truly cared for Nico. It could've been an accident, but I doubt it. Someone killed her. But why? I trudge back up the embankment. All the girls stand there, clutching at each other.

Joanna throws her arms around me and hugs tightly. It's a hug that reminds me of Willow, and my tears break free for the third time tonight. But I'm not weak for crying. I'm strong for facing the truth of our situation. I whisper quietly into her ear. "If you and Nova"—my voice breaks a little at her name—"are part of some kind of resistance group, then I need to be a part of it too."

She steps back, nodding once, her eyes shining with pride and grief and a million things unsaid. She takes my hands in hers. I'm not sure how I'm going to make a difference. Who am I? I'm only one girl. One *human* girl.

But I'll find a way.

To Be Continued in Lies of the Blood Moon...

LIES OF THE BLOOD MOON

NEW WORLD SHIFTERS
BOOK TWO

NINA WALKER

KIMBERLY LOTH

Prologue

JOANNA

I've always been a risk-taker. As a kid, I swam where I shouldn't swim, climbed where I shouldn't climb, and asked too many questions––until the day my parents sat me down and explained the importance of weighing my risks before taking them. They said I was old enough to understand that I needed to stop being reckless. I didn't like the lecture, but when my mother left the room to get supper started, my father said something that I've never forgotten. He kneeled down, looked me square in the eye, and said that one day risks would outweigh staying safe, and when that happened, I needed to be brave.

Today is that day.

And so was yesterday, and the day before, and every day since I was claimed by the Carolina Pack. I will *not* go down without a fight.

"There is no way in hell that Nova's death was an accident. None," I whisper angrily, my voice carrying over the water more than I'd like.

"But it's not possible they found out," Lexi whispers back as she scrambles into the boat behind me.

We go quiet as we untie it from the dock and let it drift out into the black water for a few minutes. Once I'm sure it's safe, I start the engine. I keep thinking about her response but don't bother to answer because it's totally possible the wolves found out about Nova. Not only possible, it's *probable*. Nova fell in love with one of them––not that I can really talk. I fell in love with Grady, but he has no idea the danger I put myself in every day. And I'll never tell him.

Maybe Nova told Nico.

Then again, maybe it really was an accident, or she killed herself like they want everyone to believe. I shake my head at the thought, and the night breeze bites at my cheeks.

The boat hums along softly as we head into town. I always worry about getting caught, but since we're going toward the city and not away from it, we're less likely to look suspicious. Lexi and I can both say we are sneaking out to visit the betas, but then we'll have to explain how we know how to operate a boat. We could say we learned it in our villages, but that argument is flimsy considering I'm from the textile village, and she was a farmer. And of course Madame Delphine would have to punish us, but we wouldn't be killed. That's the main thing.

And anyway, her punishment would only be for show since she's one of us.

I guide the boat to a dock near a nice house on the outskirts of town. We tug our hoods up and hurry for the house. We usually do this close to the new moon, when there's hardly any light, and it's unlikely we'll be seen. Tonight, however, the moon is a few days from when it was full. I resent that it lights up the landscape. Maybe it doesn't matter either way. Light or no light, it won't help us if one of the wolves roaming the outskirts sees us. Monsters can see in the dark.

The floral scent hits me as we approach the house. Shauna loves her flowers. My mother would be so jealous of her long-lost sister. Mom never could get anything to bloom so early in the season.

We skirt around the house and head for the greenhouse in the back. Each member's arrival time is staggered so no one will become suspicious. We don't want any neighbors to take notice. Lexi and I are always the last to arrive, which is nice because that means we don't have to wait for the meetings to start, but I wish I had more time to spend with Shauna. She reminds me of home.

A large man looms next to the greenhouse. He's so still that he could almost be mistaken for a tree in the darkness. He's a wolf. And he's the only one who knows about us. At least, I think he's the only one who knows. Sure, plenty of wolves know *of* us, and many are trying to hunt us down, but Shauna's husband is the only one we can trust. I'm still pretty low in the ranks of the Resistance, but I've been assured there aren't other wolves involved. That's good, because how can we really trust them?

I even wonder about Grady sometimes...

And then I feel guilty because he's proven himself more devoted to me than I ever thought possible. I have no doubt that he's madly in love with me. But what would he do if he knew the truth? Would he still feel the same? Still protect me? Or would his loyalties lie with the pack?

Our resistance group has about twenty women, and there are other groups that meet all over the city, in other wolf cities, and even out in the wilds. That's all I know about our numbers——we have to be careful. It wouldn't be safe for the other groups to know too much about us or vice versa. All it takes is one weak link, and the whole chain breaks to pieces.

But Nova was one of us, so we can't delay this. We need to come up with a plan.

"Hey, kids," Amos whispers as we approach. He ruffles Lexi's hair but knows better than to do that to me, even though I'm his niece. We shake hands. "You doing okay?"

Lexi and I nod.

And all things considered, we are. I've got Grady, and Lexi is consistently on top of the scoreboard. She's the smartest of the claimed girls, so she aces every class.

"Any word from the other cities?" I ask. I always ask even though the answer stays the same. I think we should band together and revolt.

"Go on inside and find out for yourself." He chuckles, avoiding my question yet again. "You know how she is about things. I keep my mouth shut and stand guard, and that's it."

I roll my eyes. He's talking about Shauna. Apparently there's some secret way she communicates with the other leaders so that we all have the same information, but she doesn't share how many women are involved or all the little details. My parents are a part of the Resistance. When I was claimed, they wanted me to go willingly and stay safe until they could think of something. Yeah, right. I'd fought those bastards on day one, but I ended up with Grady, so I guess Mom and Dad got their wish.

Or not... because I found the Resistance as soon as I got here.

We enter the greenhouse and find the trapdoor in the back. It's been propped open, and a ladder sticks out the top. I eye it wearily. It's not far down, but I still get a little claustrophobic descending the rungs. I sigh and climb down quickly, and my feet hit hard earth.

I duck into the cramped stone tunnel and then out into a large room lit with lanterns. This hiding place is quite brilliant, but Amos and Shauna can't claim it as their idea. It belongs to the brave humans from hundreds of years ago, those good people who smuggled slaves to safety.

The room is nearly full. Several women are crying while others are consoling them. I should be among the women crying--Nova was my friend--but anger forced the tears away.

Someone murdered her. I know it.

Shauna's head snaps up when she hears us. "Oh good, you're here." She hurries over and hugs me, kissing me once on the cheek. It's weird having her in my life suddenly, but also comforting. She was taken by the claiming before I was born, so to find her here was a small miracle in all of this. She steps away and gives me one of her winning smiles. She's a pretty middle-aged woman and looks so much like my mom sometimes it hurts.

"Ladies, we need to get started." She walks to the head of the crowd, her head low for a moment, but then raises it. A few tears glisten on her cheeks. "Two nights ago, we lost one of our own. It's not the first time a woman in the Resistance has been murdered, and it will likely not be the last."

"We should find and kill the bastard who did this to her," I call out.

Shauna glowers at me. "That's not our way, and you know it."

I cross my arms and frown. The Resistance has always moved slower than I would like. They focus on rescuing women and getting them away from the wolves, but it's not like they can do very much of that. I think we should be attacking. In fact, we should burn the whole city to the ground.

But no one listens to me.

I keep my mouth shut as Shauna continues. "Delphine, you knew her best. Do you think we've been compromised?"

Madame Delphine steps from the shadows. She knows Lexi and I come here, but she always travels on her own by town car. I wish she wouldn't. I'd feel safer if we all came together, but she says this is better. And she'll *never* talk about anything back at the manor, so it's not like I have much time to convince her otherwise. "No. I knew Nova, and there is no way she told anyone, including Nico."

And I would agree if it weren't for all the times I've wanted to tell Grady. I understand how hard it is to keep something like this from a fated mate. But then again, I saw Nico's reaction when Nova's body was pulled from the river. He was completely shocked.

And he was heartbroken. Can't fake that.

Shauna purses her lips and nods. "Okay, then onto business. Who needs rescuing this week?"

"Everyone," I snort quietly to myself. Then I tune out as they talk. They never let Lexi or me assist with any of the rescue missions. Madame

Delphine always puts a stop to it when I volunteer. I'm so sick of doing nothing. Even back in the textile village, I had more of a role than this nonsense.

After a while, the conversation dies, and I see my opening.

"I have a new recruit."

Madame Delphine raises her eyebrows but doesn't say anything.

"Who?" Shauna asks.

"My friend Poppy."

A few of the women look at me from the sides of their eyes. Everyone knows who Poppy is because of the stunt Ryne pulled on the Wolf Moon. Gossip travels fast even in the mating houses.

"Haven't you tried to get her out of the city a couple of times?"

I clench my fists. Those failures were not my fault. "Yes. She's decided she wants to join us instead."

"Absolutely not," Madame Delphine cuts in.

"Why not?" I protest. Poppy is ready for this. She has motive and is an incredible fighter. If you ask me, we should be recruiting more heavily than we are. The more we have, the better chance we'll have to fight them.

"Because she's too young. You and Lexi shouldn't be a part of this either. I will not allow another one of my girls to join. If, after the Harvest Moon Festival, she still feels the same way, then she can join."

"After the harvest, she might be in the mating house, if not earlier. If she's part of the Resistance, then she'll have an easier time escaping if she needs to--before she's been raped by a hundred wolves."

A few women flinch, but no one says anything. We should use that word more freely, if you ask me. Why not call it what it is?

"I will see to it that she doesn't end up in a mating house, but she cannot join us." Madame Delphine presses her lips tight.

"She's ready. We need—"

"Joanna," Shauna snaps. "We saw what happened at the wolf moon. The alpha either has a special interest in her, or he's saving her for his number two, but either way, Poppy isn't someone we can bring into our fold. What would happen if she were caught by one of them? She could lead them right to us, even unwittingly."

"But--"

"That's enough." Her voice is understanding but stern.

I don't argue because it's pointless, but this isn't over.

Poppy will become one of us.

Chapter One

POPPY

Unlike so many other humans who've been lost to this bleak city, Nova actually gets a funeral. I stand along with the other girls, bracing against the cold, on the edge of Nico's family plot. We're a line of modest black, our heads down, as Nico drops a handful of clumpy dirt into Nova's grave. The late January sky is a blanket of white, and the air smells of ice and salt. The wind bites through our wool coats, and it seems unfair that the cold would come out and be so distracting on Nova's day. Most of the girls are crying, but my tears seemed to have frozen with the winter. A few words are said. A prayer is offered. And then it's time to go.

We're ushered to Anders's home for refreshments. His estate is at the edge of town, and it's especially grand, almost as grand as Ryne's, but I don't care. This last week following Madame Nova's death has been the most somber of them all. That is two house mothers who have died since coming here, not to mention the girls we've lost. It's such a tragic accident, though whispers suggest it could've been something more. Classes were canceled all week, and we barely saw Madame Delphine until today.

The betas—and Ryne—never came to see us. Joanna hasn't said anything more to me about the resistance movement, and I haven't asked. Grief has overtaken us all. I stand in the corner of Anders's living room, hoping to be invisible while peering through the window out toward the horizon. Nova shouldn't have died. What possessed her to go out to the river, anyway? Maybe she just needed time to think. Or maybe she was meeting with a member of the Resistance. Some say she killed herself, but I don't think so. And others say she was murdered.

Whatever happened, Nico deserved better, and so did she.

People mingle in small circles, whispering in hushed voices. Wolves come and go, offering Nico their condolences. Some of the wolves flirt with the girls, but I stay back. I won't be caught flirting at a funeral. And I can't help but wonder if anyone will notify Nova's family back in her village.

Probably not.

She's been gone from them for so long anyway; they've likely mourned her already. I wonder if my family has mourned me.

Ryne is there, but he doesn't look at me. I avoid him anyway. Everytime I think of him, I think of that kiss and how desperately I want another one. And then I feel guilty because I should be thinking of Nova, not him.

Sometime later, we're loaded up and brought back to Drayton Hall. It may be the first time I'm grateful to be taken here. All I want to do is crawl into bed and go back to sleep. Nova's death has reignited the feelings of loss and guilt I have about Willow. I don't think I've uttered a single word all day, and I don't want to. What is there to say? It's a tragedy. I'm going to miss my friend, I desperately miss my sister, and everything is unfair. We eat dinner, and they send us to the sitting room to keep each other company. I just want to be alone.

It's late Sunday evening, and tomorrow we start classes again. As much as I hate what's happened, I'm relieved to get back to some semblance of normalcy. Joanna and I sit in the corner and read. This time, I'm able to get most of the words. Even though I'm slow, reading is a nice distraction from the pain and thoughts of Ryne. The other girls spend their time gossiping. Joy, one of the distillery girls, mutters something about Nova that catches my ear, especially when everyone else in the room goes quiet and stares at her. No one had uttered Nova's name in here since she died.

"What?" Joy furrows her dark eyebrows and glances around at all the stares.

"What did you say about Nova?" Joanna asks since no one else does. She's not being accusatory, just curious.

"What no one else will. Now that she's gone, Nico will choose one of us. It's a blessing really."

I jump up, but Joanna jerks me back down. She has no right to think those things right now. Nova's barely in the ground.

Joy sniffs. "What? Not all of us have bewitched the alpha's best friend and can count on a kiss to save us from the mating house. We need all the chances we can get."

A few of the other girls nod in agreement.

Katelyn clears her throat, and everyone looks at her. I don't think I've ever heard her say a word. She's now at the bottom of the board. Well, just above me. "But if Nico was so bad that Nova had to kill herself to get away from him, do we really want him?"

"Nova didn't kill herself. She loved Nico," I snap.

"How do you know?" Faye asks, with her arms crossed.

"Because she told me."

"If she didn't kill herself, you know what that means, right?"

"What?"

"She was murdered." Faye smirks like it's obvious. "Nova accidentally falling into the river makes no sense."

"Who would murder her?" I ask, but I'm not sure I want the answer.

Faye scoffs. "Duh. Who had the most motive? It had to be one of us."

Every single one of us had a motive to kill Nova, but are any of the girls that ruthless? Maybe, if they know what is coming. I shiver at the thought of what Ivy and Callista must be going through right now in the mating house. That should've been me. But I would never kill someone.

We all look at each other, uncomfortable and suspicious. I take a deep breath, the scent of polish and perfume and fear filling me up. This is bad. Really bad. If some of these girls start thinking their best way to get a beta is to kill someone, then it'll turn into a bloodbath. I squeeze Joanna's hand, and she squeezes right back. Footsteps pound up the stairs, and Madame Delphine enters the room in a flourish. We all stare at her, and none of us says a word about murder, though I'm sure we're all thinking it. Joanna is the only one in the room who had no motive to kill Nova.

"Ladies, classes resume tomorrow. Your new instructor will arrive late this evening, and I hope you will show her the same courtesy you showed Madame Nova. She's the daughter of an old friend of mine from the Chicago Pack. Also, the betas will be by in the morning as well. They'll be spending more time here. Now that the first cut has happened, and you've all had some training, they want the opportunity to get to know you individually, not just on group dates. I will be creating a schedule so you all get time with each beta."

I don't want to spend any time alone with Anders. Truthfully, Ryne is the only one I want to be around. And I know how wrong that is--he's the Alpha. He's forcing us to be baby-makers against our will. It's all evil, and he should've stopped it a long time ago. And I should hate him, but try telling that to my heart. That kiss was everything.

"What about Grady?" Faye asks, and Joanna stiffens next to me. I know she's in love with him, even if she pretends she's not.

"Well, as we saw with Madame Nova, nothing is guaranteed, so he will be on the rotation." She waves her hand in a circle.

My stomach sinks. I didn't think about what Nova's murder would mean for Joanna. If one of the girls did kill her, then Joanna could be next. I squeeze her hand again, but this time she doesn't squeeze back. Her lips are set in a thin line, and her eyes narrow on Faye. My best friend is mad as hell.

"It's time for bed. You've had far too long of a break, so be ready to run at six tomorrow."

A collective groan goes out among the girls, but I like to run.

Joanna and I escape to our room, and as soon as the door clicks shut, I pounce on her. "You have to be careful."

She strips off her shirt and digs in a drawer for pajamas. "Why? If you ask me, Faye is the one who should be careful. I seriously hate that girl."

"I mean it, Joanna. Whoever killed Nova might come after you next. It's got to be a girl who understands what happens in the mating houses and wants to make sure she doesn't go. And for all we know, that could be Faye."

Joanna slips a nightgown over her head. "That's ridiculous. These girls don't have the nerve."

"You're telling me that you think Madame Nova killed herself?"

"No way. But none of the girls here killed her. It was one of the wolves." My heart stills. I suppose it's possible, but I think Faye had a better idea. Not that I'd ever tell her that.

"Why would they kill her?"

"Because they are all assholes."

"I don't think so. They had no reason to. But the girls here all did. If she was killed because she took one of our betas, then that girl will have reason to kill you as well. And if she managed to kill Nova, then she's got skill."

Joanna sits on her bed and leans forward. "Listen, I know you're worried about me, but you shouldn't be. You should be worried about the girls who are going to spend one-on-one time with Grady."

"Why?"

"Because if one so much as bats an eyelash at him, I'm going to kick her ass. I don't need points, so I don't care if I end up at the bottom."

I want to laugh at her snarkiness, but I can't. She's not seeing the real danger here. But Grady will. I have to tell him.

I really hope that Joanna won't hate me for doing so.

"I'm serious, Joanna. I think one of the girls did it." And we need to figure out who before she kills someone else. Like Joanna.

She snorts. "Think about it. Nova went outside alone on a night when all the wolves were out. One of them probably killed her simply because they saw the opportunity and took it."

I look down at my hands. I'm not sure the pack's telepathic link works like that. If a wolf killed her, he'd have to be really good at keeping his secrets. Maybe I should ask Ryne about all this. I sit down on my bed. "Either way, don't you think she deserves to have her murderer outed?"

Joanna stills. "What are you saying?"

"We should investigate."

She folds a shirt, avoiding my eyes for a moment. "Okay. But we have differing opinions on who did it, so why don't you take the girls, and I'll see if I can find out any information on the wolves."

I think she's wrong, but at least she's on board. Even if she won't investigate the girls with me, I'll be able to talk things through with her at night.

I let out a breath.

Never in a million imaginations did I ever think I'd be hunting a killer.

* * *

My shoes pound the dirt running path as I push my body to move faster. My muscles scream from the exertion, and my face burns from the cold. It's bitter out and early enough that the sun hasn't fully risen. The black sky lifts away with each step I take, the horizon slowly transforming to pink. I know the running path well enough that I don't worry about tripping, so I forge ahead until I've left all the other girls in my wake. I don't mind being alone. I don't want to talk to any of them, and Joanna refused to get out of bed this morning.

She insisted she started her period and is having terrible cramps, but I wonder if that's true. Every time Joanna strays from the group, I'm going

to assume it's got something to do with the Resistance. I'm a little hurt
that she hasn't talked to me about the organization more, but I trust that
she will when the time is right. She knows I want in. That hasn't changed
in spite of my feelings for Ryne.

How large is the Resistance movement? Do they have any chance
against the wolves? It might be so small that nothing will happen for a
very long time, but I don't care. I want to take down the wolves. They've
ruined my life and countless others. And I don't care if I die in the
process.

Maybe it's because of Nova's death, but Madame Delphine didn't
make Joanna get out of bed. I worried a little bit about leaving her alone
because it would be the perfect opportunity for whoever killed Nova to
attack her, but she insisted I leave. I have to talk to Grady before it's too
late. He'll be better at protecting her than I am.

Not that he should have to. This whole pack dynamic is wrong, and
nobody should be forced to fight for a beta or spend their days in a
mating house. This has to change. *It has to.*

All I can hope is that in the process of revolution, Ryne makes it out
alive. I can't undo my feelings for him, as much as my mind knows he's
hurt me and others. I still think––still know––that there's a part of him
that wants things to change as much as I do. Is he a bad guy? Or is he
forced to be bad, but he wants to be good?

It's all so confusing.

I push myself to go even faster, because it forces the thoughts away.
It's hard, but I love it. I love the cold air, the rushing blood, and the
pumping muscles. And I even love running alone, but that quickly
changes when a streak of silver darts right in front of me and out across
the grass. I stop abruptly, my heartbeat pounding against my eardrums.
What was that? I peer into the field, but there's nothing there.

Did I imagine it?

I shake my head and begin running again, this time even faster. I feel
like something is chasing me. That's silly though. There's nothing there.

But what if there is?

My mind races, thinking about the lycans, but it's not the full moon.
A wolf then? Are wolves silver? I've seen quite a few over the last three
months, and they're always black or brown or sometimes dark gray. This
was definitely silver, as bright as the moon. I shiver at Joanna's word that
it was a wolf that killed Nova, not another girl. What if that wolf is
after me?

But that's silly because I have about as much chance at scoring a Beta as Madame Vivien does. And she's probably sixty already.

Another flash passes through the field, this time black. I don't think it sees me, but I definitely see it well enough to know it's a wolf. The wolves all look similar to each other, but I swear that's Ryne's wolf. He's heading in the same direction that the silver went, up over a hill and into the forest. I should turn back and find the other girls, but curiosity gets the better of me, and I race after them.

I creep into the trees and listen intently, pushing away feelings of foolishness and worry. I want to see what Ryne's doing here more than I care about any of those feelings. I'm pretty sure that silver flash was a wolf. Are they fighting? Is Ryne in trouble? That thought gives me speed, and I race through the trees. The sound of a wolf excitedly barking stops me. I peer around a tree and find them in a clearing.

Ryne's big black wolf circles a smaller silver one. His blue eyes stare into the other's amber ones. They bark and then pounce. At first I think they're fighting, but then I realize they're playing. The smaller wolf pins Ryne down and howls. It steps off him, and they stand on all fours one second, and then with a flash of light and fur, they're shifting into their human forms--completely naked. I shouldn't look, but I can't stop myself because I'm surprised by what I see.

The wolf is a woman.

Chapter Two

"Elle Montgomery," Ryne laughs. "I knew that was you." He pulls her into a hug, still naked as the day he was born, and the two laugh. His eyes shine with excitement and what I think could be love when he looks at her. And why not? She might be the most beautiful woman I've ever seen. She's petite and curvy all at once. She's got smooth ebony skin that seems to glow gold in the sunrise. Her long black hair is braided down her back, and her sparkling eyes are the exact color of my mama's homemade caramel.

She's a wolf. I can't seem to wrap my head around that. I thought all wolves were men. I can't stop staring at her. Her presence changes everything. If women can be wolves, then what do they need us for?

"It's good to see you too, Ryne. Look at you, all grown up." Even her voice is perfect.

I can't stay here. Jealousy claws at my heart and shreds my stomach. The two start talking animatedly, and I back away slowly until I can safely turn away without getting caught. I meet up with the running path again, and the other girls are just catching up.

Faye rolls her eyes when she sees me. "Did you have to pee?" The others laugh and pass me. Joy blows me a kiss. I guess she's Faye's new sidekick now that Ivy is gone.

I don't try to pass them. I do a slow jog. My mind is a mess of questions, but the biggest is this: What is Elle Montgomery doing here?

The mystery of Elle distracts me from what I really should be thinking about--who killed Nova--but I can't help myself.

Wolves are never female. That's why they have to take the claimed in the first place, to keep their race from dying off. My mind races through the lessons we've had about wolves, and I stumble when the truth hits me. One out of a hundred wolves is born female. We've never met one, but that doesn't mean they're not out there. And this one seems to know Ryne quite well.

I hit the showers and try to think of anything but Ryne and Elle. I'm unsuccessful. The image of the two hugging while naked is burned into my brain. I have no claim on Ryne, but after the kiss we shared, I feel like I do, and I don't want another woman anywhere near him. I walk back into our room wrapped in a towel, and Joanna grins at me. She holds up two dresses. "What do you think, the black or the black?"

They are exactly the same. I force a smile. "The black definitely."

She doesn't seem to notice that I'm not all there. So much for her having cramps and not being able to get out of bed. We dress, and I stick close to Joanna as we head down to breakfast. I haven't forgotten there is possibly a murderer among us, and that Joanna could be the next victim. I have to keep an eye on her until Grady can. He'll protect her. But first, I have to warn him.

If I can pinpoint the murderer, it will be easier to protect Joanna. Katelyn is the most obvious suspect since she is near the bottom of the board, but really it could be anyone, because this isn't about those who get sent to the mating houses at the festivals. This is about who gets a mate come the harvest.

Hopefully we'll have combat again soon, and I can keep an eye on girls who do well. They'd have been more likely to overpower Nova than a girl who can't even punch someone in the gut.

Madame Delphine walks into the room with Elle Montgomery. She's managed to find clothes. Somehow, she even looks good in the black wool dresses we often wear on the days the betas aren't coming around. Has she come to join us in our training? If a female wolf is getting added to our crew, she's bound to get a beta. I grimace, wondering what that means for the rest of us.

"Ladies, I want you to meet Madame Elle. She will be your new house mother." Madame Delphine beams at her.

Elle gives us a wide toothy smile and a small wave. I release a breath, grateful I'm not going to have to compete against this beauty. She looks to be no older than any of us, but her energy is worldly and mature. I find it strange that they would bring in another barren woman after

Nova's death. Is she barren? I have no way to know. I thought all the house mothers were, but there's something different about Elle, that's for sure.

Aside from the obvious wolf thing.

"Like I said last night, she's the daughter of a dear friend of mine, and I want you all to welcome her to our little family."

I snort. Some family. We keep getting killed.

"What you don't know about Elle is that she's a luna. That means she's one of the rare female wolves. She's here to offer extra protection and will be living among us."

The girls are especially excited by that and start to applaud Elle, who responds with a little curtsy. I can't help but roll my eyes at the way the others suck up to her. Joanna and I sit down at breakfast in our usual spots, and Elle finds a place right across from us, where Nova used to sit. I want to tell her to go away, that that seat should always remain empty in honor of Nova, but she's our fancy new house mother, so I don't.

"Did you come from a mating house or what?" Joanna shovels a big bite of biscuits and gravy into her mouth. I want to say something about Elle being a wolf, which means she's probably treated like a princess. All I can think of is what I saw between her and Ryne this morning. It replays in my mind in a loop. I fork my meal with a little too much ferocity.

Elle's ever-present smile falters. "I've never stepped foot in a mating house. Why would you think that?"

Joanna chews and swallows. "Because I thought the house mothers were either barren or done having children. You're young, and I don't see a ring on your finger. I assumed you were like our old house mother, Nova. She came from the mating houses. Right, Poppy?" Joanna nudges me.

"Right."

Elle drops her eyes and swallows. "Oh, no, I hope I'm not barren. I've never been to a mating house or with a man for that matter, so I wouldn't know."

Joanna nods. "Yeah, I thought all fertile women were to be out there making babies for whoever wants them. No offense, but you've got to be prime real estate to these men."

She sits up tall. "I'm a luna, and I make my own choices."

"Lunas can make their own choices?" Joanna asks, disbelief lacing her tone. Not for the first time am I grateful that Joanna is my friend. She asks all the questions that I wish I could. That girl is fearless.

"Uh, duh. She's a female wolf," Katelyn says from the other side of Elle. "She's special enough to get to do whatever she wants."

Elle looks away at that, and I wonder how much Katelyn's statement is actually true. Either way, I'd argue we're all special and should be able to make our own choices. I keep the thought to myself.

Joanna's lips curl into a wicked grin. "That's pretty amazing. Welcome to our dysfunctional family where you and the other house mothers prepare us for a life of whoring."

Half of us laugh, and half of us stare at Joanna like she's lost her mind. Elle frowns.

"My mother and father thought it would be good for me to get out of the city for a little bit," she confesses with a sigh. "I think they were tired of the parade of men who came to our door every day. Quite frankly, I was a little tired of it as well." She plays with her food before meeting Joanna's eye. "Tell me about the girls. You seem to be very knowledgeable about the goings-on in this house."

I nearly roll my eyes——again. Joanna will love this woman. Being a know-it-all and being recognized for it? It's her only flaw.

Elle seems very nice, and I want to like her, but my stomach burns every time I look at her. I saw the way Ryne looked at her, like her arrival was the best thing to happen to him in ages. And they were naked!

My jealous musings are interrupted by Joanna. She's good for that.

"Well, let's recount, shall we? There were twenty-two of us to start, but two got kidnapped by lycans on our very first day. A month later, one of our girls turned into a lycan herself, killing two more girls, one of our house mothers, and biting a third girl who had to be put down." She uses air quotes for that last part, giving a little scowl. "She got away in the end. Then we lost two more girls to the mating houses at the last festival, not to mention that our beloved new house mother, Nova, turned up dead in the river." Joanna bats her eyelashes. "So, Elle, are you sure you want to be here?"

Elle gapes at Joanna and motions to all of us sitting at the tables. "I'm already aware of the deaths. I meant the girls who are still here. I'm supposed to help protect you guys."

Joanna winks. "Oh, I know. I just thought you should be aware of what you're getting yourself into." She takes a deep breath. "Okay, so at the end of the table, closest to the door, you have Faye, Joy, Blair, and Emma. They are the distillery girls, meaning they came from that village and think they're better than all of us. They sit over there because they want to be able to spring on the betas when they arrive. Next to them are the wannabe distillery girls, Raven, Alyssa, and Abi. Then there's Lexi and Samantha. Those two are the teachers' pet types. They couldn't care less about the actual betas. They only want to be top of the leaderboards to prove they're the smartest. My bet is they end up taking each other down before this is all over."

Joanna pauses for a moment to scan for any girls she missed. "Oh,"— she points to a back corner of the room—"and that one with her nose stuck in a book is Bailey. She's really nice, but she's super shy with the guys and really good at tuning the rest of us out with all that reading." And she's right. Bailey leans over a novel as she eats her breakfast, her eyes glued to the book. The girl is completely unaware that we're even talking about her.

"Then you'll notice several empty seats in the middle of the room. No one sits there because we don't want to be near each other. Down here, you have me and Poppy. I'm Grady's fated mate or whatever, so I can do whatever I want. Poppy is my best friend and at the bottom of that disgusting board, so if you wanna hang with us, you have to promise to help her."

Elle's smile grows even wider. "I'll remember that. I like you, Joanna, so I will do what I can to help Poppy. But you missed these two lovely ladies." She points to the other side of her to the two girls who always sit on this side of the room near us, as well.

"Oh, that's Katelyn and Harlow. They're wannabe rebels like me and Poppy."

"Hey, that's not true," Katelyn says. "We just don't want to be like them." She nods to all the girls sitting by the door and gossiping among themselves.

Elle nods. "Fair enough. So we have the distillery girls, the wannabes, the teachers' pets, the book girl, and of course, the rebels." She tilts her head at me and smiles brightly. "Tell me, Poppy, what are your best subjects?"

I'm having a hard time warming up to this woman because of Ryne, but she *is* trying. "Anything physical besides yoga. Combat is my favorite."

"Yeah," Joanna adds, "Poppy is our resident athlete. She keeps us all on our toes."

"Well then, I will mention to Ryne that you girls need some more serious combat training. That should help you move up the board."

Katelyn groans because she stinks at combat, but we ignore her. I don't know how I feel about Elle talking to Ryne about anything, least of all about me.

"How do you know Ryne?" Joanna asks. I'm grateful to her once again for peppering Elle with the questions I can't bring myself to ask.

She giggles, and her eyes sparkle with memories. "He used to visit my family when we were kids. He teased me horribly. I see him every time he visits Chicago, though he hasn't been there in years. But we talk on the phone all the time. He's probably the closest thing I have to a best friend. There aren't many girls my age, and all the men I know want to marry me." If she had mentioned a phone to me a few months ago, I wouldn't have the foggiest what she meant. But Madame Delphine has a phone she uses all the time, so I've since been schooled on the technology.

"Does Ryne want to marry you?" Joanna asks. She plays it off nonchalantly, but Katelyn, Harlow, and I wait for her answer.

Elle scowls. "I don't know how Ryne feels, but our fathers certainly want us to marry. Mine's been planning on it for years. It might be the one thing I won't get a choice on, and if I didn't like Ryne so much, I'd probably hate him."

Her words tunnel in on me, and I set my fork down, no longer hungry. I don't care how nice Elle is, and I don't care that she's a beautiful luna--*Ryne is mine*. I shake my head, trying to clear the possessive thought away, but it clings to me like static. I'm not sure where it came from, but I still can't shake the feeling that Ryne and I are fated mates. That would explain the insane jealousy I'm feeling. I know I should be thinking about Nova and who killed her, worried about the leaderboard, planning my next step with the betas, but in this moment all I can think of is that kiss and how badly I want to punch Elle in the nose for even entertaining the thought that she could be with Ryne.

And I have to know the truth about Ryne and me.

The need to take action is so strong that I can no longer sit here and listen to another woman speak Ryne's name, especially not one who's known him since childhood, who makes him laugh and smile, who's been *naked* with him, and who will probably marry him. The chair screeches as I get up to take my plate to the kitchen. I'm shocked by my own feelings.

"What's her problem?" Emma questions mockingly as I pass by them.

"She's obviously jealous. Poor girl thought Ryne liked her and I know all about Elle. She's Ryne's fated." Faye's voice follows me as I push my way into the kitchen. I clean my plate and give it to the staff and then head out the back door. There are still a few minutes before we're due to class, and I need to think.

Better yet, I need to find Ryne.

<h1 style="text-align:center">Chapter Three</h1>

It's cold without my coat. The bitter air bites every inch of my exposed skin. I almost turn back, but then I catch some wolves racing through the nearby field, and I run after them.

"Ryne!" I yell at the big black one with the glacial eyes. "I need to talk to you right now!"

A couple of the other wolves bark and grow quiet. It's as if some kind of communication is passing between the alpha and his betas, because they look at him for a long moment and then scamper off all at the same time. Ryne changes into his human form. I should turn away while he grabs some shorts from a nearby pile of clothing. I've always been shy in the past, but this time I don't. He belongs to me, anyway. I know it.

Funny how it took jealousy over Elle to realize it.

He grabs my arm and drags me away from listening ears. "You can't summon me like that. It makes me look weak. Besides, we can't talk about this right now, Poppy."

"You've been avoiding me ever since our kiss."

His expression turns stony. "You're going on a date today with Justin. And then you'll be dating the others."

"But--"

"But nothing," he growls. "I saved you, and you should show an ounce of gratitude for that."

But *he* kissed *me,* and it wasn't for Anders like he told everyone. I've been going over it again and again in my head. I think he used Anders's infatuation with me as an excuse to save me, for his sake, not for Anders.

When we were at his house that night, he caught Joanna and me trying to run away, but he didn't punish us. No, he held me and told me he would be kissing me when the time was right. Saving me from the mating house certainly wasn't because of his betas.

He wants me as much as I want him, so why is he denying us?

"I don't know what to say," my voice cracks.

"Don't make this harder than it has to be."

My heart squeezes, but I'm not the same timid girl I was back in September. Something has changed within me over the last few months, and I'm no longer going to let others stop me from taking what I need. I may not be able to find the right words, but I can use actions to show him how I feel. I step forward, grab his face, and bring his lips to mine.

The weight of him crashes over me in a wave of relief. His lips are quick to move against mine, to claim me as his. He growls and deepens our kiss. See? This is exactly what I've been talking about. I know he feels it too. This feeling isn't normal. It's not just an infatuated kiss. It's fate. But all too quickly, he rips away and takes several steps back.

"When are you going to understand, Poppy? My betas are the best I can offer you." His voice thickens. "I can't keep saving you. You need to step up and do your part to save yourself. Now get inside before you catch your death."

Then he turns away and shifts back into his wolf, his clothes ripping to shreds in the process. I guess he cares more about getting away from me than he does for his belongings.

He runs off after his betas, and I storm back into the house. All the while, I press my fingers to my lips and try to memorize the kiss. If I could tattoo the feel of him to my lips, I would. Ryne says the best he can do is offer me a beta. I know it must have something to do with Elle and his father, with being an alpha, with everything that's expected of him and that he expects for himself. Well, a beta for my husband is not going to be good enough for me. Maybe in the past, but not anymore. Living with anyone other than my mate would be a false life, and I'm not going to settle for less than the real thing.

I don't care what it takes. I'm going to get Ryne to admit the truth, and then I'm going to make him do something about it.

I find Bailey reading in the library. It's as good a time as any to get started on my investigation, even if I am still mad as hell at Ryne. Anyway, I doubt Bailey's the killer, but I'm not ruling anyone out. She's a good person to start with because she won't get upset with me for asking questions. And I need to do something else besides obsess about Ryne right now, or I'll lose my mind.

I go over my plan in my head again. I'm telling the girls that I'm collecting stories about Nova to share with Nico. This would be more believable if I could write, but the villagers have been telling stories for years orally, so it's not that far-fetched. Last night I asked Joanna for help interviewing the girls, but she flat out refused and reminded me that our plan was for me to talk to the girls and that she was handling the wolves.

I squeeze my hands into fists and then stretch my fingers out. I don't know why I'm so nervous. Maybe it's because a part of me is afraid I'm going to find the killer and that she'll know that I know. And then what? Will she come after me?

I sit in the chair next to Bailey. She doesn't look up from her book. Lucky little thing learned to read in her village but never had access to as many books as we do now. She's probably worked her way through half the library. She reads like she's running out of time. Maybe she is.

"Hey, Bailey," I say gently.

She tears her eyes away from the page. "Yeah?"

I watch her carefully. "Listen, I'm collecting nice stories about Nova to share with Nico. Do you have any?"

It's a good alibi. At least, I hope so.

At first she just looks at me with a blank stare. Then a single tear rolls down her cheek. "She was always so nice to me, recommending books to read and talking to me. Almost everyone else ignores me. Even the teachers, but she didn't."

I nod, believing every word. That sounds like Nova.

"What was her favorite book?" I ask. I can already tell there is no way Bailey killed Nova, so that's one girl off the list. Well, three because it wasn't me or Joanna either.

"*Emma* by Jane Austen," she says and drops her eyes again. I don't know that book, but I make a mental note to read it as soon as I'm able.

I place a hand over hers. "She was my friend too."

She sniffs. "This is really nice of you to do for Nico."

I nod and stand. Time to hunt down the other girls. Even if I don't find out another single thing about who might've killed her, I'll have stories to share with Nico.

* * *

Katelyn and Harlow were also easy to cross off my list. They both had good stories about Nova and cried when telling them. I suppose they could be acting, but it's the initial reactions that I'm looking for, and I'm not finding any reason to suspect them. They also don't seem like the murderous type.

It's hard to get Faye and the other distillery girls alone, so I approach them as a group. They are sitting at a table in the dining room, painting each other's nails. The stench in the room is a little overwhelming.

I sit next to Blair, and she glares at me. "I'm not painting your nails, so shove off."

"I don't want my nails painted. I have a question."

Faye scoffs. "We probably don't have the answer."

My initial inclination is to look down, but I have to watch their reactions.

I look Faye right in the eyes. "I'm collecting nice stories for Nico about Nova and was wondering if you had any."

Faye doesn't react. Joy drops her eyes, and Emma fidgets with a bottle of paint, but no one acts suspiciously.

Then Faye laughs out loud. "I knew you were a sneaky one." She leans back and crosses her arms. "You killed her, and now you're going to use your friendship with her to get in good with Nico. You know, if you were my friend, I'd be impressed, but you're not, so get out of here." Shame burns in my stomach even though she's wrong about the motive. Because I see how it might be taken and I don't want everyone else thinking the same thing.

"Are you kidding? I'd never kill Nova. I'd never kill anyone."

Faye glares. "I said get out of here, and I meant it."

I want to argue, but I'm never going to get anything out of them. I should know that by now, but her accusation still stings. I shove my chair back and storm out of the room. I'm getting nowhere. I head out the back door because I need some air.

Lexi is painting at an easel in the middle of the grassy lawn. She's got quite the talent for it and has been painting every spare moment she can get. I watch her for a minute, finally deciding that just because those girls made me mad doesn't mean I can quit. The killer is likely one of the distillery girls, so right now all I have to do is rule everyone else out. Even if they think I'm doing this just to get to Nico.

I jog across the field and approach Lexi. She jerks her head up when she sees me. "What do you want?" she asks. She sounds more defensive than unhappy to see me. Maybe she can sense what I'm here for.

I can't see what she's painting because she's facing me, and the easel is between us. She's always been a little grumpy though, so the tone of her question doesn't catch me off guard. I don't move any closer.

"I just wanted to ask you if you knew any nice stories about Nova."

"Why would I know anything about her," she snaps.

"I'm asking everyone," I say.

Her whole body tenses.

"For Nico," I continue. "I want stories about her for Nico."

"Well, I don't have any," she says with more force than necessary.

"Are you sure? She was your teacher too."

"No. I don't know anything, and I have no idea why you think I would."

I think back to the scoreboard. She's always been fairly high up on the board because she's good at lessons, but she's never seemed to catch any of the beta's attention––except Nico. I'd forgotten about it until now, but before Nova arrived, he always sat next to Lexi. She's a smart girl, and they seemed to get along well, talking about the kind of stuff that goes way over my head. But it doesn't matter how smart you are. The scores on the board mean nothing if one of the betas doesn't choose you in the end. We all know that. Lexi knows that.

"Okay, well, if you think of anything, let me know," I say brightly. Then I turn and walk away. I don't run, even though I want to. I act like everything is normal, like I have no idea what Lexi has done.

Because I'm pretty sure I've found Nova's killer.

Chapter Four

The boat rocks, and I grip the edges, trying not to get sick. But the rowboat is tiny, and the waves are rough. At least they seem that way to me. Justin whips his fishing pole back and flings the tiny fish on a hook into the water. The movement reminds me of going fishing with my dad. Inevitably, Willow would jump into the water, and Dad always said that she scared the fish away. The memories flood me, and I force myself to refocus on Justin before my eyes fill up, and he wonders what's wrong with me.

This isn't exactly my type of romantic date, but then again, I'm not looking for anything romantic with him, even though I should be. He's said hardly anything to me, and we've been on the water for thirty minutes now. I have a cloak wrapped around myself, but it's still cold on the water.

"Do you fish often?" I ask.

"When I have time, which, no, isn't often. The older claimed women do a lot of our cooking for us, so there is no need for me to come out and catch my own, but I do enjoy it. I figured we'd catch a few and then cook them over a fire on the beach."

So maybe that is slightly more romantic. But still. Any conversation that includes the claimed doing his cooking for him isn't attractive. The longer I'm here, the more I see this evil for what it really is. But I need to stay focused, so I continue the conversation.

"How did you learn to fish if you grew up here?"

"Oh, my mom is from one of the fishing villages. She taught me when I was a child, and we still go out sometimes."

"You still keep in touch with her?"

"Of course. We all do. You know Ryne sees his mom all the time." It's not a secret anymore that Madame Delphine is the alpha's mother.

I didn't realize that if I had a child with a beta, I'd still get to see him as an adult. That makes me want it even more. But at this point, I'd only want it with Ryne.

"I wish I could see my mom again," I mutter. And my dad and little Evan. I wonder how much has changed since I've left. Maybe everything. Maybe nothing.

He sticks his fishing pole into a slot and plops down next to me, rocking the boat way too much for comfort. He slides his arm around me and tugs me close. "I know. I wish you could too, but that's simply not the way it's done."

The line of his fishing pole suddenly goes taut, and he hops up. He wrestles with the pole a little bit, and a large shiny green fish pops out of the water, thrashing.

"Grab the bucket," he yells.

I glance around, find the bucket, and hold it out. He drops the fish, and its tail flicks me. I jump and nearly drop the bucket. Justin laughs. "It's only a mahi-mahi. It won't hurt you, but it tastes amazing."

I peek into the bucket and grimace. It doesn't look very tasty. "I'll take your word for it." I adamantly refused to eat fish growing up, which drove my parents mad. Luckily, Willow ate enough for both of us.

He laughs again. This is the happiest I've ever seen Justin. I can't help but smile.

"No. You'll love it, I promise. We'll go back to my mom and dad's house, and I'll have her cook it. I won't do so hot cooking it on a fire out on a beach, and you deserve to taste mahi-mahi as it was meant to be."

"Your parents are still together?"

His face softens, laugh lines bunching around his pale green eyes. His blonde hair shines under the sunlight, and I suddenly realize how attractive this man actually is.

"Yeah. They are fated mates. No way Dad would ditch her now."

"Won't it be weird, taking me to meet them?"

"Why would it be? You're potentially my wife. It makes sense that I would introduce them to the girl I like."

I swallow. This escalated fast. "Wife? I thought you were going after Faye."

He raises an eyebrow. "She's definitely still a contender, but there's still a long way until the harvest moon. Ryne saved you. That must mean you've got something special. And I didn't realize it before, but you do. You're much easier to be around than Faye, and I doubt she'd be willing to hold the bucket while I fished."

We both laugh at that.

Faye's a challenge, and I have a suspicion that's exactly what Justin likes about her. And maybe that's why he's suddenly developed an interest in me--because now I'm a shiny prize to be won too. I'd much rather be won by him than Anders, but my heart tells me that's wrong. I belong to Ryne.

Justin catches two more fish, so we finish up and head out to his parents' place. A driver takes us across town, and we sit in the backseat and talk on the way. The fish are in a cooler in the trunk, but I can smell them anyway. I hate that smell, and after the seasickness from the little rowboat, my stomach isn't liking the idea of dinner. Hopefully his mom is good at preparing them to mask the taste. Considering we live near the coast, I probably can't avoid fish my whole life. Maybe eighteen years is all I'm going to get.

Justin and I don't have a lot in common, so the conversation is a little forced. He's used to girls fawning over him, so he goes for the ones who don't make it easy. I don't know how to do either of those things. All I can manage to be is myself, and maybe he finds that boring because at one point, he yawns.

"Do you have any brothers and sisters?" I ask, hoping to liven things up. One thing I've learned is that these guys love it when the conversation is focused on them. I expect this question to perk Justin right up, but his face goes ashen.

"Why? Has anyone said anything?"

"Uhh--no," I falter. "I'm just curious."

He relaxes and leans back in his seat. "Sorry. I didn't mean to get so defensive about my little brother."

"I understand. I'm defensive about mine too."

"Oh?" He frowns as if he's not put much thought into the fact that the girls who come here have families back home. But maybe I'm being too hard on him.

"Yeah, he's a cute kid. I miss him." And I do. He was always running around after me and Willow. A weight settles in my stomach.

He looks out the window, his mind somewhere else. This is about him, not me.

"Can I ask why you got defensive?" Okay, that was inappropriate. I hold up my hands. "Sorry, you don't have to answer that. Sometimes my curiosity gets the best of me."

"No, it's okay. I can't expect you to know everything about pack culture." He thinks through his words for a moment before speaking. "The thing is, there can only be so many betas at any given time. We can't have too many because we need a lot more deltas and gammas. So it's only the first-born son of a beta wolf who can get a beta spot, and that's only if there's availability. More often than not, those boys still have to fight it out. And as for second borns, well, they're always sent to the gamma barracks when they come of age."

"So I take it your little brother is a gamma."

Justin stares at his hands. "He was for three years, but he was killed last year when he tried to fight for a position as a beta."

My stomach turns, and my vision is filled with memories of the battle arena and all those bodies piled up. It's all so senseless, especially for an organization that claims it's doing everything it can to grow its numbers. And each of those dead? They might not all have families, but they all have someone who cares about them. And if they don't, well, that's a damn shame.

"Most betas have a lot of kids, but my parents only had two, and Dad refused to take another mate." He frowns. "So now it's just me."

"I'm really sorry, Justin." Even though our lives are wildly different, this is something I feel in my soul. I lost my sister and he lost his brother. There's a connection there that wasn't before.

He shakes his head and smiles. "Let's not talk about this anymore. We're here to have fun, remember?"

"Right." And Justin is a fun-loving kind of guy. He doesn't want a date who brings up the grief in his life. If I'm going to land a beta, I'd better learn to have fun.

I can't forget what the betas want. They want pretty. They want refined. And they want talented, strong, and subservient. Sometimes I worry that I'll never be those things, and now that Justin is taking me to his parents' place, that worry surfaces. Surely, his mother is perfect if she landed a beta. Will she judge me? My heart begins to speed as the realization hits me. If I don't impress his parents, I'll lose this chance with Justin for good.

Chapter Five

We arrive at the house, and I can't help but grin, my fears slightly dissolving. "It's really pretty."

His smile quirks as we get out of the car. "Thanks. I'll tell my mom you said that. This place is her pride and joy."

"Oh, you're not her pride and joy?" I tease.

He laughs and leads me to the front door. I stop right before we get there, leaning down to sniff a bright yellow rose. I didn't even know roses could look like this in winter. They're not always easy to grow. It offers a rare moment of magic in an otherwise drab world. I stand, and Justin smirks at me.

"What?" I ask.

He leans over and whispers in my ear, "Mom's watching from the window, and you just sniffed her roses."

"Was I not supposed to?"

But before he can answer, the door flings open, and the largest man I've ever seen ducks under the frame and steps out. He's all bulky muscle and towers over us like a mountain. "Son, another one? Your mother isn't going to be happy."

But his face splits into a grin, and he embraces Justin. He lets go and eyes me. "Just kidding. I'm Amos. Welcome to my home. What's your name?"

"Poppy." My voice cracks.

"Isn't that a flower?"

I nod, and Justin flinches. I have no idea what's going on. A tiny woman shoves past Amos and Justin and peers up at me. She's pretty with bright blonde hair and a friendly face. She must've gotten pregnant with Justin when she was first married because she doesn't look a day over forty. And maybe that means Justin isn't as old as some of the other betas. I never thought to ask. Or maybe this woman looks young because she's lived a life of luxury, and I'm used to being around women who labor.

"I'm Shauna. Did I hear you say your name is Poppy?" she asks excitedly. Her eyes dance a bit, and they remind me of her son's.

"Yes."

She grabs my hand and pulls me away from the house and into the yard.

"See you in a few hours," Justin calls with a laugh.

I'm still thoroughly confused, but his mom doesn't let go of my hand as we wind through bushes and flower beds out to a greenhouse. She drops my hand as we go inside and brings a small plant over to me with a bright red flower. She hands it to me. "For you. A poppy."

My chest warms. I've never even seen the flower I was named for. "Thank you. I didn't know what they looked like."

"Well, now you do. Do you like flowers?"

"I do, though I don't know much about them."

"I saw you admiring my Julia Child."

"I thought that was a rose."

She scoffs. "There are hundreds of different kinds of roses. I've managed to grow forty-three. Every night Amos and I come out and cover them up so they don't freeze. It keeps them blooming all year long."

"Wow. Will you show them to me?"

Her eyes light up. "That would take all day, and I assume Justin expects me to cook for everyone. But next time, for sure. If I give you a book about roses, will you study it? Then maybe you can tell me what they are when you come back."

"Of course." The idea of being quizzed makes me a little nervous, but I'm glad she seems to like me.

I don't know why, but I want to impress this woman. I don't tell her I can't read very well, but I'll have Joanna help me. Then again, Shauna's been in my shoes. I wonder what fishing village she's from.

We walk slowly back to the house and onto a deck with a sliding door that opens right into the large kitchen with deep black countertops and shiny appliances. I think back to my own mother cooking over a fire. This world still shocks me sometimes.

Justin and his dad are standing at the counter, dropping the fish into some kind of batter. "Stop," his mom shrieks.

She rushes forward to take over, but Amos catches her.

"Let me through," she demands. "You're going to ruin it."

He leans down and gives her a long kiss. It's a little uncomfortable to watch, but at the same time, I can't draw my eyes away.

Justin groans. "You get used to it. Seriously, do you have to gross her out?"

They break away, and his mom giggles while she brushes her hair out of her face. "It's been thirty years, and I'm still not used to it."

My insides sour. I want that. I want to be with Ryne, whose kisses I'll never get used to. Instead, I'm here with Justin, who is turning out to be a good guy, but I doubt he'd ever make me feel like that. And quite honestly, I think he wants it as bad as I do. He's a ladies' man with us, but seeing him here with his parents makes me wonder if that's a cover for something more genuine. And now I really hope he doesn't end up with Faye. If I were in his shoes, seeing my parents as fated mates, I'd probably wait until I found mine. Justin is young, so it's not like he has to take a mate yet. I wonder why he chose now to do so.

"I want to teach you something," Shauna says. She shoos the boys away and begins to rummage through her cupboards. "I know I have some somewhere." She pulls out a little jar of black seeds and grins triumphantly. "Poppy seeds!"

I can't help but mirror her smile. The black seeds are so small, and it's hard to imagine that something so stunning can come from something so small and seemingly insignificant. "What are those for?"

She finds a few more ingredients and shows me how to make her favorite salad dressing. We mix it in with the fresh greens from the greenhouse garden right on time for the fish to be finished. And then she does something unexpected. She hands me the jar with the seeds.

"These are for you. I know there is a greenhouse out at Drayton Hall. Find an old pot and plant them. You can move them outside in a few weeks. And then when they start to wilt, harvest the seeds for yourself."

I can feel my lips tugging at my ears, my smile so big. "Thank you. That's such a kind gesture." I set the little jar down on the counter for later. "Do you grow all your own food? I thought that's what we used the villages for?"

"Most of it. That's why I had Amos build me the greenhouse. So that I could have fresh vegetables year-round." She pinches her lips in thought.

"Honestly, I don't like to add any strife to the villages. I know how hard those people work. I was one of them, same as you."

Nobody really talks about the villages and everything we had to give up when we left home as the claimed. I can't help but ask, "Do you miss it?"

She sighs. "Yes and no. I miss my family. The people. I don't miss the hardship or the cold winter nights without much to keep me warm. And I can't imagine my life without Amos or my children." She shakes her head. "Did Justin tell you about his little brother, Jonathan?"

"Yes. I'm really sorry."

She wipes a tear. "Me too." The room has gone quiet. Something thuds outside, and she peers out the window. The men are out chopping wood. "Good, I'd hoped we'd get a chance to be alone after I got to know you a little better."

I stare at her, and she turns to me with a knowing gaze. "Your friend Joanna is my niece," she says, catching me completely off guard. I don't know what to say. Her cheeks pink, and she rushes on. "My little sister got married to Joanna's father and moved to the textile village around the same time I was brought here as one of the claimed. I didn't even know my niece existed for a long time. I had no contact with anyone back home for years. It was lonely." Her eyes shine. "Don't mistake me. I love my family here very much, but there's always been a separate hole for the ones I lost to the claiming."

I smile sadly. "Yes, I know what you mean. I think we all do. Have you seen her?"

Her smile falters, and she drops her eyes. "No, I haven't," she says a little too quickly. There's something in her tone that doesn't quite match her words.

"I'm sorry."

She shrugs. "That's the way of things. What does she look like?"

I step back. "Well, for starters, her hair is short." Shauna doesn't look up at me. That surprises me because most people are shocked by Joanna's short hair. We are supposed to leave it long. "She cut it off and said she would rather die than become claimed, but her fated mate saved her life. The short hair actually suits her, although they're making her grow it out. Joanna is pretty and feisty and my best friend since coming here, not to mention she's the best-dressed girl in our house. Sometimes she—"

"Please don't say anything to anyone," Shauna cuts me off. "I can't let people know that I found out about her. They'd have questions, and I don't want to bring my family into things that could come back to hurt them later." She twists her hands together and goes back to the food, plating it carefully so that it looks perfect on the bright white china. "Did you know it's quite difficult for a beta to lie to his alpha? Some say it's impossible, but that's not true."

"So does Justin know?"

She shakes her head. I want to ask about Amos, but I expect the answer is the same.

She studies me for a long moment, as if deciding how much she can trust me. I don't know how much I can trust her either. I want to ask if she's with the Resistance, but I don't dare take the risk. If she's not, it could be disastrous. But somehow, I think maybe she is.

"Of course I'll keep it a secret," I whisper.

We take the plates to the table right as the men step back into the house. "Wow, Mom, it smells amazing in here," Justin says, and when he grins at me, his father waggles his eyebrows, and his mother winks. The two men must have been talking about me out there. What did they say? Whatever it was, I'm sure it couldn't have been as dangerous as the words Shauna and I exchanged tonight.

We eat the amazing dinner, one that doesn't even taste like the fish I've had before, and then Justin drives me home. He walks me to the doorstep and leaves me with a whisper-soft kiss. His lips are cold. I kiss him back because it's what I'm supposed to do. It doesn't seem to matter. My mind is elsewhere. All I can think about is the Resistance.

Is Shauna one of them? Does Justin know?

The wolves can take us from our villages and strip us of our dignity, they can divide us and pit us against each other, but at the end of the day, we're still village girls in our hearts. If a beta's wife living in a grand house is missing her family enough to break the rules and risk her life, how many other women in this city would be willing to fight to obliterate those rules completely?

Chapter Six

I t's a sunny Tuesday afternoon when I finally find the time to go out to the run-down greenhouse. It's smaller than Shauna's and hasn't been touched in years, but I instantly love it. I vow to fix it up and get it running again during my free time. The walls are dirty, the plants are dead, and the watering system is probably busted. It's going to be a lot of work.

I'm one million percent up for the challenge.

I start by washing out a few pots and filling them with rich, dark soil. The earthy smells and thick humidity remind me of home, and I feel like a kid again. My mind fills with memories of the fields that stretched out around my village, of those magical blue-skied springs when we'd plant the seeds for the new year. It was hard work, but I loved having a role to play and getting to do it alongside my family. The best part was watching a tiny seed turn into something people needed. Maybe sometimes that's how change happens; maybe everything starts out small and seemingly insignificant and turns into something worthwhile.

And maybe that's why the Resistance will eventually succeed.

But there's nothing I can do about the resistance until Joanna lets me. For now, I should focus on what I can do.

Take care of Nova's murderer.

I wonder how I can get Lexi to confess.

Joanna pops her head in the door. I told her about my suspicions last night, and she thought I was jumping to conclusions. I think I have pretty solid evidence, but she just doesn't want it to be one of the girls because that puts her in danger. I also have to find a way to warn Grady about this.

She's dressed in a cute white tennis skirt and leans against one of the tables with a long sigh, a racket in her hand. "We've been looking all over for you."

"We?" I ask.

Grady and Justin tromp in next, also dressed in athletic gear.

"Yeah, we wanted to play a game of tennis and need a fourth."

"Sure." Tennis is one of the games we've learned since arriving here, and I'm pretty good at it. There's a court in the field out back, and it's become one of the most popular activities for the girls during free time as the weather has started to warm. I like it too, but right now my mind is set on my task.

Justin comes over and wraps his arms around me from behind, resting his chin on my shoulder. I tense at his sudden affection. It doesn't feel wrong exactly, but it doesn't feel right either. "You're planting the seeds Mom gave you?"

I nod and try to think of how I can gracefully get away from him. Then again, maybe I don't want to. The more time I can spend with him, the less time I'll have to spend with Anders.

Joanna scoots closer. "How long will they take to grow?"

I'd told her all about our date, but I left out the part about learning she's Shauna's niece. I have to be careful about what I tell her. Joanna has a mouth and a short temper, and I don't want to break my promise to Shauna. The last thing I'd want to do would be to get someone in trouble. But part of me wonders if these two women already know about each other. If my suspicions are correct and they're both Resistance, then it stands to reason that they do.

"As long as I take care of them, they should start sprouting in a week or two," I say, hoping it's true. I'd love to see those bright red poppies here. I'll plant them along the wood's edge for future claimed girls to enjoy.

Joanna pops up on the table next to me and peers down into the pot. "Well, hurry up with all this. I want to get my blood flowing."

Grady stands next to her and nuzzles her neck. "I can think of a few things we can do to get your blood flowing."

She giggles and swats him away. Then she jumps down off of the table. "We're going to go get started. Come join us as soon as you're done."

"Okay." As soon as they leave the greenhouse, Justin lets go of me and takes Joanna's vacant spot. He seems more serious today. It's not something I've seen on him before.

"Mom wants me to bring you back to the house."

I smile. "I barely saw them, what... A week ago?"

"I know. But they like you." He scoots closer to me and brushes a stray piece of hair away from my face. "I like you."

I don't want to put him off. He's exactly who I should be going for and someone who can save me from a life at the mating house or with Anders. But his touch isn't Ryne's. I hate that I have to fake it with him, but I do. And I need to do it well.

I lean into his touch and move a little closer to him. "I like you too," I whisper. He visibly relaxes and tugs me away from the pots I'm working on. I stand between his legs, and he brings me close. I wrap my arms around his back and close my eyes.

When his lips meet mine, I try to lose myself in the kiss. I really do. It's nice, but it doesn't have the fire that I feel with Ryne. I wonder if I can grow to love Justin. Probably. I wonder if I'll ever stop comparing him to Ryne. Probably not. But I have to. Ryne has made that clear. My life depends on me moving on with another beta and letting Ryne move on with Elle. Because I've finally accepted that Elle's the reason why Ryne doesn't want me.

Justin breaks away and smiles sheepishly before jumping off the table and grabbing my hand. "It's time to go kick Grady's ass at tennis."

"We're playing Joanna too."

"I've watched you. You're good at anything athletic. Joanna doesn't stand a chance. She'll probably stand back and let Grady do all the work."

"Don't let her hear you say that." I giggle and lean into him because that's what I'm supposed to do.

We exit the greenhouse, and I spot Faye and a few of her friends playing croquet with Anders and Nico. She sees us, and I swear her face turns several shades of red. As if I don't need another reason for Faye to despise me, now I've got her favorite beta holding onto my hand like it means something. I drop my eyes and cling tighter to Justin.

* * *

"Keep your grimy paws off my man," Joanna says, brushing out my hair. She'd bounded back into the room a few minutes before and snatched my brush out of my hands. It's the weekend, and we have dates again tonight, but I hadn't known who I was going out with.

I guess I do now.

"Don't worry. Grady knows I'd kill him if I ever caught him so much as looking at another girl that isn't you."

"That's my girl." Joanna winks at me in the mirror.

All things considered, it's been a pretty decent week. Elle made good on her promise, and we had combat twice more than normal. Add that to the points Justin gave me on our date last week, and I am now middle of the board. This is a step in the right direction, but my heart still lurches every time Ryne enters the room.

Which he does nearly every day now. He's with Elle a lot, but I feel his eyes on me all the time. And I can't help but look at him. It's like we're magnets, but we're forced apart because of their unofficial betrothal. But what hurts the most is that Ryne hasn't tried to call it off with Elle. So I guess I have my answer.

At least nobody else has died since Nova. At least, not yet. I still worry about Joanna.

"What do you know about tonight?" I ask her, but I already know the answer.

"Only that you're going out with Grady. I made him promise to give you a good score, but seriously, keep your hands off of him."

It's a joke, of course, but she doesn't have anything to worry about. I'm glad I'm going out with him because then I can warn him about Joanna's safety. I hadn't had any time to do that yet. This would be the perfect time for us to discuss it.

I wink back at her. "Who knows, maybe by the end of the night, he'll forget that you're his fated mate and take me as his wife instead."

She swats me on the arm. "That's not funny."

"Ow. I'm just joking. Better me out there with him than Faye."

Faye had actually been on a date with Grady earlier in the week, and Joanna and I spied on them when they came home. Faye tried to kiss him, but he turned his head, and she got his cheek instead. I had to lock Joanna in our room for the night to keep her from trying to fight with Faye. I'm pretty sure Faye knew we were watching, and that's the only reason why she did it. Everyone knows Grady's taken, but Faye loves to push Joanna's buttons.

"I swear. I should punch that girl," Joanna says, "or better yet, let's shave her head while she's sleeping. You know she's obsessed with her hair."

"Ah, let her be. She's already upset because Justin obviously prefers me over her." As much as I hate Faye, she's still a part of something that shouldn't even exist. If we didn't have to compete, maybe all of us girls could be friends. Okay, maybe not, but we could at least be civil.

This is only my second date since we started the one-on-one dates. Elle is in charge of setting them up, and Joanna told her not to put me with Anders. Unfortunately, Elle said she couldn't do that, but she could put him last on the rotation with me.

"Which means Faye's looking for a new man. She's going out with Nico tonight. Poor guy won't know what hit him."

Nico continued to give girls low scores on their dates, and Katelyn said when she went out with him, they didn't do anything. He took her back to his house, left her in his drawing room alone, and then had a driver bring her home. I feel bad for him. He's grieving and shouldn't be put in this position, but I also understand the girls' point of view. None of it is fair.

I enter the foyer with Faye, Harlow, Abi, and Lexi. Joanna followed me down as well, even though she doesn't have a date tonight. The betas stand in the foyer, and I look for Ryne, but he's nowhere to be seen. Joanna races up to Grady and plants a kiss on his lips. He whispers something in her ear, and she giggles.

I approach them, and she gives me the stink eye. "No hanky panky, you two," she says.

Grady reaches around and wraps an arm around my waist, planting a wet kiss on my cheek.

"Hey," Joanna screeches, and Grady laughs.

"I love making her jealous."

I shove away from him. "Well, I don't. So, hands off."

"Yeah, hands off my girl," Justin yells from behind me. I flush but don't turn around. Faye meets my eyes and glowers at me as she stalks over to Nico. She loops her arm through his, but he shakes her off. If things keep going poorly for Faye, it's only a matter of time until she retaliates. If she's actually the one behind Nova's murder, I'd better watch my back.

We'll be getting a couple of one-on-one dates a week, and I'm dreading the date that's inevitably coming with Anders. But Anders isn't here tonight either, so I push him from my mind and decide to have fun tonight. It's not often in this place that a girl gets to go on a date with a guy just as friends.

"So where are we going?" I ask as we head out to the car. It snowed a little last night, and the day never warmed up enough to melt it off. We get a few snowfalls every year, but something about this one felt different. Maybe because it was my first big storm in the wolf city instead of being bundled up at home with my family in the village.

"How do you like ice skating?" he asks, as if the words should mean something to me.

"What's that?"

Grady stops and turns to me with a boyish grin. "Did I find a sport that the infamous Poppy doesn't know how to do? Hmm, this should be interesting."

Twenty minutes later, we pull up to a massive circular building. I've never seen such a thing before.

He opens the door, and the icy night air greets me. We walk through the doors and the inside of the building isn't much warmer than the outside. We enter a small room lined with shelves full of boots, except these boots have blades on the bottom. Grady takes a pair of white ones off a shelf and holds them out for me to see. "This is an ice skate." He grins like he's discovered gold.

"It looks like a weapon."

He laughs and retrieves a black pair for himself. Sitting on a bench, he shows me how to get the skates on and then helps me up.

When we walk out of the small room, I gasp at the size of the massive space. It's wide open with a shiny white floor.

"What's that?" I ask.

"That's an ice rink, come on."

He pulls me to the edge of the floor and then takes to the ice like a crane landing on water—graceful and smooth. He's obviously done this many times before. Grady does a long turn about the ice and then comes back to teach me. As with all of my other athletic endeavors, I expect this one to come naturally. Five minutes later, I'm flat on my back and realizing it most certainly is not easy.

This ice is rock hard, and my butt kills, but I'm not one to give up, so I climb to my feet and keep trying. I'm terrible, but at least I can say I tried. Grady gives me some tips, and soon I'm doing a decent job—not good—but decent. He skates circles around me as we talk.

"I'm worried about Joanna," I blurt out. I can't help it, and she'll kill me if she finds out, but I can't keep this to myself.

His face falls. "What's wrong?"

I jump right into my theory about Nova's death, that I think she was murdered and that someone might be targeting the fated mates of the betas. Grady's face turns stark white, worry casting a garish hue across his handsome features.

"She's not taking her safety seriously," I finish up, "so I need your help protecting her without her knowing I said anything." I almost tell him about Lexi, but since I don't have irrefutable evidence, I don't want to go accusing her just in case I'm wrong.

"I'll make sure she stays safe." There's an edge to his tone that I know I put there, but I don't feel bad. I'm glad he knows. I need his help.

Voices float across the ice and I spin, nearly falling over in the process.

Two figures appear with skates in hand—Ryne and Elle.

Chapter Seven

I manage to ease myself to the edge of the rink and lean against the wall, since I can't even stay up on my own two feet. Elle leans into Ryne, and the green-eyed monster rears in my chest. I watch them. I shouldn't, but I do. Ryne seems so easy with her. They laugh and talk like they've known each other for years—which they have—but it seems so odd to see Ryne this happy and relaxed. He's normally brooding and grumpy.

Maybe he's making the right decision. That thought alone breaks my heart into a million razored pieces.

Grady skates up to them, pulling Ryne aside. Elle takes off across the ice like she was born on it. She picks up speed, jumps and spins in the air, and lands gracefully on one skate. Ryne whoops, and she beams.

She meets my eye and glides over to me.

"Poppy, why aren't you skating?" Concern shines in her coppery eyes.

"Because I can't seem to stay upright." I shrug helplessly.

She giggles and holds out her hands. "I'll teach you."

I let her pull me a little ways out.

"How did you learn to jump like that?" I ask.

"Oh, it's freezing all winter in Chicago, so I skate often. It's one of my favorite things. I begged Ryne to find me a place to go. I didn't think I'd be able to skate here. He said as soon as I arrived, he put some wolves on getting this place up and running again. Isn't that sweet?"

She doesn't know about me and Ryne, so she doesn't know about the knife she's twisting. I smile and let it go. She holds tight to my hand as we wobble--correction, I wobble--onto the ice. I think about this rink and what it must have cost to get it fixed up and running again, and compare it to my family at home making do without electricity. Some things really aren't fair.

"I thought you were supposed to be good at anything athletic," she teases, her tone playful. She's impossible not to like.

"I thought so too." I roll my eyes. "Turns out ice doesn't like me."

Elle spins around so she's skating backward and grabs my other hand. At least I can stay upright with her hauling me across the ice, but I feel like a fool.

We pass Ryne and Grady, who are speaking in low voices, both serious. I hope he's not telling Ryne what I told him about Joanna. She's going to be angry enough that I told Grady when she inevitably finds out.

Elle doesn't even look at them as she turns and looks longingly at the ice.

"I think I've got it now. You can go," I offer.

"Are you sure?"

No. I'm going to fall on my butt the second she lets go, but I don't want her to know that. The girl wants to skate, and I'm slowing her down. "Positive."

She nods once and releases my hands. As long as I don't try to move my feet, I'll be fine. I stand there for a few moments, shivering. I have to move, or I'm going to freeze. Maybe I can just go back to the car.

I shuffle my feet forward a few inches and immediately lose my balance. But before I can hit the ice, strong arms catch me. I inhale the woody scent of Ryne and try to keep my composure.

"You're not very good at this, are you?" He keeps one arm tight around my waist, and I try not to notice how much I appreciate his body next to mine.

"No. I think I'm going to ask Grady to take me home."

I twist my head around looking for Grady, but he's gone.

"He's going to take care of Joanna. I told him Elle and I can get you home. Don't worry, he's still going to give you full points for this date."

"What? Why?" And also, why would he leave me here? Being the third wheel on a date between Elle and Ryne is a special kind of torture.

"Joanna's in danger. Isn't that what you told him? I'm letting him keep her at his house now. She'll come for classes like Nova did during the day, but that's all."

Dread fills my stomach. Joanna is going to kill me. I groan.

"I thought you'd be happy about that," he says.

"I am, and I'm not. Of course, I want her to be safe. But Nova was staying with Nico when she got killed, so it's not like it's a guarantee of safety. And you and I both know Joanna won't like this at all. She's going to be angry that I blabbed."

Ryne doesn't respond. We both watch Elle spin circles for a few moments. Ryne tightens his grip on me. "You're shivering. Come on, I'll take you back to the car. We can wait in there while Elle gets her skating fix in."

I meet his eyes. The electricity between us is undeniable. "Do you really think that's a good idea?"

He swallows. "No. But I'm not going to let you freeze to death either."

He breaks the gaze and shouts out over the rink. "Hey, Elle, we're going to wait in the car."

She waves us on, and he turns me around. We shuffle to the edge of the rink, change back into our regular shoes, and escape the freezing building. Outdoors is just as cold, but I'm sure Ryne's car is much warmer.

Nerves dance in my stomach. I have no idea what's about to happen. Ryne and I haven't been alone since the night of the brawl.

We near the car, and Knox rushes out to open the back door. He meets my eye but doesn't say anything.

I guess we're not really going to be alone.

But having Knox around won't stop Ryne from doing anything. Ryne might treat Knox with respect, but he's still a slave and a human. And Ryne doesn't know the history between us. Would he keep Knox around if he did?

We slide into the backseat, and I'm immediately grateful for the blast of hot air coming from within. I'm acutely aware of Ryne next to me, but I don't look at him. I pull my hat and gloves off. My braids are a mess, so I untie them and shake out my hair, combing my fingers through the unruly locks. I close my eyes for a second and let out a long sigh of relief. I'm never going ice skating again.

"Knox, do me a favor," Ryne says. "Go take a walk."

My eyes pop open, and I meet Knox's gaze in the rearview mirror. His cheeks are red, and his jaw is set. I've never seen those sweet brown eyes of his looking so dark and heated. He holds me there for a minute, as if daring me to speak up, and then he tears his gaze away and follows Ryne's orders. The door slams, and the alpha prince and I are alone. The temperature in the car rises by ten degrees. Or at least it feels like it does.

"Why'd you send him away like that?" It's a baiting question, but I need to know. I want to hear him tell me all the things I've been longing to hear, like that he can't live without me, and that I'm his fated mate. But those silly ideas are probably all in my head.

Ryne growls low and slides in close, his large frame trapping me against the seat. Everything about having him near feels right.

"I didn't like the way he was looking at you. And I especially didn't like the way you were looking at him."

I shudder and try to deflect because I'm suddenly nervous. As much as I want Ryne, I don't want Knox getting into any trouble because of me. "I wasn't looking at him. I had my eyes closed and was trying to untangle my hair."

I'm such a liar. Can Ryne sense that in me?

"And that's the other reason I sent him away," Ryne responds. "So I could get five minutes alone with you." He reaches up and grips long fingers against my scalp, threading them into my hair and messing it all over again. I'm caught in his hands--in him--and all I can do is stare. His own black hair hangs around his chin. He's still got his beanie on. It's tugged low, framing the stormy blue of his eyes. There's something so completely male about him, so alluring and dangerous, and *mine*. I can't bear to be apart from him for another second. My gaze drifts to his lips. They're a little chapped from the cold.

He growls again—this time I can hear the wolf in him, and then those red lips are on mine.

I sink into him as he pushes me flat on the seat and covers my body with his. He's too tall for it, which makes the space tighter and forces our bodies even closer. If our first kiss was a confession, and our second was a refusal, this one is a promise. He tastes and smells and feels like everything my mama warned me about. But he also feels right, and I can't help from wanting more.

His hands slide under the hem of my shirt to grip my waist, and they are so hot, hotter than a human's, but I like it. It spreads a warmth through me that has nothing to do with the heat and everything to do with instinct. Ryne and I--we are meant to be together. I know it. He knows it. How could either of us deny that? My heart is open to him. It's not smart or logical, but it's the truth, and it fills me with a million wondrous emotions.

His mouth explores mine, and my hands explore him--his arms, his shoulders, his face, his chest, his back . . .

Someone knocks on the door, giving us just enough warning to pull apart before it opens. Elle pops her head in. Her nose is rosy, and her eyes are round as saucers. She doesn't look shocked. She doesn't even look mad. She looks annoyed.

And hurt.

"You know, Ryne, I didn't come all the way from Chicago for this," she snaps. "And I certainly don't think it's what either of our fathers had in mind when they brokered our betrothal."

Ryne doesn't say a word. He locks eyes with me for one moment more, and then he sits up and peels me away from him. I didn't even realize I was holding onto him until he separates us, and that action alone stings. But that's nothing compared to the pain of the words coming out of Elle's mouth. The pieces have fallen into place, and realizing Ryne's future doesn't include me is like a slap to the face. So much for being his fated. If I were, he wouldn't have even had Elle brought out here. The second he laid eyes on me, he would've called things off with her.

I'm a silly girl who thinks the sexy bad boy wants me. But he's just using me.

"Listen, Elle, I can explain," Ryne finally speaks.

"Save it." She holds up a hand. "You wolves are all the same. I really shouldn't be surprised, but I do have to admit that I expected more from you."

He shakes his head. "But Poppy isn't who you think--"

"This isn't about Poppy." She looks at me for the first time. "I can see why you like her. But the fact is she's not here for you, Ryne. Think about how you're disrespecting your role. You're not a beta. You're an alpha and a prince. I'm a luna from one of the strongest bloodlines in all the wolf cities, and we both know that our fathers will end up battling for alpha king if you and I don't get married and you become the sole heir to that role."

I gulp. There's so much more to unpack here than I could've realized.

"But more than that, we're friends. Maybe think about how you'd feel if you caught me making out with some human in the middle of our date." She raises her eyebrows. "Because I'm not going to go through with this if you're not going to be faithful."

Then she slams the door shut, and the last of my hope slams shut with it.

Chapter Eight

We arrive home right before dinner, but I've lost my appetite. The only thing I want is Ryne, as much as I know I shouldn't. Knowing I can't have him only makes me want him more. He consumes my thoughts and fills my body with desire. On the way home, Elle and I sat in the back of the car while Ryne sat up front with Knox.

No one said a word.

I escape to my room and collapse onto my bed. The door bangs open seconds later, and Joanna stomps in.

"Thanks a lot," she says, flinging open the closet door. I sit up and see a suitcase on the floor.

"What's going on?" My mind is a mess from everything that just happened.

She spins on me, her eyes blazing. "You told Grady that you thought whoever murdered Nova killed her because she stole Nico from us and that I'm next."

I sigh heavily. "Joanna. You weren't taking this seriously. He can protect you better than anyone."

She tosses her dresses into the suitcase and rips open the dresser drawers. "Well, thanks to you, now I'm never going to be let out of his sight. I have to move into his house." Her voice goes low. "I was trying to get you into the Resistance, and now I won't be able to."

I blink at her. "Wait. What? I've been waiting for you to say something about it. I'm ready. I want in."

She shrugs. "Good luck then, because your one and only contact has officially been benched. You know I love Grady, but I really needed this year to figure out some stuff before getting married to him."

"You still can."

"No, I can't. Because Ryne has given Grady permission to take me as his mate at the next moon festival. He doesn't have to wait until the harvest. That's six months early, Poppy."

"You'll be married..." My eyes start to water. I don't want to lose her yet. She was the only thing that made this place bearable.

"He says I can come back here for classes if I want. But I don't know. He sure made it sound like by the time we're married, we won't be leaving each other's sides for the first year, and I won't be interested in classes anyway. I'll probably be pregnant within a few months." Her body goes rigid. "Pregnant! Do you know I never wanted to have children? Who would in this world? What a perfect way to trap me here."

I rub the tears from my eyes. "This wasn't my intent. I only wanted to keep you safe."

"Well, maybe you should think before you speak." She slams the suitcase shut and zips it up. "This ruins everything."

"Really, Joanna, it doesn't. You love him, and he loves you. Some of us would kill for that kind of marriage." The words are out of my mouth before I even realize what I said.

Her eyes narrow. "Well, thanks to you, no one's going to kill me for it." She says it like it's a problem, but I'm not going to apologize for saving her life. I do feel bad about the Resistance stuff though.

She jerks the suitcase off the bed and leaves the room, slamming the door. I don't know if she'll forgive me for this, and I don't have the energy to fight with her. I never want to get out of bed again.

I don't want to think about death and murder, or the Resistance, or any of it.

Instead, I close my eyes and relive the kiss from this afternoon. It was so much better than the ones before, and there is no way Ryne could play our first kiss off as something for Anders's benefit. Or our second kiss as a mistake. This was real. And he was in it as much as I was––as much as I still am.

A soft knock comes at the door. "Come in," I call, not wanting to get up. Elle appears, carrying a tray of sandwiches and chips. She's the last person I expected, and my face immediately warms.

She sets the tray on my dresser. "You didn't come to dinner."

"I didn't feel like facing anyone." I sit up, and she sinks onto Joanna's bed.

"I'm sorry about the outburst in the car. I was. . . disappointed to find Ryne behaving like every other wolf I know. I thought he was better than that."

I curl into a ball and retreat into myself. I don't want to talk about this. Especially not with her. She moves from Joanna's bed to mine and puts an arm around my shoulder. I'm so shocked that I don't even push her away. I want to hate her, but I can't. This isn't her fault.

"I want you to know that I don't blame you at all. For one thing, you couldn't have known about the seriousness of our betrothal. Nothing has been announced, and nobody's told you a thing about our family dynamics. For another, I get it. He's Ryne Tremaine, the alpha prince. No one says no to the alpha prince. I thought he was just being nice to you because your date bailed." She scoffs. "I should've known. I'm sorry." She lets go of me and lies back against the pillows. "I don't even love him. I mean, I think I probably could love him at some point, but I don't. He's too much like a brother. We've never even kissed. But I've known for a while that we were going to get married. You've met the alpha king, right?"

I nod, my body instantly going cold at the thought of Thorn Tremaine. Part of me wants to tell Elle to go away, but another part is totally entranced by her story.

"Well, my father is his second in command and itching to take over. He's nearly challenged Thorn on multiple occasions. He hasn't because there's no guarantee he could win, and it would be a bloodbath. Others would rise to challenge the victor, and it would weaken the entire wolf shifter packs for a while. But he chafes under Thorn's rule. Our mothers actually intervened and proposed the marriage. Of course, neither one of them consulted with me or Ryne. But that's the way of things, I suppose."

I go stiff at that comment, and she frowns. "What's wrong?"

I eye her for a long minute, hoping I can trust her. She has a calming yet powerful energy, and something about that makes me want to be around her. "It's what you said about the way of things. Aren't you tired of it?"

"Of course, I'm tired of it." Intensity sparks in her eyes. "I've had my entire life dictated to me from the moment I was born––from where I went to school and what I could learn, to when I could shift and what I could do. Even down to who I'm going to marry." She takes my hands in hers. They're hot, a reminder of the wolf on the inside. "But as frustrating as that is, I know it's nothing compared to what you girls have to go through, especially the ones who won't get matched with a beta, and I'm sorry."

She's earnest––means every word––and I'm suddenly overcome with the urge to cry and rage all at the same time. Why does she have to be so nice and so perfect for Ryne? I squeeze her hands back. "Elle, we don't need to compare our pain. Yours is just as legitimate as mine, even if it looks different." I'm struck with a thought. I should keep it to myself, but I can't help sharing it. "Are you sure you want to marry Ryne? You said you didn't love him. Don't you want to be with someone you love? And what's more, don't you want to find your fated mate?"

She drops my hands and stands, pacing the floor, her sunshine yellow dress brushing her thighs as she moves. "Of course I want to marry for love or find my fated," she laments. "What's more, I want the freedom to change at will and be my wolf whenever I choose, to hunt and do my duty to the pack in the ways that are denied to me. But there's so many layers to this, and that's what I'm trying to get you to understand." She stops and turns on me, her face growing stern. "I must marry Ryne. If I don't, my father will challenge Thorn, and he'll probably lose. Thorn will destroy my family if that happens. He'll kill us all. My mother, my brothers, and me. And I'll do anything to make sure that doesn't happen."

And now I feel terrible for goading her. "I understand." I swallow hard. "I would do anything to go back and save the family I lost to the wolves. I'd sacrifice my life if I had to."

"We're two sides to the same coin." She smiles sadly before reaching over and grabbing my hand again. "I'm still sorry I caught you with him. It's probably not a good idea for you to fool around with him anymore. I know your date ditched you, but your only chance at a decent life is to fight for a beta, and they won't want a girl who's been with the alpha because then they'll think you belong to him." Her cheeks redden. "They want you to be virgins for the betas. I'm under the same hypocritical rules too."

I look down at my hands, unsure of what to say. I wasn't just fooling around with him, and this isn't about lust. It's so much more––maybe even love, maybe even fate. "What if I do belong to him?" My voice is small. Up until that kiss, I wasn't sure what I felt for Ryne, but now, I feel as if I'll die without him.

She lets out a laugh. "Come on, Poppy, I thought you were smarter than this. Ryne belongs to no one. Don't set yourself up for heartbreak."

Exactly. He belongs to no one, which means he doesn't belong to her either.

I stare at her. I haven't admitted this to anyone. But I haven't been able to make sense of the way I feel, and here is Elle, sweet and open and willing to listen. My words tumble out of my mouth without warning. "I'm not a fool, but there is something about Ryne. I'm drawn to him, and it feels like he's drawn to me too. From the first moment I met him, he hasn't been able to keep his eyes off of me. And when we kiss, everything else falls away."

Her face loses all expression. "What are you saying? Do you think you're his fated mate?" Her voice rises three notches, giving me pause.

"No, nothing like that." I backtrack. Maybe this confession was a bad idea, because what if I am his fated mate? That would change everything, for her included. Either way, I'm not sure I'm ready to confess it to her. I hope she can be trusted, but if there's anything I've learned these past months, it's that the wolves aren't always what they seem.

She continues pacing in front of me. "Good. Because if you were Ryne's fated, he'd have said something by now." Her voice shakes as she speaks, and I can tell she's starting to doubt herself. She's not even looking at me anymore, and she's muttering to herself. "If you were his fated, he would have called off the betrothal. Wolves don't deny their fated mates, Poppy. They just don't. I'm sorry."

She finally looks at me, desperation in her eyes.

"I didn't say that. But there's a lot of chemistry between us, and I like him a lot."

She gives a stiff nod. "Right. Chemistry. It's all lust or physical attraction or whatever. There's no way you're his fated." Her body stiffens, and she faces me with crossed arms and narrowed eyes. "I would appreciate if you stayed away from him now though. You understand what's at stake, right? If I don't marry him, then my whole family will die. Please, Poppy."

I nod even though I don't mean it. Because the more she talks, the less I believe her.

Ryne is my fated.

As much as I want to help save her family, it's impossible for me to stay away from Ryne. I don't even feel like I have a choice anymore. The thought alone makes me sick.

She rushes from the room, and I collapse onto my bed, my emotions swirling with guilt and worry. I already miss Joanna. She'd be able to help me figure this out.

I don't know what's worse--not being Ryne's fated mate or being his mate and still being rejected. And I stupidly confessed my feelings to Elle—the perfect luna who is supposed to marry him. Sure, I denied thinking he was my fated, but I'm pretty sure she saw right through that. I allowed my emotions to be flayed wide open for her judgment. Any other girl in this house would use that against me. All I can do now is pray that Elle isn't like the other girls here.

I groan, pushing my palms into my eyes. What was I thinking?

Chapter Nine

A scream wrenches through the air, and I jerk awake. I look at Joanna's bed, but it's empty. Someone screams again, and I leap from the cocoon of blankets. Where's Joanna? Is she okay? My mind races with images of her floating in the water, her body replacing Nova's. But then reality catches up to me.

She's safe at Grady's house.

But that doesn't explain the screaming.

I wrench open my door to find several other girls have done the same, everyone looking as equally confused and scared as I am. It's dark, and it feels like the middle of the night, but the adrenaline has us all wide awake. My eyes have quickly adjusted to the dark, and I survey the hall, looking for signs of trouble.

The screaming continues, loud and desperate. I'm pretty sure it's coming from Abi and Lexi's room. I rush to their door and stumble inside, flipping on the light. What I find will forever be burned into my brain. Blood is everywhere. Abi sits in the middle of the room, still screaming, her hands and nightdress stained crimson. My eyes scan the room, and I find Lexi's mutilated body on the floor next to the closet. Her throat has been slit, and her face scratched up. I can't even tell definitively if it's Lexi's body, but there's no mistaking that curly black hair. It was her signature, and now it's matted with blood.

Someone pushes past me. Madame Delphine and Madame Vivien stop two steps into the room. Then Madame Delphine grabs Abi by the shoulders. "What happened?"

Abi continues to scream. Madame shakes her and asks again, this time louder. "What happened?"

Abi collapses into Madame Delphine's arms, sobbing incoherently. Madame Vivien looks around the room, and then her eyes land on mine. "Can you tell me what happened?"

Ever since the Wolf Moon Festival, the woman has taken it easier on me, but tonight the edge has returned to her voice and the venom to her eyes. Does she suspect I had something to do with this?

"No. I just got here." I hold up my hands and shake my head. "I have no idea." A few girls crowd in behind me, and several of them begin to cry.

There's no denying Lexi was murdered.

She was never very kind to me, and she'd made enemies with a lot of the claimed in the house with her snooty attitude, but nobody deserves this kind of death. Lexi was easily the smartest girl in the house. She excelled in every subject and was top of the leaderboard. She had so much promise. No wonder she was killed. She was practically guaranteed a beta.

My mind reels with the implications as I stare at her mutilated body, unable to take my eyes off of her. I can't believe I thought she was the murderer. I'm a horrible detective and no closer to finding the killer. Joanna was right. No girl could possibly have inflicted that kind of damage to a body. But a lycan could.

I step back into the hallway and look around at my fellow claimed, my mind racing through the very real possibility that one of them could be next. I used to look at all of them like suspects, and now I see them as future victims. Someone is after us. The distillery girls huddle together, their faces ashen as they whisper to each other. The rest of the girls appear to be in shock, none of them speaking at all.

I press myself up against the wall and listen when Abi finally speaks. Her voice is so overcome by sobs that it's hard to understand her. "I––I had to go to the bathroom and... and when I came back, I didn't want to turn on the lights and wake up Lexi, so I just came in, but then I tripped over something, and it was her body and..." She's overcome with hysterics, and once again her voice is lost to the horror of it all.

Madame Delphine closes the door, leaving us out here to speculate.

"Did you see the body?" Blair appears next to me. She's one of the distillery girls, and I think this might be the first time she's addressed me personally.

I blink and turn to her. "Yeah."

"Well?" Faye comes to Blair's side and threads her arm through her friend's. "What did it look like? Someone slit her throat."

I open and close my mouth a few times, remembering again exactly what I saw. This wasn't a clean death. "Actually, it looked like Lexi was attacked by a lycan."

"That's impossible," Faye scoffs. "It's not a full moon, you idiot."

"Do you think the lycan can turn on nights that aren't full moons?" Alyssa approaches. At least she doesn't call me an idiot. Everyone is listening to our conversation now, and that question alone increases the tension tenfold.

Faye sends Alyssa a scathing look. "Don't be stupid. Of course, it wasn't a lycan. It had to have been one of us." She turns on me. "You were the first one in there, weren't you, Poppy? Hmm, can you explain why you got there so fast when your room is literally on the other end of the floor?"

I shake my head, unprepared to defend myself.

"That's what I thought." She glares. "Everyone needs to stay away from you. Don't think you're fooling us with this innocent act."

"That's enough, girls." Madame Vivien slips into the hall. Her hands are streaked with blood, and her eyes are rimmed in tears. "Go back to bed. We'll conduct interviews in the morning to see if anyone saw anything. For now, it's best if you don't talk among yourselves anymore. We wouldn't want anyone's stories to get tainted by false information."

We disperse, but I can still hear Faye whispering. "See, they definitely think it was one of us."

She's going to convince them all to turn on me, that's if she hasn't already done so. I can feel it deep down to my center. Maybe I should have gone to stay with Joanna and Grady. Maybe I still can. This whole time I was worried about Joanna getting targeted, and now Lexi is dead. If that's the case, that any of us could be murdered, then I need to be extra careful. Everyone here hates me.

But I don't need to worry about being blamed for this one by anyone who saw the body. Everyone who stepped in that room knows the truth as well as I do. How could a human girl do that to someone in such a short amount of time? Answer: she couldn't. There isn't a girl in this house who could inflict deadly wounds with claws and teeth. And if a lycan couldn't have been here since it's not the full moon, then there's only one reasonable explanation.

A wolf did this.

* * *

I lie awake for hours. There is no way I can sleep after seeing Lexi's body. What wolf would want her dead and why? I think about all the times I saw Lexi with one of the betas. She always stayed near them but was never overbearing like Faye. Her single dates had been with Anders and Justin.

Justin wouldn't do this. He was too nice.

But Anders.

Maybe.

The question still remains as to why. Not to mention that he'd have to sneak in here in the middle of the night and risk getting caught. She went on a date with him ages ago, so if she did something to make him mad, this would've been a delayed reaction.

I roll over and punch the pillow. Sleep will never come for me now. I sit up and flick on the light, grabbing the book about roses that Justin's mom gave me, trying to read it. I understand most of the words, but some of the bigger ones still elude me. It's not exciting, but at least I'm not constantly picturing Lexi's blood all over the place. I read for an hour or so and then peek outside my window. It's still dark, but maybe I can go for a run.

I shiver.

Whoever killed Lexi might still be out there. I think I'll wait for daylight hours and company. But I can't stay in my room anymore. I want to crawl out of my skin. Instead I head for the showers. I'll have to take another one after we workout, but at least I can get out of my room.

I push open the door to hear sobbing coming from one of the stalls.

"Hello," I call, but no one responds. I find the stall where the crying is coming from. "Are you okay?"

Whoever is in there continues to cry. I pull the shower curtain back an inch and peek in. Abi is sitting on the floor in the corner, her limp black hair hanging in sheets around her face. She's curled into a tiny ball, and I can't see her face, but her whole body is shaking. She's still wearing her bloodstained nightgown, and water pours from the showerhead. She's sopping wet but doesn't seem to notice or care.

I sink down onto the floor and wrap my arms around her tiny frame. She jerks her head up and then collapses into me. I hold her while she cries, and eventually she pulls away and wipes at her face. Her wide almond eyes are rimmed red, and her lips are puffy.

"I . . . I . . . I'm sorry," she says, her breath still heaving.

"It's okay. If that had been Joanna, I'd be a mess too."

"They took her body away, and Madame Vivien helped me clean up the blood, but they wanted me to just sleep there. I couldn't."

"Of course you couldn't. Listen, Joanna isn't staying in my room anymore. You can stay there. You don't ever have to go back into that room again. If you want, I'll even go get your clothes and stuff for you."

She nods, but her gaze is unfocused.

"How long have you been here?" I ask.

She shrugs. "I don't know. A while."

"You need sleep. Come on."

I help her up and back to my room. I get her clothes and even help her change. She falls onto Joanna's bed, and I tuck her under the covers. She starts to cry again, so I climb in with her and hold her until she falls asleep. Once she's settled, I extract myself from her and sit back on my own bed. I really do want a shower, but I don't want to leave Abi alone. She looks so small and broken.

If Joanna had been the one murdered, would anyone have been as nice to me?

I seriously doubt it.

But this isn't about me, and I realize I've been so wrapped up in my drama with Ryne that I've lost focus on what's important. These girls need my help. I don't know how, but one way or another, I'm going to find a way to save them.

Chapter Ten

The door flings open early the next morning, and Joanna bounces in. "You are totally forgiven," she announces. "Grady's bed is the most comfortable place I've ever slept in my life."

I raise my eyebrows at her. "Grady's bed?"

She climbs into my bed and smacks me on the shoulder. "Shut up. But yeah." Her face flushes. This is the first time I've ever seen her embarrassed. Are the rules different because Joanna and Grady are fated? Probably.

"Don't tell anyone, okay?" she whispers. "I don't want them to ruin this for me."

I understand because I'd feel the same way in her position. "So what happened? Did you, you know?" I ask in a hushed voice, raising my eyebrows.

"We're going to wait until the wedding, but we still fooled around a little," she admits with a wide smile. "I can't help myself, Poppy. He's too perfect."

"I'm happy for you."

She rolls onto her back, and I spot a necklace I've never seen her wear before. "What's that?" I ask. It's got a pretty gold chain with a white jeweled heart.

Joanna's fingers fly to it. "Oh, it's from Grady. It was his mom's."

My eyes flick over to her bed where Abi still sleeps. In spite of Joanna's noise, she hasn't stirred. Either that, or she's pretending to sleep while listening, but I don't think so. Abi isn't the type.

Joanna follows my gaze. "You've replaced me already?"

She pulls a bag out of her pocket and offers me a piece of red candy. I shake my head. "Something happened last night," I confess. "Something bad."

I tell her about Lexi's murder and everything I saw. Her face goes ashen, and her hands shake as I tell the story. "She had to have been targeted," I conclude, cuddling into Joanna's side and wishing she could somehow wipe my memory so we didn't have to have this conversation. "There's no other explanation for Lexi being killed like that."

Joanna finally speaks, her voice much calmer than her trembling hands. "So someone must have been waiting in or near the house, watching for Abi to leave Lexi alone in the room. Then he went in there, shifted into his wolf, ripped her throat out, and then left before anyone saw him."

"That's what I think. As much as I wish it weren't true, it's the only thing that makes sense."

"And he was fast, too," Abi's scratchy voice filters from across the room. She rolls over, stretching her arms over her head and wiping at her puffy eyes. "I couldn't have been gone for more than four or five minutes."

We all sit up and stare at each other from across the room. "Did you see anything weird lately with Lexi?" I ask.

Next to me, Joanna's hands continue to tremble. She brushes her hair out of her face but doesn't say anything.

Abi shakes her head. "I dunno, maybe. Lexi mostly kept to herself. I didn't hang out with her enough to know if something was going on. We were only roommates, you know?"

Abi's one of the wannabe distillery girls who's been trying, and failing, to get in with Faye's crew. I wonder what she thinks about being in here with me. Maybe she'll act like Charlotte did and ditch me the first chance she gets.

"What about Samantha? Do you think she'd know anything?" Samantha is Lexi's best friend in the house.

Abi shakes her head. "She and Samantha had a falling out recently. I would suspect she had something to do with it if I hadn't seen the evidence of a wolf attack."

The sun brightens through the windowpane, and there's no more time to chat. We get dressed in our workout gear and head out for our morning exercises. Joanna's movements are jumpy, and she keeps a close eye on Abi.

"You okay?" I ask as we tromp down the stairs behind everyone else. No one will get close to Abi now.

"What? Yeah. Of course I am."

I nudge her. "Is this about last night at Grady's? Did something else happen?"

She sighs dramatically. "Nothing happened beyond what we talked about. I told you I'm fine."

She moves in front of me and shoves a few other girls out of the way. She's not fine, but I don't know what her problem is. She's probably still thrown off by Lexi's death. We all are. I loop my arm through Abi's, and she gives me a forced smile.

I wonder if Madame Vivien is going to go easy on me, or if she'll single me out again like she did after Charlotte turned. Or maybe she'll go after another unsuspecting victim.

But she's not there.

Ryne is.

No betas. No madames. Only the alpha.

"Ladies, please take a seat on the grass. No talking among yourselves. You're welcome to exercise if you'd like or sit and relax. Please spread out so you aren't near anyone else. I'm going to be personally conducting interviews regarding Lexi's death."

Ryne's expression is guarded, but I can see that his eyes are haunted and tired. If there's nobody else here to conduct interviews, that must mean he's considering everyone to be a suspect. This must be hard on him. I want to go to him and comfort him, but that's Elle's job. She's not here either.

I lie flat on the grass and stare up into the blue sky. It's cold, but spring is fast approaching, and with only a few months until the next festival, I know I should be focusing on the leaderboard and the betas. But it's like my body is attuned to Ryne. Even though I'm not watching him, I can feel as he walks from girl to girl, sitting down with them to quietly discuss what they know of last night.

Eventually, he sits next to me. The tips of our fingers touch, not enough for anyone to notice, but enough to send my mind spinning.

"Can you tell me about what you experienced last night?" His voice is gentle, and I look over to meet his eyes. This is the man who kissed me so passionately and then acted like I meant nothing the second his intended opened the car door. I should be angry with him. No, I *am* angry with him. I snatch my hand away and fold it over my chest, then tell him everything he wants to know.

"How can you be sure it was a wolf?" he asks.

"Because her throat was ripped out, and her face was all scratched up. She looked exactly like the girls who were killed by the lycans. Well, not exactly. This seemed a little more controlled."

"Someone could've tried to make it look like a wolf attack."

"But Abi said it was fast, less than five minutes. If someone was trying to make it look like that, they'd have to take more time."

"Unless it was Abi," he retorts.

I sit up and look him straight in the eyes, ready to argue that there is no way Abi did it, but as I meet the stormy blue, I lose my words. Both my mind and my body betray me. I want nothing more than to climb into his lap and feel him press up against me. I want to kiss those lips and run my fingers through his unruly hair.

I want him to ask about us or to give me any indication that he feels the same feelings I do. But he drops his eyes.

"Is there anything else you saw?" he asks.

I fling myself back onto the ground, knowing if I keep looking at him, I'll do something stupid.

"No. That was it. It was a wolf. I know it."

He drops down next to me and brings his lips right up to my ear. "I believe you. But be careful who you share that with." He stays there for a brief moment, his breath hot on the side of my face.

Then he's gone, leaving me for the next girl.

Chapter Eleven

Elle sits across from me at the table. After Ryne finished interrogating us, he sent us on a quick run around the field and then straight on to breakfast. He kept his eyes on me the whole time, and I couldn't help but look back. I don't even care if anyone notices my feelings anymore, least of all him. He should know how I feel and be held accountable for leading me on. But now he's gone, replaced by the watchful eye of Madame Delphine. The girls are quiet, most staring blankly into their breakfasts. I stir the oatmeal around listlessly.

"I heard you found Lexi," Elle addresses Abi in a tender voice.

Joanna stiffens. "So?" she says accusingly, jumping in to defend Abi.

It doesn't faze Elle one bit. She keeps her compassionate gaze locked on Abi and continues. "So, that must've been hard for Abi."

Abi stiffens next to me, and I look over. Tears slip from her eyes. She hasn't stopped crying all morning. I hand her my napkin to use as a tissue, and she takes it from me. She's a pretty girl with lovely Asian features, and I hate to see her so upset. But I don't blame her, nor do I judge her. She could cry for days and days, and I'd understand. I did the same thing when Willow died. Growing up, we weren't strangers to death, and it was always sad. But to see it happen violently with my own two eyes––to smell the blood and hear pleading screams snuffed out? That's different. It changes a person forever.

Faye comes over and sits next to Elle, twirling her auburn hair around her finger as if it's any normal morning. She's never sat with us before, and I immediately suspect her motives. Elle gives her a tight smile. I expect Joanna to say something snarky, but she doesn't. I want to get her alone so she can tell me what's going on with her because she's definitely been acting strange ever since she found out about Lexi. I think she knows something.

"Everyone thinks you and Abi killed Lexi." Faye looks right at me, daring me to argue with her.

Abi gasps and collapses into sobs again.

"What are you talking about?" I ask, putting an arm around Abi.

"Oh, don't play stupid. I saw you leave the room. You two were in on it together."

"That's not what happened." This is so ridiculous. I can't believe she thinks those accusations will stick.

"Oh really? Because Lexi was about to land Cade, and you couldn't stand it. And Abi has always been jealous of her." By this point, several of the distillery girls are standing behind Faye as if to back her up. "You're both going down."

I want to jump in and tell them that they're wrong, that it was a wolf who did it, but I remember what Ryne asked and force myself to keep my mouth shut. Abi peels herself from my arms and sprints from the room, Elle and Joanna following close behind. I know they want to make sure she's okay, but I'm left here with no backup.

I stack their plates on my own and stand to carry everything to the kitchen.

"What?" Emma steps in front of me to block my path. "Aren't you going to defend yourself?"

I try to move past her, but she won't let me.

"She can't," Joy interjects. "She knows she's guilty." They're surrounding me on all sides now. The only way to get past would be to shove them, which is probably what Faye wants. She knows how to provoke me. I close my eyes and count to ten.

"We're not going to let you get away with this," Blair adds. "We already told Ryne everything."

That does it. My eyes pop open. "It wasn't me," I snap. "And it wasn't Abi. And Ryne knows it."

"Hmm—well, I guess we'll see about that," Faye says. "You know, someone really ought to warn the betas about you, Poppy."

That makes my cheeks go hot. I hadn't thought of that. I know Ryne will believe me, but what if these girls are successful in poisoning the betas against me?

"Why do you hate me so much?" I'm shaking now. A fork clatters to the hardwood.

But I think I already know the answer. It's because they can tell there's a strong connection between me and Ryne, and Faye has sensed it since the first day. That and she's a bully who recruits other bullies. They want to take everyone else down so that all the distillery girls get to stick together and end up as the beta wives. If the alpha likes me, there's a good chance he'll save me from the mating houses. Faye can't have that.

Right as Faye's about to open her mouth to answer, Madame Delphine sweeps into the room. "Alright, girls," she announces, "it's time to move on to your chores, and then we'll start the lessons. Don't bother changing out of your workout gear into your dresses though," she adds. "Today we're having a special combat session downstairs in the gym."

We disperse, and my mind whirls. Part of me is still caught up in the altercation I just had, but the other part of me is thinking ahead to the future. After Charlotte died, I argued with the shifters about our combat training but had been stonewalled. Truth is, we haven't been learning enough. We don't only need to know hand-to-hand combat. We need to know how to use weapons. We can't properly protect ourselves and can't count on others to do it for us.

We need to learn how to fight off lycans . . . and wolves.

Last night proved it.

* * *

As we take our positions in the gym, I study the betas with new eyes. One of them probably killed Lexi. Sure, it could've been any wolf, but the more I think about it, the more I think it was one of our betas. Who else knows the manor like the betas? Who else even knew Lexi? It only makes sense that it would've been one of them, and now I want to figure out who it is before they do it again.

Of course, my first thought is Anders. Even though he hasn't been around much lately, I still wouldn't put it past him. But that could just be because I hate him, and I know how violent he can be. I can't let my prejudice cloud my judgment if I'm going to find the killer.

Fact is, all these men are trained killers.

Every. Single. One.

So who was it and why? Did Lexi know something she shouldn't have? Did she see something? Do something?

"Poppy! Pay attention!" Ryne snaps, and I shake myself into the present. A few of the girls snicker, and I make sure to send him a glare that he promptly ignores. We're lined up along one side of the gym, in front of a myriad of silver weapons laid out on the floor.

Ryne clears his throat. "As I was saying, it takes incredible skill to kill a lycan. Bullets are mostly useless. While they are in their monster form, the only way to kill them is to sever the head from the body." He paces across the room. "You may have heard rumors that silver can kill them." Most of us nod in agreement. "Don't believe everything you hear. Silver will burn them, and if pierced with silver, it can sometimes turn them back into a human––their weakest state––but it doesn't kill them. You need to physically separate the head from the body to do that." I grimace, and he continues. "The best way to kill them is while they're in their human form, which is why we always have units out looking for their camps. They don't stay in one place for long and are excellent at staying hidden, but we've got trackers out there at all times." He nods in the direction of the wilderness, and I shiver.

What must it be like for the lycanthropes? Does the sickness affect them during the other phases of the moon or just the full moons? And most of all, I wonder if Charlotte is still out there in the wilds somewhere, living her new life in a hidden encampment.

"Wolfsbane is poisonous to their kind, making them sick. It's another tool we can use against them, which is why our kind grows it in mass quantities up north." He stops and stares us down, lifting a dried purple flower between his fingers. "It doesn't grow in our soil, so we don't have that advantage here. Never underestimate a lycan. They heal faster than shifters. They're bigger and stronger and bloodthirsty. If you are fortunate enough to weaken one, do not hesitate to kill it."

Ryne hands the dried wolfsbane to Elle, tosses a long sword to Grady, then picks up another and lunges for him. Joanna jerks forward, but I grip her arm and pull her back. Elle grabs her other side. "Let me go," Joanna growls.

"No, watch," I say, pointing at them. They dance around each other with the swords. "He's showing us how they work. Ryne's not going to hurt Grady."

Joanna calms, and we watch them, mesmerized by their violent dance. It's almost elegant, the way they move, but there's an aggression there that I wouldn't want to be on the other side of. Eventually, Grady gains the upper hand and flings the sword out of Ryne's grip. Grady lowers his own sword and steps back.

Ryne hunches over, breathing hard, and then claps Grady on the shoulder. "As you can see, Grady is my swordsman. He has bested anyone he's ever taken on. He's beheaded his share of lycans as well. He'll be showing you how to use the sword. Anders has the axe, Justin the pair of long daggers, Nico is best with a bow and arrow, and Cade will show you how to throw stars. Once we are comfortable with your skill levels with the weapons, you will all be given one to sleep with. We don't want any of you vulnerable again."

For about an hour, they have us test the various weapons. I do best with the sword and the axe, and I'm awful at the stars.

Ryne gathers us all back together. "You'll train in all weapons, but you'll start with the ones you're strongest in."

My hand shoots in the air.

"Yes, Poppy?" he says slowly.

"If a lycan can only be killed by decapitation, then why are we using some of these smaller weapons?"

He studies me for a second. "Close hand-to-hand combat will be useful for you. No more questions." He walks away.

I frown at his back, then go with Faye, Harlow, Samantha, and Blair to learn swords with Grady. I'm not all that crazy about being in a group with Faye, but at least I didn't have to be in Anders's group.

"I didn't hear Ryne call your name," I say to Elle.

She smirks. "I'm a house mother here, remember? Plus, I already know how to wield all those weapons."

Of course she does. I try not to get any more jealous than I already am of her. "What's your favorite?"

"The daggers. But against a lycan, I'd rather wield an axe."

Exactly. She just made my point.

Some of the weapons we're learning don't make sense with his lecture about the lycans. Because Ryne isn't only worried about lycans attacking us. Of course not. It was a wolf who killed Lexi. Maybe our enemies are more widespread than I know. Besides, I overheard Ryne tell his father that he wanted to expand into panther shifter territory. I don't know how many species of shifters are out there, but I'd wager there are more than wolves and panthers.

The thought strikes me that perhaps one of them killed Lexi, but then I shake it away. That wouldn't make sense. Why would any of them care about her? Or Nova, for that matter.

The fact that Ryne is arming us all makes me feel a little better. It means he doesn't necessarily believe it was one of us girls who is to blame. I hope he's finally taking my pleas for help seriously.

Grady goes over basic sword handling and maneuvering. He gives us sticks to practice with and then puts us in pairs. Since there is an odd number, he partners with Harlow and pairs me with Faye, which I cannot figure out because he knows I can't stand her.

He hands me a stick and leans over to whisper in my ear. "Kick her ass."

I grin. I'm going to be better than her, and he knows it.

Grady backs up and stiffens, dropping the rest of the sticks he's holding, and shoving roughly past me. I spin to see him rushing for Anders's group, where he's teaching the girls how to wield an axe. Anders is fighting with one of the girls, axes in hand, and my stomach tightens. It's Joanna, and he's much stronger than she is. If he's not careful, he's going to kill her.

Grady jumps between Anders and Joanna, knocking the axe out of Anders's hand. It falls to the floor with a metallic thud. "What are you trying to do?" he accuses. Everyone in the room freezes and turns to watch. The energy is thick with aggression—wolves are close at hand.

"You really think that if she goes up against a lycan, they are going to go easy on her?" Anders spits. "I'm trying to teach her to be strong and fight."

"That won't happen if you kill her first."

His words hang as heavy as the axes, and the room goes silent.

Chapter Twelve

"You're both right," Ryne interjects, striding to stand between them. "Anders needs to be careful with the women, especially a fated mate like Joanna." He glares at the man. "It would be wise to remember your strength and keep your temper in check."

I scoff. If only Anders had managed that on the harvest day, Willow would still be alive.

"And you." Ryne points to Grady. "You need to stop coddling your mate and stop assuming everyone is out to get her. If you really believe she's a target, then why not get her prepared to fight off anyone who could hurt her? You and I both know you're not always going to be there to protect her."

The men are practically dripping with anger, but they nod and bow their heads to their alpha. Then everything goes back to normal, or as much as it can after that outburst. Maybe stuff like that is normal in the pack, but it's not normal to me. Arguments always had a way of stirring up trouble back home, and I wonder if the same will happen among the betas. As we go back to training, I can't stop thinking about what just happened. This place is brutal. Back home, nobody died from lycan attacks, and we certainly didn't need to train in weapons, but we were told that we needed the shifters' protection against the lycans. Maybe they simply took care of it, and I took it for granted.

I turn back to Faye, my priority shifting to knocking the snot out of her with this stick. I guess this place has rubbed off on me more than I thought.

I raise an eyebrow. "Are you ready?"

She doesn't even bother to answer before diving forward and knocking me on the shins. I wince, falling to my knees. I don't have time to worry about the pain. I whip my stick up, misjudging where she is.

Her stick flies at my face, but I roll out of the way right as it swishes past me and cracks against the gym floor. I kick out, using my combat training to swipe her off her feet. We're on the ground in a tumble of sticks and punches and grunts. I jab the end of my stick into her stomach, and she screams, then bobs her head toward me and bites my arm. Actually bites me!

"Are you crazy?" I scream, ripping my arm away from her. Blood beads along the wound. She spits the blood out with a sadistic grin. Okay, I'm done going easy on her. I jump up, but so does she. We circle each other. In my periphery, I can tell people are watching, but they're nothing to me. All my focus is on Faye.

Faye, who tried to get me sent to the mating house.

Faye, who's treated me and so many others like garbage from day one.

Faye, who said my sister was a whore who deserved to die.

Anger burns inside, growing to an inferno, and I lash out with a battle cry. Her eyes widen, and she screeches, stumbling back. I swing my stick forward, prepared to take her down and take her out, but someone catches it.

Justin.

"Alright, you two." He laughs, as if this whole thing is hilarious. "Settle down. We wouldn't want anyone getting hurt."

I'm not sure if he's protecting me because of our recent date or Faye because they've been all over each other on more than one occasion. Either way, I couldn't care what Justin thinks at this moment. Faye is going down.

I jerk my stick from his hands and nod to Faye. "You giving up?"

She scoffs. "No. I'm not scared of you."

"Then let's fight." I glare at Justin. "It's wood. We're not going to kill each other. We need to learn, like your alpha said." I search for Ryne, but he's deep in conversation with Anders and not paying attention to us. All the better.

Justin shakes his head, "Nope, not on my watch."

"You're not our group leader. Grady is." I use my free hand to brush the hair that fell from its braid out of my face.

"Do you see Grady anywhere?" He looks around, and I notice that he's gone. So is Joanna. Go figure.

I throw my stick to the ground. "Fine. Whatever."

Faye laughs. "Why do you always have to be so dramatic?" She bats her eyelashes at Justin. "She's always like this. If you want to know who causes the most problems in the house, look no further. Not to mention, she's obviously dangerous. I'm pretty sure she wants to take all the girls out. You heard about Lexi, right?"

"I'm not listening to your garbage," I argue. "I'm finding a new weapon."

I turn to survey the weapons training happening all around me. All the while, my hands are shaking, and my heart is pounding. I'm so angry I could scream, but I can't. If all I can do is throw weapons around, then so be it. Elle had said the daggers weren't the best for lycans, but if I can cut one with silver daggers, then I could weaken it enough to kill it, right? And anyway, I could certainly use it if someone comes to kill me in my sleep. Since Justin seems to have given up on the daggers to take over for Grady, I head over to Elle.

I catch her eye and hold up the daggers. They're thin and about as long as my hand, reminding me of sharpened nails. "I'm all yours now," I say. "Teach me your ways."

Elle laughs, but we get to work. The entire time I can feel Ryne watching us. I'm kind of proud of myself though. One, for not watching him back. Two, for walking away from the situation with Faye instead of letting her provoke me further in front of everyone. And three, for staying down here at all. Because there had been a moment when I wanted to walk away, to storm from the gym and take the point deduction for the day.

The old Poppy would've done just that, but I'm trying to be better these days. I need to keep my head on straight and my emotions in check if I'm going to figure out who this murderer is. I need to find them. Because if I don't, it's very possible I could be next.

* * *

That night, Abi shuts our door as soon as we go to bed.

"I know who killed Lexi," she blurts.

"What? How?"

"I didn't realize it until today. Like, I don't know. I was a bitch, and I never paid much attention to Lexi, right? Anyway, after her date with

Cade, she came home crying and said he'd taken advantage of her. Of course I didn't ask how or why. I was tired, so I told her to go to bed and stop making so much noise." Abi chokes out a sob and covers her mouth. I stand and wrap her in a tight hug, waiting for her to calm down.

She sucks in a few breaths. "I was so horrible to her."

We sit down on the bed, and once her breathing slows, I ask her the most important question. "Why do you think Cade killed her?" Because honestly, Cade hasn't come across my radar at all. He's a flirt, but he always seemed harmless to me. But now that I know he took advantage of Lexi, my opinion of him sours. Did he rape her? I still didn't follow why he would've killed her over something like that, but maybe there was more to the story.

"Isn't it obvious? She was probably going to tell Ryne about what happened. I didn't think about it until Bailey mentioned today that if a beta has sex with one of the claimed before they're married, then he's exiled."

My mouth pops open. I didn't know that. I know we are supposed to stay virginal and that the wolves get to be hypocrites about sex. I know that the king acts like he is above the rules. I know he wants me to be sent to a mating house, and when that didn't happen, he roughed Faye up. "Are you sure that's one of the rules?"

She nods vigorously. "Yeah, Bailey found some old book about it in the library. That's when I put it all together. Don't you see? We're supposed to be virgins for the beta who picks us, just in case of possible pregnancies. They don't want to risk anything happening with their little heirs."

This news makes my stomach lurch. I think I'm going to be sick.

Because of my instant connection to Ryne, I've allowed myself to be blinded to many of the atrocities happening here. I'm embarrassed by my behavior and decide I need to talk to Joanna again. She said she's out of the Resistance now that she's staying with Grady, but I wonder how much of that is true. Maybe she could at least point me in the right direction. A thought strikes me. *Maybe that direction is here in this house...*

"What happens to the girl?" I ask softly.

"She's ruined. They send her to a mating house."

My hands fist into angry balls. "Then Lexi had no incentive to tell Ryne." I hate to say it, but it's true. A woman would be forced to keep quiet or risk losing her chances at a somewhat normal life. And the wolves? I'm sure they know that. Cade could've easily taken advantage.

"Cade didn't care what he did to her." Abi's voice goes hard. "Lexi wasn't the type to sweep something like that under the rug. What if she confronted him? He would've done anything to avoid being exiled, even killing her to keep her mouth shut."

A sinking feeling settles into my stomach.

I bet she's right.

"We have to tell Ryne," I say.

She clutches at me. "We can't."

"Why not?"

"Because if he doesn't believe us, then Cade will come after us next."

"If Cade killed Lexi, do you think he killed Nova as well?"

She nods. "That night at the festival, when Nova left, Cade left too. I remember because I was dancing with him, and he cut us off right in the middle of the song. I didn't think of it at the time, but now it makes sense. What if he tried to start something with Nova? He saw she was alone, and he wanted a taste, and when she resisted, he killed her."

I don't know if it's true, but her story adds up. Either way, he's dangerous.

I squeeze her hand. "Don't worry. We won't let him get away with this."

Chapter Thirteen

Before we can go to Ryne, Abi makes me promise to find solid proof first. She's terrified about retaliation and wants to lie low. Her guilt over what happened puts her into a terrible depression, and her scores fall a little more every day. I'm worried about her, but I don't know what to do. The full moon comes and goes without any incidents, which kind of feels like a miracle. Then we're back to classes and dating.

Tonight I'm scheduled to go on a one-on-one date with Anders.

I've spent the entire day terrified of what could happen with him. When it's time, I get dressed in the most modest outfit I can find. It's a casual date, so I'm in loose jeans, boots, and a heavy wool sweater. It's not quite weather appropriate for the sunny days we've been having, but it'll have to do. It's almost time to go downstairs to meet him when a knock sounds on the door, and Madame Delphine peeks her head in. "Poppy, can I talk to you for a minute?"

It must have something to do with Anders. My heart races as I lead her inside. Abi sits up from where she's lying on the bed. "I'll leave," she says, and then scurries out the door.

"This won't take long," Madame Delphine turns to me. "I'm sorry, but Anders is indisposed. He won't be able to take you on a date. As this isn't your fault, it won't affect your scores."

I plop onto the bed, relief flooding me. Anders is the only beta that's been gone more often than not, and I wonder what could be so important. Maybe all this dating is boring him, and he'll show up at the harvest and select from who's left. Wouldn't that be something?

"I'm sorry. You must be disappointed," she continues, but even I can hear the sarcasm in her voice. It's no secret I hate the guy.

I smile up at her, suppressing a little laugh. "This is the best news I've heard all month."

She waves me away and heads to the door.

"Madame Delphine, can I ask you something?"

She turns to me with curious eyes. I don't wait, don't let myself chicken out. I've been wanting to have this conversation and haven't had an opportunity. "What can you tell me more about the Resistance?"

She freezes, her expression tightening. "Don't speak of it," she hisses low. "Never speak of it."

"Someone has to," I retort. "It's real, isn't it?"

She holds up her hand to stop me. "I have an idea. Why don't you and Abi go outside and find a place for those poppies you're growing in the greenhouse. They should be ready to be replanted."

And with that, she's gone, the door banging closed behind her.

"That was weird," I grumble to myself.

It was also stupid. What if she can't be trusted? But I don't know, my gut keeps telling me she can. I go to the door and find Abi waiting in the hall. "Come on," I say, "let's go plant some flowers."

Hours later, when our work is done, we stand arm in arm and survey it with pride. The little green sprouts litter the entire area next to the woods. There's room for them to grow here, and hopefully spread their seeds through the field. The sepals protect the red buds as the soft wind tests them in their new homes, blowing them gently. I can't wait to see them bloom into magnificent flowers, and I hope it happens soon. The next festival is coming up, and if there's anything I know about festivals, it's that nothing is guaranteed. I may not be around to see the flowers after that. Abi pulls me into a hug––she's probably thinking the same thing.

* * *

Before we know it, more days pass, and we're halfway to another full moon. But tonight we don't need to worry about the moon. Tonight, we need to worry about more one-on-one dates. I'm hoping I've dodged Anders for good. I'm also hoping I'll be able to do some more digging around about Nova and Lexi's deaths. So far, I haven't been able to find any evidence on Cade, and I'm growing frustrated.

And worried.

I look over to my new roommate, who has quickly become another best friend, taking Joanna and me from a duo to a trio. "I'm sorry you're going out with Cade tonight," I say to Abi, trying to be cryptic because Joanna is in the room. She's flipping through the dresses in her closet as if she doesn't have a ton of great options to wear. She does, but no dress will make her feel comfortable with that man.

She scoffs but keeps her voice light. We haven't told anyone about her suspicions yet, not even Joanna. I hate keeping secrets from her, but she's closer than ever with Grady, and I don't want her to slip up and say the wrong thing.

"Yeah, I'm nervous," Abi confesses. "We already know he's handsy, and he likes to kiss all the girls, and that's in public. I'm worried about what he'll do in private."

Our thoughts travel to poor Lexi, and we grimace.

"I'm pretty sure you're the only one he hasn't kissed," she adds.

Joanna snorts from where she's lying on my bed. "He hasn't kissed me." She stands and walks over to me. I'm trying to do my hair, but it's not going so well. The humidity has started to come back with the sunshine, and my curls aren't cooperating. She takes the brush from me and immediately snags it on a knot. I wince as she tugs it. She's dressed in a pretty blue sundress with a thin white sweater. It's new. In fact, we all have new dresses for the spring season.

I jerk my head away and snatch the brush out of Joanna's hand so I can get the knot out myself without being reduced to tears. Abi gives up on the closet and slumps down on the bed. For a minute she doesn't say anything. "I don't know why I have to go out with any of them. Everyone knows I'm heading to the mating house at the Pink Moon Festival."

I whip around. "What are you talking about?"

"Ever since Lexi died, I can't seem to concentrate on anything. I'm at the bottom of the board."

Since we've had more combat training, and I'd finally mastered reading, I've been dead smack in the middle of the board and I haven't been paying attention to the last few slots. I feel bad that she's at the bottom, but I'm not sure how to help her. Everyone keeps saying the Pink Moon Festival is supposed to be fun. It's done outside in a garden, and everyone welcomes in the spring by dressing in pastels and dancing around barefoot on the grass. But I can't imagine it being fun when my friend is going to end up shipped off to a mating house by the end of it.

"Don't worry. We've gotten Poppy out of the bottom. We can do it for you too," Joanna says encouragingly, grabbing a dress out of Abi's closet. "Wear this one. Cade likes green."

Abi grabs the dress absentmindedly and disappears out the door to go shower. "How do you know Cade likes green?" I ask.

She snorts. "I don't. But that dress shows off quite a bit of her cleavage, and I know Cade will appreciate that."

I want to scream, because that's the last thing Abi needs, but Joanna doesn't know what I know. So I let it go, trusting Abi to make her own choices. After we finish getting ready, we head down the stairs. I'm not nervous about my date with Nico. A handful of girls have been out with him since Nova died, and they all said basically the same thing––that he took them to his house and left them with his housekeeper to eat dinner. Then he'd bring them back and give them full points. At least he's stopped giving zero points, so I won't mind the leg up on the board.

I wonder if he'll even choose anyone at the harvest moon. Is it possible to back out?

Nico meets me at the door. He's wearing a black suit, including a black shirt and tie. He is handsome, but in a different way than Ryne. He's thin with an angular face and curly chestnut hair. He keeps the sides shaved, but it's long on the top, so hair is always falling into his stormy gray eyes. His complexion is the opposite of Anders, but now that I know the relation, I can't help but see the resemblances. They have the same build, the same face structure, and even some of the same mannerisms.

He gives me a forced smile and holds out his arm. "Shall we?" he asks.

I nod and glance over at the other girls. Joanna greets Grady with a long kiss, and Cade can't keep his eyes off of Abi's cleavage. She wore the green dress. Anders is with Faye, and Justin looks uncomfortable with Bailey, who won't even meet his eyes.

Nico and I get into a waiting car. This one is smaller than Ryne's but prettier. It's bright red and all curves. Nico drives, and I kind of want to learn. What was it like for Knox to learn to drive? I wish he and I could actually have a conversation about it. I wish I could have a conversation with him about anything, for that matter.

"I thought you all had drivers," I say, running my fingers along the smooth leather.

Nico gives me a quick glance. "I like to drive. You might want to buckle up."

I slip on the seatbelt and take a deep breath.

"Are you ready?" he asks.

I nod. The car takes off, flying down the road, and I scream. I had no idea cars could go this fast. Nico lets out a whoop, and the gorgeous machine goes even faster. The engine is so much louder than the one in Ryne's black car. It vibrates to the point that I can feel it in my bones.

I let out a nervous laugh. This is the first time I've seen Nico smile since Nova died. We arrive in town faster than I even thought was possible, and Nico slows the car down.

"Fun, huh?" There's something about him that is so entirely different from his father, and I realize I've been tense around him for reasons that aren't his fault. Maybe he's nothing like Anders.

"A little. It was scary." I offer him a genuine smile.

"You'll get used to it."

He pulls up in front of a bright blue house right on the water. "Where are we?" I ask.

"My house."

I deflate. Looks like I'll be eating with his housekeeper. At least he doesn't live with Anders anymore. Since they buried Nova on Anders's property at the family graveyard, I wondered if that meant he still lived there.

"We won't stay long, but I want to introduce you to Mattie, my housekeeper. Then we'll join all the others for dinner at Ryne's house."

I blink at him because none of what he said makes an ounce of sense. "Why do you want to introduce me to Mattie?"

He bites his bottom lip. "Well, I've had a difficult time since Nova died, but I'm obligated to choose a wife. Nova confided in me your fears of being sent to the mating house and of my father. She told me that you deserved better and made me promise to help you if I could." He clears his throat. "So that's why I've chosen you to be my wife. We'll have to keep up appearances of course, and we can't tell anyone." He takes both of my hands in his. "I don't expect this to be a marriage of love at all. Maybe eventually, but it will be a deep friendship. I hope that is acceptable to you."

When I don't say anything, he smiles conspiratorially. Then he jumps out of the car and comes around to open my door. I sit there in stunned silence, and he squats next to me. "You okay? You look a little pale."

I blink at him. "Did you just propose to me?"

He chuckles and runs a hand through his hair. "I guess so, yeah. Well, what do you say? Be my wife?"

Chapter Fourteen

"I don't even know *what* to say," I sputter. "Are you allowed to ask me this early? Don't you have to wait until the Harvest Moon Festival?"

He grimaces. "I take it, that's a no?"

Is it? I would be stupid to say no. This is exactly what I've been wanting. Nico would be perfect. He is looking for a friendship and someone to give him space to grieve his true mate. Marrying him would keep me out of so many dangerous situations that could ruin my life.

Ryne's face pops into my head.

Ryne—who wants to marry Elle.

This is not what my heart has longed for, but he is my best option. Justin's face flashes in my mind. He would be a good mate as well, but there's no guarantee he'll choose me. Nico could still change his mind by the fall, but if he doesn't, this could be what I've been waiting for.

"It's a yes," I say at last.

"Good." He hugs me awkwardly. We don't kiss, thank goodness.

He takes me inside the beautiful home and explains that we can't tell anyone we're secretly engaged because it might put a target on my head. I have to agree with him there, but I don't tell him why. I'm not sure I'm ready to open up to him about my sad little investigation, not to mention the fact that Ryne asked me to keep things quiet. If Nico knew what I knew, he'd go mad trying to find Nova's killer. It might be better for him not to know.

But Ryne has been ignoring me for ages, spending all his free time dating Elle, and I'm growing tired of nursing my broken heart.

Maybe I should confide in Nico after all.

We go from room to room of his home, and he shows me his library and music room. He avoids the master bedroom. I wonder if he and Nova slept in the same bed together. I suspect they did. She loved him. They were fated and going to get married.

We head down to the kitchen, where a stout woman stands at the counter, her hands covered in flour. "What do we have here?" the woman asks.

"This is Poppy. She was a friend of Nova's. Poppy, meet Mattie."

She grabs a towel and wipes off her hands, but instead of shaking my hand, she wraps me in a tight embrace and whispers in my ear. "Any friend of Nova's is a friend of mine."

She lets me go, and tears glisten in her eyes. She wipes them with the back of her hands. "Goodness me, I'm sorry. I didn't mean to go all weepy."

Nico reaches over and squeezes her hand. "We all miss her."

Mattie clears her throat and busies herself with whatever it is she is making. "Tell me about yourself, Poppy. Where are you from?"

"Northwest. My village grew and harvested the cotton."

"Ah, nice. So you like to work outside."

"Very much so." I can't help but smile at the memories. If only I could relive them, I'd be so grateful for all of it, even the hardest days.

"What of your family?"

It's odd. She's the first person to ask me about my family since I've arrived. A twinge of homesickness pricks my heart. "My mother and father are good people. I have a little brother and a twin sister." My voice catches at the mention of Willow.

"Twins, huh? I bet that was fun. So you were born first?"

I shake my head. "No. She died."

Mattie's smile falls, and her eyes fill with sympathy. "I'm sorry, my dear. Were you close?"

I drop my eyes. "She was my best friend."

Silence fills the room, and I blink back my own tears.

Nico rests his hand on my back. "We have to go. Dinner will be starting soon, and no one wants to be late for one of Ryne's dinners."

* * *

Dinner is an awkward and uncomfortable affair. A long table with white cloth has been set up in Ryne's beautiful backyard. The swimming pool reflects the moonlight in the background. It's the first time I've seen one up close, and the clear water sparkles under the stars.

We're at the end of the table, and Anders sits next to Nico, speaking too loudly the entire time and monopolizing the conversation. And his date, Faye, laughs at all his inappropriate jokes. I sit quietly through it all and pick at my food, trying and failing to avoid looking at the couple directly across from me--Ryne and Elle.

I hate that they're eating with us, but I'm also secretly happy to have Ryne so close. I could reach out and touch him if things were different. When Anders and Faye leave immediately following dessert, everyone nearby seems to be grateful. We finish up, and the other couples start to clear out. I keep waiting for Nico to suggest we leave as well, but he doesn't seem to be in any hurry.

Before I know it, it's the two of us with Elle and Ryne. And it hurts, because last time I was in this house, Ryne held me close, telling me that he wanted to kiss me.

Now, he is with his unofficial fiancée, and I guess I am too.

"Let's have drinks in the living room, shall we," Elle offers. There's no denying the tension in the air, but she does an excellent job of smoothing things over.

"Of course." I fake a smile.

I've had a hard time keeping my eyes off of Ryne all night, and he glanced at me quite a bit too. I have no idea what it means, except that I know it's not fair to Elle and Nico. Whatever's going on between me and Ryne didn't end the day of the ice-skating date, even though it should have.

We travel into the warm house. Ryne and Elle both sit in armchairs, so Nico and I take the plush couch. He slings his arm casually around me, and Ryne narrows his eyes. I snuggle into Nico, not because I want to be close to him, but simply because I want to see Ryne's reaction.

I shouldn't do it--again, it's not fair--but I can't help myself. I notice how his hands clench at the armrests on his chair, and a vein pops up in his neck. I almost laugh. He has no claim on me, and yet the slightest attention from one of the betas, and he's ready to pounce.

Nico swirls his wine in his glass. "So, Ryne, I have a question for you."

Ryne tears his eyes away from me and glowers at Nico. "Yes?"

"Well, you gave me permission to marry Nova at the wolf moon, and Poppy and I have come to an agreement, so what do you say about letting me take her on the pink moon?"

Ryne's face turns pale, then red, and then purple. He jumps out of his seat.

"What is with this girl?" he asks, and no one responds. Ryne paces in front of us, clenching and unclenching his fists. He points at me with an accusing finger. "First, Anders asked me if he could take you on the wolf moon, and then Justin asked me a couple of weeks ago for permission to marry you earlier than the harvest, and now Nico. What sorcery is this? How have you bewitched all my men?" He locks eyes on me, and I meet them defiantly. I'm not scared of him.

I keep my seat next to Nico and lay a hand on his knee. "Nico is the first man to ask me properly. You know how I feel about Anders, and I thought Justin wanted to marry Faye. Justin certainly never said a word to me about marriage." I swallow and steal a glance at Nico. His face is a mask of indifference. So much for help from him. I straighten my shoulders. If marrying Nico gets me out of the possible clutches of Anders or a mating house, I'm not going to turn that down. "I like Nico. He's a good man who will treat me right. I see no reason to wait."

Ryne jams his hands into his hair, his eyes wild. They land on Nico, sharp as an axe splitting wood. "No. Absolutely not. I only gave permission for Nova because she wasn't a claimed woman, and she was your fated mate. Poppy is neither of those things."

I raise a defiant eyebrow. "And how do you know I'm not Nico's fated as well?"

"Because he was fated to Nova, and no wolf has ever had more than one."

Elle clears her throat. "But what of Justin or Anders. Perhaps she is their fated?"

"She's not," Ryne snarls. "That's impossible."

Elle narrows her eyes but doesn't respond.

Ryne spins back and hovers over Nico. "It's already an anomaly that so many mates have been found this year. I don't expect any more. You're going to have to battle it out with the others for Poppy's hand when the harvest moon comes this autumn. What is that? Eight months?" He motions between us. "Whatever this is between you two, it can wait eight months. Now get out of my sight."

Ryne storms back to his chair and throws his weight into it. He picks up his glass from a side table and downs it with a shaking hand.

Nico stands and offers me his hand. "I think we've overstayed our welcome."

"No, not Poppy," he growls. He doesn't look up, and a sheath of black hair covers his face. "She'll go back to the house with Elle. I don't trust you alone with her tonight." He grumbles into his drink, "Or ever."

Nico looks like he wants to argue, but he doesn't. Instead he leans down and places a gentle kiss on my cheek and squeezes both of my hands with his. "I can wait eight months, but you'll have to keep working hard to stay out of the bottom two positions on the board."

I don't like that. He doesn't either. It would be so much easier to just get married now. But that's not what I want. Deep down, Nico is a consolation prize. Which is fine considering I'm the same thing to him.

"Goodnight, Nico."

"And don't you dare announce your intentions to anyone," Ryne says as Nico makes for the door. "You will both continue with the claiming as normal."

As if any of this is normal.

Nico glares invisible daggers at Ryne and leaves.

Ryne won't meet my eyes, but I can't look away. It's as if I'm daring him to look at me. Somehow, I know that if he does, he won't be able to hide the truth any longer.

Elle must sense it. She's no fool. The second we're alone, she drops her pleasantries, striding into the middle of the living room, hands on her hips and long braids swinging. "Ryne," she snaps, "tell me the truth right now, or so help me, I will leave the Carolina Pack and never look back."

He has the audacity to try to look confused, but he doesn't say anything.

"Tell me." Her tone goes dry. "Just tell me."

He shakes his head once and takes another drink.

I'm riveted, watching this whole thing unfold, glued to the couch but wanting to interrupt. I have enough common sense to keep my mouth shut. I've never been able to get Ryne to admit his true feelings for me, nor the reason behind those feelings, but I'm also not Elle.

Elle is a force of nature, a luna with confidence and power radiating from her every pore. She's not someone to be messed with, and I don't think he could lie to her even if he wanted to. He said that wolves can't lie to each other about fated mates, which is exactly what I suspect we are. And what I'm pretty sure Elle suspects as well.

She lunges for me, and I scramble back onto my couch. Part of her begins to shift, her teeth elongating, her eyes changing shape. She snarls savagely, like she's going to kill me!

Ryne is there in seconds, ripping her away and tossing her across the room. He turns on her and growls, prepared to defend me. His wolf is practically bursting to the surface.

And just like that, she's back to herself, part of her silk dress shredded. "I knew it!" She gasps. "She's your fated mate!"

Ryne has nothing to say, but he doesn't shake his head.

"She has to be," Elle continues. "There's no way you'd defend her over me if she wasn't."

This is it. Finally. Ryne's been caught, and now that the truth is out there, he'll have to accept me. "You're right," he says at last. The words rip through him as if they cause him physical pain. I sink farther into the couch.

"But I wish she weren't."

The adrenaline racing through my veins turns to ice and my heart breaks.

Elle holds his gaze. "And why's that? She's beautiful, and you obviously like her. Don't forget that I caught you guys making out."

"I can't help my attraction to her, but she's not you," he says. "I made a promise to you, Elle. And I intend to keep it."

And at that, my heart doesn't just break--it shatters.

Chapter Fifteen

"That man, I swear. I thought his father was stubborn," Elle says. We're in the car heading home. Ryne didn't utter another word to us after he said he was still going to marry Elle even though we are fated.

I don't even know how to respond. Part of me is still in shock, I think.

Knox meets my eyes in the rearview mirror. They are laced with concern. He wasn't present for the confession in the living room, but he had to have felt our energy the second we got into the car. Elle hasn't said aloud that Ryne and I are fated, but if she keeps going, she's bound to let it slip. What does he think is going on? More than that, what would he do if he knew I was fated to Ryne? Would he forgive me? Would he help me?

"We'll figure this out," Elle says, patting my leg.

"There's nothing to figure out," I choke on the words. What's done is done. If Ryne doesn't want me, then I don't want him.

Period.

Her mouth drops open in surprise. "What on earth do you mean? Of course there is. I will not stand between you. That will not end well, no matter what Ryne said back there."

I peer out the window into the darkness. I don't want to look at Elle or Knox right now. I don't even want to be having this conversation.

"I'm serious," Elle goes on. "There's got to be a way to make this work."

I let out a laugh. "What about all that stuff you said before, about needing the marriage to bring your families together or whatever?" I don't know why I'm not fighting for him at this point. Yes, I do. It's because he rejected me. Who wants to fight for someone that doesn't want you? Not me. That's for sure.

Except... I do.

I want him with my whole soul. Something about hearing him say the words changed everything. He is *my* fated. I belong with him, and he belongs to me. How could he not want me? His actions have harmed me worse than he could ever know, and I doubt I'll ever get over it.

"Knox," she says, catching me off guard. "Can you stop the car, please? Poppy and I need to continue this conversation in private."

Knox does exactly as she says, his face stony as he leaves the car.

Elle turns on me. "Listen, Poppy. None of that stuff with our parents matters now. Those things have a way of sorting themselves out when fated mates come into the picture. We'll get Thorn to understand, and my parents too."

I snort. She's losing her mind if she thinks that will go over smoothly. Who am I to them? Nothing but a stupid human girl. And Elle is a powerful luna. Together Elle and Ryne could change the course of history. They're perfect for each other.

"If I found my fated mate, I wouldn't be denying him," she says softly, "and Ryne would totally support me in that. He's been my friend for years. I can't deny him his happiness." She crosses her arms. "Don't you want to be with him?"

"Of course I do, but you heard him. He doesn't want to be with me." I try to keep the pain out of my voice.

She gives a short laugh. "That is so not true. I've suspected this for a while now. I see how he watches you. He's denying it over some sense of stupid duty. I need to talk to Madame Delphine. She'll see reason, and if anyone can convince him, it's going to be her."

I'm pretty sure Madame Delphine already knows, so Elle's little plan is useless, but I grip her arm anyway, just in case I'm wrong. "You can't tell her. You can't tell anyone."

She gapes at me. "Why the hell not?"

"Because Ryne wouldn't want you to. He obviously wants to keep this a secret, or he would've told her himself. Look, if he doesn't want me, Nico is my best option. I don't want to mess that up."

"Nico won't care."

"Yes, he will! He won't want me if he knows I'm meant for his alpha. Think about it. That's dangerous territory."

"So, what? We go on pretending?"

I nod and slink back into the seat.

She rolls her eyes. "Oh yes, I can see us all a few years from now. Both Nico and I are trapped in loveless marriages, while you and Ryne screw on the side. No thank you. Nico might not care, but I do."

I flinch away from her. I would never . . .

Maybe I don't know what I would or wouldn't do. If Ryne were to come to me even after I was married, I'm not sure I'd be able to resist him. My face burns at the thought of being a woman like that. And I'd never want to hurt Nico. Would it hurt Nico though? He doesn't want to be physical with me; he needs a wife who will leave him alone. But it would hurt Elle.

"I think you're missing your chance at happiness," Elle says. There's something in her voice that she's not telling me. I study her for a minute. I can't believe I didn't see it before.

"You don't actually want to marry Ryne, do you?"

Her face stills, and the answer is obvious. She's hoping we get together so she can have an out.

She throws the door open without answering and orders Knox back into position.

The rest of the drive is silent until the car stops in front of the manor. Knox's eyes catch mine again, and this time they're pleading, but he doesn't say anything. I wish we could talk about this. By now he's figured out the truth about my relationship with Ryne. In another life, it would have been the two of us together, but in this one, he's going to be forced to serve the man who's fated to his first love. If only I could help him get out of here, or maybe find a love of his own. But that's impossible.

So many unsaid words pass between us until he breaks our gaze.

He gets out of the car and opens our door. Elle climbs out first, still huffing, and I follow. Knox meets my eye. "I'm so sorry," he mouths to me. I nod because I don't know what else to say.

At least he doesn't hate me.

I follow Elle into the house, and she turns to me in the entryway. "I'll keep this quiet for now, but only because you asked me to. After I think this through, I might tell Delphine anyway."

"She can't make her son do anything." The only person who can do that is the alpha king, and he'd rage if his son defied him.

"Well, I have to think of what is best for me and my family. You understand, right?"

I nod, even though I'm not sure I do. I thought the best thing for her family was to marry Ryne. If this ends up in a war between her father and Thorn, there's no telling what could happen.

But I'm just a dumb claimed girl.

What do I know?

* * *

Nothing changes.

Days pass in endless monotony. The truth is out there, but Elle and Ryne continue on as if nothing happened. Neither of them is even talking to me anymore. It's as if I no longer exist. I get placed with Cade during weapons training even though I try getting in with Elle's group. Ryne thinks I need to learn the other weapons first. I don't want to be with Cade. I'm ninety percent certain he's a murderer, but out of respect for Abi, I can't say anything. I'm not too worried about him killing anyone else in our group--since he has no motive, but I don't want to go on a date with him.

At meals, Elle sits with the other groups now, forging bonds with them that feel like little knives in my back. I even tried to corner Ryne when I found him alone during one of my morning runs, but he shifted and took off into the forest before I could get a word out.

I know he saw me.

At first I was angry, but now I realize they've decided it's best to forget about me entirely, and I refuse to let them see my anger. I also refuse to be sad. Instead, I grow bitter. I shouldn't be surprised by their actions, but I am. Elle must have come to her senses about outing the situation, and Ryne is stubborn as a mule. What a match.

There's a full moon tonight, and we're only another moon cycle away from the next festival, so everyone is extra antsy in the house. Me more so than the rest of the girls because tonight is my first one-on-one date with Anders. That day he canceled and Abi and I planted the poppies instead was one of the happiest days I've had since coming here, but I guess this date had to happen eventually.

"Let me fix your hair and makeup," Joanna offers, her voice pitying. I frown at that.

"And I can pick out your outfit," Abi adds.

I'm grateful for my friends, and I know they're worried about my bitter attitude lately, but I shake my head. "I don't want to look good for

Anders. He's already going to try something, so the last thing I need is to look good because he'll probably blame whatever happens on me. I just know it."

Abi's eyes widen. "He can't. He'll get exiled if he takes your innocence."

I snort at that silly word. From my trip to the mating house, I know the wolves couldn't care less about innocence.

"You mean virginity?" I question. She goes pale, and Joanna laughs. "Do you really think he would be exiled? He's the head of the betas. Trust me, Anders has gotten away with worse." My mind flashes to images of Willow's severed body, her blood seeping into the September soil, and I don't say anything more.

I run a brush through my hair only once, skip the makeup entirely, and dress in my most unflattering gown. It's a bulky cut and lime green, casting my skin in a sickly complexion. The whole thing rustles like dead leaves when I walk.

I grin to myself. Perfect.

Chapter Sixteen

Anders takes a tight grip on my arm as we make our way down the steps and out to the ferry boat. I've decided I hate going anywhere by boat and much prefer a car, but the shifters seem to love the old-world quality of these damned boats. I sigh and climb aboard. At least we're not alone. It seems we're going on a group date today because everyone else climbs in after us.

Anders settles beside me and leans down, whispering hot breath into my ear. "You think I don't know what you're doing? No makeup and an ugly dress? It's going to take far more than that to dissuade my affections for you. In fact, knowing how desperately you want me away from you, makes me want you even more."

I try to pull away, but he tugs me closer and wraps his arm around my waist, his fingers digging into my hips. Since it's the full moon tonight, we're doing our dates in broad daylight. Madame Delphine made all the betas promise to have us back before dusk.

The boat rocks gently as Anders leads us to the back, far from the driver. Everyone else takes seats up front. We're practically alone, which makes me panic a little, but I hope that he has the decency not to try anything too awful right now. I also hope that he's not taking me back to his estate where he could get away with anything. But he can't, right? We're going on a date somewhere with everyone. And then he's bringing me back to the manor.

Maybe.

What would I do if he took me back to his estate? Would I fight or just let him have his way with me? I know if I fight, he'll kill me. But I don't know if I could bring myself to let him have me. My thoughts race to Ryne, wishing he would have the guts to accept me as his mate. Or at least keep me away from Anders. But Ryne has abandoned me.

Anders squeezes me up against his side, and I stare out over the water so I don't have to look at him. I try not to think about his disgusting body pressed against mine. He brings his face to my neck and kisses me along my hairline. I feel his hot breath under my hair and squirm. He laughs at that and kisses my jaw. Another woman might find him attractive, but I know better. Every cell in my body is screaming at me to run, but where would I go? He yanks me to him and presses his lips against mine. I keep my mouth closed and try not to cry.

This date will not end well.

Think of something else, anything else. My mind lands on the book Justin's mom gave me, and I start to recall the names of all the roses. I want to check on the poppies tomorrow. And maybe I can start growing some other plants in the greenhouse. What about irises? I wonder if Shauna could help me with those. And I'm sure the vegetable garden will need to be planted soon too. Maybe I can request it as part of my daily chores.

Anders's lips part, and I expect to feel his slimy tongue, but instead he moves back to my neck, and his teeth graze the skin. He bites down hard, and I yelp, jumping away from him. He tightens his grip on me and bites down even harder. Tears fall unbidden from my eyes, and I cry out again. I thought I was with a wolf, not a vampire. Granted, all paranormals, except for the shifters and lycans, died during the wars, but Anders would've made an excellent vampire. He's so cold and awful. Mercifully, he pulls away. I bring my hand up to my neck, expecting to find blood, but I don't.

"Good," he growls. "That will bruise nicely. Now everyone will know you're mine."

I want to protest. To tell him that I'll never be his. But I know that will only provoke him. Instead, I keep my face turned down and wipe away the tears.

He grips my chin with his free hand and forces me to look at him. His dark eyes bore into mine. There's nothing there but hate and anger. "Oh, poor Poppy, did that hurt?"

I don't give him the satisfaction of an answer.

He smashes his lips against mine again. I try to keep them shut, but he forces them open with his tongue. He shoves his long tongue into my mouth, and I gag, wiggling to get away from him. He doesn't let go.

Once again, I let myself get lost in the thoughts of the different kinds of roses––the Bonica is a light pink rose that smells amazing, the Falstaff is a huge dark red rose, the French Lace is a pretty white one . . . Rose after rose comes unbidden to my mind as Anders continues to assault my mouth.

The boat shudders against a dock, and he pulls away. My mouth feels bruised and my lips sore. Anders gives me a wicked grin. "Perhaps after the show, we'll retire to my home for a few hours. As you will be my wife, I see no reason to wait until after the harvest festival."

I don't think there are enough roses in that book for a few hours at Anders's house. I'll never agree to go with him. I'd rather die.

He leads me along a cobblestone street, and the other couples join us. Everyone is walking the same direction, and there's a general sense of excitement among the crowd. I wish my friends were here. Since there's only five betas, the other girls today aren't the type to look out for me. Maybe Anders really will try to take me back to his place.

"Where are we going?" I ask, my voice cracking.

"The Manhattan Pack has a traveling show. They are excellent performers. I never miss them when they come into town."

"Seems like everyone else enjoys them as well," I say, pointing to the other couples.

"It is a treat," he says. "You're lucky I picked you for this date, Poppy. But then again, you should get used to it. I expect my wife to be submissive and agreeable, and in return, I will lavish her with the finer things in life."

I try not to sneer at that.

The line is long once we reach the theater. I expect Anders to cut to the front, but he doesn't. Though perhaps that is because those in line are other betas and their wives. A woman walks through the crowd with a basket of flowers. She stops at each couple and puts a flower in the woman's hair and another in the lapel of the man's coat. She reaches us. "What would you like?" she asks.

I spot a poppy among the flowers and point. She grins at me, offers a knowing nod, and tucks it behind my ear.

"And you?" she asks Anders. Her smile turns fake.

He selects a yellow rose, which I recognize as a Landora.

She tucks it into his lapel and moves on.

We enter the theater, and an usher leads us up to a box with an excellent view. Moments after we sit down, Nico and Faye join us. I meet Nico's eyes, pleading with him to rescue me, but he only gives me a stiff nod.

Are we still engaged? Were we ever?

Apparently Anders thinks we're engaged, and he never even asked me. I glare at him when he's not looking, hating everything about him. I don't care that he's conventionally attractive, that he has a high title, that he's strong and wealthy. He's a bad man, and he deserves to pay for all the women he's hurt.

Grady sits down next to Bailey, and he gives me a little frown, his eyes darting to the bruise on my neck. I shake my head, and he looks away, but I can tell by the set of his jaw that he's angry. I wish Joanna were here. It's stupid that she doesn't get to come on all the dates with him, even though everyone thinks she should. What's the point otherwise? But Bailey is a nice and quiet girl, so she's perfect for something like this. Her eyes twinkle with excitement, gazing out toward the curtain. I'm happy for her.

"Pathetic," Anders grumbles, glaring right at the poor girl.

My courage sparks. "What's pathetic?" Because I can think of someone, and he's sitting right next to me.

"Bailey ought to be sent to a mating house." Anders turns on me with a low voice. "She's clearly not attractive, nor athletic, but because she's smart, she keeps her name up on the leaderboard."

I snort. "Didn't know you cared so much, Anders."

"Of course I care. All beta men care about their wives." Anders shifts a little in his seat. I can't forget that he's had several wives over the years. "And as the top beta, who my men marry is of great importance to me."

"Well, I don't think Grady minds this date," I snap back. "And Bailey is a catch."

His nostrils flare as if he smells something rancid. "Do you remember what I said the first day I met you? We want subservient and submissive. We want refined and elegant." His eyes travel down my body, as if he can see right through my ugly dress. "We want sexy and strong."

I glare because how could I not remember the first time I met this devil?

"Bailey is none of those things. But maybe you're right, and Grady doesn't mind, considering he's so infatuated with that loud-mouthed

Joanna." He grimaces. "If you ask me, she's the least desirable woman in the house. Betas should have strong wives to create strong bloodlines. Ryne should've sent her off to the mating house ages ago."

"Well, nobody asked you," I spit. I want to go on, to argue that Joanna is literally the best, but the lights flicker and dim.

Just before the show begins, Ryne and Elle slip into the back of the box. I spin, and Ryne's gaze lands on the bite mark on my neck. His eyes go dark, but before he says anything, the lights in the theater go off, and the stage lights up.

Chapter Seventeen

The next hour is filled with singing and dancing--a wonderful story unfolding between talented actors, unlike anything I've seen before. It's a kind of magic that I didn't even know existed. Everything fades into the background as I watch the stage with rapt attention. The show is a reenactment of the common fairy tale known as "Little Red Riding Hood," but in this case, the wolf is a real shifter. He shifts between man and wolf and has a love story with the girl, but she doesn't know about his wolf side. The huntsman is the girl's other love interest, who actually turns out to be the villain. The poor wolf shifter is so misunderstood, so afraid to tell Red the truth of his identity.

Just as things are getting good, the lights lift.

"What?" I squawk. "It's over?"

Anders chuckles. His arm is on the back of my chair, and he curls it around my shoulders, pulling me in. "This is only a little intermission. Don't worry. In ten minutes they'll start the rest of the show."

"Oh, good." My voice trails off when I notice his ice blue eyes staring at the mark he inflicted on my neck like it's his own personal brand.

"I have to go to the bathroom." I jump up and run out of the theater box. I don't really have to go, but ten minutes away from Anders is just what I need right now.

The second I step outside, however, I think leaving was a mistake.

The lobby is filled with large shifter men and their stylish wives, and there are far more men than women. They're not all married, I know that. I also know I'm not safe here. Not with men like these. The crowd thickens, and I catch Anders among them. He's looking for me. My heart rate speeds as I duck into the crowd, dodging bodies as I go. I bump into a few people who shoot me scathing looks. My cheeks prickle, but I don't stop to apologize. I need to get out of here. I don't want him to show me off to these people... or worse. I spot a dark hallway and hurry inside. Hopefully I can hide out here until the intermission is over. It's empty in here and cold and perfect. I lean against the wall, closing my eyes and catching my breath.

Someone grabs my arm, and I jump. "Hey!" My training kicks in, and I jerk away, readying my stance.

"It's only me." Ryne looms over me. His eyes flick to the poppy behind my ear, and his gaze softens for a brief moment. That one look sends my mind reeling. I'm angry. I'm thrilled. I don't know what I am.

"You've been avoiding me." I say the thing I've wanted to say for what feels like forever. "Why?"

He stares at me for a long moment, and I think maybe he won't answer me at all. "Because I want to keep you safe," he whispers at last. And then he glares at me, but it's not as though any of this is my problem.

I roll my eyes, fed up with his games. "How is avoiding me keeping me safe?"

He shakes his head. "You don't understand anything."

"So enlighten me."

He pauses for a second, his stormy gaze lingering on my lips before traveling over to my neck. "Did Anders do that?" His jaw pops.

I ball my hands into fists. He suddenly cares? He doesn't get to have it both ways.

"I said, did Anders do that?" His words are clipped, eyes glued to the bite mark.

"What do you think?" I spit out. "Of course he did. And he has big plans to take me back to his house tonight too."

"The hell he does." Ryne slams his fist into the plaster, bits of it breaking and falling to the ground.

And then he's gone.

I'm back to being angry. I can never get what I want from this man. Maybe I never will. Tears well in my eyes, and I wipe them away and gather myself. Now that my nerves have had a chance to calm down, I realize I'm foolish to be hiding out back here. What if it hadn't been Ryne who found me?

So I leave and wander around the lobby for the rest of the intermission, weaving through the crowds, catching bits and pieces of people's conversations. Most of it means nothing to me. A lot of the people here keep staring at me, but I try to ignore them. A few women seem interested in the poppy. Maybe it's unfashionable and childish to have a flower tucked behind my ear, but I don't care. I've recently decided they're my favorite flower.

The lights flash, and I head back to the box. I'm excited to see what happens to Red and the wolf, but I'm not excited to spend more time with Anders or to face Ryne and Elle. I find my seat, and Anders is waiting for me with a suave smile and a bag of buttery popcorn. I haven't had popcorn in ages. It was a special treat we made only on special occasions back home. I liked it okay, but it was Willow's favorite, so I take the bag and try to forget about her murderer at my side, imagining that I'm here with my sister instead. What would she have thought of all this? Would she have liked any of these betas? Would she have ended up in a mating house?

I don't know, but I'm certain she'd have fought tooth and nail to change things.

I want that to be me. I want to do something.

Nova's face flashes through my mind. After she died, I made a promise to myself that I would do something, but it's been two months, and I'm no closer to making a difference around here. I have to talk to Abi again and see if she'll finally let me go to Ryne with her suspicions about Cade. My biggest problem is that even though Cade had a motive to kill Lexi, he didn't with Nova. Unless it's like Abi said, and when he ditched her on the dance floor, it was to follow Nova. Seems unlikely. Maybe we've got nothing here. Maybe accusing Cade will only get us targeted. I don't know what to do.

The lights dim, and the show resumes. I'm not pulled into the story as quickly this time around. Instead, I study the men around me: Anders, Nico, Cade, Justin, Grady, and Ryne.

Unlike the twisted fairy tale playing out on stage, the one playing out in my life is much closer to the original story. One of these men is the Big Bad Wolf--now I need to figure out who.

Before I know it, the show is over. Despite my racing thoughts, I still found it a delightful experience. I hope that Nico and I are able to get married, and he'll bring me to the theater every time they are in town. I swallow hard. I don't much like thinking about marrying Nico because I want to be with Ryne, but he made it very clear that that'll never happen.

After that weird little exchange we had in the hallway, he went right back to ignoring me.

I stand and stretch. Anders puts a hand on my back and leans in to whisper in my ear. "Tonight is the full moon. Let's go back to my house and lose track of time so you have to stay with me all night."

I throw up a little in my mouth, then crane my neck around and meet Ryne's eyes. He very much looks like he wants to kill Anders. Well, at least Ryne's paying attention to me again, and I would gladly step aside and let him tear Anders limb from limb.

Instead, he calls out to the betas. All five men turn to him. The power Ryne wields over them is incredible. It's as if they couldn't disobey him even if they wanted to. Maybe they can't.

I use the opportunity to take a couple of steps away from Anders and run right into Nico. He glances at my neck and gives me a strained smile. I reach over and squeeze his hand. I don't want him to think that I want anyone but him.

Ryne continues. "It's still a few hours from dusk, so I've arranged to send your dates back in the cars. We need to prepare for the lycans."

I expect Anders to protest, but he doesn't. Relief fills my chest. I wonder how often I can get away with this. At some point, I'll have a private date with him that I won't be able to get out of. There are roughly seven months until the next harvest. A lot can happen in seven months.

We leave the men in the box, and Elle leads us to the cars. One is Ryne's, and Knox opens the door for me. I climb in back and get stuck between Faye and Bailey. Elle rides up front. We start to drive, and I lean back into my seat, letting my eyes drift shut. Maybe I can finally relax. That's when Faye presses her pointy finger against the mark on my neck. I flinch.

"Ooooh, looky there. Somebody's been a naughty girl." She cackles, and Bailey averts her eyes.

I slap my hand over the stupid hickey as my cheeks redden. Maybe those women weren't looking at the poppy behind my ear after all. "You're one to talk," I mutter.

She stiffens. "No, I'm not. I don't do anything with any of the betas that I don't plan to marry. Justin's the only one I've kissed."

I want to say something about Thorn and Ryne--kissing father and son in one night--but I don't because that would be unnecessarily cruel. As much as I hate her, I don't want to sink to her level.

Instead, Elle rescues me. It's the first she's spoken to me in what feels like forever. "Did you know that Justin, Nico, and Anders have all asked Ryne for permission to marry Poppy early? Looks like you might need to set your sights on Cade instead. Though I do believe he's due for a private date with Poppy next, so that might not work either."

I flush and drop my eyes. I'm not sure if that made things better or worse. Either way, Faye doesn't say another word the rest of the way home. Her anger fills up the car with her silence, and I try to inch away from her. She's definitely not happy, and an unhappy Faye is the last thing anyone needs, least of all me.

Chapter Eighteen

Joanna is staying with us tonight because Grady had to go protect the city from the lycans. She sets up a cot next to mine, and even though I hate the circumstances, I love having her back at my side. I have a long silver sword under my cot, and she has a bow and arrow. We're all armed, so if anyone tries anything tonight, they won't survive.

The full moon feels so different this time. We've been through months of these terrifying moons, but this is the first time we've actually been able to protect ourselves. Along with the sword tucked right under my cot, I have a pair of daggers under my pillow. If something comes for me, I'm not going down without a fight.

"Alright, girls," Madame Delphine says, "this is your last chance to use the restroom before we lock the door. Elle will accompany anyone who needs to go. Hurry, please. It's already starting to get dark, and the moon is rising as we speak."

Joanna widens her eyes. "Nature calls."

"I'll go too, just in case." I already went, but I drank a lot of water at dinner, and the last thing I need is to be stuck in that room with a full bladder. It used to be if someone really needed to go, she could get a chaperone, but now we're always locked in from dusk until dawn. Nobody's complained though, not after what we've witnessed.

Joanna and I stand in line to use the restroom, and Elle waits a few paces down the hallway.

Joanna goes in first, and then I do my own business. A couple of other girls were behind us. We wait with Elle, but she keeps looking at the rising moon from the little window in the hallway. "You guys head on back. I'll wait for the other two girls."

I loop my arm through Joanna's, and we head on down the stairs. We're almost to the door of the gym when Joanna stops suddenly. "What is it?" I ask, not wanting to get stuck out here.

Her hand flies to her neck, and her expression crumples. "My necklace, the one Grady gave me, it's gone."

"Maybe you left it up in the room or even in your cot? Come on, we can find it in the morning."

"No, I had it on in the bathroom. I remember looking at it in the mirror. It must've fallen off on our walk back down. It won't take long. I can't lose that necklace. It was his mother's."

Grady's parents are both dead––something he only talks to Joanna about.

The sky is fully dark now, and we can hear Elle and the other girls coming down right behind us.

"Joanna, no. We'll find it in the morning."

"I can't lose that necklace." Her voice is adamant. There's no reasoning with her when she's like this.

She shakes out of my grip and turns back to the stairs. I follow, studying the floor. A howl pierces the air, and goosebumps rise on my skin. That one sounded like a lycan, but I can't be sure. Howls freak me out no matter what.

I rush for Joanna as Elle and the other girls meet up with her. We're all standing on the steps, Elle towering over us. "Joanna, we can't be out here," Elle hisses. Her eyes are wide, and I can sense her wolf is close at hand. She could shift at any moment.

Katelyn and Alyssa rush past us and down the steps.

"It'll only take me a second," Joanna insists. "The necklace had to have fallen off between here and the bathroom."

The moon still hasn't risen above the tree line, and all the lights in the house are turned off, so it's very dark. There's no way we'll find that necklace in time.

Elle grips Joanna's arm and pushes her back. I turn and head down the stairs.

"Let me go," Joanna says frantically.

"You're putting everyone at risk by being out here. Let's go."

A growl sounds from right behind them. Something else is on the stairs with us. To think that another monster got into this house, and so soon after the moon rising, makes me whimper. I can barely make out Elle's amber eyes in the darkness, but they go cold. "Poppy, you run. Joanna, you go with her." Her determined voice lends me strength. "I'll stay and fight the lycan. Lock the door. Don't worry about me."

"What? No way. We'll stay and help," Joanna says, her words cutting off with a scream. I can barely see what's happening but manage to catch Elle shift into her silver wolf as Joanna goes down hard, a dark monster on her back.

I grab for her hand to pull her away, ignoring the growls from the huge wolf-like animal. It's so dark I can't really make out its features, but at least Elle's silver wolf is easier to see. She lunges for it, and the creature shifts off Joanna to snap at Elle. She jumps back before its jaws can close around her neck. Then it goes for her neck again, and I'm sure it's going to succeed this time. I should run, but I can't leave her like this. I take advantage of its distraction with Elle and stomp on its foot. It howls and barely misses Elle. It's enough to give her the upper hand.

"We gotta go," I cry, grabbing Joanna by the arm and dragging her toward the gym door, but she hangs equally as tight onto me, pulling me in the other direction.

"What are you doing?" I gasp.

"Trust me," she says.

The fight has moved up the stairs, so that's the last place we should go. But Joanna is determined. Against my better judgment, I follow her up the creaky steps, through the entryway, and out the front door. The cool March air hits me like a wall, and my heart slams against my ribcage.

Again, I ask her what she's doing.

"Remember when I said that the best time to run away from this place is during a full moon?" Her voice rises in excitement. "The wolves are distracted. Let's go now."

"What about that lycan that just attacked us in the house?" Or the fact that this entire area has patrols everywhere.

Joanna shakes her head. "That wasn't a lycan. That was a wolf." Her voice darkens as she says it, and goosebumps crawl across my skin. "I don't know why a wolf is targeting us girls, but it's more reason to get you out of here."

"Me? Aren't you coming too?"

She doesn't answer me. We stumble down the front steps and out into the yard. It's dead quiet, but in the distance, wolves continue to howl. Joanna hugs me and whispers low in my ear, so low that I can barely hear her. "I never lost my necklace. That was a lie to give us more time."

"You planned this?"

"Yes. And I'm sorry, but I can't leave Grady. I thought I could, but I can't do it. So I'm helping you get out of here, and then I'll come back and say that a lycan took you. All we have to do is make it to the river where the two willow trees hang out across the bank. There's a boat and someone to take you to safety waiting there. But we have to hurry."

For a second, I entertain the idea. A few months ago, I would've taken her up on it. But now I know better. Frankly, I know too much.

I wrench away from her. Running away will set off a terrible chain of events, and that's if I don't die first. And if by some miracle I make it out of here alive and go to live in this unknown place that Joanna thinks will be a safe haven, the wolves might not believe Joanna. And if they don't believe that a lycan took me, if anyone can prove that I ran away, then my family will be slaughtered.

I don't want my fate to be a warning to others. I want my fate to be what saves us all.

"No," I whisper back. "There are a lot of things I'm willing to risk, but my family isn't one of them. And besides that, I want to help the Resistance here." I can barely see her in the darkness, but the rising full moon shines across her eyes, making them sparkle. "Get me in with them *here*. Let me help *here*."

She frowns. "But I wanted to save you."

"You can't." And then I turn back to the house.

Joanna groans with frustration but follows me back. When I step inside the manor, it's even quieter than it was outside. My mind races to Elle and that wolf who attacked Joanna. Did she catch him? Stop him? Where are they now?

We tiptoe through the entryway. Part of me desperately wants to turn on a light, but I know that will alert anyone lurking about to our presence. Maybe it's safer in the dark.

"We should've brought our weapons with us," I whisper.

Joanna slips a pair of daggers from the pocket of her pajama pants. Moonlight streams in through the windows, and the daggers glint silver. "You think I wouldn't have come prepared?"

She hands me one as we step farther into the darkness.

I hold the dagger in my right hand like it's my salvation. Maybe it is. We walk as quietly and quickly as we can. Once we reach the stairs, we head down, wincing every time one of them squeaks. We reach the landing to the basement, and it's darker than ever. I step forward and nearly trip over something soft.

"Ouch," Elle's soft voice moans out. She's in her human form, naked and in pain.

We kneel down. "Are you okay?"

"Yes." But she's curled in on herself, so she's obviously not. She's holding her hands against her stomach. Something dark and sticky pools by her side.

Blood.

"You don't look okay," Joanna says.

"I'll heal fast," Elle whispers back. "Go to the gym and knock so they can let you in."

"What happened to the other guy?" I ask.

As if on cue, a low growl rumbles from the top of the stairs.

Chapter Nineteen

"Go!" Elle gasps. But I'm not leaving her here. Joanna and I pick her up and drag her toward the gym door.

"Open up!" I scream. "It's us!"

There's a scrape of metal, and a draft of cool air as the door opens. The growl turns into a snarl, and something flies toward us. We push Elle into the room, and I manage to make it in, but the wolf is back, and its jaw has a hold of Joanna's leg. It's more determined than ever.

She cries out. I throw my dagger, aiming for the beast's heart, but it's still hard to see anything. I miss and hit what I think is its shoulder, but it's enough to get him to release Joanna. We get her the rest of the way inside, and Madame Delphine slams the door shut, wrenching the lock in place. Her face pales, but she doesn't say anything. "Were any of you bit?"

I shake my head and tell her I wasn't.

"I . . . I . . . don't think so," Joanna says. It's strange seeing her scared. She's usually so fearless. But she was bit, wasn't she? It had her leg. I'm suddenly reminded of Charlotte and wonder if Joanna had been infected, if I'd have the courage to do something about it.

The lights flip on before I can find my answer.

Someone hands Elle a blanket, and she nods, "I was, but that wasn't a lycan." I've never heard her sound so angry. "That was one of ours."

Nobody knows what to say to that, and the room grows silent, the tension thick and suffocating. Everyone is awake. Some are sitting up in their beds, others are standing. Weapons are in most of their hands. They were prepared to fight a lycan. Would they fight off one of their own betas if it came down to it?

"Well, he sure got me good." Joanna hisses, lifting up her pant leg.

Madame Delphine kneels down and begins to examine her injuries. "Looks like you got a few nasty scratches, but no actual bites. I'll get you cleaned up, and then we'll go to bed. Elle, we have extra provisions. You can sleep in here tonight."

Elle laughs bitterly. "As soon as I'm healed, I'm going back out there and hunting that asshole down."

"I'm sorry, but under no circumstances am I opening this door again until sunrise," Madame Delphine returns. "You're going to have to stay here."

Elle glares, but she knows she won't win this fight.

We crawl into our beds, and Abi stares at us like we've risen from the dead.

"Are you okay?" she asks.

"We are."

A tear runs down her face. "I thought I was going to lose you the same way I lost Lexi."

"It's okay. We're here." I grab her hand and give it a squeeze. The truth is, she almost did.

"Oh, you have got to be kidding me," Joanna groans.

"What is it?"

"Grady's necklace." Her voice is angry. "I had it in my pocket. It must have fallen out when I pulled out the daggers."

Under normal circumstances, I would laugh and tell her it was karma for the lies she told. But instead, I just tell her we'll go find it first thing in the morning.

None of us sleep that night.

* * *

As soon as dawn breaks, Madame Delphine wrenches the door open. I've already folded up my cot and blankets. So has Joanna.

We're out the door before anyone else. Joanna races in front of me, studying the ground as we climb up the stairs. We don't find anything in the manor, so we go outside, our eyes scanning the grass. I can't believe after all that, she's still worried about the necklace. But I guess if Ryne had given me a necklace, I'd want to find it too.

"Found it," she cries out and bends down to grab it.

I catch up with her, and a flash of yellow catches my eye under the azalea bush next to the house. I crouch down and wrap my fingers around a yellow flower. It's a Landora rose. The petals are still tightly folded into a bud, and some of them are damaged or missing. The same exact one that Anders was given last night at the play. But before I can process what it could mean, I spot Elle. Her hair is mussed, and she bears down on us, her eyes blazing.

She reaches us and slaps Joanna across the face. Joanna and I both recoil. This is not the Elle that I know.

"You could've gotten us all killed last night. Don't think I don't know that you ran off in the opposite direction than I told you to go. You're reckless and foolish. Next time, I'll leave you to fend for yourself."

She turns on me. "And you--maybe you should get a better friend."

My mouth falls open. "Joanna is the best friend in the world. You have no idea what you're talking about." If only I could confess that Joanna only took those risks to try to get me out of here. Joanna is safe with Grady. There's no reason for her to help me, but she does because she cares about me. Maybe even cares about me more than anyone else in the world.

Elle glares. Joanna glares. I glare. We're some trio.

"Do you think you can find that wolf who attacked us?" I ask, forcing myself to change the subject before Joanna and Elle end up in a fight. My fingers still clutch the rose, a thorn pressing into my palm.

Elle shakes her head, even angrier than before. "It's been too long. I've lost his scent. But he could've killed me. Or you. Or Joanna."

"Well, that's obvious," Joanna snaps. "But why?"

It's the question none of us have an answer to.

But we have to drop it and get ready for the day. Of course, I find myself totally distracted in all my morning classes. A lot of us are, so Madame Vivien doesn't single me out during our morning exercises. She's been pulling me out for vigorous workouts less and less, which I hope means she's stopped blaming me for Charlotte killing Lucille. The day after the full moon is always like this, anyway. But I'm not distracted because of the waning moon; I'm distracted because I figured out who killed Nova and Lexi. The Landora rose said it all. It's so obvious, glaring me right in the face this whole time.

And I know his next victim: Joanna.

She was his target last night.

I have the proof sitting in my pocket. I just don't know who to trust with the information. I want to tell Elle, but she disappeared before breakfast, and I haven't seen her again.

The person I really want to tell is Ryne, but he's not around either. When is he ever?

Right before lunch, Nico and Grady poke their heads into the classroom. Nico wiggles his finger at me to come to him, and I glance up at Madame Vivien for permission. She waves her hand. Joanna is already in Grady's arms. I know I can trust Nico, but part of me is worried that I could be wrong about him. It's not like I can confide in him in the middle of class with everyone staring at me, so I get up from my seat and go to him.

He takes my hand and pulls me into the hall. "We've come to take you ladies out for the day."

"Why?" I ask, confused. "We weren't supposed to have dates today."

"We have news, and we're taking you out to celebrate."

I swallow hard. Would they be celebrating if they knew what I knew? Somehow, I don't think so.

I climb into the passenger seat of Nico's pretty red car and quickly buckle my seatbelt. He takes off, and I fly back into my seat, gripping the handle on the door. Nico laughs. I don't know that I've ever heard him laugh. It almost breaks through my undercurrent of fear.

"What's the news?" I ask.

He peels my hand away from the leather seat and weaves his fingers into mine. "Ryne has agreed to let me and Grady take you and Joanna as brides at the Pink Moon Festival."

All the blood drains from my face, and my head feels like it's a million pounds. "What? He was so against it before."

Nico smiles and shrugs. "He called the two of us into a meeting this morning and said he found a couple of betas to replace us so the rest of the girls still have a shot with a beta. Isn't this great news?"

I nod absently and fake a smile. I should be happy. Now I don't have to worry about Anders pulling a stunt with me like he did yesterday. I bet that's why Ryne is allowing this. He's protecting me, like he said. And it might even protect some of the girls who are still in the house by bringing them more betas.

I still don't understand how Ryne can let me be with another man though. We're fated.

I don't want to be with Nico, but he's my second best option.

Ryne is the first, but he's rejecting me.

I look away and blink back tears. When I've gathered my strength, I smile back at Nico and squeeze his hand. His curly chestnut hair looks golden in the sunlight. It blows in the wind of his open window, and his tanned features wrinkle when he smiles at me. I can do this. Nico will treat me kindly and we'll just avoid any interaction with Ryne and Elle. Somehow I doubt this is going to go over well with the other betas though. What's Anders going to do when he learns that he can't have me?

* * *

Lunch is a lively affair. Joanna is thrilled with the news and is excited for me. Now she probably doesn't feel like she has to help me escape. This is a win for all of us.

The rose I found this morning is still in my pocket, and I keep waiting for the right moment to bring it up. I'm not going to be able to get in front of Ryne, so these guys are my best option. But I'm not sure how Nico will react to the news, so I wait until he excuses himself to use the restroom to confess my secret to Grady and Joanna.

We're in the middle of dessert when I pull out the Landora.

"What's that?" Joanna asks.

I let out a breath. "Yesterday at the play, the flower girl gave this to Anders."

Grady raises a curious eyebrow. "Why do you have it?"

I swallow hard and look around one last time to make sure Nico is still in the bathroom. "This morning after we got out, I found this on the ground outside. Elle said the attacker was a wolf, not a lycan. Anders must have lost it off his clothes outside the manor when he shifted. I think he's the one who's killing the girls. And he tried to kill Joanna."

Grady's jaw tenses, and he turns on Joanna. "You were attacked?"

"That's not the point," she hisses, eyes going round. "Would you listen to Poppy, please?"

He turns back to me. "What are you saying?"

"I'm saying that Anders is the one who killed Nova and Lexi."

"How do you know that?"

I quickly tell him the whole story of what happened the night before. "Anders is a violent and cruel man. He killed my sister. He obviously lost that rose during his attack on Joanna. Look, someone has been killing women, and it stands to reason it's Anders. He only wants the highest

299

caliber for his betas. Anyone who he doesn't feel deserves to be a beta wife has to go, and if it's not by way of the mating house, then he'll take them out himself." I take a deep breath, my gaze landing on Grady. "He doesn't think Joanna is good enough for you. He told me that yesterday at the play. That's got to be why he attacked her."

Grady stands, his fists clenched. "I'm going to kill that son of a bitch."

Joanna puts her hand on his arm. "Calm down. We need to think through this. Poppy's evidence is pretty damning, but we can't just go running after Anders and accuse him of all this."

I'm surprised. She's usually the one jumping headfirst into danger.

Grady jams a hand through his hair and points at Joanna. "How can you say that? Did you forget that he tried to kill you last night? I can take him. He'll be dead before dinner."

I help Joanna get Grady back into his seat. "Listen, we need to figure out why he would be doing this before accusing him, right? Do you think it's safe to tell Nico?"

They exchange a look. "The bond between father and son is strong, and alpha's rule all, but *nothing* beats the bond between a wolf and his fated."

That sentence alone is like a jab to the heart.

"We have to tell Ryne," Grady says. "If we go about this the right way, none of us will get in trouble, and Anders will still be dead."

Nico returns, and we go quiet. He collapses into his chair. "What did I miss?"

I'm not sure what to do--if I should go ahead and tell him, or if it's best to wait and let things play out. I feel terrible keeping this secret. Are they right that he'd choose avenging his mate over protecting his father? It feels dangerous either way.

So I make a decision, put my fake smile back on my face, and say, "Nothing much. Do you want some of this?" I point to the plate of chocolate cake. "It's delicious, but I'm stuffed."

Grady and Joanna don't say anything. They're taking my lead on this.

Nico chuckles and leans back into his seat, stretching his arms out. "I'll have it finished in no time. Don't you worry your pretty head about it."

He's so nice. He deserves more. And all I can hope is that I'm not making a huge mistake by keeping this from him.

Chapter Twenty

Last night, after our double date, Grady pulled me aside and told me that he would take care of Anders. He asked me to keep Joanna safe and to not tell anyone.

I'm not convinced it's the best idea, and if I have the opportunity, I will explain everything to Ryne. But I'm not counting on that, so for now, I'll keep my mouth shut. I go about my morning exercise and chores with my head down, taking what enjoyment I can from the perfect spring weather. I can't stop thinking about Grady and Anders. I hope Grady is alright. There aren't any betas here today, so I have no idea what's going on.

I finish up and get dressed in one of the simple cotton dresses our closets were equipped with last week. Mine is deep navy blue, and I kind of hate myself for thinking that it looks like Ryne's eyes.

On my way into the classroom, I pass by the rankings. There should be twenty-two girls here, but there are only thirteen of us left. I'm currently ranked number six. Now I'm battling for the top, but with Nico's news, none of that will matter by the next full moon.

That's if Anders doesn't get to me first.

I slide into my seat next to Abi. She's chipper today with a grin on her face from ear to ear because we're starting a section on writing. She and Bailey are the most avid readers of the bunch here, even more so than Joanna, and to say they're excited would be an understatement.

"Do you understand what this means?" She squeezes my arm. "We'll be able to send communications to each other."

Joanna smirks from her other side and whispers. "And why would you want to do that?"

Abi goes bright red and checks to make sure nobody is listening to our conversation. "You know, in case we need to help someone." She swallows and then whispers low. "I heard--someone--talking about the Resistance. Do you know anything about it?"

Joanna sits back, her face a mask. "Nope. But you should be careful who you talk to about that stuff."

Joanna and Abi don't know that I already talked to Madame Delphine about it. Of course the house mother denied anything and left abruptly.

I'm not sure what to say here, and I almost tell them, when Madame Delphine herself strolls in and interrupts us. "Ladies, we have a real treat for you today. Ryne has arranged a dinner cruise in the harbor. He has a few exciting announcements to make. You must wear your best dresses and make sure you do your hair and makeup like you would for a festival. There will be no afternoon classes, so you will have sufficient time to get ready."

I try not to think about the announcements, even though my betrothal will likely be one of them. Our writing class flies by, and before I know it, Elle is taking the seat across from us at lunch. She pops a french fry into her mouth. "So, what do you think the announcement is?" she asks.

"You mean you don't know?" Joanna snorts. "You must know."

Elle shakes her head. "Why would I know?" She doesn't say it in a rude way like Faye would have. She seems genuinely confused. I like her, and I hate her. It's such a weird feeling.

"Because you're Ryne's bride-to-be," Joanna says.

Elle meets my eye for just a moment but doesn't say anything about Ryne and me. I should've told Joanna everything. She's my best friend, but I don't want to admit that we're fated, and he *still* rejected me. I'm not even sure I could get the words out.

They hurt too much.

Abi plops down next to Elle. "So what's Ryne going to tell us?"

Elle's mouth drops open. "I don't know why you think I know. It's not like I live with the guy. I'm a house mother *here*. Plus, this is all wolf business. He only discusses those things with Anders and a council of betas."

Joanna narrows her eyes. "Why is Anders the second? If you ask me, it should be Grady."

Elle chuckles at that. "Grady is welcome to challenge Anders for the position. Good luck."

"If something happened to Ryne, then Anders is in charge?" Her lip curls.

"He's not automatically alpha. But yes, he would step up and take Ryne's place until a new alpha surfaces. The men have to fight it out."

"And who would take over if they both died?" I ask. I'm pretty sure it's Grady because of how close they are, but then again, there are a lot of betas, and I only know a handful. Sometimes pack hierarchy can be confusing. Anders and Ryne don't seem all that close, and yet Anders is the second in command.

Elle scoffs. "If they both died, it would be a bloodbath. There isn't a direct line to anyone because Ryne doesn't have an heir yet, and King Tremaine doesn't have any other sons."

I've often wondered if Ryne has brothers. Guess not.

"There's only the alpha and his second. If they both died at the same time, then all the betas would battle for the position of alpha. I don't know if you've noticed this, but Anders and Ryne don't go to the same battles or patrol the same areas at the same time. It's not in the pack's best interest to have them together too much."

So maybe Ryne shouldn't be coming around here to oversee the claiming as much as he has this year. I can't help but wonder if that has something to do with me. It must, right? I'm his fated mate. Not that he cares. I'm looking right at the reason he won't be with me, and she's gorgeous, as always. Elle's braided hair is tied back in a long white silk ribbon, and she's wearing a silky white dress to match. It contrasts perfectly with her ebony skin, and all I can think is she'll look amazing in a wedding dress.

I shake the image clear of my head. "What about you?" I ask.

"What about me?" Her eyebrows furrow.

"You're a wolf. Could you ever be an alpha?"

She drops her eyes and swallows. "No. I'm a female. Males aren't allowed to fight me, so I could never challenge an alpha for his role."

"But what if you did?" My tone is goading, but I don't care. I want to know. I shift forward in my seat and stare her down, willing her to answer me.

"The betas would detain me. They wouldn't let me fight," she says at last.

I lean back in my seat. "Well, that doesn't seem fair."

Joanna cracks a smile. "So you've thought about this? Hmm, Princess Elle has a nice ring to it, but it's not better than Alpha Elle."

She bristles and shushes us. "Keep your voices down."

"Okay, but answer us. You'd love to be alpha, wouldn't you? I can tell. It's in your blood."

She studies us, as if weighing whether she can trust us. "When I was a kid, I told my father I'd be the alpha one day, and after beating me for my insolence, he explained why that would never happen."

"He beat you?" Abi whispers. She's been watching this conversation unfold with round saucer eyes, her food completely untouched.

Elle lifts a shoulder and drops it. "It's not a big deal. I was a spitfire of a child, and he worried that I would cross Thorn. It hurt, but at least I'm still alive. If I had told Thorn that I wanted to be an alpha, he might have killed me on the spot." She takes time to look us each in the eyes. "And he still would. So when I tell you that I do not want to be the alpha, I mean it."

"This is a dangerous world to be born a woman in, isn't it?" Joanna asks, but it's not really a question. Nobody says anything more about it.

I push my chicken salad around my plate, no longer hungry. I wonder if that's why Ryne rejected me. If his father was that cruel, and he didn't want me to be Ryne's wife, then he'd probably kill me. I just wish I knew for sure. If Ryne would sit me down and explain everything, then maybe I could let him go. Maybe I wouldn't have to hurt so much.

"Come on, ladies, it's time to get ready. Joanna needs to pick our dresses," Elle says with a smile. She's acting casual, but her smile doesn't reach her eyes, and her hand trembles a little bit.

Joanna groans, but I know she loves it.

* * *

Hours later we're still getting ready. I've swapped out the blue cotton summer dress for one of red plush velvet. The neckline plunges down both the back and front, and the slit goes all the way up to reveal my entire right leg when I walk. I don't have much cleavage––Willow was always the one with the curves––but this dress works perfectly on my shape. It's by far the sexiest thing I've ever worn, and for the first time, I allow myself to draw power from it.

It's not something I would normally wear, but when Joanna pulled it out and dared me to wear it, I couldn't resist. It's the kind of dress that gets attention, and tonight, I want attention. From one man only. But I've noticed that when other men pay attention to me, Ryne reacts strongly.

My skin has paled in winter, which contrasts nicely against the red. Elle does my hair up in a swirl of soft curls, and Abi applies my makeup, complete with blood-red lips and smokey eyes. I've even learned how to walk in high heels, so I slip into some strappy black ones that will make me tower above the other girls.

Elle leans down to whisper in my ear so the other girls can't hear. They're distracted with their own dresses anyway. "Ryne isn't going to be able to keep his eyes off of you. Maybe tonight he'll come to his senses."

I have no idea what she's talking about, or why she's even saying this, though I do wonder if maybe she's been trying to convince him to not reject me. I still think she wants out of marrying him, and I'm her ticket to freedom.

I stand and examine myself in our full-length mirror. Before coming here, I would've felt self-conscious about how I look, especially about being so tall, but I don't care anymore. The wolves are massive men, anyway. I could never be taller than them. And I've decided that confidence makes me far prettier than all the hair and makeup and dresses combined.

"You're going to show Ryne what he's missing," Joanna laughs the second Elle leaves.

I smirk and blow a kiss to myself in the mirror. "That's the plan."

And okay, maybe some of this confidence is fake, and on the inside I'm terrified about so many things, but I have to at least try. Fact is, Ryne is my fated.

And I don't want to marry Nico.

I will if it's what I have to do to save myself from Anders or the mating houses, but part of me hopes that Ryne will take one look at me and decide he doesn't want to marry Elle either.

A knock sounds on the door, and Madame Delphine slips into the room. "Poppy, this is a gift from Nico for you to wear tonight."

Joanna gasps. "I bet it's a family heirloom, same as what Grady gave me." She points to the gold necklace with the little flower of green emeralds on the end. "He said that wolves only give this type of jewelry to someone they consider part of their family." She winks and holds up her hands. "Just wait, soon we'll have engagement rings too."

Abi's smile is laced with pain. I can tell this hurts her, and I wish I could help. I vow then and there to do a better job of making sure she gets married to a beta too––a good one. Joanna and I still haven't told her that we're getting married soon, and that Ryne will be bringing a couple more betas into the season. I hope one of them is perfect for her.

I take the box from Madame Delphine and thank her. My hands shake when I slip the black ribbon from the box and peel it open. A gold necklace with a huge red sparkling stone in the shape of a teardrop winks up at me. My breath catches in my throat. I don't think I've ever seen something so beautiful.

"This is a ruby," Madame Delphine says wistfully. She clasps it to my neck. "It's a very rare and valuable gemstone. And Joanna is right. This piece belongs to Nico and Anders's family. It's going to be a very exciting night for you."

Leave it up to Anders to have a gem that looks like a huge drop of blood.

But at least he wasn't the one who gave it to me. Thank goodness I'm going to be paired with Nico. But what has happened to Anders? Did Grady really go after him? And will Nico hate me once everything comes to light? Ready or not, I may soon find out. I swallow and keep my gaze away from Joanna, feeling guilty that she doesn't know Grady has made it his mission to end Anders.

We leave, and as we walk out to the river, the necklace weighs heavy.

Chapter Twenty-One

We shuffle onto the boat, everyone trying to stay upright in our heels and tight dresses. We all look stunning tonight. Better even than on the night of the Wolf Moon Festival. All the girls understand what is at stake now, and we've gotten better at dressing ourselves and doing our makeup and hair. There are also attachments starting to form, real feelings involved for several of the girls and the betas. It's changed everything.

On the walk down to the dock, Faye eyed my and Joanna's necklaces but didn't say anything. She's the only one who doesn't look better than she did before. Her dress is a little too short and tight, and her makeup is a tad garish; her look reeks of desperation, and I'd feel bad for her if I didn't hate her so much. She's only gotten meaner through this experience, which is incredible considering how she started out. If I didn't understand her need to please the betas, I might judge her for it. But even despite our rivalry, despite the horrible things she's said about Willow, and even accusing me of killing Lexi, I still wouldn't wish her to end up in a mating house.

Though if it comes down to a beta for her or for Abi, I will fight for Abi. And the fact that the wolves have even put us into this position will never be okay. Once I'm married to Nico, I will find and join the Resistance. There's got to be a way to change things for the better. Even Ryne had a better idea about finding willing women to have the children, but I still don't like it. What's so bad about letting everyone get married?

The betas are nowhere to be seen. The sea air is cool, and we stand out on the dock much longer than usual. "Our hair is going to get messed up." Abi sighs. "Not that it matters for me, but I at least wanted them to get a look first."

Joanna laughs and pulls her into a hug.

A white boat finally putters around the corner, larger than any of the others I've been on. It has three stories, and the majority of the boat is enclosed with wide windows, though there is a walkway that seems to go all the way around the large interior room. The room has double doors that are intricately carved with gold trim. It comes in at a slow crawl and stops at the deck.

Another breeze kicks up, and goosebumps rise on my skin.

"Are they gonna let us in?" Joanna asks. "Or wait until we look a mess?"

This time Abi laughs.

Almost as if on cue, the doors open, and Knox stands on the other side wearing a tux. My heart flutters a little. I've never seen him so dressed up.

He meets my eye for a fraction of a second and then clears his throat. "Ladies, name cards have been placed at each table, so please find your seat. Ryne and the betas will be here soon."

Joanna grabs my hand and drags me to the front. Sure enough, we're sitting at a round table with six name cards. Mine, Joanna, Grady, Nico, Ryne, and Elle. Nico's name card is on my left, and Ryne's is on my right. I don't know why he would put himself right next to me, but perhaps he didn't have anything to do with the seating arrangements.

Abi is stuck at a table with Faye, Joy, and Blair. I know she'd much rather be with us or even Harlow and Katelyn. I mouth "I'm sorry" to her, and she just shrugs. She's used to it, and it's not fair. I don't know why I've received so much attention from all these betas, but it must be because I'm Ryne's fated mate. The men are probably picking up on something there, thinking I'm more special than I am. If I weren't Ryne's fated, I can't help but think I'd be at the mating house by now. I could even be pregnant.

A side door opens, and even before I see Ryne, I know he's there. I can feel his presence like an electric current, and all of my senses heighten. The connection is stronger than ever. The men all enter, each dressed in identical black tuxes. Ryne strides in last.

His cobalt eyes meet mine, and it's as if the rest of the room disappears. It's only me and him. He doesn't move from the door; he just drinks me in, and I let him. I want to get up and go to him, but even being entranced by him, I know better.

I wonder what he would do if I did. Would he kiss me or reject me? I suspect he'd kiss me. Even he can't deny it, and I understand now how hard it must be for him to resist.

A hand drops on my shoulder, breaking the spell. Nico leans in, pressing a soft kiss to my cheek before sitting down.

"You look lovely," he says.

"Thank you," I mutter, tearing my eyes away from Ryne. Which is a mistake, because they land right on Joanna and Grady, who are in the middle of a passionate kiss. I avert my eyes and look over at Nico.

He leans in. "I'm sorry I don't treat you like Grady does Joanna." His gaze flicks to the necklace, and his facade falters for a moment. This jewelry was meant for Nova, and we both know it.

I swallow. "It's okay. I'm not sure I want you to."

Hurt crosses his face, but so does understanding. This is such a hard position to be in. Still, I don't want to hurt his feelings.

"Yet," I hurry to say. "We're not there yet. You're still in love with Nova, and I would never want to take those feelings away from you."

He scoots a little closer to me and rests his arm along the back of my chair, his fingers lightly resting on my shoulder. "Thank you for being so considerate. The more I get to know you, the more I understand why Nova liked you so much." He pauses for a long second. "You're kind, and in this world there's not a lot of that, you know?"

I do know.

"I can't give you the feelings I gave so easily to Nova," he continues. "It's not in my power, and for that I apologize."

"You don't have to."

"Please, I need to say this." His voice is earnest.

I nod once, hoping whatever he says doesn't make this harder.

"I like you. You're my friend. And I wouldn't be doing this if I didn't really believe that in time, we will grow to love each other. I'd really like for us to have that chance."

"I would too," I say, but I know it's a lie.

Loving him would be like loving a shadow.

Ryne slides into the chair next to me, and I swear the temperature in the room rises by twenty degrees. I can't move, can't breathe. Did he hear our conversation?

"You look beautiful tonight, Joanna," he says, but his eyes are on me, and I know the compliment is mine. My cheeks flame, and I grab the glass of ice water and gulp it down. "Grady is a lucky man," he adds.

"The luckiest," Joanna quips back. "And I'd say the same of Elle if you weren't busy stripping another girl naked in your mind."

"Joanna!" Grady gasps, but Ryne just chuckles and leans back in his chair like it's all a silly little game of breaking hearts.

I'm mortified, about ready to strangle Joanna, and poor Nico shifts uncomfortably in his seat, his eyes going from me to Ryne and back again. I reach out and thread Nico's fingers through mine and squeeze. After a few long moments, he squeezes back. He can't know about me and Ryne. He'll break off the engagement. I'm sure of it. Or will Ryne make him marry me? He can't deny his alpha. Still, I don't want to risk anything.

Elle has been busy chatting with the other house mothers who are seated in the back, but unfortunately that couldn't last forever. When she saunters over and sits down next to Ryne, my heart drops. He leans over, whispering intimately in her ear, and she giggles. This is pure torture. Is that what I have in store for the rest of my life? I can only hope Nico and I won't have to be around the alpha too often.

Anders strolls up to Abi's table, finding his seat between Faye and Blair. He immediately pulls Faye into a kiss, and I relax a little. At least his gaze isn't on me. I don't think I could handle another beta's attention right now.

But I can't help but wonder what Anders knows or what happened between him and Grady. He obviously didn't succeed in killing Joanna two nights ago, but that doesn't mean he won't try again.

The water outside the boat twinkles under the moonlight and then ripples when the engine turns up. In the inky blackness of it, I imagine Nova's body floating aimlessly. Anders knows what really happened to her that night because he did it. What kind of person drowns someone like that?

The kind who decapitates a girl in front of her own family for no good reason.

The kind who bites a woman against her will, brandishing her for a date.

The kind who thinks women were made for men's enjoyment and nothing else.

We pull out into the water, and everyone cheers. I can't. All I can do is watch Anders, a glare deepening my gaze.

Anders meets my challenge through the midst of raised glasses and cheering, and we stare at each other. His handsome, charismatic face goes flat. There's nothing good behind his eyes. It's all fake. His expression is dark, clinging to mine. Neither of us turn away; neither of us break the spell. It's like we're in a face-off. He may be a beta wolf and used to this kind of thing, but I've spent my life fighting to survive in a terrible world. I'm no longer scared of a challenge.

And I'm no longer scared of Anders.

He nods once, raises his glass to me, and drinks.

He knows I know.

He must.

Chapter Twenty-Two

Waiters come around pouring wine, and I eagerly down my first glass. Alcohol is not something I drink much of, but I need it to take the edge off. I'd probably drink the whole bottle if I thought it would help me tonight, but I know it won't, and that's not who I am. I'm scared to lose control, even when I know I've never really had it. So I sit here, sipping my second glass of wine and trying to make small talk with Nico, all the while completely and utterly aware of Ryne by my side. It's all I can do to not look at him.

I'm not the only one who drank my first glass of wine like it'd disappear if I didn't. Both Ryne and Nico did as well.

Before long, everyone at our table is relaxed and laughing at Joanna's stories. Our delicious meal is followed up by the most decadent dessert I have ever seen. It's a ball of chocolate mousse topped with fancy whipped cream. The richness of the chocolate sits heavy in my mouth. We never had anything like this back home, never had these kinds of parties or dresses or fancy food, but at least we were mostly free to do as we pleased within the confines of our community.

I sigh, the past really is gone. This is my life now, and I want so badly to believe it'll be a good one.

"Dinner parties with you two are going to be a riot," Elle says, her voice sweet and sultry like the chocolatey dessert, and my stomach sours. She glances around the table. "I like this group. After the weddings, we should make this a weekly occurrence." So much for avoiding the alpha.

Joanna raises her glass. "Definitely. To friendship."

We all raise our glasses and utter the same words. Ryne slides his free hand over mine in my lap under the table. He squeezes my fingers, and blood rushes to my face. I want to pull away and tell him to not toy with my feelings.

But of course I can't.

He lets go quickly and stands, moving to the front of the room. Elle slides into his vacated seat. She leans over and whispers into my ear. "It's going to be okay."

I stare at my hands. "I don't see how."

She reaches over and squeezes one of them, so utterly similar to the way Ryne did but carrying a very different meaning.

I can tell she craves her freedom. And she said herself that she didn't want to marry Ryne because she was worried she'd end up married to a man with a mistress. I don't know if that will ever happen--I don't want it to happen--but how can she be so calm about the situation now?

Ryne stands on a slightly raised platform in the front of the room. His presence is so commanding that the entire room quiets before he even looks up. When he does, he smiles, and my heart melts a little bit. I want that smile to be mine. And for a fraction of a second, it is. As he shifts his eyes across the room, they hold with mine and then drop away. Pretty indicative of our entire relationship, and I'm a lost cause. How can I possibly marry Nico when I feel like this?

"Wolves and ladies, tonight I brought you here to celebrate with me. You see, a few weeks ago, I was reunited with a dear friend of mine that I wasn't expecting to see. I'd always known I'd fall in love with her, but I didn't expect it to happen so quickly." His words are rushed and rehearsed, but they still sting. I steal a quick glance at Elle. She's smiling, but it doesn't reach her eyes. "Tonight, I'm announcing my engagement. Elle, can you join me up here?"

As she makes her way up to the stage, she's the picture of grace, and every eye is on her. When she reaches Ryne, she slides a petite arm around his waist. They're the perfect couple. She's all feminine beauty, and he's masculine power. They're gorgeous and strong and everything the pack wants.

"This is my lovely bride-to-be. We shall be married at the Pink Moon Festival." Cheers erupt around the room, and Ryne holds a hand out for quiet. "I have two more weddings to announce."

Whispers spread at those words. Ryne clears his throat, and everyone quiets. "This has been an unusual year for the claiming, and so when two of my betas came and asked for permission to marry their brides early, I couldn't deny them that, especially considering how I feel for Elle. I know what it's like to desperately want to be with someone."

The tension in the room rises as the girls realize two of the betas are about to be unavailable. I can feel the eyes on our table, and my skin prickles. Is it too late? Should I stand up right now and announce that I can't marry Nico? I want to, and yet I'm frozen in place.

"But I also didn't want to have a disappointing year at the harvest festival, so at the pink moon I will be bringing two new betas to take brides this autumn." That's the news everyone wants to hear, and several of the girls clap and squeal. "Now, it's time to announce the additional weddings. Grady and Joanna."

"No surprises there," someone mutters from the table behind me.

"And Nico and Poppy."

A collective gasp circles the room followed by a shattering glass. I search for the noise and see Anders standing up, his face beet red.

"You can't do that," he shouts. "They are not fated."

Ryne clenches his fists. "Are you challenging me?"

Anders doesn't move from his spot, but his chest rises and falls rapidly. "Of course not. But you know how I feel about Poppy. You can't let my son marry her. That's needlessly cruel."

I snort at his use of the word cruel.

"Why not?" Nico stands, his arms rippling with fur. I'm afraid we're about to see a bloodbath on this boat, which now seems far too small.

"Because it's a slap to my face, and I won't allow it. Poppy is mine." Anders storms toward us. "I claimed her the day I killed her sister. She's the reason I even entered the harvest this year, and you know it."

I expect Nico to move between me and Anders, but it's Grady who gets there first.

"What are you doing?" Anders asks, peering around him to meet my eyes. There is nothing but hatred and lust in them. The two emotions shouldn't go together, but for Anders they do, and they probably always will.

"I won't let you hurt Poppy," Grady snarls. He stands taller, and the two of them face off, ready to rip each other apart.

"What makes you think I want to hurt her?" he asks. "I love her."

A muscle in Grady's jaw ticks. "Go sit back down, old man. She's Nico's now."

Anders moves so quickly that I don't even register it. He grabs Joanna by the arm, wrenching her out of her chair. "Perhaps I'll take your bride instead then."

Grady leaps onto the table, sending plates and glasses flying, and then he's on top of Anders, punching him hard in the face. Blood flies, splattering the white linens. Anders releases Joanna and kicks out at Grady, slamming him in the gut. Grady doubles over for just a moment before tackling Anders to the ground. A flash of fur ripples over both of them in light gray and dark brown. They're going to shift any second. If that happens, this probably won't end until one of them is dead.

Ryne leaps from the platform and yanks Grady off of Anders. "Enough," his voice bellows. Anders stands, wiping blood from his mouth.

"That's insubordination," Anders says. "I am second in command to the alpha. You cannot attack me."

Ryne levels a look at him. "Be reasonable. You provoked him."

Not to mention, Anders questioned his alpha.

"That is no excuse. You know the punishment for insubordination. Are you going to be a strong alpha and enforce the rules, or will you let chaos reign?"

Ryne swallows, and I see the indecision in his mind.

"What's the punishment?" I whisper to Nico.

"Exile." The word seems to echo through the space, but that's only because everyone else is whispering the same thing.

My stomach drops. I don't want my friends to be sent away, because surely Joanna would go with him. The wilds are dangerous. I'd never see them again.

Joanna's face turns frantic, and my heart hurts to see a side of her I've never seen before. She's suddenly vulnerable and small, just like the rest of us women in this world. There's nothing left to do. I have to be strong.

"I'm sorry," I whisper to Nico. I still don't know what this is going to do to him, and I hate that he's already been through so much. He questions me with a small frown. But I'm out of time.

I step forward, point at Anders, and my voice finds me. "You killed my twin sister, Willow. My best friend and other half. That does not make me yours."

He laughs, and everyone turns on me. "It brought you here, didn't it?"

I won't be bated. "And you killed Nova. And you killed Lexi. And you tried to kill Joanna."

The silence is filled with so many emotions.

I hold Anders's gaze as he glares. Finally, he speaks, but his voice doesn't carry its normal tone. "You're a liar. How dare you accuse me of such things."

"I'm not a liar." My voice is all steel now; it holds me up, and I stand straighter because of it. "And I can prove it."

I reach out my right hand, and in it, Joanna places the rose that she's been keeping tucked in her bodice. She insisted on bringing it along tonight, just in case something like this happened. The rose itself is shriveled and sad looking since it was cut days ago, but it's intact well enough to serve its purpose. The second Anders's eyes land on it, he takes a step back. That small movement is not enough for most people to even notice, but I do, and I bet Ryne and the other wolves do as well.

"Do you recognize this?" I ask. "Wait, don't answer that; it wasn't really a question. I know you do because it was the very same rose you placed on your lapel on our date to the theater."

"What does that have to do with anything?" he scoffs. He looks over to Ryne. "Are you really going to let this go on?"

Ryne raises an eyebrow as if amused, but his eyes are filled with lead, the blues of them going dark. "Let the woman finish. If you're as innocent as you say you are, then you shouldn't have anything to worry about."

"That's ridiculous. No innocent man would tolerate being accused of murdering a claimed girl and his son's fated." He looks to Nico, expression pleading. "You know I loved Nova."

The color in Nico's complexion is gone. He's completely ashen. "No, Father, I never knew that. It was actually the opposite, as I recall."

"Hmm." Ryne takes a step closer. "Isn't that interesting?"

I clear my throat. "As I was saying..." I give the men a look as if to say *let me have my moment* and continue on. "This very rose was left behind when a wolf pretended to be a lycan and attacked Joanna on the night of the full moon."

Grady widens his stance. "Which I've known about for a whole twenty-four hours. You're lucky you're not already dead, and don't think I didn't try to find you because I did. I should've known you'd be spending the night at the mating houses again." He spits on the ground.

Anders glares right back. "This is preposterous. All that because of a rose?"

"There's more," I hiss. "You had a motive to kill Nova. You told me yourself that you hated that your son wouldn't be able to have children with her."

"Nova was depressed. She drowned herself." He tugs at his collar and sweat forms on his forehead.

I shake my head. "She was excited to marry Nico. That very night she told me she loved him." I turn back and point to poor Nico. He's still stunned. "Everybody knew how much you two loved each other--you most of all."

Abi steps forward, and it's maybe the first time anyone's ever paid her attention.

"Oh, what now?" Anders snaps.

"Lexi was my roommate. She was the top of our class, the smartest of the bunch, but you didn't think she was pretty enough to be a beta's wife."

Anders gapes at her. Of all people, I'm certain he never expected Abi to have something to say.

"Don't try to deny it," Abi continues. "She told me herself that you said she'd never be a beta wife. Well, maybe you made sure of it."

"I did no such thing." He points to Abi. "For all we know, you killed Lexi."

"That's not possible," I interject. "Her wounds were from claws and teeth, and it wasn't a full moon."

That's all it takes. Grady and Nico exchange a glance, and then together, they lunge for Anders.

Chapter Twenty-Three

Pandemonium erupts.

Elle is at my side in seconds, grabbing my hand. I reach for Joanna, and we run for the back of the room. There's nowhere to go. Tables and chairs are flying as the betas all shift into their wolf forms. Girls huddle along the walls in groups. Elle stands between me and Joanna and the wolves. Every once in a while, I see her fur ripple along her arm.

"What are you doing?" I demand.

"Protecting you. All of this is about protecting you," she hisses in my ear. "Ryne and I aren't really getting married, and neither are you and Nico. We have a plan to keep you safe from Thorn, but we have to pretend like everything is normal until the last possible second. Ryne would be heartbroken if anything happened to you, so I'm making sure you stay safe."

I grip her arm, my mind still trying to catch up to what she confessed. "What plan?"

"I can't tell you."

I'm momentarily distracted by the howling wolves. Ryne gets himself between Anders and Nico, with Grady right by Nico's side. The other betas stand with Ryne. No one wants a bloodbath. But then again, they're used to that, and they'll do what they have to.

Without warning, Nico leaps over Ryne, landing on Anders, his jaws clamping on the back of his father's neck. Anders bucks, but Nico doesn't let go. He claws at Anders's face, and Anders rolls, pinning Nico underneath him. All the other betas join the fray, and for a moment all we can see is fur and gnashing teeth.

The wolves freeze.

"Anders just conceded." Elle breathes a sigh of relief, but she doesn't move away from shielding me.

The fur all changes to flesh, and now six naked men stand in the middle of the room, all breathing heavily. I keep my eyes on their heads and faces so I can concentrate on what they are saying.

Nico clenches his fist. "I do not accept that. You will die for killing Nova. How could you do that to me? Your own son."

"I concede," Anders repeats. "I will not fight my child like this. You can take my place as the alpha's second in command."

"That is acceptable to me," Ryne says loudly.

"Not to me," Nico growls. "And besides, that honor should go to Grady, shouldn't it? I won't be placated with false prizes." He points at his father, pain twisting his features. "I've lived under your claw for my entire life, doing everything you asked of me, and when the one thing came along that would actually make me happy, you had to take it away."

Anders's lips thin. He's not sorry. He's only sorry he got caught. He shakes his head at his son. "You never lived up to your potential, and you never will without my help."

Nico's face falls.

"There will be a trial," Ryne snaps in response. "We will bring King Tremaine in to exercise judgment, but for now, nobody is killing anybody."

Nico looks from Ryne to Anders and then storms off. Grady has been holding Anders, but now he lets him go, striding over to Joanna and wrapping her in a hug. He's still naked as the day he was born, but they obviously don't care. Elle shoots me a knowing look and rushes forward, picking up a couple of tablecloths. She hands them to the men and then gives one to me. "Take this to Nico to cover himself."

I take the stained white sheet and hurry out the door where I last saw Nico. He's leaning against the railing and staring down into the water. I approach and hand him the tablecloth. He takes it without a word and wraps it around his midsection.

"Are you okay?" I ask.

He shakes his head. "I can't believe my own father would kill her."

I lay my hand on his arm. "I'm so sorry."

His face crumples, and he collapses into me, sobbing. This isn't something I ever thought I'd see from one of these tough men, but it doesn't bother me. If anything, it makes me like him more. He's a good man, and he never deserved any of this. I hold him and stroke his hair, not caring that he's ruining my dress or that he's half-naked. Nico is my friend, and he's hurting.

I hope that at some point, Anders feels pain worse than this.

It would be the only way justice could be served.

* * *

The boat docks roughly at the city's edge, and we all scramble off. I want to get far away from the betas and all the trouble they bring. Plus, I need to get away from Anders. I'm the one who accused him, and I'm fairly certain he'll come after me the first chance he gets.

So when I see him being led away by Cade and Justin, I relax a little.

"Where are they taking him?" I ask anyone who might be listening.

"To the jail cells. He'll stay there until the king comes to render judgment," Elle says. "Normally this would be Ryne's choice, but Anders is ranked high enough that he gets to plead his case to Thorn."

At least I don't have to worry about Anders for now, but the thought that Thorn will be here soon makes my skin crawl.

"Elle, Poppy, you're coming with me," Ryne calls out. It's not a request; it's a command.

"Why?" I ask, now concerned. Elle shrugs, and we head for his car. Joanna watches me with worried eyes, but Grady is already ushering her to his own car.

We pile into the backseat of Ryne's car, Elle pressed up against him. I shove down my jealousy. "Why do I need to come with you?"

Ryne doesn't look at me. "You're the one who accused Anders of murdering two women. I want to hear the story from you. I need to know exactly what happened."

"The night Nova died . . ." I start.

"Not here," he whispers, his voice cracking with exhaustion. "Wait until we get back to my house, and I've cleaned up a bit."

I glance up at the rearview mirror and find Knox's eyes on me. Obviously Ryne doesn't trust Knox with this information, but I'm not sure why. Maybe he's just being careful, or maybe he really does want to get cleaned up first.

We arrive at his house, and Ryne heads up to what I assume is his room as Elle leads me to another bedroom. It's beautiful with white silk blankets across a large bed and intricately painted landscapes on the walls. She opens up a drawer and pulls out a black top and shorts similar to what we run in.

"Why do you have clothes here? I thought you stayed at the house."

"I actually sleep here more often than not lately." She hands me the clothes. "Here, you need to get out of that dress."

I glance down at what was once a beautiful dress that is now splattered with blood. I didn't even realize it got on me. I change quickly, and so does she. Then she leads me to another room on the floor. It's a library, but smaller than the one at the claimed house. Dark shelves line all four walls from floor to ceiling; there are no windows. A small table sits in the middle of the room, framed by four squashy leather chairs.

Elle examines a shelf near the door and plucks out a book. "Good luck," she says, moving for the door.

"You're not staying?" I ask.

"No. This is between you and Ryne. He wants you to be able to speak freely about what you know. Good night, Poppy. I'll see you in the morning." She winks as she leaves, which confuses me even more.

If her confession is true, then she must care for him as a friend more than anything else, and she did say that she wasn't really going to marry him. I think about Knox. We used to date, and I even thought I loved him, but I know now that we were only ever meant to be friends. Still, I'd do anything to help him.

Maybe that's how Elle feels about Ryne.

I walk around the room slowly, looking at the books on the built-in shelves. I can read all of the titles now. Sure, I might be slow, but I can do it, and pride fills me more and more with each one. These last months have been the hardest of my life, but at least I have something to show for it. I take a book from the shelf titled *Persuasion* and flip through a few of the pages. Okay, maybe this one might take me a while, but I'm intrigued by the first line, which seems to go on and on forever. I didn't know people could write like that. Maybe I could write something one day. Would I share the story of my life? Or would I want to make up something else entirely? A magical land where none of this horror exists.

The door creaks open, and I turn, meeting Ryne's stormy eyes. He still isn't wearing a shirt, and his pants hang low on his hips. He shuts the door and locks it. Ryne and I have never been so alone before, not with a locked door and no windows. A jolt of nervous excitement pulses through my entire body.

Ryne approaches me. I expect him to say something, anything. He doesn't. He places a finger on my chin and forces me to look up at him. Then his lips are on mine. They are rough and hungry as he presses his body into me, pushing me back into the bookshelf.

I drop the book I'm holding and wrap my arms around him, ignoring the wooden bookshelf biting into my back. This is the kiss I've been waiting for. It holds the promise of future and love.

And then I remember.

He's engaged to Elle.

I shove him away from me.

"Are you going to marry Elle?" I breathe. He can't kiss me until he explains himself.

He chuckles and closes the distance between us, planting a kiss on my nose. "That's a ruse," he says. He grabs my hand with his and leads me over to one of the chairs. He sits, and when I go to sit in the opposite chair, he growls a little and pulls me into his lap.

"I don't understand," I say, but I think I'm starting to, and my hope feels too good to be true.

He nuzzles my neck. "I don't want to talk tonight, Poppy. I just want to be with you."

And here I thought he brought me here to talk about Anders.

His lips feather along my jaw, and it takes all of my willpower to not melt into him. But I need answers first.

"I really need to understand what's going on. You've been ignoring me since the night you admitted we are fated." My heart hurts at the memory.

He squeezes me tighter. "I know. I'm so sorry I've kept my plan a secret from you. It's been so difficult. You have no idea how many times I've come close to ravishing you in front of everyone."

"Then why haven't you?" The words are out of my mouth before I can stop them.

He grins, and his eyes dance. "You would've liked that, huh?"

I nod because my words seemed to have escaped me at the moment.

"Because you'd be in danger from my father. Unlike Anders, he doesn't have to hide his kills. You threaten my relationship with Elle, something he's planned for years, and I have no doubt he'll kill you if he finds out."

I place my hands on his chest, spreading my fingers over the hard muscles.

"So, what's the plan?" I ask.

"Oh, it's quite brilliant. Elle came up with it. The night of the wedding, you and Elle will switch at the last possible moment, and I'll marry you instead. It's part of our shifter bond that we cannot attack another's wife, so once you're mine, my father won't be able to touch you."

A thrill races up my spine. His wife.

"What about Elle and her family?" I can't forget everything she told me about how important this marriage is to them.

"They will all be here for the wedding. And just before the ceremony, I'll initiate Elle and her family into our pack. They will have to move here, but at least they'll be protected. Thorn won't want to mess with that. Besides, it's not like any of this is Elle's fault. We're going to make it look like it was all my doing and that Elle wasn't part of the plan. My father will pity her and will be angry at me, but he won't retaliate. Oh, he'll make threats, but I'm his only heir and the child he spent decades trying to have." His face softens. "Trust me, Poppy. Everything will be okay once the dust settles."

What is it with these men and their terrible fathers? It makes me miss mine even more. I can't imagine ever having to go to such lengths to keep Papa from hurting the people I care about. I frown, overcome with immense sadness for Ryne. He deserves so much better.

"I hope it works." I don't know what else to say.

"Me too." He runs the back of his hand gently along my jawline. "You understand that after we leave this room, we have to go back to ignoring each other until the festival, and even there, we really can't even look at each other until the moment you and Elle switch places?"

"I understand."

"Good, now can we please stop talking?"

<h1 style="text-align:center">Chapter Twenty-Four</h1>

Those blue eyes glitter with mischief and then flash deeper. Longing is evident on his face as he inches his body closer to mine, and there's nothing else to say or do. I reach out and pull him close, erasing any distance between us. His mouth takes mine, and a fire ignites between us. It's hotter than it's ever been before, and I'm happy to let it burn me up. The kiss is zero to one hundred in seconds, as if we're fighting to stay alive, and the only way to do so is to stay connected.

Ryne is everything.

He works his lips against mine, and it's like the whole world is falling away. My heart is burning with a passion that makes me feel like a whole different person—like the women in our village right after they got married. They always had a way about them, as if losing their virginity gave them a knowledge and maturity the rest of us couldn't understand. And maybe that was true, or maybe that was just a shield, but I never cared. It didn't interest me. I knew one day I'd marry too and would leave my maidenhood behind, but I'd hardly thought about it much.

Now it's all I can think about.

I've never wanted someone or something as much as I want Ryne.

He must feel the same, because we go from me straddling him on the chair to him straddling me on the floor. He lifts from me for a moment, breaking the kiss, and I murmur my frustration.

He chuckles, and it's a lovely kind of wickedness. "What am I going to do with you?"

"I have a few ideas." I reach up to bring him back to me, but he holds strong, still leaning over me and caging me to the floor with those steel arms. I don't know how he can possibly wait. His hair hangs down to frame his face, so I shimmy my hands free and run my fingers through it.

He groans and rolls away.

"What's wrong?" I ask, teasing. But part of me is afraid that something really is wrong. If he rejects me now, I might die of heartbreak.

"We can't do anything but kiss, and I'm dying." He lets out a laugh.

"So if you die, then we'll die together." I move close and trail slow kisses along his neck. I've never felt so bold before, but I like it. "Because I feel the same way."

"The claimed girls have to stay virgins until marriage."

I roll my eyes. "Are you serious?" My mom drilled innocence and virtue into us until she was blue in the face, but none of that really mattered to me, and it certainly doesn't now. "We're going to be married in three weeks anyway. What's the difference?" He turns and kisses me again, long and deep, and I think he's agreed until he pulls away once more. "We don't have to tell anyone," I whisper.

And what I don't say is that I hardly think it's fair for any of these men to insist their wives come to the marriage beds as virgins considering their pastimes in the mating houses.

"It doesn't work like that," he says. "I wouldn't want to keep this a secret from my brothers in the pack. It's very hard to lie to each other because once we're in our wolf forms, so much comes through the link between us."

"I don't understand."

"We work together as a whole. Could your left hand lie to your right hand?"

"Oh . . ."

"Which is why I didn't want you to know about our future marriage until the last possible second. It's hard enough for me and Elle to keep this a secret. What if I slipped, and it got out to others? Or let's say you told Joanna, and she told Grady.–"

"You can trust Grady."

"I know. He's one of my closest friends, but it's not so simple."

"You're the alpha. Make it simple."

He growls a little and tugs me closer, placing a kiss on my temple. "And here I thought you were sweet and innocent. You're conniving."

But he's laughing, so I snuggle in closer to him––as if that were possible. "You can't blame me for that. You're the one who threw me in a house with twenty other girls and said, 'Fight for a man.' Of course I've learned to be ruthless. I didn't want to end up in a mating house."

His grip tightens on me for a moment, and then he wiggles away and stands, helping me up. Once I get a little distance, my mind clears, and I'm reminded of all the things I want to ask him. I wouldn't be able to live with myself if I didn't speak my truth.

"Ryne, why don't you make changes around here? You're the alpha. You said yourself that you wanted the mating houses to be filled with women who are there willingly, so why not do it?"

His face softens, eyes dropping to the floor.

"What's more, why not do away with the claiming altogether? The women who wants to come to the shifters city to date the wolves for a chance at a better life could, and if it didn't work out, they could either willingly go to the mating house as a means of employment, or they could return home. I've been thinking about this a lot, and I can't leave here tonight without letting you know my feelings."

His eyes pop up, and he hugs me. "I wish it were that easy."

"So that's a no?" My voice cracks.

"It's a beautiful dream, Poppy. But it's not the reality of this world."

"So what? You send innocent girls to the mating houses against their will? And what about you, do you go there? Do you sleep with women who would like nothing more than to live a normal life?"

I already know he does. He took me to one and said as much.

He lets out a long sigh. "You're right. I know that. And I would love nothing more than to be able to give you that world one day and prove myself a worthy alpha on my own terms." He takes my hands in his. "Poppy, I lied to you. I often go to the mating houses to check on the women, but I've never been with one of them like that. Not every wolf in my pack has, and I don't enforce it. Some of us don't believe in having sex with someone placed in a whorehouse against her will, even if that woman acts like she wants to."

I gape at him. Why would he keep this a big secret? All those lies to protect his image? "Ryne, this is huge. We need to talk about this."

He shakes his head. "No. It's time to go back. We've got three weeks, and then we can talk all you like." He gently kisses my lips again. "Until then, we can't let anything jeopardize the plan. Thorn will be here in less than a week to take care of Anders. I already sent a few wolves to fetch him. He's the biggest danger to you, so I'll make sure Elle keeps you close.

That way, when my eyes are inevitably drawn to you, he'll think I'm looking at her."

I smile. "Now who's the conniving one?"

He kisses me once more. "You have to go."

I pull him close. "Sure, I'll go."

Three kisses later, and we still haven't left the library.

* * *

The next morning at breakfast, Joanna sets her plate down next to mine. "What the hell happened last night?"

I flush, and my eyes flick up to Elle, who sits across the table from me. "What do you mean? Nothing happened."

Joanna raises an eyebrow. "You mean, you just went to Ryne's house and spent hours there, and nothing happened?"

"How do you know I spent hours there?"

"Because I ran into Abi when I got here, and she said you didn't come home until two in the morning."

I feel my face flaming once again as my mind flashes back to a particularly passionate kiss and Ryne's hands wandering where I'd never let a man go before.

"Why are you blushing?"

"I'm not blushing." My voice has taken on a dreamy quality, and normally I'd give in to her by this point.

"Yeah, you are. Hello! You're as red as your namesake." Then she looks at Elle, who's staring at us from across the room, and visibly swallows. "I see. We'll talk about this later."

I can't talk about it later. I promised Ryne. "There's nothing to talk about. Ryne questioned me for a while. Elle was there. I'm blushing because he's intimidating to be around, and I'm embarrassed about the whole situation. I'm not used to having his undivided attention. He wanted to know everything I know about the deaths and the attack on you."

I hate lying, but I want Ryne's plan to work. Nobody can know.

She twists that around in her mind for a long minute before relaxing. "Yeah, Grady's all up in arms about it. He and Ryne are going to question Anders this morning. Ryne showed up at our door bright and early, telling Grady he wants to understand everything before King Tremaine gets here."

Morning classes pass in a blur, and Joanna stops questioning me. Maybe she bought the story, or maybe she didn't, and we simply haven't had any more alone time for her to continue her interrogation. Either way, I'm glad to be free of it. I'll tell her everything after the Pink Moon Festival, but I can't say anything until then.

I wish I could. I want nothing more than to gush to my best friend about my man.

She catches me on the way to lunch. "The weather's nice. You want to grab our food and eat outside?"

A warning signals in my head. "Yeah, that sounds good. We'll get Abi and Elle to come as well."

She nudges me. "No, silly. Just you and me."

I don't know what I'm going to tell her. I'm not good at keeping things from her, but I can't say anything.

I'm still trying to figure out how to keep lying to Joanna when the front door flies open. Ryne stands there flanked by two men I've never seen before. "That's her," he says, his voice dark and angry, and points right at me.

Adrenaline slices through me like a knife.

The men descend on me, and I have a momentary thought to run, but none of this makes sense. I freeze. But they don't touch me. Instead they grab Joanna.

She struggles against their grip. "Let me go," she demands.

Ryne stalks toward her. "You're part of the Resistance," he spits.

I knew there was a Resistance, but it's the first I've heard of it from him. My heart rips itself in two at that moment, half with my mate and half with my friend. Because I know what he speaks is the truth. But after what he confessed last night, doesn't he understand why the Resistance even exists? Is he really so surprised and angry that women would try to take down this horrible system?

She glowers at him. I expect her to deny it, but that's never been Joanna's style. "Oh yeah? Prove it."

Another figure appears at the door, and I crane my neck around so I can see him. My blood runs cold. Anders.

He saunters into the room, a free man. "Funny that. I uncovered a group of Resistance women, and as per King Tremaine's instructions, I took care of them without bothering Ryne. The king felt it was best to work under the radar on this one. Of course I was forced to tell Ryne the whole story this morning." He winks at Joanna. "You were my last target.

I actually didn't plan on killing you right away. I planned on questioning you first to see if you could help me find the head of the movement and lead me to more kills. But as you know, Elle got in the way."

"You're lying," Joanna shouts, her eyes locked on Anders in challenge. "You killed those women because you didn't approve of them. Nova wouldn't have given your son children, and Lexi wasn't good enough in your eyes to be a beta's wife."

"Oh really? Then why would I have come after you?"

"Same reason." But her voice waivers.

"Don't flatter yourself." Anders chuckles. "Oh well. You'll be dead soon enough. Maybe Thorn will still let me do the honors."

Ryne's eyes darken. "That's enough gloating from you, Anders. I don't approve of the way you handled this. But that doesn't change the fact that Joanna is part of the Resistance. It makes sense now." He glares at her. "Don't forget I caught you trying to run away."

"Doesn't she get a trial?" I rush forward, panic settling in. I can't see another sister––because that's what Joanna has become to me––killed by these men.

Ryne doesn't even acknowledge me, and suddenly it feels like everything is falling apart. "Take her to the prison," he orders. "King Tremaine is already on his way. With matters of the Resistance, he insists on taking things into his own hands. How unfortunate for you, Joanna. I may have shown a shred more mercy."

Joanna stares up at him, disbelief in her eyes. "Where's Grady?"

"Resistance or not, he'd fight for you. We had to lock him up. We'll let him out after we've dealt with you."

My mind can't seem to comprehend what is going on. "Dealt with her? What's that supposed to mean?" I ask.

"If she's found guilty, she'll be executed for treason."

"No, you can't do that." My voice shatters into a million broken pieces.

Ryne's eyes finally turn and plead with mine. "Please, Poppy, don't make this harder than it has to be."

"Then don't take my best friend away to prison."

"I don't have a choice."

Elle grabs one of my arms and Abi the other, moments before my knees give out. Then the men drag Joanna away.

For the first time since I've known her, she doesn't fight.

It's as if she knows she's already lost.

Chapter Twenty-Five

I can't help it. I'm not usually much of a crier, but I keep finding myself in tears. I'm in that exact state when Elle comes and sits next to me at lunch days later. She wraps an arm around my shoulders but doesn't say a thing. Abi is on my other side, and she doesn't say anything either. But she gets it.

I can't eat. The words start to flow, an emotional catharsis that I can't stop once I start. "Ryne hasn't shown his face here for days, and nobody will tell us anything. Have they already sentenced her? Killed her? I have no idea what's going on. I hate this. It's wrong. Why won't anyone tell us anything?" I turn to Elle, pleading with her through watery eyes. "Do you know? Can you tell me?"

She shakes her head. "I don't know anything either."

Faye prances into the dining room. When she sees the three of us, she stops short and snorts. "Oh, not this again."

"Shut up," I growl. I always knew she was a bitch, but this is over the line. I can't believe she's being so heartless about Joanna.

"You are so pathetic. You know that, right? My goodness, if I'd known all it took to get the attention of the betas was acting like a helpless victim, I would've taken notes."

"And you still would've sucked," Abi snaps. "Why do you always pick on Poppy? She never did anything to you!"

"Ha! Has the shy little mouse finally found her voice?" Faye mocks. "Please, go back to keeping your mouth shut."

"You're jealous of Poppy." Abi stands, her glossy black hair swinging behind her. "Don't you get it, Faye? This isn't about us versus us. It's about us versus them!"

"Now you sound like one of the Resistance." Faye raises an eyebrow. She does have a point, but there's no way Abi is a part of the Resistance. She's only a girl who's waking up to the truth, the same as all of us. "Hmm, I'm sure Anders would love to hear all about this conversation on our date tonight."

"I'm not Resistance." Abi swings her arms and points to the girls all staring up at the two of them battling it out. "None of us are. But what we are is trapped in a disgusting game, and we shouldn't be trying to hurt each other any more than the wolves already are."

"You're just saying that because you can't get one," Faye replies, stalking close to Abi and hovering over her. "And everyone knows it."

There's a chorus of laughter from the area where the distillery girls sit. I wipe a few tears away and watch both girls.

Abi lunges for Faye.

She wasn't a great fighter when she came here, but it turns out, Abi's a quick study.

They both land hard on the floor, Abi on top of Faye, punching her in the gut. These aren't slaps or hair pulling––none of the things of cat fights of the past––this is real hand-to-hand combat. We've been learning this over the last three months, but now we're seeing it in action.

Everyone jumps up, and the distillery girls come running. Faye screams and punches Abi in the mouth. Blood sprays from her lips, but Abi shakes it off and retaliates by breaking Faye's nose.

"Aren't you going to do something?" Blair screams at Elle, who is watching the whole thing with a smirk on her face.

Elle shrugs. "Looks like they're figuring it out just fine."

Actually, it looks like Abi is beating the snot out of Faye, and I've never been more proud. The rest of the distillery girls finally realize nobody is going to help their friend, so they jump in, and suddenly it's a full-on brawl.

Everyone is fighting.

I'm not about to be left out. I swing my leg around and get Blair right in the kidney; she goes down with a groan.

It feels. . . amazing. I actually feel like I'm doing something with myself. I go after Emma, and after a few good hits, she squeals and runs away. I turn, ready to take on my next opponent, but everyone's stopped.

"It's a damn good thing you're already spoken for," Madame Delphine says, storming in the room and pointing right at me. "Or else you'd be back to scraping the bottom of the leaderboard again. And right before a festival, no less."

"She started it." Raven points at Abi, and a bunch of the girls call out in agreement.

Abi peels herself off of a bruised and bloody Faye. "Not even going to try to deny it." She laughs bitterly. "I already know I'm going to end up in the mating house by the end of all this. Least I can do is ugly up Faye to make myself feel better." Abi brings a hand to her mouth, and I see her wiggle a few teeth.

Faye whimpers on the ground, her nose gushing blood, and her friends slowly help her up. She's going to have black eyes for weeks.

I hate that we keep fighting. Fighting each other isn't right. But some of these girls never seem to learn. They trade insults like they're ammunition. And quite frankly, I'm tired of it.

So is Abi.

Good for her. She's acting like Joanna, and I love every second of it. Joanna has been good for all of us. My eyes prick with tears. I don't even know if she is still alive.

"You'll be getting two new betas after the next festival." Madame Delphine frowns at Abi. "What if one of them takes a liking to you?"

Abi lifts a shoulder. "Still worth it."

I hope she's right, but when everything is said and done, I have a feeling she'll change her mind.

Madame Delphine surveys the lot of us, disappointed. Except for Bailey and her book, we're all a mess. "Get yourselves cleaned up. We're going into the city tonight." She pauses for a minute, and the energy intensifies. "King Tremaine has arrived."

* * *

We get a front-row seat to Joanna's trial, but it feels like I'm walking into a funeral or another brawl where only one side can come out victorious. At least she's still alive, but it's likely she won't be for long. I'm so nervous my hands are shaking, and my stomach feels like it's been carved out with a knife. We are seated outside on long benches in front of a tall building. A double staircase leads to a landing flanked by tall columns. Underneath the landing is a set of double doors.

"What's that?" I ask, pointing at the ominous doors.

"The prison. Back before the war against the paranormal, it was a market. But the wolves bricked it all in and made it a prison for the humans who fought against them. Nowadays, it's hardly used," Elle said. "Most people who get into trouble here don't last long."

Madame Delphine stands next to Elle but doesn't add anything. She stares up at the landing where Ryne stands with Nico, Grady, and Anders. Anders is arguing with Grady, whose face is red, but Ryne is staring at me. I drop my eyes, and Elle squeezes my hand.

"Stay strong," she whispers in my ear.

A hand touches my shoulder, and I glance up to see Madame Delphine looking at me, her eyes full of concern.

"This isn't fair," I say.

"I know. But maybe she'll be acquitted. They have no proof."

I want to believe her, that they won't execute my best friend over a madman's accusations, but everything I've seen with these wolves has shown me otherwise. And what if they do have proof?

A collective howl erupts from the crowd behind us. A pretty car with dark windows has pulled up, and King Tremaine steps out from the passenger door. He's dressed in a dark suit with his hair slicked back––the picture of power and wealth. In another time I might have found him handsome, but knowing who he is makes him look harsh.

He heads up the stairs flanked by a couple of bodyguards. Thorn greets Ryne and the others with a handshake. Grady leans over and whispers something in Ryne's ear. He doesn't say anything back, but he frowns deeply, and his eyebrows furrow.

The king shakes off his jacket and looks over the crowd. It's larger than I expected. How often do they have trials like this? Maybe most of the wolves came to see the king. Or maybe they're here for blood.

The king stands at the edge of the platform and surveys us all. I wish there weren't a railing there because then all it would take was a small shove, and he'd fall to his death. Or maybe I'm being dramatic. It's not that far down.

He holds up a hand, and the crowd quiets.

"Friends, I seem to be making more trips than normal down here lately. Maybe I should relocate." A howl goes up again, and he chuckles. I glance over at Ryne, who does not look happy with that idea. "Today though, I'm here to celebrate with you. Anders, come join me, please." Anders moves to his side, and the king puts a hand on his shoulder.

"Anders discovered a plot among some of our women to kill and overtake us. Not that they could possibly succeed, but they could hurt or kill a few of us, and every wolf's life is worth protecting."

That's a lie. If it were true, then they wouldn't fight to the death for dominance, but I have a feeling most of what is going to come out of his mouth is a lie. I haven't heard of the resistance movement wanting to kill the wolves. It's more about protecting the women. And maybe there's more to it--maybe there could be equality, and maybe the dream I confessed to Ryne could come true. I swallow that down though, because too much hope hurts even more than none.

"In the process of discovering this plot, he killed two of the women involved and found a third. I was called in to decide what we will do with this woman. I have decided that we will execute her to kick off the Pink Moon Festival, and all can watch. In the meantime, Anders will head up a group of wolves who will interrogate her to root out the rest of the women involved. I will stay in town and oversee the interrogation."

The breath rushes out of me. "No," I croak. "That wasn't a trial. She's not even here."

Elle grips my hand. "Keep quiet, or they'll think you're involved as well."

Movement up on the platform distracts me. Grady rushes for the king, and they both go over the rail and plummet to the cobblestones below.

Everyone reacts. Men descend on where the two fell. Ryne changes into his wolf and leaps off the balcony, landing in the middle of the crowd. He howls, and the surging crowd retreats. I can't see what's going on because there are too many people in the way.

I try to shove forward, but Elle and Madame Delphine hold me back. "You'll get trampled."

"But I have to know," I say.

"You'll find out soon enough."

I watch the writhing crowd as they all drop to one knee. Ryne still stands there in his wolf form, but another wolf stands next to him now. He's the same color as Ryne, midnight black, but he's almost twice as large. He howls, and the men in front of us shift into wolves as well, answering his call.

Of course, King Tremaine survived his fall.

But I doubt Grady will live much longer.

The two snarl at each other, and right as Grady pounces for the king, several of the wolves lunge. The alpha king howls, and the other wolves fall to the sides. They paw at the ground, eager to jump back into the fray, but for now they'll listen to whatever the king has ordered through the shifter link. I'm not sure if it's telepathy, intuition, or what exactly, but they understand each other so well in this form, and I'm left to stand here and watch.

At least Joanna isn't here to see it. Witnessing Grady's death would break her.

There's a moment of silence. It stretches tight like a wire. And then it snaps.

The king and Grady lunge at each other, snarling as they do. Thorn's wolf is massive, but Grady is quick. He dodges Thorn's claws and gets a swipe of his own, then rolls away and jumps back up to do it again. Thorn isn't falling for it a second time. He catches Grady's paw between his teeth and bares down. Grady howls painfully. I think the arm is about to break, but the king stops, flips Grady over, and presses his other leg to Grady's neck.

Grady changes back, and then so does the king.

I look down, staring at my scuffed shoes not only because I don't want to witness their nudity, but more because I don't want to see my friend's death.

"Ryne!" the king calls out. "Grady here is your number three, is he not?"

"He is, Father," Ryne growls. Anger radiates from his voice, but still, I don't look. I can't look. I won't.

"Then why would he challenge me, his king and an alpha, if he is loyal to you? Is this your doing?"

"Never," Ryne spits. "He does it because Joanna is his fated mate." Ryne bows his head, subservient to the king.

"And you didn't even give her a chance to defend herself," Grady shouts.

Thorn chuckles madly. "Well then, that certainly makes things interesting. I was planning to kill you today for your insubordination, but I think it would be more fitting that you die at the full moon with your mate."

"I'd rather die for her than live for you," Grady snaps, and Thorn presses his face into the floor until Grady coughs.

"Don't worry, that will be arranged. But since this is my son's pack, he will be the one to do it."

Ryne's face pales. "Father--"

"You will kill them yourself, Ryne, and you will do it in front of your pack like the alpha you were born to be. End of discussion!"

With that, he storms from the grounds, and Grady is hauled away.

Chapter Twenty-Six

I can't sleep. Soon, Joanna and Grady will be executed. It's been two days since the so-called trial, and everyone is acting like nothing is wrong. I throw on my workout clothes and plan to get a run in before the monotony of classes.

Not that I've been paying much attention. I can't. Not with Joanna's death looming. I'm slipping a little on the board, but at this point, I don't care. I'll be married off soon anyway.

Everyone's still sleeping, and the sun won't be up for another hour, but I tug on a jacket, then jog quietly down the stairs. I hear voices and freeze.

"This is wrong," Elle whispers, "and you know it."

"There's nothing I can do. He won't listen to me," Madame Delphine responds. I wish I could see them, but I stay right where I am. "We're not married anymore, and even when we were, he didn't listen to me. It's a good thing I gave him Ryne, or I might not even be alive today."

A hand slams against a wall. "Thorn is going to be the death of us all," Elle growls.

Madame shushes her and then sighs. "I know."

I peek around the corner and blink into the darkness, making out their forms. They don't see me, but the despondency is clear in both their voices.

Madame Delphine places a hand on Elle's arm, but she shakes herself free. "I can't take this anymore. I'm heading over to talk to Ryne. Thorn hasn't left his side, but he's never been an early morning person. We'll see if we can come up with a solution so that Grady and Joanna will live."

Madame Delphine slips back into her room, and Elle heads out the front door. I follow, and she still doesn't notice me, or if she does, she doesn't acknowledge my presence. Surely a wolf would hear someone following. They have a heightened sense of hearing, and Elle is a powerful luna. Maybe she wants me to trail after her, or maybe she's too lost in her thoughts.

She heads down the path to the boats. I keep to the bushes and trees and manage to follow her all the way to the river. A large ferryboat waits there. She climbs aboard and heads to the front to talk to the captain. Their voices murmur good-naturedly, and I use the distraction to slip aboard and hide underneath one of the benches. I have no idea what I'm doing, but Ryne loves me. He hasn't said it yet, but he doesn't have to. I know it's true. Maybe he'll listen to me. I have to see him and convince him to not hurt Joanna or Grady.

The floor is rough on my skin and smells faintly of fish, but this will be worth it. The bumpy ride seems to take forever, but eventually the boat stops at another dock. I peek out and see Elle and the captain disembarking from the front of the boat.

I sneak out from under my bench and hit the dock from the back side. There are a lot more boats out here, so I manage to hide in between them. It's early morning, and there's no one else around. Ryne's house is visible from the docks because it's on the other side of the park. I spot Elle walking through the greenery, her shoulders back and her head high. I keep to the shadows of the surrounding houses and manage to slip up the walk to his front door.

She knocks.

Now is the time to reveal myself. It's too late to turn back.

I hop up next to her. "Hey, Elle," I say brightly.

She squeaks and jumps from me, holding her heart. "Don't scare me like that."

"Sorry." But I'm not sorry. "And don't pretend like you didn't know I was following you all along."

"Hmm . . . no comment on that." She winks and then narrows her eyes. "So I assume you're here for the same reason as me?"

"Yup. I overheard you and Madame Delphine. I wanted to talk to Ryne as well. If he gets mad that I'm here, you can always say I snuck along, and you had no idea I was following you."

Her lips quirk. "You're something else, Poppy."

The front door opens, and Knox stands there, freshly showered and dressed for the day in his slacks and button up. He takes in both me and Elle, not appearing surprised to see us. His eyes linger on my face for a second longer than they should. Will we ever get to talk? And if we do, what will he say to me?

I know what I'll say to him. I'll say that I'm sorry he's in this position, I'm sorry that we can't be together, that he's become a slave to the wolves, and that I'll do what I can to make his life better. But I won't apologize for loving Ryne.

Because I do love him.

"It's not a good time," he whispers, snapping out of his trance. "Thorn is staying here."

"I was sort of hoping he'd be out at the mating houses all night," Elle replies. She takes a step back. "Let Ryne know we came."

She turns to leave.

"No," I hiss, "I need to talk to Ryne. Now."

Knox purses his lips. "Since when did you become so stubborn?"

It's not a compliment. My mouth drops open, but I recover quickly. "Since Willow died in front of me. Since you pretended not to know me. Since I found Nova's dead body. Since--"

"Wait, you two know each other?" Elle interrupts.

An awkward silence follows, and I know I've said too much. Knox clears his throat. "Same village. That's all."

"I'm not leaving." I fold my arms over my chest and widen my stance. "So go wake up Ryne and get his wolfy butt out here."

"No need." Ryne's voice breaks through the tension, and I jump. "Me and my wolfy butt are right here." He's bounding up the front steps from the street, shirtless and sweating. Gym shorts cling to his hips, but even his feet are bare. He must have been running in his wolf form this morning. My heart jumps at the sight of him, wanting to go to him, but he doesn't look happy to see me.

He peers around for a minute, and then his eyes land on Knox. "Is my father sleeping?"

Knox nods once. "As far as I know."

The sun is cresting on the horizon, painting the sky a pale pink. Back at the manor, the girls will be waking up and preparing for their morning workouts. It stands to reason this is the hour a lot of the shifter city will be waking, and Thorn Tremaine very well may be included in that. But then again, he's the king, making him above all others. He can pretty much do whatever the hell he wants.

"We need to talk." I inch toward Ryne, the rest of the world fading away. "Please."

He flicks his eyes to Knox. "Leave us," he commands, and Knox shuts the door without an ounce of hesitation.

Ryne collapses onto the bottom step and holds his head in his hands.

I sit down on one side of him and Elle on the other. She places a hand on his shoulder, her eyes narrowing. "Why do you trust that human boy so much? Poppy and I should leave."

Ryne shakes his head. "Knox is alright. I know a lot of our kind don't like to let the claimed men get too close, but Knox saved my life when some of my own men failed me."

Elle raises her eyebrows. "How so?"

"I don't want to get into it right now. It's. . . complicated."

Now this is a story I'm dying to hear. I don't think Elle will let that go, but she does. "Are you okay?" she asks at last.

He shakes his head but doesn't look up. "Everything is falling apart. Grady is like a brother to me. I can't kill him, and if we execute Joanna, Poppy's never going to speak to me again."

He reaches out and grips my hand. I study our hands as my tears swell. His is so large compared to mine, but it fits perfectly. I'm surprised he's willing to display such affection here. It's so public. I should be grateful––I am––but I'm still as torn up as he is about all this. I swallow the angry words I want to say and remain calm. "That's not true. But surely you must see the injustice here. There's no proof that Joanna is in the Resistance. Nor do we even know if there was proof for Nova or Lexi."

But it stands to reason they could've been.

"Don't you see? It doesn't matter. My father can do what he likes, even when it's not right."

Elle lets out a snort. "Careful, Ryne, or your father might think you're in the Resistance as well."

"What is with this resistance movement in the Carolina Pack anyway?" Ryne squeezes my hand tighter. "I know we've had dissent in our past--every pack has--but nothing so organized. Are they really banding together across multiple packs? I'd never even heard of this Resistance group before Anders confessed everything, and no one can adequately explain it to me. I'm supposed to believe everything without proof?"

"It's . . ." I begin, but Elle cuts me off.

"It's a group of women and wolves who want to undermine the current system," she says, matter-of-factly. "Take solace in the fact that this isn't just happening here, Ryne."

"How the hell am I supposed to take solace in that?" he grinds out.

"Because it's all over and in Chicago too. This isn't on you."

"So what have you heard?" He turns on her.

She shrugs. "Just that they don't like the alphas in charge. They want to take over."

"That's not . . ." I start but shut up when Elle gives me a scathing look. But she's wrong. Isn't she? I thought the Resistance wanted to stop the forced mating. It has nothing to do with alphas. At least Joanna never alluded to that. Maybe Elle doesn't know what she's talking about, or maybe she doesn't want Ryne to know too much.

"In Chicago, I was part of a team trying to infiltrate and dismantle the Resistance. It threatens everything your father stands for. Which is why he's so determined to snuff it out here, even if he doesn't have proof that the women Anders targeted are truly part of it."

I still don't know if her words are entirely true or not, but with Elle shooting daggers at me, I don't dare say any more. She and I will have to have a long talk later.

"Why haven't I heard about it until now?" Ryne asks. He looks up, and I expect him to be angry, but he's not. He's shocked and frustrated with himself, as if he never believed he could miss something so big happening right under his nose.

Elle rolls her eyes. "Don't you see, Ryne? Your father feels threatened by you. You're one of the strongest alphas ever born, and if you were to join such a movement, you might be able to take him down. In fact, there are very few wolves who are aware of its existence or tasked with fighting it. I think Thorn recruited me because I'm no threat since I can't take over."

Ryne tugs me closer to him. "And he trusts Anders?" The disgust in his voice is strong. The fact that Thorn went around Ryne, right to his number two, is pretty low. I imagine this is the kind of thing that would make alphas challenge each other.

Elle stands and stretches, hovering over both of us. "I don't know why he asked Anders to be involved in taking out the resistance. I think he's tried to find one wolf in every pack to root it out in their city. But never the alpha. My guess is Anders was the most ruthless wolf he could think of."

"It should be the alpha," Ryne spits. "This is my pack. Mine."

The door behind us opens, and Ryne jumps up, dropping my hand, every exposed muscle tensing like thick cords of steel. Thorn stands there and then strides down the steps until he's standing a stair above us. He tilts his head. "Is it your pack, Ryne? Because if you ask me, you haven't been acting like a leader in quite some time."

Thorn towers above us with his oily hair slicked back and his fitted button-down shirt and pressed slacks. For all Madame Delphine said about Thorn not being a morning person, he looks as if he's been up for hours. Was Knox lying to us? Or did he simply not know? I really hope Thorn didn't overhear everything.

"Well, what do we have here?" Thorn asks, his eyes roaming over the three of us like he can see every secret written across our skin. Ryne was still holding my hand when Thorn stepped out here. Did he see it? My gut twists because I'm certain he did.

Ryne moves quickly toward Elle and slips his arm around her waist. "Elle often joins me for breakfast. Is that a problem?"

Thorn's eyes land on me.

"Poppy is my best friend," Elle says. "I hate traveling on the boats alone, so she sometimes comes with me because we get so little time to chat just us. She reads in the library while Ryne and I eat." Her voice is smooth as silk, the lie coming out clean.

The king closes the distance between me and him. He runs a thumb along my cheek. "Ah, yes, Poppy, I remember you. Last time I was here, Ryne couldn't keep his eyes off you." He jerks his head back around and chuckles. "Looks like that's still true. You are a pretty little thing, so I can see why. But I can't have you getting in the way of Elle and Ryne's relationship."

"I'm not," I sputter. "Elle's my best friend. I barely even talk to Ryne."

Thorn gives a wicked grin. He thinks this is amusing, as if I'm a mosquito that needs to be squashed. "I'm not buying that story for a second. So let's fix that, shall we? I haven't taken a wife since Delphine."

"No?" My voice is trembling. I don't even know what I'm doing, except that maybe if I ask enough questions, I can slow this down.

"I've been a single man for eight years. Delphine and I parted ways as soon as Ryne turned fifteen and came of age."

I know Ryne's twenty-three and that Thorn had a number of wives before Madame Delphine. What I don't know is what happened to those other wives. Are they even alive anymore? A knowing chill creeps over me as his eyes narrow on mine.

"I think it's time for a new one. You'll do just fine. After the Pink Moon Festival, you'll return to Chicago with me as my human queen. You'll want for nothing."

Ryne moves for me, but Elle is faster. She inserts herself between me and Thorn, pushing me back. "You can't do that."

Thorn's eyes flash. "Why not? Last I checked, you were not king."

She lets out a breath. "I know. But Nico is her fated. You can't stand between that––it's not our way."

His eyebrows raise. "I admit that I don't really keep up with the drama among Ryne's betas, but I thought I heard that Nico was fated to the woman who died at the Wolf Moon Festival."

Elle shakes her head. "He really liked her. That's why so many people assumed she killed herself. Because he was going to leave her for Poppy."

Thorn clenches his jaw. "I don't appreciate being lied to, Elle." Then he locks eyes on mine. "I don't buy this farce for a second, but even so, I will talk with Nico about this. Something is off about you, dear Poppy, and I'm determined to find out what it is. And when I do, I'm either going to marry you or kill you."

<h1 style="text-align:center">Chapter Twenty-Seven</h1>

Elle doesn't say another word to me until we are on the boat headed home. After Thorn's threat, I thought Ryne was going to challenge him right then and there, but he didn't. We ended up eating breakfast together, and it was a tense affair. Elle managed to keep the conversation flowing, but I don't think I heard a word anyone said. And I still didn't get to talk to Ryne about Joanna. She's going to die, and there is nothing I can do to stop it.

"What was all that about the Resistance?" I accuse Elle, not even bothering to hide my anger.

"Half-truths."

"Why didn't you let me talk?"

She throws her hands in the air. "You can't tell Ryne about them."

"Why not? He actually seems sympathetic."

"That's the problem. He'd understand, but he couldn't safely be a part of it. Oh, he'd want to—I know Ryne well enough to know that. But *Thorn* is his alpha, and he'd never be able to keep this big of a secret from him. Not to mention, that's his own father he'd be working to take down. Do you really think he'd be able to follow through with something like that? It's better to leave Ryne out of it."

Everything she's saying makes it sound like she's part of the Resistance, so if that's the case, her argument doesn't stand. "Isn't Thorn your alpha too?" I challenge. "You're a wolf. How are you keeping these secrets?"

She shuts her mouth and drops her eyes, the blood draining from her face.

"Oh, come on, Elle." My voice goes low. "It's obvious you're involved in this."

She sighs. "Listen, I'm stronger than most people think. They underestimate me, which I use to my advantage. And besides, Thorn hardly questions me on anything. I'm not important enough to him."

"He thinks you're going to marry his son."

"So? I'm a woman. A luna is only special to them because our sons make great alphas. I'm not even ranked. We aren't allowed to be."

I stare at her for a minute, trying to read her sour expression. I know she's probably not allowed to tell me anything, but for whatever reason, I've gotten her to open up just a crack. Time to keep prying. "Will you please tell me if you're a part of the Resistance?" I whisper. We're alone, and the waves lapping against the boat are muffling our conversation, but asking aloud is still terrifying. Doesn't matter––I need to know.

She winks at me. "Are you?"

"I'm not, but I know about it because of Joanna." Time to be brave. "And I want to be."

She grins wickedly and leans back, closing her eyes. The breeze has disappeared since this morning, and the sun is out, and it's as if she's soaking in the rays like a cat. I would join her, but my mind won't slow down.

Something Elle said earlier hits me. "Wait a second, if Ryne can't hide things from Thorn, then how can he hide his feelings for me?"

A ping of insecurity swells through me as her eyes open lazily.

"That's an interesting loophole actually. Because you're Ryne's fated mate, that means he'll do anything to protect you. That counts for this form as well as his wolf form. Thorn knowing about you is a threat to your safety, so Ryne can effectively hide all thoughts about you. It's not easy though. One loving thought or memory of you, and that's it."

"Memory?" I sit up taller. "Tell me how the link works?"

She shrugs. "It's like being part of a shared mind. Thoughts, feelings, memories, images––they all get passed around."

"Do all the packs have this?"

"I don't know about other shifters, but for wolf shifters, yes."

"Does it stay within the pack?"

She hums to herself for a second. "Well, that's tricky. The answer is yes and no. When we travel to another pack, we can't usually access their link without being initiated into the pack. But there are exceptions if the alpha brings you into the link. It's a conscious choice he makes while in wolf form."

"This is getting confusing."

She laughs. "Yeah, Ryne brought me in because he wanted the pack to respect me and see me as important, because we're supposed to get married, but also for my protection since I'm an unmarried woman. But he could just as easily change his mind about that and remove me. If I was initiated though, the only way for me to be removed from the link would be death, exile, or being initiated into a different pack."

"What's the initiation link?"

"If I told you that, I'd have to kill you." Her smile quirks. "It's a sacred ritual––meaning it's a big secret."

"So is that what they mean when they say a wolf comes of age at fifteen? They get initiated into their pack?"

She points at me. "Exactly. And just because Thorn is the alpha over Chicago, don't think he's not linked in when he comes here. He is. There are packs under his command all over the continent, and if any were to show Thorn disrespect, he'd have the alpha replaced immediately."

"And how does Thorn feel about fated mates?"

She blows out a long breath. "Do you want the scary truth or the sugar-coated version?"

"The scary truth."

"The bond toward a fated mate trumps the bond toward anything else, including higher ranks. Since it's considered sacred, and since they're rare, he allows it. But if there were too many fated mates in a pack, I don't doubt he'd feel threatened." Her face goes hard. "And, honey, the Carolina Pack has had three fated matches in a matter of months. Don't think that's gone unnoticed."

I sit back, my mind whirling with everything she explained. It sounds complicated. It also sounds like Ryne is taking huge risks to keep me safe. And as much as I hate it, I finally understand why he's tried to stay away from me and keep our interactions limited. Why he's held off kissing me in the past or stopped more from happening. But I already miss him. I wonder how much longer Ryne and I are going to have to wait. Some days it feels like I've been waiting for him forever, and others like it's only been a moment since we met.

The wedding can't come fast enough. But then that day will be ruined, because my best friend will be executed right before I'm supposed to be married. How can I survive something like that? I force my mind from all these fears and focus back on Elle. As we fly across the river, the spray of the water glistens off her dark cheeks, illuminating her high cheekbones. She's smart, strong, beautiful, and perfect for Ryne. In every way, she's perfect. And part of me wonders if at the end of this, she'll be his mate after all.

* * *

"There's got to be something we can do," I say to Abi, my voice hollow. We're lying in our beds, staring up at the dark ceiling. Outside, the moon is only two days away from waxing full, and we're not any closer to saving Joanna and Grady. I'm more determined than ever to join the Resistance, but with Joanna gone and Elle keeping her mouth shut, I can't figure out who to even talk to. Abi has been right by my side, wanting to help too, and feeling just as frustrated. I've told her some of what's happened with Ryne but not everything. I'm still keeping the secret about the weddings.

After that fateful morning where King Thorn caught Ryne holding my hand, Thorn sent word that Elle was to leave Drayton Hall and officially move in with Ryne. We haven't seen her since, and Faye keeps telling everyone it's because she's on a pre-honeymoon with Ryne. I've wanted to slap her for it, to put her in her place and tell her that Ryne loves *me*, but what can I do? I'm sworn to secrecy. And besides, we haven't seen him either. Her assumption makes sense from the outside looking in.

Abi sighs. "What about your dress fitting today? Was there anyone there that seemed like they could be part of the Resistance?"

"No," I reply miserably. "I'd hoped Elle would've been there, but she wasn't. And when I tried to talk with the seamstress about Joanna, she poked me and told me to mind my manners." The dress fitting had been a horrible experience anyway. None of the choices were close to anything I'd like to get married in, so I ended up letting the workers choose for me.

"That's it," I say, jumping from the bed. "I'm going to Madame Delphine."

At this point, I'm beyond caring who knows I want to be part of the Resistance. I'll do anything to save Joanna. There is no way I'm letting Ryne execute her. Elle said he'd do anything to protect me. Maybe I'll put myself between him and Joanna.

"I'm coming with you," Abi squeaks, and together we pad from our bedroom and down the dark hallway. The girls are supposed to be sleeping, but with the festival coming up, I doubt very many of them are. Last thing I need is for one of them to catch me out here and try to use it against me somehow.

We reach Madame Delphine's door, and I tap on it. No answer. I tap a little louder and hear her murmur from inside.

"Crap. I think you woke her up," Abi hisses.

"What's going on?" Madame Delphine peeks her head through the door and stares up at me. I'm tall, so I'm used to women looking up at me, but when she does it, it makes me feel like when Mama used to chastise me. "Are you okay?"

"May we please come in?" I ask. I don't want to answer her questions here.

She considers it for a moment and then widens the door to let us through. Her room is warm and cozy, with a big bed and rumpled blankets from where she'd clearly been sleeping. "On with it," she says. "Although I suspect I already know what this is about." Her face is irritated, but her eyes are sympathetic. "Again."

"Joanna," I confirm, trying to keep the tremble out of my voice.

She gives me a sad frown. "There's nothing I can do for the girl."

But I heard her with Elle. I know she cares about Joanna. I know she thinks Thorn is a tyrant. And if Elle is part of the Resistance, then it stands to reason Madame Delphine could be as well.

Time to gather my courage and ask.

"Are you in the Resistance?" Abi beats me to it. "Because we're pretty sure you are."

My lips twitch a little. I didn't know Abi had it in her to be so bold. It was a very Joanna-like move. But then I shouldn't be surprised, since Joanna's influence has rubbed off on us.

Madame Delphine's weary eyes grow alert and narrow. "How dare you speak of such things." Her words come out in a hiss. But she doesn't deny it. And she doesn't even sound that mad.

I inch closer to her, eager now. "You are, aren't you?"

She sputters and shifts back a few steps. I've never seen her so flustered. "Of course I'm not. Why would I be part of an organization that goes against my son?"

Abi isn't buying it, and neither am I.

"Maybe because you want to help him." I stand a little taller. "Maybe because you know first-hand, better than anybody, how dangerous Thorn is, and if someone doesn't stand up to him, eventually he's going to kill Ryne."

"Get out," she snaps.

I don't expect it, and it feels like a slap.

"But we want to help," Abi protests.

I nod. "I have an idea. One that could save Joanna."

"No." Madame Delphine's tone is hard. "I am not part of the Resistance, and you are not either. Whatever this plan is, it's foolish and dangerous and must be forgotten immediately. Joanna will die, and there is nothing you can do to stop it. It will hurt, and you will move on. You must remember your place, else you end up like her."

She ushers us to the door and into the hallway.

"But if you'd be willing to hear me out, I think--"

"Enough!" She slams the door in my face.

I turn to Abi.

"What are we going to do now?" she asks.

"We're going to save her ourselves. Are you prepared for something like that?"

Her mouth thins into a determined line. "I have nothing left to lose."

Chapter Twenty-Eight

The morning of the festival, I wake with my stomach in knots. I peer over at Abi to find her eyes wide open as well. It's early, but the showers are already going. Tonight, two new betas are going to be introduced to the remaining claimed girls, and they want to look their best.

Tonight, Abi goes to the mating house.

Tonight, we're going to save my best friend.

Or die trying.

I roll over and face Abi. "Are you ready?" I ask.

She shakes her head. "No. But I have to be."

"We got this." Dinner from the night before threatens to come up, but I swallow it down. I can't show Abi that I'm scared. Her part in the plan is crucial.

The morning passes excruciatingly slow, but at the same time speeds by. I can't figure out how that is possible. We don't have afternoon classes because we all have to get ready for the festival.

I grab Abi's hand and head to the stairs, but before we can go up to our room, Madame Delphine stops us.

"You're getting ready in the city," she says to me.

"What? Why?" I sputter.

"Because you are marrying Nico tonight, or did you forget that?"

"I didn't forget. I just had other things on my mind. Like my best friend getting executed for no reason."

"I understand." She nods. "But brides go into the city. Abi will come over with the rest of us."

Abi shoots me a panicked look. I squeeze her hand. This wasn't part of the plan, but we'll have to roll with it. "Harlow and Katelyn will help you get ready. You'll be okay." I turn to Madame Delphine. "Alright, let's do this."

She tilts her head. "The beta wives have your wedding dress ready to go, and they'll be helping you get ready. Are you prepared to behave?"

"Why wouldn't I behave?"

She doesn't answer that. Instead she says, "It's very important that you get along with them. These women will be your peers from here out."

I swallow and think of saving Joanna instead of these women I'm supposed to impress. My plan would work so much better if I had a dress I could easily move in, but the tailor saw to it that my poofy monstrosity is skintight through the bodice, and it has about a million pounds in the skirt. Too bad it may have to get torn in the process. I don't care––this plan has to work. Joanna's life depends on it.

And then once she's saved, Ryne and I will get married.

A car is waiting for me, but it's not Knox behind the wheel. I've never seen this guy before. He doesn't say a word to me as we drive into the city. That's probably for the best. He pulls up to a large white house with towering columns and round porches. Another car has just pulled up behind us. Elle gets out and gives me a nod but doesn't say anything. She's wearing white silky-looking pajamas, and her hair looks freshly braided. It feels like I haven't seen her in ages, and I want to ask her a million things all at once.

We climb the stairs together. "Where have you been?" I ask.

She shakes her head. "Not now."

We knock on the door, and a stout woman answers, squealing. There are about thirty women all laughing behind her. The woman pulls us into the room and slips elegant glasses filled with pink champagne into our hands.

She claps. "Oh, this is so exciting. Usually we don't get to do this except for the wedding season right after the Harvest Moon Festival. Ladies, by the time we are done with you, you won't recognize yourselves."

Elle and I are ushered off to different rooms. I am plucked and waxed, and it takes hours to do my makeup, hair, and nails. When they try to make my nails longer, I refuse. I already feel like I don't belong in my own body. I have to keep something normal.

I'm taken to another room, which has my huge white dress slung over the couch. Two women help me into it. It's corseted and pushes my breasts up, but even then, I don't have much cleavage. They tie the strings tight, and I can hardly breathe. Sleeves that fall off my shoulders reveal a peekaboo of skin, and the skirt poofs out like a gigantic cupcake. I swear it sticks out six feet in all directions. There is no way in hell that I'm going to be able to move in this thing, but I'm just going to have to suck it up and force it.

I nearly get stuck in the doorway on the way out, but I somehow make it down the stairs into the main room without falling onto my face. Elle stands in the entryway in a sleek cream wedding gown that looks fantastic on her. There is a slit that practically goes up to her hip, and I'm jealous because if she needs to run, she can. Why didn't they offer a dress like that for me?

Her lips twitch when she spots me.

"Nice dress," she says with a sly smile. "You look like a princess."

"Thanks," I grumble. "Maybe we should switch."

"Not happening." She nudges me and drops her lips to my ear. "Our plan is still on. Try to be happy about that."

I jerk away from her. As much as I love Ryne, I can't think about that right now. When she says "plan," all I can think of is the one with Abi, but I know she's talking about marrying Ryne. "I'm not going to be happy until Joanna is safe and sound. If he kills her, there is no way I'm going through with any wedding. How could I?"

The chatter in the room suddenly dies down. Elle chuckles, but her eyes are hard. "Ignore her. She just hates getting dressed up and is nervous about the wedding. Come on, Poppy, our carriage awaits."

She motions toward the door.

I swallow.

It's time.

After tonight, nothing will be the same. I'll either rescue my best friend or die in this horrendous dress.

* * *

It's late March, so spring is in full bloom when we arrive at the venue. I expect to be taken to one of the old city buildings or at least be getting married inside, but we're not. We're back at the very same park where I watched Ryne kill all those wolves who challenged him, the one across from his stately home. Back then, it had been cold and dreary, but today the park has been entirely transformed. My mouth falls open, and a little purr of approval comes out, despite my better judgment.

"Tell me about it," Elle says. And then we're being ushered from the safety of the town car. The other patrons haven't arrived yet, so I'm able to take it all in without distraction. The trees are flowering with buds of pink and white, tulips line the walkways, and pansies in every shade crowd the flower beds. And in the middle of it all, a series of crisp white tents have been erected. At least, I think they're tents. I'm not really sure what they are because they're so grand and pretty. They're open on all sides and big enough to fit a hundred people in each. I've never seen anything like it. At the end of the tents, out in the open field, a stage has been built. I've seen enough stages in my time here that I know it can't be good. That's probably where they're going to kill Joanna and Grady—I force myself to look away.

A waft of savory food tickles my nose, and my stomach growls. I haven't eaten in hours, and I'm used to eating three solid meals a day now. I've gained at least ten pounds of much-needed weight since arriving here. I frown, because how many times had I gone to bed hungry as a kid? And how many villagers live on the barest scraps while the shifters live in luxury?

And okay, not all the wolves live in luxury, but if I end up marrying Ryne today—or even Nico—then I will. I've been so blinded by my feelings for Ryne that I've forgotten to ask myself this one very important question: how am I going to live with myself?

How am I going to live with myself if Joanna dies?

If humans continue to be treated like slaves?

If the girls keep getting sent to the mating houses?

If Anders gets away with killing so many innocent women?

If the king continues to rule over Ryne, and Ryne continues to take it?

"No," I snap.

"What?" Elle asks. I hadn't meant to say the words out loud. She stares, and from the knowing look she gives me, I wonder if she's thinking the same questions. Maybe they've been haunting her much longer than they've been haunting me. It's no wonder she's in the Resistance. Even though she won't admit it aloud, I know it's true. I won't be able to make it much longer here without joining myself. I can't sit around and do nothing anymore.

"Nothing," I reply, and it physically hurts me to say it.

But she knows better, knows I'm a liar and that nothing is most definitely something. And I can only hope that when the time comes, she'll be on my side.

Chapter Twenty-Nine

I stare out from the little plastic window of the small tent that Elle and I are taken to and told is the bridal room. We've been swarmed with the same hair and makeup crew who are applying the final touches. "Let's fix your lipstick," one says to me, her voice pleased with herself and excited. I couldn't care less. I relax and open my lips, but I don't look at her as she glides something thick and gooey across them. My eyes are still trained on the window.

I don't care about the newcomers, the beta families all dressed up, or even our claimed girls who come prancing down the sidewalks like a row of colorful spring flowers in their special pastel Pink Moon Festival dresses. The arriving guests only keep my attention for a short moment, long enough to see if it's who I'm waiting for.

Joanna.

I don't want to miss her.

I have to help her. And I hate to think about it, but if my plan fails, I have to at least say goodbye.

My eyes start to water.

"Oh, none of that," the makeup girl chastises. "This is your special day!"

"She's just really happy," Elle lies for me.

Our eyes meet, and she nods once in understanding. She's as worried as I am. Maybe I'm not so alone. I reach out and grab her hand, and she squeezes back in solidarity. I'm reminded of how much she's risking with this too. If things go south, her family could end up dead.

"Are you ready for this?" she asks.

No.

"Yes," I lie.

I gaze back out the window to see Shauna and Amos. They look happy, which makes me a touch happier too. I wish I could've spent another evening with them, laughing around Shauna's dinner table and talking about flowers. After the engagement to Nico was announced, Justin backed off completely. We didn't even talk about it. All I got was an understanding nod from him, and that was the end of our relationship. It was time to move on.

"Look!" Elle jumps up, and her hair and makeup people scatter in protest. "That's my family. My mom and dad and my four brothers."

Sure enough, a beautiful family strolls down the sidewalk. Her mother looks so much like her, ebony-skinned and petite and absolutely beautiful. She's an aging human with some gray in her hair and wrinkles around her mouth and eyes. Her appearance is a good twenty years older than her fit-looking husband, but the man holds to her arm like he doesn't mind it at all, like he'll be proud to stay with her until her dying day, and may even stay single thereafter.

It makes me smile.

Elle's father is perhaps the largest shifter man I've ever seen. His head is shaved and shiny, which is different from the shifters I've seen who keep their hair long. Her brothers look to be both older and younger than her, but all close in age. They're copies of their handsome father but with jet-black curly hair. The boys catch the gazes of many of the men and women as they find their places among the waiting crowd below the stage. How could they not? They're gorgeous, and from the looks of it, single.

Off on a distant lawn, little white chairs are set up in rows facing an arbor decorated in white roses and shiny gold ribbons. Madame Delphine made me practice the ceremony back at the manor a couple of times this week, but it's not much different than the ones the humans use. Soon I'll be standing under that arc, proclaiming my love and sealing my fate. The question still remains as to who.

A thought strikes me——when will Ryne find the time to initiate Elle and her family into the pack? Has he already done it? He would do it before the ceremony. So maybe he already has?

No.

Because the other wolves arriving would question why they suddenly have eight new pack members. I still don't know what the initiation is, but it can't be simple. Nothing about these wolves is simple. I grimace to myself—-this isn't going to be easy to pull off. Especially not with King Thorn overseeing it all. With that final thought, the last to arrive are the grooms and the king himself. They climb out of the same car. King Thorn first, then Ryne, then Nico.

My breath catches, snagging somewhere between my heart and my head. I don't know what to do about Ryne, and I don't think he'll forgive me, but I'll never forgive myself if I don't go through with this. I can only hope that when it's over, he'll still want me as his wife.

The sun begins to set, and lights brighten the field and twinkle among the trees. The warmth of the spring day lingers, mixing with the sweet scent of all the fresh flowers. The tent flap opens, and a woman sticks her head in. "It's time," she says. She's holding two massive flower bouquets. She hands the white calla lilies to Elle and the crimson poppies to me. I take them eagerly, wondering if these were chosen from the ones I grew. I know it seems silly, but I decide that they are, and that makes me feel a little bit better.

The weddings won't be first. Starting with the gore and ending with the celebration seems to be the wolf way, and as we step out into the blinding sunset, I realize we're wanted out here for display, as if to say, "Look at our lovely brides" and "This is the prize betas earn when they stay in line."

All the other claimed girls are already next to the stage, preening and waving to the betas milling about. There are no chairs for us. Not that I'd be able to sit in this monster of a dress anyway. Ryne is talking to his father across the stage as Elle and I walk up the stairs. He lifts his gaze and meets my eye. The connection is undeniable. I couldn't break it even if I wanted to, and I don't want to.

"Stop staring at him," Elle hisses in my ear. I tear my eyes away from his, and Elle blows Ryne a kiss. Thorn's mouth presses into a straight line. I wonder if he noticed. Hopefully he thought Ryne was staring at Elle. He'd probably be unhappy to see me no matter who I was looking at; the man has it out for me. Which makes it all the more terrifying that he tried to make me his wife. Unless he was bluffing. If he knows the truth about me, I'm doomed.

We take our positions in front of the other girls, and several of them glare at me. Abi moves to stand right behind me and grips my hand, passing me the dagger that is supposed to be tucked safely under my pillow back at the manor. We'd planned to take care of this part back at

Drayton Hall before Madame Delphine had taken me away. Nobody seems to notice as I adjust the blade so it's hidden between my hands and the massive bouquet of poppies. It's part of a matching set, and Abi has the other one hidden in her bodice.

I look around at the crowd. It's mostly betas and their wives, all dressed up, standing in front of the stage. But beyond the park, swarming the streets, are the gammas and the deltas. The park is surrounded by wolves on all sides, most in their human forms, but some have shifted. I should be used to it by now, but it still makes me nervous every time I see one of them in their wolf form. They can inflict so much damage with claws and teeth.

Even if I do manage to save Joanna and Grady, the odds that they make it out alive are slim to none. Those wolves will tear me apart if their alpha commands it. They'd be more than happy to. And for the first time, I wonder if Thorn can command them, or if orders like that have to come directly from Ryne. I'm afraid I won't like the answer to that question, but I have to do something about Joanna and Grady. I can't let Ryne execute them.

I can't.

Once we are in position, Thorn takes his place at the center of the stage.

"Friends and family, tonight's festival won't only be the usual releasing of the lowest-ranked claimed women into the mating houses. Tonight, we have not one, but two special events planned. My son has chosen a bride, and he will wed her at the end of the evening, but first, we are to have a public execution of some very dangerous and equally foolish criminals. They are traitors and do not deserve to live."

A roar goes up among the crowd, and my stomach sours. King Thorn waits for them to quiet down with a smug expression on his face. He motions for one of his men to come forward. The man hands him a long sword. Thorn takes it and swishes it about a few times with that wicked grin he so often carries.

"Beheading is appropriate, is it not?"

Once again the crowd shouts their approval.

"As much as I like a good beheading, this is not my territory. The honor belongs to my son." He holds the sword out to Ryne, who takes it easily, as if he's used it before. I think I'm going to be sick.

"Bring in the prisoners," Thorn cries. He and Ryne take a step back. I crane my neck around to see. A path has formed in the street behind the stage. Several men carry a board about two feet wide and eight feet long on their shoulders. On top of the board are two people sitting back to back. My heart tightens. Joanna looks like she's been roughed up, and her eyes are blindfolded, her mouth gagged, and her hands and feet are both bound with tight cords. A rope ties her to Grady.

The men on either side of the path spit on her and Grady as they pass. One loogie hits her right in the cheek. I clench my fists. She doesn't deserve this. Neither of them does.

The men set the board down on the stage, and I can see that Joanna is trembling. Grady fights against his binds, but they are tied tight. I wonder why he can't shift and get away, but there must be something to the binding preventing it. I try to get a closer look, but he's moving so much it's hard to see. If I'm going to save either of them, I have to start with him. I've seen his wolf––I know he can fight.

Ryne steps forward, and Abi leans into me. "Now."

She launches herself across the stage with me on her heels. I can't move like I want to, but I can't think about that right now. I accidentally drop my flowers, and some of the poppies scatter across the stage. But I've still got a hold of the dagger––I cling to it like a lifeline.

Ryne glances up at us, and Abi throws herself at him, the sword falling from his hand.

"Save me from the mating house," she yells. Her mouth puckers, as if trying to kiss him, and several people in the crowd laugh. They know a kiss from the alpha could save her and are roaring at her expense.

I reach Joanna and Grady, crouching down between them and Thorn so he cannot see what is happening. My dress is good for that at least. I have no idea what's going on behind me, but at any moment someone could grab me and pull me off. The blade is sharp and slides easily through the rope on Grady's hands. I cut the rope to his feet and the one that binds him to Joanna. By now, he's ripped off his blindfold and spit out his gag.

"Thank you," he whispers as I move to Joanna.

Hands grab my shoulders, and I'm flying backward, losing my grip on the knife. I hit the stage, and my head cracks on the hardwood. Stars flash in my eyes as I sit up. I cannot afford to waste any time, nor do I know who attacked me.

I look back over at Joanna, but I'm distracted when Ryne tackles Grady, both of them tumbling off the stage. Did Ryne throw me off? Anger burns at that realization, and I scramble to right myself. Thorn is watching everything unfold intently, as is the rest of the crowd, including the betas on stage, *including* Nico. They're all a bunch of cowards. I quickly crawl back over to Joanna, but now that I have no blade, this will be much harder.

She is bucking and thrashing, trying to get free of her bindings.

"It's me," I say to her. "Calm down and let me get these off of you."

She stills, and I go to work on the ropes binding her hands. Abi crouches next to me and starts on the ones at her feet.

Elle comes up and helps me with the hands. "If anyone asks, I was trying to stop you," she whispers. I could hug her right now, but there's no time. People can see us, but I doubt they can tell what's really going on.

We manage to get Joanna's hands undone, and she rips off her blind-fold and gag.

She coughs and looks around frantically with bloodshot eyes. "Where's Grady?"

"That doesn't matter. You need to run," I say, pulling her up and shoving her toward the other girls.

"I'm going with you," Abi says.

"I'm not leaving without him." Joanna clenches her fists and cranes her neck around to see over my shoulder.

"No," she cries and shoves past me.

Her cry is swallowed by Grady's soul-crushing wail. It's so deep and painful and awful that tears instantly blur my eyes. I smell the blood before I see it.

Chapter Thirty

They didn't shift.

It's my first thought. I wonder why they didn't shift. When Ryne killed before, he shifted first. The wolves would snarl and bite and claw as wolves do. But this time, they stayed humans, and he went for Grady with that damned sword. Grady had no way to protect himself. And maybe that was the point. Maybe Grady wasn't allowed the dignity of dying in his truest form.

The cheers grow to deafening heights, and I can no longer hear any screams as I force myself to take the whole scene in.

Grady lies in the grass, and a few feet away from him, his right arm claws outward toward the stage. A line of red connects the arm to the body. My stomach twists.

Joanna runs for him, and miraculously, he sits up.

So he's not dead. Not yet, anyway.

He looks around with wide shocked eyes and then to his severed limb. He's losing so much blood and fast. Joanna falls to her knees at his side and grabs a hold of what's left of his bleeding arm. Then she goes for his pants, attempting to undo his belt with trembling fingers. The crowd of wolves from the streets has surged into the park, forming a tight half-circle around Grady and Joanna. Most are dressed in t-shirts and jeans, but a few wear hooded shirts, casting their faces in darkness.

"Leave her!" Thorn bellows. The crowd quiets, and he continues. "Let her try to save him. This should be fun."

The crowd laughs and watches gleefully as she attempts to cut off the flow of blood by cinching the belt around what's left of his bloody stump.

I run toward them. I have to help.

Arms grab me and hold me back. "Stop, Poppy. You can't." It's Nico's voice of reason in my ear, and suddenly, I hate him.

"Let me go!" I scream, my voice growing hoarse. I squirm and drop my weight, but it's no use. His hold is iron tight.

"If you go over there, Ryne will be forced to kill you too," Nico hisses in my ear. "Joanna wouldn't want that. Nobody would want that."

I stomp on his foot, not bothering to inform him that Ryne would never kill me.

"I'm bored," Thorn calls out. "And the moon is coming. Son, it's time to end this and begin the festivities."

Ryne swings his sword around, which the crowd loves even more. It shines silver and bloodied under the lights. Sometime during all that, the sun has disappeared, and the full moon rises. It's not a white or yellow moon, but rather, it's a brutal shade of red--a rare blood moon. My mama always said blood moons were a bad omen, that they brought death and destruction with them. I've only seen a few in my lifetime, and they always gave me a sense of bad things to come.

How fitting that we'd get one tonight of all nights.

I stomp on Nico's foot again, and he drops me with a curse. Then I scramble away and crawl toward my friends. Nico goes for the hem of my skirts, calling for me to wait, but I kick him again and continue forward.

"What's this?" The king laughs as I practically tumble off the stage, but his voice is filled with malice. "Has another come to die?"

My skin buzzes. My ears too. I don't allow fear to come in. I keep my eyes on Joanna and Grady. Nobody else. Not even Ryne.

I leap for them, land in a crouch, and raise my head, looking into the fuming ocean blue of Ryne's eyes.

"If you are going to kill them, you'll have to kill me first." My words come out breathy and weak.

Ryne narrows his eyes. "Step aside, Poppy," he growls, only for me to hear. "I have no choice." And then he adds louder, "I am the alpha!"

I stand up, and even though I'm still several inches shorter than him, I feel invincible. I take a step toward him, and the crowd moves closer in on us. I can practically feel them at my back. I want to shout at them to move away and not to hurt Grady, but I keep my eyes on Ryne.

"Then you'll have to kill me."

"Poppy." His low voice comes out in a strangled cry. "Don't do this."

"Kill her, son." Thorn's ugly voice slices through the crowd. "Do as she asks."

"Poppy," Ryne whispers my name, and in that moment I know I've just broken his heart. And by forcing him to put me before the pack, I'm breaking my own heart too.

But it has to be done.

"You can't, can you?" I shout my answer. "Because we're fated. You can't deny it anymore. You can't kill me because you love me, and our bond is stronger than even the call of your alpha." I look over Ryne's shoulder. Thorn's mouth is pressed into a straight line. I always knew he hated me, and now I've let everyone know why.

A hush falls over the crowd, and no one moves.

"Is this true?" Thorn asks. He steps closer as if he's shocked by this revelation. Of course that is another one of his manipulations.

Ryne hangs his head for a moment and drops the sword. He turns and faces his father.

"Yes, Father, it's true. Poppy is my fated mate. I cannot deny it."

Thorn is quiet for a very long time, and then he begins to laugh. It's a quiet laugh at first, just a snort, but within seconds, he's doubled over, roaring with laughter.

He must be mad.

I take advantage of the distraction and turn around. I come face-to-face with a large shirtless man. He's bald but has bulky muscles and smells strongly of body odor. He leers at me. "Looking for a real man, kitten? How dare you embarrass our alpha."

I take a step back and try to spot Joanna and Grady, but the crowd around me and Ryne is too thick. Everyone is pressed in, and there isn't a sign of either of them except blood on the ground.

My plan worked.

Joanna and Grady are gone.

And no one seems to notice that they've disappeared. Every eye is on me and Ryne. Thorn recovers from his outburst and stands tall, adjusting his tie. Behind him, Nico stares at me, his eyes unbelieving. I can't tell if the expression is one of sorrow or relief. He never loved me, this much I know.

"I'm disappointed in you, Ryne," Thorn says coolly. "For years I tried to have an heir. Several women failed me until I found your mother, and then she only gave me you. One child. One son who's so weak that he cannot put a woman in her place." His eyes land on me. "It disgusts me."

Thorn is circling the area, and without a moment's notice, he reaches out and grabs Elle by the arm, tugging her close to him. She cries out.

"I promised a wedding tonight, and a wedding we'll get. Ryne has been a weak alpha and will need to prove himself to me again. Is he worthy of a luna after this pathetic display? I think not!" he bellows. The crowd grows agitated. Ryne is their alpha, and it's as if they don't know how to take any of this. "Anders, come!" Anders rushes to Thorn's side. "Challenge Ryne. It's time for a new alpha of the Carolina Pack. And when you are alpha, then you can wed Elle."

Anders's face pales. He knows he cannot win. "That's . . . that's your son."

Thorn shrugs. "I like you better."

Anders is still shocked, but something bright in his eyes indicates that he's thought of this many times before. How long has he waited to be the alpha? I shiver to think what would happen to this pack if Anders were in charge.

So far, Ryne hasn't moved an inch. His body is taut like steel wires. I want to reach out and grab his hand, but I know that would be foolish. He keeps himself between me and his father so that I cannot be hurt, but I desperately want to see his face. I want him to know that I'm with him, that I love him, that I'm his... but he doesn't look at me.

Anders stares at him, not saying a single word.

Then without warning, he changes into his large brown wolf and leaps at Ryne.

Ryne reaches back and shoves me into the crowd seconds before shifting into his wolf. If I were smart, I'd run, but I can't leave Ryne. We are connected. If he dies, I'll die, because I can't imagine going on without him.

I can't...

Chapter Thirty-One

They circle each other for a moment, and the men around me jostle forward, blocking my view. I shove at hard flesh, but no one is letting me through. Snarls and thuds come from where they are fighting, but I still can't see. I drop to the ground and try to crawl forward, but my blasted dress is stuck under someone's boot.

"Stop!" Anders's voice rings out. "I don't want to do this!"

"So you concede?" Thorn replies. "So soon? What happened to the man that hunted down Resistance members so mercilessly? And now you concede after barely a minute of brawling with my pathetic son?"

I wish I could see what's going on. I tug on my dress.

"I do not wish to kill Ryne," Anders says. More like he doesn't want to die. He knows how strong Ryne is and has seen countless wolves die trying to usurp him. He's smart to refuse, but I still saw that look in his eyes. He'd do it if he knew he could win.

"Then you will be exiled," Thorn growls. "That's the price of conceding."

"Stop, Father," Ryne yells. "You've made your point. But this is my pack, and you need to stand down."

I manage to get to my feet, and they all come back into view. I'm surrounded by wolf shifters that I've never met before, and one of them grabs my wrist, but I shake him off and shove my way to the front.

"What are you going to do, Ryne?" Thorn growls. "Are you going to marry that pathetic human mate or the powerful luna I've been saving for you?"

Everyone turns to Ryne then. We all want to know.

Me the most.

The moon shines down on us, blood red lighting the planes of Ryne's face. But before he can answer, wolves begin to howl.

Not wolves--lycans.

I jerk my head around to find they're all around us, mixed into the crowd, towering on their haunches and growling with thirst. They must have come as humans, planting themselves here before the moon fully rose and took over their infected bodies. I'd always thought of the lycans as bloodthirsty creatures with no control over their actions, but here they are, organized and ready to fight. To be able to pull off something like this means they must have far more control over their human forms than I thought. My mind spins with the implications. What does it all mean?

That thought gets cut off as one of them jumps, flying over the men and women, coming directly toward me. I can see death in its red eyes. It wants to take me out. Announcing my relationship to Ryne in front of this crowd meant announcing it to the lycanthrope.

Ryne spots me, grabs my wrist, and pulls me out from the crowd. A second later, the lycan lands where I was standing and screeches out a desperate howl. With one swoop, Ryne hoists me up into his arms and leaps back up on the stage where the betas are circling the girls to protect them. He sets me down in the middle, shoves me next to Abi, and shifts back into his wolf form without a word.

All around me the men have shifted into wolves or lycan.

All of them but one.

Thorn still stands in the middle of the stage--a lone man.

His angry eyes meet mine, and I raise my head in defiance. Three lycans jump up onto the stage behind him, and I hope they tear him to shreds. But before they can reach him, he rushes for me, knocking over the betas. He wraps a strong arm around my waist and pulls me out from their protection. He spins me around and shoves me right at the three lycans.

The monster's sharp claws scratch at my arms and sides. It burns, and I scream out. That only seems to encourage them. One grabs a hold of my cupcake skirt, and it tears away from my dress, leaving me standing in a thin white slip. I can't fight them--I have no weapons. I drop to the ground and scramble to the edge of the stage, a trail of blood behind me from the claws that tore open my skin. Two shifter wolves have joined the fray. I spot Ryne a few feet from the stage battling a lycan.

I want to cry out for him, but I don't want him to get distracted.

Pain shoots up my leg, pain that burns like liquid fire. I cry out and glance back in time to see a silver wolf clamp its jaws down on the lycan that's mere inches from me. I tumble off the stage and run.

It's slow going at first. I limp from the fire in my leg, and fights are raging all over the park, but I weave my way to the edge of the fighting crowd, leaving the rest of the claimed girls on the stage.

Everyone is focused on killing each other and none seem to notice me. I have no idea where to go. Behind me is the park, and in front of me is the inky black river. It's high with the spring runoff from the mountains up north. There's no way I can safely try to cross it.

I let out a frightened cry and run toward the houses instead. I'm not really sure where I'm going, just away. I manage to pass several homes and then realize I've rounded the park, and I'm right in front of Ryne's house. This is probably not a safe place to be. Ryne is obviously a target of the lycans, but merely the sight of his home makes me want to sob with relief.

A voice calls out my name behind me, and I nearly falter. It's not the voice I want to hear, but it's a welcome one.

I slow and turn around.

"Knox," I breathe, and soon he's right in front of me.

"What happened?" he asks, his eyes searching my body for wounds. His mouth is pulled tight in worry and sweat beads along his hairline.

"I don't know," I reply. "It all happened so fast."

"You're bleeding," he says, dropping down to examine my leg. He tears off a part of his shirt and wraps it around the wound. "Come on, let's get you inside."

"No," I say a little too forcefully. "Thorn knows about me and Ryne. He'll kill me if he finds me in there."

Knox stares at me for a moment, and suddenly I wish none of this had ever happened. That Knox had not been claimed and that Willow had never died. Then we'd probably be married by now, living a peaceful life back home among the fields. And not here, not trapped in a wolf shifter war, not slaves to a broken system, not targets for crazed lycans.

But then I never would've met Ryne.

And it's true that I never did have Ryne, but I had his kisses, and I had the dream of him, the hope of us––and if I'm being honest, that means more to me than a million lifetimes with Knox ever could have.

Knox gives a short nod. "Then come with me. We'll get you in the car and wait for Ryne. He'll know what to do."

But he won't.

Because I can already feel the virus moving through me, a liquid fire thickening in my veins like a death sentence, circling right back to the pain in my leg, demanding I acknowledge the truth.

I've been bitten by a lycan.

Chapter Thirty-Two

I stare out of the window of the car and try not to cry. Knox hasn't moved the car, but he waits, leaning against the outside. He doesn't have any weapons, and I don't understand how he can be so calm. After what seems like hours, I spot Ryne striding across the grass. He looks uninjured, but his head hangs low.

Knox calls out for him, and he comes running. I can't hear what they're saying, but Knox hands him a pair of pants. He jerks them on and then yanks the car door open.

Relief floods his features as he catches sight of me. "You're alive."

"I am." But I can't find any joy in the statement.

He slides in next to me and wraps me into a hug. I try not to cry on his shoulder. Knox closes the door behind him, and within seconds the car is flying down the road.

"Are the lycans gone?" I ask.

He nods once. "Not before they took a bunch of us out. I'm pretty sure my father was their target."

I hate that I hope Thorn is dead. But I do. "And is he——"

"He's alive." His voice is sharp. "But we lost Cade. And a couple other betas. Most of those who died were my deltas and gammas. They died to protect me."

I can hear the hatred in his voice. I hope he isn't directing it at himself. The lycans organized this. They planned this. Ryne's pack was simply doing what they were born to do——defend their alpha.

We ride in silence for a while, and my aching leg starts to go numb.

"Where are we going?" I ask. My voice is shaking now. I know what I have to confess, but the words are caught in my throat.

"Away from the city where we can regroup. I don't know what's going to happen with my father and Elle and her family now. But the secret is out. You made sure of that." He chuckles for a moment. I thought he'd be mad. He pulls away and stares at me straight in the eyes. I can't help the tears that stream down my face.

He cups my cheeks and wipes at the wetness with his thumb. "Come on, Poppy, don't cry. We'll figure it out. We're together now, and that's all that matters."

"We can't be together."

"Of course we can. My father tried to have me replaced back there. He failed, and now I will never let him get between you and me ever again."

It's everything I've wanted to hear, but it's too late. I make myself stop crying, gathering my strength as I pull away from him and lift my foot into his lap.

"We can't be together because I've been bitten by a lycan. Please kill me quickly. I don't want it to hurt."

Ryne freezes. He doesn't say anything for a long moment. He just stares at the wrapped wound, a haunted sheen over his face and pain in his eyes.

"Are . . . are you sure?"

I've never heard him sound so broken, and it shatters me. "Look for yourself."

He gently unwraps the cloth and runs his fingers along the bite mark. There's no denying what it is. I shouldn't turn until the next full moon, but it doesn't matter. It's already a death sentence. I know how this works. We both do.

"Knox," he calls out in a strangled voice. "Drive us to the wilds' edge."

Then he pulls me close and holds me tight.

We stay like that for a while. As my mind clears, my eyes focus on the night outside. We're driving away from the city, and the houses grow farther and farther apart. If there are electric lights in these houses, they must be off or not working because they're all dark. More likely the homes are abandoned because they are so close to the wilds. I assume Ryne's having Knox take me away so he can kill me in private, allowing me some semblance of dignity in the act.

But then again, why take me away from the city for that?

He's not going to kill me.

I sit up, peeling myself off of him.

"Are you sure?" I ask, and he knows what I mean because he immediately nods. "Isn't that against wolf law or something?" I ask.

He shushes me seconds before his hands cup my face, and he brings my mouth to his. I don't care that Knox is here. My thoughts melt away with Ryne's kiss. And my heart aches.

I'm losing him.

We're losing each other.

And this is our goodbye, not spoken with our voices, but spoken with our lips.

I'm not ready for it to be over when he pulls away because the car has come to a stop. We climb out, and I wince when my foot hits the pavement. I can't help it; the pain is throbbing. Ryne winces too, but his face is unreadable in the darkness. Maybe that's a good thing. I'm in nothing but a slip and corseted bodice. My feet are bare. I lost my high heels ages ago. I have nothing left.

My eyes start to adjust to the moon, and I long to look at it, as if the moon and I already have a deal together, as if we've already signed the agreement in blood. I force myself to take in my surroundings instead. There's no bridge and no river--not like when I first came into the shifter city. In fact, the fields in front of me look so similar to home that my heart jumps into my throat. "Will I be able to say goodbye to my family?" I ask, but it comes out sounding like a beg.

"No, I'm sorry." Ryne is regretful. "It's too dangerous. If this is going to work, everyone must believe you're dead."

My breath catches, but I still need him to confirm. "You're not going to kill me?"

Ryne growls low. "I could never kill you, Poppy. Never."

"So what now?"

He looks to Knox. Under the moonlight, I can see their features enough to notice an unspoken agreement passing between them.

"Now you run," Ryne says roughly. "You run, and you never look back."

I open and close my mouth, unable to find a response.

"Knox is going with you," he continues. "You won't be alone. He'll make sure you make it to safety."

"Safety? Out there in the wilds? Out with the lycans?" I shake my head. "I can't leave you, Ryne. No. That won't be safe--"

"You are a lycan now," he snaps. "You know this is the only way."

"But--"

"Please don't make it any harder than it has to be."

I'm not trying to make it harder, but there has to be another way. The thought of leaving him and going, running and never looking back, becoming a lycan--it's impossible.

Ryne holds out his hand, and Knox drops the car keys in his palm.

"I'm serious, Poppy," Ryne's voice grows hard. "If you come back to my city, I will kill you myself."

"But you just said you could never kill me," I say.

"I wouldn't have a choice!" His voice booms into the night, rolling across the fields like thunder. This is it. This is the end. How could this be the end?

I don't want to believe it. I can't.

Ryne rushes forward, wraps me into a tight hug, and whispers tenderly against my ear. "I'm sorry. Please be brave for me. Please do this. You can survive out there. You're the strongest woman I know."

I don't feel strong right now. I feel angry, confused, beaten--but not strong. But I have to be, so I nod into his chest, and he lets me go. The weight of that release breaks my heart. I've never felt more alone, even though he still stands a foot away.

And then he's getting in the car, and then he's driving away, and then he's gone.

I turn to Knox. "Are you sure you want to come with me? You can go back. Or you can run away. Whatever you want, I won't judge you."

He stares at me for a long moment, his buzzed blonde hair shining pink under the glow of the blood moon, and he smiles the saddest smile I've ever seen. "I would never do that to you, Poppy."

And then the first boy I ever lost reaches out and takes my hand. His is cold, and mine is burning hot. Together, we turn to face the unknown.

RISE
OF THE
WILD
MOON

KIMBERLY LOTH

NINA WALKER

Prologue

ELLE

The blood moon shines down over the carnage as if to mock us. I've seen a lot of gore in my life, but the scene before me is by far the worst. Death hangs heavy in the air, and the stench of it makes my stomach churn. The last shred of innocence I have left urges me to run away, but I can't. I have to face this. I'm with the Resistance so I knew this attack was coming, but I never expected it to be so ruthless—— for so many to die.

The lycans are gone for now, having disappeared into the night, but they could return to finish off more wolves. They've taken out a good number of Ryne's pack, including some of the higher-ranked betas. Most of the claimed girls are huddled near the edge of the stage with tear-stained faces and glassy eyes. They're in shock. As a house mother, my duty is to go to them and offer comfort, but I can't right now.

I scan the scene for the people who are tied to my heart. My eyes first find Madame Delphine, and I sigh a breath of relief. The lycans know she's high in our ranks with the Resistance, but I can never be sure what they're going to do once they turn into monsters. Her hair is a mess, and her skirts are torn, but she's alive, and she's there, talking to the girls in a soft whisper. She'll take care of them. Not for the first time, I thank the heavens that she's my ally.

I spot my parents and brothers and nearly cry out in relief. They're walking among the dead and injured, checking for pulses and wrapping wounds. They should leave. It's not safe for them to be here anymore. I have no idea what the next few hours or days will bring, but if Thorn figures out that I was in on the plot for Poppy to marry Ryne, or that I knew this attack was coming, my parents' lives will be the first to go--after me, of course. As if my father can hear my thoughts, his eyes snap to mine.

"Go," I mouth, and he gives a stiff nod, taking my mother by the forearm and dragging her away. My brothers follow close behind. Father's actions appear rough, but that's always been a show for Thorn; my dad is one of the most gentle men I've ever met. He also probably knows that my mother won't leave me here, and he's hoping they'll be far enough away that they can't turn back when she realizes I've stayed behind.

I can't go with them. Even though my heart aches to leave, I have to stay. Our family can't afford any suspicion, and besides, I'll be alright. I'm the strongest female wolf who isn't already married off. Thorn will want me alive.

The stench of blood is thick in my nostrils as I walk through the wreckage, looking for those who I can help. I find my ripped dress and slip it back on. It barely stays put, and I consider dropping it altogether since I'm not shy about nudity, but I keep it on. It's something for me to fret about that isn't life or death, and as silly as that is, it calms me down a bit. In the back of my mind, I don't know how we'll recover from this, but in the forefront I can only deal with the here and now. I keep looking for Ryne, but he's nowhere to be found. It seems the alpha has disappeared, most likely with Poppy. I swallow a hard lump in my throat and try not to panic. That boy needs to come back immediately and take care of his pack. Otherwise his father will lose it. The king may even take control from his own son; he certainly threatened it earlier.

For now, the best I can do is damage control. There aren't many wounded left. They're all dead. The lycan were supposed to get Thorn! But this? They killed whoever they could. This wasn't the plan. I fist my hands and walk toward the far side of the stage--a place I don't want to be--where my enemies stand. Too bad I have to be the one to face them since all of my allies have fled.

Thorn stands tall, surveying the carnage with an angry frown. Of course the man is alive and well. What were the lycan thinking? Did they even try to attack him? Logically, I know they did, but I'm still mad as hell. Someone needs to get them in line, and if that person isn't going to be Madame Delphine, then it'll have to be me. They won't enjoy taking orders from a wolf, and a woman at that.

Thorn starts arguing with Anders, the angry tone in his voice rising above all the other noise. It's then that I finally take it in, as if my ears had gone deaf from sensory overload. Wolves howl all around us. Snarls and fights are still going on, but they are among each other, not the lycan. It's maddening that in a time like this, brothers can so easily turn on their own.

Ryne really needs to get back from wherever he ran off to; his pack needs him.

I put on my best smile and smooth my skirts. My heels are long gone, and I pad softly across the stage, my tattered wedding dress brushing around my ankles. I hold my head high and approach the two men. They're so enthralled with their argument they couldn't care less about me.

"You were supposed to kill him," Thorn hisses. "I gave you the chance, and you squandered it."

My blood runs cold when I realize they're talking about Ryne. Thorn really is okay with his only son dying, just to keep himself strong and in power. It goes to show how powerful Ryne is becoming if his father is afraid of him.

"I already told you the men wouldn't follow me if I did that," Anders whines.

"They wouldn't have had a choice, you idiot. You know what? I was wrong about you. You don't have the strength to lead this pack. I'll find another man."

I clear my throat, anger flaring to life. "I thought that man was Ryne, your *son*."

Thorn catches my eyes and an oily grin spreads across his lips like a stain. "Elle, love, why don't you go make sure our girls are okay? This must've been terribly traumatic for them. Go back to the house with them, and we'll come visit when we're done here."

I stand my ground. He's not going to get away with changing the subject. I know what I heard, and it makes me sick. "No. I'm a luna. I want to stay and help."

He raises an eyebrow. "Help with what? The lycan are gone, and the men are taking care of whatever comes next."

It takes everything in me not to spit at him for that comment. I'm so sick of being treated less-than because I'm a woman. "I'm just as capable as any man here, if not more so, and that includes Anders."

I can't help the dig, and Anders snorts in response.

If Thorn forces Ryne and me to marry, the first thing I will do is banish Anders. Now that he's challenged Ryne, I'm sure the others in the pack will be happy to see him leave. Sure, human wives don't have any say in what goes on in the pack. They are just pretty babymakers. But I've done some research. It turns out that before the wars, the luna wives would rule alongside their husbands as equals. In some cases, she even became the alpha.

If it happened before, it can happen again. There's a case to be made, and I plan to make it.

Thorn probably doesn't know any of this, or he would've killed me years ago. The man will do anything to preserve his power, and tonight proves it. Someday, someone will have enough power to overthrow him. That someone just may be me. Of course, if Ryne and I actually got married, there would be more of a chance of it happening. I'm not a fool though. There's no way I can stand between Ryne and his fated mate. Maybe someday I'll meet mine, assuming I even have one. I want that kind of love, but right now, love is most definitely not my priority. I eye Thorn, imagining him among the dead, and my resolve strengthens. I'd love to kill him right now, but I can't. I'd probably lose, and if I won, the pack would kill me, so I keep the fake smile on instead.

"You are likely right on that point. You are a capable young woman, aren't you?" Thorn chuckles, sliding closer to me. I nod, and my hackles rise. Something is off, but I can't quite put my finger on it. "Why don't you leave the tough stuff to the men? Even powerful lunas need their rest."

I stand a little taller. I'm not going anywhere. "I feel great, actually."

Something burns behind his eyes—a challenge? "When Ryne returns, the wedding will be performed, and you'll be in for a long night." He winks, and I have to resist the urge to punch him in the nose. "Actually, that might be a good job for you. Find Ryne and bring him back here."

I scoff. "You mean to tell me that you don't have dozens of wolves already out there looking for him?"

"I do. But according to you, you're better than they are."

"You're right, I am," I growl and move to the edge of the stage, ready to shift.

"On second thought, why don't you wait on that," Thorn calls after me, and I spin around to face him. He studies me with curious eyes and approaches. He stands way too close. His chest is bare, and blood oozes from a wound across his collarbone. His nostrils flare with every breath as he stares at me for way too long. He brings a hand up to my face and forces me to look him in the eye. I stare at him defiantly.

"You are right. You are the most powerful wolf here. You will make Ryne a very strong alpha."

I nod stiffly, his fingers still digging into my chin.

He purses his lips. "Perhaps I do not want him to be a stronger alpha anymore. You saw how he disappointed me tonight. He doesn't deserve a fine specimen such as yourself."

What is he saying?

"If you pass me on to Anders . . ." I let the unsaid threat hang in the air. I don't know what I would do, but Anders would die before he touched me.

Thorn chuckles. "I'm not going to pass you on to Anders. He's proven he's a weak wolf as well. No. I've come to a realization tonight. Can you guess what it is?" He doesn't wait for my answer. "If you want something done right, you have to do it yourself."

Dread fills my stomach, and I hope he's not saying what I think he's saying. "I don't understand." The words feel like sand in my mouth.

"Oh, I think you do. You will be married tonight, but Ryne won't be your new husband." His eyes flash with desire and greed, and he steals me into his arms. "I will."

Chapter One

I don't even have shoes. And while there are a lot of things I could probably do without here in the wilds, shoes are not one of them. About an hour into walking on my bare feet, I rip off part of my ruined slip and tie the fabric around my injured soles, but it offers little protection, and I'm still slowing us down. The blood at my ankle has stopped flowing, but two crescent moon bite marks throb next to the bone. I'm desperate to sit and rest for a while, but I can't.

I'm not even sure where we're going. Knox and I have been walking through the darkness along the edge of an abandoned road. It's overgrown with weeds, and the concrete is broken up in parts, but at least it's a landmark to go by. He doesn't want to stop, saying we need to get as far away from the city as we can, but it's grown darker, and even though the full moon brightens the landscape, it's not nearly enough light to continue by for much longer.

"I think the adrenaline has worn off," I say, my voice coming out achingly hoarse. Maybe from screaming, maybe from the lycan venom. I don't know.

"Yeah, me too," he sighs.

"We need to set up a camp."

"What camp? We don't have any equipment, and besides, walking is the smartest move right now."

I'm not so sure that's true.

"Where are we even going?" I've been afraid to ask because I've been scared of the answer.

"West, I guess," he says despondently. "We're banished. Think I don't know what happens to banished people?" He points to the moon and shivers. "They die."

"Or they get bitten." I lift up my ankle. "At least I have another full month to figure something out before I end up turning into a monster."

Even though he winces at my bluntness, I can't pretend it didn't happen. I'm a walking time bomb. A less selfish person would tell Knox to get away from me, maybe even help him find a better life. I am not that person. The truth is that being alone out here is terrifying, and as twisted as it is, I'm grateful that Knox is with me.

"I have an idea." He points into the distance. "One of the villages is just over those hills. I'm going to sneak in there and find us food, clothing, and maybe some boots for you." I wouldn't blame him if he just stayed in the village and left me here. It's his safest option.

"That's stealing," I argue. He gives me an annoyed look. Even in the moonlight, I can tell he's frustrated. "Okay, fair enough," I quickly relent, "but I'm not letting you go alone."

"Pretty sure you're less than conspicuous in that outfit."

"I guess you have a point." I stop in my tracks, glaring down at the ruined slip and what remains of the ugly bodice. "Wait, no, you can't go tonight. You'll have to go tomorrow."

"Plan is to be long gone by tomorrow."

"But wolf shifters guard the settlements on full moons."

He gives me a sad look. "When are you going to realize that most of what you were told was a lie? How many wolves did you see protecting our village when we were growing up?"

I swallow hard. "None, but that doesn't mean they weren't farther out."

"The wolves are far more concerned with protecting their city than they ever were with the villages. Trust me, I'll be fine."

I wonder for a moment how we managed to stay safe on the full moons. The villages would be easy pickings for the lycan. It makes no sense that the wolves would leave them vulnerable to attack, but I can see his point too. I don't remember seeing wolves on full moons, and the stories about the lycans were mostly just that. Stories.

I end up sitting against a thin tree trunk, hidden inside a little grove of aspen, as Knox goes off to play hero or abandon me completely. I vow to stay awake as I wait for him to get back, and for a long time I do, but eventually exhaustion overwhelms me, and I give up the fight.

Hours later? Minutes? Urgent hands shake me. My automatic reflex is to scream, but Knox is quick to palm my mouth. Once I'm aware of what's going on, he carefully removes his hand. It's sweaty--he's been running. Gratitude surges in my chest. He came back.

"Did you get anything?" I whisper, eager for those boots.

"No." His breath comes out ragged. "But we have to go. Now."

He drags me up, and we run into the nearby forest. No road. No path. Just underbrush to slice at my legs and rip my dress even further. My eyes have adjusted better to the darkness, but that advantage is short-lived once the trees grow thicker. It won't be long until one of us rolls an ankle or worse.

"Slow down," I gasp. I'm a runner, but this is madness.

He whirls on me, pushing one hand against my mouth again and holding his index finger up to his lips in a shushing motion.

That's when I hear the howls.

The adrenaline rushes back. If it's lycan, we're probably dead. If it's wolves, we may stand a chance, but that's only assuming word hasn't traveled. I'm a fugitive now. What I did to King Thorn won't be forgotten. All I can hope for is that the king believes me dead. That's not going to happen if someone reports back about seeing us out here. Thorn will follow my scent, and I'll be a goner by morning.

Knox leans close, mouth pressed against my ear. "We can't be found."

Now it's my turn for an idea. I point up. He doesn't seem to understand, and I'm too scared to say anything aloud, so I begin to climb. Up and up I go. The pine needles are scratchy and sticky, and the bark catches on everything, but the higher I climb, the safer I feel. Knox follows and is soon only an arm's length below me. Eventually, I find a large bare branch and relax onto it, my back against the trunk. Knox stops at one a few feet down and does the same. The pine has thinned enough up here that we can see the whole valley. I don't know if it will make a difference.

My mind races back to everything that transpired tonight. I made a gamble and nearly won, but the lycans showed up and ruined everything. At least I got Joanna and Grady out of there alive. Thorn was going to kill them, and I just hope Grady is okay. He lost his arm, and he might bleed out, leaving Joanna vulnerable. She's part of the Resistance though. She's got contacts and people who can help her. She'll be okay so long as she doesn't have to face Thorn ever again. The man is a monster. It's hard to believe that he had Anders challenge Ryne, and it proves he's far crueler than I ever thought possible. If he knew I was bitten and currently on the run, I'd be hunted down to the bitter end and made to suffer. I stood up to the man, and nobody does that. Even Ryne has a hard time with it. I just hope Ryne is able to convince him I died. A lump forms in my throat at the thought of my fated mate. I recall the look of sheer panic on his face when he saw I'd been bit, and my heart squeezes.

But then I remember that he was going to let our friends die. How could he think I'd marry him right after their executions? And now that we've parted ways, I don't think I'll ever understand his reasoning. He put his father before them, and it's unforgivable. I'll probably never see him again, and maybe that's okay, because he isn't the man I thought he was. Tears threaten, but I hold them in, focusing on the darkened forest below instead, listening and waiting.

Knox and I sit like this for ages. This time, I don't fall asleep.

Chapter Two

The sun peeks over the trees. Knox still sits one branch below me, his head bobbing. I understand the feeling, but if we fall asleep up here, we could plunge to our deaths. I reach down and tap him on the head. He jerks around and blinks up at me. Do I look as tired and wild as he does? His buzzed blonde hair has broken leaves and thistles stuck to it, and his face is covered in dirt and scratches.

"Is it safe?" I mouth.

He swallows and glances around. "I think so." His voice is barely above a whisper. He slowly makes his way down the tree, and I follow. We both land on the ground with a soft thud, and I nearly cry out. My feet will not survive this trip because my poor ankle is thrashed. Tears spring to my eyes because I suddenly don't know what to do. We're going to get killed because of me, and if we somehow make it out of here, I'm still going to become a lycan on the next full moon. My life is over.

"Are you okay?" Knox is obviously concerned, and I can't lie to him about this. He needs to know what he's signing up for.

I shake my head and point at the wounds.

When Knox kneels down to study them, worry settles over his features. "We'll have to fix that problem today. But first, we need to find a place to get some sleep, water, and food if we can. I don't know where we are now, but we'll figure it out."

I'm a coward because I don't say anything. If I was brave, I would insist he ditch me to save himself. Instead, we walk for what feels like hours, but is probably only thirty minutes. Each step is agony, and I don't know how much more I can take. I always thought I was strong and capable, but obviously I overestimated my abilities.

The ground becomes soft and squishy. I glance down. My feet are covered in water. It's freezing cold and brings sweet relief.

"I think we found water," I point out, smiling to myself. I think it's the first time I've smiled in what feels like ages.

Knox only nods, but I don't mind because neither one of us has the energy to talk much. After a few minutes of letting me numb my ankle, he glances around with a determined look on his face. "Stay there for a minute, and I'll see if I can find a place to rest."

I shift a little so I can lean against a tree, but I leave both feet in the water. I know it's probably going to open them up to all kinds of infection, but at the moment, I don't care. If I can get the swelling down, maybe I can go on a little longer.

After several minutes, Knox returns. His brown eyes sparkle, and I know he's found what he was looking for. "This turns into a stream not too far that way." He motions over his shoulder. "There's several trees and soft ground where we can get some rest and then figure out what to do next."

I follow him in a daze. Something scratches my arm, and I glance down. It's a bush with bright black berries. "Knox, stop." He turns and spots the berries as well.

"Do you think they're safe?"

He nods. "We had these at home. Blackberries are fine. Good catch, Poppy."

I don't hesitate to pluck several off and shove them in my mouth. The sweet and tart juice is heavenly. I glance at Knox. He's doing the same, and when he smiles at me, his teeth are stained purple. I laugh because mine probably are too.

We don't eat too many because even in our delirium, we know that it could make us sick. The area Knox found is indeed a comfortable-looking spot. We drink from the stream. Knox says it's fine since we know it comes out of the ground where we just were, and I don't think I've ever been more grateful for water. Once sated, we settle against a large tree with springy moss along the bottom. My body relaxes right away, and my feet don't hurt as bad.

"Do you think one of us should stay awake in case we're attacked?" I ask.

He chuckles, trying to hold off a yawn and failing. "Could we fight them off anyway in this state?"

"Good point."

My eyes flutter closed, and before I know it, sleep claims me.

* * *

Something snaps, and my eyes pop open. Knox and I are surrounded by people. I reach for his hand and squeeze. One of the people crouches down and stares at me. The middle-aged man is large and shirtless, with broad, tanned shoulders and enormous biceps. Scars crisscross his face and body, and his lip is curled into an intimidating scowl. The guy is creepy as hell.

He studies me. I do nothing but blink, not seeing a way out of this. I don't know if these are lycan or just people who've learned how to survive out here. Either way, this isn't good.

The man snarls, and I jump. He laughs, revealing rotting teeth and breath that smells like a latrine.

"What's your name?" he asks, his face still menacing.

"Mary," the lie rolls off my tongue easily. "And this is Frederick." Those are the names of my parents and the first ones that come to mind. "We are in love, but my parents tried to force me to marry someone else. We escaped our village but were not well prepared for the wilds."

The man sniffs and purses his lips. I'm not sure if he believes me, and a warning bell is sounding in my mind that he doesn't. He shifts on his haunches, and I take the time to check out the rest of the group. There is a mix of men and women, all powerfully built like they've spent a lot of time out here. They're dressed in worn pants and shirts, with their hair tied back with leather thongs. A few hold makeshift weapons.

"You've been eating our berries," he finally says.

"We were starving," Knox chokes out. At least I know he's awake. "But we didn't know they were yours."

I want to say something about how berries in the wild shouldn't belong to anyone, but I keep my mouth shut.

The man stands, and I let out a breath of relief that he didn't just kill us on the spot. He steps back to whisper with his people. I strain my ears, but I can't hear what they are saying.

"What should we do?" I ask Knox in a soft voice. My injured ankle is tucked under me, but if they see it, they'll know right away that I was bit. Will they kill me?

Knox's gaze drops down to where I've got my ankle hidden, and he swallows. "I'm not sure there is anything we can do. There are too many of them. Hopefully they'll just leave us alone."

"Maybe they can help us." I know it's overly optimistic of me, but if they aren't here to help us, they will hurt us. And besides, they may be our only shot of survival out here.

The man turns back. "Time to go," he announces.

They descend on me and Knox as one, and I'm suddenly afraid of them. They're rough and angry, and even though I kick and scratch and fight, it's no good. They tie up my hands and feet, the ropes searing against my wound. I cry out and am dropped. "She's been bit," one of them remarks gruffly. Tears sting my eyes when the large man lifts my foot and runs a finger across the wound. It stings so bad I nearly pass out.

"Don't touch me," I cry.

He picks me up and flings me over his shoulder.

I don't know where I'm going, and I'm certain it will be horrible, but at least I don't have to walk anymore.

"Are you going to kill me?" I ask the man.

"If you give me a reason to," he responds. "Now be quiet, or else I'll bind your mouth too."

I hate being afraid, hate the way my muscles tense and my heart speeds. I hate how my thoughts become muddled and frantic all at once. I've been in fight-or-flight mode for months, and I don't know if I can handle another second of it. I try to relax, to force the panic back, but it proves impossible. I don't know who these men and women are, but one thing I've learned about people lately is that they can't be trusted.

Not even Ryne. Not even my fated mate.

Blood rushes to my head because this mountain of a man has me tossed over his shoulder like a sack of potatoes. I try to lift my neck up but can't hold the position for long, so I end up with my head resting against his bare back. It's hot today, and his sweat sticks to my cheek. I breathe through my mouth to try and lessen his stench––he clearly hasn't bathed in a while.

Knox is forced to walk, probably because he doesn't have any injuries. He's a few paces behind us, arms tied behind his back, with guards on either side. His eyes hold mine as he mouths, "it's going to be okay."

It's a lie and an attempt to coddle me, maybe even his way to love me right now. Make me believe life can't possibly get worse, force me to think about other things. He used to do the same when we were dating, and I'd worry about his claiming. I don't need that kind of love anymore. I don't need love at all actually. I need loyalty, and I need the truth.

I look away and study the rest of the group. It's hard to count them in this position, but I'd guess there are about twenty people here. There are more men than women, but not by much. The women seem just as scary and weathered as the men do. They're nothing like the women back in the city who are constantly dressed up like dollies to be played with.

As we continue, a headache starts to build. Just when I think my brain is going to combust, the man sets me down. "I'm going to put a blindfold on you now," he says, dropping his gaze to mine. He's about my father's age, and it makes me miss the days when I could trust the adults in my life, especially the men. "If you fight me, I'll knock you out."

I see no point in fighting him. I'm too weak.

I nod wearily as a strip of fabric is tied over my eyes. I can see specs of light coming from around my nose, but it's not enough to make a difference. We must be getting close to wherever their camp is, and they don't want us to know the exact location. I want to tell him that it's pointless and that I don't know where I am anyway, but I don't. I'd like to keep all my teeth.

Even though I can't see it, I can tell my ankle has swelled up even more. It tingles and throbs like crazy, and when I try to take a step forward, I can't. I wince and fall to my knees. A few people chuckle, but not everyone. Maybe there will be someone here who is sympathetic to me, who will help me. More than likely I'll end up dead, but I can't allow my mind to think about that right now. I want to survive but I'm injured and facing the very real possibility that this could be the end for me. I'm starting to lose all fight.

Luckily, the man picks me back up and carries me again. I'll gladly take his sweat and stench over walking on this ankle. We continue on for another twenty minutes or so, and then we climb into something. From the way we rock gently and the sound of lapping water, I know we're in a boat. I expect an engine to rumble to life, but it doesn't. Maybe they don't have fuel? Someone must be rowing.

Only a few short minutes later, we hit a shoreline, and I'm carried off the boat.

So we crossed the river--I file that information away, just in case.

We're back to walking, but branches brush against us this time. We're definitely moving through some kind of well-hidden path, probably going deeper into the forest. If I were these people and had to figure out a way to survive out here, I'd do the same. I keep thinking we're going to stop, but we just keep going and going. With the blindfold on and the blood pooling in my head, I grow disoriented. Eventually, I fall asleep.

Thump! I wake up with a start as I'm dropped to the ground. I expect the pain of hard earth, but there's none. The blindfold is gone. And so are the people and Knox. All that's left is me and this burly man. But I'm not on the ground, am I? I gasp and crawl back, fear pulsing through my body. This is a tent. I'm on thick rugs, and we're all alone in here.

Is this it then? Is he going to take my virtue?

"We're not the wolves." He sneers, leering over me, obviously sensing my fear. "We don't take women to our beds against their will."

I let out a breath.

"But we don't tolerate liars, thieves, or spies either." He looks me in the eye. His are brown and ringed in yellow. "I won't hesitate to kill you if need be."

Why hasn't he already? He knows I've been bit.

And that's when it hits me. The way they smell, why they were close to the city, why they seem to hate the wolves, and most of all, why they didn't kill me the second they found my bite wound. These aren't ordinary humans.

They're lycan.

Chapter Three

"I'm not a spy. If you just let me and my friend go, we won't bother you again."

The man snorts and rocks back on his haunches. "We're not letting you go. You've been bitten. You're going to need our help."

I bristle a little bit. I don't want help from a man like this. I don't want help at all. I never want to go through my first shift because I don't want to be a lycan.

"You can't help me. I won't attack people." Even as I say it, my throat hollows.

He chuckles. "Oh yes, you will, and you'll like it, but that's a discussion for another day. Today, you will tell me who you are and where you came from. Keep in mind that my mate is asking your friend the same questions, and if your answers are different, even just a little bit, both of you will die. We will not risk our people."

I swallow. Knox and I didn't talk about this at all. I have no idea what answers Knox is giving, and the only chance we have at getting things right is to answer honestly. I'll just keep my answers as short as possible and hope for mercy.

"Fine. My real name is Poppy, and we came from the wolf city."

The man stands and paces, his brow furrowed in thought. "Are you from the mating houses, a beta wife, or one of the claimed?"

"The claimed."

"So you must have been in the city during the festival and got bitten in the raid. How did you get to the wilds before a wolf found and killed you?"

This is the part that I am unsure of how Knox will answer. I don't want to use Ryne's name if I can avoid it. I hesitate for a moment.

"Answer me," the man screams in my face.

"Knox was a driver––one of the claimed men. He got us out."

"And why would he help you?"

"Because we are from the same village, and we were . . . friends before the claiming."

The man's lips twitch. "Friends, huh? I won't kill you for that omission. Now, tell me, Poppy, why does that bodice look suspiciously like the top of a torn wedding dress? The wolves don't take wives until the harvest."

Once again, I hope Knox goes with a half-truth here as well. "One of the betas took a liking to me and asked for my hand early. The alpha agreed."

"Which beta?"

I wonder for a moment how much this man knows. If he's asking for specific names, then he must know the city. Maybe he was one of the lycan that came in and attacked. From the scratches all over him, I wouldn't be surprised.

"Nico," I say.

He stands and paces again.

"Will Nico come after you?"

"I don't know, but I doubt it. I'm not his fated mate or anything like that."

"If he loved you so much that he convinced the alpha to move up the wedding date, then why wouldn't he come after you?"

I swallow, thinking of how I can spin this. Going with half-truths seems like the best course of action. I look the man dead in the eyes and strengthen my resolve. I will not die today. "Nico knew I was bitten when I left with Knox."

"He should've killed you." He stops and stares at me, curiosity alight in his eyes.

"He should've, but he didn't."

The man cocks his head. "Hmm, that's interesting. A wolf who let his little lycan go? How romantic." He scoffs. "You're not telling me everything, but you've told me enough to keep you alive. Count yourself lucky."

He turns on his heel and exits the tent. I hang my head between my knees. My hands are still tied up behind my back, and my ankles are bound together once more. I can hardly move, and everything hurts. Now that the man is gone and my adrenaline has slowed, I can feel every ache and pain. But underneath it all is something else––a burning in my veins. I know what it is, but I can't face it yet. Instead, I focus on the man and what he could be doing next. He said I'll get to live, but he seemed quite interested in my relationship with Nico. Could he be planning to use me against the wolves?

Ugh, probably. Maybe I shouldn't have said so much.

Now that he's gone, I figure he's going to find out if Knox and I gave the same answers. If we didn't, we might die. If we did, I'll live for the time being, but I'm not sure about Knox. I don't really want to hang out with a bunch of lycan, especially if they end up killing Knox, but I don't see that I have any other choice. Maybe if I can get them to trust me, Knox and I can figure out how to run away.

I feel better now that I have a plan.

The tent flap rustles, and I tense. This time a woman enters. She's nearly as tall as the man, wearing a worn tank top and baggy pants that have a couple of holes. Her boots stomp hard on the ground, and she holds a wicked-looking knife.

There is a long scar across her face, and when she smiles at me, I notice she's missing three teeth. She lunges for me, and I jump.

She cackles up a storm.

"You should see your face. So scared."

"You're holding a knife."

She crouches in front of me, her putrid breath assaulting my nostrils. Do these people not bathe, or are they smelly because they've recently spent the night as lycans? She holds up the knife. "And I want nothing more than to carve your skin right off your body, but Laik said your stories check out, so I have to let you go. But I come with a warning."

I swallow and nod. The brutish man who carried me must be Laik.

"We have three rules in camp. One, you do your chores even if you don't like them. Two, no fighting. Three, you listen to Laik and do whatever he says without question, which is why I'm letting you go instead of cutting you up. But for you, there is a fourth rule."

"Okay." The rules seem somewhat reasonable. Though number three concerns me.

"You and your friend are not allowed to talk or interact in any way. If you accidentally make eye contact, you look away immediately. I'll be watching you, and if you fail to follow this rule, I have full permission to use this knife on you."

"For how long?" I gasp. This rule is just cruel. Knox is the only person I have left.

"Until Laik says. You should pretend your friend doesn't exist."

Running away is impossible now. If Knox and I can't even talk, we'll never be able to make any plans, and I won't leave without him. He stuck by me, and I'm going to stick by him. Rule number four can't last forever though, and when we no longer have it, we'll figure out how to get out of here. We'll live on our own or in a human village that can take us in. I will not stay with these monsters. And when it comes time for me to turn, I'll lock myself up somewhere I can't hurt anybody. It's not ideal, but I can make it work.

The woman takes the knife and slices the ropes free from my legs, then she moves behind me, nicking my wrists with the blade.

"Oops," she says with a giggle. "Better get you to medical."

I manage to climb to my feet, but I'm still limping quite a bit. I was right that my ankle swelled up. It looks like a damn balloon.

"What's your name?" I ask her while trying to hold back a sob.

"Didn't I say? I'm Wanda." Her eyes go glassy. "Wanda will be watching Poppy." She opens the tent flap, and I step out into the blinding sun. All around me people bustle about, and panic sets in. In my haste to get away from Wanda, I forgot where I am and who I'm with.

Lycan...

At least, I think they're lycan. There are about thirty of them here and they look like humans, but they're rough around the edges. Probably from living like this. The camp is made up of camouflaged tents sitting among tall pines. A babbling brook winds through it, where many of the people are washing up in various states of undress. So maybe they smelled bad because they weren't here on the full moon. Laik is among them. He's a beast of a man and completely naked.

I avert my eyes, and my cheeks warm.

"Does she think she's better than us?" someone says gruffly. "She won't be one to talk come next month."

"Go easy on her," a woman's voice cuts through. I want to look, but I keep my head down. I don't want these people to notice me, let alone think I'm watching them bathe. "Laik says she was one of the claimed girls. Don't you think she's been through enough?"

"I know she's a liar," someone bounces back.

"That's enough." Laik's voice cuts them off, and I look up. I meet his eyes, careful to avoid the rest of him. "Our lycan self has a distinct stench that hangs around until we can wash it away. And Chase is right. You will be one of us soon." He nods toward a tent. "Now, go see Callum and get yourself patched up. There's no downtime here."

I wobble over to the tent. The flap is already open with the scent of sandalwood drifting out. "Come in," a young male voice says. I don't know what I was expecting of the healer, but I assumed elderly and probably female. The last thing I want to do is go into a tent with a male, but I have to take Laik's word for it. Nobody is going to touch me against my will here.

I duck inside to find a cramped space with a couple cots, blankets, and a table covered in dried herbs. The man inside can hardly be called a man. He's got to be younger than I am. "I already know what you're thinking," he says, "I was the apprentice for three months when our medicine woman died, so here I am. Have a seat."

Settling onto a flat pillow, I try not to wince. The swelling has started to go down, but somehow that's made it worse. It's like the ligaments have loosened too much. The boy kneels before me and begins examining the ankle. "Doesn't look infected," he says. "You're lucky. A third of the bites are, and not everyone can survive an infection out here. We don't always have access to antibiotics, you know."

I swallow hard. "How do I know if it's infected?" I don't even get to the part about antibiotics. I don't know what they are, and I feel out of touch enough as it is.

He sighs, and I take the opportunity to get a better look at him. If I had to guess, I'd put him no older than seventeen. He's got edgy features and long black hair tied into a messy bun. He doesn't look like anyone from my village, but he does remind me of the men back in the wolf pack. It makes me miss Ryne, and I squash down that longing immediately. Ryne betrayed Grady and Joanna and then sent me off to die. If he really cared about me, he wouldn't have fed me to the lycan––he knows who lives out in the wilds. But then again, should I be surprised? He was going to kill our friends, all to please his father. When things get tough, it turns out Ryne chooses Thorn.

"The edges will turn red, it will start to pus, and you'll get a fever. So watch for those things. You'll need to keep it clean. Good thing is, after your first renewal, you'll be able to heal from wounds quickly."

"Renewal?"

"That's what we call it when we shift," he explains. "With each moon we become stronger than the last."

"But that doesn't really explain 'renewal.'"

He pauses for a second. "Listen, you didn't hear this from me, but you'll learn soon enough anyway, so I may as well be the first to explain it to you." He leans forward and smiles conspiratorially. He doesn't smell like the others, and his breath is fine. He must have already bathed. "We can only change into our lycan forms during full moons, but we do have extra strengths during the month. The new moon, when there is nothing in the sky, is when we're at our weakest."

"What kind of strengths?"

He shrugs a shoulder like it's nothing, but I realize he's bragging, and his eyes keep flashing to my bare legs. I hate that I'm still in this torn slip, but Callum's checking me out, which could play to my advantage.

"We're fast and strong, and we can heal quickly. It's nothing like when we're lycan, but we're still better than humans." He holds up a hand. "No offense."

"None taken." But that's not true. I am kind of offended. I don't want to become one of these brutal monsters that kill humans, and now that I know they think they're better than humans, I like them even less.

"I'm Callum, by the way," he reaches out a weathered hand, and we shake. I already know his name from Laik mentioning it, but it feels nice to be properly introduced.

Over the next few minutes, I ask him questions while he packs and binds my wound, but I don't learn anything else new. He also treats the cuts on my feet, rubbing goo into them and covering them in bandages. He hands over some slippers and tells me where I can find a set of clean clothes in another tent. On my way out, he gives me some herbs to take for the next few weeks. "Some will help you get rid of the inflammation and pain, and others will prepare your body for your renewal next month."

"Which ones work for which things?" I ask curiously.

He seems excited that I'm interested and spends the next five minutes going through each one. I listen intently and then thank him as I leave. Even though part of me knows I shouldn't, I decide I'm not going to use any of the herbs meant to help me through the renewal. I'll take the stuff for my wounds, but that's it. Maybe it's stupid, but I can't help but wonder if the lycan are wrong about me. What if I'm stronger than all of this? Maybe I'll get lucky, and my body will fight off the lycan venom on its own. If taking Callum's herbs will help me turn into a lycan, then I'm going to do the exact opposite.

Chapter Four

By lunchtime, the offensive stench of the lycan is washed away. Everyone has bathed and is wearing fresh clothes. They look a million times more put together than they did when I first met them. I catch sight of Knox every once in a while, but I avoid his eyes, and I notice that he avoids mine. I worry that they might change him on purpose. He's in far more danger than I am in this camp. Eventually we'll figure out how to talk to one another, but for now, I must keep my head down and let myself heal. At least, the bits of me that can heal. It's not just my ankle that's torn to shreds. It's my heart too, and I don't think that'll ever be the same.

I wear thick socks, boots, cargo pants, and a tight tank top. Most of the other women are dressed similarly, though they wear sandals or tennis shoes. It's getting warmer, and summer is fast approaching. The humidity will be brutal out here in the wilds, but at least my feet will be better by then. The woman who gave me clothes told me they needed time to heal and to keep them in socks until they do. I'd tried to strike up a conversation with her, but the mention of socks was all she offered. It was apparent she didn't want to talk, and I know she won't be the only one here who wants to steer clear of me. I'm the outsider, and Laik already told them I came from the wolf city. They don't trust me, and I can't say I blame them. I wouldn't trust me either if I was in their position.

After changing, I wander around the camp. I'm not really sure what to do. A few people introduce themselves, but most just go on ignoring me. They won't even share eye contact. I don't take offense or try to push them. I need to focus on staying alive, and Mama always said you catch more bees with honey than vinegar. It may kill me to keep my tongue in check while I'm here, but it may also save me.

The camp is set up in a circle. There are folding tables and an outdoor kitchen at the center surrounded by large canvas tents that groups of people sleep in. The biggest ones are for men and women, but there are a few for couples, and Laik has his own. The supply tents, medic's tent, and the tent Laik questioned me in form an outer circle. I don't go into any of the tents, but I watch as people go in and come out with supplies––food, clothes, and even a few weapons.

I don't know what to do with myself, so I sit to the side and watch, my aching feet starting to ease up a little. I think Callum's herbs are starting to work, and it sends a wave of relief through me. He's not so bad. I'm still not going to touch the ones he gave me to prepare for the next full moon, but I'm definitely sticking with the healing herbs.

Lunch rolls around, and it doesn't smell like much, but hunger has turned my stomach raw, and I need to fill it up. I walk on shaky legs and go to the line. I stand with the rest of them and get a gooey brown mush along with a roll dumped onto a metal plate. I sit at the farthest table and pick at the food. The mush looks off, and I can't even tell what's in it. My stomach turns in protest. Maybe I'm not as hungry as I thought.

"It tastes better than it looks," Callum says with a chuckle. I jerk my eyes up, and he sits next to me. He's the first person to actually look me in the eyes in hours, and I'm instantly grateful. Maybe we can be friends.

"What is it?" I ask, almost afraid of the answer.

He shrugs. "A mix of grains, vegetables, and legumes. See, there's a carrot." He points to a pale orange lump. "We add deer meat when we can get it, but there's not any in there today. All vegetarian, baby." He winks, and I think it's rather ironic that a bunch of lycans aren't eating meat. Callum's trying to lighten the mood, so I give him a small smile before returning to stare at the supposedly edible sludge. I sniff at it, take a small bite, and grimace. It does not taste better than it looks.

"Oh look, the princess thinks she's better than our food." Wanda takes the seat next to me and looks me up and down with a curled lip.

"I'm no princess," I grumble.

Callum hands me a salt shaker. "Use as much as you need."

I practically dump the whole thing on my food and choke it down. At least the roll tastes alright. Hopefully my stomach will thank me, but I'm not so sure. This is a far cry from the meals we had at the manor. Even the villages eat better than this.

"At dinner we get berries and things for dessert," he adds hopefully. "It's my favorite meal of the day."

"Is it all like this?" I ask. My voice comes out whiny, and I instantly regret the question.

"Yes," Wanda grunts. "You should be grateful you aren't starving, little girl. We don't have to feed you, let alone keep you safe. You're lucky Laik is willing to help." It's obvious she'd taken a different route if she was the leader here. The woman hates me.

But she's also right. It's not that I want to stay here with the lycan, but I can't turn my nose up at them either. And I guess it makes sense now that nobody wants to go to the wilds because they're, well, *wild.* What else are people supposed to eat out here?

"You're right. I'm sorry. I'm just not used to it."

She sniffs. "We eat for fuel here, so finish that because you're going to need the energy."

I force another mouthful and nod. Again, she's right, even if I don't like it.

"I know the wolves gotta keep their babymakers well-fed in the city." She eyes my stomach. "You aren't pregnant with one of those monsters, are you?"

Monsters? The lycan are also monsters. I've made the argument myself that the wolves are monsters too, so I guess I can see where she's coming from. But not all of them. My heart clenches. I miss Ryne more than anything and hate that I care so much about him.

"I'm not pregnant," I mutter. "Promise."

She shrugs. "Wouldn't matter anyway. You'll be a lycan soon, and the change from human to lycan wouldn't let you keep a baby anyway."

My mouth pops open. "So I'll never have children?" It's not like I want to bring a child into this world, because I certainly don't, but the idea that I'll become infertile if I turn is jarring.

"No," Callum cuts in, shooting Wanda a stern look. "Sometimes lycan women have children, but a pregnant human has never had a baby survive the first renewal. It's too hard on the body. Anyway, you won't get your chore assignments until tomorrow morning, but I was wondering if you wanna come help me sort herbs and fold dressing?" His cheeks pink slightly, and his eyes are so hopeful that I don't know how to answer.

"Poppy is coming with me," Laik's strong voice carries across from the next table over where he sits near Knox. I turn towards him and offer a thumbs up. He takes that as confirmation and returns to shoveling food into his mouth. I don't know what Laik wants with me, but whatever it is, it's not going to be nearly as pleasant as spending the afternoon with Callum, even if the boy is a little too eager.

We finish up, and I follow the others to drop my scraped-clean plate into a vat of soapy water. I ate it all, even though it tasted awful, because Wanda made a good point and also because I don't want to make anyone hate me more than they already do. The dishes reek, and I eye the water with a grimace. I really hope that I'm not assigned dish duty tomorrow.

I can't even begin to think about what it's like to eat this way day in and day out. I hope I'm not here for long.

Chapter Five

I search the group of people cleaning up and find Laik standing near the path to the forest. I approach him cautiously. Instead of saying a word to me, he grabs the handle of a wagon and tromps down the path. I have to hurry to keep up with the man. He's huge, almost as tall as Ryne, and much bulkier. I wince a little as my feet still hurt, but the boots are keeping them safe from new wounds, so I can't complain.

"Where are we going?"

"To gather wood for the dinner fire." He pulls a long saw out of the wagon. "I'll get some of the bigger pieces if you'll gather kindling."

Okay, that's not so bad.

I search the ground for small branches, and he cuts up bigger ones. We work in silence for a long time, and it's actually peaceful. If this is my job, I'll gladly scour the woods with Laik. He doesn't scare me as much as his mate does. At least, I assume that Wanda is his mate. She certainly seems possessive of him. I hope I'm right, that he isn't so bad, but a little voice in the back of my head is warning me to be careful.

"Do we get new chores every day, or is it the same?" I ask.

Laik dumps a few logs into the wagon and brushes his hands on his pants. "It depends on the job and the day. More specialized jobs, like medical, are the same every day, but things like gathering wood and dishes are rotated around. You'll be doing a little of everything to see if you have talents in any particular area. Is there anything you're good at?"

I recall my time at Drayton Hall. I learned a thing or two, but not well. The only thing I excelled at was running and fighting. I'm not sure I want to fight for the lycan, but it would get me out a little more. The people who guard the camp get to roam the outskirts, and most of them have weapons. I could use that to my advantage and get out of here.

"I'm a pretty good fighter."

Laik eyes me up and down. "You're too small to fight."

I hold my head high. "I assure you I can hold my own. I know you have patrols and guards. Let me be one of them."

He laughs, and I'm surprised by the joyfulness of the sound. He doesn't strike me as the kind of guy to take a joke. "We will see if you can fight, though I doubt you're any good. Either way, you aren't joining our guard until you prove your loyalty to me."

Oh, so he was laughing *at* me. I sniff. Fat chance of that. I'll never be loyal to them. But I don't want to be on kitchen duty the rest of my time here, either. I'll never escape that way. Considering my other training at the manor, I could try to get this guy to like me. I'm not about to flirt with him, but if he sees me as one of his own, I'll get what I want faster. "What do I have to do to prove my loyalty?"

He stares at me, scrutinizing my every word and action. Something changes between us, and I can't tell if it's more trust or less trust, but whatever it is, the man is starting to see me as more than a silly girl who ate his berries. "You're serious, aren't you?"

"I am. I have no love for the wolves who forced me from my home and then abandoned me when I got hurt." It's a half-lie. They did do all those things, but I still love Ryne. Perhaps that's the curse of being his fated mate. I'm doomed to love a man I should hate, a man I'll never trust again or see again or...

I can't think about that.

Laik nods slowly, and a muscle pops in his jaw. "Okay, give us some time, and we'll see what we can come up with. Give yourself time as well. Adjusting to being a lycan isn't easy. We can resume this conversation after your first renewal."

I swallow. I'd forgotten that I'm one of them. I don't have time for my renewal to swing around. I need to get out of here and find a cure to this curse before it takes me hostage for good. Everything has already changed in my life, but if I become a lycan, there will be no going back. Not ever.

* * *

Dinner is better than lunch but not by much. The food is bland again, and I don't have an appetite. I keep thinking about what Laik said about adjusting to being a lycan. It's only been a few hours, but the idea of a cure suddenly seems like a foolish fantasy. I've never heard of one before, and that's because there isn't one. Maybe I should take Callum's herbs, after all? I don't know what to do.

The thoughts weigh heavy on my mind, and I have a nagging feeling that there's a lot more to becoming a lycan. When Charlotte turned, she killed a bunch of people. What if that happens to me too? I don't know if I'll be able to forgive myself. I want to run away, but that could be a mistake. Maybe if I stay and have my first renewal with these people, they can help me, and once I have a better idea of what I can and cannot handle, I can make a run for it. Is that a terrible idea? Should I get out of here before it becomes impossible to leave? I don't want to go through my first shift on my own, but I don't want to trust these people either.

It's an impossible situation and has hit me like a slap to the face. I've been in denial the last few days, but I can't deny it anymore. I've been infected, and I'm going to turn into a monster.

"What's going on with the alpha?" a woman asks a man as he settles in for his meal. They're not talking to me, but I listen intently while keeping my eyes down. I don't want them to know I'm eavesdropping on them. The guy she's talking to is burly and still reeks like a beast and is covered in dirt. He must have just arrived back at camp. He surveys the group, eyes landing on me and holding. I don't meet his gaze, but I can feel it lingering on me like a shadow.

I grow hot, fear washing through me. Was he at the festival? Did he see me? Does he know about me and Ryne? If anyone here finds out I'm fated to Ryne, that knowledge will be used against me. Either that, or I'll simply be murdered for my association with their enemy.

The man looks away. "Not sure what you're talking about," he responds.

The woman gives the man a look. "Everyone knows what you were doing there. Is the alpha married or not?"

My breath catches. So then that man *was* there that night. He probably saw me and is going to tell everyone. I'll go from being the lost berry-girl to the enemy's fated mate. For the first time all day, I catch Knox's eye. He sits on the far side of another table, and he's looking at me too. He shakes his head once and returns to his plate. His ears are pink. Is he afraid? For him or for me?

Now everyone within earshot is watching him. He takes a bite of his bread and slowly chews, leaving us suspended. I feel as if I'm two seconds from exploding. Because it's an answer I need to know as well. Is the alpha married? Surely after everything, the weddings didn't happen.

The man swallows, takes a long drink from his cup, and sighs with satisfaction.

"Enough with the theatrics, Tanner." Laik sits right next to me, and I can feel the tension rolling off of his body.

Wanda slams the table with her fist and yells, "Tell us!" For once, I agree with her.

"Sorry, sorry." Tanner laughs, eyeing the whole table. "I didn't realize y'all were so eager to know." He prolongs the suspense for a few moments longer. No one is eating anymore, and every eye is on him. "Yes, despite everything, the alpha got married to the luna."

Laik drops his head. "This isn't good," he mutters.

I can't help myself. "Why not?" I instantly regret asking. I feel as if I'm suffocating––I don't know how to handle this.

"Because marriage to a luna makes his pack stronger. It hurts our mission. There are lycans tasked with taking down packs, and this one is ours."

Reality sinks in at that moment, but I have to hold it together. People pepper the man with follow-up questions, but I can't stay, can't hear the answers to a single one. I think it might kill me. I excuse myself, going for the latrine. It's gross, nothing like the flushing toilets of Drayton Hall, but I'm no stranger to rough conditions. And it's the only place I can have some privacy.

Female guards stand far enough away to let me do my business, but I don't go to the hole in the ground that is our bathroom out here. Instead, I push past the latrine area, press up against the biggest tree I can find, and burst into tears.

Ryne is married.

Chapter Six

I lose track of time, the days dragging by. Even when we move our camp farther away from the wolf city in preparation for the upcoming new moon, I couldn't care less. Laik says not staying in one spot for long is for our protection. That, and the lycan can't fight very well during the new moon. He also says I have to help carry supplies since my wounds have healed.

Great. Don't care.

I'm grieving my old life, but most of all, I'm angry. The rage is all-consuming sometimes, and after we set up camp in our new location, I beg Laik to let me join the warriors. "Please," I plead, "I need to beat someone up." No one knows my connection to Ryne, but they have learned that I'm snappy and mean. I didn't used to be, but that's who I am now.

He turns to Knox, who is standing nearby. "Is she always like this?"

It's the first time he's addressed us together and it feels like a trick. "Only since the wolf shifters murdered her twin sister in front of her and then took her in the claiming instead."

My cheeks flame, and I glare at Knox. I don't like my secrets aired out for people I don't trust, but Laik takes it all in stride. "Good." He nods to me. "Beat someone in a scrimmage, and I'll take you to the panther city with us tomorrow."

The panther city? Those three words wake me up. I didn't know there were other kinds of shifters until the conversation between Ryne and his father about overtaking the panther city. It's a conversation that feels like it happened a million years ago. That night we'd almost kissed, and then he'd kissed Faye instead to throw King Thorn off, but it had hurt all the same. I should've known then that a romance with Ryne was doomed. Of course, rumors of other shifters had abounded in my village growing up, but nobody could confirm anything. Now I know the truth, and whatever's in the panther city, I want to see it for myself.

"Deal."

"Better yet." He grins wickedly. "Knox, why don't you two fight? I don't even care who wins. I'll let you both come."

Knox scowls and backs away. "She's almost a lycan, and I'm not, which basically guarantees that she'll win. But even if she weren't, I wouldn't lay a finger on her." And then he walks away, which only makes Laik laugh. My anger isn't directed at Knox, but I'd definitely fight him if it meant we could both go tomorrow. Besides, the more the lycans see me and Knox around each other, the sooner we'll be allowed to talk again. And maybe get away from this horrible place.

I hate the camp. At first I'd thought maybe I could like it, or at least tolerate it, but the more time I spend here, the more time I want to get away. The days are monotonous—just a bunch of angry people waiting for the full moon so they can go do something. They hate the wolves, and I'm sure they're planning another attack, but they won't tell me anything. I haven't proven my loyalty to Laik, and I doubt I ever will.

I watch Knox disappear into the trees and want to scream at him to get back here, that I'm not a lycan yet, that I need him, but I don't get the chance. Someone jumps me from behind. Wanda laughs in my ear, her breath hot as she yanks on my braid. Fingers claw down my face as I throw her off me and round to face her.

"Let's see what you got, princess," she hisses. This woman is hot and cold, but the more Laik has loosened up on me, the colder she's gotten. I can't figure her out, and maybe that's the point. She doesn't want me to be able to guess what she's going to do next.

"How about a fair fight?" I snap.

She laughs at that. "You think the wolves will be fair?"

It's strange, this conversation. I had practically the same one with Ryne when I was first taken down to the basement of the manor and taught to fight. They'd jumped me then too.

"True," I say, punching her directly in the nose.

Wanda's voice drops into a low growl, and she lunges for me. I jump out of the way, and she goes stumbling in the crowd, which has now gathered around us like moths to a flame. Laik oversees us. His thick arms are crossed, and a nasty smirk mars his face.

"Beat Poppy, and you can go with us to the panther city tomorrow." He raises an eyebrow at his woman.

Their relationship is odd, and in the few seconds I've been paying attention to Laik, Wanda has regrouped. Before I can react, she tackles me to the ground.

Her putrid breath is worse than her fists pommeling my side. We have soap here and herbs to clean our teeth, but she must not care or she's done this on purpose to throw me off. I've never done well on my back, and her stench is disarming. I roll, knowing I'll take more hits, but it will also be easier for me to get up. She tumbles off me, and I jump to my feet. I don't know her strengths and weaknesses, and I don't want this fight to last long.

I don't even wait for her to get her bearings. I swing my leg up and around and manage to connect right with the side of her head. She crumples to the ground, unconscious.

My eyes flash to Laik's, and for a second I'm afraid he's going to be angry with me for taking down his mate, but instead a slow grin forms on his face.

"I told you I could fight," I say.

"Geoff and Malik, take Wanda to see Callum. Poppy, you've earned yourself a visit to the panther city. We leave at dawn."

* * *

I don't like leaving Knox behind, but I'm excited about our trip. I'm not excited about the walk, however.

"How far away is it?" I ask.

Laik adjusts his backpack. So far, it's just me and him. I was a little eager to make this journey but also a little nervous to be alone with this brute of a leader.

"About thirty miles."

I swallow down my groan. That will take all day. My feet are better, but I can already imagine the blisters I'll be dealing with soon.

Wanda approaches, glaring at me, but doesn't say anything. She has a purple bruise on the side of her face and a split lip. It makes her look even wilder than before. She runs her finger along the wounds and grins at me like she likes them. I didn't think about what it would mean to have her with us, but she might use this time to retaliate. I doubt she'd do anything in front of Laik, but she could easily make something look like an accident. What if she wants me dead?

"Who are we waiting for?" I ask Laik, turning away from Wanda.

"Just Callum. He needs to get some more medicine."

I haven't had a chance to hang out with Callum since that first day. Laik has kept me on gathering wood duty, which is nice because I get to wander in the woods. There's always another man with me, but they have all been quiet. I know it's because they don't trust me, and I normally wouldn't mind, but it has left me far too much time to think.

And the only one I ever think of is Ryne.

His betrayal eats away at my soul. I recognize that to him, I'm as good as dead, but it still hurts. I feel like I didn't know him or Elle at all. How they could do this to me——still get married despite everything——is beyond my comprehension.

Callum joins us, rubbing his eyes, and I nudge him. "Not a morning person?"

As if on cue, he yawns. "Definitely not."

Laik starts walking with Wanda right behind him. I frown, so I guess she is coming along after all. I'll have to watch my back. Callum and I follow them, and for the first twenty minutes or so, we all walk in silence. Then the path opens up a bit, and Wanda falls in next to Laik, and Callum and I walk side by side.

"Do you like it here so far?" he asks.

Absolutely not. And with the full moon fast approaching, I hate it even more. The moon haunts my dreams, keeping me awake at night. "I don't know," I say instead. "I mean, at least I'm not worried I'll be sent to the mating house." I sigh heavily.

"But?" This time he nudges me, and something inside me unlocks.

"But it's not exactly comfortable living in the wilds knowing I'm going to turn into a monster soon," I blurt out.

Callum furrows his brow. "The wolves are the monsters, not us. I've treated several women we've rescued from the mating houses. I'm glad you never went to one."

I think about that for a minute, twisting the information around in my head like a key I didn't know existed. "Rescue?" I always thought they turned them or killed them.

Callum nods as if the answer is obvious. "We work closely with the

Resistance to rescue as many women as possible."

This is the first I'm hearing about that, but I guess it makes sense considering everything I've seen. The lycans would kill the wolves, but they'd take the girls. Well, except for Charlotte. Not for the first time, I wonder if she's still alive.

"No offense, but what I've witnessed of those rescues haven't exactly gone to plan. My roommate got bit by a lycan and killed two other girls the next month during her renewal. I've also never heard of the lycan working with the Resistance, and my friend was one of them."

Callum's frown is thoughtful. "Nothing's perfect, so sometimes humans get bit, but we figure it's better they become lycan than be trapped as wolf baby-makers."

I'm not certain I agree with him, but I don't argue.

"How much do you know about the Resistance?" I ask. Maybe I can finally get the answers I've been seeking.

"Not much. I'm not in leadership. Laik is usually the only one who meets with them."

Laik turns abruptly, tromping off the path and into the dense woods. Callum and I scramble after him. We come to a small clearing where Laik is lifting a camouflaged tarp off a vehicle. There are several others here too. All hidden so well I wouldn't have realized they were here unless I was standing right in front of them.

"You have cars?" I ask, relief flooding my body.

Laik gives me a grin. "You didn't think we were walking the whole way, did you?"

Suddenly, my day just got a hundred times better.

Funny how I'd never even seen a car until I got to the city, but now I've come to expect them on long journeys. This car is different from most of the ones in the wolf city. It's large, with two seats up front and an open compartment in the back. It kinda reminds me of a small boat.

"We'll climb in the bed," Callum offers. He reaches out a hand and helps me into the back, which is apparently the bed. It's the opposite of a bed, if you ask me. Sure, it's flat, but it's metal and uncomfortable. I'm still taking it all in when he chuckles. "You've never seen a truck, have you?"

"Nope. I didn't know that's what these cars are called." I swallow hard, the memories coming at me. "The first day in the wolf city, they put us on what they called a trailer bed. It was behind one of these. Then they drove us around the city to show us off to all the men."

A shadow passes over his face, making him look years older. "See? What did I say? They're the monsters, not us."

I'm beginning to wonder if he's right. Thorn is certainly a monster. But Ryne isn't. I clench my fists. Maybe he is. After all, he did go and marry Elle even though I'm his fated. Maybe everything I know about Ryne is a lie.

We sit down, Laik starts the engine, and we pull away, following the bumpiest dirt road I've ever seen. I'm tossed about and hanging onto the side for dear life. This is still way better than walking even though the engine is loud and the metal of the truck bed hurts my butt. The discomfort is nothing compared to the worry that creeps into my thoughts about where we're going.

What am I going to find in panther city?

Chapter Seven

We have to pass through a wasteland to get to the panther city. I knew it was bad out here in the wilds, but to see it for myself is chilling. There are no more trees. For miles, there's nothing out here but barren wilderness. The humans had nuked various areas to try to take out the shifters. Turned out humans were the only ones who were affected by the bombs, but it left scars all over the landscapes. I've never crossed a radioactive field before.

"This is the most dangerous part," Callum says over the rumble of tires. "We've had a lot of scrimmages with the wolves out here because we're so open to attack."

"If they're hunting you, why stay near them at all?" It seems to me that the lycans could find everything they need in the woods. Or find a home far away from the wolf shifters, like with the panthers or some other friendly pack.

He gives me a hard stare. "It's our choice to be in the camps. We could stay with the panthers and live normal lives, but all of us have reasons to put ourselves in danger."

Two things stick out to me. One, that he said camps, meaning more than one. Could Joanna and Grady be in a different camp of lycans? But no, that doesn't make sense. Grady is a wolf shifter—they'd never take him in. And two, that Callum has a reason to be out here risking his life. I imagine what they're doing is like being on the front lines of a war. And he's so young. So many of us never had any choices, but it seems he did. He could die before ever really getting a chance to live.

We hit a big pothole, and I scream a little, then immediately feel stupid. "Is the area still radioactive?" I ask, wanting to deflect my embarrassment and because it would be good to know.

"Sure is," he says, "but you don't need to worry about that. The only ones who are affected by that are the humans, and you'll be a lycan in a few weeks anyway. When we have humans with us, we have to go around the radiation hotspots. It takes way longer, but we don't want to risk them getting sick."

My heart sinks because it's one more reminder of what I'm going to become. When I first arrived here, I hoped to find a cure to the venom. It's only taken a few weeks for me to completely give that notion up. It's happening whether I want it to or not. And now that Laik is purposely exposing me to radiation, what other choice do I have? Anger is my first emotion, but it's only on the surface. There's something much deeper hidden underneath, and that's grief.

Again, my mind returns to Joanna. Has she been exposed to something like this? I hope she's okay. My heart aches, wanting to know where they are and what they're doing. Grady lost his arm and may have bled out. For all I know, he's dead, and she could be too.

I don't ask Callum any more questions after that. The dead zone fades into the distance, and the forest returns. It's denser now, the vegetation thicker than it is on the other side of the zone. There's always humidity in the air, but I feel it growing as if we're getting closer to the ocean. Even though our rivers feed into it, I've never actually seen the ocean before. Maybe I finally will. Something about that makes me incredibly sad, missing all the people I've lost. I could be experiencing something new that they'll never get to experience with me. My little brother Evan would've loved it. Actually, my whole family would've had the time of their lives. I can picture Willow running head-first into the water like she always did, little Evan close behind her, and my parents standing watch with satisfied grins on their faces. And I'd be there too, content and happy and soaking it all in. I can see it all--a nice fantasy that will never exist.

We pull up to a guard station, and someone stops us to talk to Laik. The man has a big gun strapped across his bare chest and black shorts on. It's only April, but it's warming up, and I've learned that shifters aren't as sensitive to extreme temperatures as humans. The man waves us through, and as we pass, his dark eyes meet mine.

He pities me, and I wonder why. Is his life really so much better? We're all scrambling to survive in the same harsh world.

We drive into a city that feels much like the wolf city. Some of the buildings are abandoned and lost to the wars, but the ones that aren't are well taken care of. People come out of their homes to watch us, some of them even waving and calling out warm greetings. Is this the place that Ryne talked about with his dad? The one he wanted to take over for his pack? I shiver at the thought of these people being forced into the wolves' cruel system. As much as I'll always love Ryne, I'm not a fool. I know what they are doing there is wrong. Someone has to make it stop. Maybe the lycan aren't as bad as I thought they were. It's hard to imagine being one of them, but it's happening soon. I would stay and help, but I don't know if I can stomach fighting against Ryne. Just seeing him again would break me.

Thinking of Ryne reminds me of the wedding, and my heart stills. I can't love Ryne anymore. I have to make myself stop. It would be so much easier to hate him, but I can't seem to do that either. I'm doomed to a broken heart.

We pull to a stop next to a park, and Laik jumps out, coming around to pat the side of the truck. "Welcome to Savannah," he says, his tone lighter than I've ever heard. "The northernmost city in the panther shifter territory. Are you ready to prove your loyalty yet?"

My mouth falls open, and he laughs. "Just kidding. I'll save that for after your first renewal."

I glare, thinking of a few choice words, but I keep them to myself. If he dumps me here in this city, then I'll never see my family or friends again. Am I ready for that? It's a reality I haven't accepted yet even though I know it's one I'm currently living.

No. It's best to follow along and make him think I respect him, even though he's done nothing to earn my trust. Even if these guys have a worthy mission, I don't like the way he lords over everyone or the way he keeps me and Knox from talking. His power trip is growing exhausting, and his mate has a few screws loose. Even now, Wanda is watching me like she's planning my death. Her smile is sinister, and her eyes sparkle with mischief. "Come," he says, taking off for a nearby building. Like the little mindless followers that he thinks we are, we hurry after him.

Callum grabs my hand. "I'm going to take Poppy to get medical supplies."

Laik pulls out a few coins, giving them to Callum. "Meet back here in two hours. Get some lunch as well."

Callum nods and drags me away from Laik and Wanda. It's an immediate relief, especially when Wanda's face falls. Whatever she was planning will have to wait.

I'm a bit in awe as we walk down the street. The people here are so . . . content. No one is fearing for their lives, and men and women mingle freely. Kids run up and down the streets as well. They're not dressed as nicely as the betas and their wives, nor as poorly as the lower-ranked wolves. They remind me a lot of the people in my village, simple and hardworking. But there's a sense of happiness that I haven't seen anywhere before. I almost don't trust it.

"After we finish getting the supplies I need, we'll get some food." Callum tightens his hand around mine. "Savannah has the best shrimp and grits in the world."

"What's shrimp?" I ask.

He laughs, mirth dancing in his eyes. "You'll see."

We stop outside a shop that has a line out the door, and Callum joins it.

"What's this?" I ask, eyeing the brick building with *Pharmacy* written across the top. I don't know what it means, except that it must be something medical if Callum is here.

"We're getting more antibiotics. Savannah has one of the only labs in the area that can make them. They have a limited supply, so they only sell so much per person each day. Even the doctors in the city have to come for refills often. I wish we could travel here more often to get them, but Laik and the panthers have a deal that we can only come once a month."

"Why only once a month?"

"It's dangerous." We move up the line, and he nods toward the building. "But necessary. Even though lycans can usually fight off infections naturally, sometimes antibiotics are needed to save a life."

It's that word again, "antibiotics." Maybe I should ask him what it does, but from what I can piece together, it must be something to heal these infections he speaks of. I don't know what he means by the word "lab" either. I people-watch while we stand in line, and those questions get filtered out by more interesting ones. There is a vendor with all kinds of delicious fruits across the street. I recognize most of them––apples, oranges, and bananas. But there are others that I've never seen before. My mouth waters just looking at them.

A young couple, with a boy who looks to be about three, approaches the fruit stand and chats with the vendor. The man has his arm slung loosely over the woman's shoulder, and she laughs at something the vendor says.

It's only then that I recognize the different types of people. Some are as tall as the wolves, but most are not. People are dressed in a multitude of styles, and skin color ranges from light pale to dark brown to black. I've never seen such diversity.

I go back to watching the young couple. The little boy grabs a strawberry and shoves it in his mouth while no one is looking. His mother glances down and sees the red juice streaming down his chin.

She scolds him, and without warning, his clothes go flying, and he turns into a tiny panther. He has an adorable black face and black spots, but he growls and snaps at his mother. His father immediately shifts into a much larger panther, his coat a glossy black, and lays a heavy paw on top of the boy's head, snarling and growling.

Then, just as quickly as it began, they both shift back. The mother grumbles, handing them fresh clothing from her satchel, and they quickly dress. The little boy wipes a few tears from his face as his mother gathers him in her arms, and he buries his face in her hair. It's an embrace I've seen countless times before. Human or not, we all need our parents to love us.

Except the wolves—most of them don't have parents. They only have the pack. Maybe that's why they're so ruthless? They're raised without love.

The little family turns back and continues their conversation with the vendor as if nothing has happened.

Callum nudges me. "Panthers are taught to respect women from a very young age. It's different from the wolves, yeah?"

"It is. Is the whole city made up of panther shifters and their families?"

"It used to be, but it's become a sanctuary of sorts. The majority of the population is panther, but they welcome almost anyone, so besides humans, you'll find lycans and a few of the exiled wolves who plead their case successfully. I've even heard there are even some shifters from out west, like bears and hawks, but I've never met one."

I wonder if maybe Joanna and Grady made it here. I wish there was a way for me to search for them, but I wouldn't even know where to start.

The line moves slowly, but eventually we get inside the shop.

Two men in white coats stand behind a counter.

Callum approaches. "I'm from Laik's camp."

One of the men nods and flips through a book. He runs a finger down the page. "It says here you have about twenty people, and you are thirty miles away. Is that correct?"

"Yes, sir."

"And did you use all of your medicine?"

"No. I still have two bottles left. But last month we ran out."

"Very well. Give him four bottles."

The other man gives Callum a bag, and we head back out on the bustling street.

"You didn't give him any coins," I say.

"We don't pay for medicine. The coins Laik gave me were for food. Speaking of . . ."

Callum stops at a vendor that has small caramel-colored candies. He picks up a couple and hands me one. "These are amazing."

I taste one, and sweetness explodes in my mouth. I've had decent desserts at Drayton Hall, but candy isn't something I've eaten a lot of before. The sugar melts in my mouth and the nuts at the center stick to my teeth. Once I've managed to eat it all, I laugh. "What is that stuff?"

"Pralines." He glances at a clock on the wall. "We gotta hurry if we're going to get all that we need. You know the food we eat back at camp isn't the best, so the days we come to Savannah, we get something more tasty to bring back for dinner. It keeps the others from getting too jealous that they weren't invited to come along."

We dodge in and out of the crowd, which seems to grow thicker as we get farther into the city. I also see several panthers lounging about in the streets or sidewalks. It's just so different from the wolf city.

Everyone here is relaxed. I don't see any indication of extreme wealth or extreme poverty––just all kinds of people working and living together. I can't believe that Ryne would consider taking over this place. That would be barbaric. Maybe I've completely misjudged him.

Maybe he is the enemy.

Chapter Eight

"Why wouldn't you want to stay here?" I question Callum after we've gathered the last of our supplies and stopped to scarf down the yummy shrimp and grits. "This is so much better than living in the wilds." I motion to the lively city square. There's electricity and running water and happy people. "I don't get it."

"Someone has to protect all this."

"But why can't the panthers do that?"

He swallows hard and looks around, as if making sure nobody is eavesdropping. I don't think anyone is. We're two of many here, and nobody seems to pay us any mind. "They have a cease-fire treaty with the wolves and aren't willing to fight them unless absolutely necessary. It's why Laik says we can only come here once a month. Because he wants to keep our business with the panthers a secret."

"So you're doing their dirty work for them." It's actually pretty smart, but for some reason it irks me, and it shouldn't. I want to end the human slavery as much as these people do, but I can't help but think of Ryne getting killed by the end of all this. My alliances are muddled, and it's starting to wear on me. I need to let him go already.

Because the lycans are right.

"The panthers are run similar to the wolves with several cities working together. They have guards who protect those cities," Callum continues, "but they don't send soldiers out to fight. They want to keep the peace they have here, and part of that means not starting any wars."

"Well, maybe they should," I grumble. I realize I've come to side with the lycans over the wolves. Hopefully that doesn't change after my first renewal, but I don't think it will. Even if I don't stay with Laik's people, I'll never be able to forget everything I've been through. If it wasn't for the wolves' brutality, I'd still have my family. I'd have a normal life.

"We have a few more minutes." Callum tucks my arm in his and leads me away. "There's something I want to show you, but you have to promise not to tell Laik."

We head toward one of the unmarked buildings, and my apprehension builds at keeping a secret from Laik. He still scares me, and Wanda is his match in every way. There's something strange about those two, like they belong out in the wilds instead of in the safety of the city.

"Laik wants you to stay with our camp," Callum says, "and he doesn't want you to know that you actually have a choice in the matter."

Before I can utter a response, Callum sweeps me through a doorway and into a beautiful lobby with polished marble floors and gleaming gilded mirrors. A man and a woman stand behind a desk, smiling warmly at us. "Welcome to The Sanctuary," the woman says. "How can we help you?"

"I'm here to give my friend a tour to see if she wants to stay here instead of with us in the wilds."

Her eyes widen, and she rushes toward me. "Oh, you poor thing! When did you get out?" She pats my cheeks and peers down at my weather-worn clothing. "Have you been with the lycans for long?"

"She's one of the claimed girls and was bitten during the last moon," Callum says. "She's been with us for a little over three weeks."

The woman steps back and nods solemnly. "In that case, we'd better start on the fourth floor."

"What's on the fourth floor?" My voice trembles. I don't like the pitying way everyone is looking at me. I know my life isn't perfect, and I've been victimized, but I don't need pity from anyone. It makes me feel weaker than I already am.

"People who understand exactly what you're going through," she says, and I stiffen. How could anyone truly understand the ache of my heart? I've been alone since the moment I lost my twin, and I don't expect that to ever change. "I'm sorry, but you'll have to wait here. There are no men allowed past the lobby," she explains to Callum.

"No problem, just have her back in ten minutes if you can. We're short on time."

"In that case . . ." She turns around, her long skirt swishing at her ankles, and hurries toward the staircase while I follow. My thighs are burning by the time we get all the way up to the fourth floor, but that pain is nothing compared to my curiosity.

"The Sanctuary is for the women who come from the wolf cities. Most of them have been in the mating houses and have a lot of trauma to work through before they're comfortable around men again, which is why I asked your friend to stay behind."

Okay, so maybe they do understand bits of my heartache. My virtue was never ripped from me, but my sister and my friends were. And my love betrayed me in the most painful way. They're all wounds that can never be fully healed, but maybe these people can make it so they don't fester so badly.

The woman throws open a set of double doors, and light streams over my face, then my eyes adjust, and I take it all in. The large sitting room, the kitchen tucked to the side, the lines of doors leading to what I assume are bedrooms, and the women.

Young women.

"This floor is reserved specifically for women like you--women who've escaped the wolves but not the lycan. Everyone here has already been through a renewal. You could choose to stay if you wanted. I can tell your friend that you're not leaving with him."

I blink, letting her words sink in. It would be so easy . . .

One by one, the ladies turn toward us, some smiling and waving, others offering consolatory nods. And then one in particular turns from where she's standing at the window, her honey-blonde hair lit up like a halo.

I freeze--a torrent of emotions storming through me, anger and sadness and frustration all at once. I would recognize that girl anywhere. "Charlotte," I say at the same time she whispers my name. Something comes over me, as if I'm not myself. I march toward her and slap her clean across her face. Hard.

Time stops, and nobody moves.

And then all at once, I'm descended upon by people trying to stop me, but I don't care. All I care about is Charlotte and the horrible things she did. "How could you?" I start screaming, fighting against the strength of a powerful lycan woman holding me back. "You killed so many of us! You kept your bite a secret from me."

"Let her go," Charlotte orders the women, her voice stoic. A tear drops from her eye, and my desire to punish her weakens. "She's right. I deserved that."

"No." Someone tightens her hold on me. "You never asked to be bit."

"If you'd told anyone, you'd have died," another adds.

Charlotte glares at them, and they loosen their grip. I shake free. "Are you saying that her life is more valuable than the others who died because of her actions?" I glare at the women. If this is the attitude they have, then maybe I don't want to stay at this sanctuary. "Let's see, you ripped those girls to shreds, you killed one of our house mothers, and you bit another who had to be put down by Anders. Is there anyone else I'm forgetting? Any others you've taken out since that night?"

"You're right," Charlotte says again, stepping toward me. More tears roll down her face. This isn't the Charlotte I knew. Where's the selfishness? Where's the cold shoulder and the prissy attitude? I suddenly feel bad for the things I've said, but I shouldn't because I'm right. Why should she be forgiven so easily when she could've told someone she'd been bitten? She chose herself over all of us, and it cost several people their lives.

"I made a mistake, and it's something I will have to live the rest of my life regretting. But you're here now, so I'm guessing you've been bitten too."

I meet her eyes and harden my voice. "Yes. But I haven't killed anyone." I practically spit out the words. "And I'd rather die than do what you did."

"Then let me help you," she rushes out. "I'll make sure what happened to me doesn't happen to you also."

I step back. I want nothing to do with this woman. I've had a lot of time to think about this, and I know in my heart of hearts that I couldn't do what she did. Fortunately though, when I shift for the first time, I'll be surrounded by lycan. I don't need Charlotte. "I'm sorry, but it's too late for you to absolve yourself. Those women are already dead, and I already have people who are going to help me."

I turn back to the woman who brought me up here. Her mouth is set in an angry line. Maybe she thinks I'm being too harsh on Charlotte, and maybe I am, but I don't care. She had so many opportunities to tell the truth. And if she'd told me, I would've helped her get out of Drayton Hall somehow. It's not like I would've just turned her into the wolves. But she went into that locked room knowing full-well she was going to turn into a lycan, and in doing so, she knowingly chose her own life over so many others. If that's what they condone here at The Sanctuary, if they're okay with her living a great life without any punishment for what she did to us, then I don't want it.

"I'm ready to go back to my friend now," I say, heading for the staircase. The woman follows behind, and there's another set of footsteps behind that.

"I'm going with you," Charlotte says.

I whip back around and glare up at her.

"It's a lycan camp out in the wilds," the woman interrupts. "It's no place for a young lady, Charlotte."

"Wherever you're going and whatever you're doing," she continues, ignoring the woman and pinning her crystal-blue eyes on me. "I have to try to make up for what I did."

"I don't want you there," I spit out and bunch my hands into fists. I'll fight her if I have to.

Her eyes water again, and she clears her throat. "Too bad."

"No."

"Please," she whispers, "please, let me at least try to pay penance for what I did." Her voice cracks, and the pain is unmistakable. "I know it was wrong, okay? I know that. But I was scared and dumb, and I made a mistake. Haven't you ever made a mistake?"

Not one that got people killed.

Her pleas seep through me, but my resolve is firm. "If you come back with me, it's not because I'm okay with it or because I forgive you."

"I don't expect--"

"And my friend brought me to The Sanctuary when he wasn't supposed to. You're going to get us in trouble. Stay here, Charlotte. You're not wanted anywhere else."

Those are cruel words, and I expect her to deflate with them, but she doesn't. She stands even taller, her mind made up. "I'll tell your people that I ran into you in the city. Nobody has to know you stopped by The Sanctuary."

I roll my eyes. This girl really has an excuse for everything, doesn't she? I let her walk all over me, but I won't do it anymore. I'm done with Charlotte. However, it appears that she isn't done with me.

"You follow me, and you're going to have to convince Laik that you're worth his time. Good luck with that one."

"Who's Laik?" She folds her arms over her chest as if she's up for the challenge. But I meant what I said--I'm done. I turn to leave, fully prepared for her to follow me against my wishes. The woman has made up her mind. I can't stop her when she's like this, but I don't have to give her any warnings about Laik either, let alone Wanda. She's about to find out what it's like to be on the receiving end of a very distrustful bunch of lycans.

Chapter Nine

"**N**o, absolutely not." Laik crosses his arms over his chest. We're standing next to the truck, and I don't even bother to deal with whatever is going to come of this. I climb into the bed and wait for this conversation to be settled.

"Why not?" Charlotte asks, brows furrowing. She's got that innocent look about her that I know is complete crap, but always seems to work in her favor. "I can fight. And you people come in all the time asking for more fighters. You need me. Why would you say no?"

"Other camps might come looking for more fighters, but I don't. Our camp is different. I trust everyone, and I don't trust you."

Well, that's interesting, considering Laik has made it abundantly clear that he doesn't trust me. So why is he keeping me around? There's still something I'm missing . . .

Charlotte throws her hands in the air. "You trust Poppy? I thought she just joined your little group. If she could prove herself, then so can I."

"Hey," I call out, "leave me out of it."

"Actually, I don't trust Poppy yet." He turns to give me a scowl, and I roll my eyes. "But she'll get the opportunity to prove herself after her first renewal. She brings certain . . . qualities to our camp that I'm looking for."

My qualities? What qualities? Something about that word and the way he said it leaves me uneasy.

"Let her come," Wanda interrupts dryly.

Laik spins on her. "Why?"

"We have too many men and not enough women. It's causing fights. Another woman should ease the tensions for a bit." Her reasoning makes sense, even if it does make my skin crawl a little.

"That's not why I want to go." Charlotte's blue eyes widen, but nobody seems to care.

"Look, Poppy's already gained the attention of Callum, and now he and Delson aren't fighting over Rachel," Wanda goes on. "We need more women, you've said so yourself."

Callum's ears go pink, but I don't care about that right now. "You aren't bringing Charlotte into your camp just to use her like the wolves do at the mating houses," I growl, jumping out of the truck bed and pointing at them. "That's not why I'm there, is it?"

Laik storms up to me, getting right into my face. "We may live like wild animals in the woods, but we treat our women with respect. Not a single one is forced or coerced to do anything, and don't you dare accuse us of such brutality." He takes a step away and turns to Charlotte. "Why do you really want to join us? And don't lie to me." He looks her up and down, "A woman like you doesn't seem like the type, lycan or not."

She stands taller, and her blonde curls bounce around her shoulders. He's right. Charlotte is nothing like the people in our camp. She's way too prissy, and I know she'll be begging to leave within a week. "Because it's an opportunity to get back at the wolves," she says with conviction. "I've been hiding out here since I escaped, but I want nothing more than to bring those dogs down."

Laik studies her for a long moment, then gives a stiff nod. "Fine, you can join us. But remember that I'll be watching you. Give me one reason to doubt your loyalty, and you're gone."

Callum, Charlotte, and I climb back into the bed of the truck, which is now full of all kinds of supplies. Callum sits on the opposite side of the truck from Charlotte and I but doesn't look me in the eye. Maybe he wanted me to stay at The Sanctuary? Maybe he's upset that I have another confidant now? Or is he embarrassed that Wanda said he was interested in me? I'm not sure, but I don't have the time or the energy to figure it out.

"Are you okay?" Charlotte whispers to me once the truck starts up.

"Why wouldn't I be?" I snap, and she raises a knowing eyebrow.

"You've been bit. Also, you were at the bottom of the leaderboards before I left. Were you in the mating house?" Her voice softens. "I've heard horrible stories from those places."

I shake my head. "Not that it's any of your business, but I managed to keep myself at Drayton Hall. I was supposed to marry Nico the night I was bit." My insides go sour because that's not the whole truth. I wish I could tell her everything, but I can't, and I never will. She's not trustworthy. And if I can't talk about it, it's almost as if it never happened.

"Nico. Huh. He seemed like a nice guy. But you know they're all monsters, right? The wolf packs need to be taken out. If we can do that, we might be able to live in peace."

I wince at the thought of taking them all out. Is killing them all the answer? It seems too extreme. What about the children? Or the ones who don't hurt anybody? If we condemn them all because of what they are, then we'll become the bigger monsters.

"What about the lycans?" I ask. "It's not like they're innocent--you should know."

She shrugs, and her pretty blue eyes go cloudy. "You learn to control it. Each renewal is easier than the last. And as long as you're not a bastard like I was, you never have to bite or kill anyone except for the wolves. The first couple of shifts are really hard, but you'll have support to help you through it, and after that, it's easy."

"Then how did you get bit?" I scoff. That first night in the city was terrifying, no thanks to them. "If they have such control, why bite a human girl?"

"Because sometimes the lycan make mistakes," Callum interrupts. I didn't realize he was listening to our conversation. "We're not perfect, but we're doing the best we can."

Charlotte nods.

"I don't understand how you can defend against biting like that."

Something clicks in his jaw, like I've pushed a sensitive button. "Look, we go into the cities on the full moon to kill as many wolf shifters as we can and to rescue humans. But when you're in the midst of fighting, sometimes there are casualties. Innocent people get bit. It doesn't happen very often, but it does happen. We usually take them straight to panther city to get help."

My mind races back to that night and the two girls who were taken. "Is that what happened to those other claimed girls back on the harvest night? Were they rescued?"

"Yes." He nods, like that's a sufficient answer. "And they weren't even bit. I'm pretty sure Charlotte here was the only mistake that night."

I try to remember it, to see if he's telling the truth, but my memories of that horrible night are all muddled. Too much has happened.

"Then why didn't Laik take me to The Sanctuary?" I ask. "Why go to all the trouble of keeping me in the camp and separating me from Knox? Why enroll us into your cause without even asking us first?"

Callum considers this for a long second before finally shaking his head. "I don't know. He should've taken you to The Sanctuary right away, and Knox could've found a new life too. But whatever you said to him during your interrogation changed his mind. He obviously thinks you can help us in some way."

My heart sinks. Does he know then? Is this all because of Ryne? If Laik knows I'm Ryne's fated mate, it could change everything. All this time I've been thinking nobody knows who I really am, but what if they've been playing me? I think back to when Laik had me trapped in that tent, but I was so scared that I don't remember what I said.

"About what Wanda said about Delson and me," Callum mutters, and I wave a hand.

"It doesn't matter."

"No. It does. I don't want you to think that my friendship is manipulative."

Charlotte's lips curl into a small smile as she looks away. It's not like it's real privacy though, and I don't want to have this conversation anyway.

"I know it's not manipulative, and it's okay. We're friends." I wonder for a second what it would be like to be in a romantic relationship with someone like Callum. He's kind and cute, not brutish in any way. He's a little younger than me, but lots of girls back at the village dated younger boys. And Callum reminds me of Knox in a lot of ways, which is a good thing. But my heart still belongs to Ryne, as much as I don't want it to. And if I were to give it to anyone else, I can't help but think that person *would* be Knox. I know I'll never have Ryne, and Knox would probably take me back, but how do I turn off my feelings for someone that was chosen for me by fate? Maybe I should pursue someone else. Maybe a different man could help me remember what it's like to love for real. Even though my heart wants Ryne and my past lies with Knox, maybe Callum is the safest choice for my future. He doesn't know about my history or my secrets, doesn't have expectations of me, and is eager to please.

I don't know if my heart can move on, but I decide I'd better try because otherwise I'm afraid Ryne's betrayal is going to fester and eat me alive. I worry a little bit about what Knox might think, but since I can't talk to him right now, this is the best I'm going to do.

I leave Charlotte's side and make it over to Callum without falling over. I sit close to him, like I would if this were one of my dates with the betas. He gives me a shy smile, and I wait for that familiar swoop of desire, but it never comes.

Chapter Ten

The days leading up to the full moon are fraught with worry. I can feel the lycanthrope virus growing stronger with the phases of the moon and can't deny that I'll soon belong to it. As much as I wanted to believe I'd somehow be different––that there was no possible way I'd turn––that was wishful thinking.

I sit up on the cot, skin wet with chilly sweat, and gasp for air. The women around me stir, but none wake. They all know about my nightmares by now. The dreams always feature sharp teeth, long claws, and grotesque limbs. Sometimes Ryne is there. Or my parents. Sometimes Willow or my brother. Once, I dreamed about the claimed girls, about Joanna and Faye and the ones who'd been taken to the mating houses already. But the dreams always end the same, with me turning into a monster and hurting people.

I crawl from the tent, and my heart rate slows as the night air calms me. I wander over to the hole-in-the-ground bathroom to relieve myself and then walk back to the tent. I stare at it for several long minutes. I can't bring myself to go back to bed just yet. I can't go outside of the perimeter of the camp without getting stopped by one of Laik's guards, so I sit by the campfire instead. There's nothing left but a few glowing coals. I sink down onto a stump and let my mind go. It's been so hot lately, but right now it's not. I shiver in the chilly night air and think about starting the fire up again, but I don't have the energy.

We pack up our camp and move through the forest every five or six days. Laik says it's to stay safe from the wolves, which is probably true, but I also think it's to keep the members of the camp from fighting. We have to stay busy. Since arriving, Charlotte has become a favorite, fitting in much easier than I ever did. She's tried to reach out to me, but I want nothing to do with her. She can pay her penance to someone else. Not to mention, within hours of coming back with us from the panther city, she'd rekindled her friendship with Knox. I don't have ownership over him, but it bothers me to see them together. He should be on my side, not hers.

Footsteps approach, and Knox sits next to me. His hair is a mess of blonde haloing his head now that it's starting to grow back out, and his clothes are rumpled from sleep.

"We're not supposed to be seen together," I mutter.

"I don't care anymore." He drags his boot along the ground, forming a line in the dirt between us. "I think Laik is more bark than bite."

I snort. "Don't let him hear you say that."

He looks up, taking in the inky sky with the big round moon in the middle. "What are you going to do, Poppy?"

I look up too. The full moon is tomorrow night, but it's so big right now that I can almost pretend it's tonight and that I'm still human, that I made it out unscathed, and the bite did nothing. "I don't think there's anything I can do." I have no idea what he expects of me. I have no choice about turning, and I hate that. I'm so tired of having my choices ripped away from me. It's like no matter what I do, there will always be something else directing my fate.

"I'm not talking about becoming a lycan. I'm talking about Ryne."

At that, I shush him and look around.

"Nobody's here but you and me." He points out. "Are you going to try and go back to him?"

"What do you mean? He sent me out here and betrayed me," I say darkly. "You saw what happened. As far as I'm concerned, things with Ryne are over, and I wouldn't go back to him even if I had the chance. If I never see his face again, I won't be sad." But even as I say the words, I know they are nothing but lies. I shove away my love for Ryne and focus on my hate instead. That's easier right now.

"He also saved you. Any other wolf would've killed you the second they saw that bite."

I press my lips together. "Why are you defending him? You should hate the wolves as much as anyone."

"And I do," he says, "but this conversation isn't about me. It's about you."

"I don't get where you're going with this." But maybe I do, and my skin starts to prickle all over with awareness.

"I know you love Ryne, but are you still going to be on his side, even after your renewal tomorrow?"

He knows a lot about my relationship with the alpha and knows I'm fated to Ryne, but I'm not sure he fully understands what that means. He saw way too much, but I'm suddenly glad he did. "You were there for a lot of it, and I'm sorry for that." I swallow hard. "But you still don't know what it's like to be fated to one of them. You don't know that kind of all-consuming love."

"I don't?" he snaps, and then he's on his knees before me, grabbing my hands between his, and my world flips upside down. "Because I'd take you back in a heartbeat. I've been hurting for so long, and you're the only one who can heal my heart."

Back in our village, we had talked about running away together before he had to go to the claiming. Ultimately we didn't because our families would've been punished for it. Although we did love each other, it was a shadow of what I had with Ryne.

"Knox, I don't know . . ."

His face twists in agony. "Please, just listen to me. I've had to watch you from a distance for the last month, knowing the kind of pain you were going through and not being able to talk to you. Not only that, but from the moment I saw you in the city, I had hope that we could be together once again.

"First I had you, then I lost you, then I thought I had you again, but I had to watch you fall in love with someone else. And even though I know you'll always love him, I still don't care. I still want you. You're the girl for me. There's never been anyone else, and there never will be."

My heart speeds at his words, but my stomach goes hollow. His confession could make things easy for me. I could give into this new life without looking back. And I so desperately want to give him what he wants, but I can't. In my heart of hearts, I know he deserves better.

I pull my hands away and stand. "I'm sorry, Knox, but I'm not your girl." I'm rejecting him for his sake, not my own. Ryne will never be mine, not now that he's married to Elle, but the history between Knox and me is just too heavy. He knows too much. And as much as I could give into this, I don't want to do that to my friend.

"So, what? You're just going to find an oblivious guy like Callum?"

His voice is hollow as he stands. He's taller than me, but it's not like when Ryne towers over me. I don't feel a burning in my chest or a need to be near him. I don't love him anymore. That much I know. "Because he'll never love you the way I can. Nobody else here could possibly feel what I feel. I know you, Poppy. We're good together. I'll fix your broken heart, I swear." His voice has risen slightly, and I worry that he's going to wake someone, but I don't move away or shush him. I may never be able to love Knox romantically, but I do want to be his friend. He's the only one who could possibly understand my situation.

He reaches out and traces the line of my cheek. I don't realize I'm crying until his fingers are mopping up my hot tears. His skin is cool and perfect, and I almost give in. Maybe I could do it. Maybe I could let him try to fix me. But what happens tomorrow? Or a year from now? Ten years from now?

"I'm sorry," I whisper, "but I care about you too much to let you try. The truth is, eventually we'll both end up hurt because how can we be together when my heart is beyond repair? And even if you stayed with me, you would come to resent that I don't love you the same way. I don't want that for you, Knox. I want you to have the kind of love I thought I did. You will find it."

And with those words spoken aloud, I realize how foolish I was to think I could try to flirt with other guys and maybe date someone else. It's impossible that there could be anyone but Ryne. Maybe eventually this feeling will fade, but right now it's hot and all-consuming. Even after a month apart, it hasn't gone away. It's only grown stronger. The memory that he tried to kill my friends and then threw me out in the cold when I needed him most is the only thing that's going to get me through my renewal tomorrow night. I'm angry, and I'm starting to hate Ryne even more than I love him.

Knox's face falls in disappointment, but he doesn't look surprised either. He steps back, his head hanging low.

"And to answer your earlier question..." I clear my throat and fold my arms over my chest, resolve spreading through every inch of me. "I am *not* on the wolves' side. I never was, and I never will be."

"What's that supposed to mean? You just told me you could never love me because you still love him."

I grab his hand. "I do, but I also hate him. Can you understand that? Sometimes love and hate get tangled together."

"Yes." He swallows. My heart drops, and he squeezes my hand. "I don't hate you, Poppy. I never could. And I hate Ryne too, but I also worry about him. I know a little about what you're feeling. I was a slave, and I didn't have a choice in that, but he treated me fairly." He shrugs. "It's hard to explain, but my gut tells me Ryne isn't all bad. Still, he's the alpha, so he's responsible for what's happening there."

Is he? Or is Thorn? Either way, I don't want to talk about Ryne anymore, so I change the subject. "Are we going to listen to Laik or not?"

He drops my hand. "What do you mean?"

"Well, he said we weren't even allowed to look at each other, but here we are alone in the middle of the night. As I see it, we have three options: we could run away, we could go back to bed and pretend that we didn't have this conversation, or we can hang out here and tell Laik to jump in the lake."

Knox snorts. "My vote is number three. I'd say number one, but you are going to turn into one of them tomorrow night, and I'm not sure I want to be alone with you when that happens."

He has a point. Part of me had hoped he'd run away with me because I still don't really feel comfortable here, but it's too late for all that.

"Okay, so what do you say we start the fire up? Pretty sure I'm not getting any more sleep tonight."

Knox doesn't answer, but he starts gathering up the wood. I help him, all the while trying hopelessly not to think about what tomorrow will bring.

Chapter Eleven

I sit with Knox and Charlotte at breakfast, and it's almost like being at home again. Callum sits on the other side of me, and I don't remember ever having a more enjoyable time in the wilds. We talk and laugh about old times, and Callum tells us stories of his village as well. It turns out he's more like us than I originally thought--he was one of the humans who lived in the Carolina Pack's territory and understands what that's like. There's a story there, and I'm curious to know what it is. Has he seen his family since turning into a lycan? Was he supposed to be one of the claimed men and ran away, or was he just unlucky enough to get bit?

"How old were you when you were bitten and taken from your village?" Charlotte asks.

Callum drops his eyes. "Twelve."

"What happened?" Charlotte presses. This is personal, and the energy in the group goes cold.

"I don't want to talk about it." He abruptly picks up his plate and leaves.

Charlotte stares at his back, and her eyes are filled with concern. Maybe she really has changed. The Charlotte I knew wouldn't have cared about another person's feelings so much. "Should I go after him and apologize? I didn't mean to upset him."

Knox snorts. "You really didn't think that asking him how he got bitten would make him upset?"

Her cheeks redden. Knox does have a point. "I guess not. I wasn't thinking. I don't like thinking about that night either. I'm going to talk to him."

She hurries to the medical tent where Callum has disappeared. Laik drops into Callum's abandoned seat, and Wanda takes Charlotte's. Her hair is tied into two wild buns on the top of her head, and her eyes glint with malice.

"I thought you two weren't allowed to talk to each other," she says with a sinister grin.

"Maybe we realized that you guys aren't like the wolves who would kill us for disobedience." I give her a hard glare. "We're friends. No one else here is under any restrictions. Don't you think it's been long enough?"

"No one else came to us straight from the wolf city of their own accord either," Laik adds. His lip curls as he studies us for a long minute. My heart speeds, and I try to keep my surface calm and collected, but I lose courage and drop my face to my plate. "You two don't think we know exactly where you came from? You've been the alpha's pet for some time now, haven't you?"

I jerk my head up, wondering how on earth he knows that, but he's looking at Knox.

"It's not as if I had a choice in the matter," Knox spits out. "I was claimed, remember?"

I'm both relieved and scared. I've allowed myself to get too comfortable among these people, thinking they wouldn't hurt me, but I can see now that was a terrible assumption.

"Doesn't matter. It gives us a reason to doubt your loyalty. Both of you. Talk all you want today because tomorrow everything will be different. We may not be the wolves, but we don't tolerate disobedience either. Every action has a consequence." His gaze lands on me. "Remember that tonight during the full moon."

Wanda cackles, and they both get up and leave.

"What do you suppose that means?" Knox demands. He looks around, and his voice goes low. "Maybe we should run away."

I shake my head. "Whatever it is, it can't be worse than me accidentally killing or biting you out in the wilds."

"I'm the only human here." A trace of panic enters his tone. "How long until Laik decides to do something about it?"

It's what I've feared too, but have been too afraid to say. What if Knox gets bitten tonight? Or worse, what if he gets killed? I want to get him out of here, but I don't know how. I can't forget what Callum said about a lot of bites getting infected. If he gets bitten, he might not survive. "I promise, after I learn to control my lycan, we're not staying here a second longer than we have to."

* * *

Only a few hours later, when the sun is bright and warm in the sky, my body goes cold. Shivering so hard I can barely breathe, I drop the firewood I've been collecting and hightail it to the women's tent. I'm only wearing a tank top and shorts, and I've got to get into heavier layers of clothing immediately. It rained a lot the first few weeks we were in the wilds, but I was too angry with Ryne to really care about something as trivial as the weather. Now that it's May, and the sun is shining, and the trees are budding bright green leaves, I should be comfortable working outside. In fact, it's rather hot. Everyone has been wearing as little clothing as they can get away with, and I am too, but it's as if all that means nothing now. My body thinks it's the middle of an icy winter storm, and I'm outside without a coat.

This must be the beginning of the renewal.

"Are you okay?" a woman asks. The tent is large and made from thick canvas. There's a crate in the corner where we share clothing. I wish we could keep things as our own, but Laik won't allow it. Once something is cleaned, it goes right in the crate and not back to whoever was last wearing it. That means that the women on laundry duty get first choice, and this gal is one of them. She's currently folding clothes and putting them away. She's enjoying this nice day, oblivious to how cold I feel.

I drop to my knees next to her. "I need a coat."

Her eyebrows furrow, and she looks at me knowingly. "This happens to a lot of us when we first transition," she says, then she puts her hand on my forehead. "You're burning up."

"No." I shake my head, growing frantic. "I'm freezing."

She nods toward my cot. "Honey, you have a fever. Go lie down. I'll grab Callum."

I don't know if she has the authority to let me off my duties for the day, but I don't care. If I can't get a coat, then the pile of my blankets will be even better. I crawl over to the cot and bury myself under the mound of warmth. After a few minutes, my shivers start to settle, and I drift off to sleep.

I go in and out of sleep all afternoon—sometimes because I'm having nightmares and sometimes because Callum is trying to help me. When I'm lost to the darkness, finally asleep without dreams, his hands pat my cheeks.

"Leave me," I say groggily. I've never been more tired, and my body feels like a million pounds. I can't even open my eyes.

But those damned hands keep patting at me. "You're burning up." Callum's voice drifts into my thoughts. "You're too hot. This isn't safe."

I don't answer him.

He starts to shake me. "I either give you medicine, or I carry you down to the creek and dump you in the freezing water. One way or another, I'm bringing this temperature down."

That does it. As I fight to open my eyes, my vision blurs and then clears. Callum is in the tent with me, and so are Charlotte and Laik.

"What's happening?" My voice is hoarse, and tears flood my eyes. I didn't think anything would happen to me until tonight.

"This is normal," Laik says. "You'll be fine."

"Is it though?" Charlotte's voice is more concerned than I've ever heard from her before. "I got a fever but not like this. She shouldn't be so sick that she's flat on her back. I've helped a few people through their first renewal, and I've never seen this."

"If she's meant to be one of us, then she will be okay," Laik says gruffly. "Either the fever cooks her brain, and we bury her, or she comes out the other end stronger than ever. It's up to the virus to decide. Occasionally people don't make it, and that's natural selection."

Everyone goes silent, and time seems to crawl by. I blink, and Laik is gone.

"Don't listen to him," Callum says softly. "We have medicine for a reason."

I'm not sure if he's talking to me or Charlotte. Does it matter at this point? I'm so tired, my body is covered in sweat, and my brain can't hold a thought. My eyes flutter closed again, but Callum shakes me and forces me to sit up.

"You need to drink this." He presses a little cup to my lips, and a gooey liquid fills my mouth. It tastes bitter and sweet and horrible. I cough, trying to get it out, but Charlotte covers my mouth and stares at me hard.

"We're serious," she says. "We have to get your fever down. You won't be human much longer, and then you'll feel so much better." Her eyes start to water, tears forming. "I won't let you down, I promise."

I want to tell her that she's changed, that I don't hate her anymore, but to speak now would be too difficult. With their help, I manage to swallow the medicine. Then they're making me drink water, and soon I'm plummeting back to sleep.

It's restless and endless, and I'm certain I'm going to die.

Everyone dies. It's part of life. I never thought this would be my time, that I'd go so early, but I should've known this would happen. I never took Callum's herbs to help me through this process, and given everything that's happened in the last year, *I should've seen this coming*. If I'd known, would I have done something different? Yes. I would've gone to see my family. I would've said goodbye to the ones I love. I would've found Ryne and told him exactly how I felt. I would've––

Searing, burning, unimaginable pain slices through my core. I bolt up, wide awake, and a bone-deep scream erupts from within.

Chapter Twelve

My eyes pop open. My first thought, before I even register where I am, is that I'm naked. I'm alone. I'm outside. It's dark and——all thoughts are replaced with blinding pain. My head feels like it's too big for my body, like it's about to burst. I squeeze my eyes shut because I can't stand it.

Keeping my eyes closed, I gingerly reach my hands to my face, but they're stopped by a long snout. I jerk my hands away and scream. Only, it doesn't sound like a scream. It sounds like a howl. The pain that started in my head suddenly radiates through my bones and joints. My sense of hearing is strong, and every crack and pop of my hands and feet and bones are magnified. I groan because I know what's happening, and I still can't believe it.

And the pain... Oh my, the sheer pain of this is too much. It's all I can feel. It's as if every inch of my body has been bitten by a fire ant. I scream out.

Again, another howl.

Miraculously, the pain starts to lessen a little until it's a dull ache. Everything still hurts, but it's manageable. I wait another few moments, and it fades even more. I open my eyes, moaning, and scramble up to my knees. My legs don't bend under me like they should, and I stand instead. I'm so tall. The ground is at least two feet farther away than it should be.

I stare at my hands because I can't stand the thought of looking at the rest of my body. My hands are covered in thick brown fur, which is bothersome, but it's my fingers that really horrify me. They are thick, dark, and curl under, and there is a massive yellow claw at the end of each one.

A hunger forms in my throat, and I feel the need to bite, claw, kill something.

I shrink at the thought. I am not a monster. I've never killed anything in my life, and I'm certainly not going to start now.

But the hunger is raw and dry and demanding. I grip at my throat and then remember my creepy hands, and I drop them, now staring at my wolflike feet. I'm a monster.

Welcome to the pack.

I jerk my head up. I didn't realize the lycan could speak telepathically like the wolf shifters. Nobody told me, or maybe it's a secret the lycan keep. Either way, the monsters are all around me.

So, I'm not alone after all.

They move in at once, forming a tight circle. We're somewhere in the woods in a small clearing, and the bright moon hangs overhead, a light in the darkness. There are thick trees beyond the lycan, but here the ground is grassy and damp. And it's just us. I have nowhere to run.

How do you feel? That voice is different from the first, and I can recognize it, but not completely. Callum perhaps.

"Not . . ." But my voice doesn't come out. It's more like a strangled cry.

You have to speak to us through your mind. It's okay, go ahead. Has the pain gone away?

I can't be sure who is talking at this point. The sounds aren't the same as human sounds, and the thoughts come at me against my will. I'm not part of this pack so lycan must be able to communicate to any other lycan. It's not like the wolves, where they're so connected through their links they can anticipate each other's moves. But still, it's eerie.

Answer the question, another voice cuts in uninvited.

I shake my head, and shaggy fur falls into my eyes.

A large lycan steps out from the circle, and the rest close in so there are no gaps. At least they are keeping me here instead of letting me run wild and hurt someone. The need to feed is growing stronger every second. It's getting harder and harder to focus on anything else. I've never been this hungry before. I didn't even know it was possible.

The massive lycan stands in front of me, at least three feet taller and twice as wide as my monster. His stance radiates dominance, and I keep my eyes plastered to the ground. He takes a giant paw with gnarled fingers and forces my snout up to look at him.

I am your alpha. Pledge your allegiance.

This must be Laik.

Is giving him what he wants the best thing to do? I don't know this man very well, and I certainly don't know what his plans are. So far, he's done nothing to show me that he's trustworthy. I didn't even know that the lycan had alphas until now. The fact that they have alphas at all is unsettling. And they can communicate telepathically? That would allow them to be far more organized than I realized. I stare at this man, this creature who I want nothing to do with, and gather my courage.

No.

He howls, and I jerk back, the sound filling me with fear. It was the same sound that came every full moon and stole away our friends.

Why not? he bellows.

Because I don't know you. I don't know this. I hold up my paw, surprised at how clear my thoughts are. He inches closer, and I'm hit with an overwhelming fear of what he could do to me in this form. My fight or flight instinct so badly wants to kick in but either choice could end up with me dead. *Let me have a few moons to understand what I am before joining your pack.*

He bares his teeth, and I'm certain he's about to attack, but instead, he steps away. *I thought you might feel that way. It's a shame, but perhaps after tonight, you'll feel differently about what it means to disobey me.*

I'm waiting for the punchline. I know it's coming.

Enjoy your meal.

He goes back to his place in the circle, and I can't figure out what he means, but I am hungry. So, so hungry.

All at once, they howl, and I stumble back, tripping over something.

I land flat on my back, but it doesn't hurt like it should. I shake it off and scramble onto all fours. There is no more pain, only raw unfiltered hunger. I'm desperate for something, anything to feed on. I smell it before I see it––warm, savory, and begging to be mine. But when I locate the object of the smell, horror fills my chest. Lying right beneath my snout, hands and feet tied up and mouth gagged, is Knox.

The lycans howl once again. As a human, their howling was chaotic screeching to my ears and nothing more. But now, something about the howls call to me, luring me into a trance. The hunger keeps growing, and

I force myself to step away from Knox. I want to give in. I want to feed. But I can't do that to Knox. Not my first love. Not him.

The hunger claws at my stomach, a beast tearing me apart from the inside out.

No, I scream through the telepathic link, *I won't touch him.*

Are you sure? Another's voice snaps back. *We saved him just for you.*

Saliva drips down my jaw, matting my fur. It would be so easy. Knox lies there, eyes wide, shaking his head back and forth. I wish I could talk to him, tell him this isn't my fault. I would never willingly choose this, but now that I'm here, I don't know how I can resist. My choices were stripped away from me too.

I just wish I could ask him to forgive me.

My thoughts melt away, and the hunger takes control, his human scent filling my nostrils. Saliva pools in my mouth, and I open it, the spit rolling out and dripping on Knox. I snap my jaws shut. The desire to bite him is all-consuming, and soon I can't remember why I wouldn't want to.

I shake my head again. I can't hurt Knox. I reach my hand out to untie the rope that binds his feet, but instead my claw rips open his skin, the blood pouring out. He bellows, but it's muffled by his gag.

I try to clear my nostrils of the scent of his blood, but it's useless. Every cell in my body wants to bite.

Bite. Bite. Bite.

The chant fills my brain, and I glance around. Each and every monster in the circle is watching me with intensity, stomping their feet to the rhythm of the chant in my head.

Bite. Bite. Bite.

But I don't want to. This is Knox. I can't hurt him.

I run to the edge of the circle, needing to get away from Knox, but rough paws and snapping jaws shove me back toward him.

The warm salty smell of his blood calls to me, and for a moment my mind clears. Why is that? Before the last world war killed them off, vampires were the bloodsuckers. But now, here I am, here we are, no better.

As quickly as the thoughts come, they leave, replaced by fantasies of sinking my fangs into Knox's flesh and tasting that sweet blood. I lunge, and then I bite, and then I'm lost to the bliss of his flesh.

Chapter Thirteen

I bolt awake to the morning sun. My memories are hazy, and my bones ache, but at least I'm not burning up anymore. The fever is long gone, but there is a stench around me that makes me gag.

I roll over with a groan and press my face into the dewy grass. *What happened last night?* I'm naked, and my head is pounding. I stand, trying to shake off the weakness in my limbs. I brush myself off, searching for something to tell me where I am. I'm back to my human form, but that's almost worse. Because my hands and legs and everything are covered in blood.

The night resurfaces in my mind like a slingshot and I cry out in horror. What have I done to Knox? I stare at my hands. *No.*

I crumple to my knees, overcome with sobs. As much as I want to think last night didn't happen, it did. It was real. The memories come in flashes. The way his flesh felt in my teeth. The blood spurting around my jaw. His horrified scream. After that, the memory is gone, but I know it happened, and I'll never forget what I've done.

I killed Knox—they made me kill him. There's no other explanation for all the blood. I don't know exactly how it all happened, but I did lunge for him. And that was my decision. I wasn't strong enough to resist the hunger.

My grief gives way to rage, and I jump up, tearing through the forest. I'm barefoot and naked as the day I was born, but right now I couldn't care less. As soon as I find the camp, I'm going to kill Laik. He is responsible for this! He punished me by making me kill the one person who he knew I had left in this miserable world. And for what? Because I wouldn't instantly join his stupid pack? Or was it because Knox and I defied him by talking? *Talking!* I don't care that he's bigger than me or that he's the alpha of this ramshackle encampment. He set me up, and he has to pay for what he did.

My senses are stronger, and my body is faster as I maneuver through the brush with ease. When I catch the smell of something cooking on a fire, I head in that direction. Someone's making eggs for breakfast, which is considered a treat out here. I'm not hungry. I don't know if I'll ever be hungry after what I did last night. It's sick to even think about. As I catch sight of a trail of smoke twirling up into the morning sky, someone tackles me to the ground.

I growl and lash out, my fist colliding with a jaw. "Get off me!"

"Relax," Charlotte growls back. "I'm trying to help you."

I roll off her and stand. She's already clothed and is rubbing her jaw. She glances at the ground and points to the clothes that are now scattered around us. "I brought these for you."

I glare, but I gather up the clothes. I turn so my back is toward her and hurry to dress, suddenly feeling awkward. I've never really been naked around anyone before. My hands shake as I slip on my shirt, my mind still on Knox and what I did. When my feet miss the hole of the pants, I trip and fall. And then I start crying.

"Hey, it's okay," she says, sitting next to me.

"No. It's not." I finish up sliding into the pants, ready to go find Laik, but the tears won't stop. They burn trails of anger down my cheeks. "I have every right to cry after what you guys did to me." My voice cracks. "And to Knox."

The forest grows silent as we sit there. She doesn't know what to say, and I don't either. I wonder if she was there last night, watching me devour my friend. And suddenly, I hate her. Because I understand her now, I'm no better than she is. I'm a murderer, and I don't think I can survive with the knowledge of what I've done.

"Finish getting dressed," she says softly. "Last night was not what you think it was. I have something to show you."

I snort. Not what I think it was? I remember tearing into Knox's flesh. There is no other way to interpret what I did.

I follow her, not because I want to, but because I know she'll lead me back to Laik, and I can kill him for what he did to me. Then I'm going to find out who else was in that circle and hunt them down. They will all pay for forcing me to kill my friend. I'll never forgive myself, but maybe revenge will help me survive this.

I hate that I'm more like Charlotte than I thought I was. I should've taken Knox and gotten out of that situation, found shelter somewhere else, or at the very least, set him free. I could have. He even suggested it yesterday. The other lycans didn't open my jaws and make me bite. I did that all on my own, and now it's too late.

We stride into the encampment, and I'm ready to raise hell. There's not a stream near this one, but there's been so much rain that we've collected it in big bins, using filters supplied by the panthers to keep our source clean. Several of the people are using that water to wash the lycan stench off. I should want to, but I'm more bent on revenge. I look around for Laik, but I don't see him yet. There are more lycan in the camp than there had been in the circle last night, and as I glance around, I wonder who was there. Who watched me murder another soul? Who treated my first renewal like a sport? It's sick.

Charlotte pushes me toward the medic tent. "Go on in."

"I don't want to see Callum right now," I snap angrily.

"I heard that," Callum calls from the inside. "Now get in here."

I pull the tent flap back. Callum hovers over someone, wiping their brow with a cloth. Apparently, I'm not the only one who had a rough night.

"I'm not sick. I don't know why . . ." My words die off when Callum moves off to the side.

Knox lies there, still and pale and unmoving.

I drop to my knees and cry out. "Why would you show me this?" I swivel my head so I don't have to look at him.

Charlotte points. "Because he's not dead."

"What?" Turning so fast that I nearly fall over, I crawl to the bed. His chest rises and falls a tiny bit with his breath. Tears of relief stream down my face, and I reach for his hand, but he's still unconscious, so it hangs limp and cold in mine.

"You bit him," Charlotte says, joining us. "But it's not your fault." She points to his bare chest, where an angry red welt is rising.

"Laik was going to bite him if you didn't," Callum adds. "It was inevitable."

I find my voice. "That still doesn't make this okay."

I stare at my friend's beautifully broken face. It's scratched up, swollen, and there's a bruise on his cheek. I bring his cold hand to my cheek and just watch him, afraid that at any moment he's going to die on me. My body is tired, and I really should go wash up, but I'm not leaving until Knox wakes.

He's going to be angry with me. I just turned him into a monster, but at least he's alive.

Charlotte and Callum whisper behind me. I ignore them. It doesn't matter what they have to say to me now. Knox is alive, and I'm going to do whatever it takes to keep him that way.

"Poppy, let's go wash up," Charlotte says, laying a hand on my shoulder.

"No. I'm staying right here."

Callum chuckles. "No offense, but you stink. I'll stay here with him. When he wakes, you don't want him passing out again from the stench, do you?"

He has a point, but I'm still reluctant to go. "Were you there last night?" I ask, eyeing him with mistrust.

"Where?"

"In the circle with Laik."

He shakes his head adamantly. "No. I didn't even know what he planned to do. Charlotte and I found out this morning when they returned."

"I was so pissed when he brought you outside without me," Charlotte says. "I wanted to be there to help you, but after you passed out, Laik and a few others took you. They told us if we followed, we'd be dead meat."

I don't know if I believe them, but I want to. I need someone on my side here. I decide their story is good enough for me. If they weren't there, then they aren't the enemy.

"Okay, I'm going to wash up right outside the tent. If anything changes with him at all, you call for me."

"We'll be right here waiting for you," Callum says.

I step back out into the muggy air and find a bin of water. There are clean rags next to it, and I dip one in and start to clean off the lycan stench. I keep my eyes peeled for Laik, but I don't see him anywhere.

Guilt still crawls through my insides, but at least Knox is still alive. He'll become a monster, but he'll get to live a full life. Even though I hate the lycan that lives inside of me, I'd rather have it than be dead.

I rush through the washing and then hurry back into the tent. Knox still lies there just like he did before. Callum stands and lets me take his place. Charlotte rests in the corner, her gaze watchful and alert. She looks just as worried as I do. I'm not surprised, she's always had a thing for Knox. Callum kneels next to me, placing a gentle hand on my back.

"He's going to be okay. He just had a rough night."

Okay? Being bitten by a lycan is never okay. "What if he hates me?" I ask with a small voice.

"He won't. He loves you," Charlotte says. "He told me that you wouldn't give him a second chance. He's been whining about it ever since I joined up with you guys."

I ignore the obvious irritation in her voice. "Look what I did to him." I run my fingers along the angry welt on his chest.

"I told you before, if you hadn't, Laik would've," Callum argues. "It was inevitable. Don't you wonder why Knox wasn't taken to the panther city straight away? Laik doesn't take care of someone for no reason."

"But why not let Knox be human? He wasn't hurting anything. Laik didn't need another lycan. He's worse than the wolves."

Charlotte shakes her head, suddenly defensive. "No way. He's not enslaving women." Her change in tone catches me off guard.

"But he still made me turn Knox. That's cruel."

Charlotte scoffs. "But it's not worse than what the wolf shifters are doing."

"What did Knox ever do to Laik?" I press.

"He's that wolf alpha's lackey, which makes him far from innocent," Laik barks from behind me as he steps into the tent. I whip around to face my newest enemy.

Chapter Fourteen

"If you cause trouble," Laik says, towering over me, "I will enjoy putting you in your place, but you won't like it. You may even end up in the medic tent next to your little friend."

But he doesn't know what I'm fully capable of. He never let me join his guards, stating he couldn't trust me yet. I use his underestimation of me to my advantage and whip out a leg, kicking him in the shin. When he looks down, I punch him square in the face, and he tumbles out of the tent onto his back.

"You sure about that, old man?" I ask, following.

Now it's me who's towering over him, every bit of anger I've felt over the last month on display for the whole camp to see. Blood drips from his nostrils and into his mouth, making his teeth pink when he smiles. And then he laughs, a manic sound that sends a shiver through my body. "Don't say I didn't warn you, little girl."

He dives for me, taking me around the middle and flattening me on my back. He's a huge man, but he's not as big as the wolf shifters, and I trained with them for months. I can do this. My mind goes clear, and my attention zeroes in on what I'm about to do. I've never killed anyone before, but I'm willing to kill him for what he's done. If this pack works anything like the wolves, that will make me the alpha. I'll be able to make some decisions around here and finally be let in on all the nitty-gritty secrets.

He rolls over and pushes me off him with so much force that I go flying back. I'm quick to recover, and then we're both up on our feet. The rest of the camp has realized what's going on, and they run over. When a couple of them go for me, Laik yells at them to stop. "She's mine." His chuckle is low. "Let's see what she's got."

"My pleasure." I go for him again, this time aiming to knee him between the legs. I will play as dirty as I have to in order to win this fight. As far as I'm concerned, anything goes, but I miss, and he clocks me on the back of the head. My vision blurs for a second, and I drop to my knees.

Breathe, I tell myself. *Just breathe.*

"I should kill you for what you did last night," Laik says against my ear.

"Are you kidding me?" I gasp. "I didn't do anything."

"You refused to recognize me as your alpha. You embarrassed me in front of my pack, and you're doing it again." And then his meaty arm is around my neck, and he's pulling tight. My oxygen is cut off, and I have limited time. The people are wildly chanting his name. They're angry that I didn't accept him. They must see it as though I rejected everyone here, but that's not it--if only they realized how deranged their leader really is, surely they wouldn't follow him.

I don't simply claw and bite and kick and punch. I use my skills to gain control of the situation by twisting from his hold and breaking free. He comes for me again, but this time I know what I'm looking for and create space between us at the perfect moment. Catching him off guard, I lock him in a chokehold of my own. I've got one arm around his neck, compressing his esophagus, and my other arm is locked to secure the hold. I squeeze as tight as I can, my muscles burning with the effort. If he wasn't so big, I'd be able to stay this way until he passes out, but the man is a beast, and he rips from me after a few short seconds.

"You're going to regret that," he snarls, knocking me down and sitting on my chest. He shifts a leg to press down on my neck, and once again, I can't breathe. I fight with everything I have, but it's no use. He's just so much bigger and stronger than me. Impossibly strong. Even more so than the wolves, despite being the size of a human. I realize why as the world begins to fade away. It's because of the moon--lycan are strongest around the full moons and weakest at the new moons. Of all the times I could've chosen to fight Laik, this was possibly the worst.

But I'm a lycan too.

I'm stronger now, and I can't give up.

With all the strength I have left, I twist around. I'm on my stomach now, and he's still on top of me, but I have more space to breathe. I suck in a deep breath, and then I rear my head back, slamming it into his nose. It cracks, and he bellows, dropping his weight off me for just a moment, but it's enough for me to scramble away. I'm back on my feet in an instant, ready for round three, when he jumps up and glares at me. Blood streams down his face, and a sick sense of satisfaction fills me. If I hadn't broken it before, there's no doubt I just finished the job. I fist my hands and bare my teeth, something primal taking over me. I'm ready to fight this man to the death. There isn't an ounce of fear left in my body. No matter what happens next, I have to try.

"Stop!" A familiar voice cuts through the crowd, and I turn to find Knox. He's barely standing, hanging off of Charlotte's arm. He looks terrible, but at least he's awake. "Both of you, just stop."

"I'm doing this for you," I snap back. "I never would've bitten you if it wasn't for him."

"You don't understand, Poppy. I asked to be bitten. I wanted this." Knox's face twists in pain as he stands taller. I blink at him, stunned. Why would anyone want to be a lycan? It doesn't make sense. "I've thought about it all month, and when the moon came, and they took you away for your renewal, I asked Laik to bite me. I didn't know they were going to tie me up and throw me to a new lycan though." He glares at Laik, and Wanda laughs maniacally.

"He's right." Laik mops the blood up with his shirt and smiles down at me smugly. "He wants to be stronger. Can't say I blame him."

"She could've killed me." Knox gives him a nasty look. "Don't act like what you did was okay."

He's right. It wasn't okay, and it will never be okay, but asking to become a lycan?

"There are consequences to your actions out here." Laik speaks loud enough for everyone to hear. "You should all use this as a lesson. Poppy and Knox were told not to speak to each other, and they broke that instruction. So really"—he pauses to scowl at Knox—"you did this to yourself. And I missed the part where you said thank you." Silence falls over the group, and Laik repeats himself. "I said I missed the part where you said thank you."

"Thank you," Knox mumbles.

I'm rooted in place, stunned by what just happened. Knox wants to be a lycan? Why would he do that to himself? I don't understand how

Knox could want a life at the mercy of the moon's phases. He knows how dangerous lycans are and the horrible things they can do. Was he really so frustrated that he'd resort to something drastic like this?

"He wanted to be stronger," Laik says, as if reading my mind, "but he also wanted to prove his loyalty to us. Something you have yet to do."

"What do you want from me?" I growl. I could fight him again, but the wind has been taken from my sails, and I'm suddenly weary. "Don't you think I've been through enough?"

"You didn't submit to me as your alpha, so in exchange, you're going to have to do something for me." He pauses, letting my curiosity eat me up. But I don't ask. I know he's going to keep talking. I thought the man was quiet when I first met him, but now I think it's the opposite. He loves to hear himself talk. "We're going to the wolf city tomorrow night for a little . . . mission. And you, dear Poppy, are coming with us."

Chapter Fifteen

My mind reels with the implications of Laik's declaration. *I could see Ryne again.* Do I want that? Of course I do, but I also want to break his nose like I just broke Laik's. He betrayed me, and I don't know if I love him or hate him. Maybe it'll always be both.

Callum touches my arm. "Go help Knox back to his tent. I'll take care of Laik's nose. It'll heal easily, but I need to reset it first."

I glare over at Laik, where he's mopping up his bloody nose with his shirt. He seems amused by this whole thing, and it makes me want to scream. "Am I allowed to talk to Knox now or not?"

He drops his soiled shirt, crosses his arms, and smirks. "Sure, you can talk to him, but remember the price you paid for that luxury last time."

I want to stay and argue or fight or something, but at this point, I don't think it will do any good.

Charlotte holds tight to Knox's left arm. I take his right, and he hobbles back to his tent. Once there, we gently guide him down to his bed, and he collapses onto it, breathing hard. He slowly scoots himself back to the wall.

I sit on his bed across from him, and Charlotte perches on the edge.

Knox looks back and forth between us. "Charlotte, I need you to leave us alone."

"But . . . but . . . I helped you. Don't shut me out now."

He reaches over and grabs her hand. Something about the gesture is intimate, and I'm not sure how to feel about that. I don't want Knox for myself, but I don't trust Charlotte either. Then again, maybe I shouldn't trust anyone at this point.

"I know," he says to her. "But Poppy and I have had no alone time since we arrived at the camp, and there are things we need to discuss."

"Things you don't want me to know about?" Charlotte asks, hurt lacing her words.

Knox swallows. "Please just leave us alone. I'll talk to you later."

She stands, glaring at me, and then storms from the tent. Funny how she takes her anger with Knox out on me. Some things never change.

I give Knox a knowing grin. "She's pouty today, isn't she?"

Knox nods, wincing. "She and I became pretty close while you and I weren't able to talk. I think she liked having me to herself."

I nudge his foot and give him my brightest smile. "Can't say I blame her." I want to keep the mood light because I feel like it's about to get very heavy.

Knox frowns. "Don't do that, Poppy,"

"Do what?"

"Pretend like you like me," he says abruptly. "I think after everything we've been through, you owe me the courtesy of not leading me on."

"I'm not. I just . . . You're my friend."

"That's the thing, Poppy. I don't want to just be your friend."

"I know. But I can't ignore my own feelings. My heart belongs to someone else."

He sighs and rubs a hand along his face. "Fine. But please don't give me hope where there is none."

"I understand."

"But that's not what I wanted to talk to you about. You deserve to know why I chose to become lycan and what they have on me."

"Come on, Knox, they can't have anything on you."

"Do you know why Ryne trusted me so much?"

I shake my head.

He stares down at his hands. "The night of my claiming, Ryne and his betas came to visit all the claimed boys after the festival. It was quite late and still dark. There were only three of us. While they were laying down the law––no touching any of the girls and stuff––we were attacked by a group of lycan."

I bite my lip and let that sink in. It seems like the lycan have been going after the city nearly every full moon for a while. "What happened?"

He shrugs. "I hid like a coward. They got away with the other two boys, and Ryne's betas ran after them, leaving Ryne behind alone. Then, out of nowhere, three more lycan attacked Ryne."

He pauses, and his face screws up like he's remembering everything. "The wolves are quite well armed on the full moons. They can shift, but they also have swords and knives to fight with--I know now that those are for the beta wives to protect themselves and their kin." A haunted sheen passes over his eyes. "I was hiding between two cars, and at my feet was a long sword that someone had left behind. I'd never wielded one in my life, but my brothers and I used to play with sticks, pretending we were fighting with swords. I didn't know at that time how brutal the wolves were, just all the stories we'd heard about the lycan. So, as Ryne was fighting the three lycan, I attacked them from behind, killing two. I can see now that I got lucky because there's no way I would've been successful if I hadn't snuck up on them. The third one ran away."

"You saved Ryne's life," I whisper. No wonder Ryne trusted Knox so much. What claimed person would risk their life to save their captor? It must've taken loads of courage.

"I did." He says the words like he regrets his actions.

"If you hadn't, Anders would be alpha, and you and I both know he's worse than Ryne. Knox, I'm so proud of you."

He shakes his head. "Well, it turns out that the lycan who got away was Laik."

No wonder Laik didn't trust us. We're lucky he didn't kill Knox on sight, but that explains how he knew our first story about running away from a village was a lie.

"When did you find out that Laik knew about you?"

"Yesterday, the son of a bitch kept his secret to himself until he could use it against me."

My mouth pops open. "So what did he do?"

"Well, while you were in your tent with a fever, he came to me and told me the whole story. I was backed into a corner. I told him how much I regretted protecting Ryne, and that from that day on I've been seeking a way to atone because over the last year I've seen firsthand how brutal the wolves are." His voice goes low. "He wasn't buying it, wanted to use me against you as punishment for killing two of his men, so I told him how much I wanted to become lycan. I pledged myself to his cause, to kill Ryne and the other wolves."

My heart splinters for him. "So you didn't really want to become lycan?"

"No," he whispers bitterly. "But I did ask him to do it. I couldn't see any way out. But there is an upside to this."

"What's that?" I can't see how there could be an upside to being a monster. I'd do anything to reverse what I've become.

"I can kill wolves now, and I wasn't lying when I said I wanted Ryne dead. I want them all dead."

"You can't mean that." My voice is soft, but I don't feel soft at all. I feel hard. Defensive.

"I do. Poppy, they kidnap innocent men and women and do horrific things to them. The more time I spend here with the lycan, the more I realize how wrong everything is. The lycan don't attack our villages. The wolves just make it seem like they do. The lycan are the good guys, not the wolves."

"You honestly believe Laik is a good guy?" I roll my eyes. I can't believe what I'm hearing.

"He's better than Ryne." Again, he sounds so bitter and angry. I'm angry at Ryne too, but to want him dead? I could never . . .

I stand. "You're wrong."

And I march from the tent. I can't have this conversation anymore because the awful thing is, I think he might be right.

* * *

"Nobody is telling you anything," Wanda says, "so don't ask."

"Wasn't gonna," I grumble and haul myself up into the back of the truck.

"Behave yourselves," Laik adds.

Two other lycan I don't know very well--Tanner and Christian-- load into the back. They settle down across from me, giving me horrible looks. I'm not surprised. There's no shortage of animosity toward me since I haven't accepted their alpha as my own.

"You have to put this on." Laik leans over the edge of the truck, a red bandana clutched in his meaty hand. "I don't want you knowing where we are and how to get back here. I still don't trust you."

I sigh heavily but don't protest because I already know the man isn't going to budge on this. And honestly, I can't say I blame him. If I were in his position, I would treat me with trepidation too. But I still don't trust him, especially after the stunt he pulled with Knox.

He ties the fabric tightly around my face, and everything goes dark. I'm never going to take him as my alpha, never going to officially join this strange pack, but he doesn't have to know that. The least I can do is follow through with whatever mission he has in mind and hope it's something that helps my friends back in the city. If what he said about helping humans is true, then this mission should be an easy one for me to accept.

The truck engine rumbles to life, and we're off. The metal of the truck bed had been so uncomfortable when we drove across the war-torn roads to the panther city, but it doesn't bother me anymore. It's as if turning into a lycan has made me immune to pain. At least, right now, I feel amazing, but I'm pretty sure that will change with the waxing and waning of the moon. What will I feel like in a couple of weeks when the sky is empty again? My only hope is that I won't feel worse than I did as a human. I doubt I'll be so lucky.

Tanner speaks up over the sound of the engine. "If you don't do a good job today, then you'll be tossed out on your ass and will have to fend for yourself. The wilds aren't a safe place for a little girl like you, Poppy."

Is that true though? I haven't had a chance to find out. If anything, I'll go to the panther city and ask for help. I'm pretty sure I can find my way there.

"Yeah," Christian adds in a gravelly voice. "Think about all those lone wolves. You know, the ones that your wolf city kicks out. Ever wonder what happens to them?"

Of course I've wondered about them, but I hadn't thought to ask. Now I'm interested. "Where do they go?"

"Well, most of them aren't given asylum in the panther territory. You know the wolves and the panthers are enemies, right? They have to plead their case to the panthers to be taken in and most won't take that risk. Either that or they're too proud. So what can they do but try to survive? They're out there in the forest, living on scraps and lonely for companionship. Can you imagine what one of them would do if they found a woman alone?"

I swallow hard because I can imagine, and it's not good. "I want to prove myself to your people and to Laik," I say, and I'm not entirely lying. I need safety and security. I need answers. And I need help. I don't want to kill Ryne, but I want to let him know exactly how I feel about what he did to me and my friends. I'm aching to see Joanna, but I fear I never will. And I'm sure that Abi is lost to the mating houses by now. I hope they're both still alive, and that I can make things right for them somehow.

"We'll see if you're being honest soon enough."

The truck stops, and thankfully, the blindfold is removed. I blink, taking in the brightness of the evening sunset. It paints swashes of orange and red across my vision. Then the trees come into focus. And then the people.

We're not alone.

Chapter Sixteen

I climb out of the truck with the others. I want to fold in on myself, guard myself from these new faces. There are about thirty in all, but I can't trust them. I don't think I'll trust any new person ever again. The need to run away is powerful, but I force myself to keep my arms at my sides, my shoulders square, and my head up. I need to be seen as strong.

"Welcome to the Resistance." Laik pats me on the back. "Don't embarrass me."

I barely register his words because standing across from me are two people I'd given up hope on ever seeing again. A little squeal of disbelief escapes my throat, and I nearly crumple to my knees. I'm propelled forward and into the arms of Joanna.

"Poppy!" she says into my hair as she hugs me. "You're here! What are you doing here?" She steps back, and her eyebrows crease as she studies me.

Grady gives me a look up and down, scanning me too. He doesn't exactly look happy to see me, or maybe he's unhappy because of the arm that's now a scarred-over stump above his elbow. "She's a lycan," he says. "I can smell it on her."

Joanna's face falls. "You got bit?"

Tears spring to my eyes. "The night of the festival, right after you guys left."

"You mean after you saved our lives," Grady says. He nods in appreciation but still keeps his distance. I'm just grateful he's alive.

Joanna hugs me again and whispers in my ear. "Don't mind him. It's in his nature to hate lycan, but we're both so grateful for what you did."

I know she's right, but his attitude kind of hurts. I don't feel what Grady feels. There's no inner need to not want to be around him. But as I step back, I take in the alarming fact that I'm the only lycan who feels that way. The rest of them are keeping their distance from Grady. Either there's a bias that they've learned, or something is wrong with me. I'm glad for it though. I could never hate Grady. And I don't hate all the wolves. People should be judged on their actions——and not the ones beyond their control. This ideology either makes me foolish, or it makes me wise. I haven't decided which yet.

I just hope that Grady isn't in danger here.

"Let's get started," a woman speaks up. I would know that voice anywhere. I turn around to find Madame Delphine at the head of the group. I gape at her, but she gives me a curt nod and nothing more. She's all business, here to do a job, and nothing is slowing her down. "We have limited time."

I peer around at the group and realize there's a mix of lycans and humans here. Madame Delphine obviously came from the wolf city, but I don't know about the others. Nobody else is familiar to me.

I stay close to Joanna, and Laik takes his place right next to me. "Who's your wolf friend?" he asks, motioning toward Grady. His tone is steady, but his eyes are distrustful.

"Grady. Ryne nearly killed him." I point to Grady's missing arm. "He's not part of that pack anymore."

That makes him a lone wolf, but he's got Joanna, so I know he'll never be alone, and that makes me feel slightly better about everything that went down. Laik gives Grady a stiff nod, but before anything more can be said, Madame Delphine continues her speech.

"Our mission tonight is to rescue Elle. She's been forced into a marriage that she didn't want with a man who is more cruel than I ever imagined." My heart tightens, and I find it odd that she would speak of her son in that way. I thought they were close. Maybe Thorn got to him though, and he's changed. Or maybe I didn't know him all that well in the first place, and he's always been like that. "She's taken up residence in the alpha's house, but we aren't sure exactly where. As we speak, the wolves are being lured away from the house, so you should be able to easily get her."

Her eyes roam over the group and then meet mine. She gives me a sad, regretful smile. Does she feel responsible for what's happened to me? Part of me wants to be angry with her for not preparing me better, or at least not bringing me into the Resistance while I was still at Drayton Hall, but she's easy to forgive. The woman has faced as many hardships in her life as I have, if not more. Our eyes stay locked for a long moment, as if a whole conversation is passing between us, and then she turns to find Grady.

"Everybody, this is Grady. He is one of the wolves we can count on, and I expect you all to treat him the same as you would any other member of our resistance." There are mumbles of approval and dissent, which she quickly cuts off. "Grady, you know how to get to the alpha's house and how to get in and out, so I want you to lead this mission. When it's over, please send me word as to the success or failure of Elle's rescue."

Grady inclines his head and weaves his way to the front of the group. Madame Delphine gives him a hug, tugs her hood over her head, and quietly slips away. I wish I could follow after her, to get information about what's been happening back in the city and with the other claimed girls. I want to know what Ryne has been up to, where Thorn is, and if Abi is okay. There are so many questions spinning in my head, but I'm certain she has to get back. I wonder what Thorn would do to her if he found out she was in charge of the Resistance. Perhaps she was just a messenger, but everyone listened to her, so whatever she is must be high up.

That makes me smile. One of the highest leaders––if not the highest––is King Thorn's old beta wife and the mother of Ryne. How's that for irony? It goes to show that the cunning of a wronged woman shouldn't be underestimated.

Grady looks around at our group, making eye contact with everyone. "We're going to split into four groups. If we go into the city all at once, we'll attract too much attention. One group will stay here to keep watch, one will go into the alpha's house, and the two others will be placed on our path to and from the house to offer reinforcements as needed. I will lead the group into the house. I need three others to volunteer as group leaders."

Three men raise their hands. Grady splits us up into groups, putting me, two other men, and one woman with him and Joanna. I'm the only lycan in his group.

"I go with Poppy," Laik says from behind me.

"I'm Laik." He puffs out his chest and glares. "Poppy is new to my pack. I need to keep an eye on her. She doesn't go anywhere without me."

I roll my eyes because I'm not okay with this, but I know better than to challenge Laik right now. We need to be focused on helping Elle, and he's the kind of man to let his ego get in the way of the mission.

Grady stares at him for a moment, looking like he wants to argue, but just sighs instead. "James, switch places with Laik."

We all split up and head toward the city on foot. Grady leads, and Joanna loops her arm through mine as we fall to the back of the group. Laik stays near the front with Grady. Grady's movements are stiff, but he seems to be carrying on a conversation with Laik. I wonder if Laik is trying to push Grady for information about me, or maybe it's the other way around. Does Grady still trust me? Or has everything changed now that I've succumbed to lycanthropy?

"It's so good to see you," Joanna says, nudging me in that familiar way of hers, "but I'm sorry you were bitten. What happened?"

The weight of keeping it a secret breaks. "In the chaos after you left, the lycan attacked," I whisper softly. "I got caught in the crossfire. Instead of killing me, Ryne took me to the edge of the city and banished me."

Her eyes widen and shine with tears. "If I had known, I would've taken you with us. You shouldn't have been alone. I bet you were so scared."

"I was scared, but I wasn't alone." I squeeze her hand. "He sent Knox with me."

"Knox?"

"You know, Ryne's driver." I hate that Knox was so irrelevant that she didn't know his name. He'll never be irrelevant to me.

"Oh, yeah, him. Why did he send him with you?"

"Ryne trusted him to help me, I think." I don't add that Knox and I knew each other before. It feels like a lifetime ago and no longer relevant, but really, I just don't want Joanna to question me. I kept Knox a secret from her, and I shouldn't have, but it's something I don't know how to explain after everything we've been through. "It only took one day for a lycan pack to find us." I eye the back of Laik's head warily. "I'm still not sure about them, but they helped me through my first renewal."

If help is what you would call it. I'll never forgive Laik for what he did to me and Knox that night.

"Renewal?"

"It's what they call turning into a lycan."

"Was it scary?"

I nod. "And painful."

She squeezes my arm a little tighter. "I'm so sorry."

I shrug. "It's okay. I'm surviving."

A shadow passes over her face. "Us too." There's something in her voice that tells me she's not fully okay. Maybe she's just scared, but the Joanna I know doesn't get scared easily. There's something more going on here.

"Where are you guys living?" Would it be possible to abandon Laik and join her and Grady instead? It might still be hard, but at least I'd be with people I trust and who actually care about me. I'd want Knox to come with us as well, but since he's been bitten, he'll need a group of lycan to help him through his first renewal.

"We're staying near the outskirts of the panther city with another resistance camp." She swallows hard. "It was pretty scary when we first got out. Grady almost bled to death, and then we had to find a way to get me safely through the radiation field." She smiles softly. "But we did it, somehow. Thanks to you, Poppy. We'd both be dead if it hadn't been for what you and Abi did for us."

Thinking about Abi makes my heart hurt. I hope she's okay, but I know she probably isn't. I failed her and will never forgive myself for it. When I got bit, and Ryne rushed me away from the battle, I should've demanded we retrieve Abi first. But I'd been consumed in my own pain and fear, and I selfishly left her behind. Now I'm sure it's too late.

"Can I come back with you? I don't want to go back to the lycan camp." My voice drops another octave. "They're so rough, and their alpha isn't my favorite person." I hate what he made me do to Knox, and I don't respect the group at all.

She shakes her head. "No lycan are allowed. I'm sorry."

I let out a breath, wondering if she's staying with humans or banished wolves or both. "It's okay. But I want to see you more often. I miss you."

"Me too."

Laik is just going to have to learn to trust me. I won't pledge myself to his pack, and I want the freedom to come and go. If he won't let me do it, then I'll just find a way to get into the panther city. Charlotte did it. I can too. It might have to wait until after Knox gets control of his lycan though.

She smiles, but there's something in her eyes that I've never seen there before, something I can't quite place. Regret? Fear?

Wolves patrol the city, and we go quiet the closer we get. I keep imagining that we're going to be found out and attacked at any moment. I have a knife to protect me, and I'm strong from the recent full moon, but that's it. I doubt it's enough to fight off a wolf. We move quickly, methodically, and ever so carefully. Since there's not a full moon tonight, I hope the wolves have their guard down a little. They may not know that even though we can't shift we're still strong, the moon's illumination favoring us. Maybe we can really do this.

"We have to cross the river to get to the city," Grady says. "The best way to do that will be to go over the bridge."

My heart lurches because I've seen that bridge and know it's falling apart. There's no way it's safe, but maybe it's better than trying to go by boat. Boats aren't always the quietest, and I know the docks near the betas are all heavily guarded.

We are exposed, running from the cropping of trees to the bridge, and just because it's night doesn't make it safe. Shifters can see in the dark when they're in their wolf forms, and the moon is bright enough to reveal us to anyone who could happen to look our way. A shiver runs up my spine as we get to the bridge. It's riddled with gaping holes, and the concrete is crumbling in places.

"Hang onto the rails, and no more talking," Grady instructs.

We follow, me right behind him, Joanna behind me, and the rest of the group behind her, with Laik bringing up the rear. I keep waiting for the moment that someone falls into the rushing water below. Since it's spring, the river is moving faster than it does other times of the year. I'm not sure that I'd survive a fall, lycan strength or not. Swimming was Willow's talent, not mine.

Sweat beads along my hairline, and I hold my breath for what feels like ages. I take a wrong step, and my left foot slides out from under me. Pain courses up my leg as it scrapes across the metal and concrete. I hold in a yelp and scramble to hang on, squeezing my eyes tight, but my fingers slip from the rail, and I fall.

Chapter Seventeen

Joanna is quick. She grabs hold of my arm and yanks me up. I grip the rail for a moment, tears welling in my eyes, as I gasp to catch my breath. I reach down and pat my leg. There's blood, but the cut is shallow, and though it stings, it won't affect my ability to walk. If what I've learned about lycans is true, it'll heal fast.

I'm okay... Sure, I almost died, but what's new?

My mind may make jokes, but my heart pounds and my stomach churns. I give Joanna a nod, and we continue on. Eventually, we make it to the other side, and the moment my feet are on solid ground, I want to lie down and kiss it. The thought of having to leave the city the same way makes me want to throw up. I hope we'll have a boat or that we'll get to leave another way, because I don't ever want to cross that bridge again. I hadn't realized that I was scared of heights, but now I know.

This part of the city is as equally run down as the bridge, but I understand why we came this way. We're near the nice area where Ryne lives.

And now Elle too.

Grady keeps to the back alleyways as we maneuver through the sleeping city. We cross behind a mating house at one point, and the voices of men and women laughing scatter into the night. I swallow hard, wishing I could run in there and free those women. It reminds me why I'm even here and doing this. It would be selfish to hide away when I could help people break free from this awful system.

The other two groups splinter off, and ours keeps going. I start to feel disoriented because we're in the rundown part of the city that was too far lost to the wars to bother restoring. But after a few blocks, we leave that behind and enter into the neighborhood where the betas live. Being here sends opposing emotions racing through me——fear and love, longing and hatred. I don't know the houses, but I'd recognize this neighborhood anywhere. When the back of Ryne's stately house comes into view, my heart tightens. I know he's not in there right now because Madame Delphine lured him away, but I still miss him. I miss him so much that I forget to breathe.

Then I remember that he married Elle, and apparently, he's not been kind to her. That knowledge is so at odds with the man I knew that it's hard to believe, but I must believe it because that man also hurt people—— hurt me, his own mate.

How can I love and hate him so much at the same time? *Damn you, Ryne.* And damn me for feeling this way.

I stare up with trepidation. It's late, and the house is completely dark. We scale the backyard fence, landing in the cover of mature trees. The climb was easy for me, way easier than it would've been when I was still human. I don't know what to do with that information, but I have to admit it felt amazing to scale that fence as if it was nothing.

The yard is cast in shadows, the swimming pool is a black mirror, and the trees are eerily still. It's so quiet I can hear my heart pounding. The house itself is grand and intimidating, and I can't help but question how Grady is going to get inside. He sprints over to one of the flowerbeds near the back door, overturns a rock and picks something up, then returns to us, revealing a shiny silver key. It's the strangest thing, but I instinctively want to knock the key out of his hand. Him knowing about Ryne's spare key is proof they were close friends. And now he's going to use that to break into Ryne's home and kidnap his wife. Not kidnap——rescue——but Ryne and his pack won't see it that way. I can already imagine the awful things King Thorn will say to Ryne when news of this inevitably comes out.

I clench my hands into fists and will the urge away. I must think of Elle——she needs our help, even if it means exploiting Grady's knowledge of Ryne's home.

Grady gathers us together so that we can all hear his whisper. "Joanna and Poppy take the first floor, Laik and I will take the second, and Cici and Michael will take the third. Search every room. When you are finished, you come back outside and meet by that tree." He points to a large oak on the edge of the property. "With a little luck and a lot of stealth, we'll have Elle with us."

The second floor is where the bedrooms are, and I expect that's where they will find Elle, so it makes sense that Grady would want to do that himself. I'm grateful that he trusts me with Joanna. Quite frankly, I'm a little surprised he wanted Laik with him, but maybe he's just giving Joanna and me time together. He's a good man, and I'm glad he and Joanna have each other. And knowing Grady, he also wants to keep an eye on the lycan alpha.

We sneak into the house and all go our separate ways. If my heart was pounding before, it's thrashing now. Sweat forms on my brow, and my stomach is so tight I could be sick. I'm terrified, and I need to get it together. What am I so afraid of anyway? Seeing Ryne? I won't see him since he's not here. Getting caught? That's it. If they catch me, they'll kill me without question.

I pause in the living room and just stare at the couch for a moment, my throat clogging up a bit. That's where I tended to Ryne's wounds. The memories flood me, and I'm brought right back to heartache. At least it drowns out the fear. Joanna tugs on my arm, and I shake the memories away. I need to focus.

We quickly move through the first floor, but there is no one here. I expected a guard of some sort, but Madame Delphine was right. There's nobody. Joanna waves me on, and we slip back outside and wait by the tree.

"Was it hard being back in the house?" Joanna asks, her voice soft.

I nod but don't elaborate. Confessing the details about Ryne and myself will just make things harder. I'm doing my best to put that all behind me.

We wait in silence, and soon the others are back. "No sign of Elle?" Grady asks.

We all shake our heads. Grady jams a hand through his hair. "We have to get her out of this mess. I have no idea where else she would be."

"We could just ask Ryne," Michael says with a smirk.

"What's that supposed to mean?" I ask. My voice sounds weird coming out, like it belongs to someone else.

"He's asleep upstairs in the library."

Laik's eyes sparkle. "Excellent. Let's kill him."

Something squeezes in my chest. As much as I'm upset that he betrayed me, he did let me go when he should've killed me. And he's my fated mate, so even though we'll never be together, the assurance that he's alive is a comfort to me. I can't explain why.

Grady nods. "It's the perfect opportunity."

My heart sinks even more. If Grady is on board, then it's practically a done deal. Even though they were friends, I understand why Grady would want to do it--Ryne nearly killed him and took his arm. He'll never be whole again, and that's all Ryne's fault. As much as Ryne betrayed me, he betrayed his friend even more.

I think fast, trying to find a good argument for why we shouldn't kill him.

"No. We can't do it," I say.

Grady glares at me. "Why not?" Though he knows exactly why I'm arguing with him. At least he hasn't said anything.

"Because..." My mind scrambles for an explanation. "We all know that even though Ryne is Carolina Pack's alpha, he's not the worst possible person for the job. If he dies, Anders becomes the alpha, and he's even worse."

"She has a point." Joanna looks to the others who don't know Anders from Ryne. "Anders is a vile man. He'll make the mating houses a worse hell than they already are. He's talked openly of wanting to bring more girls in, he may even start raiding the villages."

They consider this, but I can tell they're not convinced.

"Look, what if we just kidnap him?" I offer. "Bring him back to the lycan camp for interrogation and send the wolf pack into a frenzy. They might even think he's gone on a trip before they realize we took him, and by then we'll be long gone."

"Same thing, hon," Joanna frowns. "Anders will become the alpha."

I shake my head. "No, don't you remember this from our lessons? As long as Ryne's alive, the pack will instinctively know it. It will cause chaos here because they won't be able to replace him with Anders. They can't, at least not permanently until the pack bond breaks."

"That's brilliant." Cici chuckles low. "And maybe we can send another group in to kill Anders. Hell, I'll volunteer."

"So will I," Michael adds.

I nod eagerly. "And while Ryne's being interrogated, we can find out what they did with Elle. She should be here. We can come back for her once we know where they're really keeping her."

Grady's eyes are hard, but I can tell he's considering it.

Laik releases a low growl. "If we take the alpha, he's coming back to my camp, and I can't guarantee I won't end up killing him there if he doesn't cooperate."

I hate to think of what Laik will do to Ryne, but this plan gives me some time. I can find a way to get him out of Laik's clutches before they kill him. Plus, I have some questions of my own that I want to ask. He has some serious explaining to do about why he still went through with his marriage to Elle.

We all go silent for a long minute. Grady and Joanna exchange a knowing look and then turn to me. "What do you think? Can you lure him out?" Joanna asks gently.

Grady explains to the others, "Ryne has a soft spot for Poppy."

"Now why would he have a soft spot for Poppy?" Laik asks gruffly, his hooded eyes zeroed in on me.

I swallow hard because this is the last thing I want to explain to Laik of all people. "He took a liking to me during the claiming and often sought my company. I wasn't an idiot, so I encouraged it. It's the reason he sent Knox with me after I was bit, and why I wasn't immediately executed. He cares for me."

Something unreadable passes over Laik's face. "And do you care for him?"

If I lie, he'll see right through it. "I do."

"Then you will stay here while the rest of us go inside."

"No." Joanna shakes her head. "Ryne will have weapons near him, and he can shift at any moment, unlike you. He'll fight. He knows his house better than anyone else. Getting him down three flights of stairs will be impossible. If Poppy can lure him out here, we can be waiting with everything we need to knock him out and kidnap him."

I wouldn't have thought of that, but she's right.

"She could just as easily warn him, and he'll get away," Laik challenges.

"He betrayed me." I stand tall, unwavering in this. "I have no love for him anymore. I'll get him out here, and you can do whatever you need to subdue him."

Lies. All lies.

Before Laik can protest anymore, I'm running across the yard, not bothering to look back. They can't call out to stop me because that would give them away. My thoughts whirl as I run. What if Ryne hates me? I've betrayed him as much as he betrayed me. For all I know, he'll kill me the second he sees me. Maybe this wasn't a good idea after all. But I couldn't let them kill him, no matter how much he hurt me. Though, Ryne won't see it that way. I could just warn him, but Laik would take revenge out on Knox and Charlotte, and they've been through enough.

I was never clumsy before, but it's amazing how my limbs move much easier now that I'm a lycan. It's effortless to climb up the stairs and not make a sound, to slip through the halls and into the library. I close the door behind me with a soft click, and my eyes adjust to the room instantly. One of the curtains is open, and soft blue light streams in from the large waning moon, casting shadows along the floor-to-ceiling bookshelves. Ryne is on the couch, and I step forward, needing to go to him. Nerves dance in my belly, and I can't tell if they are good or bad ones.

I approach, drinking in his long black curls and sharp, smooth cheekbones. His lips are soft, and his eyelids flutter and pop open. He blinks several times. "Poppy? Am I dreaming?"

Chapter Eighteen

I shake my head, at a loss for words. Now that I'm here in front of him, every fiber of my being longs to go to him and never leave his arms. I clench my fists at my sides, angry at myself for being so weak. He's not mine anymore. He's Elle's and I need to ask him where she is.

He's out of his chair in one fluid movement. His large hands palm my cheeks, and he stares into my eyes. "I've missed you so much."

Without warning, his lips are on mine, moving furiously, and all thought and space disappears. It's just me and him. My arms clutch his neck, and his hands slip down to my side, pulling me taut against his warm body. He teases my lip with his tongue, and I let him in, hungry for more of this man. I want nothing more than for this moment to never end. All the emotions of the last month spill out into this kiss like ink seeping onto paper, messy and beautiful and permanent. It's not fair. We should've been together. It should've been us. But now he belongs to another, and I've become his worst enemy.

Something shifts between us, a softness I'm not expecting. All at once, he goes limp in my arms, his towering frame falling forward onto me. We collapse to the ground, his weight too much for me. I hit my head on the hardwood, and stars flash before my eyes. He's on top of me, his dead weight heavy, and the breath whooshes from my lungs. I'm trapped beneath his unconscious body.

I have no idea what just happened.

"Ryne?" I whisper and push against him, but it's like pushing against a brick wall. He's not moving. "Ryne?" I say louder, panic in my voice. His heady smell envelops me, rich with sleep, but there's no way this is sleep. People don't just fall asleep like that. My oxygen grows thin as I try to wiggle out from under him, but I can't move either. Panic starts to set in like claws dragging across my skin. I won't last long. He's too big.

I keep pushing. I should be stronger than this. The moon is almost full, and I'm not the girl I once was. For weeks—-months—-I've longed to be next to him, to feel his limbs tangled with mine, but this is torture. I finally get my wish, and he's going to suffocate me.

"Ryne!" I scream this time and thrash against him. He groans slightly and shifts his weight, but not in the direction I need. He's even more on top of me now, and there's no breath left to scream again. Stars are still dancing around my vision, growing dim as a black tunnel closes in, turning the ceiling into darkness.

And then Ryne is gone.

I gasp, sucking in air and coughing. My vision returns, and I sit up. The others surround us on all sides.

"What happened?" Joanna asks.

Laik kicks at Ryne's side, laughing. "Did you go ahead and kill him?"

"No." I swallow, and my throat burns. "He kissed me and then passed out."

They all give me a strange look.

"We need to get out of here. We've already taken too much time." Laik crouches down next to Ryne and begins tying up his arms and legs.

"Why can't you guys just shift when you're tied up?" I ask Grady. But he's distracted by something Joanna is whispering to him.

The way I figure it, the wolves should be able to shift out of whatever binding they're in. Keeping Ryne as our prisoner isn't going to be easy. It's not like we have other shifters with us to guard him, and I've seen what the man is capable of.

If they don't take him as a prisoner, they really will kill him. I have zero doubt it's something Laik has been trying to do for years, and I've delivered Ryne right to him.

"We're sensitive to silver, but they're sensitive to wolfsbane," Laik says as he finishes tying Ryne's limbs. "Not that they would've told you that."

"What's wolfsbane?"

He snorts. "It's a plant. It's woven into the fibers of this rope."

I eye the rope with a frown. I didn't know he'd brought it along. This action may be small to everyone else, but it's big to me, lending another reason to distrust Laik. The man is more calculating than he lets on. The mission was to free Elle--nothing that would've required wolfsbane threaded rope. I know better than to question Laik about it, but I tuck the information away for later, reminding myself to keep a close eye on things once we're back at camp.

We all gather around to carry Ryne from the house. It takes everyone helping because Ryne is so big, and I grimace when some people are less than gentle with his body. I want to talk about this—I'm practically over-flowing with the need, but we have to stay silent, and I'm distracted by Ryne's head. I'm the one who's holding it. His cheeks are warm, and his long hair is silky. I want to kiss him again, which is ridiculous. He's not my lover. He's not even my friend. We're on opposite sides of a war, and there's no defending his side anymore. He's in the wrong, and as much as I love him, I have to accept that he's the bad guy. Even if Thorn is the worst of them, even if Ryne never slept with the mating house girls, even if he dreamed of ways to make changes, even if his kiss makes me feel the most like myself, the fact remains that he's the alpha of this pack. He's made his choices.

And we're done.

Laik leads us away from the beta houses and around the deserted parts of the city until we reach the riverbank. We're so quiet as we go, so slow and methodical in our movements among the shadows. Twice people roam by, but they don't notice us. I'm grateful they're not in wolf form because I think they probably would've sensed us then.

I gaze out at the river and release a shuddering breath. "What's the plan here?" My heart has started to race--I have a bad feeling about this.

"I hope you can all swim," Laik says nonchalantly. "And if you can't, drop him. Their alpha can drown for all I care."

I'm not a good swimmer, but it's not me I'm worried about.

"No--" My voice breaks, and I'm given the death stare by everyone here. Even Joanna doesn't care if Ryne dies. "He's not valuable to us dead, remember? Anders . . ." My voice speeds up. "Anders is so much worse than Ryne and you know it. We already agreed!" I look down at Ryne, where we've set him on the dirt. How is he still unconscious?

"Wait. Will the pack be able to track him to the lycan camp?" Cici asks skeptically.

Grady answers, but I can tell he hates giving away this kind of information. He may not be a part of the pack anymore, but his roots still run deep. "We know if our alpha is dead or alive, not where he is."

"Are you sure?" Cici frowns. "I'm not lycan, so I'm not going back to the lycan camp, but I don't want to lead wolves there either."

"He's not my alpha anymore--"

"Enough," Laik cuts in. "The camp is under my protection." There's a double meaning behind his words, but I'm not sure what it is. It's almost as if he doesn't want to have this conversation in front of Grady, which is strange, but considering Grady is a wolf shifter, maybe not. "The alpha lives. For now. So let's keep his head above water, huh?" A sour grin mars his face.

A few of the others laugh, but I can't. The water is high, and the currents are dangerous. Swimming in this river could mean death, but there's no other way to get Ryne out of the city quickly. The sun will be up soon, and it's only a matter of time until we're being tracked by the wolves.

This stupid plan was all mine, but I'm pretty sure I made a mistake.

Laik must sense my trepidation. "Don't worry, little lycan, we make great swimmers. You'll see once you're in the water. And as for Ryne, the water and the wolfsbane will help mask his scent." He peers back out at the city, his jaw clenching and unclenching. "Don't forget we're moving camp again soon. I know how to stay one step ahead of these dogs." He turns back to offer Grady a cocky grin. "No offense."

Grady sighs but doesn't reply.

I hope Laik is right, but there's nothing more to say, and there's little time left. So against my better judgment, I follow them into the river and try to stay alive.

Chapter Nineteen

The river is colder than I expected. Maybe because my blood runs hotter than it did when I was a human. I don't like it one bit, but I manage to keep my head above water and Ryne's head resting on my shoulder. Laik is right that I'm a much better swimmer now that I've become a lycan, and for the first time since my renewal, I'm glad for it.

We're all soaked to the bone when we reach the other shore, but nobody is lost to the currents, and I thank my lucky stars for that. Cici and Michael splinter off to report back to the Resistance members who will be waiting for us. They'll explain that we didn't find Elle, but we hope to find answers about her once our new prisoner wakes up.

Laik refuses to go anywhere but back to his camp with Ryne in tow. Grady and Joanna insist on coming back with us even though I'm sure Grady will hate being among the lycan. Laik doesn't fight him on it, which surprises everyone.

Ryne is heavier now that we've got river water weighing us down and Cici and Michael are gone, but we manage to get to the truck. I nearly cry out in relief when we do.

By the time we drop off the truck and shuffle back into camp hours later, I'm shivering madly and ice-cold despite the May air being hot and humid. It's going to be a ferocious summer out here in the wilds, but right now I'd give just about anything for some of that warmth.

I change quickly and meet Grady, Joanna, Knox, and Charlotte outside my tent. Knowing Ryne is not far makes me itch to be near him, but I know that's not possible. I'm not even sure why I want to see him, and I'm glad my friends are here to distract me.

"Are you guys staying long?" I ask her, hopeful. If Joanna stays, I'll have my best friend back.

"Don't know yet, but I want to be here when Ryne wakes up and realizes he's been betrayed by his girl," Grady answers, giving me a bitter smirk. It's not that he wants to hurt me, but he wants to see Ryne suffer, and my heart tightens at that.

They were best friends.

"Ryne's here?" Knox asks, his face going pale. I'm still not exactly sure where Knox's loyalties lie when it comes to Ryne.

"Yeah. Poppy totally kissed him, and he passed out. Kidnapping him was easy," Joanna says with a cheeky grin. The smile is so *her* that I want to burst into tears and tackle her in a hug. I didn't realize how lonely I was.

"Why did he pass out?" Charlotte's eyebrows knit together.

"Because of Poppy's saliva," Callum announces from behind me.

I spin and find him and Laik. Callum eyes Grady's stump. I know he's just doing it because of his medical background, but Grady doesn't know that, and he gives him a hostile glare. Callum drops his eyes.

"What do you mean by my saliva?" I ask.

Callum looks at us for a long moment, as if deciding if he can trust us with this information. "It's a theory I've had for a while. We know that wolf shifters can be poisoned by our bites, but I don't think our fangs are the only thing that's venomous. I was pretty sure our saliva is dangerous for them too. Well, I was right, and you've just confirmed it."

My mouth pops open. "I poisoned him?" Of all the times lycan have tried to bite and kill him, who would've thought a kiss would've done it?

"He's alive and seems okay, so our saliva must not be as lethal as our actual bite. Either that or it's not as potent as it would've been during a full moon. He just woke up, and he's spitting mad."

I swallow. I almost killed Ryne, and I didn't even mean to. Does this mean I can never kiss him again? Of course, I can't. Our situation was already impossible to begin with, but now it feels like we're cursed. I want to cry, to scream, to break something, but I can't show that kind of emotion in front of these people, so I force myself to stay calm.

"We need you to go in there and kiss him again. But only a small one. We want him subdued, not knocked out," Laik says.

I cross my arms. "He's not going to go for that. At this point, he'll know I betrayed him."

"Actually, he won't. We're going to dump you in there all tied up, but loosely so you can get out of them easily. Then you kiss him, and we'll come in and interrogate him. You can help."

"You want my help?" I squeak. I eye Laik with skepticism. From day one we haven't seen eye to eye, but now that I'm useful to him, he suddenly needs me? *I don't think so, buddy.*

"Yeah. He'll probably talk to you before he'll talk to one of us. If he cares for you as much as you think he does, then it should be easy."

"Not if he thinks I betrayed him," I try again.

Laik shrugs. "We'll see. The sooner we get answers from him, the sooner we can kill the bastard."

I clear my throat. "If I help you, what's in it for me?"

Laik scoffs. "How about I don't kill you?"

I raise an eyebrow and nod because he does have a point. As much as I hate it, he's the one in power here. Not me. Hopefully I can do something to change that before everyone I care about ends up dead. Joanna gives me a funny look—she's probably following my train of thought and knows I'll risk my life for Ryne. I follow Laik, and Joanna slips her arm through mine.

"What's your plan?" she whispers.

"What do you mean?" I feign innocence.

"Oh, come on, I know how the bond works. There is no way in Hades you're going to let Ryne die, even if that's what everyone else wants. So what's your plan?"

"I don't have one. Not yet anyway." It feels good confiding in her even though I'm still confused. Everything moved so fast. I will find a way to get Ryne out of there before he dies. Even though he betrayed me and married Elle, I still love him.

We stop outside Laik's tent, and he glances at Joanna. "What are you still doing here?"

"Poppy's my best friend. I'm here to support her."

Laik rolls his eyes. "Poppy doesn't need any help. Go back to your dog, and Callum will get you guys set up in a tent. This will take a couple of days. Cici and Michael will let the Resistance know that we need Anders dead. Once it's confirmed that the alpha's second in command is no longer in the picture, we can kill Ryne." He gives Joanna an annoyed look. "We don't need you for that, little girl."

Joanna is stiff, and I can tell she's got fire on her tongue, just waiting to spit it out at Laik.

"It's okay. You can go," I say. "You can't come into the tent with me anyway."

Joanna gives me a strained smile and rushes back to Grady. Laik goes into his tent and comes back out with rope and a gag. I let him tie me up, and like he said, I'm bound loose enough that I can get out but tight enough to look real.

Then he hoists me over his shoulder a little too roughly. We walk about thirty feet, and he opens the tent flap. I catch a quick glance at Ryne before Laik dumps me on the ground. My head hits the packed earth, and I see stars.

As soon as Laik is gone, I sit up. Ryne has a bag over his head, and he's straining against his bonds. Muffled sounds come from under the bag. I'm guessing they have him gagged as well.

I easily slip out of the ropes tying my hands together and then rip off my gag. I have no idea why he even bothered to tie me up when Ryne can't see me. Probably his idea of a sick joke.

"It's me," I say. "I'm tied up, but I managed to get my hands out. Let me get my feet undone, and then I'll help you. We'll need to move fast."

He stills, but I have no idea what he's thinking. It takes me a little longer to untie my feet because Laik tied those ropes tighter, but within moments I have them undone as well. I think about untying Ryne and trying to run away with him now, but we'll never make it. Laik and several others stand right outside the tent door at the moment. I'll have to wait until people are sleeping, and we can slip away unnoticed. Maybe I'll get him out and stay back. Saving his life doesn't mean I have to bring myself to be around him anymore.

I pull the hood off his head, and Ryne blinks at me, his hair a mess. I get to work on the knot on the back of his gag, but it's tied tightly. My fingers slip and slide but eventually find purchase, and I'm able to undo it. I tear it off.

"Poppy, what's going on?" he asks, a razored-edge to his tone.

"I don't know, but we're going to get out of here. I've missed you so much." My voice cracks. Can he sense the torture I feel inside? I need to be strong right now. Ryne might not realize after that first kiss that I betrayed him, but he will after this one. Before I can even think about what I'm doing, I lick my lips and press them against his. It's a quick kiss because I can't risk a bigger one, and I pull away.

His taut body immediately goes limp, but he's still conscious. His sorrowful eyes meet mine. "Poppy, what did you do?"

Laik enters then, giving a slow clap. "Well done, Poppy. We couldn't have subdued him without you."

He crouches in front of Ryne. "Now, let's see what information you can give us."

A couple of other men come in. I don't remember their names because I've never spoken to them, but they are two of Laik's go-to guards. I don't know what they are going to do to Ryne, and I don't want to watch them.

One grabs my hands, and the other grabs my feet. They tie me up again, but tighter this time, and put a gag on me. I'm so startled that I don't process what's happening fast enough to fight them off.

"Now, we aren't sure what your connection to Poppy is, but based on how you reacted to her, we expect you would do anything to help her. Otherwise, why would you send your man with her out into the woods instead of just killing her? You've shown before that you're willing to kill any and all lycan," Laik says.

He just looks at them through a dazed glaze. I wonder if he can even hear them. I don't know how badly my saliva affected him.

"Tell us where Elle is."

His gaze sharpens, and I know he heard the question. Instead of answering, he spits in Laik's face.

Laik wipes the spit off and stands. "You know, if I were to return that favor, you'd be unconscious again. Lucky for you, I want you conscious."

He turns to the men standing by me. "Break her finger."

Chapter Twenty

Panic blooms in my chest as one of the men slams his boot down on my left pinky and twists. For a moment, I feel nothing but shock. No pain, no comprehension of what happened. I glance down. My pinky is bleeding and turned in the wrong direction. Then all at once, pain sears through my hand and radiates up my arm. I cry out, and Ryne yells, "No!"

Laik chuckles. "I knew you'd come around."

I try to keep from whimpering. I don't want Laik to have any more ammo to use on Ryne. As much as I want to hate Ryne, right now, I hate Laik more. This is how he wanted me to help him? This is like the sick game that he played with me and Knox. And here I am, the stupid girl who should've stopped trusting men like him long ago.

The pain is horrible, but not as bad as I expect it to be. At the back of my mind, I know I'm not human anymore. I'll heal quickly, but I'll have to get Callum to set it for me first. I don't think I can do it myself. Soon this agony will be in the past, but right now I'd love nothing more than to claw Laik's eyes out.

Ryne hesitates for a moment, searching my face before looking up at Laik with disdain. "I don't know where Elle is. After she married my father, I helped her escape, but I don't know where she went, and my father made me swear to keep her disappearance a secret."

I let out an audible gasp. He didn't marry Elle. *His father did.* I want to ask him what happened and tell him I'm sorry and beg for his forgiveness. But I can't because of the gag.

Laik studies him and then me. Tears flow from my eyes, but I can't say anything. Maybe they'll all think it's because of the pain, but the pain is only part of why I'm crying.

"Where's the king alpha?" Laik sneers, bending down to get in Ryne's face.

Ryne only shrugs. "When he's in my city, he usually stays at my house, but tonight he was called away. He's been on the hunt for Elle but not having much luck, and it's been getting to him, leading him out of the city more often than not." His eyes narrow at that. "Careful, lycan, Thorn may venture to your little camp here."

Laik grins. "I'm not worried about us. If he does somehow show up here, that will give us the opportunity to kill him."

Ryne is unchanged, but I can see his brain processing everything: these men, this cramped canvas tent, the wolfsbane bindings at his hands and feet. Everything. "Well, he usually takes my man Anders to help search for her, so you'd be fighting off two wolves."

"Why wouldn't he take you? You're his son, an alpha, a *prince*."

"Because he trusts Anders with the secret of his missing bride, and he doesn't entirely trust me after Poppy . . ." Ryne trails off, not finishing the statement, and my heart pounds.

"After Poppy what?" Laik asks.

"After she sabotaged my wedding with Elle." It's sort of true. It's better than him saying that I'm his fated. But I suppose if this keeps going on like this, Laik is bound to figure it out. I still don't know what he'll do with that information, but I'm certain it won't be good.

"Now why would she do that?" From what I've told Laik, I was encouraging Ryne's advances to get by.

"Because she's in love with me. Has been since she arrived in my city, but I always told her we could never be together. Don't mistake me. Poppy is a beautiful girl, and I dated her, but I never intended to marry her. She knew I was engaged to Elle. She didn't listen though."

He gives me a scathing look, and I wonder if anything in his expression is true. These lies are meant to help me--I know that--and yet they still twist me up inside.

"But you do care for her." Laik stands and comes to my side. "If you didn't, seeing her in pain wouldn't cause you to open your mouth."

Ryne scowls through inky strands of hair that have fallen across his face. "I don't like seeing any woman in pain. If you'd brought another in here and done the same thing, I still would have talked."

"I doubt that's true." He kicks my side. "You like this one."

Ryne sighs. "What I'm telling you isn't a secret that I need to keep from you anyway, so can we just get on with this."

Laik scratches his chin, and I know he's trying to figure out if Ryne is lying or not. "You really don't like seeing *any* woman in pain? That's the biggest lie you've told me all day, *alpha dog*." He says alpha like it's a curse word, and I know he's referring to the way the shifters treat human women.

"I'm not lying." Ryne looks at me, his eyes narrowed. "I hate the way the harvest and mating houses work. I've been trying to make changes for years, but I'm not the one in charge of these things. My job is to enforce the rules and keep order in my city and nothing more."

"Spare us the bullshit." Laik moves to tower over him, and the two lock in a glare.

"I'm serious," Ryne seethes between gritted teeth. "I was getting close to a solution, and then you kidnapped me. Now who's going to help those women? You?" He cackles. "You can't take on my father, and if you think you can, you're an idiot."

Laik kicks him then, hard and dead-center. Ryne coughs but nothing more. Everything goes quiet for what feels like ages. In that pause, my finger starts to throb again. I'm not as strong as I thought I was, but I need to be. I don't want to draw attention to myself.

Finally, Laik nods to the men guarding me. "Take Poppy to the medic's tent. We're done for today." He crouches in front of Ryne. "I have men in your city. If I find out you're lying, then I will kill Poppy right in front of you. Do you want to change your story? This is your last chance to come clean."

Ryne shakes his head, and I'm roughly brought to my feet. They drag me out of there, and Ryne just stares after me. There's so much I want to tell him, but I can't. Not right now. But after I'm healed, I'll come back here and tell him how sorry I am and that I'll get him out of here and do anything else he needs. He says he had a plan to take down Thorn, that he's been wanting to change things for years, and deep down I know that's the honest truth. I was never able to reconcile the cruel alpha with the tender man I fell for, and now I know why. My heart was right all along—Ryne isn't bad.

I can't believe I doubted him.

* * *

Ten days pass––ten long, arduous, awful days––where they don't let me see him. Ten days where I'm put to work doing manual labor that leaves my muscles burning, my sleep deep, and my free time completely consumed. I never complain, hoping that it will get me in good graces with Laik. I ask Laik to see Ryne every single day, and he always says no. Always.

It's after another one of these dead-end conversations that I find myself stalking through the woods, muttering nasty things about Laik under my breath and kicking trees.

"What did them trees ever do to you, huh?" Wanda's scratchy voice makes me jump, and I whip around to find her. She's watching me with amused eyes and a yellow smile.

I glare. "Has your boyfriend always been such an ass?"

Her smile falls. "If it weren't for Laik's generosity, you'd be long dead. I'd have killed you and your little alpha-boy and been done with the lot of you ages ago. But for some reason, Laik thinks you'll be more valuable to us alive." She shrugs her bony shoulders. "Lucky for you, I trust Laik."

"I've already proven myself to you people," I practically shout. "What more could you possibly want from me?"

She stalks in close, her sour-sweet scent wrapping me up. "You already know. Don't pretend you don't."

I still, realizing she's right. Swear loyalty and take Laik as my alpha. It's not something I ever plan on doing, but I have the sinking suspicion that's what he's waiting for. Eventually, he's going to grow tired of waiting, and then what? Will he kill me? What about Joanna and Grady? Knox? Charlotte? The man has so many of my friends under his care right now.

And not from the goodness of his heart.

"You have nothing to say?" she chuckles and walks away. "That's what I thought. We're leaving, by the way. Laik told me to come find you."

I chase after her. "What? We're leaving?"

"Yeah, caught wind of wolves nearby. We need to retreat closer to panther territory."

So maybe now I'll finally get to see Ryne, and that excites me, but I'm also filled with dread at the prospect of wolf shifters nearby. It stands to reason they're out looking for their missing alpha. Quite frankly, I'm surprised we've gone as long as we have undetected. It doesn't really make sense. The wolves are hunters, and we're not that far from their city. How are any of the lycan still alive out here? We get one day a month to be powerful, and they can call upon their beasts at any time.

"How come they can't find us out here?" I ask, hoping I'll get lucky. "There are so many more of them than us."

"They're not great at following a lycan's scent." I'm surprised she answered so quickly but grateful all the same. "Especially near the full moon. Do you believe in God?"

She turns on me again, this time pinning me against a tree. I fold my arms over my chest and stand tall. I'm not scared of her, and I don't want her to think I am. "I don't know what I believe anymore," is all I say. My parents believed in God, and Mama taught us about that stuff, but I haven't thought of God very much lately. Her mention of him now catches me by surprise.

"Well, I do," she says. "I know we're here to stop the shifters, and that includes your precious Ryne. Wanna know how I know?"

I don't ask, but she answers anyway.

"Because our saliva is their poison. Because when we bite humans, we can easily make more of us. Because God made the moon, and we're beholden to that moon. And because those dogs can't follow our scent to save their own lives."

She kind of has a point, but does God really want us to kill each other? Because if God is real, and he made us, then he also made them too.

She must think this is hysterical because she walks away, laughing the entire way back to camp. Her words stick in my mind, and I examine them at all angles. I was Ryne's fated mate, and now I'm his enemy. But what was that story Mama always told us? The one with the lion befriending the lamb?

Perhaps there's a bigger purpose here––a reason for everything that's happened to me. Ryne and I are still fated, that much I can sense to my core. Turning into a lycan didn't take my feelings away, and if anything, they've only grown stronger. Someone has to save the humans. Maybe Ryne and I are meant to do that together.

Chapter Twenty-One

The camp is in complete disarray. People are taking down tents, loading food into carts, and stuffing their backpacks. They scurry about, an air of practiced panic at their heels. We've moved several times since I've been with them, but the energy is so different now that there's a known threat in the area. The only tent still up is Ryne's, and I take a step closer to it. How is he doing? Probably not well. I asked Callum last night at dinner if he was at least getting food. Callum was vague but assured me Ryne was okay.

I find Laik talking with Grady and Joanna. Everyone shuts up when I approach, and I grow uneasy. "What do you need me to do?" I ask.

"Nothing. I thought you were gathering wood in the forest." Laik's voice is gruff.

"I was, but do you really want me to carry wood to a new camp?" I shrug. "Anyway, Wanda came and told me you needed me."

Laik runs a hand along his face. "Of course she did. That woman never listens to me."

Wanda approaches with a wicked knife in her hands. "Can I do the honors?" She shakes the blade in my face.

"What's she talking about?" I ask, now concerned.

"We can't haul Ryne with us," Laik says.

My stomach tightens. "You can't kill him!"

Laik rubs his eyes. "See, Wanda, this is why you should've left her in the woods."

I glance over at Joanna. "You guys were going to let him die?"

Grady gives me a frown. "Ryne isn't being the most cooperative prisoner, and you knew he was going to die here eventually."

"You can't mean that." I scramble for something else to say. "Besides, you guys said you wanted Anders dead first."

"Unfortunately, the Resistance didn't agree with us on that one," Laik snaps. "Fools, all of them if you ask me, but we can't execute Anders without their help. Not yet, anyway."

I hate the way he speaks about the Resistance like they're a tool for him to use, not like he's part of them, like we're all in this together. "Okay, but Anders being alive is exactly why we kept Ryne alive too. The Resistance not seeing eye to eye with us is still not a good reason to kill Ryne."

Grady points to his stump of an arm. "This is his fault, and don't forget that he would've done worse if I hadn't gotten out of there. Isn't that a good enough reason for you, Poppy?"

Joanna scowls at him but doesn't say anything to defend me either. I can't believe she's okay with this.

"But . . . but . . . he said he was working against his father. He helped Elle escape, we know that now. Why do you want to kill him?" This question is mainly for Grady, because even after everything that's happened, I suspect he must still care for his ex-best friend and alpha. There's got to be something left.

"He's a wolf, isn't he?" Joanna finally speaks up. "That makes him our enemy. I'm sorry, Poppy, but it does."

I point to Grady. "Um, excuse me, but he's a wolf too!"

"You know what I mean. Listen, we heard this morning that Anders has been doing a lot of awful things in the city." She gives me a pointed look and even more weight is added to my shoulders. "Who cares if Anders is a stand-in alpha when he now has the power to do whatever the hell he wants. Our plan backfired, so keeping Ryne alive is pointless." Tears spring to my eyes and her voice softens. "I'm sorry, but if we kill Ryne now, the shifters will be able to feel that they've lost their alpha through the pack bond, and then all hell will break loose in wolf city while they fight each other for his title."

"And one of the other wolves might stop Anders," Grady adds.

I have to admit, their logic makes sense, and I'm seconds away from falling to my knees and begging.

Laik smiles broadly. "The chaos we're about to create will give us the perfect opportunity to take them down."

"Ryne's already been kidnapped and imprisoned and who knows what else!" I throw my hands in the air. "Isn't that enough?"

"No," Grady snaps. "As long as he's alive, the pack is going to remain united. We need to do this now. Hell, we should've done it already."

"While we are at our weakest? Is that really what you want?" I turn to Laik because surely he needs to think about the safety of his people too. "If you kill Ryne, you'll have to answer to his father during a new moon." I point to the blue sky. "Have you forgotten that your precious moon will be weak tonight?"

"We can't let him go, and we can't take him with us," Laik barks. "The best option is to kill him."

"Please, don't." My voice cracks, and I dig my boot into the ground. A bead of sweat trickles down the back of my neck. "Too many people have died already."

Wanda slithers around the other side of me. "See, told you she was a snake. She's on their side, not ours."

"Just because she's sticking up for Ryne doesn't mean she's on their side," Joanna says, but Grady stiffens beside her.

Suddenly, hands grab me from behind. Two of Laik's bodyguards have a vise-like grip on my arms, their rough fingers digging into my skin.

"Come on, Grady, let's take care of him," Laik says, leaving me behind.

"No! You can't kill him!" I'm screaming and flailing, but I don't care. I need to save him. The need is as strong as my need to breathe––to live. I can't bear a world without Ryne in it.

"Joanna," I plead, but she just turns away from me. The brutes drag me away from the tent, but I can't let him die. I go limp in the hopes that they loosen their grip, but they hold on even tighter. I exhale in short little bursts, and my stomach twists. I can't lose another person that I love. I just can't.

A flash of silver shoots by us. "Wolf," someone screams, and the men holding me falter. Time seems to slow and then speed as they drop me and run after her. I do the same.

I'd know that silver wolf anywhere.

It's Elle.

She leaps onto Laik's back, and he goes down. Grady glances around, and Elle snarls at him. I reach them quickly and debate whether I should stop or head straight for Ryne.

If I leave her there, they might try to kill her.

Already, the whole place is descending on her. She's one of the strongest wolves I know, and the lycan are at our weakest with it being a new moon soon, but that doesn't mean she won't end up dead. I'll lose Ryne and Elle all in the same afternoon.

I rush forward, putting my hand on her back. "You have to change back, or they're going to kill you," I yell, knowing she can hear me, but so can the others. If I was doing a good job at hiding my alliances before, I've definitely ruined that now.

She glances at me like I'm crazy but then leaps off of Laik and shifts back into a human. She stands there, completely naked, her face livid.

"Callum," I yell. "Get her something to cover up with."

He finds a cart and grabs a blanket off of it. I hand it to Elle, who still hasn't said anything. She's lost weight since I last saw her, but her eyes have added a depth of angry bitterness that can only speak of hard times. What has she been through?

"You can't kill Ryne," she grits out as she wraps the blanket around her torso.

Laik scrambles up. "Who are you?"

"I'm Elle. Ryne saved my life, and I know you've been looking for me. I've been following you for some time." Everyone goes quiet. "You can't kill him. He's the key to the resistance movement. I've been working on him for months, and he's finally agreed to help us." Her voice hardens. "You *cannot* kill him."

"You can't tell me what to do. Now, if you'll excuse me, I have a wolf to kill."

He turns back around and marches for the tent. Elle gives me a look, and I nod. We're not going to let this be Ryne's fate.

She shifts back into a wolf, and I'm right behind her. We both attack Laik, and soon Elle is on his chest, her jaws at his throat. He looks up at me, eyes wide. Others surround us, ready to defend their alpha, but he holds them off. Maybe he has too much pride, or maybe we all know Elle would kill him before they'd be able to stop her. It would take less than a second for his throat to be in her muzzle.

"You cannot kill him," I demand again. "Give us your word, and Elle will let you go. We didn't want to attack you, but Elle's right. He's too important to the Resistance. Let him join us, or let him go. Those are your only options."

Laik glares and then sighs heavily. "Fine, I won't kill him."

"Swear it on your honor as a lycan that you won't kill him or allow anyone else here to do it. He's under your protection now."

He growls under his breath and closes his eyes for a second. He's so enraged he's panting, but we've got him by the throat.

"I swear."

It's the best we're going to get, but from the frustrated looks on the other's faces, it's enough. Elle climbs off of him and shifts back into a human. This time, Callum hands her a shirt and pants.

"But I won't work with him either." Laik gets up and spits at our feet.

Elle rolls her eyes. "You're going to have to. I'll send word to Madame Delphine, and we'll go from there. The leader of the panther city should know as well."

"It's not fair that the panthers pretend to be neutral," I grumble. "They're clearly not." My face warms when I realize I said all this aloud.

Elle purses her lips. "They might be more open about their true feelings once they find out we have Ryne on our side. Good job getting him out."

"I don't think he'll see it that way."

She shrugs. "Let's go pay him a visit, shall we?"

"Wait." Laik holds up a hand. "This is my home and my pack. You can't come in here and take over."

"Actually, I can. Madame Delphine made me her second in command of the Resistance down here, so if you're working for the Resistance, you're working for me."

Chapter Twenty-Two

The guards at the tent doors give us scathing looks but don't stop us from entering. We slide through the opening and find Ryne sitting in the back corner. I kneel down at his feet and begin fumbling with the wolfsbane ropes. I need to get them off him. Except for bathroom breaks, he's been trapped in here twenty-four-seven, and it's my fault.

He winces when I touch him, his eyes shiny and tired as they watch me through the curtain of his oily hair. "Not sure if I can trust you're actually helping me or not, but I heard what happened out there."

"You can." I bite my lip for a moment, thinking of what I could possibly say. "I didn't want to hurt you. I was trying to help."

He turns away and gazes up at Elle. "You were supposed to run away, and yet you can't be more than a day's walk from my city."

Elle shrugs. "You saved me. Now it's my turn."

I finish with the bindings and stand up.

"I could turn," he says, looking down on me. "I could turn and kill you right now, kill all your little friends too."

"These people aren't my friends," I shoot back. "Well, not all of them anyway. But we have bigger problems to worry about. Namely, your father."

"And let me guess, the lycan are magically going to help me now? How am I supposed to trust them?"

"They're with the Resistance," Elle points out. "And you don't have to trust them, but you can trust me."

"Well, that's one person," he snaps, and I deflate. He's mad at me, and I don't blame him, but it's not like he's entirely innocent here. He's the alpha in charge of the pack that killed my sister and enslaved so many. He's got blood on his hands, far more than I do. Still, I don't want him to hate me. I want to go back to what it felt like when he loved me. I want his kisses and his warmth and the promise of things to come.

"So what now?" he asks Elle.

"We move." Laik steps through the tent opening, his nostrils flaring. "We have two more weeks until the next full moon, and we're vulnerable here. Since Elle's demanding we keep you with us instead of killing you, you've become a liability."

"I didn't ask to be kidnapped." Ryne shakes his head. "I had a plan and knew what I was doing and——"

"I don't care." Laik cuts him off. "You're with us now, and I said we're moving out."

I want to say something more, or at the very least get a moment alone with Ryne to discuss everything that's happened, but he brushes past me like I'm nothing, and I'm the last to leave the tent.

Packing up is tense, but at least it's busy. There's no more time to fight. Everyone's got a job to do. I work alongside Callum and Charlotte. Elle and Ryne are on the other side of camp.

Once we start walking deeper into the woods, and the afternoon sun starts to fade, the tenseness among our ragtag group grows palpable. Everyone hates Elle, especially Laik. Everyone hates Ryne, especially Grady. And I'm pretty sure they all hate me. But at least we're alive.

We approach the camouflaged trucks, and Laik instructs half of the group to go to the panther city. "It'll be safer for you there. I'll send for you before the next full moon."

"What about him?" Someone points to Ryne. "Shouldn't he be sent away?"

"I can't go there." Ryne is quick to argue. "I'm forbidden. There's a treaty, and if I go there . . ." His voice falls away, and Elle shifts uncomfortably.

If he goes there, then that could be bad for his pack, which would actually be good for the Resistance, wouldn't it?

But nobody says anything more, and a few minutes later, our numbers are smaller than ever. There's Wanda, Laik, and four of his most trusted guards——three men and one woman. Callum also stays, and so do Charlotte and Knox. And then there's Elle, Ryne, and myself. Joanna and

Grady stay with us as well, but I don't know why. Even though Grady's allegiances have completely changed, I'm glad they're here because Joanna is my best friend. It hurts my heart that our bond is slipping, but it's undeniable that we're not the same as we once were. She cares for me, but she's madly in love with Grady. And I can't possibly talk to her about how I feel about Ryne, not with everything that's happened.

And Ryne is all I think about. He consumes me, day and night. Even now, I watch the way he moves and talks to Elle, and I'm sick with jealousy. Every cell in my body craves his touch, but he's cold and distant.

We're not any safer than we were before. In fact, we're less so, but maybe that's the point. Laik doesn't want to keep Ryne and Elle safe at the expense of his people. I can't say I blame him, knowing what I do about King Thorn.

We make camp that night, and nobody talks to me, not even when I try to lay my pack down next to Ryne. He gets up and moves to the other side of camp. That one action alone is like a twisting knife to the wound, and I only get angrier at him. He thinks he's the only one who's been hurt here? What about his actions? His choices? Why do I have to be the one to extend the olive branch? Will he ever look at me with love in his eyes like he used to? I go to bed with these questions swirling in my mind and get little rest.

The next day, we walk and walk and walk, and still, nobody talks to me. I try to make small talk with Joanna, but she keeps it surface-level and then ditches me for Grady. Charlotte and Knox seem to have some kind of budding romance happening because they are practically attached at the hip and don't give me a second thought. Elle is too busy scouting the area to pay much attention to me and my hurt feelings. I could reach out to Callum, but I feel weird about it. I don't want him to think he has a chance with me because with Ryne here, there's no question.

I want Ryne back.

Maybe it's the dumbest thing I've ever wanted, but it's eating me alive, and I can't let it go on without doing something. Sure, I'm lycan, but we can work that out. I just can't kiss him again, but even to hold his hand and hug him would mean so much. I try not to let the silent treatment bother me or let them see that I care, but my heart goes from angry to aching. I'm doing the best I can, and it's not like anyone else here is perfect. We're all making mistakes left and right. It feels like whatever I do, I'm going to make someone mad, so shouldn't I do what I think is best?

When we finally stop to set up camp the next day, I nearly cry out with exhaustion and relief. After helping set up the women's tent and foraging for firewood, I follow the little stream, hoping to find a private place to bathe. I'm pretty sure I smell like a horse.

It's warm enough for me to have some time to dry off in the sun, so I find a deep pool and strip down but keep my underwear on. There are too many people who could walk up on me to be comfortable bathing naked. I take a bit of soap from my bag with clean clothes and step into the cool water. I hiss, the water colder than I thought it would be. I'm still not used to my hot lycan blood. Sinking deep into the water, I let it soothe my aching joints. I scrub at my hair and body, getting all the dirt off. My skin becomes blissfully numb, and I lay my head back on a rock to relax and just enjoy the day.

A splash jars me out of my reverie. It's followed by laughter, but I can't see anyone. I swim across the pool and peek around the corner. If I had just walked twenty feet more, I would've found a gorgeous lake surrounded by thick trees. Elle and Ryne are splashing one another, huge smiles on their faces.

I know they aren't a couple but seeing them together makes me want to cry. They belong with one another. Even fate couldn't make me and Ryne work, but they're so easy and perfect. They match--their power, their determination, their leadership. Everything. At least they're not completely naked this time, unlike the first time I caught them together right after shifting from their wolf forms. They're in their underwear, same as me.

A tear slips down my cheek. Feeling foolish, I take a step back so they can't see me.

Too late.

"Poppy," Elle calls. Ryne's back is to me, but his whole body stiffens. Elle ignores him and swims over. She grabs my hand and pulls me into the middle of the lake with them.

Ryne swims to the other side and hoists himself onto the shore. I don't even bother trying to hide my stare. He's lost a little weight--we all have out here--but he's still ripped with muscle. The water streams down his tanned skin and tangles his black hair.

"Come on, Ryne, don't be an idiot," Elle calls after him.

Ryne spins. "Idiot? Poppy tricked me and kidnapped me."

Elle rubs her eyes. "Are you sure that's what happened?"

He crosses his arms and glares at me. "Are you saying it's not?"

"No, that's exactly what happened," I say, and Ryne scowls. "But I did it to save your life."

"I'm supposed to believe that?" His natural distrust hurts, and I want to leave. It's hard enough that we're estranged now. I don't need to be reminded.

"Of course you are," Elle says with exasperation. "Now get back in here. You and Poppy have to work this out."

For a second, I think he's going to storm away, but instead he listens to Elle and slides back into the water. I wonder if he'd ever listen to me the way he does her. Probably not, but maybe that's a good thing. Elle is his friend, and friends can be real with you in ways that lovers cannot.

And I never wanted to be Ryne's friend.

He swims over to us and stands up. The water comes up to my chest, but only his torso. He glowers down at me. I feel like there's a ten-foot glass wall between us. I can't climb over it, so I'm just going to have to break it.

"You have thirty seconds to convince me that you are not my enemy."

"Wait," Elle says, backing away. "I'm going to give you guys some privacy. I'll keep watch so no one else interrupts you either."

I appreciate her optimism, but I'm not convinced it's necessary.

We both watch Elle leave the lake and disappear into the woods. I'm both grateful and nervous that she left us. Ryne could do whatever he wanted with me, and I'm not sure I'd fight him. He could kill me. Drown me right here and run away. His pack wouldn't blame him.

But he stares at me, torment clear in his eyes. I did betray him, but only because I love him. And I've realized now, that a lot of the bad choices he made when it came to me were out of love too. We're just two messy people trying to survive a horrible situation.

"That mission wasn't supposed to have anything to do with you," I begin. "We were supposed to be rescuing Elle. I thought she was your wife, not your father's. I was so angry with you even though I know I didn't have a good reason to be. I am lycan, and you can't be with me, but I still felt betrayed and abandoned." I take a deep breath and stand a little taller. I can do this. "We found you asleep, and Laik wanted to kill you." I leave the part out about Grady wanting to kill him because he's been hurt enough as it is. "Even angry with you, I didn't want you dead, so I suggested we kidnap you instead. I was supposed to lure you out. I thought maybe you'd get away or . . . I don't know what I thought. But I didn't know that kissing you would knock you unconscious."

He steps closer to me and cups my cheek with his rough hand. It's a small gesture, but it's everything to me. My toes curl into the mud, and I long to wrap myself around him. "But the second time you did," he says, his voice hardening. "You sedated me for them."

I swallow, knowing there is no way out of this. "I did. But again, I was doing the best I could to keep us both alive. I was stuck between two hard choices."

"Would you have made that same choice again knowing that I'm not married to Elle?"

"I would do anything to save you, married or not. Can't you see that?" I inch forward, spreading my hands on his bare chest. When he doesn't flinch or pull away, hope fires within me. "I still love you, and it hurts so badly that we can't be together."

He hesitates for a moment and then crushes me in a hug. "I've missed you so much," he whispers in my hair.

Tears prick my eyes, and I clutch at his back. I didn't think I'd ever hold Ryne again, but here we are in the middle of a lake, clinging to one another like there is no tomorrow.

And maybe there isn't.

Especially when Laik finds out.

Ryne drops his head and kisses my neck, trailing his lips up along my jaw and across my cheek. Everywhere his lip touch burns, and I crave more and more. No one else in the world matters except me and Ryne. Whatever happens after this, at least we will be in it together.

Then his mouth is on mine, and I open my mouth and run my tongue along his lips. A half a second later, my mind clears, and I remember that I can't kiss him. He's about to pass out in the middle of the lake. He's too big for me to carry on my own. He'll drown!

Maybe I'll kill him after all.

Chapter Twenty-Three

I rip away from him and squeeze around his middle. "Come on," I grunt. "It's not safe here."

He chuckles. "Poppy."

I can't move him. The man is practically twice my size, and my lycan strength has waned with the moon.

"Poppy," he says again, crouching down and peeling my arms away from him. "I'm okay. I feel completely normal." He chuckles again. "Well, I do feel like I want to kiss you, but you know what I mean."

I blink at him, relief flooding me. "My kiss didn't hurt you?" I can't figure out what's changed.

He shakes his head. "But just in case, we'd better test it again."

His lips return to mine, and I want to shake him off, to tell him we should try this on the shore, but my mind blanks when he deepens the kiss. Fear of my saliva doesn't deter him or slow him down, and if anything he's more energized from kissing me. It's the validation I need. I float my legs up to wrap around his torso and press myself closer. I could stay like this forever.

"You're shivering," he says. "Let's get out of here."

We swim over to his clothes and then walk up the trail to retrieve mine.

"Laik said that lycan saliva is what poisons you, so this doesn't make any sense."

"It does," he replies. "Your bite is deadly, but only when you're in lycan form. Your saliva acts similarly to the wolfsbane. It weakens us but I don't think it's deadly."

I raise an eyebrow at him. "You don't look weak to me, and let's not forget you just had your tongue down my throat."

"When you put it that way, I don't sound very romantic, do I?" He grins sheepishly.

I snort out a laugh and shimmy into my clothes, then run my fingers through my hair in a pathetic attempt to brush it. "You know what I mean." And then it dawns on me. "Lycan are stronger the closer we get to the full moon, so that means I can't kiss you before or after it."

He smirks. "What's that? Five or six days every twenty-eight?"

"Something like that. I don't know for sure."

He wraps me in a hug. "Good thing we have plenty of time to figure it out."

"Do we?" I wish we did, but we both know what a mess we've gotten ourselves into. It feels surreal to be here, kissing and acting like lovestruck kids who have nothing to worry about but each other. But that's not our reality, and I'm not sure it ever will be.

"Maybe not, so we'd better make the most of it while we still can."

That's all I needed to hear to meet his lips again and pick up where we left off out in the lake. Too bad we don't have more privacy here and have to resort to making out in the woods, but at this point, I'll take whatever I can get. I want Ryne. I love him. And lycan or not, he's my fated mate. We'll figure the details out later.

Someone clears their throat, and we spring apart. Elle peeks her head out from behind a tree, a satisfied smirk on her pretty mouth. "Sorry to interrupt, but we have to get back before Laik sends out a search party."

I thread my fingers with Ryne's. "So what are we going to do? Do we pretend that we're not together or––" It's also my way of asking if we *are* together, but I'm not always as brave as I'd like to think.

"They're not keeping us apart anymore," he replies quickly.

"They could use our status against us."

"Like I said..." He squeezes my hand. "They're not keeping us apart anymore." I appreciate his confidence, but I'm not so sure we can pull it off.

"They don't trust any of us," Elle points out.

"She's right," I add. "At the very least, we can't let them know that we're fated." That's dangerous knowledge even in the hands of friends. In the hands of enemies, it's deadly.

"Fine." But he doesn't sound fine. He sounds angry. "But those people kept me tied up with painful wolfsbane rope for two weeks. If they want my help, the least they can do is leave you and me alone."

I agree, but I have a sinking feeling not everyone is going to see it the same way. Even my allies might not be so friendly about it. I shudder to think of what Joanna and Grady will say. I'm going to have to warn him about them.

Elle rolls her eyes. "You two are disgustingly cute, do you know that?"

I blush and squeeze Ryne's hand a little tighter.

"Nobody has ever called me disgustingly cute before," Ryne grumbles. We grow silent for a long second before we all burst out laughing.

* * *

We're halfway back to the camp when something zips out of the forest, tackling Ryne to the ground. My first thought is that we've been ambushed, but then I recognize the wolf with a missing limb. Grady. Despite the loss of a leg, his movements are still swift and precise. More importantly, his teeth are still razor-sharp, and right now they're clasped around Ryne's neck.

"No!" I scream, rushing forward, pulling at Grady's fur, but he's already on top of Ryne, saliva dripping onto his face. I claw and grab, but it's useless.

Elle shifts, her clothes ripping to pieces. I jump back, giving her space to help. Joanna stumbles onto the trail and grabs my hand. Tears shine on her cheeks, and her mouth is set in a grim line. "I told him not to go after you guys."

Time slows down. Grady lets go of Ryne's neck seconds before Elle collides with him. I expect Ryne to shift into his wolf, but he doesn't. Instead, Grady changes back and falls onto his knees. "Fight me!" he screams. "Turn and fight me, damn it!"

Ryne shakes his head and stands, brushing off his pants. Grady gets right into his face. "What's the matter? Are you a coward when dear old dad isn't here to instruct you?"

Grady shoves at Ryne, and he stumbles back a step but doesn't fall. I grip Joanna's arm and she mine. Elle still circles both of them in her wolf form. I've no doubt she'd take Grady down if he really hurt Ryne.

"I'm so sorry," Ryne says. "I didn't have a choice."

"There's always a choice." Underneath all that anger is the vulnerability of betrayal.

"You got out of there alive."

Grady sniffs. "Because of Poppy. Don't pretend you had anything to do with that. You would've killed me."

Ryne's eyes flick to where Grady should have an arm. Grady catches Ryne's gaze and hauls off, punching him in the jaw. Ryne's head jerks back, and I flinch. Elle stops her pacing and crouches into a fighter's stance.

Ryne recovers and rubs his jaw. "I deserved that."

"You sure as hell did."

"Are you done?"

Grady shakes his head and punches him in the gut. Ryne doubles over, and I move to go to him, but Joanna holds tight to me. "If they are ever going to get out of this as friends, we have to let them fight it out," she hisses in my ear.

"But Ryne's not fighting."

"I know. And that's okay. Grady needs this. Let him have it."

"By using Ryne as a punching bag?" I squeak just as Grady throws another punch, blood exploding from Ryne's nose.

"Please, forgive me," Ryne says, his voice thick.

Grady stands there, breathing heavily, and then gives a stiff nod. He holds his hand out, and Ryne takes it. "You were my best friend and I trusted you."

"I know."

"We'll never be friends again, but I will work with you to take down Thorn."

Ryne nods once.

"After that," Grady continues, "I don't ever want to see your face again."

Ryne's mouth thins, and his eyes soften. As much as it hurts, he gets it. Too much damage has been done.

Joanna bounces up on her toes. "I think that's the best we're going to get."

Elle shifts back, and we walk back to camp in tense silence. Well, until Elle starts chattering. She rambles on about the girls with Madame Delphine, about how she wants to help them before more get shipped off to the mating houses. Ryne keeps a tight hold of my hand, and Joanna has her hand tucked into Grady's remaining arm. He and Ryne both walk on the outside of our group, farthest away from each other, but at least they agreed they were on the same side.

Camp is noisy when we return, with lunch well underway.

We get in line for food, and the cook plops a little less on Ryne, Elle, and Grady's plates, but none of them complain. We find Knox, Charlotte, and Callum sitting on a large fallen log and join them.

Callum eyes Ryne's arm around my back but doesn't say anything. Knox won't look up from his plate. This is exactly what I was worried about. Knox told me he thinks the wolves should die, that Ryne should die. What if he tries something?

"Hey, Knox," Ryne says, and Knox barely lifts his eyes.

"Yeah?" He clears his throat. "Hi."

"Thanks for taking care of Poppy for me. I owe you one."

"I did it for Poppy, not you."

"Right," he says, "understandable."

I haven't been sure if I should tell Ryne the truth about Knox's feelings toward him or not. I don't want to get Knox into trouble for no reason. Ryne still doesn't know about our dating history, but I don't want to keep it a secret anymore. I'm tired of secrets. I'll tell him all about it once we have a chance to be alone. Surely Ryne wouldn't hold my past with Knox against him, especially since Knox doesn't have a chance with me anymore, and Knox helped me get out of the city.

"We should plan our next move," Elle declares. "The full moon is only ten days away, and you all are the strongest on those days."

"You should be talking to Laik and Wanda about that, not us," Callum replies.

Elle creases her eyebrows. "Why? Are they the only ones who can help?" She scoffs. "They're working for the Resistance, same as all of us."

Callum shakes his head. "But Laik is the alpha. We don't do anything without his permission."

Elle rolls her eyes. "He's not my alpha. I'm no lycan." She scrunches her nose. "No offense."

"You know what I mean . . ." His voice drops. "I don't do anything unless it's okay with my alpha. That's the way it works around here."

I have a thought then––what if the alpha-hierarchy here isn't as strong as Laik wants me to believe? In the shifter pack, the wolves can change at will and are connected to each other through their senses and the telepathic link. Lycan are similar, but I've never seen the lycan here treat Laik even close to the way that Ryne's pack treated him. Maybe Laik is just a bully who calls himself an alpha because he wants power, not because he actually has it. If I'm right, it could change everything, and it could also explain why Callum just got all weird.

"Well, guess what." Elle has that knowing gleam in her eyes she gets whenever she's passionate about something. "I'm in charge of the Resistance, so he'll have to listen to me, and I value your contribution far more than Laik's."

We all stare at her, and I can't help but grin. When I met her, I really thought she'd be my enemy. Thank heavens I was so wrong.

"Why?" Callum asks.

"You're the healer, right? You have much more of a sense on how to attack with the least amount of life lost. You're safe, not reckless. I want you to be my liaison between us and the lycan, not Laik."

She winks at me, and I wonder what she's up to. Perhaps it's just that she wants to undermine Laik's authority. Or she could be telling the truth. Or she could simply have a crush on Callum. I'm kinda hoping it's the last one, as far-fetched as it could be. I've never seen her crush on anyone, but if they did get together, then maybe Callum will talk to me like he's a friend and not a jilted lover.

"I can't do that."

"Why not?" Elle pops a wilted strawberry into her mouth and frowns.

"Because Laik is my alpha. I cannot defy him." But his voice wobbles a little, and again, I wonder how much control Laik actually has over his pack. This is an interesting development, and I can't wait to have some alone time to talk with Ryne about it.

"I'm not asking you to defy him. I'm simply asking that you be my go-between. You know Laik and I are going to have conflicts. This eases that."

Callum snorts. "For you maybe, but not for me."

"Fine, then Charlotte can be my liaison."

"Nope. Laik isn't my alpha. I barely know the guy." Charlotte holds up her hands, a half-eaten apple still in her right palm. "I can't help you with that one."

Elle looks at me.

"I didn't swear allegiance to him," I say. Beside me, Ryne's shoulders relax.

"See, Callum," Elle says. "It has to be you."

Callum twists his lips and gets up to leave, but he doesn't say no again, and I'm pretty sure Elle's got him on the hook.

Chapter Twenty-Four

Ryne and I spend as much time together as possible over the following days, testing the strength of my kiss whenever we're alone. The moon grows a sliver larger each night, but so far we've been fine. My saliva isn't hurting him. He still has his own tent because Laik doesn't trust him to sleep near the others, and I find myself sneaking in to be with him after the other women fall asleep and returning hours later. Our romance isn't a secret, but I don't want the extra attention that moving into his tent permanently would create. We're playing a dangerous game, a game of deep kisses and blissful temptation and shifting alliances--I never want it to end.

Three days before the night of the full moon, I wake up with a sense of urgency coursing through my veins. I slip from my blankets and hurry outside to help with breakfast. Looking around, I can tell I'm not the only one here who feels what I'm feeling. There's an intensity in the air that wasn't present yesterday. Even though the lycan here have gotten along with the wolf shifters well enough, I worry that may not last as the full moon draws closer.

"There you are." Ryne drops a kiss on my cheek and wraps an arm around my waist. "How did you sleep?"

"Honestly? Great." I look up at him, and he leans in to peck me on the lips, but I duck away and step back. "But I feel different today."

"Different?"

"Charged somehow." I swallow hard. "I don't think we should kiss again until three days after the full moon. I don't want to hurt you."

He lets out a breath and nods. That's a whole week every moon cycle that we're going to have to be extra careful. It stinks, but at least it's not every day.

"What are you telling him our secrets for, huh?" Wanda strides right up to me, squaring her shoulders and getting in my face. I'm taller than her and probably a better fighter, but she's unpredictable.

"I don't know your secrets. And besides, he's on our side," I reply. "You have a problem? Take it up with Laik."

"No," Ryne interrupts. "Take it up with Elle. She's the highest-ranked here right now." I smile at him, and not for the first time, I wonder how he feels about not being the alpha. Technically he's still the alpha of his pack. They won't fight for a new one until they can sense he's dead through the pack bond, but Elle was never one of his, so she's not bound to him. She's all Resistance now, and seeing her out here is witnessing her in her element. She's an exceptional leader.

"Whatever." Wanda's tone completely changes, going light and sweet. It would catch me off guard except that I'm used to her erratic behavior. "That might change today."

"Why do you say that?" I study her, trying to gauge if she's bluffing, but I can never tell with her.

She falls silent as Laik approaches. "We're going on a little field trip today," he announces loud enough that everyone in earshot can hear. "It's time we take this matter of Elle's disruption to the source."

"The source?" I question.

"The Resistance, you dummy." Wanda cackles. She twirls away and follows Laik over to the morning campfire.

"This should be interesting," Ryne says with a long sigh. Something lingers in his eyes. Fear? No, not fear, but he's nervous, and I can't say I blame him for that.

* * *

"Anyone who hasn't sworn loyalty to us has to wear a blindfold." Laik's eyes dart to those of us who aren't part of his little pack. We've hiked to the three trucks, and Elle's helping with seating arrangements when he decides to make this announcement.

"Oh, not this again," I mutter.

"I'm not putting that thing on," Joanna snaps.

"If you want to come, you will wear it." Laik straightens, his face stern.

"We're all part of the Resistance," Elle argues. "And haven't we already discussed this? You don't make the rules."

"But I make the rules about the safety of my camp, and I have a right to keep its location hidden."

"A little late for that, don't you think?" Grady chuckles. "Most of us know where we are, genius."

A few in the group stiffen, but most seem unfazed. Hope blooms in my chest. Maybe they're starting to realize that Laik isn't all that great.

"It's true," Joanna adds. "You're not the only one who has a strong sense of direction."

Laik growls but throws the blindfolds into the back of the closest truck. "Let's roll," he calls out before climbing into the driver's seat and slamming the door.

"We're not going in his vehicle," Joanna says, peering up at Grady. We split up, and Laik's people end up either with him or in the second truck, while the rest of us squash into the third. Knox drives with Charlotte in the cab while the wolves, Joanna, and I sit in the back. It's the closest Ryne and Grady have been to each other since their fight, and Elle eyes them carefully.

Grady sets Joanna in his lap and then whispers something in her ear. She giggles. He turns to look away from me and Ryne but keeps talking low to her. They're so often in their own little world, and I hate that I find myself jealous. I have Ryne, but it's not like we can just run away together. Grady and Joanna could. They could leave right now and never look back.

"Comfortable?" Ryne asks, his fingers sliding along the little sliver of exposed skin above my shorts.

"Not really," I laugh. "But I'm not complaining." I lean back into him and close my eyes, allowing the next hour to go by in relaxing silence. I don't even mind the bumpy war-torn roads because I've got Ryne to keep me comfortable.

* * *

The little room is packed with people. Even though my senses are slightly enhanced, I can't tell who is what. There are lycan, humans, and panther shifters all around us. Pretty sure Grady, Ryne, and Elle are the only wolf shifters, but maybe not.

Several people have poppies stuck to their shirts or in their hair.

"What's with the poppies?" I hiss to Elle.

She grins at me. "Don't you know? You're famous. The girl who stood up to King Thorn. Since you left, your namesake has become a symbol of solidarity."

I don't even know how to respond to that. Instead, I glance down at my shoes, avoiding the eyes of those around us. How many people had these boots before me? There's a small hole growing in the toe.

Elle drags us all the way to the front of the room, where Laik is talking with another man. He's tall, with bronzed golden skin even darker than the wolves, vibrant yellow eyes, and black cropped hair. He's not much older than Ryne and is stunning to look at. I can't help but wonder who he could be--someone with power, if I had to guess.

Laik glares at Ryne as we approach. "He's not leadership," he growls.

The other man ignores Laik and holds his hand out to Ryne. "Welcome, we've been waiting a long time for you to join our side. I'll admit I was skeptical, but Delphine and Elle insisted you'd do it. I'm Derek, leader of the panther pack."

Ryne tilts his head and studies the leader. "I know who you are. Gotta say, I shouldn't be surprised to see you here, but I am."

Derek nods. "This is the closest we come to wolf territory. We aid the Resistance and nothing more."

"If my father knew--"

"War would break out," Derek finishes. "We know. And we don't want that for our people. I'm glad you're on the right side of history now."

"My mother always had more faith in me than I had in myself. Elle did too," Ryne says.

"I'm glad they did." He turns to Laik, who's got his arms folded over his broad chest, still glaring daggers at Ryne. "Come now, Laik, there is no reason to be like that. Ryne offers a unique perspective into the wolf shifter dynamics."

"Fine. Put him out there with all the other shifters. He doesn't need to be up here."

"Actually, he does," Elle says.

"Why?" Laik challenges. His nostrils flare as if he smells something vile. "We've got too many wolves here as it is."

"Because he's the one who'll have to take down his dad at some point. We can't do this without him."

The two begin a stare off, and the tension builds. Someone has to back down, or else there will be a fight any second. I've never seen Elle like this. Her leadership skills are unmatched.

"Fine," Laik growls at last, stepping back. "Let's get started."

I turn and find that Joanna and Grady aren't behind me. I search the crowd and see them talking and laughing with another couple. Joanna doesn't laugh with me like that anymore. Callum, Knox, and Charlotte are with them as well. Maybe I shouldn't be up here either.

I extract myself from Ryne. "I'm going to go be with them."

Elle laughs. "Absolutely not. You're in this with us."

Laik opens his mouth to argue, but Derek cuts him off. "Let's get this started then, shall we?"

He steps forward, holding his hands up. It takes a few moments, but the crowd quiets. "Before we begin, I want to introduce you to some new faces up here with me. Prince Ryne Tremaine, alpha of the Carolina Pack, has finally joined us."

A cheer goes up.

"Yes, he plans to assassinate his father." The crowd silences with that declaration, and Ryne's face goes red. I can see the pain in his eyes and wonder if I'm the only one. No son should have to kill his own father, no matter how evil the father is. I wish I could take this from him, but there are too many people depending on Ryne to do the right thing. These are all things we've talked about in our time alone together the past few days, and his plan before we kidnapped him hasn't gone away. As one of the only men allowed close to Thorn on a regular basis, Ryne is committed to seeing this through.

"And we will do anything we can to help him with that," Derek continues. Everyone nods, and murmurs of agreement circle the room. He talks as if he's used to giving speeches, and he motions to me with confidence. "Standing at his side is someone you've all heard of by now. I'm honored to introduce you to Poppy."

A hush falls over the room, and red-hot embarrassment spreads across my cheeks.

"Poppy has become a symbol for our cause," he continues. "We fight for her and all the other girls she represents. She is one of the lucky ones. She was turned lycan, but she escaped Thorn's clutches. We will not rest until everyone is free from the tyranny of the wolves."

Another cheer. I still don't understand what's going on, but I let myself look at these people, meeting their eyes. They care about this as much as I do. They're committed--we're going to make this happen.

Derek waits for the crowd to quiet once more. "Before we talk about the plan for the upcoming full moon, I want updates from all of you. What have you done that has aided the Resistance? What have you seen that has weakened their stronghold? Who needs rescuing?"

Several hands shoot up all over the room, and Derek calls on them one by one. They all tell tales of things they've done and accomplished, but there are also stories of wolves who've done unspeakable things. When those stories are told, Ryne tightens his grip on my hand. I know he blames himself, and others in this room probably blame him too. But I don't blame him anymore. For a long time I did, but I know who he really is——I know his heart. It's not his fault he was born to be the alpha, but he's changing his fate, despite the odds. I admire him for that.

Once they are done, Derek waves Laik forward.

"What is the plan for the lycans on this full moon?"

"We're going to go into the city and take down as many of those bastards as possible." He speaks like the answer is obvious and that he'll be successful. I'm not so sure.

"That's not going to work," Ryne says sharply. He rakes a hand through his hair, and his mouth thins. Everyone turns on him, and whispers ripple through the crowd.

Chapter Twenty-Five

"Why not?" Laik growls. His fists are clenched, and I'm a little nervous he's going to attack Ryne on the spot. From the looks of it, he wouldn't be the only one.

Ryne takes it all in stride, seemingly unafraid. "Because since the last festival, they've become far more vigilant. They don't let anyone into the city on the full moon or even a few days before. And considering you kidnapped me the day after the full moon, I can only imagine security has grown tighter."

"We have ways of getting into the city undetected," Laik insists, and I have to fight to roll my eyes. Ways? We crossed a ramshackle bridge on the verge of collapse.

"Explain," Ryne says, unconvinced.

"I'm not telling you our secrets. Just know that it can be done."

Ryne furrows his brow, disbelieving.

I'm acutely aware that this conversation is happening in front of everyone, but these two don't seem to care. They obviously hate each other, and the forced proximity is starting to wear thin.

"Whatever. Even if you can get into the city, the plan to just kill at random is a stupid one."

"Because you're protecting them."

"They're my pack!" Ryne yells, and everyone goes still. "Not every wolf is evil. I know those men. They're my brothers, and they're not in control of the laws governing our ways. Killing them serves no purpose." He takes a deep breath to steady his voice. He's got some convincing to do now, and for more than just Laik's sake. Others are starting to eye Ryne with distrust. "War is bloody, I know that, but we should avoid killing as many innocents as possible. Why not try to take out key people that are close to my father?"

"Like you?" Laik laughs.

"Not helpful," Derek mutters.

"Like Anders, and I *know* you people know how dangerous he's gotten. So start with him, and if we can also take out the ones my father brought in from Chicago, when the time comes for me to challenge him, everyone else will be on my side."

Laik grins. "Why not challenge dear old dad now? Why wait?"

I squeeze Ryne's hand because I don't want him to take the bait.

"Timing is key. I'll only get one chance, and we can't blow it."

"You're stalling."

"My father is a fearsome fighter, and I'm not as strong as I need to be. Since I arrived at the lycan camp, I've felt weak. You kept me locked up and malnourished until Elle arrived with some common sense." He gives Laik a pointed look. "I need another month, if not more, to regain my strength and prepare."

"Are we going to allow the lycan into the city when Ryne challenges Thorn?" I ask. I'm so caught up in the conversation that I don't even realize I've spoken. But I'm worried about Ryne. He could die. And if they do it on the full moon, I'm not sure I'll even be aware of what's going on. I need to be there when it all goes down, just in case there's a way I can help.

Derek speaks up. "I think we should. And as much as I hate to say this, the panthers may break the treaty to be there as well. At that point, we want to make sure the wolves have the leadership we put in place, not their own. The Resistance needs to subdue them."

Ryne shifts uncomfortably, and I can't say I blame him. We don't know these panthers, and they could hurt his people. But at the same time, we may need their help.

"But how will you know who the good guys are?" I ask. "Because not all the wolf shifters are bad."

"That is a conversation for another time. For tonight, we should focus on who the lycan should target this month. I agree with Ryne. Taking them out randomly is counterproductive and too risky." Derek raises an eyebrow. "Let's make a plan."

The conversation changes as new strategies are outlined, but it's Laik who's got my attention. The man can't be trusted, and it's only a matter of time before he lashes out.

Over the next hour, our plans all start to come together like storm clouds gathering. If everything works, we'll be successful. We're almost through when someone enters the room. She's breathing hard, like she's been running, and she has a black cloak over her head. "Sorry I'm late," she says, removing the hood. It's Madame Delphine.

Her eyes lock on Ryne, and then she's rushing through the crowd and climbing onto the stage to wrap her son into a tight hug. "I knew you were alive, but I was so worried."

"I'm okay." They pull apart and smile at each other. It's one of the rare times I get to see them as mother and son, and it makes my heart ache for them both. Their relationship should be simple, but Thorn has made it complicated.

"I have news," she announces to everyone. "And I don't have much time, so please let me say my peace."

Derek nods, and she begins. "There was a plan to bring more betas into the claiming this year so that more of the claimed women could become beta wives. That, unfortunately, hasn't happened."

Ryne's eyes darken. "Thorn's doing?"

She nods. "I'm afraid so, but it's more than that." She swallows hard. "As you know, Anders is running the pack in Ryne's absence. Things are grim, and now he's decided that at the festival next month, more than two girls will be taken to the mating houses."

"How many more?" I breathe. There's not even that many left.

"Eight women."

"Eight!" Elle gasps. "That can't be!"

"I'm afraid it is." Madame Delphine's voice wobbles. "I can't stay for long. I'm lucky I was able to travel here at all. There are more patrols than ever, and I need to get back before my absence is noted, but I had to come beg you to save these women."

"We'll do our best," Derek replies.

"I need you to promise. Send some of your best people to Drayton Hall on the coming full moon, and I'll help you get the most vulnerable women out."

"It will spread our resources too thin," Laik interrupts. "We already have a plan."

"I don't care about your plan." She glares at him. "This Resistance is about helping the women, is it not? Well, I'm telling you that these girls need us."

"They all need us," Laik snaps. "Every single woman in that city needs us."

He has a point, but I know those women and was friends with a few of them. And even though I wasn't close with most of them, they still don't deserve to be taken to the mating houses. I wouldn't wish that on anyone; not even Faye with all her nasty comments and sabotaging actions. Nobody deserves to go to a mating house. Nobody!

I think of Abi then. I want to get her out too. I wonder where she is now. Could I find her? Could I save her? Is it too late?

Of course it's not too late. Part of me feels guilty that I think only of her and not all the other women as well. How many of them are trapped in those hellholes? This has to stop. All of it. But if we try too much at once, we will never succeed. The Resistance isn't big enough to take the whole system down quickly.

"Laik is right that they all need us," I say. Everyone stops arguing and looks at me. I swallow and lick my lips. "But how many mating houses are there? If we try to rescue the mating house women all at once, we will fail. However, we can prevent some women from the horrors of those places to begin with if we start with the claimed. The ultimate goal is to end this inhuman practice once and for all, but right now, we have enough resources to take out a couple of key players and rescue those girls."

Laik crosses his arms and glowers at me. "And then what?"

"And then we keep doing this until we save them all."

Madame Delphine beams and squeezes my shoulder. "I knew you were going places."

"I want to help with the rescue efforts," Ryne says.

Laik practically growls. "Absolutely not. I have a few guys who are good at rescue missions. We'll send them."

Ryne's eyeballs just about pop out of his head. "Are you insane? You want to send lycan after them on a full moon? They'd be totally out of control."

"Give my alpha some credit," Wanda calls out, her voice shrill above the others. "We've gotten women out of there on full moons before. We can control ourselves just fine."

Ryne wraps a protective arm around me. "How do you explain Poppy then?"

Laik considers this for a second, and something tickles at the back of my mind--a suspicion that he's not being completely honest with us.

"I'm not saying people don't get in the way and sometimes end up bitten, which is what happened with Poppy, but if there are shifters around, my men will be able to take them on better than anyone else. One bite from us, and they won't be strong enough to fight us off."

"I'll go with them," Elle volunteers. "That way Ryne can go with the group to take out the shifters. He can identify them for you."

"No. No shifters," Laik says. "I'm not working with wolves."

"Me too," I say, ignoring Laik's obvious prejudice. "I'm coming too."

"No," both Laik and Ryne say at the same time. I huff and cross my arms. I hate that the one thing they agree on is against me.

"Why not? I know these women. They might listen to me."

Ryne snorts. "Doubtful."

"Why can't I go?"

Laik eyes me like I'm stupid. "It's only your second full moon. You aren't going to have much more control than you did on your first."

He has a point, but I can't accept it. "So we'll go in before the moon fully rises. Please."

"No. I will put my foot down on this. You will stay with the shifters, and the lycan left back at camp will help you through your renewal. Charlotte is good for that. You'll need to help Knox as well."

Ryne stiffens, and I wonder if he knew that Knox had been bitten and that I was the one who did it.

"Fine. I'll stay behind." But I don't like it. Not one bit. I'm certain I can control myself. I want to go, but now is not the place to discuss this.

"I'm still going," Elle argues.

"I told you, no shifters." Laik's voice booms as if he gets the final word.

Ryne simply ignores him. "I'm with Elle on this one. We're not sitting this out."

"This is not a democracy."

Madame Delphine steps forward. "You're right. It's not. Lest you forget, I'm the one in charge, and those are my girls you're talking about. Ryne stays back at camp with Poppy." She gives him a pointed look. "I'm sorry, son, but half the shifters are out looking for you. You going puts this whole operation in jeopardy. Elle will lead the lycans to rescue the girls. She knows Drayton Hall, and I trust her. More importantly, the claimed trust her." She turns to Elle. "Get as many as you can."

"I will," Elle nods.

I want to push my case, but at least Elle gets to go. And I have to admit, I'm glad Ryne isn't going to be in danger, but can I really just stay back? I'm going to turn into my lycan self for the second time, and I don't want to do it in front of him--not before I can learn to control it, and especially not before I've accepted myself as this new monster.

But I still want to help the women back at the manor. I'll just have to figure out a more creative way to do it.

Chapter Twenty-Six

I wake the morning of the full moon sprawled out on Ryne's chest. He has his own tent since none of the lycan want to sleep next to a shifter, and last night I snuck out of the women's tent to be with him. I didn't plan to sleep in here, but I couldn't bring myself to leave the warm blankets or the comfort of his body. We couldn't kiss, so we spent the night cuddling and talking until we fell asleep. I study him now, taking in the sharp edges of his cheeks and chin, the dark hair fanning his pillowcase, and the fullness of his perfect lips. I want to lean up and kiss him, but I know that's a bad idea. Ryne needs to be at his full strength, and I'm pretty sure my saliva today would knock him out for days.

I settle for pressing myself as close to him as I can. These moments feel fleeting, and I wonder how long it is before we are separated again. I shouldn't worry about that. It doesn't seem like there is any reason we would be torn apart now, but based on everything that has happened so far, I don't think our luck will hold.

I keep my cheek pressed against his chest as it moves up and down with the rise and fall of his breath. It's long and slow. He's still asleep.

All of my senses are heightened, and I inhale Ryne's woodsy scent. It's my favorite smell in the whole wide world.

I smile at the thought of what Joanna would say if she heard the mushy thoughts in my head. She'd be mortified. Or maybe not? She's as in love as I am. My smile falls because I can't talk to her about this kind of thing anymore. We barely talk at all now that Ryne is no longer tied up. Before she and Grady were almost killed, I could've sat in our room and droned on and on about Ryne. She would've thrown a pillow at me, but she'd have still listened and offered advice.

Even though I get to see her every day, I miss her.

Ryne's arm tightens around me, and his breath changes.

"Morning, beautiful," he mumbles.

I prop my head up so I can look at him. "Good morning. I love you." The words seem so small compared to how I feel about him. But it still feels amazing to say it, and I want to keep repeating it over and over for the rest of my days.

"I love you too." He grins. My heart flutters, and I can't help but match his grin. I'll never tire of him. Never. "I would kiss you, but . . ."

"Yeah. I know."

He presses his lips against my forehead. "But I can kiss you in other places."

Then he moves his lips to my cheeks, the line of my jaw, down my neck . . . I shiver.

The tent flap flies open, and I jump back. "Time to get up," Elle says with way too much cheer for this time of day. She stops dead when she sees us and giggles. "I didn't think you guys could do that kind of thing today."

"We were testing the limits," Ryne growls.

Elle plops herself down on the bed. The woman has no shame. "Whatever, Laik is in a foul mood and wants everyone out there to go over the plan again. I have no idea what else there is to do. Everything seems pretty straightforward."

"I hate that I have to stay behind while you all head right into the middle of danger. What if something happens to one of you, and I'm not there?" I whine. "I'll forever feel guilty."

"Don't." Elle clasps my hand and squeezes gently. "You're still too unpredictable. You could just as easily kill us. You're safer away." She drops my hand to pat Ryne's leg. "Besides, someone's got to look after this one. An alpha without his pack is never a good thing."

Ryne groans and shakes his head. "You could say that again."

Guilt eats away at me because I haven't asked many questions about how he's doing. I've been so wrapped up in being together again that I forgot how hard this must be for him. He's got to be sick with worry. I've been around enough wolves to know they're not all bad. I think of Justin and Nico and hope they're okay. I wonder what women they're courting now and how the claiming is going for them. Given the circumstances, I can't imagine anyone is having fun, but maybe I'm wrong.

We spend our day moving our camp closer to the city. I hate that we keep having to move it, but I understand the reasoning. It's exhausting work, and by the time we're done, the afternoon is waning, and supper is on. Soon, most of our group will leave. Charlotte and Callum are staying back to make sure Knox and I handle the transition okay. I can feel the moon tugging on me and remember what it was like last month when the fever took hold. The day is already hot, and I worry Knox must be blistering, but when I ask him about it, he assures me he feels fine. He's been taking Callum's herbs, so maybe he's okay. I'm still not sure how I'm going to do tonight and Knox must be freaking out.

I give him a skeptical look. "Are you sure? Because––"

"I said I'm fine," he sighs. "I asked Laik for this, remember? It's what I want." He gives me a hard look, the kind that tells me not to ask any more questions, and he stomps off into the woods.

"Don't take it personally," Ryne says, coming up to wrap his arms around me from behind. "He's still mad that you didn't choose him."

I freeze at those words. We haven't talked about my connection to Knox because I didn't want there to be any unnecessary drama. I turn around in his arms and look into his eyes. "What do you know about us?"

He nods once. "That you were together before he was claimed."

"How did you find out?"

"After I took an interest in you, I did what I could to learn about your past. I found out you and Knox came from the same village, and the way he talked about you made it obvious. I wish you would've told me, but I understand why you didn't."

"Are you mad?"

"No. It happened before you met me. I can't blame you for that, and anyway, Knox is a good kid. I like him."

"You really think he's mad that I didn't choose him?" But I think Ryne's probably right. "Actually, don't answer that. It doesn't matter. He's moving on anyway."

"Already has." Ryne grins. "I saw him making out with Charlotte yesterday. They're probably in the woods doing it again right now."

I snort, and my cheeks redden, but I'm happy for them. Charlotte's not my favorite person, but I don't think she'd do anything to hurt Knox. She's had a crush on him for years, and if a relationship with her makes him happy, then more power to them both.

"I want to talk to you about something." I step back and hope this comes out right. "I don't want to spend time together tonight."

He frowns. "Do you think I'm ashamed to be with you when you're a lycan? I'm not."

"No, I don't think that, but I'm not ready for you to see this new side of me." My voice cracks, and my eyes water. "I'm sorry. I think I just need to do this one alone. I'm afraid I might hurt you."

He swallows hard. "Okay. I can give you that. But can you promise me that you'll try next month?"

I wish I could promise him that, but I can't. If I'm totally out of control, I still can't risk it. "I don't know," I mumble. "Let me think about it, okay?"

He gives me a frustrated look and Elle skips over to give us both a hug. "We're heading out. The moon will be rising before we know it."

She's right. I can feel it reaching out to me, a promise of what's to come. Over the next twenty minutes, the camp comes back together, and everyone gets what they need for the mission. It's a flurry of activity, and then it's silent all at once after they leave. There's just me, Ryne, Charlotte, Knox, and Callum. We're the leftovers, and we know it.

"We're going to spend the evening in the medic's tent if you need us," Callum says, and they leave me and Ryne standing around aimlessly.

"This is weird," I say. I suck my lip between my teeth and rock back on my heels.

"I think it's great." His smile quirks, and he runs his fingertips along my arm. "Alone time."

I shake my head. "I think I need to start *my* alone time now. I'm sorry."

His face falls, but he understands and retreats to his tent. I hightail it out of there, my heart pounding in my chest and guilt eating at me for the second time today.

I lied to Ryne.

This isn't about me needing to be alone, even though I don't want him to see me change––I don't know if I'll ever be ready for that––no, this is about me needing to go after Elle and the lycan in her group. I can't let them go to Drayton Hall without me. What if something happens? And what if my help could get one more girl out of there? I know that manor better than any of those lycan, and if they're not willing to let me come along for the ride, then I'll just have to invite myself.

<h1 style="text-align:center">Chapter Twenty-Seven</h1>

I keep to the woods as I head toward Drayton Hall. If I can find the river, then I can find the manor. I'm surprised by how easily I know the way, but with my heightened senses, it's second nature. I can practically smell it from here––smell the bread rising in the kitchen, the flowers growing out front next to the large garden, and the lavender and vanilla scented soap in the bathrooms. This is unlike anything I've experienced before, and I haven't even completed the shift yet. What will it be like my second time as a lycan? I need to hurry because I don't plan on that happening until after I'm away from the manor, just in case I lose control again.

It doesn't take me long to catch up with the rest of the group. I can see and smell them, but my scent is probably mixed in with everyone else's because nobody looks my way. I stay several hundred yards back, unmoving as I watch them from behind a thicket of trees. They are waiting on the river's edge for the moon to rise. I'm going to have to swim––as are they––but I'm sure I can manage it. The river is gentler here than in other parts, and lycan are stronger than the current. The girls won't like being dragged through water, but they'll survive, and eventually, they'll be thanking us.

I keep an eye on the darkening sky. I'd say we have maybe twenty or thirty minutes until they get the girls. I push my hearing out over the trickling of water and the brushing of wind against trees, landing on the manor. I can hear the girls hustling down into the basement, footsteps and nervous voices. If I try hard enough, I can even hear the faint pattering of their hearts.

This ability is astonishing.

Madame Delphine is going to intentionally leave their door unlocked, but how will that work without casting suspicion on her? I've seen that lock. It's huge. Maybe she'll open it when it's dark. Maybe she'll create a diversion.

I hope we can trust her. What if we're walking into a trap? Madame Delphine wouldn't do that, would she?

I swallow and try to stay grounded. The plan is for each of the lycan to grab two girls and run off with them. Meanwhile, Elle will go after four girls who are more likely to want to escape the city. I'll stay in the background and keep an eye on the lycan with girls. I don't want there to be any accidental bites, and deep down I know I could hurt someone. It's better that I stay back and watch. I'll help if they need me, but hopefully they won't.

The moon continues to rise, and I feel myself change. It happens faster than it did the first time. I fall to my knees, keenly aware that this life isn't what I wanted. My senses grow even stronger, and I'm suddenly thirsty. It's not water I need. It's human flesh. But my mind is still clear enough for me to push that horrible need away. If I get to the point that I'm close to losing control, I'll force myself to run.

My hands elongate, and thick nails form. They're like little daggers, pressing into the dark soil. My shoulders broaden with audible pops, and my face contorts and twists. I want to scream, to howl, but I refuse to let myself. It's still painful, but not as painful as last time.

I can do this.

I can do this.

I can do this.

I get back up and stand there for a second, breathing in and out. It takes a minute of concentration, but I still seem to have my whole mind. If I were human, I'd cry with relief right about now. Instead, I take a deep, steadying breath, and the scent of two lycan and Elle slide into my awareness. Elle smells horrible, like wet dog and old tomatoes. The other wolves smell similar to Elle but fainter, and the girls smell like the copper of human blood mixed with the scent of the lavender soap. Madame Delphine had said she would try to avoid having betas protecting the hall, but she might not be successful. All I can hope is that those wolves I smell aren't powerful fighters. I don't want to injure anyone, or be injured myself . . . or die. That's always a possibility too. This is the start of a war, or maybe it's the middle or the end. I don't know, but blood has been shed and will continue to be until this is finished.

One of the lycan whips around, and I drop to the ground. He sniffs and eyes the area where I am, but I don't think he can see me.

"What's wrong?" Elle asks. She's still in her human form, but I'm not sure why she asked one of the lycans anything. It's not like he can talk to her in this form.

He paces around the circle, eyes trained in my direction.

Elle merely stands there. How can she be so calm when she knows that it would be so easy for them to kill her? One bite, and she'd be a goner. She must trust them more than I do. Or she's just braver than I've ever been.

The lycan continues to look in my direction as they wait. A howl comes from the woods on the other side of the house. The wolves standing guard outside Drayton Hall take off after it.

It's time.

I keep my distance, but no one is paying attention to me now. Elle and the others take to the water, swimming so swiftly they're back out within seconds. It might be a good thing—the water will help cover their scents. They rush to Drayton Hall, lines of black and gray and white cutting through the night. They enter the manor quickly, wrenching open the front door, and a few seconds later, a chorus of screams ring out. The lycan appear with two girls each under their massive arms. I can't tell who the girls are, but they're all screaming and crying loudly. The guards are going to hear them and come running.

I don't see Elle or the other girls, but I'm not all that worried about them. Elle may have run from Thorn, but those women like her and won't want to hurt her. The lycan men pass by me, their fur dripping wet and clawed feet covered in grass and mud, and one of the girls manages to wriggle free. The lycan snaps at her, wrapping a grimy paw around her tiny waist. If he's not careful, he's going to bite her. I can smell her from here and know he must smell that delicious scent as well. Just because we have our wits about us doesn't mean our instinct isn't to bite and feed.

Out of nowhere, a wolf collides with the lycan, and two girls go flying. I'm pretty sure that's a beta, but which one? My eyesight is perfect in the dark, and I quickly recognize Justin's dusty-colored wolf. I hope he doesn't get bit. I'd feel terrible if something happened to him, but I know the lycan won't hesitate to shred him to pieces.

I can't sit here and let them kill Justin.

The other lycan rushes away, and I dash from the privacy of the woods and into the open meadow. I have a choice to make. I can go after the girls or help the beta. But if I help Justin, the people back at camp will kill me. Laik would never understand why I saved a beta over one of his men. Another wolf shows up--one I don't recognize--and engages the lycan in battle. The fighting turns fierce, and the girls are all but forgotten. They start to run back to the house. If I join the fight, they'll get away and likely be sent to a mating house after this.

Girls it is.

I expect my body to feel awkward, but it doesn't. My mind is clear, and I know just what to do. Within seconds, I've reached the girls. I grab one and then the other with no hesitation. There are more women out here but they're in the water and swimming for their lives. I can't possibly go after them and hold on to the ones I've got. I want to save more women, but two is better than zero.

I run faster than I've ever run before, holding my prize in my arms and dodging trees and fallen logs as we go. They fight back but I'm far stronger and bigger than they are. One reaches up and grabs a fistful of hair, yanking hard. I howl with pain, and she lets go. I wonder if my howl hurts her ears. I don't really care. If I could just talk to them, they'd go with me willingly. If they knew who I was, they'd thank me. Maybe we could even go back and get more girls out.

But I'm stuck in this monstrous body.

I'm only seconds away from the rendezvous point, and once I get there, others will swoop in to get us all to safety. The girls continue screaming and clawing and crying, but I've got this.

Elle is already there with her two girls, as is the other lycan with one other claimed woman. I'm so glad Elle got out of the house that I don't even bother to hide my identity. I drop the ones I saved at her feet, and Elle meets my eyes.

"You weren't supposed to come," she says with a raised eyebrow.

I'm surprised she recognizes me because she's never seen me in this form before, but then again, she knows me well. I'm not the type to stay back and let everyone else handle the important work. I grunt at her, not wanting the claimed to know who I am. I'm not ready for that. I'm still hyper aware of their scents, but I don't have a desire to bite any of them. I hadn't expected to be so in control on my second renewal. It's a good thing though, or I would've done something dumb.

We only managed to save five claimed girls. Four cry when they see Elle, thanking her for saving them and seemingly bewildered that the lycan aren't planning to eat them, that we're actually here to help. One of the girls I grabbed, however, jumps up and tries to run away.

Elle latches onto her wrist, jerking her back. "It's not safe back there."

"Yes, it is, and you can't stop me." The girl turns, clawing at Elle's hand, and I finally catch sight of her face.

I've rescued Faye.

Chapter Twenty-Eight

We go back to the camp and wait for morning. When it comes, Laik tells everyone to wash up and pack because we need to move out.

Again.

I head over to the women's tent to help. Laik stops me, pressing his finger into my sternum until I stumble back. "I should leave you here," he threatens. "How dare you disobey orders."

I want to argue, to explain my reasoning, but that will only get me in more trouble. "I'm sorry. It won't happen again," I say.

He looks me up and down. "It's been another month, you know. Are you ready to swear your allegiance to me?"

"My allegiance is to the Resistance." I choose my words carefully. "And that includes you."

It's a round-about way of giving him respect without control. He's not my alpha, and he never will be. Let him think what he wants.

He studies me for a second and then whispers low. "I saved your life, and this is how you repay me? Embarrass me again, and see what happens."

He stalks off, and I try to forget his threats while I pack. I'm dead tired and would rather our camp stay put so we can rest, but I know it's not a good idea. We're playing with fire here. It's only a matter of time before we're found by the wolf pack and attacked. We have their alpha and five of their prized women. Everyone except for Faye seems happy with our circumstances. They do as they're told, eager to get away. Charlotte promises to take them to The Sanctuary in the panther city.

"I'm not going to some sanctuary." Faye turns her nose up at Charlotte, and everyone watches her like she's lost her mind. Maybe she has.

"It's a safe place," Elle assures her. "You don't have to marry anyone or be forced to have anyone's babies. You won't be bit. You'll get to start a new life."

She shakes her head adamantly. "I don't want it. I want to go back to the manor. I had a life there. I was going to be a beta wife!"

Laik strides up to her, getting in her face. "You will do as you are told."

"And who are you to tell me what to do?" She scrunches her nose up. "You're a dirty lycan."

His lip curls, and he strikes her to the ground. I've never seen him hit a woman before.

Elle shoves him back. "Don't you dare touch her!"

Everyone is watching now, and I catch Ryne inching closer. The expression on his face is livid, but the last thing he needs to do is get involved in this quarrel.

"Let her stay with us," I interject, inwardly wanting to kick myself. What am I thinking? I should want her gone. She's never been a friend to me. "Faye can stay with us in the wilds for a while. I'm sure that after a few weeks out here, she'll be begging to go to The Sanctuary."

Faye scowls at me but doesn't say anything, and I wonder why she's suddenly grown quiet. Maybe she's scared of Laik.

"Fine," Laik relents. "But I don't want to hear another word from this ungrateful brat until she changes her attitude."

I can't say I blame him for that. "What about the rest of the plan?" I change course. "Did the Resistance take out any key players? Did any wolves die?"

At first I think he won't say, but he finally shakes his head and storms off. I guess we weren't all that successful.

I don't stick around after that. I'm covered in dirt from the night before and wearing random, ill-fitting clothing that I dug out of the women's tent early this morning. I'm dying to get clean so I hurry over to the stream, walking a ways up so I can have some privacy. Once I'm sure I'm alone, I undress and dip into the icy water to wash the lycan from my body. I've been living out here in the wilds for two months now, and I'm growing weary of it. I look down at my body though, admiring it in a new way. I've lost some fat, gained some muscle, dealt with dirt and sweat in every pore, and transformed from human to lycan twice now. I'm so much stronger than I ever thought I could be.

And I'm so ready to be done.

Then I remember the wolf city. I remember Abi and all the other humans who still need my help. This war is just getting started.

"We need to talk." Faye appears beside me, kicking a splash of water in my face. "Right now."

I glare at her. She's the last person I want to deal with. Of all the girls we could've rescued, I can't believe my luck that she's the one I brought back. Her face is still an angry red where Laik hit her. I almost feel bad for her, but she was saved when others weren't, and here she is still causing drama.

"Can I at least get dressed, or do you want to stare at my naked, shivering body?"

"Oh please, spare me the agony. Get dressed, but don't you dare go anywhere."

I climb out of the water and yank on my pants and shirt, Faye not taking her eyes off of me.

"What do you want?" I ask.

"Take me back. I was top of the leaderboard, and Justin had already promised to marry me. I've met his parents and everything. You ruined my future."

I squeeze water out of my hair. "I saved you from an unimaginably horrible future. After this, you get to *choose* who you marry. Not be forced into it by people who don't even know you."

She crosses her arms and stalks closer to me. "What if I choose Justin?"

I want to tell her that she's not Justin's first choice and that she's not good for him, but I don't. "You and I both know that things at Drayton change quickly. You could just as easily end up in a mating house or married to someone like Thorn. Look at Elle."

"And whose fault is that? Elle would be married to Ryne right now if not for you. And I would be planning my wedding. You are the one ruining everything, not the wolves."

I close my eyes and think. She's not being rational at all. Then again, Faye never has been. "Whatever. At this point, it's not my choice. Do yourself a favor and stay out of Laik's way. Honestly, it would be better if you went to The Sanctuary. Charlotte can take you there."

"No. I'm not going to The Sanctuary, and I'm not staying here. I'm going back to Drayton Hall, and you're going to help me."

She's being ridiculous. I shove past her and head back toward the camp. She grabs my arm, jerking me back. Without thinking, I use my free hand to shove her away. It breaks her grip easily, and she flies back, landing in the water.

Oops. I forgot my own strength.

She sputters, climbing back out. "You filthy rotten lycan bitch," she yells at me. I smirk and continue walking away.

"They don't know about you and Ryne," she yells.

I spin and stare at her. She's dripping wet, a few feet behind me. "Of course they know about me and Ryne. We share a tent half the time, not that it's any of your business. They're all used to us being a couple."

"But I bet they don't know you're fated mates." She pauses to gauge my reaction, an eyebrow lifting in satisfaction. "They'd never let you stay together. They can't trust you to do what's best for the group when you'll always choose each other."

I have a feeling Laik already suspects, but he hasn't said anything. Ryne and I have been very careful to keep it a secret because she's right. If the others knew for sure, who knows what they'd do. They may kill us or use that knowledge to their advantage. Blackmail wouldn't be off the table--they could hurt me to get Ryne to do just about anything they want. Being his fated is the most wonderful feeling—I wouldn't trade it for the world, but it's also dangerous.

I can't have her blabbing.

"Faye. I know you're pissed, but this is low. You can't tell them."

"Take me back to Justin, or I will."

She's serious. I know she's beautiful, but Justin doesn't seem like the type to go for the mean girl, and I really doubt they're going to be together in the end. Then again, Faye has a way of getting what she wants, and it's been two months since I left. The summer is half gone, and I know all too well how much can change in a season.

"Fine," I relent. "Let me talk to Ryne, and we'll figure out a way to get you back."

She snorts. "Oh no. You can't talk to him."

"Why not?"

"Because he'll want to find a way to keep me away from them. He ran away, right? He betrayed his own pack. He's not going to bring me back to them."

"Actually, he was kidnapped and hasn't been allowed to return yet. He cares about his men, and if Justin really loves you, Ryne will find a way to make sure you guys are together."

Faye's face falls for a nanosecond. There's something there, like insecurity or sadness, but it's gone before I can be sure. "Fine. Talk to Ryne, but don't tell him it's because I threatened you."

I doubt I'll keep that information to myself. Ryne and I have been telling each other everything lately.

"If he sabotages this at all," she adds, "I will make sure Laik knows exactly what's going on between the two of you."

I groan, nodding. It's the best I'm going to get. "Done. Give me a couple of days, and I'll let you know our plan. Laik is intense, and he doesn't like wolves or anyone who he suspects sympathizes with them, so don't be surprised if he does what he can to prevent us from talking. But I will get you back to Justin. You have my word."

She must take that as good enough because she stalks past me, shoulder-checking me in the process. I roll my eyes and groan, wishing I could get the upper hand in this situation, but I don't see how that's possible. She's got the dirt on me and doesn't care about anyone but herself.

I hurry to finish cleaning up and follow her out of the forest. We arrive back at camp, and all the girls from the night before are sitting at a table eating breakfast. The camp is almost packed up, and I'm sure we'll be leaving in a few minutes. We've saved Faye, her friend Blair, Alyssa, Bailey, and Harlow. I don't want anyone to end up in the mating houses, but I'm glad we were able to get these women out, especially Bailey. She's got a kind heart and is super smart, but she hadn't been progressing well with the betas. I want to go to the girls and see how they are doing, but I wonder how many will see me as the enemy now.

Faye plops herself down between Blair and Alyssa, and they immediately put their heads together and whisper. Elle sits across from them with a massive smile on her face. She sees me and waves me over.

Bailey scooches closer to Harlow so I can sit between her and Elle. All the girls stop talking and stare at me.

"What?" I ask.

"You're a lycan," Bailey whispers.

"So?" I meet each of their eyes with a challenge. "I think we all know now that wolves like Thorn and Anders are the enemy, not the lycans who rescued you last night."

"We all saw what Charlotte did though," Harlow adds. She shoots a look over to where Charlotte and Knox are eating together. Guilt is written all over Charlotte's face as she watches us from afar.

I don't want to defend Charlotte, but I can't help it. "Charlotte made horrible mistakes, but she didn't mean to kill anyone, and she has control now. Really, you can trust the lycan. We're not all bad."

Faye eyes Laik on the other side of the camp. "Says you," she snaps. And she's right.

"I'm still me every other day but on the full moon, and even then, I'm still pretty much me. The first time I shifted was rough, but last night I had control. I'd never hurt anyone."

The women exchange skeptical glances, and Bailey thumps the table. "Thanks for rescuing us. I was bound for the mating house, and now I get to go to a sanctuary. I'm so excited."

That perks the others up, and they nod in agreement. Part of me is a little sad they are leaving.

"I'm not going to that sanctuary," Faye bites back. "I already talked to the boss, and he's going to let me help with the Resistance."

Elle's eyes widen skeptically, and I have to force myself to keep quiet.

"Are you sure?" Alyssa asks. "Maybe I should stay back too."

"No," Elle interjects. "You're going to The Sanctuary. Don't follow Faye's example. Faye, I don't think you should stay either. I'm going to talk to Laik. Life with the lycans is dangerous. You're much safer with the panthers."

Faye rolls her eyes. "That's funny coming from you, considering you're here with them, and one bite could kill you."

"But I'm here for a bigger cause." Elle's eyebrows knit together. "Why would you knowingly put your life in danger?"

"Because I'm not a coward. I can fight just as well as you and Poppy."

"Me too," Blair pops off. "I want to stay and help."

I open my mouth to say something, but Elle interrupts. "I'm head of the Resistance here, and I'm putting my foot down. No one stays unless they are a shifter or lycan."

Faye smirks at her, twirling a lock of her auburn hair around her finger like she knows something the rest of us don't. "We'll see about that."

Then she storms off.

I'm actually hoping that she can't convince Laik to let her stay until she goes back to Justin. But she doesn't go to Laik.

She goes to Ryne.

Chapter Twenty-Nine

In the end, Faye is the only claimed girl who sticks around. Elle was livid when she found out that Ryne and Laik both gave permission for her to stay. She argued with them for well over an hour but didn't get her way. It seems that nobody has as much power as they think they do around here, not even Elle. Ryne won't talk to me about what Faye said, but I'm sure she made similar threats to Ryne as she did to me. Of course he gave in. He's not willing to risk my life, same as I'm not willing to risk his. But why would Laik keep a snarky human girl around for no reason? He must have plans for her.

I'd take any of the other claimed girls over Faye, but they all left for The Sanctuary the next day while the rest of us moved camp again. And a week later, we moved again. And a week after that, same story. It's time we make a change because we can't keep living like this.

Until then, I'm enjoying Ryne as much as I can.

Our tent is small but perfect for the two of us. Humid summer air keeps us warm instead of the blankets we've opted to lie on top of, and he's opened a corner of the door so that we can gaze at the stars. We can see out, but it's dark enough that nobody else can see in. We're in our own little world. After the camp's last move, I gave up sleeping in the women's tent altogether to stay with Ryne. That was the first night we felt safe kissing again, and the night we took our relationship to the next level. It was gentle and perfect at first, and then it was more. So much has changed in such a short amount of time, but it also feels like I've been with him forever.

He trails his finger across my cheek, over my shoulder, and then down to his favorite places, sending lustful shivers through my body. I lean over and kiss him, and he smiles into my lips, pressing me to my back and covering me with his warmth. I'm a changed woman because of my mate. I always knew I would make love someday, but I never expected it to be so special. It's all-consuming––claiming my emotions, my body, and my very soul. He tells me it's the same for him. He looks at me like I'm the only woman in the world, touches me like nobody else exists, and confesses he'll die if he can't have me.

Tender kisses turn frantic, and I give into the blissful heat of our flesh.

Sometime later, I'm tucked under his arm. We're still and quiet, our bodies sated and our minds at ease. It's peaceful, but that peace ebbs as my thoughts return to our issues in camp. We're wasting so much time in the wilds, and as much as I want to stay cocooned in this tent with Ryne, we have a bigger mission. The longer he's away from his pack, the more people are going to need us, but he's stuck here playing house with me and keeping Laik happy.

"You need to be the alpha," I whisper to him.

"I am the alpha."

"That's not what I mean." I roll toward him and squeeze his bicep. "I'm talking about your father. I'm talking about Chicago. You need to be the King Alpha and we can't keep stalling it from happening."

He swallows hard and nods. "I know. I've known for a long time what I have to do, but it doesn't make it any easier."

"I can't imagine what you're feeling." I kiss his warm cheek and breathe him in for a minute. I wish there was something I could do to make this all simple, but there isn't. If we're going to make changes, we have to kill Thorn soon.

"His death isn't the end of it, you know," Ryne says. "Once he's gone, there will be a massive battle for his throne."

"It doesn't automatically go to you?" I thought it was implied, but I guess I shouldn't be surprised. These wolves are used to fighting to the death.

"That's not how it works. I'll have to go to Chicago to fight for the title. I'll face the most fearsome wolves from all over the continent. You know what that means, right?"

My insides clench. I can't think about him dying. My life would be over. "Well, maybe someone else could be alpha and––"

"There's no way." He shakes his head, and his long hair tickles my face. "I'll become enemy number one after Thorn is gone. This is why I've been so slow to do anything about him. I wasn't ready to put myself or my pack in that kind of danger. I can see now that I was a coward."

"I don't think you're a coward."

"Tell that to all the men and women I've failed." His voice cracks, and there's nothing I can say because he's right. My sister is dead, and my family is lost to me because of his pack and his right-hand man. But maybe when this is all over and Ryne is in charge of things, I'll get to see my parents and little brother again. Maybe everything will change. Ryne had said that he wants to allow the mating to happen by choice--whether it's women married to wolves they love or women being paid to have the children of the pack. Either would be infinitely better than what's happening now.

Ryne freezes.

"Hey, it's okay--"

"Shh," he says, sitting up slowly. "Did you hear that?"

Before I can answer, he's tearing out of the tent, shifting into his wolf as he goes. I jump up too and hurry to throw on some clothes. My heart is pounding in my chest, and my movements feel too slow. I hear the growls before I see them.

Two wolves.

They circle Ryne, and then they pounce.

The noise wakes everyone up, and one of the guards comes running. "We're under attack!"

I want to scream at him that he's too late, but there's no time for that. I need a weapon. I pick up a long stick and hurry over to what's left of the fire, holding it in.

"Please light," I mutter to myself. But it's not lighting, and I don't have time to sit around and wait for it.

"What's that going to do?" Faye appears beside me, her eyes round and hopeful. She probably thinks she's being rescued right now.

"Do you have any better ideas?" I'll admit it's not my brightest, but I don't see anything else that will make a better weapon. I want a sword or a knife.

Faye shakes her head. She has kept to herself the last few weeks and I'm pretty sure Ryne and I are the only ones who know she wants to return to the wolves. She yanks the stick from my hand and runs toward the fighting wolves. The end is glowing red but it's not on fire.

Better than nothing.

"Damn it, Faye!" I scream and run after her. Now I'm weaponless.

Our little band isn't able to turn into our lycan selves right now, but that doesn't mean we can't fight. We're small, but we're mighty––we may be able to overtake them. There are only two. The problem is that we're nearing the new moon, so that means we're weak. The wolves must know that.

Laik points a gun at the fray and starts shooting.

People scream, and I tackle Laik, the gun catapulting out of his hand and landing on the ground. "You could kill someone!"

"That's the point," he growls, throwing me off him. We don't have many firearms. They're hard to come by, even with the panthers supplying our resistance. Everything that's left is from before the wars, and most of it was destroyed.

I scramble for the gun, but Wanda beats me to it. "You want to die today?" She cackles at me, waving the gun in my face. I fully expect her to turn it on me, but she doesn't. She starts shooting at the wolves as well, but lucky for them, she's a terrible shot.

"I'm out of ammo," she whines, throwing it back to Laik.

"Yeah, and you wasted it, woman!"

She laughs and unsheathes a long knife from her belt, running head-on toward the wolves.

Elle is there now. The wolves are fighting two against two.

I look around for Joanna and Grady because we could really use his help right now, but he's nowhere to be seen. I can't believe they're not here helping. Where the hell are they?

A wolf gets his jaw around Ryne, but Ryne tosses him off, so he goes for Elle instead. She cries out when it gets her leg. It's a piercing sound that drives right to my center, but I know she'll recover. Wolves heal fast. Ryne goes for the wolf again, ripping him away from Elle and then finishes him.

Blood sprays, and the body goes limp.

The final wolf backs off with a growl but drops to its hind legs and starts to whimper.

Elle changes back to her human form, rubbing her bloodied leg. "Justin, what are you doing here?" she yells at the wolf.

I gasp. I hadn't recognized his wolf in the fray. Faye stands to my left, her burning stick hanging limp in her hands. She drops it, moving forward. Ryne stands over him, still in his wolf form as well.

Justin gives a slight shake of his head, turns, and runs away. Ryne immediately gives chase, with Faye right behind him. Elle stays behind to nurse her leg, and I groan and take off as well. I have no idea what's about to happen, but I can't let Faye get hurt, and I worry that this might be a trap for Ryne.

I've always been a good runner, and since being in the wilds, I've gotten better at dodging trees and avoiding roots. Faye runs faster than I expect, but I still overtake her. I don't stop to bother with her though. I just want to make sure that Ryne is safe.

I keep my senses tuned to the padding of his footfalls and the rustle of leaves. I'm falling behind because I can't run as fast as the wolves, but I can't give up.

All at once they stop, and I continue in the direction I last heard them. There's a clearing up ahead, and I really, really hope this isn't some trap where the wolves have Ryne cornered. I don't think I could fight them.

My saliva is useless in the middle of the month.

Just before I reach the edge of the woods, a body hits me from the side, and I go flying. I hit the ground with a thud, and for a second I see stars. A hand covers my mouth, and I jerk my head back and forth.

My vision clears.

Ryne straddles me, his eyes wide with fright.

I still, and he removes his hand, climbing off of me. He's completely naked, but I'm so used to his body by now that it doesn't faze me. He offers to help me stand, and I take it. I rise to my tiptoes and kiss him on the cheek. "Faye's right behind me," I whisper low in his ear.

He shakes his head. "She lost the trail and ran in a different direction. Elle's going after her."

"How do you know?" I ask.

He points to his head. I'd forgotten about the telepathic link, and I definitely want to know what Justin said to him, but now is not the time.

"What's going on?" I ask.

He takes my hand and leads me to the edge of the clearing. I peer through the bushes and leaves. It's another lycan camp but much bigger than ours. Several large men––lycan––patrol the area, all carrying massive guns. How did they get them? Laik acts like the few guns we have are made of gold. In the middle of the camp is a large group of people, all tied up and gagged. They look tired and beaten down. One tries to get up, but the man patrolling the area closest to him kicks him back.

Tents are set up on the far side. This looks like one of the military camps I'd seen in a book once. They're nothing like our tents.

"What is this?" I ask, keeping my voice down. "This isn't our resistance, is it?"

Ryne shakes his head. "I have no idea. But take a good sniff. Are any of them human?"

I let my senses take over. I don't smell human anywhere, just lycan.

"Why would they tie up their own kind?"

"Your guess is as good as mine, but come on, we need to get out of here before we get caught."

We retreat slowly so we don't make enough noise to attract their attention. Once I'm sure we are out of earshot, I grab Ryne's hand and pull him close to me. "I was so scared they were going to hurt you."

He chuckles. "You have little faith in my abilities."

"I have a lot of faith in your abilities, but two attacked at once, and even you aren't invincible."

He kisses my forehead. "I know."

"Did Justin say anything to you?"

"He did. Thorn wants me back, dead or alive. Justin volunteered to be on the search party. The other wolf was one of Thorn's lackeys, and Justin thinks he would've killed me if he'd gotten the chance. That right there tells you a lot about my father."

"I'm so sorry." I don't know what else to say. This isn't good.

"Justin says he and the rest of the betas are still loyal to me, but they are pretending not to be in order to keep Thorn happy." He swallows hard. "As long as I'm still alive, I'm still their alpha. Not even my father can change that."

"And what's been reported of Anders is true?"

"Justin confirmed things have gotten bad with Anders and I'm pretty sure he'll try to kill me when I go back. My betas no longer trust him, not that they ever did."

"I'm sorry."

He shrugs. "The good news is we won't have to fight alone."

"That is good news."

He tightens his hold on my hand. "The full moon will be here soon. We need a plan, and now, after seeing Justin, I think I have a good one."

Chapter Thirty

We get back to camp before I can ask Ryne to explain his plan in full, and Faye is already there, pacing like a caged tiger. She rushes up to me and drags me away from everyone.

"Where the hell is Justin?" she asks. Her hair is a mess of red around her face, and her eyes are rimmed with tears.

I hate that I'm the one to tell her this. "He's on his way back to the city."

"Why didn't you make sure he took me with him?" she hisses.

I rub my forehead. I knew Faye was going to be a problem. "Look, Justin was here trying to warn Ryne. It wasn't a good situation. I'll get you back to him, but it wouldn't have worked for us to send you now. How would you explain your sudden reappearance without having to explain about where you've been?"

"I would've lied, you idiot."

"Or you would've gotten us all killed. I'll make sure that no matter what we decide to do on the full moon, you'll be in my group. I'll get you as close to Justin's house as I can, and you can slip away."

She chews on her bottom lip, as if thinking, and then nods. "That's a good idea. His mom likes me. She'll take me in until we can figure out the next step."

I'm actually pretty surprised at that. Faye isn't exactly a sweet girl, but maybe she knows how to make it look like she is. Or is it possible she's changed?

"But if that doesn't work, your secret is out," she adds. Guess that answers that.

I gaze past her to where Ryne is arguing with Laik. The two look like they are about to come to blows, but before they do, several people enter the camp, including Madame Delphine. The fact that she traveled this far is astonishing and incredibly dangerous, but I'm too happy to see her to think about that much.

I leave Faye and rush up to her, crushing her in a hug. The woman is a motherly figure to me, and I just want her to know how much I appreciate her. She doesn't react at first, but slowly her arms come around me and tighten. Something loosens in my chest, an unburdening I've been needing. I don't know how long we stand there, but it's long enough that I start to miss my family, my father especially, and I'm no longer unburdened.

She pulls away and just looks at me without a word. Then she squeezes my hand and steps around me to give Ryne a hug.

Laik clears his throat. "What are you doing here?"

She glances over at him. "We have a monster to kill, don't we? We need a plan. We've done a decent job of rescuing some women, but we need to change the course of history if we're going to save them all."

Ryne stands a little taller. "And I know exactly how we are going to do that."

"It's a bad idea," Laik growls.

Ryne clenches his fists. "It's not. You've proven that the lycan are unpredictable. If I use my men to stage an uprising, we can kill Thorn without the risk of too many people dying."

"What are you talking about?" I ask. If Ryne's planning on leaving the lycan behind, it means he'll leave me behind as well, and I can't have that.

He turns to me. "I want to take Thorn out using the betas. If I can get Justin and my most trusted men to back me up, we can ambush my father. The festival won't be about taking girls to the mating house. It will be my return as the alpha and ending my father's tyranny. There will be a fight, but I think most of the wolves will back me up. Once Thorn is dead, we'll take out any wolves who aren't on our side and head to Chicago as a group, gathering allies along the way."

It's actually a really good plan, but Laik is glaring at him, and Madame Delphine frowns.

"You're completely leaving out the lycan," Laik scoffs.

"I'm asking that you not be involved until after I've killed Thorn and established myself as King Alpha. I don't want you in my city, but you can come with us to Chicago as our backup."

"That's the thing, Ryne. You aren't going to be the King Alpha," Madame Delphine says in a soft voice.

"Why the hell not?"

"Because the Resistance has already had a plan in place for a long time. Izaak will take over as the king, and you will remain here presiding over the Carolina Pack."

"Who's Izaak?" Laik questions.

"Elle's father. He's high up in the Resistance movement."

This is all news to me. I try to recall what I know of Elle's father, but nothing is coming to me besides what I saw of him at the last festival. He seemed like a formidable man with a strong no-nonsense type of way about him and a soft spot for his family. Elle certainly loves him, but can we trust her to be able to see past the blind spots when it comes to her own father? What if he's no better than the rest of them? Elle is still off in the woods so she isn't here right now to weigh in, but I wonder how much she knows about all this. Probably a lot more than she's let on.

"Why Izaak?" Ryne asks, his brow furrowed. "Wouldn't that cause more unrest? He's been rivals with Thorn for years. Someone new would be better."

"I'm sorry, but this plan has been in place for far longer than you have been the alpha of the Carolina Pack." It feels like a wall has gone up between mother and son, and my heart aches for them both. "We didn't know if you would be for or against your father."

"And your husband."

"He's not my husband anymore, but he will always be your father." She clears her throat and steps back. "We have to let things go on as planned. Too many people are counting on it. I do like the idea of you taking Thorn out with the help of your betas, but then you need to bring the lycan in for damage control."

"My men will never go for that," Ryne argues.

"Neither will mine," Laik says. "We're nobody's damage control."

Madame Delphine shakes her head, frustration painting her cheeks red. She points at them as she speaks. "And you two wonder why the Resistance waits until the last minute to bring you in on our plans. I don't care if you like it or not. If we are going to change the world and save women from the fate that currently exists for them, you will do as I say."

It's almost humorous watching both men stare down Madame Delphine. I know from experience how intimidating she can be. And quite frankly, she's not just talking about our city. She's talking about cities all over that need liberation. She's thinking big here, and that starts with the lycans and wolves cooperating with each other.

"I want to be the Alpha King," Ryne pushes again. "I can do far more good than Izaak. You know that. He's a fine man, but he's too wrapped up in politics and has almost as many enemies as Thorn."

"And you don't have enemies?" Laik snorts.

"Not many." Ryne glares between Laik and his mother. "My vision for the future is a fair one that I cannot enact unless I'm the one in charge."

Some may say he sounds selfish, but to me he sounds like the alpha I know him to be. Leadership runs in his veins, and he's been stomped down too many times to keep taking it.

"Ryne, can we argue about this another day? We have precious little time to make sure that we have a solid plan for the festival." Delphine gives him a pointed look.

Ryne jams his hand in his hair. "The plan will change because I'm the one going to Chicago."

"Please don't make this difficult. We can't afford to squabble among ourselves right now."

Ryne clenches and unclenches his fists, his face contorted. He's seething mad, but there's something more. There's betrayal. His own mother doesn't believe in him, and it makes me want to riot with him. "Fine," he says at last. "But this conversation is not over."

I'm so torn on what I want to happen. Part of me wants to support Ryne in this, but the other part of me really hopes he doesn't get his way. Because if he does, there's a real possibility he could die before he ever makes it to Chicago.

Chapter Thirty-One

I can feel the moon like I breathe air. I don't have to think about it—it's automatic. She grows stronger a little more each night, and so do I. We spend the time before she's full again getting everything ready for her. It's going to take the entire Resistance working together to pull this off, but it's possible. We're not just taking down Thorn. We're dismantling an entire system: a system that a lot of wolves still support.

Ryne and I decide not to confront Laik about the other lycan we saw because we're pretty sure they're not with the Resistance. There are other groups out here in the wilds, and they're not our primary concern right now. Tensions are already too high, and we need to focus on staying ahead of our enemies while building an unbreakable plan of attack.

We get together with different Resistance members several times over the following days to go over everything–weighing our options and discussing all the possible outcomes. Every last variable is accounted for—at least we hope so. Nobody's sure if Ryne's plan to use his betas is going to work, but it's the best one we've got.

Regardless, I believe in Ryne.

He wants this. I can see it in his eyes. That want is stronger than anything I've seen in him before, maybe even stronger than the love I see when he looks at me. Because that man is living with painful regrets, and this is his way to make things right again. Or at least, as close to right as he can. The damage has been done. We all know that. Nobody can fix what has happened, just like nobody can bring the dead back to life.

But someone has to make it stop.

On the day of the full moon, we split up into several groups. We're entering the city from three different points, just in case someone gets caught. The other lycan groups that are partnered with the Resistance have joined us, plus some of the lone wolves like Grady. There are far more of us than I thought. There's at least two hundred in all.

"I wish we had panthers to help us too," I say to Charlotte. She's with me, Ryne, Knox, Faye, and a few others. Joanna, Grady, and Callum are with a different group.

"That would solidify our win, wouldn't it?" She sighs. "I still don't understand why they aren't here, considering this is their battle too."

"They can't risk it," Ryne points out. "It would be seen as an act of war, and they're more inclined to hide behind the lycans now, aren't they?" He's been conflicted about them in the past, but he now thinks they're cowards for skirting around the treaty. I can't say I blame him. "We don't need them anyway."

Knox rolls his eyes and takes a long swig from his canteen. "Whatever you say, boss."

There's a friction between the two men that's grown by the day. I can't quite put my finger on it exactly, but I can sense it's there.

"We're getting closer," Wanda says. "Time to shut your traps."

I glare at her back as she continues to lead us down the forest path. I don't like Laik, but I really don't like Wanda. At this point, I'd take him leading us over her, but he's coming in from a different direction. It's all part of the plan. We have to split up our strongest fighters, just in case. We can't have any weak links.

For the next hour, everyone stays quiet. There are wolves patrolling the area, watching for us. I thank my lucky stars, yet again, that my lycan DNA makes it hard for them to sense or track me, but having Faye and Ryne with us is a big liability. We have to be extra careful.

I also thank my lucky stars that we're not crossing the bridge again—that was given to Joanna's group. No, we're coming in one of the back ways, similar to how Knox and I left the city in the first place. There's an old highway nearby that's been broken into pieces, and every once in a while, we can see it through the trees.

When we pass by one of the villages, I find myself looking at it a little too long. It's not my home, and my family isn't there, but I can imagine they are. I can see myself climbing the trees and working in the fields. Hiding out indoors during the full moons, expecting the wolf shifters to protect me from the evil lycan.

My eyes fill with hot tears. If they could see me now, I don't even know if my family would want anything to do with me. Maybe Papa. Probably Evan. But definitely not Mama. She was never one to step outside the lines, and associating with a lycan would be out of the question.

The tears fall, and Ryne squeezes my hand. He doesn't ask if I'm okay —he knows I'm not. And he doesn't ask me why I'm crying. Being fated to him is similar to being beholden to the moon. I couldn't stop it if I tried. It's who I am now.

Wanda picks up the pace, and nobody complains. The sun has just set, and the moon is still behind the horizon, but it won't be much longer. Once that light peeks over the horizon we're goners. It grows darker, and we start to run. It doesn't matter if we're monsters when we enter the city, but the farther we can get away from the villages, the better.

"Are you sure you want to do this?" Ryne whispers to me one last time. He's asked it before, and I've done the same. I don't respond because he already knows my answer.

There's no turning back now.

We come to the first house and stop in a cropping of nearby trees. "This is it," Wanda says. "Don't let the Resistance down, or I'll kill you myself."

"Gee--nice pep talk." I roll my eyes.

I know this house on the outskirts of the city. It's Justin's family home, located on the river. They have a pontoon waiting for us on their dock. We run to it and climb aboard, staying silent as Ryne starts the engine. This will get us downtown the fastest, and we need to be fast if we're going to get into position before the moon rises.

At the last second, Faye jumps off the boat and sprints for the house.

"What are you doing?" Wanda hisses after her.

"It's okay." I hold up my hands. "Let her go. She never wanted to fight. She just used us to get back to her beta wolf."

I can tell Wanda wants to tear after her and pull her back by her hair, but we're running out of time. Faye disappears around the corner of the house and is quickly forgotten. We have way more important things to worry about than her.

As if reading my thoughts, Ryne looks up toward the starry sky where a faint light is hovering near the horizon, and he winces. "I'm going to use the highest speed. Everybody hang on."

We start by bouncing across the waves to soon flying across them. It's going to draw attention to our boat, but hopefully not too much. The Buck Moon Festival is tonight, and the July heat will linger all night long. My skin is sticky from it, but also from my lycan--she's ready to be released. I can feel her digging at my muscles and heating my blood.

When we get to the dock, two guards come running.

"Prince Ryne?" One of them lets out a gasp. "You're back?"

The other gives our party a curious glance, his lip curling when he catches our scent.

"You will speak of this to no one," Ryne says hastily. "I'm still your alpha, and you cannot defy me."

"But--"

"Unless you wish to fight for my title right now?" He raises an eyebrow. "I'll admit a delta has never been alpha before, but there is a first for everything."

"I would never," one says as the other shakes his head. Then they bow to their alpha.

"Now tell me if the festival has started," Ryne says, and they nod. "Is my father there yet?" They nod again.

"You both stay and watch this boat. Make sure nobody takes it," he instructs them. They don't argue in the slightest as we scramble from the boat and up the dock, leaving them behind.

Wanda's eyes are wide and angry, but she doesn't say anything. Knox and Charlotte exchange an unreadable glance, and the other two lycan stare at the alpha wolf with newfound interest--probably because Laik doesn't have this kind of power even though he claims to be their alpha. It's clear to me now that he's taken his power by force and nothing else. He makes people pledge loyalty to him, but it's only words. He must hate that the wolves have something he'll never have.

Our group is supposed to wait nearby until Ryne gives the signal that it's time to move. I don't like waiting on the sidelines and want to go in there to kill Thorn myself, but I've never taken a life, and I'm not sure I would have the guts to do it. It's better if Ryne does it. His pack needs to see he's still the one in power. We'll come in as reinforcements.

This will change everything.

The other groups are assembling outside the festival as well, but at different vantage points. Madame Delphine and Elle are going to sever the phone lines to the city and plan to take off the moment Thorn is dead. They have to go to Chicago to deliver the news and make sure Izaak takes the throne. All of the packs under Thorn's rule will feel the moment he is dead, but they won't know what happened or why. Brawls will break out, but it's important to the Resistance that Elle's father is the one to gain favor and become the ruling family. Anyone else, and we could be in an even worse situation than we already are. Deep down, I fear it won't be that easy. If Ryne is right, and Izaak has a lot of enemies, then he'll face challenges not only to take the throne, but to keep it.

If things don't work out, Ryne is fully prepared to go to Chicago. He hasn't told me as much, but I know him, and I know he will do what needs to be done.

The festival is happening in the same park where the spring one took place. There are no weddings this time, but there is dancing underway. The lively orchestra music filters through the trees as we get into position.

Ryne gives me a tight hug and whispers in my ear. "No matter what, I want you to stick to the plan."

I don't agree or say anything. He should know me better than that. This plan isn't perfect, and neither are the people implementing it, so if need be, I'll throw it all aside like a scrap of paper. He's the same, and maybe that's why fate put us together. He presses a kiss to the top of my head, squeezes my hand, and then he's gone, dashing through the trees.

"Do you feel that?" Wanda sighs blissfully. "It's almost time for our renewal."

I find the best shadow I can and strip down to my underwear. I doubt I'll still be in the city when the moon sets tomorrow morning, but just in case, I want to have clothing and shoes somewhere waiting for me. I'm still not used to all this nudity and doubt I ever will be.

Just as I finish undressing, the moon makes her appearance, and my bones crack.

Chapter Thirty-Two

I stand taller and broader in this form, and my senses come alive with pristine clarity. My thoughts are my own. It's better than it was last time and completely different than it was on my first renewal. I still feel like myself. And what's more--I don't feel like a monster. I feel like a goddess. I'm powerful and free and amazing.

I like it.

The park is huge, and the festival is taking place in the center. We're in a cluster of trees for cover, but that's all. There's not much to keep us from being discovered, and I'm sure this place is crawling with guards, not to mention all the wolves here to attend the festival.

One wrong move, and it's over before it even starts.

I look to the others, thankful that we're all keeping still in our new forms, waiting. It's not easy to wait when we're like this, and it's only Knox's second renewal, but he seems to be holding up okay.

I stay the shadows and wait for Ryne's signal. Once he howls, then we'll howl back and descend on the party. But what if Ryne never howls? I tell myself to be patient, but time crawls by slowly, and I'm antsy for action. I feel like something should've happened by now. What if he needs my help?

I can't wait.

I can't get a good enough view of the festival, and I don't like it, so I dig my claws into the thickest tree of the group and climb. The others follow my lead, which wasn't my intention. I tell the lycans nearest me to stop through our telepathic link, but they ignore me, and I can't exactly make them do anything.

Before I know it, I'm in the tops of the trees with the others below me, all scrambling to get a better view, but I forget them and watch the scene on the stage. It's still hard to see, but I know it must be Ryne in a heated battle with his father. Snarls and thumps sound regularly over the orchestra music, but the view is obscured by the beta wolves who are crowding. Someone screams, and the music stops. It takes a minute for people to realize what's going on, but once they do, they're quick to run toward the stage.

Suddenly, a wolf goes flying out of the middle of the crowd and lands with a thud on the grass. Nobody moves to help and they all back away. There's a ripple of confusion in the crowd. A few of them shift. I squint, and a calm understanding washes through me at the same time as complete horror. It's Ryne--he's not moving.

My heart plummets.

I leap from the tree, landing hard on my feet, but it doesn't hurt. A few men around me cry out, but I ignore them and rush for Ryne, praying that he's not dead. I reach him at the same time that a giant black wolf with a white stripe across his nose lands near him. He snarls and leaps for Ryne, his jaws open, going for the neck. I've seen this move too many times before. If he reaches Ryne, he'll tear his throat right out.

I rush in front of Ryne, my own jaws snapping. Thorn crushes me on top of Ryne, and I flail, not knowing which end is up. My jaws connect with flesh above me, and I clamp down, hoping that my venom will kill Thorn. All at once, I'm thrown in the air and land on my stomach as my face snaps down on the ground, causing stars to flash behind my eyes.

I shake my head and crawl onto all fours. Ryne still lies on the ground, blood pouring from various wounds. Thorn stands over him, about to go in for the kill. He's determined, and nothing will stop him, not even a lycan. A sword glints on the ground, and I don't know how it got there, but I don't hesitate.

I grab the sword in my clawed hands and rush for Thorn. We trained hard with swords at Drayton Hall, and I remember my lessons on using solid footing. It's different being in this form, but it's still familiar enough that I know what to do. I raise the sword over my head, but before I can bring it down, someone collides with me from the side. We both hit the stage, and the sword clatters out of my hand.

The wolf snaps his jaws at me, and I growl. I only need to get one bite in to sign his death warrant. It won't kill him instantly, but it will slow him down enough that I can finish the job. But he's good. He manages to avoid my teeth. Out of the corner of my eye, I glimpse the sword just beyond my reach. I wiggle to the side and lurch over like I'm going to bite his paw, and the distraction is enough for me to grab the sword. I snatch it up and drive it right into the wolf's heart.

He goes limp, and I shove him off of me, leaping back up.

Ryne has gotten to his feet and is fighting with Thorn again, but he's weak and is losing badly. They're in their wolf forms, but I know exactly what I'm seeing, a father and son fighting to the death. My heart shatters. Ryne never should've had to do this. It's not fair, and now he's going to die at his father's hands.

No.

I won't let that happen. I can't.

I rush toward them, raise my sword, and arc it toward Thorn's neck. It slices hard, and hot blood spurts in all directions. His wolf body crumples to the ground, his snarling head landing a few paces away. I don't think I can cry in this form, but if I was my normal self, I know I'd be sobbing.

Ryne collapses on the other side of his father's corpse, and I rush for him. There is a huge bite on his flank, blood matted with fur, and horror sets in when I realize that it's a lycan bite.

My lycan bite. I didn't bite Thorn as intended.

I bit Ryne.

Chapter Thirty-Three

He's not dead yet. He's not dead yet. He's not dead yet.

It's a mantra that rings through my mind as I watch Ryne, while breaking into a million razor-edged pieces. Lycan venom takes time to kill a wolf--two or three days. But it's not Ryne's only wound, and the pain he's going to experience will undo us both. The compassionate thing to do would be to end his life now, to spare him from his fate. But I can't. I release my own howl--an ugly screech that echoes into the night. My insides feel hollow. I know I've killed Thorn, but when Ryne dies, I'll be alone.

I gather up his wolf body and run into the frenzied crowd. The other lycans have descended, and the world is in pure chaos. I don't care about any of that though. I only want to spend time with Ryne away from everyone else before he dies. A few wolves fall into step with me, and I automatically growl. But I recognize Justin and Nico, and I swallow hard. Are they going to kill me for this? Do they understand it was an accident? I can't forgive myself, I never will, so I can't expect them to either.

They were loyal to their alpha to the end, and here they are, loyal still. We run together, the three of us with Ryne's limp body in my arms. Pain wells in my chest, but I can't lose it yet. I need to wait until I'm human again. Not as much time has passed as I thought. We still have hours before the moon sets.

The other lycans are wrangling the crowd now. The next part of the plan is in full swing, but I can't think about that right now. All I can think about is Ryne.

He's still alive.

He's still alive, and I'm going to keep him that way as long as I can.

We manage to get out of town without incident and escape into the woods near the village we had passed earlier. It's exhausting, and my lycan body isn't as strong as I expected, but I don't even care. I have to get to privacy. I catch sight of a clearing and run to it, finally letting myself stop.

I carefully lay Ryne on the ground and assess his wounds. It's so hard with my overly large lycan hands and sharp claws. Tears course down my gross snout, and I sit back on my haunches. Everything about me is wrong right now. This isn't *me*!

Justin and Nico both turn back into humans and push me aside. They must know who I am or at least suspect it because they don't seem bothered that I'm here. At least I have that. I'm grateful they don't act as if they're going to hurt me because I couldn't stand to fight one of them.

"I'm going to run into the village and see if they have bandages," Nico says. I nod since I can't respond, and he takes off, shifting into his wolf as he goes.

Justin just stares at Ryne. "You know, we really should just put him out of his misery."

I shake my head fiercely.

"Poppy. He's going to die slowly and painfully. You really want him to suffer?"

I don't respond. I don't want to accept that Ryne's going to die. He can't. Not yet.

Justin looks around and grabs a large stick. "Fine, if you won't do it, then I will." He raises it high over his head.

I howl and throw myself over Ryne. Justin just glares at me, but I don't move. I won't let him hurt my mate. Maybe I'm selfish, or maybe I'm foolish, but I can't accept that this is the end. Ryne can't die. He just can't.

Ryne whimpers and twists, and then he shifts back into his human body. He's naked and vulnerable, but it allows me to get a better look at his wounds. They're worse than I thought. The angry bite mark on his torso festers, and he clutches at it but doesn't regain consciousness. I stay where I am, fully prepared to fight Justin off if I must.

A few minutes later, Nico jogs up empty-handed. "Poppy, you have to see this."

I want to ask what "this" is, but of course I can't. I can't even argue with him. I gather Ryne back up in my arms. I would never be able to do this as a human, but as a lycan it's easy. It would also be easy to end his pain. It would be as quick as a kiss.

"Leave him with Justin. We'll be back in a second," Nico says.

I give a fierce shake of my head. Nico looks between me and Justin, who has stayed strangely quiet. I long to tell Nico what Justin attempted to do while he was gone, but of course I can't. Nico is smart though. He assesses Justin with a scowl but doesn't address it.

"Fine. Follow me," he says, motioning for us to get up.

I lift Ryne again, and this time his eyes open, and he blinks rapidly. "Poppy?" His voice is scratchy with anguish. "Poppy––" He coughs, blood splatters down his chest, and then he passes out again.

"Once he's dead, the alpha bond will break, and the betas will begin to fight over our pack," Justin says to Nico. "Your father will likely win the spot. Are you sure you don't want to go back for that?"

Nico laughs bitterly. "I'd rather not see that, but thanks." He nods toward the direction he came from. "Now, come on before they're gone."

I'm curious who he's talking about. Tucking Ryne closer to my body and ducking under the low-hanging branches, I follow him as quietly as I can. He and Justin shift back into their wolves and slip through the forest like water through a brook. It's so natural and easy for them. I soon find that it's the same way for me, despite Ryne's dripping blood that tickles my senses. The moon's power is stronger than anything I've felt before.

That's not true.

I've felt grief much stronger than this.

And heartache. I'm feeling that now.

And a little bit of denial.

After a few minutes, we come upon the water's edge and duck into the tall grass to watch. There's a large boat, with lycan standing on the shore. The moonlight seems to favor them compared to the humans they're with.

Wait, why are they with humans?

This was never part of the plan. Then again, I don't recognize any of the lycan. Several of the humans are already on the boat, crying. Another lycan approaches, dragging two humans with him. They're women I don't recognize. Could they be saving them from the mating houses?

They must be.

I start to relax, and then the lycan bears down on the women and bites them both in quick succession. They scream, and my world flips upside down.

Chapter Thirty-Four

I have to stop them. But I'm holding Ryne, and he's losing blood quickly. Do I save these women? Can I save them? It might be too late, but I can't just watch and do nothing. before I can make my decision, the last of them are on the boat, and they're moving out. We sink back into the shadows. The wolves growl, as do I. In this, we're together.

I want to kill those lycan. They took the choice from those women. It wasn't an accident. It was planned. How long has this been going on? A memory surfaces––the other group of lycan Ryne and I saw in the woods a few weeks ago. They'd had several lycan with them who were tied up. They smelled like lycan to me at the time, but maybe they were humans who were on their way to their first renewal? They could have easily been people who'd been bitten on the previous full moon. I know what it's like to feel your life draining slowly away between full moons. Imagine having to go through that knowing your bite wasn't an accident but was intentional.

I look to the wolves and hold Ryne up to them. They nod in understanding. We have to tend to Ryne's wounds before we can do anything else. He can't travel much farther, so I move away from the shoreline to a quiet place in the trees and sit with him while they go. I don't know how long it takes for them to get medical supplies because I get lost looking at the man I love––the man I've sentenced to an early and horrific death.

I can't say goodbye to him. Not yet. Not like this while I'm still trapped in this monster's body.

They return, wearing clothes and carrying supplies. Faye is with them, holding hands with Justin. I guess she wasn't lying after all. She gives me a little wave and a sad smile. The men kneel before us and get to work patching Ryne's wounds. Normally he'd have healed on his own by now, but the lycan venom must be slowing down that process.

He cries out in his sleep when they stitch him up, the shiny needle and black thread piercing through his skin like claws. Then they apply ointment and wrap bandages around the rest of the wounds.

"Where to?" Nico asks, and Justin raises his eyebrow. "What? I'm not leaving my alpha until I have to."

"Same," Justin says grimly.

So I pick Ryne up, and together the five of us head toward the lycan camp. It's going to take a few hours of walking, and I have no idea what to expect when I get there, but I can't imagine things could get any worse than they already have.

The camp is in disarray when we arrive just after the moon sets. I hand Ryne off to Justin and Nico right before my body transitions to its human form. Normally I'd be happy about that, but I can't think about anything except Ryne right now. I hurry and slip into some clothing and go looking for help, the two men follow close behind.

Our plan didn't go as we'd hoped, considering Ryne's state, but at least Thorn is dead. I've never killed before, and I never want to do it again, but part of me is glad I was the one to do it. Ryne never should've had to kill his own father, And I'd do anything to save Ryne.

I shake my head, angry at myself for the thought. I didn't save Ryne. That's the last thing I did. I'll never forgive myself for my mistake. I ignore all the craziness in camp and find the medic tent still set up.

We slip in, and the guys set Ryne down on a cot. I cover him up with a blanket and smooth his hair back from his face. A body slumps down next to mine.

"What happened to him?" Callum asks. He gives Nico and Justin a skeptical look, his nostrils flaring.

"I bit him by accident." I cringe and look away.

Callum puts an arm around my shoulder. "I'm so sorry. Is there anything I can do?"

I wipe the tears that dot my face. "I know it's supposed to be painful. Can you give him something?"

"Yeah, let me see what I can find."

"You should put him out of his misery," Justin says again, sinking onto the cot across from us.

I shake my head fiercely. "No. What if you're wrong, and the venom doesn't actually kill him?"

"It will. No one has ever survived."

"Maybe. But you usually kill them before they even have a fighting chance, don't you?" They don't answer. "Well, I'm going to give him that chance."

"Fine," he grinds out. "But don't come crying to me when he's in so much pain you can't stand watching it."

I can feel Justin's anger, and I know it's deeper than that. He's heart-broken too. Nico still doesn't speak. His eyes are closed, and he's frozen in place, as if he's trying to imagine he's anywhere but here.

The tent flap opens, and several more people enter. I don't even bother to look up. I only have eyes for Ryne.

"What the hell did you do?" Laik booms and I jump. He grabs me by my hair and pulls me from the tent, throwing me to the dirt. Everyone surrounds us, but Nico and Justin stay by the tent door, protecting the entrance to Ryne.

I jump up and spin on Laik. "I killed Thorn. Wasn't that the plan?"

He jams his hand through his filthy hair. "No. The plan was for Ryne to kill Thorn and take control over his pack again. Do you realize what a mess you made back there?"

"But Ryne--"

"And now we have to leave the territory because there's no telling who will win the battles for alpha and what they will do. Ryne was more inter-ested in protecting his soldiers than trying to hunt us down out here. How do we know the next son of a bitch won't be?" He shakes his head violently. "I'm certain that there's going to be an extensive manhunt to find whoever killed the Alpha King."

"But Ryne's not dead yet. No one should be taking over for his pack."

Laik glares at me. "They know he's on his way. They saw the bite, Poppy! We had to retreat because Anders all but incited a riot."

I glance at Justin and Nico. "You two should go back. Fight for your alpha."

Justin shakes his head. "Nope. You decided to keep him alive. I'm staying with him until he dies."

"Me too," Nico says. "And besides, I'm happy being a beta. I don't want to be an alpha, and I won't fight my father to get it."

I take in the rest of the crowd. Faye sits down. Charlotte and Knox hover behind her. Joanna and Grady stand near the entrance of the tent. There's a funny look on Grady's face—like he's both heartbroken and relieved at the same time.

"Kill him now. We have to move, and we can't be slowed down by a dying wolf," Laik says.

I stand and face Laik. "I'm sorry, who put you in charge? I don't remember swearing allegiance to you, and you're not a real alpha."

"What did you just say to me?"

"You're not! Lycan don't have pack bonds like the wolves do. There's a difference between loyalty and blood, and you know it."

He takes a long breath, a blood vessel popping along his sweaty forehead. "Delphine and Elle are headed up to Chicago to smooth things over and to make sure Elle's father takes control as the King Alpha. That leaves me as the leader of the Resistance down here."

"Wouldn't that be Derek?" I scoff, thinking of the intelligent panther who would be a far better leader than Laik. It's too bad the panthers didn't join us because it could've changed things for the better.

"Do you see that spineless panther anywhere?" Laik shouts in my face, and I rear back. He thinks he's the leader now, huh? Rage rises in my chest as I remember what the lycan were doing on the banks of the river.

"Okay. Leader. Explain the fact that several lycan were turning humans against their will tonight."

Laik's face is smooth and expressionless. "What are you talking about?" he asks, but there's obvious deciet in his tone, and I want to slap him for them.

Wanda cackles. "She's no dummy, that one. You've discovered our master plan."

"Shut up, Wanda," he spits out, and she clams up.

"What's your master plan?" I ask. No one around me seems confused. Callum drops his head, and several others back up.

Laik sighs. "The only way we can defeat the wolves is with an army. Humans are useless."

"Humans are useless?" I gasp. "Their freedom is what you're fighting for!"

"In the future, sure. But right now, humans are either collateral damage, or they're weapons. Which would you rather have in a war?"

The realization of what he's saying hits me hard. "So you're forcing them to become lycan? How is that any better than the mating houses?" My eyes water, and my fists clench. I want to kill him for this.

"At least then they can defend themselves," Charlotte says with a shrug. "Being a lycan isn't so bad. I'd rather be a lycan than stuck in my old life."

I glare at her. "You agree with him?"

"The wolves need to be annihilated, Poppy. Surely you see that?" Knox says. He straightens next to her and puts an arm around her shoulders.

Justin and Nico have gone stony still, but they're staring at the lycans with as much hatred in their eyes as I currently feel. This is evil. Pure evil.

I shake my head. "Absolutely not. The point of the Resistance is to take out the bad wolves, not the entire race."

"Well, that's our plan." Laik rolls his eyes as if he's talking to a naïve child. "I'm sorry if you don't like it. The wolves who join us will be spared, but none of the rest. We need to move. If you don't kill Ryne this instant, I will."

"You can't!"

"You're not thinking clearly." He sneers. "I know what you are. I've known what you were since the day I brought you back here." He swings his arms wide and looks at the others. "Don't listen to her. She'll never be fair when it comes to that dog. She's his fated mate!"

Chapter Thirty-Five

I hurry to the entrance of the tent to stand with Justin and Nico. Justin shifts to his wolf form and growls, and Nico takes on a fighter's stance. "You will not touch him," he spits.

Laik laughs, but he shouldn't. He's no longer a lycan, and these men could rip him to shreds.

"So you've known all this time about me and Ryne, and you said nothing?" I give him a glare.

"I was waiting for the perfect timing. Are you really so dumb that you'd think none of us knew about your stunt at the last festival? I gave you so many chances, Poppy. I should've known you were never going to be reasonable until someone manned up and killed your mate." Laik's followers nod their heads as if he's making perfect sense.

"No matter what happens to Ryne, I will never follow you," I say slowly, enunciating every word. "I refuse to buy into a plan where you force people to do something against their will, no matter how noble you think it is. What you are doing is sick and wrong."

Laik closes his eyes. "Fine. You and your little wolf buddies can stay here and fight off the Carolina Pack on your own. We're moving out." He points at me, his finger jabbing into my sternum. I stand tall, not giving even an inch. "You are no longer part of the Resistance."

"That's not your choice to make." I glare. "In fact, I could say the same to you."

Laik snorts. "You're not in charge of anything."

"I am now. Madame Delphine and Elle left for Chicago and I'm guessing they don't know about your plans or what you've been doing behind the scenes, do they?"

His lips curl into a predatory smile. "They don't need to know everything."

It takes all my self-control not to scream. "The Resistance is not about what you're doing. We are about saving people from slavery, not putting them right into another form."

"Poppy's right," Nico says. "We will follow her and not you." Justin pads his feet in the dirt and bares his teeth.

"Me too." Callum surprises everyone, moving to stand next to Nico.

Laik begins to pace in front of us, breathing hard for a few minutes. "Fine. You pathetic lot can stay here and nurse your pitiful wolf. But if you don't come with us now, don't bother searching for us later. We will kill you."

He turns and storms away, Wanda following closely behind him. Knox and Charlotte give me one last look, and then they go too. My heart hurts a little to watch them walk away, but I find I'm not all that surprised.

Grady and Joanna approach us. "Why won't you kill him?" Grady asks, his voice cracking. "I don't like it, but it's the right thing to do."

"Because I have to believe there is some hope." And maybe I'm foolish to think so. He may have days left or hours. And I'm signing up to watch.

Grady glowers. "I can't do this anymore. I can't sit around and watch this place fall apart. Ryne tried to kill me, and even though I forgive him, it doesn't mean I'm okay with what happened. I'm sorry, Poppy, but we're going with our best chance of survival, and that's with Laik."

"He's a monster." I throw up my hands.

"So is he," Grady says, pointing to Ryne's tent. "So are you. So am I. None of us are innocent anymore, but my job is to keep my mate alive, and I'll do whatever it takes to give Joanna a future."

He turns and slumps away. Joanna stares at me for a long moment, her eyes red and shining with tears. I want to beg her to stay, but I know I can't. She wouldn't leave Grady any more than I'd leave Ryne. She rushes forward and wraps me in a tight hug. As I breathe her in, the dam breaks loose. I finally let myself cry. For her, for me, and for all we've lost.

"Take care of yourself, Poppy," she says shakily. then she turns and runs into the early morning darkness, disappearing into the woods.

I go back to sit with Ryne, staring at him as he sleeps restlessly, and then I look at my companions. They've all joined me, huddled around our dying friend. From the looks on our faces, none of us know what's going to happen.

"We're here because it's the right thing to do," I say, gathering my strength. "Because the one thing we have left in this forsaken world is our freedom to choose, and we're not going to choose the wrong side."

"How do we know what side is right and wrong?" Callum asks. "It seems like they're all wrong if you ask me."

"Because we refuse to take away that choice. Because we believe in freedom and in helping the people who need it most. And that whether you're born a wolf or a human, have become infected like I have, or whatever you are—you shouldn't have to hurt innocent people to get what you want."

They all nod, and it gives me the first spark of true hope that I've felt in a long time.

"So what now, boss?" Faye says, and I just blink at her for several moments. She's being serious. There's no snark, no hatred, no tricks. She means it. She's been quiet and her words shake me out of my misery for the tiniest second.

"You sorta signed yourself up for this," Nico chuckles.

"Right . . ." My voice trails off, and I take a moment to gather my thoughts, looking each of them in the eyes. There are only five of us, plus Ryne, but we're all stronger than we ever could've imagined. And I'm proud of us. "I'll be honest. I don't know what's next, and I don't know how to be a leader. But I've come to realize that the best leaders put others first, and they care about their people." I smile softly. "Believe it or not, I care about all of you, and I'm going to fight for your rights just as hard as I'm going to fight for all the men and women who need our help."

I point to Ryne. "But first, we need to save him." I can tell they want to argue, but they don't. "Listen, maybe it's wishful thinking, but we've got to try." I widen my eyes. "The Carolina Pack needs Ryne, and you know it."

"You're right," Justin says, "but I don't know how you can possibly save him. He's as good as dead."

I shake my head. "I refuse to accept that. And it's not because I'm in denial, and it's not because I love him, which I do. It's because he's the strongest alpha that his pack has ever known. He's still alive despite all he's been through tonight. He's trying—he's fighting—so we have to too."

They give me pitying looks. They don't believe it's possible.

"Okay," Justin gives in. "We'll try."

"We're the Resistance now," I say, taking this small victory and running with it. "Not Laik and his people. Not the panthers. Us. Now it's time we start acting like it." I stand up and brush myself off. We have a lot of work to do and countless people depending on us. "Let's get started."

FALL OF THE HARVEST MOON

NEW WORLD SHIFTERS
BOOK FOUR

NINA WALKER

KIMBERLY LOTH

Prologue

People have been taking choices away from me for as long as I can remember. I was raised by a community that treated me as less than everyone else. I was Abigail, the unimportant claimed girl everyone would soon forget. Not Abi, the girl who had ambitions for herself. When I came to the wolf city, I had foolish hopes that things would change for the better, but they only changed for the worse. Despite the lessons in pack hierarchy, I had no real idea what was in store for me, and when I learned what I had to do, I didn't sleep for three days.

How could I be expected to fight for a beta when I hated them? To become the wife of somebody I didn't love? To raise children with a man who would most likely frequent brothels, only to set me aside once I aged beyond fertility? Not that it mattered——none of those men liked me any more than I liked them. I was never going to get engaged. That was a fate left to the prettier and more flirtatious girls. Flirting has never been my strength. Even now, when I know it might get me kinder men, I still can't figure it out.

I'm actually lucky to still be alive, considering what I've done. But maybe it would've been better to die instead of rotting in the mating house. Cutting through Joanna's and Grady's ropes had been more than just an act of setting them free; it had been an act of defiance. My personal rebellion. I took back my power in that moment. Finally making a choice worth living for.

That's the memory I cling to every time I think I can't possibly endure another day in this mating house. I stare at the ceiling above my bed. There's a water stain that looks like a bunny rabbit. We raised rabbits back home. I was never allowed to get attached to them because they were food, but I still liked cuddling them.

"Earth to Abi." Jasmine snaps her fingers in front of my face, and I startle. "Are you alive in there?"

I blink and refocus on the task at hand, preparing myself for the day ahead. I need to get up and get going. The older women make the wolf city run, but we mating-house girls make the wolf city grow. I sit up and stretch, reaching for the dress I had laid out earlier when I had come to bed. It's short and form-fitting, easy to get on and off.

"Sorry," I mutter. "Can you pass me the lipstick?"

Jasmine rummages around in a makeup bag and retrieves the lightest color. She knows I hate the dark stuff. Of the twenty girls who live in our mating house, she's my closest friend here. She's funny, kind, and optimistic. And she's also so deep in denial about what's going on here that her mind isn't always with us. Some of the others make fun of her for it, but it makes me want to protect her. She's been in the house longer than anyone else and is getting close to retirement. The worst part is the way she talks about her children as if she'll see them once she leaves this house. She must know it's not true, but still, she pretends.

"Do you think Henry and Luke are together? I had them in the same year. Irish twins. I bet they're together. They're probably reading by now. Do you think they know they're brothers?"

I swallow hard and then smile at her. "I'm sure they do."

It's a lie. I'm certain that they're being raised like all the other wolf shifter boys, grouped by age until they're old enough to be ranked and given assignments. On the rare occasion that a girl is born, she's whisked away to Chicago to be raised with the other lunas, never to be seen again. The only exceptions are the children the betas have with their wives. Motherhood isn't something we mating-house girls will ever get to experience, no matter how many Henrys and Lukes we have. Those are the sixth and seventh names I've heard her talk about. I wonder how many kids she's had in total, or if she even knows.

Jasmine hums wistfully to herself and leans toward the mirror, applying a swipe of mascara across her already dark lashes. It makes her brown eyes impossibly beautiful. Why didn't she get picked for a beta's wife? She's so pretty, so kind and sweet. She pats her belly gently. "I think I might be pregnant again." Her voice is filled with excitement. "I love being pregnant."

Her pronouncement makes my own stomach twist. I knew what I was getting myself into, and still, this is worse than I could've imagined. And the rumor is that our house isn't even the worst one. Here, the men are punished for being violent toward us, though we still go to bed with bruises some nights, and there are limits to how many men can frequent our beds each day. Some of the other houses have no rules or limits. It's wrong. It's all so wrong.

"I hope I never get pregnant," I say with conviction. What I don't say is that giving up children against my will to be raised by other people would be worse than giving up my body to these men who care nothing for me. To give the pack a child would be to give them what they want, like some kind of sick reward for what they're doing here. I know that having a child means I'd be able to leave the mating house for the duration of the pregnancy, but still. I don't want to have a child just to give it up.

"Oh, but pregnancy is the best," Jasmine argues. "You get to live in the fancy house, and they treat you like a queen for the entire nine months, plus a month after while you're healing from delivery."

I scoff. "And isn't delivery terrible? Some women die."

She shrugs as if death wouldn't be the worst thing, but given the circumstances, maybe it wouldn't be. She finishes with her makeup and helps me with my hair, and we go down to the parlor room where we're to meet our "dates" for the evening.

"Abigail..." Madame Lindy, our housemistress, stops me at the stairs with a cross expression. She's never been very kind to me, and I wonder what I did wrong now. Yesterday, she scolded me for trying to get out of my date. But it's not my fault that I ate something bad and puked all day. Thankfully, my date was quick, and I didn't throw up on him. Though, that would've been amusing. "You're a week late. Why didn't you say something?" She raises a notebook as if to hit me with it.

"Late to what?" My stomach twists again, and I wonder what it is I've been eating.

Jasmine claps her hands, and Madame Lindy shushes her. Jasmine quiets and fusses with her dress.

"Your period is late, Abi. You were due to start seven days ago."

Her words ring in my ears. They don't make sense. I'm not late. I can't be late. But then again, I haven't been keeping track––I didn't want to face the reality of a late menstrual cycle. My whole body goes rigid, and my knees weaken. *I'm late . . .*

"Back upstairs." She points. "No dates for you until we can confirm that you're not pregnant."

"And if you are, you know what that means," Jasmine practically cheers.

"A baby," I say, my voice flat and emotionless, not at all reflecting the torment I feel inside. I can't be pregnant. I just can't be. I've only been here for three months, and that seems too fast for it to have already happened.

"It means the good life!" Jasmine giggles manically, turning on our mistress. "I think I'm pregnant too, Madame Lindy. Should I go upstairs with Abi?"

"No," our mistress barks back. "You're not due to bleed for another two weeks."

Jasmine grabs her breasts and flops her head to the side dreamily. "But I can tell. My boobs always hurt when I'm pregnant, and they've been hurting all day today."

Madame Lindy rolls her eyes. "Back to work with you, Jasmine. We can't keep your date waiting."

My mind races as I climb back up the stairs. Pregnant. I remember when my older brother's wife got pregnant. She was so excited. But then, three months later, she wasn't pregnant anymore. Maybe that's what'll happen to me. My body will reject the baby, and I'll never have to hand him over. I barely make it back to my room when Madame Lindy pokes her head in.

She tosses me a stick. "Here, you need to pee on this."

"What is it?"

"A test to tell whether you're pregnant or not."

She follows me into the bathroom.

"Are you going to watch me?" I ask, mortified.

"Yes. Too many girls have learned how to fake the results. I have to watch you all now."

I don't look at her while I take care of things. It's too embarrassing. Though, after all the things I've done with men, I shouldn't be embarrassed to have my body on display for anyone anymore.

I hand her back the stick, and she sets it on the counter.

"Now what?" I ask.

"Now we wait. If two lines appear, you go pack your stuff. If just one, then I'll make some calls and get another man down here for you tonight."

I should want those two blue lines, but I don't. I'd rather she make the call.

After what seems like ages, she picks up the stick and shows it to me. "Congratulations. You're growing the pack. Go get your stuff."

I put my hand on my stomach.

I'm growing a monster.

Chapter One

It's been three days since Ryne was bitten, and I haven't left his side. I know there is so much going on outside, so much I should be worrying about with the Resistance and the lycans and wolf-pack hierarchy, but I can't leave my mate. I have to wait with him. I've banished both Justin and Nico from the tent. They keep telling me it would be more merciful to kill Ryne, but I can't let them do it. He's still alive, and they thought he'd be dead by now.

Callum keeps giving him herbs for the pain, but I don't think it's doing much. His body writhes most of the time. Occasionally, he comes to, looking me in the eye and telling me that he loves me. And then I lose him again.

It's the middle of the night, and I'm lying next to him, my head on his sweaty shoulder.

"Poppy." Ryne's voice cuts through the darkness even though it's soft. I jerk up and look him in the eyes, to search them for a sign that he's getting better. They're brighter than they were last night, but he's very pale.

"It's okay. You can go back to sleep."

He shakes his head. "I don't think I'll be alive much longer. I can feel myself slipping away. Poppy, I love you. Promise me you'll take care of yourself."

I lean over him. "Don't talk like that."

His hand grips my waist. "I mean it. You need to fight for your freedom." He's more coherent than I've seen him since I bit him. That has to be the sign I need, right?

I shake my head. "You're not dying."

"Yes, I am. No one survives the bite. Even me. You need to let me go."

Tears fall onto his chest. "Not yet." I know I'm going to lose him, but I'm not ready. Not by a long shot.

He pulls me closer. I'm surprised he has the strength. He places a hand on the back of my head and presses his lips against mine. For a moment, I forget that he's dying. Forget that he's writhing in pain. Forget that I may never kiss him again. Our lips and tongues move furiously against one another. The desperate last kiss of a dying man.

And then he falls limp in my arms.

A sob bursts from my lungs. This is it. This is the end. His breathing stops, and his body goes impossibly still, as if it's not a body anymore, as if he's not Ryne anymore.

"No, no, no," I cry out, shaking him. "Don't go. Don't leave me."

But it's useless . . . Ryne is dead.

I don't want to believe it. I can't possibly accept it. But deep down, I know it's true, and no amount of crying or pleading is going to bring him back. After all the death and trauma I've had to endure, this one will break me. I will never be the same. I cling to his body, knowing it will soon grow cold, but this is a luxury I never had with my sister. I can hold him for as long as I want.

I should go get Callum and the others. We're going to need to prepare the body for burial. Or will they want to burn it? The thought of his beautiful body being engulfed in flames makes my stomach pinch, and I lie down again, returning my head to his shoulder, and whisper confessions of love and regret into his ear. I never want to leave him—this beautiful man who I killed.

And so I don't.

Sometime later, when the birds begin to greet the dawn, I get up the nerve to face reality. I'm unable to look at Ryne's face as I hurry from the tent. I have to find Ryne's packmates to let them know what's happened. They were right about him dying, so they won't be surprised, but I need to get this over with before they find him in there.

"Poppy, are you okay?" Justin asks, standing up near the long-dead campfire. I briefly wonder when it went out. Did it die around the same time Ryne did?

A labored inhalation later and Nico is at my side, catching me as my knees buckle. Hoarse sobs rip from my body as the grief hits me all at once. "He's dead," I gasp. "Ryne's dead."

Nico steadies me and then looks me right in the eye, his voice careful. "Are you sure?"

I don't know why, but that asinine question sends rage through my core. "Am I sure?" I bite out, pushing him off me. "Am I sure? I don't know, Nico. Ryne took his last breath in my arms last night, but maybe I was mistaken." My voice doesn't sound like me. This is some other Poppy, the Poppy who has been ruined by death. First, I lost Willow, and I only survived it because I found Joanna and Ryne. And now she's left me for our enemies, and Ryne is gone forever. This angry Poppy, this rageful Poppy, *she's* the new me, and *this* is my life now.

"Poppy." Justin inches forward, his eyes flashing to the tent and then back to me. "We'd have felt his death through the pack bond. But we felt nothing."

I stare at them, wondering how they could be so cruel.

"According to our bond, he's not dead yet," Nico insists.

Time seems to still, hanging like a question mark in midair. I know what happened.

Together, they sprint past me and into the tent. I follow them in, barely registering that Callum and Faye are awake and in the tent now too. It seems everyone has to see for themselves that Ryne is really dead; they can't take my word for it.

"I don't know what's going on with the pack bond, but I know what happened last night." Tears pour down my face, sadness lapping over the anger. Ryne left me. He stopped breathing. He stopped moving. His body grew cold. *He's gone.*

I can't even bear to look at him anymore, knowing that his soul is no longer there. But I have to. I have to prove to the others that I'm not crazy.

"Here, let me." Callum kneels next to Ryne and presses his fingers to Ryne's neck. It's the first time I've let myself look at Ryne's face in death. He looks the same but different. Right but wrong. Here but not.

Another sob wracks me.

"I'm so sorry, Poppy," Faye whispers, standing at my side in the entrance to the tent. It's perhaps the first kind thing she's ever said to me, but it does nothing to make me feel better. Nothing ever could or ever will. Not without Ryne. She grips my hand, but I shake her off.

"He's got a pulse," Callum says, disbelieving.

"But he's obviously not breathing," I state woodenly, pointing to his chest. "How can there be a pulse?"

"I don't know. None of this makes sense." Callum looks up at me and shakes his head. "But since when did wolf shifters or lycanthropes make sense?"

Could he really be alive? I drop to my knees on Ryne's other side, pushing Justin out of my way, and briefly press my lips to Ryne's. They're cold. Too cold. Cruelly cold. "What's happening here? Are you dead or not?" I whisper to him, wondering if perhaps he can hear me. He doesn't look like himself. He has to be dead. Pulse or no pulse.

"Our bond indicates he's not dead," Justin insists. "Trust me, we'd know if our alpha was gone."

Hope burns through my every cell, and I pray it's not false hope because I don't think I could handle this being some cruel twist of fate. "But he's so cold . . ."

"I don't understand," Faye interrupts, hands on her hips and glowering down at all of us. "He was burning up, but now he's cold? He was dead, but just kidding, he's alive? Which is it?"

There she is. I glare daggers at her, and she holds her hands up. "Hey, don't shoot the messenger. I'm just stating the obvious here." She's right. I know she is, but I don't have to like it.

"Let's look at the facts." Callum goes into doctor-scientist mode, pacing the tent. "Ryne was bitten by a lycan, and no wolf shifter has ever survived a lycan bite before."

"Fact," Justin and Nico say in unison.

"But, the difference here is that Poppy was the one to bite him, and she's kissed him several times since, even though it's close to the full moon, and she shouldn't have."

Blood drains from my face. I can't believe I didn't remember not to do that. We'd been so careful not to kiss near the full moon since my lycan saliva sedates him, but I was so distracted and desperate over these last three days that I forgot. "What are you saying?"

"You're not just anyone to Ryne." A ring of excitement lightens Callum's voice, and he bounces on the balls of his feet. "You're his fated mate."

"Which means?" I'm not following his line of thinking.

"Which means, if my theory is correct, that your bite and your saliva, however painful and dangerous they may be, won't actually kill him."

"And why on earth not?" Faye asks incredulously, and I squeeze

Ryne's hand, hoping that Callum could somehow be right. His heart is still beating, so he's still here when he shouldn't be.

"We can't intentionally kill our fated mates. It's one of the things we're taught as pups," Nico says bluntly to Faye and then looks at me. "I thought you could accidentally kill him, but perhaps fate won't allow that either."

Callum agrees. "And maybe because it was you and not someone else who bit him . . ."

I finish his thought. "Ryne might be the first wolf shifter to survive the lycan virus."

And in that moment, that glorious death-defying moment, Ryne's eyes fly open.

Chapter Two

Ryne leaps off the cot, eyes blazing and fists clenched. "Where's my father?" he growls.

No one utters a word. The others move away from him, but I step closer. He flicks his gaze around the tent.

"Wait, where am I?"

I reach for his hand, but he jerks it away. My heart stills, but I recognize he's disoriented. I take another step closer to him but don't try to touch him. "You're in the wilds. The medical tent. Remember, we brought you here after . . . after you got hurt." I don't want to alarm him with too much information even though we've been through so much over the last few months, especially during the last festival.

He frowns. "The last thing I remember was fighting with my father. He didn't kill me?"

I blink back tears as I recall that awful moment. "No. He didn't."

"So what happened?"

All of his muscles are taut, and a vein in his neck twitches. He's ready to attack. "You . . . you got hurt. We brought you out here."

He finally meets my eye. "And my father?"

"Dead."

"How long was I out?"

"A few days." I can't believe he's forgotten it all. He was awake and lucid for some of it. We talked, he begged me to let him go, and he told me he loved me, that it wasn't my fault. But all that seems to have been erased from his mind in the last few hours.

He nods and finally relaxes. He sinks down onto the cot, and I risk sitting next to him. He doesn't move away from me, so I reach for his hand again, and he threads his fingers through mine. I lean my head on his shoulder.

"Tell me everything," he says, looking at Justin. "Did the Resistance fail? What happened to the other lycans?"

"They have abandoned the Resistance." Justin winces. "In fact, they're infecting humans on purpose now."

Ryne looks around the tent. "Where's Grady?"

My heart sinks at that question, for myself, for Joanna, for Ryne . . . for all of us.

Justin leans back on his heels. "He went with Laik. He thinks he'll have a better chance of keeping Joanna alive if he sides with them. Knox and Charlotte went too."

Ryne's face is horror-struck, and nobody moves a muscle for a long, tense moment until Callum crouches in front of us.

"How do you feel?" Callum asks, his voice smooth and gentle.

"It doesn't matter. I need to know what's going on. We should go to Chicago."

"Delphine and Elle are already there," Nico assures him. "Hopefully, Izaak is already the alpha."

"That's right. I forgot about the plan to put Elle's father on the throne. Everything is fuzzy. Why are we here instead of at my house?"

Justin sighs. "We thought this was safer. We didn't think you were going to make it."

"Why the hell not?" Ryne growls. "What happened to me?"

I hold my breath, and my stomach goes hard.

Callum's eyes sparkle as he examines Ryne. "You were bitten by a lycan." I wonder why he intentionally left my name out of it, but I can't help but be a little relieved, even if it's temporary.

Ryne leaps up. "And you didn't kill me right away?"

Justin shrugs. "We wanted to. Poppy wouldn't let us."

He glares down at me. "You would have me suffer?"

"I couldn't let you go." I stand to meet him, praying he'll understand. "And look. You're alive."

He jams a hand through his tangled hair. "How?"

Nico chuckles. "Well, you can't kill your fated mate. Remember?"

"What does that have to do with . . ." His voice fades away, and he turns to me, his jaw clenched. "*You* bit me?"

My face goes hot. "I didn't mean to. Your dad was going to kill you. I thought it was him that I was biting, not you."

"That was stupid and reckless. You could've gotten killed."

It's my turn to be angry now. I saved his life, and he's acting like I did something wrong. Which I guess I did, but still.

"You're alive, aren't you? If I hadn't intervened, you'd be dead."

"You should've killed me." Anger laces his voice.

How could he say something like that to me? "It was an accident." I reach for him, but he backs away as if I'm going to bite him all over again.

"How did my father die?" He looks at Justin, but I answer the question.

"I beheaded him," I confess. He's not going to get away with ignoring me. I get that he's angry that I bit him, but I didn't do it on purpose. And does he really think I would've allowed the others to kill him? He seems even angrier that I didn't, but I won't apologize for keeping my own mate alive. He did the same thing when I was the one who'd been bitten.

Ryne taps his teeth, and I can see the wheels in his head turning. "Who all knows it was you?"

"The other lycan that were on the mission and the people in this tent. Nobody else would've known it was me."

He nods once. "Good. I'm glad he's dead. It's time for me to go back to my pack. Things will be tense now without a king, and we don't need Anders doing anything stupid. Justin, Nico, let's go."

"Wait," Callum and I say at the same time.

"What?" Ryne asks.

Callum speaks before I do. "We have no idea what the lycan virus has done to your body."

"You're right. You can come with us. You're a competent doctor, and I trust you to keep me on track. We'll cut your hair to look like a claimed boy, and nobody else can know you're a lycan. But you will have to agree to be locked up during the full moons."

Callum looks pained at the idea, but he agrees anyway.

"What about me?" I ask. Ryne hasn't looked at me since he found out I bit him.

"You stay here. I don't ever want to see you again."

And with that, he leaves the tent.

Shock burns through me, a fire that is doused by shame. I can feel the pitying stares of everyone in the tent, and I refuse to meet their gazes. I don't know if I've ever been as angry with Ryne as I am right now. I jump up and storm after him, fists clenching and stomach a hollow pit. I might say something I'll regret, but at this point, who the hell cares? I've got nothing else to lose.

"You don't get to treat me like this," I yell at his back. "I saved your life!"

He ignores me, stalking off into the forest. He's already got his shirt off and is unbuttoning his pants when I catch up to him.

"Going to shift into your wolf and run away, huh?" I push his hard chest, but it's like pushing a tall unmovable wall. "I never knew you to be a coward, but I guess I should've known, considering how you never stood up to your father."

The second the words are out, I know I shouldn't have said them. He turns on me, knotted hair hanging to his shoulders and stormy blue eyes filled with malice. "I tried to kill my father according to the plan, but why should I have bothered when you did it for me?"

"So things didn't go according to your precious plan, and now you're going to take it out on me?" I throw my hands in the air. "I get that it would've been better for the pack hierarchy if you'd been the one to kill him, but, Ryne, you were losing the brawl. You needed my help." My voice softens at those last words, and I remember how scared I was that I was going to lose him.

He scoffs at that. "I was fine."

I meet his eyes. His breaths are short and fast, and his fists are clenched. I'm not used to seeing so much anger on him. I'm not scared of him, but I'm scared for him and for us. "Are you really so prideful that you'd have rather died and let him continue on as alpha king?"

His face becomes as unreadable as a mask. It would be easier if I could read him, if there was fury in his eyes or sadness in the turn of his lips, but there's nothing. His next words come out slowly, as if he wants me to consider them carefully. "I'm glad you're not dead, Poppy, and I'm angry that you could've died, but most of all, it hurts to look at you knowing how you betrayed me--how you *bit* me."

So this is about the bite? Is he serious right now? "The bite was an accident, but if I had to choose between biting you and you surviving the suffering it caused,"—I motion to his clearly intact and healed body—"or watching you die at the hands of your own father, then I would choose to see you alive." My voice cracks. "I love you, Ryne. You're my mate."

He winces and steps back. "And what *my mate* did to me is worse than death."

"How can you say that?" Tears blur my vision. My anger is all used up now. All I feel is desperation. If he leaves me, I don't think I can go on. I already lost him once. I was certain he was dead, and to have him back only to lose him by his own choice would break me.

"Because you should've let my betas kill me. Because I can feel the moon even now," he growls, his voice low and panicked. "It's already got a hold of me, and if I turn into a lycan next month, I'll lose my pack. There's no way they won't sense my new form if that happens."

And that's worse than dying? I don't understand how he could be upset by this. "Do you know what I went through last night? I was sure you were dead, and it destroyed me." My voice cracks, and I steady myself, peering up into his storm-cloud eyes. "So I get that you're afraid of what will happen if you become some kind of lycan, but I'll never regret that you're still alive."

His jaw clenches, and he leans closer. We're only inches apart now, so close I could touch him, kiss him, but I don't know that he'll ever let me do that again. "If I lose my pack, I'd rather be dead."

Those words rip my heart in two. "And what about me? No matter what you are, I love you. You wouldn't want to live for me? The woman who loves you?"

"You'd have me lose my pack to be with you?" His eyes travel up and down my face, searching for something that must be lacking, but I'm not sure what else he wants from me. "You call that love?"

"It's not like that."

He shakes his head and steps away, the space between us feeling like a million miles already. "Well, I don't give a damn about fate anymore. Fate may make it so I can't kill you, but it can't stop me from rejecting you."

The tears are pouring down my cheeks at this point, and I double over, heartbreak wracking through my body and searing deep down into my soul. Never would I have expected Ryne to be so cruel. There's no excuse for it. He doesn't love me, not like I love him, because if he did, he would never reject me like this. He would never be so harsh. So cold. It's as if that bite changed him in every single way. The Ryne I knew is gone.

"Don't come back to the city." Then he shifts into his wolf form and disappears into the forest before I can say another word.

Chapter Three

I storm back to the camp and into Callum's tent. Nico is gone, but Justin, Faye, and Callum are packing up.

"Where's Nico?" I demand.

"He ran after Ryne. We'll follow after we get this packed up. You should head to the panther city. You'll be safe there," Justin offers regretfully.

"Uh, no. I'm coming with you." Ryne may think he can boss me around all he wants, but I'm not the same girl I was when I came to the wolf city. I've been through it all, and I'm done taking orders.

Justin shakes his head. "No. Ryne doesn't want you to come back to the city. The Sanctuary is a good idea. You won't be safe with the wolves."

I snort. He thinks that Ryne is somehow looking out for me by keeping me away? Yeah, right.

"Why wouldn't I be safe?" I challenge.

He looks at me like it's obvious. "Because you're a lycan. You're not safe among wolves."

"Callum is going, and he's a lycan, remember? Besides, no one in that city knows what I really am except for you guys. I'm not going to be sent off just when I'm needed most." Everyone is quiet. I can't just let this go. I can't just leave them. "Where is Faye going?"

Faye juts her chin. "I'm going back to Drayton Hall. Those girls need my help. With Madame Delphine gone and Anders being Anders, things have to be a mess there."

I nod. That makes sense, but I'm surprised to see Faye doing something selfless. I figured she'd be taking the first chance she got to marry a beta, but since Ryne hasn't signed off on an early marriage to Justin yet, maybe she's just saving face. "That's a good idea. I'll help you." A thought springs to mind. "I'm not totally opposed to the panthers, you know. We can sneak girls out of the city and get them to The Sanctuary."

I expect an argument, for the old Faye to surface, but she gives me a conspiratorial grin and nudges me. "I like it. Who knew you and I would team up one day?"

I force a grin. I'm still reeling over Ryne being so angry with me, but I have to pretend like everything is fine. If I let on that Ryne doesn't want me around because he's mad at me, then they really won't let me come with.

Justin meets my eyes. "Look, I know it's hard to understand right now, but Ryne cares about you and would want to keep you safe. The panthers will be able to provide that."

Faye snorts. "He also said he never wants to see her again. You call that caring?"

Justin shakes his head. "He was just angry in the moment. He still loves her."

I don't tell him that Faye's right, that what Justin is calling protection and love is clearly rejection and betrayal. "Look, the only beta left in the claiming that I need to worry about is Anders, and he's going to be busy trying to either fight it out or suck up to Ryne once he returns. It's going to be a shock to the pack to have their alpha back. Let me at least come to Drayton so I can get a few girls out to The Sanctuary with me."

What I don't tell him is that I have no intention of staying with the panthers. No matter what, I'm staying in the wolf city. I have to see this through to the end, even if Ryne wants nothing to do with me. I can't help the claimed women if I'm not there. And if I have to be locked up on full moons with Callum, so be it.

Justin clenches his jaw. "Okay fine. But you leave as soon as you can. We won't tell Ryne that you came back with Faye. He'll be so busy with the pack that he won't worry about Drayton Hall at all. But get all the girls out. War is about to break out, and the last thing we need is to worry about what will happen to them, especially with Delphine gone. Poppy, you take them to The Sanctuary with you, and Faye, you go to my parents' house." He briefly hesitates. "Unless you want to go with Poppy and the other girls to The Sanctuary. I would understand."

Faye grasps his hand. "No way. I'm sticking with you. And I'm not going to your parents' house. I'm staying at the manor until Ryne gives us his blessing."

I still can't tell if whatever is going on between them is real or not. Does Faye actually love him? That would explain why she's willing to give up The Sanctuary for him, but then again, she was willing to do just about anything to live an extravagant life as a beta wife. Maybe she's still hoping things will go back to the way they were, and if that's the case, it would be foolish to trust her.

Justin lets out a breath. "Okay. Let's go."

It's not exactly how I would've planned it, but at least I get to go back to the city. Once I'm there, I'll figure out my next steps.

And Ryne is just going to have to live with it.

* * *

Faye and I stare up at the manor. My whole world changed three months ago when I was bitten, Joanna ran off with Grady, and Abi got sent to a mating house. In those following months, we managed to rescue a handful of claimed girls, but last I heard, Anders was making things worse for the ones left behind. That, and they were supposed to bring in more betas to court the remaining girls. Did that ever happen? Probably not without Ryne there to oversee it, but I'm not really sure.

Truth is, I have no idea what to expect when I walk through those doors.

"Did they ever bring in more betas?" I ask the question aloud.

Faye shakes her head. "I don't think so. They kept talking about it, but it never happened while I was there."

"Do we even know who's left?"

She shrugs. "That depends on who actually got sent to the mating houses."

"But Madame Delphine and Elle went to Chicago. Who's even running the manor now?"

"Vivien would be my best guess. But you forget, I've been out in the woods with you since you 'rescued' me." She rolls her eyes. "Things have probably changed."

Vivien has never been a fan of mine. I don't know how she's going to take to me telling her that we're sending all the girls to The Sanctuary.

"What's the plan?" I ask because I don't have one. I was so worried about getting back into the city that it never occurred to me what I would do when I got there. It's dark, the middle of the night, but there are still lights on.

Faye shrugs. "No clue. This was your plan, remember? Mine was just to get back to a warm bed and keep dating Justin until we can get married."

She tromps in front of me, and I scramble after her. I don't like going in blind, but we are going to have to improvise anyway. We have no idea who is even here.

Faye bangs on the door until it opens, and a surprised Madame Vivien scrambles back with her hand on her chest. "Oh, thank goodness. I thought you were Anders."

Faye creases her eyebrows. "Why?"

Vivien wrings her hands but ushers us inside and locks the door behind us. "He was so upset that Delphine brought all the girls back here after the fight instead of sending them to the mating houses, but he had so many other things going on that he didn't push her. I literally haven't slept because I've been so worried that he's going to march in here and take them all."

She sinks down into a chair, and I notice the flash of red pinned to her dress.

It's a poppy.

Chapter Four

"You're part of the Resistance," I breathe out, suddenly so relieved I could cry.

She glances up. "And so are you. Do you really think Delphine would have women working for her that were not?" She stares at Faye for a second. "I didn't think you were in on it, though."

"I wasn't. But Justin and his family are, and I go where he goes. Speaking of. We've come to rescue the girls. Poppy is going to take them to The Sanctuary in Panther City."

Vivien shakes her head. "No. Delphine sent word earlier; she's on her way back. No one goes anywhere without her approval first."

"And if Anders shows up?"

Vivien pulls a wicked-looking knife from a sheath on her side that I didn't even see. "We are all well-armed."

I wouldn't mind using that on Anders myself. I thought that killing someone would irrevocably place a black stain on my soul, but if anything, I feel better now that Thorn is gone. Lighter. Freer. And I'm willing to kill bad people if it means saving the good ones, especially the ones I love. Ryne may not like it, but I'm glad I was the one to kill his father.

"Anders isn't the alpha," I state. "You don't have to worry about him anymore."

Madame Vivien stands and walks to the window, peering out into the darkness. "I would ask you where you two have been, but Madame Delphine already told me. As far as everyone else is concerned"––she turns back to us —"as far as *Anders* is concerned, you were kidnapped by a rogue group of lone wolves, the same wolves who also kidnapped Ryne, but you were all rescued by Justin and Nico. Nobody can know you've been around the lycan, is that understood?"

"Oh, we understand perfectly," Faye agrees. "And we've already talked through our story with Justin and Nico ten times over on the way back to the city. You don't need to worry about us."

I nod along, but a prickle of fear goes through me anyway. The wolves can't tell I'm lycan in this form, but what if I somehow give myself away since we're still so close to the previous full moon? I'll be dead before anyone can ask questions. Maybe this is why Ryne didn't want me to come back. At least, I know they can't smell the renewal on me since I washed it away the next morning. If it was something they could smell in this form, Justin wouldn't have let me return.

"There's a large bounty for any information that could lead to the capture of our alpha king's killer." She gives us a hard look, me in particular. "Do you happen to know anything about that?"

My mouth pops open, but Faye beats me to it. "Of course not, but we can't say we're unhappy he's dead, now can we?"

My mind flashes to the night the king roughed up Faye, the way the light in her eyes dimmed after spending time alone with him. Maybe she really can be trusted. But I've been betrayed by people I love too many times to trust anyone at all. I'm keeping my guard up.

"Yes, I happen to agree with you, but I just wanted to make sure you knew that the lycan who killed King Tremaine has a target on his *or her* back now."

I'm not about to confess it was me. Madame Vivien probably knows I'm a lycan, but I can't be sure. If she were to also find out I killed the king, who's to say she wouldn't turn me in for the bounty? She may be with the Resistance, but I'm not sure that means she's on my side. She blames me for her friend's death and could still want retaliation beyond all those grueling workouts she put me through last spring. I guess I'll just have to get used to walking around with a target on my back and hope that nobody stabs it.

"You two take Poppy's old room and go on to bed."

I want to stay and ask questions, wondering who's still here, if more betas ever showed up to court, how we can get more women out, and what Anders has been up to lately. I open my mouth to speak because I can't stand not knowing, but Madame Vivien shoots me an exasperated look and points to the stairs. "We'll talk more later. Right now, it'd be best if you went upstairs."

Because she's expecting Anders, and even though I'm not her favorite person, she's still trying to protect me. I should appreciate it, but I'm tired of other people telling me to go away as a form of protection.

I swallow hard, not wanting to leave, but I do as my house mother asks anyway. I'm not the same girl I was when she last saw me, not by a million miles, but I'm exhausted. It's been several days and nights of pure hell, months of living in a tent, and the thought of sleeping in a real bed makes me want to cry with happiness. Faye must feel the same way because she's up the stairs before me.

"I'm taking a shower first," she announces.

Now *that* sounds even better than sleeping right now. I follow her to the shared showers, and we quickly clean ourselves under the hot pelt of water before changing into clean pajamas and crawling into our beds. Seeing Faye in my friends' old bed is wrong, but I don't argue with it. My head barely hits the pillow before sleep claims me.

* * *

Bang! I bolt upright and immediately go into defensive mode. *Bang! Bang! Bang!*

"Faye, wake up," I hiss, but she's already awake.

"I'm not going down there."

Someone is pounding on the manor's front door, and from the sounds of it, they're eager to get inside.

"Well, I'm not hiding up here," I say back. I dig under the mattress and find the dagger I hid there ages ago, still waiting for me, then run for the door.

"Are you sure that's a good idea?" She tries to block me. "Not many people even know we're up here. That could be a good thing. Maybe we should hide?" Faye never struck me as a coward, but then again, she was never one to protect others either.

"You hide. I'm leaving." And with that, I throw open the door and sprint down the stairs, taking them two at a time, ignoring the heads peeking from the other doorways and the whispers that follow.

"Madame Vivien, let me in or face the consequences." I hear Anders call through the locked front door.

She's standing in the darkened room, the shine of that nasty knife gleaming silver in her hand.

"He's going to find a way in either way," I whisper. "You know he will."

"There's been a change of plans," he calls again. "Either open this door, or I'll break it down."

He starts banging again and then goes quiet. Eerily so. That's when the window shatters, and a large gray wolf lands in the center of the room. He growls as he turns on us, and then he pauses, his eyes zeroing in on me. It's the perfect opportunity for Madame Vivien to strike.

She sees her opening and slashes her knife at his neck. I take advantage of the moment and plunge my dagger into his side. He howls and flings Vivien into the wall with his giant paw. She crumples to the ground, her knife still in hand.

He turns on me, blood dripping from his neck and ribs, and bares his razor-sharp teeth. I back up a few feet. I don't have any good angles to strike from, and I wish that I had a sword instead of a measly dagger. He lunges for me, but before he can get his jaws around my neck, two more wolves leap through the window and knock him down.

He scrambles back to his feet and growls at them.

Then they all turn into very large naked men. I flick my eyes up so I don't have to look at them. It's Justin and Nico who've come to save me, and my heart drops a little that it isn't Ryne. Hope can be so cruel.

"We just rescued her, and now you're trying to kill her?" Nico asks, breathing hard.

Anders presses a hand to his side, blood seeping out between his fingers. "She attacked me first."

"Looks like she was just protecting herself like we taught her to. Good job, Poppy," Justin adds.

Footsteps scramble down the stairs, and Faye flings herself into Justin's arms as if they haven't seen each other in ages. It's beyond ridiculous. Anders just glares at all of us.

"Fine, protect your pets. I didn't come here for them anyway. When Ryne finally dies, and I become alpha, I'll kill her. You better pick another wife, Nico."

"I'm not interested in any of the others," Nico lies. We both know there's nothing between us, that our sham engagement was never about love, but right now I'm so grateful to Nico that I could kiss him. It wouldn't mean anything, but to see him stand up to his own father for me?

It's what Ryne should've done . . .

Anders shrugs. "Suit yourself. Go gather the rest of the girls."

"For what?" Justin asks.

Anders pinches the bridge of his nose and squeezes his eyes shut. "We're losing good wolves from our pack because they want more women. They're threatening to leave for Chicago to fight for the position of alpha king since the position is still vacant. I'm going to release the rest of the girls to the mating houses as an incentive for them to stay. In addition, I'm sending men out to the surrounding villages to gather more women. Then, hopefully, we can keep the pack together."

"You can't do that," I shout.

He rolls his eyes. "I can, and I will."

"It's not your place. You're not the alpha." Justin glares.

"Not yet. But I am second in command, and until Ryne returns, I'm in charge. I'm only doing what's best for the pack."

Justin and Nico exchange glances, and a grin spreads over Nico's face. He turns around, unlocks the front door, and turns back to the group. He crosses his arms and smirks at Anders. "Suit yourself, but I'm not helping you anymore, *Father*."

Anders bears down on him, growling. "I am in charge, and you will obey me, *son*."

Nico chuckles. "No, I won't. You have no control in my life anymore."

The door flings open suddenly, and we all spin. Ryne stands there, breathing heavily. He's clean and has on fresh clothes, and his hair is brushed back into a low ponytail. I want to go to him, but I can't. Not after what he said to me. Not after what he *did*.

He glances around the room, taking in everything. His eyes stop at mine and narrow, but he doesn't say anything.

"What's going on?" he asks Anders.

"Ryne, you're looking healthy. I thought you were left for dead."

"I survived."

"I see. Well, the men are hungry for fresh meat, so I came to get it for them."

"These girls are not yours for the taking, Anders. They are still going through the process of matching with a beta. You cannot take that from them."

"Oh, please. The betas have already made their choices. Cade is dead. Justin wants Faye. I'll back down to let Nico have Poppy, considering you don't want her, and she's probably used goods after what those lone wolves did with her." His lip curls as he looks at me and then at his son. "I don't want any of the ones who are left, so I'm backing out of the claiming this year."

"And your point?" Ryne seethes between clenched teeth.

"Give the men what they want."

"That's not your call. Remember, I'm your alpha."

"Not for long."

Ryne takes a step forward. "You're challenging me?"

Anders snorts. "No. I have bigger ambitions than just that. If you won't be reasonable and give your own men what they deserve, then I'm going to Chicago to fight for alpha king myself." He puffs up his chest. "Then I'll come down and remove you from your post, and the Carolina Pack will run the way it's supposed to."

He shoulder-checks Ryne as he stalks away, turning into a wolf as soon as he clears the doorway. Nico and Justin stare at Ryne. Justin's lips are thin, and Nico looks like he's about ready to murder his father himself.

"No. We aren't going to chase him down," Ryne announces. "Let him go to Chicago and get himself killed. Good riddance. Nico, stay here and protect the girls tonight. I'll send some more betas over to help. Justin, come with me."

"What are we going to do?" Justin questions.

"We're going to take control of the pack once more and try to keep as many men as we can from following Anders to Chicago."

"Aren't you going up there to fight for alpha king?"

Just the thought of it makes me feel ill. Ryne's not weak, but he nearly died twice in the last few days, and he might not be in a position to battle for that title right now. Luckily, he shakes his head. "I'll worry about the alpha king later. Izaak is strong enough to win the throne, and we already trust him. If he fails, however, and if it ends up going to someone we can't trust, well, only then will I fight for the crown."

It's something we talked about a lot, something I wanted for him, and he knows it. His eyes meet mine again, but once again, he has no words for me. He and Justin leave without another word or even a backward glance. Nico strides over to Vivien and helps her to her feet. She's shaky but otherwise unharmed.

"What now?" I ask.

Vivien stands tall. "Now, we go back to normal."

Chapter Five

I turn that word over and over in my head, trying to make sense of it. *Normal.* It seems like a joke that we could go back to normal around here, but then again, nothing about the last nine months could be described as normal. Anders brutally murdering my sister and then forcing me to come here in her place wasn't normal. The forced breeding in order to keep the pack growing and competing to marry a beta wolf wasn't normal. Falling in love with the alpha, a man I should hate, wasn't normal. And becoming a lycan certainly wasn't normal. I never would've guessed that I could thrive as a lycan, but during that last renewal, I'd finally been able to take back my control, to protect myself, to be strong, and to fight.

And I won. I killed King Thorn Tremaine.

All that, and I am now expected to get prettied up and pretend as if none of it happened?

Because that's exactly what we did after we went back upstairs, only this time with Faye as my roommate instead of Charlotte or Joanna or Abi. Maybe for Vivien, this is normal. This is the way things have been her entire life, but for me, this seems like a cosmic joke.

Faye smirks at me from across the room, smoothing out her skirts. "What are you going to tell the other girls?"

I adjust my own skirts and study myself in the mirror. I feel like so much has changed, *I've changed*, but I look the exact same as I did when I left here. How can that possibly be? "Just what Madame Vivien requested. That we were captured by lone wolves, and then we were rescued. Nobody needs to know anything else."

And if Faye brings up my being a lycan to the wrong person, I'm as good as dead. I'm expecting her to blackmail me with that right about now, but instead, she rolls her eyes. "Aren't you forgetting what happened at your sham wedding? You confessed to being Ryne's fated mate. Everyone knows about you two now. And not only that, I know you're no innocent virgin anymore."

Blood drains from my face. I hadn't thought about that. One of the rules for the claiming is that none of the girls are allowed to lose their virtue before marriage, and if they do, they'll be sent to the mating houses. And now that everyone knows about Ryne, they're going to treat me differently, especially the betas.

"Pretty sure they're going to think neither of us are virgins, considering we were supposedly taken by lone wolves," I state. "But none of that matters anymore. We're not actually going through with the claiming, and it's not for another three months anyway. There's going to be a new king, a better one, and Ryne is going to make changes around here. And don't forget we're supposed to be leaving for The Sanctuary soon."

"Not me. I'm marrying Justin."

So she says, but I'm still not sure if those two are the real deal.

"Well, some of us will be leaving, whether or not we're still virgins."

"I guess we'll see what happens but I'm not counting on that plan."

I don't say anything more because she's right and also because I don't want to leave the city either. Running away isn't going to solve whatever went wrong between me and Ryne. And besides, I need to stick around in case he needs me. He's acting like he isn't infected with the lycanthrope virus, but I know, come this next full moon, something is going to change. Something big. I'm just not sure what yet.

We go down to breakfast, making a dramatic entrance as is Faye's way. And she's right. Everyone swarms us with questions and suspicions. They especially want to know all about my interactions with Ryne, of which I lie and pretend there are few. The whole time, Faye has this knowing smirk on her face like she could spill my secrets at any moment. And maybe she will.

There aren't many original claimed girls left. So many have died, and the ones who are still alive aren't all here. Charlotte is off with the lycans, who think it's okay to turn humans against their will, and now so is Joanna because Grady believes it's the safest place for them. Faye's distillery friend Joy is still here, though she's a shell of the girl she was before, and I wonder what happened to her. Katelyn was sent to the mating house at the last festival, as was Emma. My stomach twists thinking about the others who've been at the mating houses for even longer, like Abi. Especially Abi. We saved Alyssa, Bailey, Harlow, and Blair for the panther city, so they're safe for now. Samantha is here and is probably still top of the leaderboard. She and Raven look like they've become best friends in the months since I've been away, and I wonder if they'd be willing to leave all this for The Sanctuary. Joy is still here. And then there's me and Faye.

Five women.

Five women, but what of the betas who were supposed to choose a bride?

Cade is dead.

Grady is long gone.

Anders left for Chicago––thank goodness. I hope he dies there.

Justin has apparently picked Faye to be his future wife.

Nico might still be courting after our botched wedding, though people seem to think we're still engaged. He'll forever be heartbroken over Nova—his fated mate who was murdered by his own father—and I don't think Ryne will make him get married. I'm certainly not going to marry him.

So why are we even still here?

A feeling of hopelessness settles over me as I eat the first decent meal I've had in months. Not even sugary pancakes can cheer me up. I don't know what to do next. Do I really leave the city and take the girls with me? Do I leave Ryne? Or do I stay here and pretend that things are back to normal when I know they'll never be normal again?

Samantha settles in next to me, nudging me on the shoulder. "We all know about the Resistance," she whispers low, "and we're on your side. We're going to get through this together."

I turn to meet her bright amber eyes, this girl who I've barely spoken two words to, this girl who I thought I had little in common with, who is now nodding and giving me a knowing look of encouragement. She reminds me to remember how far I've come. I can't back down now. I can't give up. There are still so many lives at stake, and just because women are in the mating houses now doesn't mean they aren't important. If anything, saving them is more crucial than saving the girls in the manor.

"I need to talk to Ryne," I announce, standing up.

Everyone quiets and stares at me.

"I'm afraid the alpha doesn't take requests," Madame Vivien says, arching her thin brow over her morning cup of coffee, "not even from his fated mate."

But before I can argue with her, the door swings open, and everyone holds in a collective gasp. I almost expect it to be Ryne––but it's better.

It's Elle.

Chapter Six

I rush out of my seat and fling my arms around her. She holds me tight for a minute before letting go, keeping me at arm's length to study me. "Are you okay?" she asks softly. Her eyes carry dark circles and a haunted look--her eyes have seen too much.

I nod, but my face probably betrays me because she purses her lips.

"What happened in Chicago?" I question.

She shakes her head, her mouth trembling in a grief-stricken way that's nothing like the girl I know. "Nothing good. My father is dead."

I let out a little gasp as pain rakes through me. Pain for Elle, for the Resistance, for Ryne, for myself, for all of us. Izaak being dead was not in our plans.

"My family went into hiding," she continues, "but I couldn't leave Delphine alone. She needed help getting back safely with..." She falters.

"With what?"

But before she answers, a girl I don't recognize pushes past her. "Is there food? I'm starving."

Elle steps aside, and several more girls enter the room. They're of varying ages, and they're all beautiful like Elle, but other than that, none of them look alike. One has bright red curls and is covered in freckles, and another has long, shiny blonde hair. A third is short and curvy with warm brown skin and thick glasses. I can't figure out who they are. None of them are dressed like the girls from the villages, but where else could they be from?

Elle grins. "Ladies, meet the lunas."

We all go silent.

There are more than I expected, but if they are sent to Chicago from all the packs, that would make sense. I do a quick count. Including Elle, there are nine lunas. The youngest appears to only be about five years old, and the oldest seems my age. We have room for them here, of course, but no one knows what to expect from these new women. We all love Elle, so hopefully, they are just as wonderful as she is, but I've learned to never expect anything from anyone. Not that I'm worried about the little ones, but there are three who look like young women, and from my experience with the claiming, that could mean more women who hate me.

The redhead plops herself down next to Faye, takes her plate of food, and helps herself. A couple of the other girls do the same, several jumping in to help out the younger ones. The pretty blonde luna looks down her nose at Samantha. "What are you waiting for? We need food."

Samantha just gapes at her, but Faye leans forward with a nasty glint in her eye. "We're not your servants. Go into the kitchen and get it yourself." Then she snatches her plate back from the redhead.

The redhead whips her hand back and slaps Faye right across the face. "I am a luna and will not be talked to that way."

For a second, nothing happens—the sound of that slap seems to echo in the room, though I know it doesn't really.

Faye lifts her hand to her cheek, and then without warning, she growls and attacks the girl, both of them falling to the floor.

Elle rushes past me, Delphine on her heels. They yank the girls apart, but the girls are still glaring daggers at each other. Elle gets right in the redhead's face. "Violet, I know you were raised like a princess, but you're no better than these girls. You cannot slap them or demand things from them."

Violet sniffs. "They're humans, aren't they? They're only here to serve and make babies. Of course I'm better than them."

My jaw drops, and anger roils the pancakes in my stomach. I'll never forget what it felt like to be a helpless human in this world. Never.

Madame Delphine pushes past Elle. "You will not speak of humans in that way. If you do not change your attitude, you are welcome to go back to Chicago and fend for yourself."

Violet's eyes widen. "You wouldn't dare send me back there. Chicago is dangerous for lunas right now."

"Try me."

Violet lets out an exasperated huff. "Fine. I'll be nice. But I am starving."

Something tells me she will not be nice. This is exactly why I need to talk to Ryne––these prejudices against humans need to be corrected. Especially now that Izaak is dead and the Resistance has been cut off at the knees. Ryne's the only one who can demand change around here, so where is he?

"Elle, why don't you show them where the kitchen is so they can help themselves to food? Then get them set up in rooms and see if Vivien can find clothes for them. We'll work the rest out later." Madame Delphine turns on me, her lips thinning. "Poppy, we need to talk."

She brushes past me, and I follow her to her office.

Madame Delphine shuts the door and leans against her desk. She brushes the hair away from her aging face with shaky hands. "Please tell me what happened. I've heard the rumors, of course, but I want to hear everything from you. I know Thorn is dead, but they're saying Ryne didn't do it."

I shake my head. "That's because I did."

She gasps. "Well, that complicates things, doesn't it? I want the whole story."

She sinks into a chair, and I sit on the couch and spill everything. From renewing as a lycan, to killing Thorn, to accidentally biting Ryne.

"Thank goodness he's alive, but he's not talking to me. I don't know what will happen to him on the full moon."

"That's a lot to process." She offers a small grin. "I'll talk to Ryne this afternoon about his pigheadedness. You should be staying with him at his home, not here." She tilts her head at me, her eyes looking me up and down. "Have you two been intimate?"

"I'm useful here," I blurt out. "I want to stay at the manor."

"Okay." But her knowing eyes catch it all, and once again I'm prickling with shame. I gave Ryne everything, and he left me in the wilds.

"What's happening in Chicago?" I ask.

She sighs. "It's a bloodbath. When we left, they were still fighting to be the alpha king. And new wolves arrive every day, wanting to fight for the throne." She swallows hard. "They're willing to fight to the death. When Elle's father died yesterday morning in battle, we knew we had to get out of there."

"I still can't believe it," I whisper. "I thought he was going to win."

"We all did," Madame Delphine says. "The Resistance was counting on it."

My heart is breaking for our cause, but most of all, it's sinking for Elle. I can tell she's trying to be strong, to act like she's okay, but I know what it feels like to have your world ripped apart like that. She's not okay. "And the lunas?"

"They were vulnerable. Wolves kept coming to their academy to try and steal them away, thinking being married to a luna would make them stronger for the throne."

I shake my head, horrified to imagine it. Most of those lunas are far too young to be married. And to be married to someone who only wants them to strengthen their position?

It's wrong.

"So we offered them refuge with us. At least here they won't be used as pawns. They all trust Elle, and Elle trusts Ryne, so they agreed to come with us."

"They aren't very nice."

Her lips thin, and she lets out a long sigh. "From the time they were babies, they've been raised to think they're better than other women. Each will be married off to the most powerful alphas in the kingdom. They have been waited on hand and foot and never told they were wrong. The only person they ever feared was Thorn, and you can imagine why."

"But Elle's not like that," I argue.

"Elle is a special soul, but she was also raised by a wonderful beta family." Delphine stands. "All of these girls were raised in the academy. Their tutelage was overseen by the king himself. They're not as lucky as Elle."

I nod in understanding.

"I'm going to see Ryne. Would you like to come with me?" Delphine asks.

I'm out of my chair before she can change her mind.

She chuckles. "Let's go."

* * *

There are things Ryne and I need to talk about besides our messy relationship. As much as I want to demand he take me back, my heart isn't what's most important right now. Saving the women in the mating houses is.

We're driven over to Ryne's house by a new driver, a burly wolf shifter with a mean expression. I keep expecting to see Knox's kind eyes watching me through the rearview mirror, but of course, Knox is long gone. I would be happy for him and Charlotte if they hadn't sided with Laik and Wanda. I wonder where they're at now, what they're doing, and if they're going to attack the Carolina Pack soon. Laik's people have gone rogue, biting humans to build their army, and some of my best friends willingly went with them. What does this mean for the Resistance? Delphine and I don't even get a chance to talk about that in detail, but I explain the basics despite there being so much going on at the moment that I can't even think straight.

The car pulls to a stop in front of Ryne's beautiful white home, and I swallow back my nerves. Delphine doesn't bother to knock; she walks right inside the alpha's home, calling out to her son.

Ryne rounds the corner, barely giving me a second glance. He gives his mother a kiss on the cheek. "I was just leaving. I can come down to the manor later."

Madame Delphine isn't having it. "You don't have time for your mother?"

I want to add "and your fated mate" to that sentence but keep my mouth shut.

"I'm needed in the villages." He finally meets my gaze but breaks away quickly. "There's no time. We can talk later, Poppy."

"We're coming with you," I demand. It's been nine months since I've seen my parents, since I left little Evan and my father without saying goodbye. I never thought I'd see them again. This is my chance.

"No." Ryne's tone is sharp. Final. How quickly he forgot that we fought together out in the wilds and even against his father. I have just as much right to go.

"Which village?" I beg. I don't know if I want him to say Northwest or not. I'd give anything to see them again, but I don't want them to be in any kind of trouble.

"Southeast," he says. "There's a rumor that they were visited by lycans at the last moon."

We both know what that means. People were turned. Laik must be working with more lycans who share his mindset. Ryne doesn't stick around to address the horror in his mother's eyes.

He tears out the door, and I chase after him. "We can ride with you," I call out. "Explain your plan on the way. Maybe we can help."

Ryne turns back. "You'll only get in the way. You're not even supposed to be here."

Delphine marches up to him, getting right in his face. "I know you're angry with Poppy, but that doesn't give you the right to talk to her that way or boss her around like that. This sounds like a problem for the Resistance, so we will be joining you, whether you like it or not."

Ryne gives me a glare but nods to his mother. "Just don't get in the way."

Chapter Seven

We follow him out the front door, and I try to ignore the sting of his continued rejections. Right now, I need to be less concerned with our happily-ever-after and more concerned with the things that need to change.

With Thorn dead, there is no reason to have the mating houses or the claiming anymore. Ryne promised he'd get rid of them, and I have every intention of making sure he sticks to his word.

Two trucks are waiting out front now, both beds filled with wolf shifter men, some in their human forms and some more comfortable in their wolves. Ryne climbs into the driver's seat of one truck, and Nico is already driving the other. Madame Delphine climbs in with Ryne, leaving me with Nico.

I don't hesitate to join him––I'm not getting left behind––but I am nervous. Nico and I haven't been alone since I abandoned him at our sham wedding.

Nico gives me a tight grin and puts the truck into gear, following Ryne down the street.

Neither one of us says anything for several minutes.

"I'm sorry I lied to you about the wedding."

Nico sighs. "I wish you would've been honest with me about the whole thing, but I get it. And we both knew there was no romantic love between us. At this point, I'm not sure I'm going to take a bride, and I'm happier that way. Someday, when the pain is gone, I might. But for now, I'm going to focus on being a warrior beta."

I want to argue with him about not taking a bride, which means forcing one more girl to go to a mating house, but if Ryne sticks to his word, then it won't matter. Besides, who am I to deny Nico his wishes?

I stare out the window as the city drops away. "Thank you for not hating me."

He reaches over and squeezes my hand. "I may not have loved you, but I do care for you and your wellbeing. I promised Nova I would look out for you, and I intend to keep that promise. At least, until Ryne's speaking to you again. Then he can look out for you." He chuckles, but I don't see the humor in it.

"You really think he'll forgive me?"

"He's alive, isn't he?"

"Yeah."

"Then he'll forgive you. We can't stay away from our fated mates, no matter how badly we want to."

I clench my fists. "I don't want him to come back to me because he feels obligated."

"He won't. It'll be because he loves you and wants you around. Just give him some time."

I roll my window down and let my hand hang in the wind. I don't know how much more my heart can take. "That's what everyone keeps saying, but I just want to fast forward to the part where he loves me again."

"I know."

Then I realize how selfish I'm being. Here I am, whining about how Ryne isn't talking to me, and Nico's fated mate is dead. Sometimes I marvel at my own stupidity. We need to talk about something else.

"What do you know about what happened to the village?"

"Not much. A man came into the city today, claiming that lycans came and took his wife. We're going to investigate."

"Where's the man?"

"He's staying with Shauna and Amos for now."

"Do you think the whole Carolina Pack will join the Resistance or not?"

"Of course not, but many will once things become public. Ryne's just waiting for the alpha king to be named before making his move. It could be weeks or even months. Now that Izaak is dead, there's more chaos in Chicago than ever."

I hate the uncertainty of everything. Things seem even bleaker now than when Thorn was alpha king. Between Laik and his turning people against their will to the lack of leadership among the wolves, nobody knows what's going to happen. Not for the first time, I long for the days before I was claimed. Where I climbed trees with Willow, worked the fields, and teased my little brother about the neighbor girl. At least, Evan is safe.

Or I hope he is. If Laik is attacking the villages, maybe he's not. Goosebumps rake across my skin. I'll have to see what I can do about checking on my family.

We drive for another thirty minutes and then pull into the middle of the village. People cautiously come out to look. I wave at a little girl who peers through a window. These people have likely never even seen a truck or a car before, and I know how disconcerting that can feel.

Ryne stops in front of us, and I scramble out of the car. Delphine and Nico join him as well. The other wolves stay in the truck bed.

A man approaches Ryne, hat in hand and head bowed.

Ryne speaks softly to him. "Tim from your village came to us and told us about his wife. He was pretty shaken up, so we decided to see what happened for ourselves."

The man runs a hand over his short hair. "They came out of nowhere, grabbed men, women, and children. Some from the same families, some not. We lost thirty-two souls that night."

My stomach drops. Thirty-two people.

Most of them will wish they were dead, come the next full moon, and not everyone will survive the renewal. I pray that those who do will be able to come to terms with their new lives. Except that's not why they were turned, was it? They're meant to be weapons against the shifters. They won't have a choice in the matter, especially the first time they become one of us. They'll be lost to the bloodlust.

"Do you think they're dead?" the man asks mournfully.

"We don't know," Ryne answers. "But we're leaving six wolves to protect your village and more come the next full moon. We're going to spend between now and then hunting down the lycan that took your people." He peers around at the shabby village and swallows. "Will you be able to feed and house the six?"

The man's face pales. "Yes, but what happened to the two wolves that were supposed to be protecting my village on the full moon?"

"They're gone," Ryne admits. "The lycans don't leave bodies behind, but as alpha, I can tell when anyone in my pack is cut away from me."

What must that be like? To have that kind of connection to so many people? It's no wonder Ryne has always put the needs of his pack above all else.

"I'm sorry to hear that. Thank you for coming and for bringing more wolves."

People have come out of their houses now and surround our company. I spot a girl about my age sneaking toward the front. She's pretty and graceful but has a scowl on her face. She catches me looking at her and waves me over.

"What's your name?" she asks in a whisper.

"Poppy, and yours?"

"Laura. Are you a claimed girl?"

"I am." My stomach hardens because I'm pretty sure I know where this conversation is going.

"I'm the only one from my village going at the next harvest moon. The women who help me prepare don't tell me anything other than to explain the pack hierarchy and proper behavior. But I don't know why I'm going to the city in the first place." She sneaks an awed look at Ryne then back to me. "I can't believe the alpha came all the way out here to help us. Is he going to be there when I get claimed?"

I want to give her some reassurance, but if I told her the truth, what would she do? Would she try to run? Would it help her to know or hurt her? I bite my lip and consider. "Listen carefully," I say. "Things should be better by the time you arrive, but if they're not, you need to remember that the other claimed women are not your enemy."

Confusion sparks in her eyes. "Why would they be my enemy?"

I take her hand and squeeze it tight. "That's the point. They're not, and don't let anyone make you believe differently. You got that?"

She nods once.

"I wish I could tell you more." I suck in a breath. The claiming is in less than three months. I can't believe it's almost time for another one. "Honestly, if your whole family can run and get to the panther city down south, they have a sanctuary there, and you could—"

"Panthers?" She drops my hand and steps back. If she looked confused before, she's positively bewildered now. And unnerved. I've scared her, and I want to kick myself for that. Of course, she doesn't know about the panthers. I should've just kept my mouth shut.

"That's enough," Ryne cuts in. "It's time to go."

He grabs my upper arm and marches me back to the truck, setting me in the front seat next to him. There aren't any shifters coming back with us, so he must have sent them out after the lycans and left his six to protect the village. My mouth flattens into a thin line. If he'd kept his promise from the beginning and actually protected this village properly, none of those innocent humans would've been taken.

My relationship with Ryne has been complicated from day one.

I love him, and I hate him.

Both emotions shouldn't exist together, but they do, and right now, I'm ready to let them out.

Chapter Eight

"**S**o what's the plan, alpha?" I ask the question without an ounce of civility. Talking to Laura and seeing the hope in her eyes quickly slip into fear has surfaced the anger I've been holding inside. "Are you going to let those people fend for themselves out there in the wilds with Laik's crew, or are you going to hunt them down and kill them all?"

Ryne's long fingers tighten on the steering wheel as he maneuvers us back to the road. We're on the complete opposite side of the wolf city from my village. Northwest isn't accessible by car because of the river with its crumbling bridge, and my heart twists as I recall the times I made it over that bridge or across that river, but never once to see my family.

"If you must know, I gave them a no-kill order for newly bitten," he says at last, and then he adds, "at least until the full moon when we can see what we're dealing with."

"Being a lycan isn't what you think."

"The bite is the one thing that can kill my people," he growls. "What would you have me do?"

"Have mercy," I state. "And are you forgetting that you're––"

He cuts me off. "Don't say it. Don't you dare."

I throw my hands up. "Fine, stay in denial, but it won't change what happened to you or that you were bitten too. Trust me, I should know."

He turns to glare at me, and I glare back. He's incredibly sexy when he's angry, and I have half a mind to do something about that, to bring him back to me, back to us, to remind him why he loves me so much. And just forget about all the bad blood between us.

But I have to be strong. What I'm about to say is far more important.

I inhale a steadying breath and let it out slowly. "Remember when we were back in the tent, and we talked about all the ways we could fix the city once your father was dead?" I don't wait for him to answer because, of course, he remembers. "It's time to start doing those things, Ryne, beginning with shutting down the mating houses."

No more forced breeding. No more rape. No more claiming. He owes me and the girls that much.

Ryne doesn't say anything for a long time, and my already broken heart begins to shatter because I know him. *I know him.* And if he's not agreeing with me, it's because he's changed his mind.

"Say it," I snap. "I want to hear you say it."

He sighs heavily. "It's not so simple."

"It is, though." All he has to do is say no more. His wolves have to listen to him. They don't have a choice. "That's what being the alpha means. You're in control."

"Being an alpha means so much more than control, Poppy. Just because I'm not making these changes now doesn't mean I never will. I just barely returned to my pack, and if I start making massive changes right now, it will be worse for everyone. Especially the girls. I'm going to do it when it's safest."

"You're waiting for it to be safe?" I laugh bitterly. "Take a look around, Ryne. It's never going to be safe. This world is a terrible place for humans, and what you're doing is making it so much worse. The lycans wouldn't hate you so much if there weren't mating houses and slaves. Maybe none of those people would've been kidnapped on the full moon if you'd made the necessary changes already."

"Don't pin what Laik did on me." His voice is low and murderous. Maybe I deserve that, but he's being completely unreasonable.

"I know you weren't there that night, and I know Anders was acting as stand-in alpha at the time, but tell me why I never saw wolves patrolling my village during the full moons. Was it all a lie? Because the other lycans told me that the humans were never their enemies or their targets. It was always you guys."

"We were the enemies? Have you already forgotten what just happened during the last full moon?" he seethes. "And what about all the other people who were bitten by lycans? And are you forgetting about yourself? About what Laik did to you?"

"I could never forget what happened to me and the terror of becoming a lycan, but that's not the point I'm making."

We sit in silence for a long minute, and it nearly kills me not to say anything, but it's his turn to explain himself. And he needs to because, as far as I can tell, he's a hypocrite. If I thought my heart was broken before, it's utterly decimated now.

"It's my job to protect my pack," he says. "You have no idea the pressure of that. I do protect the villages when it's needed, but it wasn't needed for a long time. You're right. I didn't have men out patrolling on full moons until recently, but now that there's been an attack on a village, I've got more men out in the field than I've ever had before." He's driving faster. Too fast. His anger is fueling the truck's speed. I grab onto my seat belt and squeeze. "I've got young wolves out there as we speak, wolves far younger than I've ever had to send out before. Many of them are searching the wilds and putting their lives at risk. How do you think that makes me feel?"

Part of me wants to hit him. "How dare you make this all about yourself. It's not about how you feel. What about the feelings of the humans who got bitten or lost their loved ones? What about how the claimed feel?" I'm squeezing the seatbelt so damn tight that it's practically biting into my hands, but I don't let up, and he doesn't slow the truck. "And what about *me*?"

"Everything I ever did was for my pack before you came along and got in the way."

He says it like I'm some kind of stain, like I'm not the love of his life but the curse of it. All those tender touches. All those kisses. The way we burned together in the dark of night inside that tent. Our whispered "I love yous" and the stolen glances. All of it comes tumbling down around me.

"I can't believe you would go back on your word like this. I thought you cared about what happens to the women."

"I'll set everything right when I can, once I know who the alpha king is and how to position our pack. And before you tell me to go fight for king, I'm not leaving my pack to do that. Not when they need me most."

Tears burn in my eyes, blurring my vision.

"Don't cry," he says softly, a shadow of my lover returning to me. But it's only a shadow––not the real thing.

"Don't worry. I won't give you any more of my tears," I whisper back. "I've already given you far too many."

He winces, and we don't say anything more after that. I stare out the window as the world passes by, so completely broken inside at the hands of the one person who was supposed to hold me together. Ryne was supposed to choose me. To love me the most. But once again, he's not the devoted fated mate. He's the alpha wolf putting the needs of his pack above all else, even when it's wrong. *Because this is wrong.* I made excuses for him before because of his father, but even with Thorn gone, things are still the same. He'll never be willing to risk his pack for the humans. I truly thought I could trust Ryne after everything we've been through, but it turns out I was wrong.

He drives me straight to the manor.

"One more thing," he says as he slows to a stop, but I don't wait for him to finish. I tear from the truck, slamming the door behind me, and sprint toward the manor. As far as I'm concerned, he had plenty of time to talk during the last half hour of our pained silence. I'm not sticking around another minute to let him break me more than he already has.

Ryne and I are officially done.

Chapter Nine

A pillow hits my head. "Get up." Faye's voice is too loud. I promised myself I wouldn't cry anymore, but I failed, crying myself to sleep last night. How could I not? I still can't believe what Ryne is doing. And how could I have been so fooled? I saw a man in him who didn't actually exist, not when it mattered anyway.

"What's the point?" I mutter and use the pillow she hit me with to cover my eyes.

She rips the pillow away. "The point is that Madame Delphine said we have to get up and get dressed. The betas are coming, and she wants it to look like everything is normal."

"Betas? You mean Justin and Nico? They already know everything, so who cares?"

She grabs my arm and pulls. "It's not just Justin and Nico. Madame Delphine won't say what's going on, only that wolves are coming here who aren't part of the Resistance, so the manor and everyone in it have to look normal."

I sit up and rub my eyes. "Normal?" I snort. "With only six of us claimed girls left? Hardly."

"It's not just us anymore. The lunas are here as well."

"They aren't part of the claiming." I point out the obvious. Those girls still act like the world owes them something just for being born, and it's getting old fast.

"You think that'll stop them from snatching up our men? You are lucky you're fated to Ryne. I still have no guarantees with Justin."

I roll my eyes, but as I look at Faye with her little pout and troubled expression, I realize she's being serious. She's actually worried about the lunas stealing her man. "Justin loves you," I whisper. "I wouldn't worry about that. And Ryne and I are finished. Fated mate means nothing to Ryne."

She means more to Justin than I do to Ryne.

Faye stands and pulls her dress down a little so her cleavage sticks out more. She assesses herself in the mirror for another full minute until she's satisfied, and then she grabs a dress out of the closet and tosses it to me. "You really believe that, huh? Fine. Whatever. But Ryne will be here with them, and this will show him what he's missing. Put it on, and let's go see what all the fuss is about."

I put on the dress only because I don't want to argue with her anymore. It's fitted tight in the bodice and way shorter than anything I'd normally wear, but she has a point about showing Ryne what he's missing.

She glances up at the clock then returns to the mirror yet again to smooth out her already silky auburn hair. Faye has a way of looking gorgeous under every circumstance, even when we were in the wilds. I thought maybe she'd have a facial scar from when Abi beat the snot out of her, but she healed up perfectly and went right back to looking like a future beta wife. "Sit. If we skip breakfast, I can do your hair and makeup."

I don't want to skip breakfast, but I oblige and watch her work. We don't talk. It's not like we're magically friends now, and I don't know what we'd say even if we were. We don't know why Ryne is showing up with a bunch of betas who aren't part of the Resistance, but I'm sure it's all for the good of his pack. I nearly roll my eyes. That's the only thing he cares about, apparently.

Faye loops her arm through mine when it's time to go downstairs. "We're friends now," she says as if able to read my thoughts. "Don't think too hard about it, okay? People can be enemies and then become friends. It happens. It's called character growth."

I snort but don't correct her and don't tug my arm away. It's surreal, and I don't trust it, but at least I'm not alone. I miss Joanna, though. Fiercely. I miss her almost as much as I miss Willow. And then there's my family and Abi--I don't think I can take another loss. Becoming friends with Faye puts me at risk for more pain.

We hit the entryway just as the door is opening. Justin is the first to enter, followed closely by Callum. It's strange seeing Callum here, especially with his head now buzzcut to look like a claimed boy. Three more men that I don't know enter, and Ryne is the last inside. Justin makes a beeline for Faye, swinging her around. She giggles and holds tight to him.

Callum comes up and gives me a kiss on the cheek. "Nice dress," he mutters and backs away, giving Ryne a glance, who glares at him.

Good.

"You let a claimed boy near these women?" One of the new wolves questions his alpha.

"I do not," Ryne says, and Callum blanches, stepping back against the far wall. Very few people know what he really is, and the last thing he needs to do is draw attention to himself. Still, I can't shake the image of Ryne's possessive glare when Callum kissed my cheek. Maybe there's something to Faye's plan of making Ryne jealous. At this point, I'll do anything if it means getting through to him. He needs to honor his word, to be the man I know he can be, the man he talked of being in the wilds.

Vivien enters from a side door. "What are you two doing out here? You should be with the other girls out on the lawn."

Faye grabs my hand and pulls me away from the men. Two of them are checking me out. Maybe Faye knows what she's doing. Not that I'd give Ryne the time of day unless he does what he promised.

We join the other four claimed girls. I can't believe it's come down to just us. Elle and the three lunas around our age are here as well, including my least favorite, Violet. I stride up to Elle.

"What's going on?"

She crosses her arms and glares at the men as they descend the steps onto the lawn. "Nothing good. Ryne thinks he's doing the right thing, but this is a stupid distraction."

"What is he doing?"

But before she can answer, Ryne waves us all closer. Delphine and Vivien have joined them.

"Ladies, it's been a rough year. We've lost too many girls. Cade died in battle. Grady and Joanna have run off. Nico lost his fated, and Anders has left our pack for Chicago. It's not been fair to you. In an effort to make things a bit better, I'm bringing in three more betas."

This was talked about before I was bitten, but it never came to fruition, and it's not a solution. It's the same old thing, and my fists ball tightly as I glare at Ryne. He doesn't even flinch.

"That's enough for each of us," Samantha hisses next to me.

I can do the math as well, but it only twists the knife in deeper because it looks like Ryne has written me off once and for all. So that's it? He proclaims his love for me, we sleep together, and then it's back to the claiming for me? I'm a lycan now. Sure, I can hide what I am during the full moons for now with careful planning, but that won't happen if I get married off to the wrong guy.

Ryne chuckles. "What Samantha said is only partially true. It wouldn't be a good claiming if there wasn't a little competition."

"What are you talking about?" I ask, forgetting that I vowed to never speak to him again.

"The lunas who are of age," he says, pointing at the three of them and Elle, "will be dating the betas as well. In the end, the betas will choose. If they choose you humans, then you don't have to worry about the mating houses. If they choose a luna, then . . ." He lets his words trail off.

"A luna doesn't have to agree to marry a beta. She can choose to say no," Elle says harshly. "No offense, but I'm not marrying any of you." She drops her voice low and nods toward us claimed. "And no way would I steal a man from one of you girls."

Violet scoffs. "She's right. I'm only marrying an alpha."

The curvy one, Marissa, folds her arms over her chest and studies the men with interest, but otherwise, she stays quiet. That seems to be her way, but I wonder how long she'll stay like that if she ends up liking one of these guys.

"Me too," the blonde one, Cecily, adds. "Ryne, if you're interested, let's chat. Otherwise, why bother?"

I have to bite my tongue at that comment.

"I'm gonna be alpha someday," one of the new betas says. His muscles ripple under his shirt, and aside from Ryne, he's probably the most handsome man I've ever seen, with a strong jaw and devastating smile that he's throwing at Cecily.

She doesn't look impressed.

"So if one of the lunas gets picked by a beta, and one of us doesn't, that means we're heading to the mating house. Including me?" I cross my arms and challenge him. I need to know how serious this is.

"Including you. Good luck, Poppy." He turns to his betas. "While Poppy is my fated mate, I recognize the need to strengthen my pack. I'll be choosing one of the lunas. Poppy is a strong woman and would make a fine wife for any of you."

My mouth turns to ash. I can't believe what I'm hearing. "Where's Nico?" I ask, voice cracking. He's the only other one I'd consider, but considering our conversation the other day, I'm pretty sure he's already backed out. I suddenly wish he hadn't.

"I released him from his pledge. He deserves time to mourn losing Nova."

"Oh, so he's devastated to lose his mate, but you're just fine losing yours?"

"I'm an alpha," he snaps. "I do what's best for my pack at all times."

I grit my teeth and back down. I don't know what else to say. There's nothing left. But it looks like we're fighting a losing battle once again.

Chapter Ten

I'm not going through with this harvest. No way am I marrying some random beta or getting stuck in a mating house. If I have to, I'll run for The Sanctuary. In the meantime, the Resistance still needs my help. They started using the poppy as a symbol of solidarity with each other, a simple way to know who's on their side, because I stood up for what is right in front of everyone. Who would I be if I backed down now? So I'll be quiet, and I'll pretend, but it won't last long.

"We've prepared a picnic brunch for you all to get to know each other," Madame Delphine says. I notice she doesn't have her usual enthusiasm, and I wonder if she's as angry with Ryne as I am. "Please, enjoy yourselves."

The August heat is already too much. I'm sweating and want to get out of the sun. Luckily, the tables are set up underneath the shade of the weeping willows, and I hurry to them, plopping myself down with folded arms, still glaring at Ryne. I have no interest in putting on a pretty smile and acting as if any of this is okay. Too much has changed for us. And it's not as if I'm going to marry another man anyway. The Carolina Pack can forget all about me.

I'll be long gone before they can touch me.

The lunas are quick to surround Ryne, except for Elle. She sits down next to me and whispers under her breath. "This is all a bunch of bullshit."

I let out a startled laugh. I don't know if I've ever heard Elle curse before, but I don't blame her. She's lost so much for this to be the outcome, almost as much as I have, and for what? For us to prance around for a bunch of entitled men to "pick" us like we're livestock? I'm so over this.

"Hi there." An attractive man sits down right next to me. "I'm Bellamy. And you are?"

It's not the gorgeous guy who claimed he would be an alpha one day. That guy is still busy trying to get the lunas' attention. But this man isn't easy to overlook either. He's got curly black hair and smooth dark skin, the greenest eyes I've ever seen, and a relaxed smile.

Bellamy . . . a nice name too.

I don't say anything because I assume he's talking to Elle, but when she doesn't answer and elbows me in the ribcage, I startle. "Uh, I'm Poppy, but you probably already know that."

"Oh, because everyone knows who you are, is that right?" he teases.

I don't know if this is supposed to be flirty, but I'm not buying it. "I'm your alpha's fated mate, and I was very publicly engaged to another beta before getting kidnapped. Of course you know who I am." These games we're all playing are ridiculous.

He chuckles low and raises a shiny glass of ice water to me before taking a long drink. I can't help but notice the way his throat bobs as he swallows. It's sexy, and I shoot Elle a "he's all yours" look because, really, they would look fantastic together, but she just winks.

"You're right," he says. "I do know who you are, but that doesn't mean I know you." His gaze holds mine, interest swirling behind those bright green eyes. "But I'd like to."

My cheeks flush, and Elle coughs. "I'm going to go mingle." Then she leaves me alone with this man I'm now certain is flirting with me.

"Why are you flirting with me?" I blurt out. He raises an amused eyebrow, and I backtrack. "I just mean, there are other women here, and lunas at that. Why would you single out a rejected mate?"

He sets his glass down and leans in so our noses are only an inch apart, swamping me with his distinct spicy scent. It's so male, but it's also so different from Ryne's woodsy musk that it's jarring. I never thought I'd be this close to another man again. "You're special, and just because Ryne's too blinded by his position as alpha to see it doesn't mean I don't."

"Sure." I roll my eyes, but I don't back down or lean away. This is an intriguing game we're playing, and maybe Elle's right that this is all a stupid distraction, but at least, it's a distraction. I need that now more than ever.

"It's true. I've been at all the festivals and have watched you every time, kicking myself for not pursuing you when I had the chance." He catches a strand of my hair between his fingers and twirls it. "And I only signed up for this because I knew you were back."

My mouth pops open, and I inadvertently sigh. Why can't Ryne be like this? Bellamy is more forward than any man I've ever met. He knows exactly what he wants: me.

I'm still a little thrown by him and his forwardness. I'm of two minds, and I don't know which one will win today. The first is to tell him to go to hell and stick with my plan of helping as many girls as possible get to The Sanctuary, staying single in the process. It's not going to be easy, and I know that it means a life of hardship and heartache, but it's also a life spent helping others.

But the other part of me wonders what it would be like to just give in. To let this beautiful man love me. To not have to worry about Ryne and death and lycans. Of course, the fact that I am one is a problem.

I glance over at him and catch a flash of red on his lapel.

I reach out and run my fingers over the soft petals. "You have a poppy." I wonder if he knows what it means or if he just has one because it shares my name.

He grins. "I do. Shauna gave it to me."

My eyes flash up to his. If Shauna gave it to him, that means he's in the Resistance.

"So you know . . ." I let my words trail off.

He glances up to where Ryne is chatting with Madame Delphine. A dark look shadows his face.

"I do. And it seems to me that Ryne is never going to be fully in even if he says he is."

"What's that supposed to mean?" But I'm pretty sure I already know. Ryne had me fooled too. Maybe he fooled the whole Resistance.

Bellamy shakes his head. "Not here. We'll talk about it on our date tomorrow night."

He's so sure of himself, but not in the arrogant way Ryne is.

"Date?" I ask.

He nods. "They're speeding up the process since we new betas have less than three months to make our choices. You'll have dates almost every night."

The other betas are leaving their tables, and Ryne walks away from Madame Delphine toward the house. Bellamy stands. "I guess it's time to go."

"I guess it is." I'm staring into his eyes, and I can't seem to look away. I'm so broken, and I doubt any man will be able to put me back together; I'm going to have to do it myself. But if someone wants to try, maybe I should let him.

He tears his gaze away and takes a step from the table. I reach out and grab his hand.

He glances down. "You okay?"

"Bellamy. If you're serious, tell Delphine that all my dates are with you."

His worried face splits into a wide smile, and a dimple appears on his left cheek. "I wouldn't have it any other way."

Then he squeezes my hand once more and strides across the lawn. I watch his retreating back for a moment, unsure of what I've just done. Then I glance up at the house. Ryne stands on the balcony, staring at me, a storm of torment brewing in his eyes. I recognize that possessive expression. I've seen it time and again when we're together. But I'm tired of the false hope, of the games and broken promises, so this time when our gazes meet, I'm the first to look away.

Chapter Eleven

"**Y**ou're really going to date Bellamy?" Elle lies on my bed, watching me and Faye dress and get ready for our dates. I nod and thumb through my dresses. I have no idea what to expect tonight, so I'm not sure what to wear.

"You're an idiot," Faye says. "But at least you'll make Ryne jealous."

"She's not wrong," Elle adds.

"What am I supposed to do? Wait around for Ryne to decide I'm worthy again? It's stupid. He's made it clear how he feels about me, and I'm not exactly on board with his 'let's keep things the same' agenda."

"Did you forget what you are? You can't date a wolf," Faye says.

"Didn't stop Ryne from declaring I would," I snap.

"She shouldn't be dating anyone." Elle sits up. "A little harmless flirting is one thing, but dating someone else puts your relationship at risk. Do you have any idea how lucky you are to be fated? I would kill for that."

"It obviously doesn't mean anything." I pick out a dress that Joanna had modified for me. It's fitted in the bodice with a flowy, feminine skirt, and it makes me miss her in the worst way.

"But it does. Ryne's acting like a fool now, but he will come around. And it's not fair of you to string Bellamy along because you and I both know that, if Ryne were to come back to you now, apologize, and get rid of the mating houses, you'd jump right back into his arms."

I think about her words for a moment, wondering if they're true. I don't know. I don't want to admit that she's probably right. Because wouldn't that make me weak?

"But he's not going to do that, so why should I wait around?"

Faye shakes her head. "Y'all are focusing on the wrong thing. What are you going to do come the full moon?"

"Madame Delphine will think of something—she always does." Besides, it doesn't seem that complicated to me. Just sneak me off to be somewhere by myself and lock me in. I have enough control over my lycan that it's not as if I'll be howling and drawing attention, and I won't leave to go off and bite people either. It won't be the most fun night, but it wouldn't be any worse than sleeping in that dark basement, fearing for my life.

Except even as I think about that sensible plan, I know what I really want to do. I want to run away from Drayton Hall so I can hunt down Laik and his cronies. I'd do anything to take those evil lycans out. They need to be stopped, and I'm pretty fearsome in my own lycan form, but then again, so are they. And there are far more of them than there are of me.

"And is she going to think of something for the rest of your life? If you hook up with Bellamy, this won't be just for this month."

"If things get that far." Which, to be honest, they probably won't. Once Bellamy sees how broken I am, he's sure to bail on me for one of the better options. "But I'm not going to worry about that yet. I've got too many other things on my mind."

"Whatever. Just don't say we didn't warn you. What do you think we'll be doing tonight?" Faye changes the subject. "Justin and I haven't been out in ages. I hope we get to go off alone, no offense."

I don't know what to expect for my first date with Bellamy. Maybe it'll be a dinner out, dancing, or even a stroll along the riverside. Whatever it is, I hope Faye is wrong and we're not sent off alone with the men. Bellamy seems okay, but I don't know him––I can't trust the men I do know, let alone someone new.

We all gather in the hallway, but the betas are nowhere in sight. Elle hangs back. She's no longer dressed like a house mother but is instead wearing one of the boring black day dresses we claimed girls have to wear sometimes. She insisted she's not dating anyone, but I have a feeling she's not going to get a choice in the matter.

Madame Delphine looks her over. "You have a date tonight."

Elle glowers at her. "I told you I'm not going."

"Please, don't make this harder than it already is—for all of us."

Elle crosses her arms. "I'm a luna, so I don't have to date them if I don't want to." Madame Delphine opens her mouth to argue, but Elle rushes on. "But in the interest of not making your life more difficult, I'll agree to date Ryne, Justin, or Bellamy. Just not Dante or Lev."

Dante is the handsome wolf who boasted that he's going to become an alpha, and Lev isn't much better. They're clearly here to land a luna, which is exactly why Elle wants to keep them at arm's length.

Madame Delphine rubs her eyes. "I can work with that. You still need to put something else on, though. Tonight is a group date."

Faye groans, and I chuckle.

Elle comes back downstairs in a plain white dress. I'm sure she thought it would make it look like she didn't care about the date, but she still looks gorgeous. The color makes her inky skin pop and her braided hair stand out.

Three cars are waiting for us, and I manage to snag one with Faye, Delphine, and Elle, thank goodness. None of us say much on the drive over, though, because the driver isn't someone we know. Well, Delphine probably does know him, and we take our cues from her and keep our mouths shut.

In no time at all, we slide from the cars, decked out in gorgeous dresses as usual, and are met with a row of handsome smiles. I zero in on Bellamy because I can't bear to look at Ryne and his date, Violet. She's been all over him the second she laid eyes on him, and even more so since he declared he's looking to marry a luna, so apparently she doesn't care about fated mates any more than he does.

They're a match made in my own personal hell, and I refuse to watch their courtship unfold.

"Do you like popcorn?" Bellamy cuts into my thoughts.

"I love it, actually." Mostly because it reminds me of home and so many better memories than the ones I've made in this city, but he doesn't have to know that. It was the one snack we could have as often as we wanted at home because we were never short on corn. I can still remember the sound of the kernels popping on the hot stove and the anticipation of the salt coating my tongue.

"And what about movies?" he adds. "Any favorite movies I should know about?"

I blink at him in disbelief. I've heard about movies—we all have—but I didn't know they still existed. "I've never seen one."

Bellamy raises his dark eyebrows and smirks, making my stomach swoop a little. "Just you wait."

We're ushered inside the building and taken to a huge room with row after row of padded seats facing a vast white wall that almost looks like it could be a window if it wasn't so opaque. I settle in next to Bellamy, and he slings his arm around the back of my chair, tugging me into his warmth.

A couple of middle-aged claimed women come around to distribute bowls of salty popcorn and tall cups of water to each couple. I hardly notice as the couples spread out because I'm too distracted by Ryne and his date. In spite of not wanting to see them, I can't keep my eyes off the pair. They're several rows ahead of us and talking to each other in low voices, their faces close. When Violet runs her fingers along his neck, I see red and clutch the armrest.

"You want to know something about me?" Bellamy's whisper is hot against my ear, and a shiver zaps down my spine. "I love a good challenge."

That snaps me out of it. I turn to glower at him, taking in his wild green eyes and the flirtation in his smile. "I don't think you realize how much of a challenge it's going to be to come between fated mates," I confess. This is not fair to him at all. "Even if we're broken up."

He leans back, relaxing, and gives me a wink. "I'm not worried, Poppy. By the Harvest Moon Festival, Ryne will be a distant memory, and I'll be the one you look for in a crowded room."

"Oh, you really think so?" Maybe I'm flirting a little too.

Maybe I like it. Maybe I need something to keep my mind off the budding romance between Ryne and Violet by having one of my own.

"Oh, I know so."

The lights dim, and before I process everything going on between us, the screen lights up. I gasp, stunned by all that brightness seemingly coming from nowhere. It flickers to a scene of people larger than life, humans from a distant place and time, long before the world was lost to the shifters and lycans. As the movie starts, a miracle unfolds: I forget all about Bellamy *and* Ryne.

Chapter Twelve

I may get lost in the movie, but I don't stay there. After the novelty wears off, my eyes roam to the back of Ryne's head. He's got his arm tight around Violet's shoulders, and my stomach sours.

Bellamy's hand finds my chin, and he slowly turns my face so I'm looking at him. There's concern in his eyes, but he doesn't acknowledge Ryne at all. "Do you trust me?" he whispers through the dark.

"No," I admit. "I don't trust any men these days."

"Fair enough. Who is your closest friend in the house?"

"Elle."

I crane my head around, looking for her, and then chuckle when I find her sitting with Justin and Faye. She's two seats away from them, shoveling popcorn in her mouth. They are making out. I have no idea where her date went, but she probably already scared him off. The woman is not interested in dating, let alone marriage. And although Madame Delphine made it seem like Elle would be getting her way tonight, she still ended up sitting next to Lev until he disappeared.

Bellamy follows my eyes. "Okay. Well then, would you be okay taking a walk with me as long as we bring Elle along?"

"Sure."

Despite the interesting movie, I want to get away from Violet and Ryne.

We leave the theater after getting permission from Madame Delphine. Bellamy holds out his arms, so Elle and I both tuck our hands in the crook of his elbows. Elle looks at me and winks. She seems more than happy to get away from Faye and Justin.

"And where'd your date go?" I tease her.

She shrugs. "He went home after I told him I'd kill him if he so much as breathed on me."

Everyone laughs, and I turn to Bellamy. "Where are we going?" I ask.

"The best-kept secret in town. My house."

I balk for a second. I don't want to go to his house, even with Elle around.

"Don't worry. It's not what you think. There are many people at my house that I want you to meet. I probably have more claimed servants than any other beta."

I snort. "If you think that's gonna make me like you more, then you have no idea who I am."

"But I do know who you are, and I can guarantee this is going to make you like me more."

Elle helps me out. "You know. You're a little too confident for your own good. Poppy's heart really isn't for the taking."

His eyes sparkle. "Fine. I'm willing to put my money where my mouth is, so to speak."

"Go on," Elle says.

"If by the end of the evening I have impressed Poppy, then I get a kiss from her."

"And if you don't?" I ask, my cheeks already burning at the thought of kissing him.

"Then I get a kiss from Elle."

Elle gasps and shoves him away, and he laughs. I stumble a little, and he catches me, his eyes sparkling. Either way, he ends the night with a kiss. The man is smarter than I thought and an even bigger flirt than Faye.

"I'll go for that," I say, actually liking the idea of Elle having a guy to distract her from her grief. "What about you, Elle? Will you take his wager?"

She stares at me for a long time, sadness in her eyes, and then she nods, and her face splits into a fake grin. "Guess I'll be getting a kiss tonight, so I probably should get to know you a little more." She takes his other arm once again and then begins to pepper him with questions about his past.

He tells us that he grew up in the pack houses and fought his way to beta. He's been a beta warrior for ten years and planned for many more before he took an interest in me. That part makes me blush even more, and I ignore Elle's raised eyebrows.

The walk doesn't take long, and soon we are standing in front of a huge southern mansion. It's almost as big as Ryne's place, which must mean Bellamy is a well-respected beta within the pack.

He pushes the oak front door open, and I walk inside, followed by Elle.

The entrance hall is wide with large rooms on both sides. Each is furnished with squashy couches and chairs. And there are women everywhere.

Some are asleep under blankets; others are chatting in low voices. A few have books in their hands.

A few more are sprawled out on the floor, playing board games.

Elle looks at me with her brow furrowed. "I don't understand what I'm looking at."

"Me neither," I admit.

Bellamy leans forward, keeping his voice low. "I'm not a fan of the mating houses. My mother once lived in them, was raped by wolves on a nightly basis. Obviously, I never knew her, but these women are living reminders of who she was. Betas sometimes take women home for a week or two if both parties agree. So I do the same thing. I bring home two or three women at a time for a couple of weeks from several different mating houses in the city. But I don't sleep with them. I let them rest and relax. My staff of retired women feed them well and care for them. We have a formal dinner almost every night. Most nights, I have between thirty and forty girls here."

My mind immediately goes to Abi, and I wonder if she's found sanctuary here. I had no idea things like this existed in the city, and I'm completely overcome by it. Bellamy really is what he says he is—resistance. And a good man at that.

"Does Ryne know about this?" I ask.

"He does."

"And he's okay with it?"

The answer to that question might kill me, but I have to know the truth. I don't know why I'm looking for redemption for him, but I can't help it.

"He tolerates it. Now, come meet everyone over dessert."

Elle doesn't wait. She's quick to make her rounds, chatting with the other women as if they're all old friends, though I'm sure she's never met them. I'm a little more reserved while I search for Abi's face. I need to find her, to make sure she's okay. "Do you know what happened to Abi?" I ask as Bellamy pulls out a seat for me at his long dining table.

"Who?" He sits next to me at the head of the table, and women begin bringing out trays of decadent sweets. I grab one of the chocolate tarts and set it on my plate.

"She's new. She went to the mating house back in April."

His eyes spark. "Oh, the girl who distracted the wolves long enough for Grady to run off with his mate. How could I forget? But I'm sorry. I haven't seen her."

My heart plummets, fear trickling through my body. What if she's dead? Thorn probably had her killed. It's something he would do––end her life for being defiant and forget all about her the next day. Just another girl who failed, another girl who died at his hands. My eyes start to water, and my stomach goes hollow. Somehow, I just know Abi isn't doing well and probably isn't even alive.

"Hey, don't worry. I'll find her for you, okay? And when I do, I'll bring her to the house, and you can come out for dinner to make sure she's doing alright."

I meet his eyes, searching for sincerity. I still don't know if I can really trust him, if there's another angle he's playing here. Maybe he's like that other beta, Dante, who joined the claiming, acting like he'd become an alpha someday. If Bellamy fought to get this position in the pack, who's to say he isn't trying to take Ryne out, using me as part of his plan?

"I know you don't trust me," he supplies as if reading my mind. "But you will. I promise."

Elle plops down in the seat on his other side, directly across from me, her smile bright and her tone joyful. It's the happiest I've seen her since her father was killed. "I have to hand it to you, Bellamy. You're the real deal. If Poppy won't give you a kiss at the end of the night, I will. Heck, I'll even slip you some tongue."

She's joking, right? I've never seen her be so forward with a man. Ever. But then she bursts out laughing, and so do I, Bellamy's tanned face flushing scarlet.

"Elle and Bell, it has a nice ring to it," I tease.

She waves her hand and gives Bellamy a more serious expression. "Oh please, you should know that I never want to get married. Not to an alpha or a beta or anyone, for that matter. Don't waste your time trying with me because the only way I'm getting married is if someone drags me down the aisle."

"Practice dragging lunas down aisles," he jokes. "Got it."

She laughs at that. "And don't say I didn't warn you about Poppy. She's already spoken for."

His eyes go dark, still trained on her. "We'll see about that."

My chest burns. I'm not sure how to parcel out my feelings. He's doing everything I wish Ryne would. And he's treating me better too. But I thought Ryne was a good man as well, and there was a time when he was sweet to me, when he made me promises and treated me like I was his world. I don't know that I can trust my own judgment.

After dessert, Elle stays in the house with the other women, talking about her hopes for the future after the alpha king is in place. Apparently there are a lot more Resistance shifters out there than I originally thought, and more pop up every day. Several are planning to fight for the throne. She believes one will win, and even though she's heartbroken her father didn't succeed, she's hopeful for the future of the kingdom. To see her so open about it makes me nervous but gives me hope, too, like maybe it's going to actually happen. It can't come soon enough. We've got less than three months until the harvest festival, and I've still got to figure out what to do about the coming full moons.

"I want to show you something," Bellamy whispers, taking my hand and leading me back outside. I don't really want to leave Elle behind, but Bellamy has given me no reason not to trust him after tonight. We go through the front door and around to a little side yard bursting with roses. The house has low lights, casting the garden into a golden haze. The scene is beautiful and smells even better than it looks.

He leads me up to another garden bed, this one brimming with bright red poppies. He picks one and hands it to me. "I thought about you for months after I first saw you, wishing I'd entered the claiming so I could court you."

Twirling the flower between my fingers, I stare at it, not knowing what to say and scared of what I'll find in Bellamy's face if I look at him. I never expected something like this. For a man to be so open with me, to want me this much. Not even Knox was like this when we first started dating. And Ryne did everything he could to fight our bond, only truly giving in to fate when we were out in the wilds.

Bellamy continues. "These roses have been here for ages, but this is the first year I cared about the garden." His thumb brushes under my chin and tilts my face up to his. "And the first year I planted poppies."

Worries of him using me to get to Ryne drift away on the summer breeze. My lips part as he leans forward, our faces mere inches apart. "Can I kiss you?" he asks softly. It's different than with Ryne, who aggressively takes what he wants. Ryne would kiss me without waiting for permission.

This isn't better. Not worse. Just different.

It's to be expected––the wound is still so fresh. My broken heart has nothing to do with the potential for Bellamy to make me happy. He could heal it in time. And if anyone can help me move on, surely it's someone as attentive and determined as this handsome man. I know it's not fair to him to be my second choice, but he obviously doesn't care. He wants me anyway, I'm his number one, and I deserve to be happy after everything I've been through.

At least, that's what I tell myself as I nod consent, and Bellamy's lips brush against mine. He's soft at first, tentative, until I open my mouth to him. A low groan rumbles through his core, and the kiss turns passionate and exploring, our tongues pulling and prodding, our lips bruising. He presses me up against the house, and though he's not Ryne, and it's not the same, my body still responds, and my thoughts still float away.

But my heart?

My heart is back there in that theater, being ripped to shreds.

Chapter Thirteen

Elle sits across from me at breakfast the next day, her eyes sparkling. I didn't tell her about the kiss with Bellamy last night. She spent the car ride home prattling on about the different girls she met and things we could do to help them. I barely heard what she said. My mind was on Bellamy and Ryne.

It still is. I can't quite seem to wrap my head around the fact that Ryne has written me off completely. I could probably be happy with Bellamy. Logically, it makes sense, and my body responded to his touch, but my heart will always ache for what could've been. Can I really defy fate?

Elle doesn't say anything until everyone else sits down. Our little group is not one I would've imagined at the beginning of the year. Faye and Samantha have their heads pressed together, whispering about something. Joy sits next to me, and while she seems to be doing better now that Faye is back, she's still withdrawn and reluctant to engage. Raven sinks down next to Elle, looking defeated, and picks at her food.

The lunas all sit together on the other side of the room, the older girls taking care of the younger. Violet and Cecily seem to be the leaders of their little group, which makes sense since they are the oldest. They don't have any interest in mingling with us, almost acting as if we don't even exist. Marissa is unaffected by it all, and poor Elle is stuck in the middle, not that she seems to mind. Elle has always been the type to do whatever she wants.

"So, Poppy," Elle begins with a smirk. "I didn't get a kiss from Bellamy last night, so that means you must've."

"What?" Faye gasps, turning on me with a huge grin. "You kissed him?"

I glare at Elle. "Yes. I did." I don't want to talk about this. I still don't understand it myself.

"And?" Elle asks, practically bouncing in her seat.

I blush and stare at my food.

Joy nudges me, which is surprising because Joy has been quiet as a mouse since I returned from the wilds. "Come on, we all want to know."

If I don't tell them, they'll never stop asking. "It was nice. He's not Ryne, obviously, but he's sweet."

"Is he a good kisser?" Raven raises her eyebrows suggestively.

I nod, and the table erupts with laughter.

Faye drops her voice to a whisper. "Excuse me, little princess, but weren't you and Ryne sleeping together?"

My blush deepens, and a few of the nearby girls gasp.

"I don't see how that's relevant." I drop my eyes. That's the least of my worries, actually. It's the lycan problem that I don't think we'll be able to get past. I can't be with Bellamy––he would never want to marry a woman who could kill him once a month.

"We're supposed to be pure." Samantha narrows her eyes. "If you're not a virgin, you're supposed to be sent to a mating house."

My whole body goes cold at her words, and I want to throttle Faye for blabbing.

Elle waves a hand. "You were with Ryne though. It's different because he's the alpha, so he's the one that gives his blessing for the weddings. Honestly, I doubt most of the wolves care about purity."

All the girls stare at me, but I don't have anything to say. It took two of us to do what we did, and I don't see Ryne apologizing for it.

"Some of them care about purity. It's a double standard." Faye rolls her eyes.

"Faye, I'm pretty sure you have no room to talk," Elle points out.

Faye straightens in her chair. "Justin and I are going to be married, so it doesn't matter what we do in private."

"Poppy thought that too."

Faye glares at Elle. "What Justin and I do when we're alone is nobody's business."

"Wait a minute, you too? Seriously, am I the only one who follows the rules?" Samantha asks, and Raven giggles.

Elle wiggles her eyebrows. "Now, you guys understand how this works. Bellamy has all but proposed to Poppy, so that leaves you three to battle it out for Dante and Lev." Elle points her fork at Joy, Samantha, and Raven.

"They're going to go for the lunas." Raven sighs. "We don't stand a chance."

"But the lunas have no interest in the betas at all. Marissa is like me and doesn't want to get married. And Violet and Cecily are going after Ryne because he's the alpha." Elle's insistence is like a knife to the heart. What if Ryne wants one of them back?

"I don't want to get married either." Raven grips her fork. "I hate this whole system."

"Well, that certainly makes this easier." Elle winks. "Raven, we'll work on getting you out to The Sanctuary, and the same goes for anyone else who wishes to leave. But I'll have a conversation with Delphine about dates and make sure the ladies who stay get plenty of one-on-one time with Dante and Lev." A small smile creeps over Samantha's face, and it's sort of wonderful that we can talk about these things in the open like this.

I don't want to get their hopes up. "Maybe we should be looking at getting all four of you to The Sanctuary. I'll go with you."

Even as I say the words, I'm not sure I mean them. I'd likely go and come crawling right back.

Elle grins at me. "And break poor Bellamy's heart? No way. But if the rest of you want to go, that can be arranged."

I don't know how she can be in such a good mood and talk about all this so nonchalantly. This is all so heavy, and I'm tired of it. I want Ryne to do what he said and make the mating houses and the claiming a thing of the past. He says that breeding can be done by paying women from the villages to come to the city, and I think he's probably right so long as they're treated with respect. It's not a perfect solution to the shifters' population problems, but it's certainly better than rape.

"Does going mean we'll never get to visit our village?" Joy speaks up, and we all turn to her. "It's not like I'm expecting to see my family again, but what if things change, and we can? I don't want to miss that opportunity. I'm not sure the panthers will be any better than the wolves, and if that's the case, then I'd rather stay closer to home."

We're all homesick, and her question makes my chest burn.

Elle offers a sad smile. "I don't have the answer to that, Joy. I'm sorry."

"I think I'll stay then." Joy shrugs, turning back to our food, and the rest of us exchange worried glances just as Madame Delphine enters the room, cutting off all conversation.

"Ladies, classes will resume after chores today. I expect my girls to show the lunas how we do things around here. Anyone sixteen and older will attend the same classes, and I'm bringing in another woman to teach the younger girls. There will be no more rankings as this is the last quarter and is highly unnecessary. As you know, the betas will be here each evening to take you out." She glances at her watch. "You have ten minutes until chores."

And just like that, life is *normal* again.

Chapter Fourteen

The next few weeks pass in a blur. It's classes, chores, and dealing with obnoxious lunas during the days and romantic dates with Bellamy most nights. Sometimes we go out with other couples, but half the time we're alone. Elle joins us quite a bit. She still refuses to date Lev or Dante, so she only goes out with Bellamy or Ryne––just as she said she would. The girl is great at getting her way, and I kinda envy her for that.

Ryne rarely even looks at me. Though, one night, I didn't realize he was on the porch when Bellamy brought me home and gave me a long goodnight kiss. I found Ryne glaring at us before shifting into his wolf form and running away. I almost went after him, but my pride wouldn't let me. Why should I care? I'm the one who got dumped.

The whole thing is wearing on me.

A week before the full moon, I'm on the front porch, waiting for Bellamy to arrive, wondering what on earth I'm going to do about us.

"You okay?" Bellamy asks as he approaches. We're well past small talk, but I'm still not sure if I'm ready to open up to him emotionally.

"Yeah, why?"

"You look sad." Those words hurt because they're true. I am sad.

I shrug it off. "I'm just worried about things, you know. There is still no alpha king, and I'm tired of trying to keep the Resistance a secret. I'm ready for change." And I want Ryne back, but I don't say that.

He grabs my hand. "I know. It seems like everything is in limbo, but it won't last forever. Besides, I have a surprise for you."

I give him a small grin. "You have a surprise for me almost every day."

"Yeah, but this is something I think you'll really enjoy." He takes my hand and leads me to his car. There's no driver tonight, and I ride in the front as we travel through the center of the city. I don't like this area. It's where most of the mating houses are located, reminding me of all the disappointments I've had since coming here. But I'm one of the lucky ones, right? This is such a horrible world we live in that I should consider myself lucky...

I expect him to park here, but when we keep going, my spirits lift. I was worried he was going to take me to see some of the women in the mating houses. It feels selfish that I didn't want to do that. We finally end up on the other side of the wolf city––on the outskirts, the opposite end of Drayton Hall. He pulls up to a beautiful estate with wolf shifters stationed all around it. It's got far more protection than even the claimed girls get. They nod to Bellamy as we drive up to the entrance.

"What is this place?" I ask.

But Bellamy stops the car and opens the door for me, and I get my answer. A group of four pregnant women strolls through a rose garden in the distance. They gaze over at us with lifted hands to shade the sunset's glare from their eyes, casting their faces in dark shadows. I imagine their expressions are filled with distrust at the sight of us. I'd never look at any man the same if I had to go through what they've gone through to end up here.

We should go.

It isn't right to come here on a date; it's like we're rubbing it in their faces that we're parading around on dates while they're here––not beta wives but baby makers all the same. If I ever have kids, I'll do anything to keep them with me. Being a beta wife would do that for me. Is pregnancy even possible now that I'm a lycan? Maybe I'm infertile, and I don't even know it yet. I want to say something to Bellamy, and my stomach churns at the thought of seeing what's inside this estate home, but I bite my tongue out of curiosity. It's good to know what the Resistance is dealing with, and I'd love to see if the pregnant mating-house women are treated as well as Ryne said they are.

"Unfortunately, we can't go inside." Bellamy seems to read my mind. "Well, you probably could, but this is the one place the women are allowed respite from the men. Only women inside unless they call on us for protection."

"Can't say I blame them," I mumble as we round the corner of the back of the house instead of heading inside.

A woman sits with her hands resting on her belly, though the belly in question is as flat as mine. Her hair hangs around her face, and when she looks up at us with that familiar blue gaze, my heart flutters.

"Abi," I gasp. I drop Bell's hand and race to my friend.

She rises from her chair and catches me in a hug. When I pull back, her eyes are round with disbelief. "I thought you were dead. I heard you got taken by lone wolves and assumed they had killed you. What are you doing here?" She stares at me like she's seen a ghost.

I shake my head. "I'm fine, but enough about me. How are you?" My voice cracks, and I wonder if I should've asked another question instead. Of course she's not doing well. She's been in a mating house for months, and now she's here, pregnant. I know that's the point, that eventually we're all going to have babies, or at least try, but to see it happen so fast is a shock.

"I'm okay." Her eyes dart to Bellamy.

I turn to mouth a big "thank you" to him.

"I'll be waiting in the car when you're ready to leave, but no rush. We've got all night."

I'm grateful for his thoughtfulness.

And then he's gone, and it's just me and Abi on this stupid huge porch, and everything comes flooding in at once. She must feel the same way because we fall into each other's arms, sobbing. I don't know how long we stay like that, but long enough for the tears to dry up into salty streaks down our cheeks. Then we sit on the porch swing, gently swaying, as we tell each other everything that's happened over the last four months.

Well, almost everything.

Abi can't handle explaining the details about the mating house, and I can't explain what it felt like to become a lycan and bite Knox the way I did. She's not happy about being pregnant because she doesn't want to contribute to the wolf city. She doesn't care that she gets better treatment away from the men for the next nine months. And I'm not happy about Ryne and everything he's put me through recently.

And when I tell her about Joanna, how she went with Grady to be with the horrible lycans that are biting humans, she becomes angry with shock. "I just can't believe they would do that," she keeps repeating. And I feel the same way, though I have a hard time blaming Joanna for anything. Grady demanded it, and she wasn't willing to leave her mate.

I take Abi's small hand in mine and squeeze. "If there's one thing I've learned this year, it's that people aren't always who they say they are."

"And sometimes people are exactly who they say they are," she replies, her voice dark and filled with unknown horrors.

"Things are going to change," I whisper. "I'll get you out of here, and you can take your baby with you, or you can leave the baby with someone else to adopt, but I promise you're going to live in the panther sanctuary before you ever step foot in another mating house."

She scoffs and points to the men at the perimeter. "Do you see the security around here? I don't think I'm leaving until I have the baby, and as soon as I'm healed, it's back to the mating house for me."

"No." I'm adamant. "Don't think that. Trust me. I'll find a way. Between Madame Delphine and Elle and Bellamy, we can work it out. And if those bastards out there"—I point to the men on the perimeter—"won't let you out, I'll take it up with Ryne. He owes you that much for protecting us."

She nods, but I can tell she doesn't believe it's possible, and that only makes me more determined to keep my promise.

On the way home, my thoughts are all over the place, and I stare out the window, unable to say a word.

Bellamy holds my hand and gives it a squeeze. "You okay in there? I thought for sure seeing Abi would make you happy."

I give him a smile, a genuine one that I seem to only reserve for him these days. "I am so grateful for what you did, but seeing Abi was hard," I confess. "She's been through a lot, and now she's going to have to give up her baby. It's just one more reminder that this isn't right."

He goes still, his jaw ticking. "I wish there was more we could do." He's quiet for a long, drawn-out moment, which is rare for him. One of the things I enjoy about Bellamy is his constant chatter. He keeps matters light and my mind off of heavier things.

"I want to talk to you about something."

"Sure."

He hesitates again, and now I'm worried. "We've been at this for a month now and only have two left. How . . . how are you feeling about us? I mean, me, specifically. And please be honest. Don't just tell me what you think I want to hear."

My heart clenches. I owe him the truth, even if that means possibly losing him. "I'm not sure. I mean, you're probably the most genuinely good man I've ever met, and I care for you deeply. I enjoy our time together, I'm physically attracted to you, and I desperately want to love you, but I worry the fated mate bond between me and Ryne makes that impossible. I think I will always long for him even if I hate him too." I can't look at Bellamy while I speak. "I'm yours if you're willing to accept only part of my soul. If you're willing to understand that I'll never love you the way you love me but that I'll love you as much as I'm able and give you everything I can give."

The words tumble out, and I can feel the silent tears falling down my cheeks. Ryne has robbed me of this as well. The ability to love fully. The chance to be enough for someone as wonderful as Bell.

"What if Ryne were dead?" His voice goes dark.

I gasp and turn on him. "Are you planning on killing him?"

He backpedals. "No, no, no. Nothing like that. I was just wondering if that would change your feelings."

I stare at him for a long moment, afraid of saying the wrong thing. "I honestly don't know."

"But is it easier when he's not around?"

"Yeah. It is," I confess. "But if he were to die because of me, I'd break for good."

Bellamy nods. "Okay then. Don't worry. We're not killing Ryne." He worries that full bottom lip between his teeth, and I wonder where he's going with this. "I've heard of a pack out west where things are different. They're so far removed from this side of the kingdom that they barely even recognize the alpha king. They don't have mating houses, and they live openly with the humans. Once this is over, and we're married, I'm sure Ryne will release me from the Carolina Pack. And we can head out west, and you'll never have to see him again. Poppy, any part of your soul is worth more than you know. I'm willing to accept whatever you have to give."

My eyes water, and I can't think of what I've done to possibly deserve such a kind man in my life. "I think I would like that. But do you think maybe we can go find my family and bring them along as well?"

"We can bring whoever you want. Well, except Ryne."

I smile and squeeze his hand once again. It's hard to think about what comes after marrying Bellamy, but for the first time in a long time, I have hope that maybe my life won't always be horrible.

And then I see the waxing moon rising over the horizon, and I remember––I can never be with Bellamy, because I'm a lycan.

Chapter Fifteen

The next morning, Madame Delphine calls me into her office.

"How are things going with Bellamy?" Her mouth is pressed in a straight line. She doesn't really approve of me dating him when I'm already fated to her son, but there is nothing I can do about that. Ryne's the one being an idiot. Not me.

"He's very good to me."

"Do you kiss him?"

I frown. "Yes." But I don't elaborate.

Madame Delphine sinks down into her chair. "I was afraid of that. How long before and after the full moon does your venom take them out?"

I swallow. I don't like thinking about my lycan form. "Three days."

"Okay. Then we need to get you out of town for a week. I'll need a couple of days to organize things, but you'll take Raven to The Sanctuary."

"What about Joy and Samantha?"

"They haven't agreed to leave yet, but we'll see if I can change their minds. Either way, you'll stay there through the full moon and come back three days later. We won't tell Bellamy until after you've left because, if we tell him before, he'll insist on going with you."

"Okay."

It's the best solution. I hate deceiving Bellamy, and I dread the day I have to tell him what I am. That will likely be the end of us, and I'll be alone again.

* * *

Three days before the full moon, Elle takes me, Raven, and four of the mating-house women to the panther sanctuary. It's an all-day journey. The others find it grueling, especially when we have to don the heavy protective gear required for humans to cross the contamination zone, but it's no trouble for me. I put it on myself because I don't need the other women questioning what I am, but my lycan-self is growing stronger with the coming moon, and carrying gear is no issue. In fact, I suspect I may be getting stronger with each moon that passes, which makes sense considering what I've learned about lycans. I have increased stamina, my senses are clearer than ever, and I still have three days until the next renewal. It feels incredible, and I would consider myself lucky if I weren't in such a dangerous position. I'm hunted, and if anyone else finds out what I am, I could be killed. Elle is the only one in our group of seven who knows the truth, but she doesn't comment on it, and I'm not willing to reveal my secret to the others.

"This is where I'll leave you," Elle says, parking the jeep a half mile from the perimeter of the panther territory. "We've already sent word that you're coming. They're expecting all of you."

"But Derek is on our side," I argue, sliding from the passenger seat and helping the other ladies remove their protective gear. "You should come with us and see what it's like in Savannah. It's so much better than what the wolves have created in your kingdom. The panthers have the freedom to live how they want, they mix species without prejudice, and people share enough that nobody is in poverty."

The other women stare at me with dazed expressions. I get it. I would hardly believe it myself if I hadn't seen it with my own eyes.

"It's really that good, huh?" Elle asks skeptically.

"It's wonderful. We could have something like that in our pack if Ryne would pull his head out of his ass and take control the way he promised he would."

Raven snorts. "I was wondering when you were going to stop being so forgiving of that man. Not that it matters. We're never going back there, and I hope to never see his disgustingly handsome face again."

My stomach clenches at the thought of never seeing him again, and I shake my head. "You already know I'm going back. I'm only here to make sure you guys are set up and have everything you need."

"You really want to go back to the wolves?" Raven asks. "After everything you've been through?"

"Yes, I really do."

The women stare at me like I've grown a second head. "But why?" Raven presses. "We're here now and get to start a new life. Do you know how lucky that is? Chances like these don't come around often."

They barely come around at all, but my mind is made up. "This isn't where I'm meant to be," is all I say. But what I'm thinking is that I can't bear to leave Ryne or Bellamy. Not so suddenly. Maybe one day, I'll come back here to live with the panthers or go out west with Bell if he'll be willing to marry a lycan, but that day is not today. Besides, I still need to see things through with the mating houses, and I want to reunite with my family. I have too many responsibilities, too much hanging in the balance, to leave right now.

"You really think you're meant to stay in that pack?" one of the mating-house women says, frowning deeply. "You won't be thinking that when you end up where I did."

"If I left now, I'd always wonder."

Her eyes narrow. "Wonder what? How many babies you wouldn't get to raise? How many men would get to have your body?"

"Wonder if I could've fixed things," I reply, agitated. "That's my goal. I want to end the mating houses altogether, and I can't do that if I leave. I'm not going back to get a mate. I'm going back to help more of you."

Elle nods because she gets it, but the rest shake their heads.

"Sure looks like you're going back for Ryne." Raven frowns. "Whatever. Your loss. Let's go." And with that, the girl turns on her heels and stomps in the direction of the panthers.

She doesn't look back.

I say a quick goodbye to Elle. She promises to see me in seven days then returns to the jeep and drives off, the dust from her tires kicking into the air.

Seven days...

No way I'm sitting around here for seven critical days. Ryne is about to go through some kind of wolf-lycan hybrid renewal, Laik's pack is probably planning to bite more humans against their will, and what's left of my family is back home in their village, oblivious to the danger they're in. I won't stand for it. What kind of person would I be if I stayed here?

That's the question that spurs me on the day of the full moon, and after making sure the women are settled and happy in The Sanctuary, I leave the city, hours before sundown. I'm on foot, but I don't have to worry about the radiation zone, and I'm fast. When the moon rises, I shift into my lycan as easily as breathing.

And then I'm even faster--impossibly fast.

The forest comes alive under my heightened senses, my claws slicing through any branches that get in my way, my mind clearing, my ears attuned to every small sound. It only takes an hour to get to my village. When I finally see it after all this time, I want to cry, and if I could, I absolutely would.

I spot the white church and the little schoolhouse and the huge tree that I often climbed with Willow . . . And there, in the middle of the town square, stand the other lycans.

My stomach hardens at the sight of them. Somehow, deep in my gut, I knew they'd come here tonight. I hate that I was right. There aren't many of them. Only three. But three is already too many.

And there isn't a wolf shifter in sight.

At least, Laik isn't here with dozens of lycan--I can handle three.

I hope . . .

I do a quick glance around and listen intently, but the people are all tucked into their homes. I watch the lycans and wonder if they can sense me. Maybe they don't even register it. They seem to be conferring about something, and if I wanted to, I could listen in on the conversation, but I deliberately keep myself out of it so they can't sense me.

Then they split up, all heading for different houses. A large male heads for my old house, the little one next to the big tree, and I don't even think. I sprint out in the open and leap up on him. There is no way I'm letting him get my family.

He bucks under my grip, but I've taken him by surprise. Without thinking, I bite down on the back of his neck, his sinewy flesh tearing in my jaws. He howls and throws me off. I go flying and land in the dirt, pain snapping at my right shoulder, but I'm up in two seconds flat, shaking the stars out of my eyes.

My plan worked though. He's heading straight for me, blood pouring down his back, my family forgotten.

Who are you? The lycan stands over me, breathing heavily. I can't believe that after I attacked him, he still wants to talk, but I'm not playing that game.

I lunge for him again, this time using my claws to slice open his stomach. He howls and drops to the ground, his eyes pleading with mine.

Why are you doing this? he demands

I'll not let you hurt the people in this village, I reply.

Hurt them? I'm protecting them from the wolf shifters.

The fact that he thinks that is ludicrous. *By turning them? That's hardly protection.*

The lycan shakes his head. *We don't turn them.*

The wheels spin in my head. I wonder if the man is telling the truth or if he is just deceived by what's really going on. I know, for a fact, that humans are being bitten against their will. I also know not every human will survive the virus. And if they do, they'll still have lost their families and the lives they once knew.

What do you do with them after you kidnap them? I challenge.

Laik disperses them to safe houses.

Laik does no such thing. You're a fool for believing him. He puts them in camps and turns them all into lycan. Now get out of here, or I will kill you.

The lycan slowly rises to his feet and trudges from the village, but I have half a mind to go after him for being so foolish to begin with. I glance around for the other two lycans, but they're nowhere to be found. I'm sure they took people back with them, but there are too many possibilities for where they could have gone.

So Laik is smart enough to wait to bite the humans. He's got his pack out here doing his dirty work. I wonder how many actually know what's going on and how many are blind to the truth.

I stop under the tree by my own house, wondering if they are all hiding in the back corner, my dad ready to fight to protect his wife and son. Is Evan crying, or did he sleep through the whole thing? Is Mama praying with her eyes closed right now, or is she right there with Papa, ready to fight to the death? If I went through that door right now, they'd attack me. I have no doubt they wouldn't even hesitate to kill me—the evil lycan.

My blood boils, and anger scorches me from the inside out. Anger at Laik for what he's doing. At myself for not being able to see my family again. And also at Ryne. Especially at Ryne. I can't believe he didn't have wolves protecting the villages after last month. He made such a fuss about it, and yet I'm the only one here—another lycan, something they'd kill if they saw me. I don't know what Ryne is doing, but it's nothing good, that's for sure.

After doing one more sweep of the village just to make sure no lycans are left, I turn and head back for the wolf city. Just as I'm crossing the taxing field, memories I can't seem to forget drown me in grief. It's like

I'm right back there again, right back to the day Anders killed Willow for no good reason, and I was taken in her place. So much has happened that it feels like a lifetime ago, but right now I'm reliving it like it's happening all over again. I can still smell her coppery blood in the air, hear myself scream, and feel the rawness of it tearing my throat. I can see the horrified expressions branded on the onlookers' faces and the way my mother immediately handed me over to my sister's killer to protect herself.

I'd give anything to go back and redo that moment. Maybe I could coach Willow on how to act. Maybe I could say something right as we parted that would change the way she responded when Anders groped her. And yet, deep down, an honest part of me knows that Willow wouldn't have survived the claiming for long. She was always too proud, too headstrong, and fiercely independent. She reminds me so much of Joanna, but without a fated mate to protect her. If Grady hadn't stepped in for Joanna when he did, she'd have been lost the same way as my sister.

Anger racks me, and I want to howl and release my pent-up emotions into the night, but I hold them in because it would scare the villagers. Maybe the moon could sort my feelings out for me because, no matter how much time passes, I can't seem to do it myself. And maybe I never will.

Something hits me hard in the back, trying to push me to the ground, hard and so fast. I turn on my haunches, that horrible howl echoing from my lungs despite myself. Instinct takes over, and I ready myself for an attack. If it's another lycan, they're dead. If it's a wolf, I'll try not to kill them, but I'll do what I must. And if it's a human, I'll run to protect them.

"Don't do it," the woman yells in my face.

Not just any woman––Joanna stares up at me, a long knife in her hand and a fearsome glare in her warrior eyes.

"I've changed my mind," she goes on. "We can't take the humans to Laik. They're innocent, and he's no good."

I step back, realization taking hold. She thinks I'm one of the lycan working for Laik. I don't know what their plan was for tonight, but obviously it had something to do with taking humans to help build Laik's army. I want to tell her it's me, not the other lycan she came with, and that I'm here to help the humans. I want to beg her to come back with me to the manor so that we can hide her or take her to The Sanctuary even though I know she won't go anywhere without Grady. But most of all, I'd give anything to hug her. Just hug her.

But we can't communicate, and she has no idea who I really am.

"I mean it." She shakes her knife at me. "I'll kill you if I have to."

I step forward slowly, hoping she'll recognize the gesture as one of peace, but she spooks and takes off running, clumps of dirt kicking up behind her. Instinct tells me to make chase, but when I catch a glimpse of Grady's three-legged wolf on the edge of the woods, waiting for her, his eyes glowing in the darkness, I think better of it. I don't want anyone to get hurt, and Grady will engage me in a fight.

My heart drops, desperate for her to know who I am. But I can't risk trying, and the moon will be in the sky for several more hours at least. I'm stuck in this form.

I'm stuck.

So I let them go and head back toward the wolf city in search of Ryne, and when I find a band of young wolf shifters with their throats cut a mile outside of my village, I get the answer to my earlier question. Ryne *did* send wolves out here to protect these humans, but the lycans must have killed them. How many more wolves were killed tonight? And how many humans were taken?

No doubt, this was a coordinated attack, and Laik is planning something big.

Chapter Sixteen

I'm careful to keep myself hidden once I get to the city. If a wolf shifter spots me, I'm in serious trouble, and while I could wait until sunup, this night is too important. I'll get to Ryne's house and just wait outside until I shift back, but hopefully I can catch a glimpse of whatever is going on with him.

Because, surely, something has happened. He didn't survive my bite for nothing.

I manage to keep to the alleys, and I spot the park by Ryne's house with its many trees. Great hiding spots for me. I edge my way there, keeping to the shadows, slow and methodical. Someone yells, and I narrow my vision at a group of wolves that have gathered in the middle of the park. I know what this is about, and I nearly roll my eyes. They should be out there protecting the villages, worried about the lycans, fighting for the humans, for their own brothers--instead, they are here, fighting Ryne for his title of alpha. Did they wait until the full moon when they knew he'd be distracted?

It's a clever tactic, but as angry as I am with Ryne, I hope it doesn't work. I know where things stand with Ryne. A new alpha would be too unpredictable. I creep close enough to hear everything and scale a tree until I have a clear view of the wolves surrounding Ryne. He's covered in scratches and bite marks and blood. How many wolves have challenged him so far? How many does he have to kill or banish before they give up and accept he's too strong?

He shifts back into his human form and prowls in front of the group, naked and menacing. The fact that he can still shift like normal is good news—the best news, actually. He'd hate me forever if he lost his wolf-self to his lycan, and I watch him, completely unable to look away. He's beautiful like this, with the moon lighting him up like a beacon. He's radiant and terrifying, and he'll never be mine.

"Who challenges me now?" he roars. "I have been merciful so far, simply banishing the three wolves who fought me instead of killing them. But I'm done. If anyone else thinks they can beat me, it will be a fight to the death."

I wonder if Bellamy is in the crowd of wolves or out protecting a village somewhere. If he could see me now, would he still want me? I snort. Highly unlikely.

A large man steps forward, and recognition hits me. It's Dante, the handsome beta who claimed he would be an alpha someday. I wonder if he's taking the chance now that he's got lunas he's after. "Someone needs to fix your mistakes," he snarls. "It might as well be me."

"Dante. Are you sure about this?" Ryne sounds hurt. Betrayed. I would be too.

"It's time for a new alpha." Dante's voice echoes through the night, and then he shifts into a huge brown wolf. Ryne wastes no time shifting and lunging for him. I've seen Ryne fight before, but I've never seen him move so ruthlessly. His claws are out, shining like sharpened knives, and he's fighting like a madman. Within seconds, Dante's wolf is flat on his back, snarling and snapping his jaw. Ryne jerks Dante's neck around and bites him on the flank. The brown wolf immediately goes limp.

Ryne shifts back into his human form, and even from this distance, I can see the shock in his eyes. He wipes blood from his mouth. The wolf doesn't move.

Dante's dead.

"Anyone else?" Ryne snarls, and the whole crowd disperses, leaving Ryne alone with the dead wolf. Ryne limps in the direction of his house, and I stay in the tree, watching him go. He glances back at the dead wolf every once in a while, confusion and pain evident on his face. He may not understand what just happened, but I do.

His bite *alone* killed Dante.

He's part lycan now, and just like us, he can end wolf shifters with a single full-moon bite.

I drop back to the ground and keep to the shadows, following Ryne. I manage to make it to his gate, without being seen, just as he's climbing his porch steps.

Can you hear me? I ask through the lycan-communication link.

I hold my breath and wait. If he can hear me, then my theory is correct, and he really is part lycanthrope. He spins around, anger warring on his face.

"Get out of my head," he shouts. His eyes search his yard, but he doesn't move, and I'm hidden behind a bush.

But you can hear me. How interesting. You know what this means, don't you?

"Get out of my head, or I will find you and kill you."

You would kill your fated mate? I thought that wasn't allowed.

"Poppy?" His voice softens. I peek out around the edge of the bush. He's sunk onto the steps, and his head hangs low.

I want nothing more than to comfort him, but that's not possible in this form. I glance up at the sky. The sun will be rising soon, and the moon will no longer have her hold on me. Thankfully it's the middle of the summer instead of the winter, or I'd be out here for several more hours.

Yeah, it's me. I'll come see you when the sun rises.

He stands, and for a second, I'm scared he's going to come after me, but instead, he turns around and slumps inside, leaving the door cracked open. It's the first time since he found out what I did to him that he's shown any indication that he wants anything to do with me. Not that I'd go running back into his arms.

There's too much bad blood there, but he does need to accept what happened tonight.

The sun is up about thirty minutes later, and I find myself back in my own body. I'm as naked as the day I was born, but it's nothing Ryne hasn't seen before.

I rush up to the front door, push it open, and close it quickly behind me.

"Poppy?"

I spin, but instead of finding Ryne, it's Callum who is waiting for me. He's got pants on and nothing else, and even from here I can smell the lycan on him. I wonder where he stayed last night, assuming he must have been locked in this house somewhere. He's lucky to have made it through the night. He quickly averts his eyes, but my nakedness is honestly nothing he hasn't seen either, considering how many times he's tended to my wounds.

"Let me get you some clothes." He disappears, and I stand awkwardly in the foyer. I wonder if it's just Callum and Ryne here or if there are others. I hope Ryne doesn't have a girl in his bed. That would be the worst. Would Ryne do that to me? Surely not, but I don't even know anymore. Ryne isn't who I thought he was.

Callum returns with a long shirt. "I can't find any shorts that will fit you."

"This'll work."

The shirt hits me mid-thigh, so I'll be careful when I sit down, but for now, it covers everything. It's a button-down collared shirt, and it takes me a minute to button it all up. I roll up the sleeves so they don't hang down over my hands. The shirt smells like Ryne, and my stomach churns. I miss him so much—but I'm also so damn angry. It's a horrible feeling.

I follow Callum into the living room and find Ryne there alone. He glances up at me and gives me a once over in his shirt. I worry about what he might think, but his lips curl into a small smile, and he drops his eyes. Callum leans over and whispers in my ear. "That's the first time I've seen him smile in a month."

I don't respond and sink down onto the opposite side of the couch from Ryne, careful to keep myself covered up. I need to shower and get the lycan stench off me, need better clothes, need a lot of things, actually, but first, I must have this conversation.

"I told Callum what happened," Ryne says, not looking at me. Something about that stings, even though it shouldn't. He let Callum in, a boy he hardly knows, and he pushed me out like I'm the stranger.

"Including that we can talk telepathically and that you killed a wolf with a single bite?"

Ryne nods, his long hair hiding his face from me. I imagine that if I could see his eyes, they'd be even more haunted than my own.

"What do you think?" I turn to Callum.

Callum leans back in his own chair and rubs his chin. "Honestly, I think Ryne is some kind of hybrid. We've never seen this before," His voice grows excited. "But it's a good thing. It might mean he can lead both the shifters and the lycan."

Ryne winces at that, saying nothing more.

"But do the lycans have to follow him like the shifters do?" I ask, thinking over the implications of this. "Like, could he become an alpha for us too?" I imagine Ryne stepping in and bossing Laik and Wanda around, telling them to leave the humans and wolves alone.

"I'm not sure. It's something we'll have to test on the next moon. You'd be perfect for it."

"If the lycans in this area have to follow him, that would solve a lot of problems, but I kind of doubt we'd get so lucky. You know our pack bonds are nothing like the wolf shifters'. They're more about intimidation than anything else."

"Yeah, but can you imagine how good that would be?" Callum smiles.

I nod because it would be good, but probably too good to be true. We're not wolf shifters. We never will be. "You're right, but we need to have someone else test it. I'm not good for that."

"Why not?"

"Because I'm his fated mate." I shrug, hating those two words. They don't mean anything anymore, and yet they always will. "I think the rules are different for us."

"That's fine. I'll test it myself then." Callum shoves his hand through his hair, and I can tell he's thinking hard, that scientific brain of his categorizing everything he knows. "I wish these rules were written down somewhere. No one really understands how all of this works."

"You can write it down."

"I am, but there is so much that doesn't make sense."

He's right, and talking about it is getting us nowhere. "There are other problems as well. I was at my village last night."

Ryne's head pops up, and he glares at me. "I thought you were at The Sanctuary."

Oh, so now he speaks? I glare right back. "I obviously left. Since when do I stay where I'm told?" I ask, realizing that I have more Joanna in me than I thought.

His lips twitch. "Truth. I hope you found it well guarded. I was worried about the villages last night and sent out some of my best men. Which is how I ended up being challenged. The ones who don't listen well stayed behind and got it in their heads that I needed to be taken out. They were some of Anders's cronies that got left behind."

"No. I did not find them well-guarded. In fact, I found wolf shifters on the edge of my village with their throats slit. They never saw it coming. I'm surprised you didn't know, considering you're their alpha."

Ryne jumps up and lets out a stream of curses. "You're right, but I was distracted by the challenges to my title. Callum, call Justin and the other betas. We need to figure out exactly what happened last night."

Callum rushes from the room, and Ryne approaches me, kneeling and taking my hands in his. There's no lingering scent of lycan on him, as if his infection never happened. He's still the wolf shifter I met nearly a year ago. He's still Ryne. "Poppy, I'm so sorry for what I've done. When I get back, can we talk?"

His words are like being drenched in ice water. I jerk my hands from his and shake my head. "You hurt me, Ryne. Deeply. And then you threw your betas at me like it would all be okay."

"About the betas––"

I hold up my hand. "We're through, Ryne. I'm with Bellamy now."

I don't know if I mean the words or not, but he cannot just expect me to be okay with him now that he's realized he's not going to shift into a monster. I don't wait for him to respond. I push him back and stand, heading in the direction that Callum went. I trust Callum to help me find a shower and women's clothing, and then I'm going back to the manor and getting on with my life.

Chapter Seventeen

I don't talk to Ryne in the weeks that follow. For three days, I avoided Bellamy, and then I let him right back in where we left off, spending more time together than ever. Although I'm not falling in love the way I fell for Ryne, I do feel myself falling a different way. With Ryne, love felt like an exhilarating free fall, but with Bell, it's like jumping––I just have to make that choice to step off the edge into the unknown. Because of him, I'm changing. My heart is opening. Most of all, my mind is accepting that I could have a different life with Bell, a happy one. Maybe even a better one as long as we don't have to be around Ryne.

Except for one problem—Bellamy doesn't know the real me.

He doesn't know that I'm a lycan or that I'm not a virgin, both things that could be non-negotiable for a beta wolf shifter in search of a wife. Faye insists I should take these secrets to my grave, and Elle says Bell deserves the truth, that he's a good guy and will accept me for me.

But I don't know.

My palms sweat, and my knee won't stop bouncing as we sit at dinner in his manor one warm September night. It's become one of my favorite dates with him, to join him and several of the mating-house women here. Now that I know Abi is okay, at least for now, I can talk to these women without the incredible guilt I had the first time he brought me here.

"What's wrong?" Bellamy asks, steadying my knee. His large hand is warm and comforting, but I'm still beyond nervous. "Is the food not to your liking? You've barely touched it."

I stare down at the full plate of cold food and sigh, knowing I can't keep these secrets another day. We're together too much, he wants me too much, and things are progressing without the truth. It's time. If he hates me for it, then so be it. If he tries to have me executed, I should have enough allies around to hopefully save my life and get me to the panther sanctuary. But if he accepts me, if he really is okay with all of me, lycan and everything, then maybe it's time to let myself love him the way he deserves. To make that leap.

"Can we go somewhere and talk?" I ask.

"Outside?"

"More private." As much as his yard seems private, there are neighbors, and I can't take any risks with this information. This has to be just him and me. Though, in some ways I'm risking my life that way too. He might try to kill me. It's a risk I have to take.

His lovely green eyes widen, and he stands, taking my hand and leading me into a wing of the house I haven't been in before. "All the bedrooms are occupied, and I can't guarantee privacy in the common areas. Is it okay that we go to my bedroom?"

I swallow hard and nod. "I need to talk to you about something," I reiterate. "It's nothing more—"

He squeezes my hand to cut me off. "I'd never assume anything was going to happen between us before marriage, and I swear I won't try."

That stings a little, but I trust him enough to take him at his word and follow him into the large room. It's more modest than the rest of the house, not what I expected, but I kind of love it. He has a large bed with a white comforter, an oak dresser, and a closed door that probably leads to a private bathroom. I sit on the edge of the bed and then think better of it and stand, pacing from one side of the room to the other.

"Are you okay?" Concern laces his tone. Only concern. Not suspicion. Not expectation. And not judgment. He's such a good man.

This is it. Now or never.

I turn to him. "I'm not who you think I am."

His smile quirks. "And who are you then?" He stands and approaches. I don't move, allowing him to tuck a strand of hair behind my ear and cup my face gently. "Because I'm pretty sure I have a good idea by now, and I'll tell you, I like you, Poppy. A lot."

"I'm not a virgin," I blurt out, expecting him to flinch away from me like I've just burned him.

He only shrugs. "I figured you weren't, knowing the way Ryne looks at you." He clears his throat. "And I know you were taken by lone wolves. I figured they might have . . ."

"I've only been with Ryne," I say quickly. "And you're okay with that? I thought betas required that wives come to them virginal."

"Some do, and some women would prefer it that way too, but it's not important to me." He peers into my eyes. "I care about your heart, your tenacity, and your drive—all things that matter way more to me than your virginity."

Relief floods me, but it's short-lived. "There's one more thing."

One more big thing. One more thing that could ruin us forever, that could make him see me as a monster. Make him hate me.

"What is it?" He arches a brow. "I can take it."

Oh, I'm not sure you can, Bell.

I step back and wring my hands. This is not going to go over nearly as well as the virginity confession. But he doesn't let me stay there. He steps forward, placing his hand on my cheek again. He wants to reassure me, to make me feel like I can trust him, but there's no way he's expecting I'm a monster—his greatest enemy. I take a deep breath and proceed. "When I was kidnapped, it wasn't by lone wolves. It was by the lycan. I was with a pack of lycan for three whole months before I was rescued."

He nods slowly, his eyes creasing in alarm. "And if I ever catch the bastards who took you, I'll kill them for what they did."

I wince. "Except, they didn't *take* me. They took me in. I had been banished when they caught me in the wilds."

He freezes at that, his warm hand still cupping my cheek. It doesn't move, but I expect it will with what I say next. "I had been bitten by one of them during the blood moon attack. Ryne sent me away for it instead of killing me."

His lips part, but besides that, he's still frozen.

"So you see, I'm one of them now. I'm a lycan."

Chapter Eighteen

Just as I expected, Bellamy's hand drops from my face, and he sinks down onto the edge of his bed. He stares at the floor, not saying a word. I shouldn't be surprised, but his reaction doesn't hurt as much as I feared.

If this were Ryne, I'd be right next to him, begging him to understand, to love me, to want me. But this isn't Ryne. It's Bellamy, and as much as I like him, I don't love him yet. If this is a deal breaker for him, I'll understand. And I won't even be angry. How could I blame him for rejecting me? Any other wolf would. Even my own mate did in the end.

He finally glances up at me, and his eyes are a little haunted. "What does that mean for us?"

It's not the question I was planning to answer. "What do you mean?"

"You could kill me on the full moon."

"I could, but I can control my lycan form, so I'm not worried about hurting anyone. And I'll keep to myself; no wolves will ever see me. Oh, and kissing is off-limits three days before and after."

"You know this because of Ryne?" His fists clench on the bed's comforter.

"Yes. Kissing would cause him to pass out."

His fists clench even harder. "Thinking of that bastard kissing you always makes me see red."

I crease my eyebrows together. "I thought you liked Ryne."

"I do. He's my alpha. But I hate what he did to you, and the thought of you two together kills me. And sometimes . . . sometimes, I think maybe I hate him."

Unfortunately, I know the feeling.

I know Bell likes me, but to hate his own alpha on my behalf, to call him a bastard? It's everything I need at this moment, the kind of validation that I haven't gotten from a man before. Not ever.

And it feels so good.

"Tell me something," Bellamy asks in a low voice. "If Ryne was willing to be with you even though he knew you were a lycan, what changed?"

I swallow. This I cannot tell. Ryne has kept this from his wolves for good reason. Who knows how they'll react? Maybe they'll rise up and kill him for it, or maybe they won't, but either way, it's his secret to share when he's ready.

"We had a fight about how to handle the Resistance, and he decided that he'd be better off with a luna." I hate lying to Bell, but it's close enough to the truth. And honestly, Ryne abandoning me for accidentally biting him isn't fair. He may as well have dumped me for a luna.

Bellamy approaches me again and, to my surprise, slides a hand behind my back, tugging me close to him. He rests his forehead on mine. "You're lying. I can tell, but that's okay. I'm guessing you're hiding something for him. You being a lycan definitely makes things more complicated for us, but I don't care, Poppy. I want you to be mine, and I'll be there for you, no matter what."

Then he smashes his lips against mine. I return the kiss eagerly, grateful for his instant acceptance of who I am. I'm a lycan who is not a virgin and who is fated to someone else, and he still wants me. Against all the odds, we're here together. Choosing each other. Jumping together.

And maybe that's better than fate.

We tumble onto his bed, and the kissing goes beyond what we've done before, our bodies exploring each other. We don't have sex, but it's only a matter of time if things progress. I fall into the warmth of his skin, the strength of his long, lean muscles, and the taste of his mouth. We're wrapped up in a fiery heat. It's not as hot as it was with Ryne, but it doesn't burn me either. It's just enough to keep me safe and make me feel loved.

Suddenly, he pulls away, breathing heavily. "I should take you home."

I collapse back onto his bed, my own feelings of desire swirling. "Or I could just stay. I'm not ready to give myself to you yet, but that doesn't mean we can't share a bed. It's late."

I want to stay here, for me and for him. And a voice in my head also wants Ryne to hear about it. He hurt me, so why shouldn't I hurt him too?

Bell chuckles and slides a hand across my stomach. "It's not that late, but I will not turn down that offer. I promise to be good." But the devilish way he says "good" tells me he'd be open for more if I was too. He drops his head to my neck and kisses it slowly, working his way to my collarbone. I weave my fingers through his thick hair and lose myself in the sensations.

This is definitely better than going home and worrying about everything, and I realize, in this moment, exactly why I like Bellamy. He not only makes me feel safe, but I trust him with every fiber of my being. If he says he's going to be good, he'll be good. When I'm with him, I don't have to be Poppy––the savior of the Resistance, or Poppy––the fearsome lycan, or Poppy––the rejected mate. I'm just a normal girl who enjoys kissing and cuddling, who wants to be wanted, to be loved, the same as everyone else.

* * *

The next morning, I wake in Bellamy's arms. I know I should go home, but I want to stay here forever and be the mistress of the house that helps the girls in the mating houses. I could be so much more effective here. I don't need more classes or lunas glaring at me. I don't need to date around or watch my fated mate fall for someone else.

This is what I need.

"Morning, gorgeous," Bellamy says, his voice raspy from sleep. I jerk my head around. I hadn't realized he was awake.

"Good morning." I cuddle even closer to him.

"We should get you back."

"I've been thinking about that. What if I don't want to go back? I could just stay here with you and help you with the girls."

He tightens his grip on me. "As much as I'd love that, Madame Delphine needs you for the Resistance, and I don't want to cross her."

I shake my head at that. "She wants what's best for me as much as she wants what's best for the other women. I'm sure she'd agree that I should stay here if it makes me happy. I can still help the Resistance from here."

His lips thin as he rakes a hand through that unruly hair of his. "And what about Ryne? You really think he'll just let you move in with me?"

I shrug and sit up. "Ryne doesn't get a say in my life anymore."

"Except that he does. He has to approve all the beta marriages, and it's going to be hard enough to get him to agree to us being together." His face stills, and he studies me for a long minute, neither of us saying anything.

"Why would he disagree with us being together? I thought that's what he wanted. It's what he told everyone."

Bellamy gives a dark chuckle. "Sure he did. But as soon as he saw that you and I were getting close, he had words with me."

My eyebrows rise. I hadn't heard about this. "And what exactly were those words?"

"He told me to back off. That he had changed his mind about you marrying a beta."

My body goes cold and hot all at once. "He can go to hell."

"He'll never approve of our marriage. I know I should've told you before." He gives a sheepish grin. "But I was afraid you'd go running back to him."

I grab his hand. "I'm not. It's you I want." Even as I say the words, I'm still not convinced that they're true.

"I could challenge him for alpha. That would solve all of this."

Tears blur my vision. "That's the last thing I want because one of you would die, and it would be my fault."

"One of us would die," he agrees, "but it wouldn't be your fault. None of this is your fault. Still, I couldn't do that to you. And honestly, I don't want to challenge Ryne, and I have no interest in being the alpha, at least, not in this pack. I'd only fight for it if I had to, and I don't think I do."

"I still believe Ryne will do the right thing when the alpha king is named, but if he doesn't, let someone else fight him." But the thought of someone else, anyone else, hurting Ryne makes me want to burst into tears.

"It's okay, Poppy. We only have to wait a little longer, and then I can choose you as my bride at the harvest festival. If Ryne doesn't agree, we'll run away together."

"If Ryne agrees, then what happens?" My voice cracks.

"Then you decide what comes next. We can stay here and keep doing what we're doing, helping the mating-house women, or we can go out west and join that other pack I told you about. Either way, I promise to keep you safe." He shifts in bed until he's sitting across from me, taking my hands between his. "But I want you to be mine. I don't want to watch you wish you were with another man. Do you ever think you'll be able to give him up?"

As I'm confronted with the question, panic grips me, but I force myself to calm and squeeze his hands back. Then I answer the question I have no business answering. "Yes," I say softly. And then more forcefully. "Yes."

Chapter Nineteen

"You slept with him."

It's the first sentence Ryne has spoken to me in more than two weeks. I'm out on my morning run by myself after having returned from Bell's house, sweat dripping down my face and lungs burning in my chest.

I whip around to find Ryne standing a few feet away from me. He's completely naked, covered in dirt, with a murderous expression etched onto his rugged face. His dark hair hangs around his shoulders, tangled and wind-swept. He hasn't looked this unkempt since the wilds. And his eyes——his eyes are as bright blue as I've ever seen them.

"Where are your clothes?" I squeak. It appears he shifted and ran all the way over here this morning instead of driving like normal.

He doesn't answer my question as he stalks in close. He catches my face in his hand and forces me to look into his savage gaze. "Did you have sex with him?" he asks.

I swallow hard, my heart pounding in my chest. I knew this confrontation could be a possibility if I stayed with Bellamy last night. I knew it, and I stayed anyway because I wanted to see Ryne angry and jealous. Why should I have to sit around and watch him move on with somebody new while he's telling Bellamy to back off from me? Love works both ways, and so does heartbreak.

"That's none of your business," I spit.

"The hell it isn't." He runs his nose along my neck, and goosebumps erupt, memories flooding of the last time he did something like that. "You smell like him. You reek of lust."

"We didn't have sex!" I grind out and snap back, pushing him off me. "But we're going to soon, and there's not a damn thing you can do about it. You dumped me, remember?"

His cold eyes burn into a raging inferno. "And it was a mistake!"

Those words pierce through my heart, but I don't let them stay for long. I'll deal with the wound later. "And what about dating the lunas? That a mistake too? Or do you have another one lined up for tonight, same as all the other nights?"

"I want you back," he states. "I don't care about the lunas. I never did."

"And why should I believe you? You've put me through more than enough heartbreak already. Bellamy treats me like a queen. You treated me like a burden."

He winces, but I don't take it back. It's true. He knows it's true.

"You are not to have sex again until you're married," he says at last, as if he has any right to tell me what to do with my body. "And if you still want him, come time for the harvest moon proposals, then so be it."

"And what if I don't wait? Would you stop wanting me back if I have sex with someone else?"

"No matter what you do or where you go or who you're with, I will always want you," he growls. His face softens, and he inches closer to me. I stand motionless as his hands run up my arms to cup my face. I'm very much aware that he's naked right now. "I love you, Poppy."

"You have a funny way of showing it."

"I'm sorry--"

"How long until the Harvest Moon Festival?" I interrupt.

He blinks, surprised. "Six weeks, give or take a day."

I rip myself away, and it's like ripping my heart in two all over again. "Fine. What's another six weeks to wait for Bellamy, a man who has loved me from day one with his *actions* and not just his *words*?"

And then I turn and sprint away, hoping that I can make it six weeks without crumbling under the pressure of such a huge decision. Because as much as I adore Bellamy, I'm still hopelessly in love with Ryne, but I meant what I said. Actions matter more to me now than ever. Words be damned.

* * *

I return to my room and find both Faye and Elle sitting on my bed, giggling about something. Faye had been asleep when I'd changed into my workout clothes this morning, and it still catches me off guard sometimes to see her being so nice to my friends. But it's nice. Really nice, actually.

Elle meets my gaze. "So. Here we thought you spent the night at Bellamy's and were both ready to milk you for every detail, but I think this is even juicier."

"I did stay at Bellamy's."

Faye gapes. "Girl. You've some nerve." She drops her voice. "Are you sleeping with both of them?"

"Both of whom?"

Elle points to the window. "We saw you and Ryne at the edge of the woods."

"I've never seen him naked. That is one fine man." Faye fans her face. "Please tell me Bellamy is just as hot."

"Faye. What about Justin?"

"What about him?"

Faye flushes. "I haven't seen him naked."

"Wait a minute, you two aren't sleeping together?" Elle asks. "Because you sure have made it sound like you are."

"Yeah, in front of the other women because they need to back off my man." Faye winks. "Justin wants to wait until after we're married. So I have to live vicariously through Miss I'm-sleeping-with-two-incredibly-hot-wolves."

I drop down onto Faye's bed and face them. My shower will have to wait. It might be good for me to get out my messy emotions.

"Bellamy and I aren't having sex, but I did spend the night with him. And Ryne and I aren't back together, but he wants to be."

Elle blinks at me for a moment. "We need more details than that."

I spill everything to them, including Ryne's secret since they already know I bit him and that he survived. They can be trusted. And they are surprisingly good listeners. It's almost as good as talking with Joanna or Willow.

Once the story is all out, I wait.

"I think you should get back together with Ryne. You know it's going to happen anyway. Why postpone the inevitable?" Faye says matter-of-factly.

"No way. Ryne's an asshole. He didn't want her back until she was with someone else. Someone that makes her happy. She deserves someone like Bellamy." Elle crosses her arms and glares at Faye.

"Excuse me, Miss Elle." I point at her. "You've been team Ryne since the second you found out we were fated. What changed?"

"What's changed is Ryne hurt you, and Bellamy put you back together. Bell's a really good man."

"But he's not her mate," Faye points out.

They bicker back and forth about who I should be with, and I find that I like this. My friends are amazing. If nothing else, I've learned that bonds with women are stronger than my messed-up relationships. I still can't believe Faye and I went from hating to trusting each other, but here we are. I don't know if I'll ever forget the things she said about Willow or the way she blackmailed me in the wilds, but things are different between us. I've forgiven her. Not that she asked––she's still not the type to ask for forgiveness or apologize for anything.

"You don't know what you're talking about," Faye argues. "You don't have a fated mate."

"Neither do you."

"That's what I'm telling you. I've seen fated relationships. Look at Shauna and Amos. There's no breaking that bond. Look at Nico and Nova. Look at Joanna and Grady. She abandoned all of us just to be with him. Joanna. The strongest of all of us. You can't break the fated bonds. Ryne didn't come back to Poppy because he got jealous of Bellamy. He came back to her because he can't live without her, and Poppy's eventually going to realize that she can't live without him either. It's not fair to put Bellamy through that. Surely, even you can see that."

No one says anything for a long moment. Then Elle meets my eye. "I think she's right."

I grit my teeth and grab my clothes out of my dresser then storm into the shower.

That's not what I want to hear.

<h1 style="text-align:center">Chapter Twenty</h1>

At lunch, Faye sits down with a silly grin on her face. "Guess where Justin is taking me on our date tonight?"

"Where?" I ask, glad to be talking about her love life instead of mine.

"We're going to look at houses."

"Houses?"

"Yeah. You know, for after we're married? He said we can stay at his, or we can choose a different one. He wants it to be our house. I'm so excited."

"That sounds super fun." I'll admit it took me a while to accept that Justin was serious about Faye, or that she wasn't just using him. They've both surprised me, and I can't help but wonder how the other women feel about it. Are they happy for Faye, or do they secretly want to take Justin away?

"What are you and Bellamy doing tonight?" Samantha turns to me with a sad crease between her eyes. She hasn't made a solid connection with any of the betas. Even Lev hasn't given her the time of day. She liked Dante, but since his death, she's been thinking more about The Sanctuary. The schooling part of our time here isn't what it used to be, which was where she thrived. Now that it's all about dating, I can't say I blame her.

I shake my thoughts free and refocus on her question. "It's Elle's night with him."

"We're just having dinner at his place and hanging out with the girls from the mating houses, same as always," Elle cuts in. "You can come along if you want, Poppy. You know he'd rather be with you anyway."

"That sounds like fun." I shrug. I had planned to do some reading in bed tonight, but I do like Bell's place, and it's always great to have Elle around. She gets along so well with everyone.

"Boring." Violet snorts from where she's sitting with the other lunas. I'll admit I haven't made an effort to befriend them, but they haven't either. They still act like we're beneath them.

Faye shoots her a wicked glare. "What? Do you have something to say?"

I bristle, wishing Faye didn't have to be so . . . Faye. Now that she's decided we're friends, she's turned her vitriol toward the three lunas who are eligible to date. And although Cecily and Marissa haven't been a basket of fun, she hates Violet the most. Not that I like Violet with her nose-in-the-air attitude, but still, those girls can turn into scary, fearsome wolves.

And Faye? That girl is more bark than bite.

"As a matter of fact, I do," Violet announces. "Last night, I went to Ryne and demanded that the lunas get better treatment from the betas. You're all acting as if you're already engaged, but you're not."

"I thought you didn't want a beta," Faye retorts.

Violet shrugs. "Maybe, maybe not, but I'm tired of sitting around while you humans have all the fun." She fluffs her hair.

"Haven't you been out with Ryne lately? Or did he get sick of you?" Samantha asks, and Violet's face turns almost as red as her hair.

"He's not dating anyone right now. He's decided he's too busy with pack stuff."

That makes my cheeks prickle, and everyone looks at me expectantly. "What?" I blurt. "Ryne and I aren't together. You know that."

"Anyway," Violet cuts back in sharply. "Ryne assured me that things are changing, and I'll have all the dates I can dream of with the other betas. Marissa here has already got Lev drooling all over her." That's news to me, but nobody else seems surprised by it. She points her fingers at me and Faye. "Which means you two better watch out because Cecily and I are coming for Bellamy and Justin."

Marissa is completely unaffected by this conversation, eating her lunch as if it's not even happening, but Cecily has a smug grin on her face. She's excited for the challenge––in fact, she wants nothing more than to take us down.

Faye smirks. "Good luck with that."

But I don't smirk. I don't like this, not one bit. The lunas don't have much to lose, not like we remaining humans do. What if the betas can't resist the lunas' charms? We'll be sent to the mating houses if we can't get to The Sanctuary in time. Right now it's still a possibility, but things can change quickly here, and someday our safe haven may be gone.

* * *

I spend the night at Bellamy's again.

And the next.

And the next.

We don't get close to having sex, but we do thoroughly enjoy each other. He brings me home early each morning, and each morning, Ryne is hiding in the shadows of the woods, watching. Ryne doesn't run off anymore, but I don't go over to talk to him either. We're at an impasse.

Faye and Elle don't say much about the situation anymore, but I know they disapprove. Even now that Bellamy has to date the other women, and I have to date the other men, he still has me come over at night. And I always go. Maybe I shouldn't, maybe Faye and Elle are right to judge me, maybe Bell is using me––more likely I'm using him, but my heart is too broken not to try to fix it. I keep expecting Madame Delphine or Ryne to put a stop to our sleepovers, but they never do. It's as if Ryne is finally letting me make my own choices . . . I'm not sure how to feel about that.

"Excuse me, ladies," Madame Delphine announces one afternoon while we're in the middle of a particularly excruciating singing lesson. We all jerk our heads toward her, and the room goes eerily silent. "Ryne has called a pack-wide meeting. It will be at seven o'clock tonight at the arena. He wants us all there. Please wear a nice dress, but no need to be fancy. We will eat before we leave in case it goes late. Any dates for tonight will be postponed to tomorrow."

She gives a quick nod and then leaves the room.

"See?" Violet is the first to speak. "This is what I've been saying. Things are changing around here."

Elle, Faye, and I all stare at each other. Then we all scramble up and go after Madame Delphine. I reach her first before she escapes into her office. "What's the meeting about?" I ask more forcefully than I meant.

"I have no idea. It's with the entire pack except those who are out on guard duty. Whatever it is, it's big."

"Do you think we have a new alpha king?" Elle asks. Her eyes drift away, and I know her father is on her mind. It makes me want to give her a big hug.

"That's what I'm thinking, but I'm not positive." Madame Delphine wrings her hands.

The doorknob on the front door jiggles, and I jump. We all move back a few inches, and the door swings open. I expect it to be anyone but who it is.

Joanna.

She stands there, staring at all of us, her eyes wild, her hair tangled.

"I need help," she says.

And then she collapses into my arms, sobbing.

Chapter Twenty-One

Seeing Joanna again is a total shock. I squeeze her tightly as Madame Delphine ushers us into the office, Elle and Faye slipping in as well. Joanna sinks to the floor in the middle of the room, and I sink with her, refusing to let her go. She's unkempt, even more so than when I saw her in the wilds, and has cuts and bruises that look fresh. Her glossy eyes dart around to each of us as she murmurs a string of unintelligible nonsense. She's hyperventilating so hard that we can't understand her.

"Take a deep breath," I coach. "Look at me, talk to me, just me."

Her gaze holds mine, and I recognize the heartache and panic there—— it's the same look I saw in the mirror my first night in the manor.

Something happened.

Something bad.

"Is it Grady?" I whisper and then hold my breath, waiting for the bad news that is surely coming, but she shakes her head.

"Grady is in hiding," she says. "He's alive. It's not Grady. It's my parents."

"What happened to them?"

"They're going to be kidnapped at the next full moon. Laik is still targeting the villages, and when I tried to reason with him, he said he would go get my parents next. And then he attacked me. Grady nearly died defending me. That's when we fled."

"Does Laik know you're here?" Elle interrupts, her voice on edge.

Joanna blinks at her but shakes her head. "We ran off in the opposite direction and then doubled back down here."

"That was smart," Madame Delphine says. "If Laik suspects we know his plans, he'll change them."

"He's gone completely rogue," Elle adds. "His crew is no longer with the Resistance."

"I know." Joanna nods, a dazed and horrified look coming over her face.

"And yet you and your mate went with them." Faye throws her hands in the air and widens her eyes at me. "Am I going to be the only one to say it? You can't trust her. This could be a trap."

"It's not," Joanna cries out. "If you won't help the humans, who will? The full moon is coming up, and Laik has more lycans now than ever."

"And yet you're not a lycan," Faye challenges. "Or are you? How would we even know?"

"She's *not* a lycan," I cut in, but nobody seems to care what I have to say.

Joanna glares at Faye and then addresses Madame Delphine. "What is she even doing here? Get her out."

"I'm with the Resistance now, actually," Faye huffs. "Which is more than you can say, considering your recent actions."

Elle says nothing, Madame Delphine appears conflicted, and Faye is out for blood.

"Enough." I stand and bring Joanna up with me, keeping my arm around her. "Joanna is one of our own, and if she needs help, then we're going to help her."

"That's not up to you to decide," Madame Delphine says with a resolute sigh. "But we can go to Ryne and ask for help."

I'm not sure where Ryne's feelings are going to fall on this. I know he was upset that his guards were killed. I know he hates Laik. But Joanna and Grady made their choice . . .

"I promise I'm not a lycan," Joanna tries. "Ryne can trust me."

"I'm not so sure he'll see it that way." Madame Delphine sighs.

Joanna stiffens, and I speak up. "If Ryne won't help you, I will. I know what went down at the last full moon, Joanna, because I was there. I saw you. I know you're still human, and I know you're not with Laik anymore."

"That was you?" she asks, and I take the time to explain to everyone what I saw that night.

"Don't you see? Joanna doesn't support stealing someone's agency like that. We should protect her."

"That's not up to us," Faye says. She's still prickly and not wanting to soften up. "That's up to Ryne."

I turn to Joanna, tuning everyone else out. "Don't worry. I won't let anything happen to you or your family."

"You promise?"

"I swear on my life."

* * *

The stadium is packed with wolves. I'm reminded of the last time I was here, when the wolves were fighting for dominance and rank, even to the death. And then I met Thorn, who wanted me sent to the mating house for his enjoyment. Thorn, who nearly ruined his son's life. Thorn, whose death I thought would mean the end of the mating houses. I bristle and push the memories aside because he's dead, and I'm stronger now.

One small section is left unoccupied and is guarded by a few beta wolves, keeping people out. Madame Delphine guides us down to that section, and we sit in the very front row. Faye sits between Elle and me. Once the meeting is over, we're going to Ryne's house to see what he can do about Joanna's family and village. For now, she's hiding out at the manor, probably worried sick, but at least, she's safe.

Ryne is nowhere to be seen. Once everyone is settled, anticipation crackles through the air. The door behind the section where we are sitting opens, and Justin and Bellamy walk in. They hold the doors wide, and a woman walks through, followed by several others. A hush falls over the stadium. They walk down the stairs and sit in the rows behind us. I stare at them and realize these are the women from the mating houses. I recognize several from my nights out at Bell's house, but there are far more than I even knew.

Eventually, a very pregnant woman comes through the door, followed by others with baby bumps of various sizes. My heart leaps when I catch sight of Abi. She's starting to show. There are too many people, so I doubt she can see me, but I watch as she navigates the bleachers and sits down. Ryne is the last one in.

He looks happier than I've seen him in a long time. His hair is tied back, his eyes are clear, and there is a light smile on his lips.

Once he hits the ground, he picks up a microphone, his eyes locking on mine for a long, tense moment before roaming the crowd.

A hush falls over the arena before he speaks. "Wolves and women, I'm sure you are curious why I brought you here. Tonight, some of you are going to hear things you don't like, but I'll not apologize for it." My heart speeds, and I grip the edge of my seat as he takes command. "Things need to change, and I've been reluctant to make these changes because I've been afraid of the consequences. As the new alpha king remains undecided, and the wolf kingdom grows more unstable by the day, I'm choosing to run our pack independently. We may or may not align ourselves with the new king, depending on his goals."

Murmurs ripple among the crowd, but I just want them to shut up so that I can hear what else he has to say.

"I understand that what I'm about to announce will displease some of you. If you wish to leave the pack, you are free to go. There are many packs that will continue with old traditions, and if those appeal to you, we will not come after you."

I'm hanging onto his every word, hope igniting within my soul.

Is this it? Is this finally the end?

"The mating houses have been a tradition among our people since the virus mutated our fertility after the great wars. We were a dying race, and we had to take action to correct that. But now we are thriving, thanks to the many women who have sacrificed their freedom unwillingly." He gives the many women a slight nod, and a few of them bristle while others perk up. "I recognize that this is not something that will be easily changed overnight, but effective immediately, the mating houses as you know them no longer exist in the Carolina Pack."

The rumbling increases, and I'm dumbfounded. Faye grips my hand, and Elle meets my eye. "He's doing this for you," she whispers.

Maybe Elle's right, but I don't think so. He talked about this before. He's doing this because he knows it's the right thing to do, and he's planned this out for a long time. He was waiting for the alpha king to be established, but if he's right, that the kingdom is growing unstable, then now is the perfect way to set his pack apart from the rest. And doing it quickly makes it harder for people to plan counter moves against him.

They're either with him, or they're not.

"You can't do that," someone shouts angrily.

"I can, and I will," Ryne snaps back, his voice echoing through the stadium. "This is the first opportunity you have to leave if you wish. I will explain how this will be done, and you will likely still get as much sex as you want, but right now, if you refuse, you will no longer be welcome here. Anyone who wishes to leave may do so now. The Capital City Pack is the closest geographically, but I expect if you really want your pick of mating houses, you'll have to head to Chicago and fight for alpha king yourself."

That shuts everyone up.

The king still hasn't been decided because every time someone rises to power, they're immediately killed. It's a bloodbath up there.

Ryne clears his throat. "I've spoken with the alphas of the surrounding packs, and they are willing to accept you if Carolina is no longer to be your home." The man is serious, maybe more so than I've ever seen him before, as his calm demeanor turns thunderous. "If you're going to go, you need to go now. Don't look back!"

Silence descends. Then a handful of wolves get up and start to leave, then a few more. Then a stampede starts.

Ryne just lost half his pack within minutes.

But most of his betas are still by his side, protecting him, loyal as ever.

I would be uneasy about the loss of the wolves, but I'm too flooded with excitement. And I'm not the only one——every single woman in the stadium has an expression of either stunned disbelief, immense relief, or knowing satisfaction. This is the day we've all been praying for, hoping for, *fighting* for.

"Some of you might feel that we are weakened now, but I disagree. We just lost half of the pack who aren't willing to fight for what is right, and that is what I intend to do. We will fight to make a better life for all of us. Now that those who are not willing to adapt have left, I will explain exactly what I'm planning. But first, a story.

"A young delta wolf came to me several weeks ago and explained that he had fallen in love. That is a privilege that right now is afforded only to betas, though it is my understanding that at some of the mating houses, something like monogamy does occur. Unfortunately, the woman he is in love with is not in one of those houses. I visited with her a couple of days ago, and she confirmed the story the delta told me. She's absolutely in love with him. And so, the first change that will take place is that any wolf—— regardless of place in the pack——is allowed to take a wife or girlfriend. This must be a consensual relationship. You are not allowed to take a woman home and keep her if she doesn't want to go. This will take place immediately."

A squeal erupts a few rows behind me, and a woman crawls over all the others, shoves past the betas guarding them, and flings herself into the arms of a man a couple of sections over. Then a half-dozen more women do the same.

It shifts the energy in the stadium, and Faye snorts under her breath, but she's also grinning.

"A couple of other changes will take place immediately as well. Women will be allowed to raise any children they bear." At this, several women start audibly sobbing, and Ryne has to speak up to be heard over them. "They can give children up to the pack if they wish them to be raised as they are now, but if not, all women will be given a safe place to raise their children alone or with a partner. These children will still be required to attend daily classes with the others but will go home at night to their mothers."

This is huge.

None of these wolves, save for the betas, were raised this way. Not in this pack, and as far as I know, not in the entire wolf shifter kingdom. Everyone stares at Ryne as if he's just grown a second head, but I look at him like he's the man I always knew he could be.

And I'm so damn proud.

"All claimed men and women will be compensated for their labors, and you wolves will have to pay for services yourselves, whatever it is you want from the claimed, be it sex or labor. Effective immediately, all sex will be consensual, and all sex in the mating houses will be fairly compensated. And all my shifters will be receiving wage increases to meet the demand."

That sends a wave of whispers through the crowd, and people aren't so uneasy anymore. This can work. I know it can work.

"Women can choose to use this money to help their families back home in the villages, or they can spend it on themselves or on whatever else they desire. The pack will still provide free lodging in the mating houses should you choose to stay there." He turns to the women, smiling gently. "But if you would like, you may go home." Even more women burst into tears, and my own vision blurs. "Tell your villages that all adult human men and women are welcome to come work in the wolf city for a better life, but we will also be taking measures to ensure a better quality of life out in the villages and hope most humans will stay put. We will continue to protect the villages during the full moons."

I hope that's true because the lycans are only getting stronger, and I have a feeling Laik isn't going to stop, no matter how many changes Ryne makes. As wonderful as all this is, those lycans want the wolves dead and gone. It's as simple as that.

"Actual relationships used to be our way of life, and it is my intention that we return to it." Ryne's eyes quickly flash to mine before moving on. "But since we need to keep growing the pack, the mating houses will stay open, and my hope is that they will continue to be fruitful for generations." He motions to the betas, and most of the ones who are left stand up. "I've already recruited many of my betas who are prepared to enforce our new laws."

Bellamy is one of them.

His green gaze meets mine––his eyes are brimming with determination, with the love he feels for me, the life we've talked about, and I no longer know what to do. Now that Ryne is making these changes, can I forgive him? Take him back? Or have I already moved on?

Chapter Twenty-Two

Ryne is swarmed with questions, prolonging the meeting well into the night, and we decide not to go to his house to bombard him with the news from Joanna. I expect to be wired by the time we get back to the manor, but as soon as my head hits the pillow, I fall into a deep sleep.

I wake to a soft knock on the door and sit up as Faye rolls over and covers her head with a pillow. Long auburn curls stick up at odd angles against the backdrop of her fluffy white blankets, and I smile to myself. I pad to the door and open it to find a disheveled Bellamy.

And I don't know how to feel about seeing him.

"Hi," I croak. "What are you doing here?"

He takes my hand. "Can we talk?"

I agree, and he leads me out into the quiet sitting room. The soft morning sunrise filters through the curtains, and we sit down next to each other on the sofa.

"You didn't come over last night," he states.

"The announcements went late, and I figured you'd be busy helping enforce everything."

His lips curve into a satisfied smile. "I was."

"How did it go?"

"Better than expected," he says, and then those expressive eyes darken. "It helped that Ryne sent so many of the wolves away like that. They're probably halfway to new packs by now, and good riddance."

It's not enough that the other packs are still going to carry on as if things don't need to change, but maybe our pack can be the start of a revolution.

I've never thought of it as our pack until now.

"Any dissenters?" I ask.

He nods. "Some of the betas, as we expected."

"Why's that?"

"Pack loyalty is stronger for betas. Most of us had to fight our way to this rank, and some of us have wives and families. Leaving isn't so easy. They don't want to start over somewhere else when they're happy and well established already."

"So they can pay for their prostitutes," I snap. "They'll still get plenty of sex."

"They don't want to start paying for something that they've always gotten for free. Besides, there will be fewer women to choose from now. These men are going to have to start respecting the women that do stay, and I don't think some of our betas know the meaning of the word."

He's right. I hate that some of those men regularly visit the mating houses even though they're married. A trickle of fear goes through me, and I wonder how many of them are going to make a play for Ryne's alpha position. If someone takes him down, everything could go back to the way it was––or worse.

Bell squeezes my hand. "Hey, don't worry. Things are changing, and that's what matters."

I gaze at our hands and look back up at him. "You're right. I just still can't believe it. I think I'm in shock."

His eyes search mine. "I want to kiss you so badly right now, but I know I can't."

I frown at that. "Because?"

"Because the full moon is in three days, and we can't risk it." Oh, yeah. Right. *That.* "But if there wasn't the full moon coming up, would you want me to kiss you after last night?"

That's the question of the day, and it would be so easy to say yes to him, but I have to be honest. He deserves the truth. We both do.

"I'm confused," I whisper. "I don't know what to do."

His face falls, but he doesn't release my hand. "I expected that. It's okay. You don't have to make a decision now, but I meant what I said before. I need to know you want me and only me if we're getting engaged at the festival next month."

The fact that we're still having a festival at all was one of the questions from last night. I don't like it. As far as I'm concerned, we should be done with everything having to do with the claiming. But the beta wolves insisted that it makes sense to still hold it since we're already so close to the engagements. And Ryne announced that next year's claiming will be on a voluntary basis--an opportunity for human women over the age of eighteen to date betas for a year, to learn about pack life and what it means to be a beta's wife, without the fear of the mating houses.

Some of the lower ranks wanted to know if they could join the claiming to find a wife as well, and Ryne said he'd consider it. I'm not even sure what that would look like. It's hard to imagine. How many more women would there need to be? And how many more men would sign up? It's still an unanswered question. Something like that would've saved Knox before it was too late.

Although allowing the claimed men and women to carry on here isn't my preference, I'm okay with it. These changes certainly would've made the last year of my life a million times better.

But again, it's all too late.

I walk Bellamy out. He didn't bring his car today but rode in on his boat instead. He kisses me gently on the cheek before motoring off down the river. I sit down on the bank and lie in the tall grass, my silk pajamas soft on my skin and the canopy of trees for cover.

Some of the trees are starting to change colors already, a few of the green leaves giving way to hues of yellow and orange. I'm reminded of my first date with Ryne, of riding that horse out to the forest, his body pressed to mine. Of climbing the tree and all the red leaves that surrounded us when he tried to kiss me for the first time, and I refused him.

So much has changed--and yet here we are, right back where we started.

Him wanting me--and me not feeling sure I can trust him.

"So that's it, huh?" Ryne's voice breaks me from my daydreams, and I jump up to find him standing tall a few feet away. His hands are stuffed into the pockets of the same clothing he wore yesterday. His hair is still tied back, though bits of it have pulled free to frame his face, and his eyes are red from weeks without proper sleep.

"What's it?" I ask.

"You're choosing Bell." It's not a question. It's a statement.

"I don't know." I throw my hands up. "We've already discussed this,

Ryne. I have until the harvest moon to make my decision."

He inches closer. "You asked me to show you my true feelings for you with my actions, so I have. Can't you see I'm fighting for you here? That I love you? That I'm sorry?"

"That's the thing. Did you do this just for me? If so, that's not enough."

Ryne jabs a hand through his hair. "No. I didn't do it just for you. I was planning on doing it anyway but was waiting for the alpha king to be chosen before deciding how I was going to make this work. But I did do it early just for you. I want to prove to you that I'm the man you deserve. Poppy, you cannot deny this." He invades my space and grabs my hands. "We're fated. Don't you see that we're meant to be? There is no choice needed here. It's you and me, not you and Bellamy."

I jerk my hands away from him. "And that's the point of it all, isn't it? Choice. I didn't get a choice when Willow was murdered right in front of me. I didn't get a choice when Anders ripped me from my family. I didn't get a choice when Laik bit me. And when I finally did get to make a choice––to save you––you used that against me and then practically forced me to date your betas again. Now you're telling me that I don't have a choice in who I marry. You're wrong. I can choose to deny the fated bond if I want to. And I just might."

I turn and race back into the house, slamming the door behind me. I couldn't stay out there because, if I had, he'd have seen the tears. I sink onto the floor, entirely overcome with this decision. The sobs wrack my body painfully, like a punishment. It's true I have a choice here, but never before has it been so hard to make one. This choice will forever change my life.

If I choose Bellamy, there is no way we can stay here. Ryne proved last night that he will continue to fight for me, no matter what, and I won't put Bellamy through that.

And if I choose Ryne, is it really a choice at all?

Chapter Twenty-Three

After breakfast, I gather the women I trust most: Madame Delphine, Elle, Joanna, and Faye. I need to talk about this, to get some solid advice. I realize I only have just over a month to make a decision, but I'm going to make sure it's mine.

We sit in Madame Delphine's office. Joanna is perched on the couch beside me with a pillow in her arms. She's been so quiet since she got back. She roomed by herself last night, and this is the first I've seen of her since, but she won't look at me. Not *really* look. It's like we don't even know each other anymore.

I lay it all out. I tell them just about everything that has happened with both Ryne and Bellamy and how I feel about them both. "And now I don't know what to do."

Faye snorts. "Why are you still denying it? Look at what that man did for you. He risked his whole pack and his life. And you're still making him fight for it?"

Elle shakes her head. "I'm starting to go back to my original opinion on this one. Bellamy has been far better to you than Ryne has. He's such a good man too. Perfect, really. He'd never hurt you like Ryne has. If you love him, you should go with him."

I look at Joanna, but she's not exactly paying attention.

Madame Delphine clears her throat. "You still have one month, give or take a few days, so why not take that time to figure it out? Obviously, this is an unusual situation, and my choice would be Ryne, but you deserve to make this decision for yourself. Date them both. Go out with

Ryne one night and Bellamy the next for the whole month. I would recommend not spending the night at either house as that could get out of hand quickly."

That's not a bad idea.

"I think I could do that. Do you think they'll be okay with it?"

"If they want a shot with you, they will be," Faye says.

Joanna shifts in her seat and shoots me a very serious expression. "I don't like any of this. I have no love for Ryne, but he is your fated, and I think he's right. You won't be able to deny it. So do Bellamy a favor, and when you realize that you want Ryne, don't drag it out any longer."

Elle shakes her head. "Or if you decide on Bellamy early, then you should end things with Ryne once and for all."

I sit back, unsure of how to take this information.

The door crashes open, and we all jump. Ryne bursts into the room, face pale, and he's panting. When he sees Joanna, his eyes go wide.

Her hands fly up in surrender, and she jumps off the couch, her pillow flying across the room. "You were right about Laik, Grady was wrong, and I'm here because we must stop the lycans during the next full moon when they attack the villages again. Don't shoot the messenger."

"Where's Grady? Is he okay?"

"He's in hiding, but he's fine."

Ryne nods. "He's welcome back in my pack and as my beta. That's if he wants to come."

Joanna's mouth trembles. "Thank you."

"But we have bigger problems than the lycan," Ryne says, his eyes passing from each of us and finally landing on me. Fear clenches in my gut. Something is wrong. "The new alpha king has been chosen."

He sinks onto the couch Joanna just vacated. I can feel his heat from here and also his anxiety. A haunted look takes over his face.

"And who is it?" Madame Delphine asks carefully.

"Anders."

Of all the names he could've said, this one hurts the most.

Bile rises in my throat, and I clutch at my abdomen. Panic sweeps through me, and so do the unwanted memories. They bombard me one after another, no matter how hard I wish them away. Anders groping my sister and then decapitating her for rejecting his advance. Anders taking me to the claiming in her place and then forcing me to date him, talking about marriage and sex, intimidating me into pretending I was okay with all of it. And then when we figured out that he killed Nova and Lexi, he turned everything around on us and convinced Thorn that Joanna and Grady were the problem. That they needed to die.

I hated Thorn. From the moment I met him, he made my skin crawl, and I'm not sorry he's dead.

But Anders? Anders is the true villain in my story.

I hate him with everything in me, with every breath, with every thought, with all of me--*I hate him*. But worst of all is the fear because, if I'm being honest with myself, I'm downright terrified of Anders. Even despite the gruesome lycan hiding under my skin, even despite the amazing friends at my side and the powerful shifters to protect me, I'm afraid. Nothing else matters because Anders will always be the one who hurt me the most. And the very thought of him as the alpha king and what that will mean for the future of this kingdom sends me into a tailspin.

He'll hurt my friends.

He'll kill Ryne.

And he'll rape me.

I sink to my knees, pressing my face into the rug as my vision blurs and my throat tightens.

"What the hell is wrong with her?" Faye squeals. I try to look up at her, but my neck won't move. Tears slip from my eyes.

I'm so hot. I'm shaking--and then Ryne is with me. Hand on my back. I can feel his calming presence, but I can't see him. I wish I could see him.

But all I can see is Anders and the terrible things he'll do now that he's king.

"She's having a panic attack."

I vaguely make out Madame Delphine's voice as the fear carries me into the dark.

* * *

I wake in familiar arms. I blink rapidly and sit up as everything comes back to me. I'm in my room, and Ryne is lying with me on my small bed. He's asleep, despite the sun filtering through the curtains. And we're alone in here. How long was I out? I've never had something like that happen to me before, and my cheeks warm at the memory.

"Are you okay?" Ryne's eyes pop open and run over my body. "Are you thirsty? Do you need something to eat?"

I shush him. "Just tired. Looks like you're pretty tired yourself."

He tugs me back into his arms, his woodsy scent enveloping me, calming me. I know I shouldn't, but I let him do it. I need the comfort I find there, even if it's only for a few minutes.

"Things are tense and busy," he mutters. "I haven't been sleeping well."

"Well, I'm glad you napped with me. How long was I out?"

"A few hours."

I shake my head. "I still can't believe it."

He squeezes my upper arm and pulls me in closer, brushing a kiss on my forehead. "You had a panic attack. Do you know what that is?"

I think about it for a moment, remembering an old neighbor who used to talk about those. It wasn't something my childhood brain needed to understand, so I never asked. "Vaguely."

"Everything that's happened is like someone piling rocks on your back. Eventually, you weren't going to be able to carry the weight anymore." He runs the tips of his fingers up my arm, leaving a trail of goosebumps. "I'm so sorry. It's all my fault."

My immediate reaction is to tell him that it's not his fault, but truthfully, a big part of it is. He's hurt me, abandoned me, and hasn't treated me the way I deserve. He's been one of the people piling those rocks up. And now with Bellamy, I know what it's like to have a man treat a woman well, to have someone take the rocks away.

I just wish I could love Bell the way I love Ryne.

I sit up again, scooting back on the bed to make some distance, and choose my words carefully. "I think we need to talk." He nods, brushing the hair from his face, and sits up too. "We have a lot of things to take care of before we worry about our relationship. First of all, Joanna needs our help. She has information on the next lycan attack, and if we're smart, we may be able to get rid of Laik and his cronies for good."

"She and I had a long conversation while you were asleep. Nico is already on his way to the panther pack to see if we can get their help. With the Carolina Pack being so vulnerable right now, we're going to need an ally, and since I've made the changes Derek wanted, I really think he might help us this time."

I nod, hopeful for the support but worried the panther leader will keep his neutral position.

"And then there's the matter of Anders."

His gaze turns murderous, blue eyes like thunderclouds about to unleash lightning. "You let me worry about Anders."

What I'm about to say might come as a shock, but it needs to be said. "I know you don't want to leave the Carolina Pack, but you have to. Who else is going to stand up for the women all over the wolf kingdom? You're making a great start here, but if change is going to spread to the other packs, we need a good man as alpha king. Not Anders. He'll come here and put things back to the way your father had them or worse. The wolves that left have probably already told him what happened."

"Like I said, I'll take care of Anders." He stares at me for a long moment. "But I'm not making any moves against him right away, not when we're still adjusting to change here and have a vigilante group of lycans attacking our villages. If, in the end, we have to take the whole pack and move them out of Anders's reach, we will."

He's right. We have to worry about Laik right now. That's priority number one. Still, we can't run from Anders forever.

"But I really don't think Anders will show his face here anytime soon." He smirks. "He's always been afraid of me. He was only my number two because my father wanted a spy. I'm stronger than he is, and he knows it. And he also knows that I'll kill him if he tries to come here and take what's mine."

I sit back on my heels. "Okay, that's fair, but you need to accept the truth about yourself, Ryne. You're a hybrid now. Your wolf bite contains the lycanthrope virus and will kill any wolf shifter during the full moon. That's valuable. You could use that to kill Anders."

His face drains of color, and he's quiet for so long that I'm not sure he heard me. "I already know that," he finally whispers. "But you can't tell a soul, not even Bellamy or Elle or anyone else. If it gets out, I'll be hunted down and executed."

I frown, unable to believe that his most trusted friends would hurt him. "Would they really do that to you?"

"Without a doubt." There's no hesitation in his voice. "If not my own pack, then certainly one of the other packs. And the more people who know, the more likely it is to get out. You and Callum are the only people who know about my bite. Callum has been a big help."

I nod because, even though I disagree that he needs to be so secretive, I understand. I have to hide my real self now too. We're the same in that, and it doesn't feel good, but it's better than the alternative. "Okay, and last thing . . . I still don't know how to forgive you for hurting me. I want to, and I'm grateful for all you're doing to help the claimed men and women, but I'm not sure I can trust you with my heart again."

"Poppy, please——"

"So I've decided that I'm going to date both you and Bellamy," I cut him off.

Heartbreak splinters across his face. I don't know if I've ever seen him so vulnerable, so hurt. The alpha is used to fighting for what he wants and getting it, but this time, he might not win, and he knows it. I recognize that with Anders being alpha king, I'm actually safer with Bellamy. Together, we can run away. Ryne can't. He has his whole pack to worry about. I will never be his number one priority.

"I have to be sure, and I'm just not there yet, so I would like to alternate dates between the two of you until the harvest festival. If I choose you, you'll get all of me, forever, and I'll never look back."

His eyes drift down to my mouth, and I have the sudden urge to kiss him. But I won't, not only because of the full moon coming up but because he needs to internalize what I'm about to say to him, to understand how serious I am with this decision. "But if I choose Bellamy, you must respect that. You can't hurt him, and you can't try to stop us if we get married and move to a new pack."

It's like we're frozen, staring at each other, the world going cold around us.

And then he moves so fast that I barely see it happen. One second, I'm sitting on the end of the bed, and the next, I'm flat on my back, and he's lying on top of me, caging me with his arms. He inhales deeply then drags his mouth from my temple to my jaw and down to my collarbone, peppering my skin with soft open kisses——but nothing else about him feels soft.

"Fine, we'll do it your way," he whispers against my ear, and my core burns hot, the frost gone in an instant. "But I'm going to give this little plan of yours my all, so you better prepare yourself, Poppy. Bellamy doesn't stand a chance. By the harvest moon, you won't even remember his name, but you'll be consumed with mine."

Chapter Twenty-Four

I bounce back and forth on both feet.

"Would you calm down?" Joanna presses a hand to my arm.

"Oh, come on, like you aren't just as excited."

We're standing on Ryne's porch, watching the road. Any second now, a car is going to pull up, and if all goes as planned, my family and Joanna's parents will be inside.

"I really wish we had another week," she says. "I'm not excited. I'm nervous."

"I know, but the full moon is tonight whether we like it or not."

The panther pack showed up early yesterday morning. Since half of Ryne's pack deserted him, there is plenty of room in the city. We spent a couple of hours going over a plan to take out Laik and his followers. First, we wanted to get everyone in a central location so they will be easier to protect. All the villagers will be transported into the city, and the wolves and panthers will guard it. Then, Ryne, Derek, me, Joanna, Grady, and a few others will go hunt down Laik. Any lycans who surrender will be restrained until the full moon is over and then allowed to go free. Ryne's wolves didn't like that idea, but Derek insisted that the lycans be protected if they didn't fight, and for once, I actually liked the guy.

My family is staying at Ryne's, and Joanna's parents are staying at Shauna's, but they're meeting us here. Women from all over the city are anxiously awaiting to see their relatives again. I wanted to go with the wolves to get them, but Ryne said it would be faster and easier if it was just the wolves since they could communicate with each other telepathically and because weepy reunions would slow things down.

He was probably right.

A car pulls up, and I straighten my skirt. Nerves dance in my stomach. "How do I look?"

Joanna laughs. "You look just as good as you did fifteen minutes ago when you asked. What about me?"

"Stunning as always." And she does. It's as if life was breathed back into her when Grady finally returned to the pack last night. He even got his old house back. Joanna's supposed to move in with him as soon as they're married, but I'm not sure she'll wait that long. Ryne won't care. He's just glad to have his old friend back. I'm unsure if Grady will ever truly forgive Ryne for the loss of his arm, but I hope they can become the brothers they once were.

Joanna grabs my hand, and we run for the car. Ryne climbs out first, and I wonder if he told my parents anything about our relationship. He extends a hand and helps my mother out of the car. She falls back a few inches when she sees me, her hand on her mouth. Ryne helps steady her, and I rush for her. She collapses into my arms, hugging me tighter than she ever has before. Another set of arms engulfs us, and I spot my dad out of the corner of my eye.

Then, two little arms wrap around my waist, and I nearly lose it. Mama pulls away, her hands on my cheeks. "I thought I'd never see you again."

I nod, sniffling, not sure what to say. It hasn't even been a year, but it feels like eons have passed.

"Poppy!" Evan squeals, and I pick him up.

He squirms. "I'm not a baby. Put me down."

I hold him close to me and kiss his cheek before setting him down. "We have food ready if you're hungry. You're staying here tonight. This is the alpha's house, so you know it's extra secure." I point up to the gorgeous house, and my mother's face pales.

"Aren't you staying with us?"

I shake my head. "No. I have to help protect the city." I won't tell her that I'm a lycan, not yet, but I can fight, and that's going to be my excuse.

"But you're just a girl. Is that what they brought you here for, to be warriors?"

Joanna, who'd been standing nearby with her parents, snorts. "Hardly. But we were taught to fight, and Poppy and I decided that we weren't going to sit back, defenseless. This is our home, our pack, and we will protect it."

My mom looks at Joanna suspiciously and takes Evan's hand. My dad hasn't said much, but he puts his arm around my shoulders. "We're so glad to be with you again. Ryne said, if we want, we can live in the city with you now."

It's hard to picture Papa living anywhere other than the farmland he loves, but the selfish part of me wants them to stay and make a life here.

"Yeah. You can."

"Do you live here?" he asks, marveling at the big home.

"If she wants to," Ryne says.

Evan looks from Ryne to me. "Is Ryne your boooyfriend?" he asks with a giggle.

Ryne plants a sloppy kiss on my cheek. "I am."

I push him away. I do not want to have that conversation right now. Evan creases his eyebrows. "I thought Knox was your boyfriend."

Everyone goes silent for a moment.

"Well, boyfriends can change," Mama says.

Evan shakes his head. "No way. Sarah is going to be my girlfriend forever. Can she live here too?"

Sarah is the little girl next door, and when I left, they couldn't stand each other. Willow and I used to tease him that they'd fall in love one day. Maybe we were right.

Before any of the rest of us say anything, Ryne adds, "Maybe. But not tonight. Tonight, everyone needs to stay where they are so they can be safe. We'll see about finding Sarah and her family tomorrow."

Sarah's older sister was claimed a few years ago. I hope they managed to find her tonight and are staying with her, but I'm not sure she's even alive.

"You all can go on inside. I have a few things to take care of. Poppy, I'll see you and Joanna in a couple of hours. I'll send someone to come and get you."

I watch him leave, then I lead my parents into his house.

"Ryne said that you could live here if you want, so where do you live now?" Mama asks.

"For the last year, I've lived in a home on the outskirts of the city with the rest of the claimed girls. I'll explain that all later. But for now, I want news from home."

The news turns out to be ordinary small-town things: couples getting married, breaking up, or having children. There's been a successful crop this year, but with all of us having to leave, it's unlikely all the available cotton will be harvested before it goes bad. I can tell that part bothers my father more than he lets on, but he doesn't say much about it.

"Oh, and a terrible flu swept through the village back in February. It nearly killed Old Man Lancaster, but he survived in the end. He always does." Mama adds, "Did you guys catch it here?"

I shake my head. "Wolves can't get sick, and not many humans are permitted to come and go from the wolf city, so I don't think we were ever exposed to it."

She nods thoughtfully. "Well, that's all going to change now."

I don't think lycan get sick either, but I don't mention it.

"I can hardly believe it," Papa sighs, his eyes going glossy, and I know he's thinking of Willow. I am too.

It's wonderful to be reunited with my family, but it's also a reminder of what we've lost, and that wound has been reopened now that we're together again. Or maybe it didn't heal for them, the same as it still hasn't for me. I'll never forget what happened to her, will never be okay with the brutality of her murder, but I hope the work we're doing now to make changes can help honor her memory. Because things are changing, just like Mama said. Papa may not believe it, but I do. I've fought way too hard to get to this point.

"Knock, knock," Bellamy says as he pushes open the front door. He's dressed in his best suit, and a little part of me stirs at the sight of him. His eyes go wide when he sees us all sitting in the front room, and then they soften, and he smiles. "You must be Poppy's family. You've raised a wonderful woman."

I jump to my feet, a blush forming on my cheeks. After I told Bellamy that I wanted to date both him and Ryne leading up to the harvest, I expected him to be angry or hurt, but he wasn't. True to his personality, he was warm and understanding. But just like Ryne, he insisted he'd be the one to win me over in the end. He's so charming, so kind, so perfect--he just might.

"Who are you?" Evan asks. He shifts to stand in front of me with his legs spread and his arms crossed over his chest.

Joanna snorts. "That's your sister's *other* boyfriend."

I shoot her a death-glare, and she shrugs. "Hey, it wasn't my idea, remember?"

Papa appears a little confused, and my mother shoots me a look that I've only ever seen her give to a woman who cheated on her husband.

"Umm, well, you see, the thing is," I mumble. I've no idea how to explain all of this to them. It took me a few weeks to fully comprehend it all. This is such a different world from the one I was raised in.

"I'll explain," Bellamy says smoothly, shooting me a little wink and turning to my parents. "Dating multiple people is normal here. It's how we do things when a human woman is first brought into the city. She dates multiple shifter men and may even end up marrying one of them. I happen to be one of the two men Poppy is currently dating before she decides what she wants to do about a future spouse."

Mama and Papa nod, Joanna rolls her eyes, Evan frowns, and I just stand there, relieved. Mama's face still betrays her true feelings, but at least, she doesn't seem to feel the need to say anything. I'm glad he explained that so well because I obviously didn't know what to say. And I'm also glad that he didn't go into details about what else happens to the claimed women, although my parents might already know by now. If I were to explain to them what the claiming really meant, they'd be horrified. They'd hate the shifters, and who knows if they'd even stay here tonight. And I need them to stay because as long as they're safe, I won't be worrying about them while I'm off hunting down Laik.

"Okay, that's a good enough explanation for now," I insist. "Mama, Papa, Evan, this is Bellamy."

As soon as the introductions are complete, I'm ready to go, but Papa is already badgering Bellamy with questions. Where does he live? What does he do? Does he want children? I already know Bell's answers to the questions.

Papa leans back in his chair. "Do you date other women too?"

Bellamy shakes his head. "I'm required to, but it's not serious with anyone else. Not since I met Poppy. I'm really hoping she'll choose me over Ryne."

"What do you think of Ryne?"

That one shocks me, and I'll admit I'm curious to know the answer. "Ryne is a great alpha. I'm not sure if he'll be a great husband—I can't speak to that—but I will say he loves your daughter. Same as how I've fallen in love with her."

My cheeks flame, and his words shut everyone up, me the most. Bellamy hasn't told me he loves me yet, and hearing him say those words to my father makes this all so real.

"Aw." Joanna breaks the silence. "Maybe I'm team Belly after all."

I raise my eyebrows at that because Joanna has been a strong proponent of the mating bond up until now, but when I catch her playful smirk, I know she's teasing me. I could kill her--now is really not the time.

"Team Belly?" Mama questions.

"You know, Bellamy plus Poppy equals Belly."

Evan laughs and pats his stomach. "Belly!"

"Alright, that's enough of that. We've really got to go," I interrupt, fighting back the embarrassment. Besides, I can already feel the moon calling to me even though it's hours until its light will be strong enough to turn me, and between that and everything else on my mind, I can't handle where this interrogation is headed. I give my parents one more hug each. Then I kneel in front of Evan and squeeze his hands with mine. "You stay safe tonight, okay? Promise to stay inside, and the wolves will protect you."

His eyes water. "And who will protect you?"

"I'll protect her," Bellamy says.

"We all will," Joanna adds. "We're going to look out for each other, okay? Same as you need to look out for your mom and dad."

He nods up at my friends, and I wrap him in a tight hug and leave before my family can see me cry. The truth is I don't know if Bellamy or Joanna or Ryne or Elle or *anyone* can protect me tonight. There's a pit in my stomach, one that's warning me things aren't going to be easy. Who knows how many lycans will be out there tonight attacking the villages? And of those lycans, how many will be going through their first transitions?

I shiver, just remembering how it felt to be so bloodthirsty, so unbelievably out of my mind that I was willing to feed on Knox. I would've killed him if they hadn't pulled me off. And Charlotte--she did kill during her first transition. She killed ruthlessly, without care, and would've taken out an entire basement of innocent women if given the chance. This virus makes us incredibly dangerous, and the newly turned lycans are the most dangerous of us all.

Chapter Twenty-Five

The army of wolves and panthers protecting the city is pretty epic. They're everywhere––their coats shining bright in the dying sunlight, a mix of shaggy brown massive dogs and slick black powerful cats. I can hardly look away. If the lycans can see this now, they've got to be terrified. I would be. But knowing some of those lycans as I do, this sight is probably hyping them up.

More blood for them to spill.

Ryne had scouts out all day, who discovered that Laik and his people have mostly gathered near a fishing village. It's one of the farthest from the city, splitting us from the bulk of the army if we decide to go to them instead of waiting for them to come to us. It makes me uneasy, and I'm not sure what Laik is playing at. He obviously changed his plan to attack the textile village, which is much closer and honestly made more sense. He must know we've taken all the humans into the city, so then why gather his troops so far away?

We're standing on the dock preparing to leave for battle, and I turn back to gaze at the betas' homes and the high-rise buildings in the distance. At least, the main ways into the city are by boat or bridge. The bridge is so heavily guarded that there's no way the enemy could cross it. The back-roads are all being guarded too, as is the shoreline. The entire territory is crawling with wolves and panthers, but that won't stop Laik from trying to take us down. I hope the defenses hold because I won't be there to protect those inside the city if it falls, and it makes me sick just thinking about it.

"It's not too late to stay back. You're going to get hurt," Grady pleads with Joanna.

She widens her stance. "No way. We've been over this before. Where you go, I go. I've got two swords and knives hidden on my body. I'm going to fight with you."

I don't want Joanna to come either. It's so risky. The most vulnerable people need to be behind the army for protection, not out in front of it, and she's going to be target number one since she betrayed Laik.

"But what if you get bitten by a lycan?" His voice sounds as haunted as I feel.

"Poppy and Ryne worked it out. We can too."

"You know that's not totally true," I interject, tired of their argument. Joanna is being foolish, but she has a right to make her own choices. "I was lucky to survive the bite. Not everybody does. *And* I could still end up with Bellamy." We're leaving him at the bridge as he's in charge of the wolves guarding it. He was just here to give me a big hug and a kiss on the cheek and made me promise to be safe, and Ryne is already acting icy about it.

"You and Bellamy are only dating because Ryne messed up," Joanna points out. "It's not because you're a lycan."

Ryne shoots her a scathing look, but she only rolls her eyes.

I give her a hard glare. "There's a good chance you're not walking away from tonight still a human. Is that what you want?"

"See," Grady implores. "Poppy gets it."

Joanna holds up a hand. "That's enough, you two. I've made up my mind."

"Are you ready for this?" Derek asks gently, untying the boat from the dock. I nod, and he takes my hand, helping me climb aboard. I don't let myself think too hard as the rest of the boat fills, and Ryne starts the engine.

We take it to the inlet near the fishing village and hide it in the endless marshes that filter the rivers from the sea. From here, it's only another mile on foot, and as we near the village, Joanna and Grady start bickering about her coming along again. I smile because it's great to have them back even if the reunion between Grady and the pack was less than welcoming. Ryne was ecstatic, but everyone else? Not so much. It's going to take time to heal those wounds, but I'm confident Ryne will make sure they do heal.

After a while of hiking, Ryne steps up between us, and we all stop. He looks up at the sky. It's clear tonight, not a cloud in sight, and the sunset has cast everything in wild shades of orange. "Quit arguing, you two," he shoots at the couple. "She's here, the moon's almost up, and it's nearly go time."

"Remember, he is our goal," Derek instructs his number two, a quiet man named Ace. I can't help but wonder if Ace is his real name or his nickname.

Ace nods, and Ryne continues, "We avoid fights with any and all of the others unless it's self-defense. Once Laik is dead, I will try to persuade them to stop."

A few minutes later, we find a stand of trees just outside the village that makes for a good hiding spot. From here, we can see people prowling around, but we're too far away to make out their faces. I wonder if I know any of them. Ryne emptied the village already, so they're definitely all lycan. The last rays of sun dip behind the trees, the full moon taking center stage.

My bones crack.

"Here we go," I say, hurrying to slip from my human clothing. Callum and the shifters do the same.

This transition is even easier than the last, and my mind is totally clear within seconds.

"See," Joanna whispers. "Look how badass she looks. I could totally do that."

Grady shakes his head and growls. "You stay with me, and don't even think about letting yourself get bit."

Ryne, Derek, Ace, and Grady all shift. Joanna scrambles onto Grady's back. We discovered earlier that Ryne and Derek can communicate in their shifted forms, so they'll be able to relay messages back and forth between the packs. But it's an alpha thing only, so if one of them is killed, our plan could dissolve into chaos.

I allow my mind to relax so I can hear what's going on with the lycans. I thought it would be difficult to find Laik, but apparently, he doesn't think we'd be listening because in moments, he's broadcasting to all the lycan. *The wolves have taken all humans into their city . . .*

Poppy, are you ready? Ryne interrupts the thoughts from Laik.

I am, I reply so only Ryne can hear me.

I will be going into the village first since I'm a lycan, and unless I come across someone who knew me well from the wilds, no one else will recognize me or think anything of me moving among them. Callum is going to stay with Ryne and the others. Once I find Laik, I'll notify the others where I am, and only then will we reveal ourselves to him and fight.

I prowl through the village, which is much larger than mine. Rounding a corner, I nearly falter when I catch sight of the glittering ocean. I've never seen the ocean before, only heard stories. It's an endless stretch of rolling water leading into nothing but inky black. An old lighthouse stands vigil over everything on a cropping of rocks farther out. The smell of salt and fish permeates everything, heightened by my lycan senses.

Several lycans take off toward the wolf city. On foot, it would take a human three hours, but the lycans are incredibly fast, and I know they'll be there in one. It's difficult for me not to want to try and stop them. My family is in the city, and I want to protect them, but taking out Laik is our primary goal, so I don't. I trust that the wolves and panthers guarding the city will do their jobs.

I follow Laik's voice. I'm pretty sure he's stationary, and I wonder why he's not going into the city with the rest of them. Maybe he's letting them fight first so he doesn't risk his own life.

Coward.

I turn a corner and then back up. He's there with a dozen other lycan, all of whom look like they are waiting for something, though what exactly that is, I don't know.

Steadying myself, I peek around the corner. I recognize Laik's and Wanda's lycan forms, but not the others. Aside from Wanda, they are all very big and bulky, so they're probably male. Laik stands in the middle of them, and when Wanda darts off into the village, I become uneasy.

I send the location back to Ryne. *Something is off, though. It's like he's waiting for us. This could be a bloodbath. He's got too many guards.*

We're better than they are. We can beat them.

I want to argue, but I know Ryne. He's already on his way. *See you soon.*

I stay hidden while I wait. And wait. No reason to make myself known and ruin any chance we have at a surprise, but I'm growing impatient. I can hear them rustling around. Maybe I should move a little farther away. I'm not that well hidden.

Suddenly, a lycan jumps in front of me, and I glance up to meet his cruel eyes.

Laik.

Hello, Poppy. We've been waiting for you.

Chapter Twenty-Six

S*urrender now, Laik,* I demand. But really, I'm trying to buy myself time. Laik isn't the type to surrender under any circumstance. Not now. Not ever. And I'm not the type to take such a horrible person prisoner when he deserves death.

His laugh penetrates my mind. *Why would I surrender when I've already won?*

There's not enough of you to take down the wolf pack, I say, *even if you've bitten a bunch of humans, there still won't be enough to stop us. You're just going to get innocent people killed.*

I might die, but we're going to win.

We have to.

I don't want to reveal that we've got panthers on our side yet--that our numbers have grown exponentially for this battle. He'll find out soon enough if he doesn't already know.

Because of the panthers? He guesses, stalking in close as several other lycan appear behind him. They've backed me into a corner, and if they wanted to kill me now, there's enough of them that they could. I will Ryne and the others to hurry. I can feel it all the way to my bones--my time is short. He bares his teeth. *Oh, we know all about those traitors. In fact, we've already taken Derek out.*

I stare at his grotesque lycan form silhouetted in the moonlight, unwilling to accept what he just said. I just saw him minutes ago. How could he be dead already? Ryne and Grady were with him. If he's dead, then so are they.

My heart sinks.

That's not possible. The words slip through the telepathic bond without me even realizing, and he laughs again.

Turns out, not every panther is as soft and pathetic as their leader. I already got confirmation from Wanda that our panther on the inside took him out. I believe you've met Ace already? My mate was there to see it happen.

Ace is a traitor? Oh no. No, no, no. A horrible vision of Wanda tearing through Ryne's house and finding my family flashes through my mind. She won't even hesitate——she'll kill them, and she'll like it. If I don't stop this, I have no doubt she'll be on her way to the wolf city soon.

Now stand back, Laik says to his lackeys. *I've been waiting for this moment.*

And then he attacks.

I duck as his body comes barreling toward me. I swing up on his other side and jump onto the roof of the nearby structure then take off running. I can't fight him when he's got backup, and I don't. I need to give my team more time to get to me.

I'm running toward the lighthouse, I tell Ryne, hoping he's still alive to hear me. *I've got Laik chasing me. Meet me there?*

Already on the way. I can hear his strained voice, the worry that wasn't there minutes ago. But it's nothing compared to the relief I feel that he's still alive.

Do you already know about Derek?

He's dead. Ace turned on us. Grady was quick, though. He killed Ace after it happened.

Quick. But not quick enough.

What does this mean for the panther pack?

Careful, I add. *Wanda will be on your tail.*

In all of two minutes, I've bounded from the rooftops to the beach and over to the rocky coastline where the aging lighthouse waits. Up close, I can tell that the thing is half-crumbling and about ready to topple over.

You want me? Come get me! I call out to everyone in the vicinity and sprint toward the lighthouse, tearing the door clear off its rusty hinges and climbing the old spiraling staircase. The metal groans under my weight.

I'm going to enjoy this, Laik sneers. He's only a few yards behind me, his claws outstretched and teeth gleaming. He's bigger than I am and gaining ground, and my muscles burn as I push myself to the very top of the lighthouse. There's a large broken light inside a dome and a circular walkway around the whole thing. We're completely exposed to the elements. There's nowhere else to go.

I've got you now, Poppy. You're dead.

We circle the broken light, and I edge to the railing, the cold wind whipping against my face. I'm taller in this form, which makes the height seem even worse. I can't believe I thought coming up here was a good idea. Laik pounces, and I quickly dodge him, but then I slip, grabbing onto the edge of the railing. It bends, and then I'm swinging, dangling off the edge.

He crouches low. *It's a long fall down, and those rocks look sharp, don't they?*

No, please don't. My voice quivers as my claws begin to slide. One slips free, and then I'm hanging by only a few claws and nothing else. I'm about to die.

I'm so glad I got to hear you beg before I killed you, Laik taunts.

And then he slams down on my paw, and I can't help it--I let go.

I never imagined this would be how I would die. I didn't actually think about death all that much until this last year when I started to think about it constantly. I would be torn apart by lycans or wolves. I would be murdered by someone like Anders, strangled or drowned or beaten to death. Maybe one of the other claimed women would poison me. Or maybe I'd die of a broken heart. There were so many possibilities. But falling?

And I do fall. It's fast and horrifying.

But when I land, pain doesn't explode through my body.

Because another lycan has caught me. I blink up into his face, trying to place him, but my vision is blurred, and my heart is pounding.

Are you okay? Knox's voice asks.

I nod, stunned.

Oh, thank goodness, Charlotte adds over his shoulder.

Knox sets me down, and we step back as several other lycans surround us. *Traitors,* one of them calls to the others. *Knox and Charlotte are traitors.*

You're the traitors, Knox spits. *You know the changes that have been made to the Carolina Pack, and you still want to kill them all in cold blood.*

I'm thrilled to see my friends have returned to me, but a murderous growl sounds from above, distracting everyone. Laik still stands up there, but he's not alone. Ryne's black wolf circles him, his growl darker and more threatening than ever before. In moments, the two predators are on each other, snarling and howling. We lose them from view for a second, and my heart races all over again. If Ryne dies, I don't know what we'll do.

All the lycans scramble back to get a better view of the fight, but some break away from the group to charge toward the lighthouse.

However, they're met with Callum, the wolves, and Joanna.

She really is covered in knives.

"Try me," she hisses through gritted teeth, holding up two long knives. "I'd love some target practice."

One of the lycan pounces, and she throws the knife so fast he doesn't see it coming. It slices straight through his neck, and the creature slumps to the ground.

"Who's next?" she asks, and Grady growls at her side.

Nobody moves.

Then a lycan breaks free and manages to make it through the door, dodging our people and all of Joanna's knives. I recognize her at once.

Wanda.

I race back up the stairs after her. We make it to the top and see Ryne and Laik locked in battle. Wanda leaps, but I'm on top of her before she can reach them. Her body cracks the wall of bricks, and when she fights to flip over, I make sure we turn into the lighthouse so I don't go flying off the edge again. She's all teeth and claws, and it's all I can do to keep her from tearing my neck out. My back is to the glass of the lighthouse. It's weak, but it's holding. I manage to get a leg up, and I shove with all my might, and her body goes flying right off the edge.

At the same time, I hear a loud snarling sound, and another body flies through the air.

I glance over and see Ryne peering down to where both bodies landed, torn up by rocks.

Laik and Wanda are dead.

<h1 style="text-align:center">Chapter Twenty-Seven</h1>

I turn to head back down the stairs, but Ryne stops me.

We need to get our stories straight, he says.

What do you mean? We're moving fast. There's not a lot of time to come up with a story, and I'm not even sure we need to.

Well, I don't know how the hierarchy works for the lycans, but if it's similar to the way things work for wolves, then whoever killed Laik will be the next alpha.

But they don't have to listen to their alpha, I reason. *They choose an alpha. It's not like with you shifters.*

Exactly. They won't know which one of us killed him, so you should assert yourself as alpha.

Excuse me? This wasn't the plan.

You're more than capable of leading them. His wolf form is majestic, and all I can think is that he's the one who people will want to follow, not me. Never me.

If I try to bring lycans into my pack, he continues, *my wolves might revolt. This way, we can still have some semblance of peace.*

The last thing I want is for the wolves to revolt, but the thought of outing myself is terrifying. *Very few people know I'm a lycan. Wouldn't it be too dangerous? You said yourself there are wolves who would kill you if they found out you were a hybrid, and I'm the full thing.*

His voice comes through our link, rough and determined. *You're right. And that's why we're not going to let everyone know your true identity. For now, I'm going to head back to the city, corral the panthers and my men, and you're going to get the lycans under control. You can do this, Poppy. I know you can. I believe in you.*

But I don't believe in myself––I'm not meant for leadership.

It's a good idea, though. And as long as I make it through the night, Ryne and I can figure out the details later. And if I can convince the other lycans to call off the attack, so many lives will be spared.

Silence surrounds us once we hit the bottom of the stairs. There are so many more lycans than there were before, and everyone has gathered around the bodies, just staring.

No one is fighting.

No one seems to know exactly what to do now.

One of the lycan turns and spots us. He nudges the one next to him, and soon they're all turning to face us.

The wolf killed our alpha. He dies now.

As the lycans descend on us, I step in front of Ryne. *No. I killed your alpha. That means you answer to me.*

They all stop, the few in front breathing hard. I recognize a few of them from Laik's pack. I wonder if they recognize me.

We don't have to listen to you, Poppy, the one in front says, and my insides squeeze. The lycans knowing me is one thing, but what if they are able to somehow tell the wolves? Things just got so much more complicated. But then Callum, Charlotte, and Knox step up next to me, and I feel like maybe I'll be okay.

We have an alpha so that we can be organized like the wolves and not descend into chaos, Callum says. *She killed Laik. She's the new alpha of this pack. If you don't like it, you can leave. But if you try to hurt anyone in the city or surrounding villages, we will kill you.*

No one moves for a moment. Then something unexpected happens. The lycan in front drops to his knees and bows his head like I'm some sort of queen.

Then slowly, the others follow suit, including Callum, Charlotte, and Knox.

You know, my wolves don't even bow to me, Ryne says so only I can hear, and I catch the laughter in his voice. If I was human right now, no doubt, I'd be bright red.

Get out of here while you can. I'll see what I can do about stopping the others on their way to the city.

Ryne leaves with Grady, Joanna, and the other wolves, and I plan to wait until they are out of sight before I address the lycans again. I wonder if Ryne will hear my projection. I'm still not sure how to open communication to him and the others at the same time. I nudge Callum and Knox, who are on either side of me, and they stand. There are a couple hundred lycans on the beach by now, way more than I've ever seen gathered together before. I don't know how many more are heading into the city, but I pray they hear what I have to say––for all our sakes.

Who was Laik's second in command?

The lycan in front of me stands as well. *Wanda. After her, it was me.*

What's your name? I ask, but his voice is vaguely familiar.

Christian. You know me.

And I do. He was one of the people I spent those three months with. I didn't particularly care for him, but I didn't hate him either.

What was the plan tonight? I ask.

He sent all the new lycans into the city and kept the experienced ones out here. We were going to go in after the initial bloodbath.

I can picture it now, the screams and chaos and death. We're not out of the woods yet. Those new lycans are going to be thirsty, no matter who is the alpha. *How many were there?* I ask.

About fifty. Maybe more.

I project my voice to all the lycans I possibly can, not knowing how far it will travel. At least I know these ones will follow me. *I do not agree with Laik's plan to turn innocent humans into lycan to build an army, and I'm sorry if you were bitten against your will. I know how that feels as the previous alpha did the same thing to me. But he's dead, and as your new alpha, I want you to understand that biting innocent humans against their will is not tolerated.* A few lycan shift uneasily, but nobody argues, so I continue. *Prince Ryne and the Carolina Pack are not our enemy. They are working to make changes to their system for the betterment of all species. The time will come when you will likely have to fight wolves again, but not tonight, and not this pack.*

The lycans near me agree. I can feel their support.

This might work . . .

Thoughts from the new lycans bombard my mind from all angles, harsh bits of their cruel bloodlust. They're not going to heed me–– they're already set on their course. And the worst part is I can't blame them. I know what it feels like to be going through your first renewal, to be dying for flesh, to be willing to do anything to get that first taste. And the second and the third.

We have to stop them, even if it means killing them, and maybe this decision is what it means to be an alpha. Protect the many even at the cost of the one.

Tonight, we will protect the humans and shifters from the newborn lycans. We are to go into the city and bring any lycan who cannot control themselves out. We will get hurt, and if we must kill to protect ourselves or others, then that's what we'll do. We will not attack a wolf or panther unless in self-defense. Any questions?

What if we don't agree with you? someone calls out.

Then you may leave. The woods are that way. I point away from the city.

I expect a few to leave, maybe even most. But none do.

I turn and run toward the city, my new pack following close behind.

* * *

I sleep until noon the next day. It's not enough sleep, but it'll have to do. I have people to see and plans to sort out. Ryne convinced the wolves and panthers to not attack the lycan before we arrived, and together, we were able to protect all the humans. As far as I could tell, no one was bitten, and aside from Derek, Ace, Laik, and Wanda, no one else died. Once the lycans shifted back, most of them left with the panthers for The Sanctuary, but a few decided to stay. Ryne's ordered nobody to touch them, but I fear that won't hold up against prejudices that run deep.

I collapsed into bed as soon as daybreak hit.

"You reek." Faye shakes me awake.

I blink at her. "I know. Hazard of the job."

"Take a shower before coming into *our* room next time," she huffs. "Anyway, Madame Delphine asked me to give you this."

I look at the paper in her hand. It's a calendar.

"Thirty days until the harvest moon," she says. "It's the dating schedule."

I roll my eyes. "All the changes we've gone through, and the claiming is still happening."

Faye shrugs. "Some of us like it. And it's not like those who don't get chosen are going to the mating houses. And we all can say no if we want to. But you know I want Justin, and I'm pretty sure Lev is angling for Marissa. If you don't end up with Bellamy, I think he'll drop out."

I glance at the calendar. I'm on dates every night, alternating between

Bellamy and Ryne, as expected. Elle is actually with Bell or Ryne on all of the nights I'm not, and nobody else gets any dates with Ryne. Just then, Elle bursts into the room, waving another copy of that stupid calendar around.

"You're welcome," she says, beaming at me.

"For what?"

"For not allowing lunas to go after your men. This dating schedule is a waste of time for most of us, but Madame Delphine is insistent upon it, so I convinced her to just let you and me date your guys. We all know Bell's not interested in anyone but you, and I'm never going to be Ryne's sloppy seconds, so I'm no threat."

I laugh and slide out of bed. "Who says you're not going to try to steal one of them?"

She wiggles her eyebrows. "You never know, do you?"

Faye gapes at her. "How did you manage that? I still have to share Justin."

"I asked." She bats her eyelashes. "That and I'm Madame Delphine's favorite."

Faye shoves her out of the way and storms down the hall.

"And you're her favorite too, you know." Elle wrinkles her nose. "You need to shower."

"So I've been told."

After I shifted back into my human body early this morning, I went over to Ryne's to make sure my family was okay. Dad was awake and sitting on the porch steps as if waiting for me. He didn't ask about what happened—he just patted me on the back and told me that they'd already decided to head back home. They have no interest in moving to the city, and while I wasn't surprised, I was a little disappointed. Once things are settled here, I'm going to visit home for a few weeks. Of course, we spent a few hours catching up before they left, but there's no denying that things are different than they used to be. Our family has been through trauma, and we just aren't bonded in the same way anymore. I hope we can repair things later because right now I have to stay in the city.

At least, I'm with Ryne tonight, which is good because we have a ton to discuss. We need to figure out what the next steps are, how we're going to keep my lycan identity a secret, and what to do about Anders. There's so much going on that dating seems almost comical at this point. Being an alpha is harder than I thought it was, and now that I'm alpha to the Carolina Pack's enemy, I'm afraid our future is more doomed than ever.

Chapter Twenty-Eight

The tight floor-length gown wraps around my body like a second skin, accentuating my small curves. Ryne had delivered it to me earlier, and when I pulled it out of its velvet box, I gasped. I've never loved a dress so much. It's black as midnight with sparkling blue thread woven throughout like starlight. As I stare at it in the mirror, I can't stop thinking about the way the blue reminds me of Ryne's eyes. It's stunning. I love it, and I look great in it, but I don't know why I need to dress so extravagantly for a date the night after such a big event. I'm still processing everything, and I plan to use this time with Ryne to strategize.

"He's here," Faye says, popping her head into our room. "Go get your man."

I roll my eyes but head down to him, suddenly nervous.

He meets me at the door, his step faltering and his breath catching when he sees me. "You look stunning," he whispers, and those cobalt eyes are bright as he stares at me, taking me in. He has no shame, his eyes admiring every curve. It sends a flutter of longing through me.

"You planned this." I motion to his perfectly tailored blue suit, the same color as the sparkles in my dress.

"We're fated mates. It's only right that we match."

My lips quirk into a smile, and he leads me out to the car, opening my door. There's no driver today. It's just us. When he slides into the driver's seat, I'm the first to speak.

"Have you heard anything from the panther pack yet?" They're going to have to pick a new alpha, and we're not sure what that's going to mean for The Sanctuary.

Ryne squeezes my hand, threading our fingers together. He brings our clasped hand up to his mouth and drops a soft kiss on my knuckles. "After a period of mourning, they will vote on their leadership. It's not like here. Don't worry. The panthers overwhelmingly support The Sanctuary, so whoever the alpha ends up being, we can count on them."

I release a breath. "Okay, and what about the lycans who stayed here? You really think they're not going to be hunted down and killed?"

His eyes flash. "Not on my watch. . . . Poppy, I want this date to be like any other normal date between a man and a woman, not like two alphas in the middle of a war. Can you do that for me? Can we not talk about anything related to the war and our roles in it?"

I frown, immediately anxious. "But there's so much to discuss." And really, this whole dating thing seems silly. We've got things to do and people to protect.

"And we will discuss everything tomorrow. Tonight, it's just about Poppy and Ryne."

"Poppy and Ryne," I repeat, my voice wobbly. "Okay, I can do that." But I'm not sure I can. Ryne and I have been through so much, and yet, my soul yearns for him.

He smiles, truly smiles. And when Ryne smiles, the whole world turns golden.

We drive to the downtown area. I'm a little uneasy because this is where most of the mating and pack houses are located. I haven't been down here since he announced the changes. But I don't say anything as Ryne leads me to the tallest building, and we slip into the elevator.

He pushes the button for the highest floor, and then as we're riding up, the inertia tugs at my belly. He cages me in the corner of the small elevator. His mouth hovers near my ear, his scent surrounds me, and my heart speeds. I think he's going to whisper something in my ear, but he growls instead and kisses my neck. And that's even better. If I focus on the way he makes me feel physically, then I don't have to think about the things we need to talk about. Not just the problems in our world but the problems that happened between us.

The doors open, and he steps back. "This way."

There's a metal door at the end of the hallway, and he opens it to a set of stairs. Up we go, right up to a flat rooftop. A small round table is set up with dinner, and soft music plays on the wind.

"Some say this is the best view in the city," he brags.

I step forward to take it all in, my mouth popping open at the blanket of city lights. Just like the stars, they sparkle. And just like my dress, they remind me of my mate.

"I would have to agree with that statement."

He studies me, his eyes brimming with so many emotions, so much love and grief and passion and hope, that it's impossible to look away. "I've always loved this view," he confesses, "but it's so much more beautiful with you in it."

I step forward and play with his suit jacket, thinking. If Bellamy weren't in the picture, would I be hesitating at all? Or would I have moved into Ryne's house? He hurt me. A lot. But he also came back to me. And the truth is my heart never really left.

"What's on your mind?" he prods gently.

I fiddle with his shirt, my fingers grazing over the buttons. "I don't know. You said you wanted this to be about Poppy and Ryne, and I'm so glad it is. I desperately want to move past the hurt and pain we have between us. I want to forget that you deserted me when I needed you most."

Ryne stiffens. "Poppy, I'm trying so hard here. What else can I do to prove my love? I've done everything you've asked. And I've given you space to explore things with Bellamy—something that takes a lot more self-control than you think. I know I've messed up. I'm truly sorry, but I was scared. I didn't want you anywhere near me if I was about to be overthrown by my own pack, and I was angry that I wasn't strong enough to beat my father myself. I never should've pushed you away like I did, and I want to spend the rest of my life making it up to you."

He places a finger on my chin and lifts my face so I'm looking into his eyes. They search mine, pleading for forgiveness, and something inside of me snaps. All the hurt and pain disappears. I love this man. Deeply. I want nothing more than to be his forever.

I close the distance between us, pressing my lips against his, and he tugs me closer, deepening the kiss. So much pain is washed away in that kiss. I feel the tears slipping down my cheeks, relief and sorrow mingled together.

Ryne pulls back and wipes the tears away. "What's the matter?"

I shake my head, unable to speak.

He places light kisses on my cheeks. "I love you, Poppy."

"I love you too." My voice cracks. I'm so overcome by this man, by this love.

It's all-consuming.

He gives me a crooked grin. "Look at that. It's the night after the full moon, you kissed me, and I'm still standing."

"Maybe that bite was good for something after all."

"Maybe it was."

He takes my hand and leads me over to the table. We eat and talk and laugh. It's the most relaxed I've ever been with him, and it takes every ounce of will not to go home with him that night.

I make him take me back to Drayton Hall, where I lie in bed for a long time, wondering if I've just made my choice, but I'll never know if I don't see Bellamy too.

Yet, I find that I don't want to.

I want Ryne and only Ryne.

* * *

The next three weeks pass in a blur. I continue dates with both Bellamy and Ryne, but Bellamy seems to be falling further and further away from my heart, and I think he knows it.

I arrive home early in the morning from an overnight date with Bellamy. He took me out to the panther city to visit with the few lycans who know I'm their alpha. It wasn't terribly romantic, and we didn't share a bed, but it was necessary, and I appreciated his willingness to take me.

He walks me to the front door. I lean up and give him a kiss on the cheek. "Thanks for that. It was fun."

He chuckles. "Fun is not a word I'd use to describe it. But it was productive. Ryne asked me to take you out there and do some recon while I was at it."

I cock my head. I hadn't realized that.

"He did? I didn't realize you and he were so close." In fact, Ryne won't even speak his name around me anymore. When we're together on our dates, it's just us. Every time.

"Ryne made me his second."

I hadn't seen that coming, and I don't know how I missed it. Well, yes, I do. It's because I'm too busy with all the other things on my mind.

"I did not know that. Congratulations. Though, I do wonder what

Ryne is thinking. That gives you even more incentive to want him dead. If something happens to him, you get me, and you become acting alpha."

"We talked about that, actually. But he recognizes that I've been working with getting the women out of the mating houses for far longer than he has, and so I'm less likely to rebel against him than anyone else now that he's doing the right thing."

"That makes sense." It still makes me uneasy. I trust Bellamy—I do—but so much has happened that it's hard not to be worried.

He slips his hands into his pockets and looks at me, his eyes searching mine. "Poppy, have you made your decision?"

My insides go cold, and I swallow. I don't want to talk about this; I'm too much of a coward to break his heart. I fiddle with my hair. "I have another week before I have to do that."

"I know. But I'm just asking. If you've made up your mind, then why bother keeping up this charade?"

"I . . . I . . . don't know."

He steps forward, trapping me between his body and the front door. He places both hands on either side of me.

"You know I would make you happy. You would always be my first priority."

I nod but don't say anything. Now that I'm an alpha myself, I understand Ryne so much better. I would do just about anything to make sure my pack is protected, even at the expense of my own interests, and maybe even my own heart.

Bell's lips press to mine, full of hunger and need and want. A month ago, I would've melted into this kiss. But today, it feels wrong. Broken. A mere shadow compared to the real thing.

He pulls away, and the tortured look in those green eyes says it all.

"That's what I thought. Goodbye, Poppy."

I trudge up the stairs, both relieved and a little sad. Though, my stomach buzzes at the thought of what Ryne's going to say when I tell him. I doubt I'll be spending the night in my own room tonight. I should probably get some sleep today.

I push open the door and find Elle sitting on my bed. She's fiddling with a pillow.

"You had a date with Bellamy last night."

I nod. "Yeah. You have fun with Ryne?"

She rolls her eyes. "By fun, you mean listening to him whine about you all night? No way."

I chuckle and sit down next to her, resting my head on her shoulder. Suddenly, I'm exhausted.

"You spent the night with Bellamy." Her voice is stiff and angry. It's new for her——Elle is one of the most levelheaded people I've ever met. Even with the loss of her father, she's been so strong.

"Not really. He took me out to the panther sanctuary to meet with a few of the lycan. It was a long drive. Mostly, we were with other people all night, and we didn't share a bed."

She relaxes next to me. "Oh. I see."

I want to tell her about my decision. The one I hadn't even realized I'd made. But Ryne deserves to hear it first.

"I need some sleep," I yawn.

"You're going to break one of their hearts."

I swallow. "We've been over this before. They both knew the risks, and so did I."

She slides off the bed. "Whatever. Get some sleep. I'll see you later."

I slip under the covers and wonder why she's suddenly cold and angry with me, but I don't have the energy to deal with it. Instead, I let my eyes close, dreaming of the night to come.

Chapter Twenty-Nine

Every date with Ryne is special, but this one is going to be unforgettable, and I can't keep the grin off my face all afternoon as Joanna helps me get ready. She still has her own room in the manor, but she's with Grady most of the time, and I rarely get to see her, so it's nice to have her for the afternoon.

"How dare you?" Faye's shrill voice comes from the library, and we run out to see what's going on.

She's standing head-to-head with Violet and Cecily. Violet has a triumphant smirk on her face, and Cecily twirls her long blonde hair. They're both dressed up for their dates tonight with Lev and Justin, looking as beautiful as ever, but that's nothing new.

Violet pops her hip and folds her arms over her ample cleavage. "We have as much right to date the betas as you do."

"Actually, we have more of a right," Cecily adds. "We're lunas."

"What's going on?" Joanna asks, and I set my hand on Faye's shoulder to let her know we're here for her. It's not like the lunas haven't gone on dates with betas before, including Justin.

"Oh, Faye's just feeling insecure because Justin kissed Cecily on their last date," Violet says, her eyes shooting to Faye. "And I'm sure he will again on their date tonight."

"That's not what happened." Faye clenches her fists and glares at Cecily, who stands there with her chest out and a winning smirk on her painted lips. "He came to me today saying that you kissed him, and he stopped it. And now you're trying to make me think he cheated on me, but I know that's a lie."

"They just want to come between you," I say. "Don't listen to them."

"Oh, really? Maybe she deserves to know the truth so she isn't surprised when Justin chooses someone else next week," Violet interjects.

"That's if I'll even have him." Cecily yawns playfully. "I'm not sure he's my type, and he wasn't that great of a kisser."

I have to fight not to roll my eyes.

"That's funny, considering he probably had to push you off of him," Joanna says.

"Have you ever considered that we're not the enemy here?" Violet's words drip with toxicity as she glares at us. "You humans know nothing. Second to fated mates, wolves are drawn to lunas. That's just the way it is. If they can have one of us, they're going to take that opportunity. Justin may say he loves Faye, but he's playing her."

"You're a liar!" Faye jumps on Violet, and both lunas immediately shift, their dresses ripping free and their white wolves growling up at us. If we don't get away, they might rip us to shreds before the house mothers arrive. I drag Joanna and Faye to our room before they get themselves killed.

Faye wipes tears from her eyes, and her face is nearly as auburn as her hair. "What if they're telling the truth?"

I hug her, and the three of us sit on her bed.

"I don't believe they are, but even if Justin does betray you, you're going to be okay," Joanna says, and I'm proud of my friend for forgiving Faye since she's returned. I know it wasn't easy.

"But I love him." Faye's voice cracks. "And he's the only man who's ever loved me back. Sure, I've had lots of attention from men for years..." Faye wrings her hands, and Joanna rolls her eyes behind Faye's back. "But they never saw the real me. And then Justin did."

"And he still does." I squeeze her hand. "And you know what? So do I."

She scoffs at that.

"It's true. You're one of my best friends, which is saying something considering that we used to hate each other."

"Yeah," she sighs. "I was a mean bitch, but I've changed, you know?"

"I do know, but guess what? You're still one of the strongest people I've ever met, and if Justin breaks your heart, you're going to heal and be stronger than ever. It's just in your nature."

"She's right, you know," Joanna agrees. "You're a mean bitch for a reason."

Faye laughs and nods once. "You're right. If he's stupid enough to choose one of those stuck-up lunas over me, then that's his loss, not mine."

"What will you do?" Joanna asks, and I want to elbow her in the ribs for that, but Faye doesn't seem to mind.

"Maybe I'll go home or go work in a new village, date human men for a while. But honestly, I love the city, and I could see myself joining one of the mating houses and making great money while I help grow the pack. And then I'll raise my boys myself, making sure they're ten times better than all the wolves we've had to date."

The crazy thing is I could see her being happy doing just that.

We all hug again, and I take solace in the fact that every single word I said to her today is the truth. I don't think Justin is going to mess up, but sometimes men are idiots, and if he loses her, then she's going to move on to bigger and better things. She doesn't need a man to survive in this world. The pack has changed. There's no more need to fear the mating houses, and Faye has options now. We all do.

* * *

Ryne takes me to his house for dinner, and from the moment I step inside, my entire body buzzes. The aroma of an expertly prepared meal greets us, but I'm not hungry for food. I turn on him. He's so much bigger than me, but I don't care because right now I feel powerful. I push him back against the closed front door.

His eyes flare, and his large hands tighten around my waist. "What's this about?"

"I forgive you," I whisper. "And I love you. And I choose you."

The man doesn't need me to say anything more because the next second his mouth is on mine, and he's lifting me up so that my legs are wrapped tightly around him. My chest burns as passion and love swells within me, pouring out into our kiss. I grip his long hair, pulling it back from his face, and he groans into my mouth, biting at my bottom lip.

"So does this mean it's over with him?" he asks, pulling back slightly to gaze into my eyes. There's always been so much hidden in those ocean-blue depths, but now everything is right there on the surface--his want, his need, his love.

"Yes. Bell is just a friend, and he knows that now," I whisper, my voice growing husky with need. "It's always been you, Ryne. And it will always be you."

And then we're kissing again, less desperate this time, but more untamed. He carries me upstairs to his bedroom, and we spend the rest of the night making up for lost time. Love-making is nothing new for us, but it feels like it is. It's different somehow--it's better. There's an ease to the way we touch each other, a level of trust that we never really had before. He's never going to hurt me again, and I'm never going to doubt him. We promise forever to each other with our words and our mouths and our bodies.

When I wake the next morning cocooned in his arms, I feel safer than I ever have in my life. My whole being is satiated and calm, and I'm overcome with gratitude. After everything I've been through this last year, it's a welcomed relief. Tears spring to my eyes.

"Don't cry." He shifts toward me and kisses my temple, burying his face against my hair. "Everything will be okay. We'll figure it all out. I promise."

"I'm crying because I'm so happy," I confess, and then I laugh and let the tears fall freely. "I feel like we've been given a new beginning."

He kisses each tear away and then moves to settle his body over top of mine, pinning me to the mattress in the most delicious way. "I'm the one who should be crying about new beginnings, but I have better ideas."

"Oh, and what might those ideas be?" I tease.

"I would tell you, but I think it's better if I show you."

We start to kiss again, but he pulls back before we can take things further. "I love you so much. I can't wait to marry you. Only one more week, and we'll be an engaged couple."

I smirk. "You really want to talk about marriage right now?"

"I want to do a lot of things right now, and talking about us is one of them," he confesses. "Do you want to live here after we're married, or do you want a different house?"

"I never really thought about it." And I probably should, considering it's likely I'll be getting pregnant soon. Even though we use protection, if things between us continue like they did last night, I won't be surprised if we end up having lots of babies. My mind isn't sure how ready I am to become a mother, but my heart wants to build a family with Ryne--to make his pack bigger and stronger, to give him all the things he deserves in a mate.

"Well, think about it, because it's up to you. And the wedding, what do you want to do for it? Any big plans?"

"I don't care as long as it's to you. That's all that matters."

He tsks under his breath. "I want you to have everything you could possibly want in this life, including your dream wedding, so you'd better get planning. We'll have all your favorite people there, and dancing, great food, your favorite flowers, and a huge chocolate cake because I know how much you like chocolate."

"Gotta have chocolate," I agree. "But we can decide on all that after the harvest moon. Right now, I need you to stop talking." I nip at his bruised lips to entice his mouth back down to mine. I'd like nothing more than a repeat of last night before I have to return to the manor.

"Such a bossy woman," he says between long slow kisses, but he must not mind because we don't talk again until breakfast.

I'm happier than I've ever been, but in the back of my mind, I'm terrified that something is going to come and rip that happiness away from me. The fact remains that I'm a lycan, and now that I'm the alpha to many more like me, I'm not going to be able to keep my secret hidden from the wolves for long. There are people who will kill me without hesitation if they discover the truth, and some of those people might belong to this pack, may even be living in the very same manor.

And once I'm dead, they'll come for Ryne next.

Chapter Thirty

The day before the harvest moon, Ryne invites the couples over to his place to celebrate and discuss the upcoming nuptials. We have tables set up in the backyard, and the women who cook for Ryne make a beautiful charcuterie table for appetizers.

Justin and Faye show up first, followed quickly by Joanna and Grady, and then Marissa and Lev. Away from her snobby counterparts, Marissa's personality finally comes out, and she's actually really nice. I can see why Lev chose her; they make a great couple. As we mingle, I realize these will likely be the women I spend my days with. My kids will grow up with their kids.

"You get to have a wedding after all," I say, nudging Joanna.

"Yeah." She sighs wistfully, watching Grady, who is talking with Ryne and Lev across the yard. Faye and Justin stand at one end of the table, snacking and chatting peacefully with Marissa.

"See, she had nothing to worry about," I comment.

Joanna sniffs. "Says you. Cecily was still going on this morning about how Justin was just waiting until the last minute to reveal his true choice and that he's not at all happy about Ryne inviting him here with Faye as his date."

"She's just bitter because she didn't get picked."

"Violet is too." Joanna's eyes crinkle at the sides. "That girl is the new Faye. They even look alike with the red hair."

We laugh. "True, but at least none of the girls have the threat of the mating houses anymore. They'll be fine."

"Yup, since Joy announced she's moving back to her village after the claiming, she's seemed so much happier. And I think Samantha will end up going back to her village too."

Nothing makes me happier than to know they're not going to be forced into sexual slavery, but I'm still going to miss them. Maybe I'll be able to visit, or maybe they'll come visit me in the city. Same goes for all the women currently with the panthers. I won't be surprised if several of them move home soon too.

The door opens, and I jerk my head up. All the couples are already here. Bellamy comes through the door, and my stomach drops. I haven't seen him since I told him I made my choice, and I did not expect him to choose a mate. This party is for solidified couples only.

He holds the door open, and out comes Elle. She wraps her arm around his waist and beams up at him.

I thump Joanna on the shoulder. "What the . . ."

She laughs. "Yeah. Elle made me promise not to tell you. She wanted to see your face."

I look up, and Elle meets my eyes. Then she takes Bellamy by the hand and drags him over to us. She bounces on her toes.

"Worth it," she says.

"What was?" I breathe, hardly able to believe my eyes. They look so good together, though. So happy. So *obvious.*

"Waiting until now to see your face. Seriously. That reaction was exactly what I'd hoped for."

I rub my forehead. "But when? Up until a week ago, Bell and I were talking about marriage."

"So were we. Once Ryne wanted you back, Bellamy pretty much knew he didn't have a chance. We talked about it at length several times, actually. I've pretty much been in love with him since we met."

Bellamy gazes down at her with complete adoration. "Elle was a good listener, and for the most part, we were just friends, but I'm not going to lie. I developed feelings for her some time ago. I thought it was just friendship and respect, but a few weeks ago, she kissed me. And you know, I wasn't really all that upset when you made your choice."

I reach up and give him a hug. "I'm really happy for you guys."

Then I reach for Elle. "But I don't understand why you kept pushing me toward him."

"I wanted to see you happy, and I saw how great Bell would be for someone. At that time, I didn't think he was interested in me at all."

Her eyes water. "That, and I was afraid of facing my own feelings for him."

"I totally understand." And I do because I went through similar circumstances myself. She was dealing with the recent loss of her father, and a possible rejection from a man who was dating someone else must have been too painful to risk.

But I'm so glad she did risk it because look at them now.

I grin as he plants a soft kiss on her mouth. Her entire body melts, relaxing in a way I've never seen before. I have always admired Elle. From the first time I met her, I wanted to hate her for being a rival, but I simply couldn't. She's impossible not to love. She's fierce and loyal and devoted to doing the right thing—exactly like Bellamy.

They're a perfect match.

A rustling comes from behind me, and Bellamy grabs both mine and Elle's arms and jerks us back. A wolf lands right in the middle of the table, sending cheese and meat everywhere.

He scrambles up, and Ryne rushes toward him. The wolf shifts, and I realize he's young, maybe fifteen or sixteen. His eyes widen as he takes us all in.

"I'm sorry. I didn't know you were having a party. I just saw them and thought you ought to know."

Ryne stares at the boy intently.

"Know what?" I whisper, dread building in my stomach.

The boy's lips turn into a frown, and his entire demeanor stiffens. "Anders is back, and he's brought an army with him."

No one moves for a second—it's like we can't move—until Elle grabs a towel off a chair and hands it to the boy.

"Where is he now?" Ryne asks.

"He's on his way to you. He'll be here any minute."

Ryne shakes his head in frustration. "There's no time; if there was, I'd send all the women back to Drayton Hall. But he's likely outside the front door as we speak. Men, prepare to protect your mates. I'll warn the rest of the pack, but don't engage unless it's absolutely necessary. We don't want a war breaking out if we can avoid it. Technically, he's the alpha king, so I have to obey direct orders from him, but none of you do. You only answer to me."

"We can't let him find you then," Justin says.

Ryne nods. "I think we can work around this, given a little bit of time, but Poppy's staying with me, no matter what."

I want to ask more questions, but the door flies open, and Anders saunters out, followed by several others. He's dressed in full military regalia and even wears a damn crown on his head. I've never seen someone so blatantly boastful, but leave it to Anders to do just that.

He takes in the scene around him and smirks, and then he stalks toward Ryne. "I hear you've been making some changes around here without my permission. You've made some of your wolves very unhappy. They've come to me and begged me to fix their problem. Lucky for them, I know how to deal with you."

"You can try." Ryne glares. "But my pack is loyal *only* to me."

Anders laughs. "As of this moment, my men are taking control of the mating houses. We raided a few villages on the way to supply them with new girls. I want to make sure the Carolina Pack wolves are happy––all of them, even the ones you so foolishly kicked out."

"I gave them a choice to stay. They chose to leave. That's on them that they're no longer welcome in my pack."

"A choice? Oh, you mean taking away their rights?"

"Their right to rape women? Nobody has that right," I snap, stepping forward. "Not even you."

Anders's mouth thins as he takes me in, his nostrils flaring, before looking back to Ryne. "And tomorrow at the harvest moon, my betas will be taking the claimed girls as wives, not yours. I've brought a beta for every girl." Then Anders meets my eyes, his gaze victorious and vile. "And your dear Poppy will become my bride. That's an order, by the way, so you cannot defy it."

"Never," I say just as Ryne growls, "She's mine."

"And then, once the weddings are over," Anders speaks over us, "One of my men will become the new alpha of the Carolina Pack. I've brought dozens, and they all plan to fight. You might win the first few fights, but after that, you'll be so tired that one of them will kill you. Enjoy your last night of mortality."

He snaps his fingers, and the men he brought with him rush toward him, surrounding Anders on all sides. Protecting him. I'm not surprised; he always was afraid of Ryne.

"Stay here and guard the perimeter of this house," he instructs several of them. "No one leaves or enters. Tomorrow, you will escort them to the arena for the festival. I've got a few favorite women who have been missing me that I need to visit." Anders gives Ryne and his betas one final scathing look. "And if they're not in the mating houses, then maybe I'll have to come back here and let your whores entertain me."

Then he saunters back into the house, and everyone is so quiet we hear the front door slam.

Chapter Thirty-One

"He can't do that." Faye is the first to speak. "Ryne's still the alpha of this pack."

But Anders is the alpha of the entire kingdom, and unless Ryne plans to separate from the other packs and face massive fallout, then Anders can dole out orders as he pleases, and Ryne will have to pass them down the chain. The Carolina Pack might be able to leave the kingdom in the future, but that's not going to help us tonight.

"Sounds like I might not be the alpha much longer," Ryne breathes out. His entire body is shaking with rage, and I'm certain he's about to take off after Anders.

Bellamy growls. "Don't let him win before you've even fought."

"It's too late," Ryne says. "I showed my hand too early."

I swallow hard because I know he's referring to all the wonderful things he did to get me back. Things he promised, things that should've been done ages ago but that he wanted to wait on. I refused to forgive him until I got my way, and now look what's happened to the pack. Maybe I should've trusted him and been patient.

Ryne was right.

But so was I.

"To hell with that." Justin steps forward. "It's not too late until we're dead, and do any of us look dead to you?"

"They're right," Grady adds, bowing to his alpha. It's the first true act of loyalty I've seen from Grady since his banishment. I shoot a glance at

Joanna, who's tearing up. "You're not alone, Ryne. We're with you. You're our alpha. Nobody else. We fight with you."

Ryne looks to his betas and nods once, resolved. "Then let's go." The fur ripples over his chest, ripping his shirt clean off him.

"Don't!" I grab onto his biceps, stopping him from completing the shift. Everyone turns toward us. "Don't you see? Anders wants you to lose your temper while things are uncertain. If you guys go after him tonight while the pack is in disarray and people are scared, it'll be so much easier for him to finally kill you."

"He won't kill me," Ryne hisses. "But he can try."

"He'd have to take on all of us." Justin puffs up his chest. "We're not afraid."

"So?" I throw my hands up. Why do these men have to be so stupid sometimes? Oh, that's right, because they're territorial wolf shifters who give into instinct before reason. "How many wolves do you think Anders brought with him tonight? Because I'm going to guess it's enough to kill you all ten times over. He has too many men, and there is no way for you to get him alone."

"What would you have us do?" Ryne cups my face in his warm hands. His voice is soft, but his eyes are frantic, and his bare chest heaves with labored breath. I hate to see him this way, but the fact that he is seriously asking for my opinion right now makes me so proud of my man. He really has changed.

But I understand why he's scared--it's not just his life on the line here. It's so many others. It's the wolves he's spent years loving. It's the humans he swore to make reparations for, to finally give them the life and the protection that was promised to them all those years ago. And it's the lycans who remained here as vulnerable humans counting on his protection.

They'll be the first to go.

"Ryne, the lycans," I whisper. "What if someone in the pack reveals them to Anders?"

There are twenty-nine who stayed after the last full moon, thirty including myself. We have too many people here who we love and didn't want to leave. The rest went back to the panther territory, Charlotte and Knox included. It's a very real possibility that the ones who stayed behind will be murdered. So many of the wolves don't want lycans here, not even after the battle at the last full moon, not even when things are mostly settled between our kinds.

I'm their alpha, which has felt like a lie considering not all of them even know who I am in my human form. I'm supposed to protect them, but I've chosen to protect myself first, and now I'm unable to help them. Luckily the wolves can't smell the lycan virus while we're human, or they'd be dead by now, and I'd have been killed months ago.

And so would've Ryne.

I stop to question that thought, because what if it's not actually true? What if his pack actually accepts him for who he is now? Like a flower rising from the frost, hope blooms within my chest. Maybe being a lycan isn't the curse I thought it was, and maybe it's not for Ryne either. This could be exactly what we need.

I take in our group one by one, grateful to be going through this with true friends––and fierce warriors. Everyone here has earned my trust. They all have so much to lose if Anders follows through on his threats at tomorrow's festival. If there's anyone who is going to help me stop that madman, it's this group. And I honestly couldn't think of anyone I'd rather follow into battle.

"Listen up. I have an idea." My voice is low as they surround me in a tight, unbreakable circle.

* * *

The next morning, we're taken from Ryne's house, returned to the manor to be dressed by the house mothers, and guarded by even more of Anders's men. Nobody wants to talk, and we don't act like this is the exciting affair it's supposed to be, but rather a solemn one—because we want Anders to think we're afraid. And we are afraid.

But we're also fighting for love, and love outweighs fear every single time.

If anyone should be afraid, it should be him.

We wear gorgeous dresses in an array of colors, each paired perfectly to bring out the beauty in the individual woman. Elle is a vision in daffodil yellow. Joanna is ravishing in navy blue. Faye wears emerald green like it was made for her. Marissa's skin tone glows coppery against the pastel pink. And I'm glad the dress I slide into is as red as my namesake because, tonight, I feel like shedding wolf blood and inciting a revolution.

Tonight, we fight, and we win, or we die. Either way, we'll have escaped the horror that Anders would inflict on us.

"Enough is enough," I say to these women whom I've grown to love and admire. They nod their agreement, we give each other tight hugs, and then we're ushered to the boat waiting to take us downtown.

Of course it's a boat—it's only fitting. One year ago, we were brought in a boat to this house of horror, terrified and traumatized, and then forced to compete for men and to witness our friends die or be sent away to be raped.

We've come full circle.

But if things go our way, then this will be the last time claimed women have to go through a harvest festival like this one. The time has come for it to end.

Chapter Thirty-Two

I've never seen so much red. The space around me seems to be filled with it, in every shade, in every corner, and on almost every person. It's part of the plan so we know who is on our side. The wolves wear long red scarves that will hopefully stay on when they shift. We tested it a bit last night, and it seemed to work, so Ryne put out the call for his pack to wear a scarf to tonight's festival if they were with him.

It's the one thing we were certain Anders would notice. And I hope it intimidates him. He brought his angry army, but there are more of us than there are of his people. By a lot.

And we're just as angry as they are—maybe even more so.

The sun hangs low in the sky, painting it in vibrant brushstrokes of orange. The Harvest Moon Festival always starts at sunset, and we'll have about twenty minutes before the moon rises enough to trigger the renewals. Once that happens, the fight begins.

Elle grips my hand. "Are you ready?"

"Yes. You?"

She smooths her dress and looks across the stage. The new claimed girls Anders brought in last night are with us, as are Samantha, Violet, and Cecily. Madame Delphine and a few others will get them to a safe house once the fighting begins, but they don't know that. They don't know anything of what's to come. There are twice as many claimed women as last year, so many whom I've never even met before, and very few are meant to get husbands today. Anders only brought them here to feed them to the mating houses tonight. Because despite so many girls being here in pretty dresses, the number of betas taking wives is the same. Instead of Ryne, Justin, Grady, Bellamy, and Lev standing on the edge of the stage in suits and ties, it's Anders and four of his cronies. They leer at us, and it doesn't take much to imagine what they might be thinking.

"We're doing this for them," Elle reminds me, looking toward the frightened women surrounding us. Samantha catches my eye and frowns. Her face is tight with worry, and I know she regrets staying here when she had the opportunity to go to The Sanctuary more than once—but now it's too late.

"We're doing this for all of us," I say.

And then I look back behind the stage to where the new claimed girls are standing, twenty innocent young women forcefully gathered from the villages by Anders's men. That was me last year, but so much has happened in a year that it feels like a lifetime ago. I recognize the girl I met, Laura, among them. She nods to me, a solemn expression on her face. I return the hello and quickly turn away. She didn't know what to expect when I had first met her, but she sure does now. They all do—the secrets are out, and everyone is horrified. These girls are only here to be turned into baby makers and wives and whores.

Not if I can help it.

Joanna steps between us and wiggles her eyebrows at Elle. "Have fun with Bellamy last night?"

Elle flushes. "How can you talk about things like that right now?"

Joanna bounces back and forth on her feet and rubs the back of her neck. "The tension is too much. Gotta do something, right? I know I had fun last night. I hope you two did as well."

"We were too busy preparing for today." I sigh. "I didn't even sleep."

Joanna giggles. "Neither did I. And neither did Elle, based on that blush."

Faye puts her arm around Elle. "It's okay. You can talk about it. Justin and I . . ."

"It's time." Madame Delphine interrupts us. "Come up front, Poppy."

I gather my skirts and make my way to the front of the group to stand next to Samantha and Joy, careful not to twist my ankles in these shoes. They'll be destroyed when I shift into my lycan form, which I'm not sad about. But the dress. The dress, I love. Joanna promised to make me another once this is all over. I squeeze both Samantha's and Joy's hands, and they give me terrified expressions. I wish I could tell them I have a plan to save them from the mating houses, but I can't risk it, so I just squeeze their hands again and hope they'll stay out of the way when the time comes.

Ryne stands at the front of the stage, and Anders joins him, his body-guard betas right there with him every step of the way. Ryne tries to speak, but Anders cuts him off then starts droning on about the changes Ryne made, how he's going to put things back to the way they were, and how Ryne is a disgraced alpha. I have to resist rolling my eyes.

"And so, as alpha king, it is my privilege to choose a bride from among your women, and I've always been partial to Poppy. And my men, well, they want brides, and I don't think anyone who has remained loyal to Ryne in his madness deserves them." The new betas descend on us, grabbing us roughly by the arms and dragging us to the front of the stage. We don't fight it. Not yet anyway.

The beta who has my arm shoves me next to Anders, who puts his sleazy arm around me. I hold my tongue. I have to be docile for just a few more minutes. Ryne is only a few paces away, and he glowers at us like he wants to rip Anders's head off. Anders squeezes me tighter into his body, taunting Ryne. But Ryne doesn't take the bait.

He turns back to the crowd. "You all know my stance on this. I will not go quietly. Poppy is my fated mate; I will not let Anders take her. There will be a fight, and you will have a new alpha king by morning."

Anders pulls me in even tighter, crushing my body against his. My left shoulder screams in protest, but still, I don't move. Ryne continues, "But first, you know the marriage bond is the strongest thing we have. Once a woman is married, she's not allowed to be with another wolf. Anders, you support the old ways, so you respect that tradition, yes?"

Anders rolls his eyes. "Of course I do. Which is why, once I marry Poppy, you can't have her."

"Okay, then." Ryne steps toward us. Justin, Bellamy, Lev, and Grady jump up onto the stage to back Ryne. They're all dressed in suits, and I must say they look far more handsome than Anders's crew. "See, last night, you made it so we couldn't leave my home, so we had a little fun of our own."

Anders scoffs, and his hands begin to roam my body. "I think you've had enough fun with this one, Ryne. It's about time I show her how a real man should be entertained."

He pinches my backside, and I squirm, heat rushing through me. It takes everything I have not to punch him right here and throw him off me. My mind fills with images of the first time I saw him do this to someone—to Willow—and how I was forced to do nothing. I'm not going to sit around this time. Only a few more minutes . . .

Ryne steps toward us, his voice going dangerously low. "Get your hands off my wife."

Anders stills. "Wife? What are you talking about?"

"We married our women last night, so you can't have them."

A hush falls over the crowd, and Anders goes unsteady on his feet. He's been bested. There's nothing he can do to claim me now, and he knows it. I grin, wanting to fall right back into Ryne's arms, but I don't. Not yet. I do lock eyes with him, though, and he grins right back at me.

After explaining the plan last night, Ryne married the others, and Grady married us. The ceremonies were beautiful and simple. All that was needed was the alpha's blessing and a special exchange of vows with a kiss. None of us wore fancy dresses. There wasn't chocolate cake or bouquets of flowers. We didn't even dance, but the kiss Ryne gave me was sweeter than any before. It was a promise of forever even if forever was only a day, and a promise I'll never forget.

Anders shoves me to the floor. I play along, falling to my knees. Soon after, my girlfriends are all shoved down as well. Our men are with us instantly, lifting us to our feet. Ryne wraps me in his embrace, shielding me with his body.

"All you accomplished was making sure that these women will be widows." Anders sneers at Ryne. "Because it won't be long until you're no longer the alpha of the Carolina Pack, and once you're gone, your traitors will be disposed of. No more banishment. I'll kill them myself if I have to."

Several wolves cheer, and others growl as the tension grows. There are two opposing sides, and we're at the breaking point. Only one can win this.

My bones creak, and I panic for a second. The moon is rising faster than we thought. But this could be a good thing, it could mean that none of Ryne's pack has turned on my lycans. There's no way Anders knows we're even here and about to attack his men because, even now, I can spot several of my people scattered among the crowd. This also means that Ryne's pack is loyal because, last night when he used his telepathic link to command them not to reveal the lycans' identities, they followed his orders. They want Anders dead. They want the new way of life Ryne has offered them. And they know the lycans can help them get it.

Change is in the air.

I widen my eyes at Ryne. He nods to show he's gotten the message, and then, without warning, my body expands, and my dress rips to shreds.

Anders staggers backward and gapes at me. "What? How?"

Down among the wolves, the bloodbath begins.

My lycans have returned, this time prepared to fight for freedom from the tyranny of Anders and his wolves. After tonight, nothing will be the same.

Ryne shifts into his wolf form and pounces on Anders before Anders can shift. The alpha king lands flat on his back and quickly shifts into his wolf, pushing Ryne away and scrambling to his haunches. I back up to see that Madame Delphine and the claimed girls are already gone. Ryne's betas and all the lunas stand behind him, an arsenal of snarling wolves.

Anders stares at all of them for a second.

And then the coward turns and flings himself off the stage, running from the fight.

Chapter Thirty-Three

*K*ill *him*, Ryne says to me as we make chase, but those two words come as a shock.

But you need to do it so you're the next alpha king, I argue. *That's the plan.*

Anders is fast, running through the streets at full speed, darting between buildings, his brown coat gleaming under the moonlight before falling back into the shadows. But we're faster.

Do you want to be the wife of the alpha king? Ryne challenges. *Do you want to move to Chicago where we'll always be looking over our shoulders? Have wolves constantly arguing that a lycan isn't fit to be queen or that a hybrid can't be king? Because I don't want that life for you, Poppy. And I've already made up my mind to tell my pack the truth about my lycan once this is over.*

Well, when he puts it that way, I guess he's right, but I'd do all those things and more for the people I love. If it means protecting the humans and getting to be with Ryne, then I'm happy to be the next queen, even a queen that half the kingdom would want dead. Whatever it takes.

I have an idea that will put someone else in the position of alpha king, someone who will be much better at it than I ever could be, but first, we need Anders dead.

Anders being dead is all I can think about at this point. I remember all the times he groped me, all the lewd comments he made, the way his eyes would linger on me just to make me uncomfortable, the countless women he raped over the years, the poor wives he's buried too young. I think about sweet innocent Nova and her cold body floating lifelessly in the river, a woman who was fated to his son, a son he should've loved. I think of Lexi and the way he brutalized her in her own bedroom while she slept, then how he turned on Joanna and Grady and even Ryne.

And then I think of my Willow—and that's all I need.

Fueled by rage, I leap harder and faster than I ever have, landing on Anders's back. He snarls, but I don't even stop to think about it. I attack, clamping down on his neck with my razor-sharp teeth, and I throw myself back so that his wolf body twists. He howls, and I do it again, grabbing onto his hind legs this time to twist him into an odd angle. His neck snaps, but I don't stop until his head is clean off his body. I toss it to the ground, an arc of blood spraying across the alleyway. And then I drop his body.

Finally.

Ryne and I stand there, breathing deeply for a long minute, staring at the decapitated body. It's only fair that Anders went this way—though, he deserved far worse.

You know what? I tell Ryne. *I actually feel a lot better.*

He chuckles, and then side by side, we race back to the battleground.

It's a total mess. There are more casualties on both sides than we expected. Everyone must have felt the alpha king die, but since a wolf didn't kill him, they're not bowing down to Ryne. I should've thought this through before I took him up on his offer. It's the same issue we had when I killed his father. Now there will be battles for a new alpha king— and the cycle will just continue on and on.

I was a fool, letting revenge get the better of me, and Ryne was thinking of our relationship before the betterment of the pack. We made a mistake.

"Oh, no you don't!"

I hear a familiar voice in the fight—Faye's voice. She's not supposed to be here. All the human women were supposed to get to safety with Madame Delphine. But sure enough, I follow the sound of her shrill yelling to find her fighting off an angry wolf. She's got two long swords in her hands, each already dripping with blood. I'm not sure where she got them, but she handles them expertly, slicing them toward her opponent.

Joanna is at her side.

And with them are Grady, with his three legs, and Justin—both in their wolf forms.

The group of wolves they are fighting are bigger and angrier than most of the others, fueled by the death of their alpha, or perhaps they were some who belonged to this pack before Ryne kicked them out, and now they're back for revenge. But it doesn't matter. Whoever they are, they're out for blood—so they must be stopped.

I sprint toward them, prepared to defend my friends, when one of them breaks past Faye's swords and catches her belly with his nasty teeth. He slices her abdomen to ribbons, and she slumps over, blood pooling before falling flat on her back, dropping the swords altogether.

No. This can't be happening.

I leap forward, ready to help. I'll bite her if I have to. She can become a lycan and might even like it, but she can't die. She can't.

Justin beats me to her. He throws the wolf from his wife and howls, nudging her with his muzzle. But she doesn't move. Her eyes stare up into nothingness, glossy and unblinking. The Faye we all know, the Faye I learned to love like a sister, is gone.

His cry shatters my heart, and then he's turning on her murderer. But he's distracted and doesn't see the second wolf that pounces from behind. In all of two seconds, Justin's neck is sliced open, and he's bleeding out too. In his final moments, he shifts back into his human form and crawls to Faye, resting his bloodied body against her, adding more red to her already-stained emerald gown. Suddenly, I hate red more than anything because he's gone too.

I can't believe it.

No.

"Justin was my cousin, you bastard!" Joanna screams, dashing toward the wolves. While it's true that he was her cousin, Joanna barely got to spend time with him, and now he's gone forever. I'm right there with her, and so are Grady and Ryne. We make quick work of the remaining wolves, adding them to the list of casualties, but this time, I don't feel any better. I just feel empty.

We look around us, and all we see is loss. The battle continues to rage all around, and there are still several hours before the sun rises. Many more will be killed before the night is over. How many more of us have to die? When will it be enough? Ryne leaves my side, and I follow, not daring to let him out of my sight.

He leaps for the empty stage, and I stay back. He needs to do this part alone.

WOLVES. LYCANS. STOP. His voice hits my mind with so much

power that there is no question. It reverberates through my brain. Most of the fighting stops, but some still continues. He repeats his words three more times, each time more powerful than the last. My head aches with the pressure.

Until it's done. Nobody moves. All the fighting has stopped, and everyone—wolves and lycans—gathers near the stage. It's strange seeing them all intermingled together, blood matted in fur and dropping from wounds. We're all so different, but our blood is the same.

We have fought valiantly tonight for the things we believe in. We fight against each other, and we barely even know what we're fighting for. It's time for a change. Many of you have recognized that, and some of you wish to cling to traditions and things of the past. But nothing ever stays the same. Once again, we have lost our alpha king without a new one being chosen, and he won't be chosen tonight.

Tonight, we rest. Go home and sleep. Mourn your losses. Tomorrow morning, we will meet at the arena. All are welcome—lycan, wolves, and humans—and together, we'll find a way to coexist, or I will die fighting for it. I don't know about you, but I cannot bear the loss of another friend.

His shoulders fall a little, and then he jumps from the stage. I worry that someone will attack him, especially since he just spoke to wolves *and* lycans, but nobody does. The crowd parts to let him trudge toward me. Together, lycan and wolf, we head toward his home. A few bow, publicly declaring their allegiance, and I wonder at his words earlier.

He may not want to be alpha king, but his pack wants him to be. Despite everything, they believe he's the best leader for the job, and they're right.

I'm not sure I'm willing to let him sacrifice that for me.

Chapter Thirty-Four

The plan is to start the meeting at nine. At eight-thirty, all of Ryne's betas, Madame Delphine, and everyone from Drayton Hall meet outside Ryne's house. My house now too, I guess. It's strange to think of it that way. I never really pictured myself somewhere so grand, but wherever my husband goes, I go.

We pile into several cars and slowly make our way over to the arena. Ryne and I are alone in his car. Callum was going to drive us, but he's still tending to the wounded and hasn't come back yet. Neither one of us has really spoken this morning, both lost in our own thoughts.

"Your betas know," I say.

"Know what?"

"That I'm a lycan and that you are too. And they still follow you."

"How can they know?"

"Everyone saw me change last night, and you were able to speak to them all. They know."

Ryne flexes his fingers around the steering wheel. "That makes today all the more dangerous. They could kill you. And me."

"But they won't. They would've last night. Ryne. I don't know what you have planned for this morning, but I think you should fight for alpha king. You are the only one who can make the changes stick. They'll follow you. All of them."

Ryne shakes his head. "No. I won't do it. You deserve a better life than that after all that you've been through. I'll keep my little pack here if they'll have me, but I'm not fighting for alpha king."

"Ryne. This is stupid. If you don't fight for it and win, then we could end up exactly where we were before. I've been through enough that I can handle that life."

He shakes his head. "No. Poppy, I'm not doing it."

"You're not your father, Ryne. Things will be different if it's you."

He pulls to the side of the road and parks then takes my hand, threading our fingers together. "That kind of power corrupts. I can't risk going back to who I was, and I can't risk putting a target on your back either."

"But it will be different this time—"

"Look at me," he grinds out, and I do, taking in his beaten-down expression and wanting nothing more than to see him smile again. He squeezes my hand. "I allowed horrible things to happen within my pack for years because I was afraid to challenge my father. I know I'm not him, but I'll never put myself into a position to become like him again. Ultimately, I'm responsible for what happened here since the day I became alpha, and I need to take accountability."

I shake my head. He's not getting it.

"All I want is you, Poppy. And us. I love my pack, and I love being an alpha, but I love you the most. You're my life now. My family. My wife."

My eyes water. I never asked for any of this, and I'll always mourn what could have been if Willow had lived, but getting to be loved by Ryne is the best thing that ever happened to me. "I love you too," I whisper.

A hot tear releases, and he kisses it away. "Trust me," he whispers. "I'm going to make things as right as I can, and that means I can't be the next alpha king. I have too much blood on my hands."

I hate that he blames himself for so much, but it doesn't make it untrue. Maybe he'll never forgive himself, maybe the humans he hurt will never forgive him, but I do.

"Okay, I trust you." I kiss him softly and release a long sigh. "Let's go."

As we near the arena, we see people everywhere crowding around it. When Ryne steps out of the car, a hush falls over the crowd. We make our way through the group. In the daylight it's impossible to tell who's shifter, lycan, or human. But I think they are all mixed together.

The arena is completely full, and after we make our way to the podium, we see more and more people piling in. They squeeze together, fill the stairs, and crowd along the top. How many of these were Anders's men? Are they all even from the Carolina Pack? I've never seen it like this before, and it makes me uneasy. This could be it. This could be where we all die.

Grady and Joanna appear at our side. "These aren't just wolves from Carolina," Grady confirms. "Word got out. Neighboring packs are here too."

That turns the trickle of fear within me into an all-out downpour, but I force myself to push it aside. I have to be strong; too many people are counting on me.

Ryne waits until it's not possible for another person to get through the door, and then he steps up to the stage on the arena field, pulling me up with him.

"I've never been comfortable with the mating houses and our lifestyle." His strong voice echoes over the microphone as everyone quiets. "But given who my father was, I felt powerless to make any changes. Plus, I knew once I tried, I'd be killed for it. And so I was a coward, and I bear responsibility for so much pain." He trails off, and people exchange nervous glances. "But at the last claiming, something incredible happened. I found my fated mate."

He smiles at me, and I have to resist rolling my eyes. He's going to use me as an excuse not to take the mantle he was meant for. But I smile back.

"And she showed me that there are some things worth fighting for. We've had some bumps along the way. She was bitten by a lycan, and then in the middle of the fight to take out my father, she accidentally bit me."

Every single person in the room hangs on his words. I hadn't realized that he was going to lay our secrets bare to be judged, and it terrifies me.

"Lycans have far more control over themselves than us wolves give them credit for. In fact, it's only the first shift that they are bloodthirsty. I've recently learned that most of the attacks during the full moons were to rescue the women we'd enslaved, not kill them. Because of the bite Poppy gave me, I have lycan blood running through my veins, and it did not kill me. I suspect that is because of the bond Poppy and I share as mates.

"We need change. We need peace, and we need freedom for all— shifters, lycans, and humans. And for ourselves, we need to stop fighting to the death. We're losing too many good wolves that way."

A cheer goes up in the crowd, and I realize that many of the wolves feel the same way. Maybe no fight will be necessary today.

"That is why I will not fight for alpha king."

No one says anything for a moment, and then a few people begin to chant. "Ryne. Ryne. Ryne."

And it grows until it fills the whole stadium.

I nudge him and lean up to speak into his ear. "No fight will be necessary. But you will be alpha king if they have any say in it."

He shakes his head, and we wait for the chanting to die off. "You would have a king with no fight?" he asks into the microphone, and a roar fills our ears.

"You would have me be your king?"

Again, a cheer goes up.

He swivels around and searches the small group that came with us today. He jumps off the podium, makes his way to Elle, and drags her back up here with us. Her eyes are wide, and her lips are pulled into a tight smile. She clearly doesn't know what he's doing, but I think I do, and pride wells in my chest.

"What are you doing?" she hisses, but he doesn't say anything at all. He just grins.

"I meant it when I said we need change. Most of you know the luna, Elle Montgomery. She's been a driving force for change and a key leader of the Resistance. Would you have a queen instead of a king?"

Elle's face pales, but she doesn't falter. There is a cheer again, but this time it's distinctly female, and murmurs have broken out among the crowd.

"I think you overestimated their ability to accept change," Elle whispers. But Ryne shakes his head.

"Just wait a moment for them to think through this."

A chant begins again, but this time, it's not Ryne's name. It's Elle's.

"Elle. Elle. Elle."

And just like that.

Without another death.

Ryne waves his hand toward Elle. "Get ready, because now we march to Chicago together to put Elle on the throne."

She's stunned, but she nods, and then the crowd erupts into a frenzy. There's no stopping us—there's no stopping Elle.

We will have an alpha queen.

Epilogue

FIVE YEARS LATER

The harvest festival is tonight, and I can't wait. More matches were made this year than any previous, and so many of the girls are head over heels in love with their wolves. We're sure to have an incredible wedding season soon, which is always fun for the pack.

There were also an unusual number of fated mate pairs that popped up this year. It reminded me of my claimed year, though I try not to think about that if I can help it. I used to have nightmares about the horrors I went through, but time has soothed those into unhappy memories better left to the past. And every year since we put Elle on the throne has been better than the last.

"There you are." Abi plops down onto the blanket beside me, reaching for my picnic basket. "I'm famished. What did you bring?"

"Practically my whole garden." I laugh. "I had to harvest the last of it this week."

"Mama, I'm not hungry," her son Orien complains with a pout, his huge chocolate brown eyes blinking at his mother. "Can I go play with Faye and Willow?" He looks around, confused. "Where are they?"

My twin daughters are currently hiding among the array of autumn leaves, but even from here, I can hear their sweet voices giggling. Just like me and my sister, they love to climb trees, and even at three years old, they're already experts. I attribute their natural athleticism to Ryne's alpha genes, but their taste for adventure is mine.

I point to a nearby tree. "They're up there."

Abi rolls her eyes and pats her son on the head. "Fine, go play, but you're not getting dessert until you eat something healthy." He's gone before she can even finish her sentence.

We laugh and get to work on setting up the picnic, and soon the others are joining us, blankets spread throughout the lawn in a patchwork of friendship. It's something we claimed women do often but especially on the days of the festivals. So many of us are haunted by the memories of the things that happened during those dark times, and we don't want anyone to be alone on days like today.

The park fills with mothers and their children—some are the beta wives, but many are not. The children play, and we women chat among ourselves, happy to enjoy the crisp autumn under these circumstances. The shifter men aren't invited to these quarterly picnics. These are just for us.

"Hi, Jasmine," Abi says to a woman setting up her picnic near us. "It's great to see you. How are your sons?"

The woman is about fifteen years older than us and endured so much more than we ever had to. Abi once told me that Jasmine was one of the only friends she made during her time in the mating house. Nobody thought Jasmine would ever see her children again, but Jasmine always believed. Luckily, the pack kept records of which women had which children, and Jasmine was reunited with all eleven of hers.

Eleven.

Just the thought of bearing that many children makes my body ache.

"They're doing great. Only my youngest four could come out today, though. The others are too old for games." She rolls her eyes, and we chat merrily as she finishes setting up her picnic. Then she's running off to play with her kids, her own childlike nature having never left her, despite everything.

"Eleven kids," Abi whispers. "And most of them were teenagers before she ever got to see them again."

I take her hand and squeeze because we're thinking the same thing. That could have been us.

"Anything new with you two?" Joanna asks as she sits down between me and Abi. She waggles her eyes at our friend. "Any new romantic prospects?"

It's a nice distraction. Joanna always did have the best timing.

Abi shrugs and shakes her head. After her son was born, she vowed never to touch another man again. So far, she's kept that promise. "I'm happier staying single. Orien is enough for me, anyway. He's my world."

Joanna and I nod because we understand in our own ways. Grady is Joanna's world, and when she told him she didn't want to have children, he was fine with that. All he wanted was whatever made her happiest. She practically runs that textile village now, but she always makes a point to come to the city for the festival picnics.

And as for me, Ryne and the twins are my world—as is the child currently growing in my womb, a child who is sure to be another girl.

That was the surprise of a lifetime. Soon after things settled down and people started coupling, we discovered that shifter men and lycan women nearly always have female shifter offspring.

That changed everything.

The mating houses still exist, but they're voluntary and are starting to die out. The claiming, however, has grown exponentially. So much so that three more manors have had to be opened to accommodate everyone just in the Carolina Pack. Many human women and female lycans elect to spend a year dating wolf men. Some are betas, but lower ranks are also invited to come date women. Marriages are encouraged but not required. Anyone can walk away at any time. If a couple does get engaged under Ryne's blessing, then they can live together in the city, usually raising a family together. Or they can go live among the villages with the humans.

My own parents stayed in our village, but Evan says he's going to become a lycan when he grows up, just like his sister. It scares me to think about that, but it's also not my place to stop him. Same as it's not my place to stop so many humans from taking on the lycan virus, despite the risks. Turns out lycans also age slower than humans, and a lot of people want that opportunity. What worries me most about Evan is that he'll leave us for another pack or to live among the panthers like so many others did. Charlotte and Knox moved south, and we've only heard from them twice in the years since. They wanted to start over, and I can't say I blame them, but that doesn't mean I don't miss them from time to time.

Our pack has thrived, and so have all the others, as far as I know. In the five years since Elle enforced the changes Ryne started, the kingdom has exploded with new babies—male and female wolf shifters and more lunas than ever. Of course there were dissenters, but they left for the wilds or got in line, and no more abuse is tolerated in any of the packs. Elle and Bellamy are the best thing that ever could've happened to the kingdom, and I wonder how many little luna girls want to grow up to be just like their fearless queen. My daughters certainly do.

But I don't . . .

Ryne was right not to put us on that throne. We're so happy where we're at, living in a restored farmhouse on the edge of town. I spend my days tending our gardens and raising our children while he takes care of the pack. Only on full-moon nights does adventure still call to me, and that's when I roam the forest with my own pack—a pack that I turned the title of alpha over to Callum years ago. Otherwise, it's a quiet life for me, filled with love and family and friends. It's all I ever wanted.

I lie back, hands on my large belly, listening to my friends chat merrily as they devour the food from my garden. The blue sky seems to stretch on forever, a reminder of the bluest eyes I've ever seen and the man that fate chose for me. But I know that even if fate hadn't intervened, I still would've chosen him, and he would've chosen me. And that's a choice nobody can take from us. Not ever.

The End

What a wild ride, huh? We're so pleased with the way Poppy's story concluded--these characters sure made it interesting! Thank you for reading the series and we hope you'll continue to enjoy our books. If you haven't already, please write us a written review. As indie authors, reviews make a big difference and mean a lot. By the way, if you haven't read The Alpha's Kiss bonus scene yet, access is available by going to both of our Facebook reader groups:

FB.com/groups/ninasreadingparty

FB.com/groups/kimberlylothreleaseparty

We love you guys! Thank you for going on this journey with us.

Yours,

Nina & Kimberly

Also By Nina Walker

YA DYSTOPIAN FANTASY
THE COLOR ALCHEMIST SERIES

NA PARANORMAL & ROMANTIC FANTASY
THE DRAGON BLESSED SERIES

URBAN FANTASY
THE VAMPIRES & VICES SERIES

YA DYSTOPIAN FANTASY STANDALONE
DARK OCEAN PRINCESS

ADULT ROMANTIC COMEDY BY GRACE COSTELLO
TWINFLUENCE
IVY LEAGUE LIARS

Acknowledgments

Thank you to all the readers who championed this series. We love you! And thank you to our cover designer MiblArt, editors Ailene Kubricky and Cookie Lynn Publishing, our proof readers, arc readers, and so many others. Special thanks to Virginia Wall and Phi Pilgrim, and to our amazing friends and family. We couldn't have done this without your continued support.

You're the best!

About the Authors

Nina Walker is a USA Today and Amazon Top 100 Bestselling author. Living near the beautiful red mountains of Southern Utah, she writes across multiple fantasy genres and co-writes under the romantic comedy pen name, Grace Costello.

Kimberly Loth has lived all over the world. From the isolated woods of the Ozarks to exotic city of Cairo. Currently she resides in the Missouri Ozarks with her husband and their spunky dog, Maisy. She's the author of the Amazon bestselling series The Dragon Kings. In her free time she volunteers at church, reads, and travels as often as possible.